MODERN CLASSIC
SHORT
NOVELS OF SCIENCE
FICTION

MODERN CLASSIC SHORT NOVELS OF SCIENCE FICTION

EDITED BY GARDNER DOZOIS

St. Martin's Press
New York

MODERN CLASSIC SHORT NOVELS OF SCIENCE FICTION. Copyright © 1993 by Gardner Dozois. All rights reserved. Printed in the United States of America. No part of this book may be used or reproduced in any manner whatsoever without written permission except in the case of brief quotations embodied in critical articles or reviews. For information, address St. Martin's Press, 175 Fifth Avenue, New York, N.Y. 10010.

Library of Congress Cataloging-in-Publication Data

Modern classic short novels of science fiction / Gardner Dozois, editor.
p.   cm.
ISBN 0-312-11317-X (pbk.)
1. Science fiction, American.   I. Dozois, Gardner R.
[PS648.S3M58   1994b]
813′.0876208—dc20   94-12800   CIP

First Paperback Edition: September 1994
10 9 8 7 6 5 4 3 2 1

ACKNOWLEDGMENTS

·————————————————·

Acknowledgment is made for permission to print the following material:

The Miracle Workers, copyright © 1958 by Street & Smith Publications, Inc. First published in *Astounding Science Fiction,* July, 1958. Reprinted by permission of the author and the author's agent, Ralph M. Vicinanza, Ltd.

The Longest Voyage, by Poul Anderson. Copyright © 1960 by Street and Smith Publications, Inc. First published in *Analog,* December 1960. Reprinted by permission of the author.

On the Storm Planet, by Cordwainer Smith. Copyright © 1965 by Galaxy Publishing Corp. First published in *Galaxy,* February 1965. Reprinted by permission of the author's estate and the agents for the estate, Scott Meredith Literary Associates, Inc., 845 Third Avenue, New York, N.Y. 10022.

The Star Pit, by Samuel R. Delany. Copyright © 1966 by Galaxy Publishing Corp. First published in *Worlds of Tomorrow,* February 1967. Reprinted by permission of the author.

Total Environment, by Brian W. Aldiss. Copyright © 1968 by Galaxy Publishing Corp. First published in *Galaxy,* February 1968. Reprinted by permission of the author.

The Merchants of Venus, by Frederik Pohl. Copyright © 1972 by U.P.D. First published in *If,* August 1972. Reprinted by permission of the author.

The Death of Doctor Island, by Gene Wolfe. Copyright © 1973 by Gene Wolfe. First published in *Universe 3* (Random House). Reprinted by permission of the author and the author's agent, Virginia Kidd.

Where Late the Sweet Birds Sang, by Kate Wilhelm. Copyright © 1974 by Kate Wilhelm. First published in *Orbit 15* (Harper & Row). Reprinted by permission of the author.

Souls, by Joanna Russ. Copyright © 1981 by Mercury Press, Inc.

CONTENTS

Preface ix

The Miracle Workers *Jack Vance* 1

The Longest Voyage *Poul Anderson* 65

On the Storm Planet *Cordwainer Smith* 94

The Star Pit *Samuel R. Delany* 164

Total Environment *Brian W. Aldiss* 221

The Merchants of Venus *Frederik Pohl* 260

The Death of Doctor Island *Gene Wolfe* 321

Where Late the Sweet Birds Sang *Kate Wilhelm* 373

Souls *Joanna Russ* 415

A Traveler's Tale *Lucius Shepard* 459

Sailing to Byzantium *Robert Silverberg* 504

Mr. Boy *James Patrick Kelly* 561

And Wild for to Hold *Nancy Kress* 617

PREFACE

.———————.

The short novel—or the novella, as it is usually referred to in the science fiction field—is something of a literary Endangered Species, and although it once flourished in the general marketplace, it is a form rarely encountered these days—*except* in science fiction. The novella is alive and well in the science fiction world, and while you can peruse issue after issue of most little literary magazines or those few remaining mainstream magazines that still include fiction in their editorial mix without ever finding a story more than a few pages long, there are still usually a dozen or more novellas published in the science fiction genre every year.

Perhaps this is because, in many ways, the novella is a perfect length for a science fiction story: long enough to enable you to flesh out the details of a strange alien world or a bizarre future society, to give such a setting some depth, complexity, and *heft* . . . and yet, still *short* enough for the story to pack a real punch, some power and elegance and bite, unblunted and unobscured by padding. Unlike many of today's novels, most of which strike me as novellas grossly padded-out to be five hundred pages long, there are rarely any wasted words in a good novella, a quality they share with good short stories. A good novella is no longer than it *needs* to be. It does what it has to do, what it is designed to do, and then it *stops*. That novellas need to be as long as they are is a measure of just how complicated and difficult are the tasks that they are designed to *do*: to create a whole fictional world, a universe that no one has ever explored before, to set that world forth in intricate detail, to people it with living characters, and then to use the tumbling interactions of that world and those people to tell a story that could not be told without *both* those elements being present. This is a formidable task to accomplish even in the space of a five-hundred-page novel— and yet, most of the novellas here are marvels of compression, in spite of the amount of ground they have to cover, and it would be hard to find a page of slack to cut out of any of them, or to end them one page earlier than they do.

Whatever the reason, the novella form has always been popular with science fiction writers (and, to answer the cynics out there, it's *not* because you get paid more for a longer story when you're paid by the word; traditionally, there's a drop in word-rates after a certain length in most genre markets, so you'd actually make *more* money writing a couple of short stories than writing a novella, in most cases), and much of the best work of the past fifty years has been done at novella length.

There are so *many* good novellas, in fact, that even a huge anthology such as this one can't come remotely close to including them all, or even the bulk of them. Some arbitrary decisions clearly needed to be made, and, arbitrarily, I made them.

First, I decided to concentrate on a period ranging from the beginning of the sixties to the beginning of the nineties, rationalizing this by the observation that the "Golden Age" of the 1940s and the *Galaxy* era of the 1950s were the periods of science fiction history that were already covered the most extensively by other anthologists—but this decision did lose me stories that I would have liked, in the multidimensional, infinitely extensible version of this book, to include, such as C. L. Moore's *Vintage Season*, Damon Knight's *The Earth Quarter*, L. Sprague de Camp's *Divide and Rule*, Theodore Sturgeon's *Baby Is Three* and *Killdozer*, and many more.

My next task, and a ticklish one it was, too, was to determine how famous a story could get before it became *too* famous. The stories needed to have generated enough of a reputation to justify being included in a book called *Modern Classic Short Novels of Science Fiction*, after all, but, at the same time, I wanted to avoid stories that had been over-anthologized and over-exposed, and would thus be already too familiar to the reader, such as Harlan Ellison's *A Boy and His Dog* or Ursula K. Le Guin's *The Word for World Is Forest*. As with everything else about this anthology, this was a subjective judgment call, but I think that most of the stories here, even the award-winners, are stories that have been generally unavailable for some time now to the average reader with the average reader's resources. The shelf life for books is so short now, and things come back into print so rarely once they go *out* of it (and back-issue copies of magazines and second-hand copies of old anthologies are so difficult to find, even in dealer's rooms at science fiction conventions), that many younger readers may have never had a chance to read some of the stories here, even the Hugo Award–winners. Historical memory being what it now is in the field, many younger readers may never even have *heard* of some of these stories before, even the Hugo-winners; I know, because I've *asked* many of them (as, for instance, the bright and literate young readers I ran across the other day, who, even though they considered themselves to be hardcore SF fans and read voraciously, had never heard of Cordwainer Smith or Jack Vance).

Next, this anthology being assembled in the real world rather than in some ideal one, there were practical difficulties to constrain me, stories that I would have liked to include—such as Geoff Ryman's *The Unconquered Country* or Michael Swanwick's *Griffin's Egg*—but that I was unable to use because the reprint rights were encumbered in some way, or stories that I couldn't use because they had just appeared in somebody *else's* anthology, and I didn't want to duplicate the stories in a competing volume.

All of this *still* left me with a very large field of novellas to choose from, dozens and dozens of them, in fact—and here we have to fall back on personal taste.

As was true of my 1991 anthology *Modern Classics of Science Fiction*, none of the stories here were selected because they help buttress some polemic or aesthetic argument about the nature of the field, or because they express some critical theory, or because they grind some particular political axe. Instead, they were selected on the appallingly naïve basis that I *liked* them.

These are the stories that spoke to me, as a reader, that touched me, that moved me, on a purely instinctive and emotional level—they are the stories that, when I read them again, sometimes after a lapse of many years, could still make me say "Wow!," could make my pulse race faster, or the sweat start on my forehead, or totally absorb me, or scare me, or touch my heart. Stories that I *enjoyed*—uncritically, instinctively—as a *reader*. Stories that I would want to read again.

So, as I warned you, it all comes down to one person's taste, my own. These are the novellas that *I* liked best . . . although that doesn't look as good on the cover as the firmly authoritative *Modern Classic Short Novels of Science Fiction*. Although even *that*—novellas that I liked best—is subjective, to some extent. There are so many good novellas that I could easily have assembled two or three other volumes of this size with no discernable letdown in quality, and which Table of Contents I liked the best would vary from day to day, depending entirely on the mood I happened to be in on the day when I was considering the question. Perhaps someday I'll be able to bring you some of those other volumes as well.

In the meantime, taste being the subjective thing that it is, I can't promise you that these novellas are the best science fiction novellas published since the beginning of the sixties—I think I *can* promise you, though, that they are certainly *among* the best.

I also hope that, at the very least, this book serves to demonstrate some of the amazing range, diversity, and vitality of modern science fiction, as well as the durability of the best of its stories—the oldest story here will be thirty-six years old by the time you read these words, and it is still as fresh and vivid as it was on the day it was written. I like to think that thiry-six years from *now*, long after I'm dead, these stories will prove to be still as timeless as they are today, and it is my fond hope that this book will continue to provide enjoyment for generations of readers yet to come, far into the unknown and unknowable future.

JACK VANCE
The Miracle Workers

A seminal figure, Jack Vance has produced some of the very best work of the last forty years in several different genres, and is of immense evolutionary importance to the development both of modern fantasy *and* of modern science fiction.

Born in San Francisco in 1920, Vance served throughout World War II in the U.S. Merchant Navy. Most of the individual stories that would later be melded into his first novel, *The Dying Earth*, were written while Vance was at sea—he was unable to sell them, a problem he would also have with the book itself, the market for fantasy being almost non-existent at the time. *The Dying Earth* was eventually published in an obscure edition in 1950 by a small semi-professional press, went out of print almost immediately, and remained out of print for more than a decade thereafter. Nevertheless, it became an underground cult classic, and its effect on future generations of writers is incalculable: for one example, out of many, *The Dying Earth* is one of the most recognizable influences on Gene Wolfe's *The Book of the New Sun* (Wolfe has said, for instance, that *The Book of Gold* which is mentioned by Severian is supposed to be *The Dying Earth*). Vance returned to this *milieu* in 1965, with a series of stories that would be melded into *The Eyes of the Overworld*, and, in the early eighties, returned yet again with *Cugel's Saga* and *Rhialto the Marvellous*—taken together, *The Dying Earth* stories represent one of the most impressive achievements in science-fantasy.

In science fiction itself, Vance would do some of his best early work for magazines such as *Thrilling Wonder Stories* and *Startling Stories* and the short-lived *Worlds Beyond* in the mid-fifties—"The Five Gold Bands," "Abercrombie Station," "The Houses of Izam," "The Kokod Warriors," "The New Prime," and the magazine version of "Big Planet," among others. Vance was also appearing in *Astounding* from time to time during this period, but most of his work for *Astounding* would be rather bland by Vance's standards, with only one story there, the wonderfully evocative, marvelously strange, and bizarrely imaginative novella that follows, *The Miracle Workers*, being full-throated Vancian Future Baroque.

But that was a somewhat atypical style for *Astounding*, and by the late fifties and early sixties, Vance was doing most of his best work, and some of the very best work of the period, for *Galaxy* and *F&SF*—the magnificent "The Dragon Masters," "The Men Return," the underrated *The Langues of Pao* (one of only a handful of books even today to deal with semantics as a science; Delany's *Babel-17* and Ian Watson's *The Embedding* are two later examples), the wonderful *The Star King* and *The Killing Machine* (two of the best hybrids of SF and the mystery/espionage novel ever written), "Green Magic," *The Blue World*, "The Last Castle."

Vance is reminiscent of R. A. Lafferty in that both men break all the supposed rules of writing, and get away with it. Both eschew naturalism, each using a mannered and highly idiosyncratic prose style (baroque and stiffly elegant in Vance's case, energetically informal and folksy in Lafferty's), and both have their characters spout theatrical, deliberately non-naturalistic, hieratic dialogue of a sort that never actually came out of anyone's mouth—if you were to film their work, no mumbling Method actors would need to apply; only someone with the flamboyant grandiloquence of a John Barrymore would do. Vance also—and here comes an even stranger comparison—reminds me of Philip K. Dick: each author relies heavily on a personal formula of his own, using the same basic frameworks, plots, and types of characters and situations again and again (what is important in each is not creating new motifs, but refining and developing variations on their obsessive themes); each man's style is limited in technical range, but, within that range, they are the best in the business at what they do well; both emphasize how manners and *mores* change from society to society; and, although neither is thought of as a humorist, the work of both is suffused with a dry, understated wit—Vance's humor is somewhat drier than Dick's, Dick's more surreal than Vance's, but both tend toward black humor, sly satire, a bitterly sardonic view of life and human nature, and to grotesque and macabrely ironic set-pieces. Both men have trouble ending novels, both frequently just letting the story peter away, as though they had gradually lost interest in what they were writing. And, with each, their impact on the field rests more on the aggregate effect of their work than on any particular story or novel—or, to adapt a remark of Thomas Disch's concerning Dick which is equally valid for Vance, their novels are more impressive collectively than each by each.

And, much as SF authors writing today about phenomenology or the nature of reality write inevitably in the shadow of Philip K. Dick, so writers describing distant worlds and alien societies with strange alien customs write in the shadow of Vance. No one in the history of the field has brought more intelligence, imagination, or inexhaustible fertility of invention to that theme than Vance; even ostensible potboilers such as his *Planet of Adventure* series are full of vivid and richly portrayed alien societies, and bizarre and often profoundly disturbing insights into the ways in which human psychology might be altered by immersion in alien values and cultural systems. No one is better than Vance is at delivering that quintessential "sense of wonder" that is at the heart of science fiction, and reading him has left me a legacy of evocative images that will stay with me forever.

Vance has won two Hugo Awards, a Nebula Award, two World Fantasy Awards (one the prestigious Life Achievement Award), and the Edgar Award for best mystery novel. His other books include *Emphyrio* (one of the best novels of the late sixties, up until the disappointing ending), *The Anome, The Palace of Love, The Face, The Book of Dreams, City of the Chasch, The Dirdir, The Pnume, The Brave Free Men, Lyonesse, The Green Pearl, Trullion: Alastor 2262, Wyst: Alastor 1716*, and *Araminta Station*, among many others. His short fiction has been collected in *Eight Fantasms and Magics, The Best of Jack Vance, Green Magic, Lost Moons, The Complete Magnus Ridolph, The World Between and Other Stories, The Dark Side of the Moon*, and *The Narrow Land*. His most recent book is the novel *Throy*.

I

The war party from Faide Keep moved eastward across the downs; a column of a hundred armored knights, five hundred foot soldiers, a train of wagons. In the lead rode Lord Faide, a tall man in his early maturity, spare and catlike, with a sallow dyspeptic face. He sat in the ancestral car of the Faides, a boat-shaped vehicle floating two feet above the moss, and carried, in addition to his sword and dagger, his ancestral side weapons.

An hour before sunset a pair of scouts came racing back to the column, their club-headed horses loping like dogs. Lord Faide braked the motion of his car. Behind him the Faide kinsmen, the lesser knights, the leather-capped foot soldiers halted; to the rear the baggage train and the high-wheeled wagons of the jinxmen creaked to a stop.

The scouts approached at breakneck speed, at the last instant flinging their horses sidewise. Long shaggy legs kicked out, padlike hooves plowed through the moss. The scouts jumped to the ground, ran forward. "The way to Ballant Keep is blocked!"

Lord Faide rose in his seat, stood staring eastward over the gray-green downs. "How many knights? How many men?"

"No knights, no men, Lord Faide. The First Folk have planted a forest between North and South Wildwood."

Lord Faide stood a moment in reflection, then seated himself, pushed the control knob. The car wheezed, jerked, moved forward. The knights touched up their horses; the foot soldiers resumed their slouching gait. At the rear the baggage train creaked into motion, together with the six wagons of the jinxmen.

The sun, large, pale and faintly pink, sank in the west. North Wildwood loomed down from the left, separated from South Wildwood by an area of stony ground, only sparsely patched with moss. As the sun passed behind the horizon, the new planting became visible: a frail new growth connecting the tracts of woodland like a canal between two seas.

Lord Faide halted his car, stepped down to the moss. He appraised the landscape, then gave the signal to make camp. The wagons were ranged in a circle, the gear unloaded. Lord Faide watched the activity for a moment, eyes sharp and critical, then turned and walked out across the downs through the lavender and green twilight. Fifteen miles to the east his last enemy awaited him: Lord Ballant of Ballant Keep. Contemplating tomorrow's battle, Lord Faide felt reasonably confident of the outcome. His troops had been tempered by a dozen campaigns; his kinsmen were loyal and single-hearted. Head Jinxman to Faide Keep was Hein Huss, and associated with him were three of the most powerful jinxmen of Pangborn: Isak Comandore, Adam McAdam and the remarkable Enterlin, together with their separate troupes of cabalmen, spellbinders and apprentices. Altogether, an impressive assemblage. Certainly there were obstacles to be overcome: Ballant Keep was strong; Lord Ballant would fight obstinately; Anderson Grimes, the Ballant jinxman, was efficient and highly respected. There was also this nuisance of the First Folk and the new planting which closed the gap between North and South Wildwood. The First Folk were a pale and feeble race, no match for human beings in single combat, but they guarded their forests with traps and deadfalls. Lord Faide cursed softly under his breath. To circle either North or South Wildwood meant a delay of three days, which could not be tolerated.

Lord Faide returned to the camp. Fires were alight, pots bubbled, orderly rows of sleep-holes had been dug into the moss. The knights groomed their horses within the corral of wagons; Lord Faide's own tent had been erected on a hummock, beside the ancient car.

Lord Faide made a quick round of inspection, noting every detail, speaking no word. The jinxmen were encamped a little distance apart from the troops. The apprentices and lesser spell-binders prepared food, while the jinxmen and cabalmen worked inside their tents, arranging cabinets and cases, correcting whatever disorder had been caused by the jolting of the wagons.

Lord Faide entered the tent of his Head Jinxman. Hein Huss was an enormous man, with arms and legs heavy as tree trunks, a torso like a barrel. His face was pink and placid, his eyes were water-clear; a stiff gray brush rose from his head, which was innocent of the cap jinxmen customarily wore against the loss of hair. Hein Huss disdained such precautions; it was his habit, showing his teeth in a face-splitting grin, to rumble, "Why should anyone hoodoo me, old Hein Huss? I am so inoffensive. Whoever tried would surely die, of shame and remorse."

Lord Faide found Huss busy at his cabinet. The doors stood wide, revealing hundreds of mannikins, each tied with a lock of hair, a bit of cloth, a fingernail clipping, daubed with grease, sputum, excrement, blood. Lord Faide knew well that one of these mannikins represented himself. He also knew that should he request it Hein Huss would deliver it without hesitation. Part of Huss's *mana* derived from his enormous confidence, the effortless ease of his power. He glanced at Lord Faide and read the question in his mind. "Lord Ballant did not know of the new planting. Anderson Grimes has now informed him, and Lord Ballant expects that you will be delayed. Grimes has communicated with Gisborne Keep and Castle Cloud. Three hundred men march tonight to reinforce Ballant Keep. They will arrive in two days. Lord Ballant is much elated."

Lord Faide paced back and forth across the tent. "Can we cross this planting?"

Hein Huss made a heavy sound of disapproval. "There are many futures. In certain of these futures you pass. In others you do not pass. I cannot ordain these futures."

Lord Faide had long learned to control his impatience at what sometimes seemed to be pedantic obfuscation. He grumbled, "They are either very stupid or very bold, planting across the downs in this fashion. I cannot imagine what they intend."

Hein Huss considered, then grudgingly volunteered an idea. "What if they plant west from North Wildwood to Sarrow Copse? What if they plant west from South Wildwood to Old Forest?"

Lord Faide stood stock-still, his eyes narrow and thoughtful. "Faide Keep would be surrounded by forest. We would be imprisoned. . . . These plantings, do they proceed?"

"They proceed, so I have been told."

"What do they hope to gain?"

"I do not know. Perhaps they hope to isolate the keeps, to rid the planet of men. Perhaps they merely want secure avenues between the forests."

Lord Faide considered. Huss's final suggestion was reasonable enough. During the first centuries of human settlement, sportive young men had hunted the First Folk with clubs and lances, eventually had driven them from their native downs into the forests. "Evidently they are more clever than we realize. Adam McAdam asserts that they do not think, but it seems that he is mistaken."

Hein Huss shrugged. "Adam McAdam equates thought to the human cerebral process. He cannot telepathize with the First Folk, hence he deduced that they do not 'think.' But I have watched them at Forest Market, and they trade intelligently enough." He raised his head, appeared to listen, then reached into his cabinet, delicately tightened a noose around the neck of one of the mannikins. From outside the tent came a sudden cough and a whooping gasp for air. Huss grinned, twitched open the noose. "That is Isak Comandore's apprentice. He hopes to complete a Hein Huss mannikin. I must say he works diligently, going so far as to touch its feet into my footprints whenever possible."

Lord Faide went to the flap of the tent. "We break camp early. Be alert, I may require your help." Lord Faide departed the tent.

* * *

Hein Huss continued the ordering of the cabinet. Presently he sensed the approach of his rival, Jinxman Isak Comandore, who coveted the office of Head Jinxman with all-consuming passion. Huss closed the cabinet and hoisted himself to his feet.

Comandore entered the tent, a man tall, crooked and spindly. His wedge-shaped head was covered with coarse russet ringlets; hot red-brown eyes peered from under his red eyebrows. "I offer my complete rights to Keyril, and will include the masks, the head-dress, and amulets. Of all the demons ever contrived he has won the widest public acceptance. To utter the name Keyril is to complete half the work of a possession. Keyril is a valuable property. I can give no more."

But Huss shook his head. Comandore's desire was the full simulacrum of Tharon Faide, Lord Faide's oldest son, complete with clothes, hair, skin, eyelashes, tears, excreta, sweat and sputum—the only one in existence, for Lord Faide guarded his son much more jealously than he did himself. "You offer convincingly," said Huss, "but my own demons suffice. The name Dant conveys fully as much terror as Keyril."

"I will add five hairs from the head of Jinxman Clarence Sears; they are the last, for he is now stark bald."

"Let us drop the matter; I will keep the simulacrum."

"As you please," said Comandore with asperity. He glanced out the flap of the tent. "That blundering apprentice. He puts the feet of the mannikin backwards into your prints."

Huss opened his cabinet, thumped a mannikin with his finger. From outside the tent came a grunt of surprise. Huss grinned. "He is young and earnest, and perhaps he is clever, who knows?" He went to the flap of the tent, called outside. "Hey, Sam Salazar, what do you do? Come inside."

Apprentice Sam Salazar came blinking into the tent, a thick-set youth with a round florid face, overhung with a rather untidy mass of straw-colored hair. In one hand he carried a crude pot-bellied mannikin, evidently intended to represent Hein Huss.

"You puzzle both your master and myself," said Huss. "There must be method in your folly, but we fail to perceive it. For instance, this moment you place my simulacrum backwards into my track. I feel a tug on my foot, and you pay for your clumsiness."

Sam Salazar showed small evidence of abashment. "Jinxman Comandore has warned that we must expect to suffer for our ambitions."

"If your ambition is jinxmanship," Comandore declared sharply, "you had best mend your ways."

"The lad is craftier than you know," said Hein Huss. "Look now." He took the mannikin, spit into its mouth, plucked a hair from his head, thrust it into a convenient crevice. "He has a Hein Huss mannikin, achieved at very small cost. Now, Apprentice Salazar, how will you hoodoo me?"

"Naturally I would never dare. I merely want to fill the bare spaces in my cabinet."

Hein Huss nodded his approval. "As good a reason as any. Of course you own a simulacrum of Isak Comandore?"

Sam Salazar glanced uneasily sidewise at Isak Comandore. "He leaves none of his traces. If there is so much as an open bottle in the room, he breathes behind his hand."

"Ridiculous!" exclaimed Hein Huss. "Comandore, what do you fear?"

"I am conservative," said Comandore drily. "You make a fine gesture, but some day an enemy may own that simulacrum; then you will regret your bravado."

"Bah. My enemies are all dead, save one or two who dare not reveal themselves." He clapped Sam Salazar a great buffet on the shoulder. "Tomorrow, Apprentice Salazar, great things are in store for you."

"What manner of great things?"

"Honor, noble self-sacrifice. Lord Faide must beg permission to pass Wildwood from the First Folk, which galls him. But beg he must. Tomorrow, Sam Salazar, I will elect you to lead the way to the parley, to deflect deadfalls, scythes and nettle-traps from the more important person who follows."

Sam Salazar shook his head and drew back. "There must be others more worthy; I prefer to ride in the rear with the wagons."

Comandore waved him from the tent. "You will do as ordered. Leave us; we have had enough apprentice talk."

Sam Salazar departed. Comandore turned back to Hein Huss. "In connection with tomorrow's battle, Anderson Grimes is especially adept with demons. As I recall, he has developed and successfully publicized Font, who spreads sleep; Everid, a being of wrath, Deigne, a force of fear. We must take care that in countering these effects we do not neutralize each other."

"True," rumbled Huss. "I have long maintained to Lord Faide that a single jinxman—the Head Jinxman in fact—is more effective than a group at cross-purposes. But he is consumed by ambition and does not listen."

"Perhaps he wants to be sure that should advancing years overtake the Head Jinxman other equally effective jinxmen are at hand."

"The future has many paths," agreed Hein Huss. "Lord Faide is well-advised to seek early for my successor, so that I may train him over the years. I plan to assess all the subsidiary jinxmen, and select the most promising. Tomorrow I relegate to you the demons of Anderson Grimes."

Isak Comandore nodded politely. "You are wise to give over responsibility. When I feel the weight of my years I hope I may act with similar forethought. Good night, Hein Huss. I go to arrange my demon masks. Tomorrow Keyril must walk like a giant."

"Good night, Isak Comandore."

Comandore swept from the tent, and Huss settled himself on his stool. Sam Salazar scratched at the flap. "Well, lad?" growled Huss. "Why do you loiter?"

Sam Salazar placed the Hein Huss mannikin on the table. "I have no wish to keep this doll."

"Throw it in a ditch, then," Hein Huss spoke gruffly. "You must stop annoying me with stupid tricks. You efficiently obtrude yourself upon my attention, but you cannot transfer from Comandore's troupe without his express consent."

"If I gain his consent?"

"You will incur his enmity, he will open his cabinet against you. Unlike myself, you are vulnerable to a hoodoo. I advise you to be content. Isak Comandore is highly skilled and can teach you much."

Sam Salazar still hesitated. "Jinxman Comandore, though skilled, is intolerant of new thoughts."

Hein Huss shifted ponderously on his stool, examined Sam Salazar with his water-clear eyes. "What new thoughts are these? Your own?"

"The thoughts are new to me, and for all I know new to Isak Comandore. But he will say neither yes nor no."

Hein Huss sighed, settled his monumental bulk more comfortably. "Speak then, describe these thoughts, and I will assess their novelty."

"First, I have wondered about trees. They are sensitive to light, to moisture, to wind, to pressure. Sensitivity implies sensation. Might a man feel into the soul of a tree for these sensations? If a tree were capable of awareness, this faculty might prove useful. A man might select trees as sentinels in strategic sites, and enter into them as he chose."

Hein Huss was skeptical. "An amusing notion, but practically not feasible. The reading of minds, the act of possession, televoyance, similar interplay requires psychic congruence as a basic condition. The minds must be able to become identities at some particular stratum. Unless there is sympathy, there is no linkage. A tree is at opposite poles from a man; the images of tree and man are incommensurable. Hence, anything more than the most trifling flicker of comprehension must be a true miracle of jinxmanship."

Sam Salazar nodded mournfully "I realize this, and at one time hoped to equip myself with the necessary identification."

"To do this you must become a vegetable. Certainly the tree will never become a man."

"So I reasoned," said Sam Salazar. "I went alone into a grove of trees, where I chose a tall conifer. I buried my feet in the mold, I stood silent and naked—in the sunlight, in the rain; at dawn, noon, dusk, midnight. I closed my mind to man-thoughts, I closed my eyes to vision, my ears to sound. I took no nourishment except from rain and sun. I sent roots forth from my feet and branches from my torso. Thirty hours I stood, and two days later, another thirty hours, and after two days another thirty hours. I made myself a tree, as nearly as possible to one of flesh and blood."

Hein Huss gave the great inward gurgle which signalized his amusement. "And you achieved sympathy?"

"Nothing useful," Sam Salazar admitted. "I felt something of the tree's sensations—the activity of light, the peace of dark, the coolness of rain. But visual and auditory experience—nothing. However, I do not regret the trial. It was a useful discipline."

"An interesting effort, even if inconclusive. The idea is by no means of startling originality, but the empiricism—to use an archaic word—of your method is bold, and no doubt antagonized Isak Comandore, who has no patience with the superstitions of our ancestors. I suspect that he harangued you against frivolity, metaphysics, and inspirationalism."

"True," said Sam Salazar. "He spoke at length."

"You should take the lesson to heart. Isak Comandore is sometimes unable to make the most obvious truth seem credible. However, I cite you the example of Lord Faide who considers himself an enlightened man, free from superstition. Still, he rides in the feeble car, he carries a pistol sixteen hundred years old, he relies on Hellmouth to protect Faide Keep."

"Perhaps—unconsciously—he longs for the old magical times," suggested Sam Salazar thoughtfully.

"Perhaps," agreed Hein Huss. "And you do likewise?"

Sam Salazar hesitated. "There is an aura of romance, a kind of wild grandeur to the old days—but of course," he added quickly, "mysticism is no substitute for orthodox logic."

"Naturally not," agreed Hein Huss. "Now go; I must consider the events of tomorrow."

Sam Salazar departed, and Hein Huss, rumbling and groaning, hoisted himself to his feet. He went to the flap of his tent, surveyed the camp. All now was quiet. The fires were embers, the warriors lay in the pits they had cut into the moss. To the north and south spread the woodlands. Among the trees and out on the downs were faint flickering luminosities, where the First Folk gathered spore-pods from the moss.

Hein Huss became aware of a nearby personality. He turned his head and saw approaching the shrouded form of Jinxman Enterlin, who concealed his face, who spoke only in whispers, who disguised his natural gait with a stiff stiltlike motion. By this means he hoped to reduce his vulnerability to hostile jinxmanship. The admission carelessly let fall of failing eyesight, of stiff joints, forgetfulness, melancholy, nausea might be of critical significance in controversy by hoodoo. Jinxmen therefore maintained the pose of absolute health and virility, even though they must grope blindly or limp doubled up from cramps.

Hein Huss called out to Enterlin, lifted back the flap to the tent. Enterlin entered; Huss went to the cabinet, brought forth a flask, poured liquor into a pair of stone cups. "A cordial only, free of covert significance."

"Good," whispered Enterlin, selecting the cup farthest from him. "After all, we jinxmen must relax into the guise of men from time to time." Turning his back on Huss, he introduced the cup through the folds of his hood, drank. "Refreshing," he whispered. "We need refreshment: tomorrow we must work."

Huss issued his reverberating chuckle. "Tomorrow Isak Comandore matches demons with Anderson Grimes. We others perform only subsidiary duties."

Enterlin seemed to make a quizzical inspection of Hein Huss through the black gauze before his eyes. "Comandore will relish this opportunity. His vehemence oppresses me, and his is a power which feeds on success. He is a man of fire, you are a man of ice."

"Ice quenches fire."

"Fire sometimes melts ice."

Hein Huss shrugged. "No matter. I grow weary. Time has passed all of us by. Only a moment ago a young apprentice showed me to myself."

"As a powerful jinxman, as Head Jinxman to the Faides, you have cause for pride."

Hein Huss drained the stone cup, set it aside. "No. I see myself at the top of my profession, with nowhere else to go. Only Sam Salazar the apprentice thinks to search for more universal lore: he comes to me for counsel, and I do not know what to tell him."

"Strange talk, strange talk!" whispered Enterlin. He moved to the flap of the tent. "I go now," he whispered. "I go to walk on the downs. Perhaps I will see the future."

"There are many futures."

Enterlin rustled away and was lost in the dark. Hein Huss groaned and grumbled, then took himself to his couch, where he instantly fell asleep.

II

The night passed. The sun, flickering with films of pink and green, lifted over the horizon. The new planting of the First Folk was silhouetted, a sparse stubble of saplings, against the green and lavender sky. The troops broke camp with practiced efficiency. Lord Faide marched to his car, leaped within; the machine sagged under his weight. He pushed a button, the car drifted forward, heavy as a waterlogged timber.

A mile from the new planting he halted, sent a messenger back to the wagons of the jinxmen. Hein Huss walked ponderously forward, followed by Isak Comandore, Adam McAdam, and Enterlin; Lord Faide spoke to Hein Huss. "Send someone to speak to the First Folk. Inform them we wish to pass, offering them no harm, but that we will react savagely to any hostility."

"I will go myself," said Hein Huss. He turned to Comandore. "Lend me, if you will, your brash young apprentice. I can put him to good use."

"If he unmasks a nettle trap by blundering into it, his first useful deed will be done," said Comandore. He signaled to Sam Salazar, who came reluctantly forward. "Walk in front of Head Jinxman Hein Huss that he may encounter no traps or scythes. Take a staff to probe the moss."

Without enthusiasm Sam Salazar borrowed a lance from one of the foot soldiers. He and Huss set forth, along the low rise that previously had separated North from South Wildwood. Occasionally outcroppings of stone penetrated the cover of moss; here and there grew bayberry trees, clumps of tarplant, ginger-tea, and rosewort.

A half mile from the planting Huss halted. "Now take care, for here the traps will begin. Walk clear of hummocks, these often conceal swing-scythes; avoid moss which shows a pale blue; it is dying or sickly and may cover a deadfall or a nettle trap."

"Why cannot you locate the traps by clairvoyance?" asked Sam

Salazar in a rather sullen voice. "It appears an excellent occasion for the use of these faculties."

"The question is natural," said Hein Huss with composure. "However, you must know that when a jinxman's own profit or security is at stake his emotions play tricks on him. I would see traps everywhere and would never know whether clairvoyance or fear prompted me. In this case, that lance is a more reliable instrument than my mind."

Sam Salazar made a salute of understanding and set forth, with Hein Huss stumping behind him. At first he prodded with care, uncovering two traps, then advanced more jauntily; so swiftly indeed that Huss called out in exasperation, "Caution, unless you court death!"

Sam Salazar obligingly slowed his pace. "There are traps all around us, but I detect the pattern, or so I believe."

"Ah, ha, you do? Reveal it to me, if you will. I am only Head Jinxman, and ignorant."

"Notice. If we walk where the spore-pods have recently been harvested, then we are secure."

Hein Huss grunted. "Forward then. Why do you dally? We must do battle at Ballant Keep today."

Two hundred yards farther, Sam Salazar stopped short. "Go on, boy, go on!" grumbled Hein Huss.

"The savages threaten us. You can see them just inside the planting. They hold tubes which they point toward us."

Hein Huss peered, then raised his head and called out in the sibilant language of the First Folk.

A moment or two passed, then one of the creatures came forth, a naked humanoid figure, ugly as a demonmask. Foam-sacs bulged under its arms, orange-lipped foam-vents pointed forward. Its back was wrinkled and loose, the skin serving as a bellows to blow air through the foam-sacs. The fingers of the enormous hands ended in chisel-shaped blades, the head was sheathed in chitin. Billion-faceted eyes swelled from either side of the head, glowing like black opals, merging without definite limit into the chitin. This was a representative of the original inhabitants of the planet, who until the coming of man had inhabited the downs, burrowing in the moss, protecting themselves behind masses of foam exuded from the underarm sacs.

The creature wandered close, halted. "I speak for Lord Faide of Faide Keep," said Huss. "Your planting bars his way. He wishes that you guide him through, so that his men do not damage the trees, or spring the traps you have set against your enemies."

"Men are our enemies," responded the autochthon. "You may spring as many traps as you care to; that is their purpose." It backed away.

"One moment," said Hein Huss sternly. "Lord Faide must pass. He goes to battle Lord Ballant. He does not wish to battle the First Folk. Therefore it is wise to guide him across the planting without hindrance."

The creature considered a second or two. "I will guide him." He stalked across the moss toward the war party.

Behind followed Hein Huss and Sam Salazar. The autochthon, legs articulated more flexibly than a man's, seemed to weave and wander, occasionally pausing to study the ground ahead.

"I am puzzled," Sam Salazar told Hein Huss. "I cannot understand the creature's actions."

"Small wonder," grunted Hein Huss. "He is one of the First Folk, you are human. There is no basis for understanding."

"I disagree," said Sam Salazar seriously.

"Eh?" Hein Huss inspected the apprentice with vast disapproval. "You engage in contention with me, Head Jinxman Hein Huss?"

"Only in a limited sense," said Sam Salazar. "I see a basis for understanding with the First Folk in our common ambition to survive."

"A truism," grumbled Hein Huss. "Granting this community of interests with the First Folk, what is your perplexity?"

"The fact that it first refused, then agreed to conduct us across the planting."

Hein Huss nodded. "Evidently the information which intervened, that we go to fight at Ballant Keep, occasioned the change."

"This is clear," said Sam Salazar. "But think—"

"You exhort me to think?" roared Hein Huss.

"—here is one of the First Folk, apparently without distinction, who makes an important decision instantly. Is he one of their leaders? Do they live in anarchy?"

"It is easy to put questions," Hein Huss said gruffly. "It is not as easy to answer them."

"In short—"

"In short, I do not know. In any event, they are pleased to see us killing one another."

III

The passage through the planting was made without incident. A mile to the east the autochthon stepped aside and without formality returned to the forest. The war party, which had been marching in single file, regrouped into its usual formation. Lord Faide called Hein Huss and made the unusual gesture of inviting him up into the seat beside him. The ancient car dipped and sagged; the power-mechanism whined and chattered. Lord Faide, in high good spirits, ignored the noise. "I feared that we might be forced into a time-consuming wrangle. What of Lord Ballant? Can you read his thoughts?"

Hein Huss cast his mind forth. "Not clearly. He knows of our passage. He is disturbed."

Lord Faide laughed sardonically. "For excellent reasons! Listen now, I will explain the plan of battle so that all may coordinate their efforts."

"Very well."

"We approach in a wide line. Ballant's great weapon is of course Volcano. A decoy must wear my armor and ride in the lead. The yellow-haired apprentice is perhaps the most expendable member of the party. In this way we will learn the potentialities of Volcano. Like our own Hellmouth, it was built to repel vessels from space and cannot command the ground immediately under the keep. Therefore we will advance in dispersed formation, to regroup two hundred yards from the keep. At this point the jinxmen will impel Lord Ballant forth from the keep. You no doubt have made plans to this end."

Hein Huss gruffly admitted that such was the case. Like other jinxmen, he enjoyed the pose that his power sufficed for extemporaneous control of any situation.

Lord Faide was in no mood for niceties and pressed for further information. Grudging each word, Hein Huss disclosed his arrangements. "I have prepared certain influences to discomfit the Ballant defenders and drive them forth. Jinxman Enterlin will sit at his cabinet, ready to retaliate if Lord Ballant orders a spell against you. Anderson Grimes undoubtedly will cast a demon—probably Everid—into the Ballant warriors; in return, Jinxman Comandore will possess an equal or a greater number of Faide warriors with the demon Keyril, who is even more ghastly and horrifying."

"Good. What more?"

"There is need for no more, if your men fight well."

"Can you see the future? How does today end?"

"There are many futures. Certain jinxmen—Enterlin for instance—profess to see the thread which leads through the maze; they are seldom correct."

"Call Enterlin here."

Hein Huss rumbled his disapproval. "Unwise, if you desire victory over Ballant Keep."

Lord Faide inspected the massive jinxman from under his black saturnine brows. "Why do you say this?"

"If Enterlin foretells defeat, you will be dispirited and fight poorly. If he predicts victory, you become overconfident and likewise fight poorly."

Lord Faide made a petulant gesture. "The jinxmen are loud in their boasts until the test is made. Then they always find reasons to retract, to qualify."

"Ha, ha!" barked Hein Huss. "You expect miracles, not honest jinxmanship. I spit—" he spat. "I predict that the spittle will strike the moss. The probabilities are high. But an insect might fly in the way. One of the First Folk might raise through the moss. The chances are slight. In the next instant there is only one future. A minute hence there are four futures. Five minutes hence, twenty futures. A billion futures could not express all the possibilities of tomorrow. Of these billion, certain are more probable than others. It is true that these probable futures sometimes send a delicate influence into the jinxman's brain. But unless he is completely impersonal and disinterested, his own desires overwhelm this influence. Enterlin is a strange man. He hides himself, he has no appetites. Occasionally his auguries are exact. Nevertheless, I advise against consulting him. You do better to rely on the practical and real uses of jinxmanship."

Lord Faide said nothing. The column had been marching along the bottom of a low swale; the car had been sliding easily downslope. Now they came to a rise, and the power-mechanism complained so vigorously that Lord Faide was compelled to stop the car. He considered. "Once over the crest we will be in view of Ballant Keep. Now we must disperse. Send the least valuable man in your troupe forward—the apprentice who tested out the moss. He must wear my helmet and corselet and ride in the car."

Hein Huss alighted, returned to the wagons, and presently Sam Salazar came forward. Lord Faide eyed the round, florid face with distaste. "Come close," he said crisply. Sam Salazar obeyed. "You will now ride in my place," said Lord Faide. "Notice carefully. This rod impels a forward motion. This arm steers—to right, to left. To stop, return the rod to its first position."

Sam Salazar pointed to some of the other arms, toggles, switches, and buttons. "What of these?"

"They are never used."

"And these dials, what is their meaning?"

Lord Faide curled his lip, on the brink of one of his quick furies. "Since their use is unimportant to me, it is twenty times unimportant to you. Now. Put this cap on your head, and this helmet. See to it that you do not sweat."

Sam Salazar gingerly settled the magnificent black and green crest of Faide on his head, with a cloth cap underneath.

"Now this corselet."

The corselet was constructed of green and black metal sequins, with a pair of scarlet dragon-heads at either side of the breast.

"Now the cloak." Lord Faide flung the black cloak over Sam Salazar's shoulders. "Do not venture too close to Ballant Keep. Your purpose is to attract the fire of Volcano. Maintain a lateral motion around the keep, outside of dart range. If you are killed by a dart, the whole purpose of the deception is thwarted."

"You prefer me to be killed by Volcano?" inquired Sam Salazar.

"No. I wish to preserve the car and the crest. These are relics of great value. Evade destruction by all means possible. The ruse probably will deceive no one; but if it does, and if it draws the fire of Volcano, I must sacrifice the Faide car. Now—sit in my place."

Sam Salazar climbed into the car, settled himself on the seat.

"Sit straight," roared Lord Faide. "Hold your head up! You are simulating Lord Faide! You must not appear to slink!"

Sam Salazar heaved himself erect in the seat. "To simulate Lord Faide most effectively, I should walk among the warriors, with someone else riding in the car."

Lord Faide glared, then grinned sourly. "No matter. Do as I have commanded."

IV

Sixteen hundred years before, with war raging through space, a group of space captains, their home bases destroyed, had taken refuge on Pangborn. To protect themselves against vengeful enemies, they built great forts armed with weapons from the dismantled spaceships.

The wars receded, Pangborn was forgotten. The newcomers drove the First Folk into the forests, planted and harvested the river valleys. Ballant Keep, like Faide Keep, Castle Cloud, Boghoten, and the rest, overlooked one of these valleys. Four squat towers of a dense black substance supported an enormous parasol roof, and were joined by walls two-thirds as high as the towers. At the peak of the roof a cupola housed Volcano, the weapon corresponding to Faide's Hellmouth.

The Faide war party advancing over the rise found the great

gates already secure, the parapets between the towers thronged with bowmen. According to Lord Faide's strategy, the war party advanced on a broad front. At the center rode Sam Salazar, resplendent in Lord Faide's armor. He made, however, small effort to simulate Lord Faide. Rather than sitting proudly erect, he crouched at the side of the seat, the crest canted at an angle. Lord Faide watched with disgust. Apprentice Salazar's reluctance to be demolished was understandable: if his impersonation failed to convince Lord Ballant, at least the Faide ancestral car might be spared. For a certainty Volcano was being manned; the Ballant weapon-tender could be seen in the cupola, and the snout protruded at a menacing angle.

Apparently, the tactic of dispersal, offering no single tempting target, was effective. The Faide war party advanced quickly to a point two hundred yards from the keep, below Volcano's effective field, without drawing fire; first the knights, then the foot soldiers, then the rumbling wagons of the magicians. The slow-moving Faide car was far outdistanced; any doubt as to the nature of the ruse must now be extinguished.

Apprentice Salazar, disliking the isolation, and hoping to increase the speed of the car, twisted one of the other switches, then another. From under the floor came a thin screeching sound; the car quivered and began to rise. Sam Salazar peered over the side, threw out a leg to jump. Lord Faide ran forward, gesturing and shouting. Sam Salazar hastily drew back his leg, returned the switches to their previous condition. The car dropped like a rock. He snapped the switches up again, cushioning the fall.

"Get out of that car!" roared Lord Faide. He snatched away the helmet, dealt Sam Salazar a buffet which toppled him head over heels. "Out of the armor; back to your duties!"

Sam Salazar hurried to the jinxmen's wagons where he helped erect Isak Comandore's black tent. Inside the tent a black carpet with red and yellow patterns was laid; Comandore's cabinet, his chair, and his chest were carried in, and incense set burning in a censer. Directly in front of the main gate Hein Huss superintended the assembly of a rolling stage, forty feet tall and sixty feet long, the surface concealed from Ballant Keep by a tarpaulin.

Meanwhile, Lord Faide had dispatched an emissary, enjoining Lord Ballant to surrender. Lord Ballant delayed his response, hoping to delay the attack as long as possible. If he could maintain himself a day and a half, reinforcements from Gisborne Keep and Castle Cloud might force Lord Faide to retreat.

Lord Faide waited only until the jinxmen had completed their preparations, then sent another messenger, offering two more minutes in which to surrender.

One minute passed, two minutes. The envoys turned on their heels, marched back to the camp.

Lord Faide spoke to Hein Huss. "You are prepared?"

"I am prepared," rumbled Hein Huss.

"Drive them forth."

Huss raised his arm; the tarpaulin dropped from the face of his great display, to reveal a painted representation of Ballant Keep.

Huss retired to his tent, and pulled the flaps together. Braziers burnt fiercely, illuminating the faces of Adam McAdam, eight cabalmen, and six of the most advanced spell-binders. Each worked at a bench supporting several dozen dolls and a small glowing brazier. The cabalmen and spell-binders worked with dolls representing Ballant men-at-arms; Huss and Adam McAdam employed simulacra of the Ballant knights. Lord Ballant would not be hoodooed unless he ordered a jinx against Lord Faide—a courtesy the keep-lords extended each other.

Huss called out: "Sebastian!"

Sebastian, one of Huss's spell-binders, waiting at the flap to the tent, replied, "Ready, sir."

"Begin the display."

Sebastian ran to the stage, struck fire to a fuse. Watchers inside Ballant Keep saw the depicted keep take fire. Flame erupted from the windows, the roof glowed and crumbled. Inside the tent the two jinxmen, the cabalmen, and the spell-binders methodically took dolls, dipped them into the heat of the braziers, concentrating, reaching out for the mind of the man whose doll they burnt. Within the keep men became uneasy. Many began to imagine burning sensations, which became more severe as their minds grew more sensitive to the idea of fire. Lord Ballant noted the uneasiness. He signaled to his chief jinxman Anderson Grimes. "Begin the counterspell."

Down the front of the keep unrolled a display even larger than Hein Huss's, depicting a hideous beast. It stood on four legs and was shown picking up two men in a pair of hands, biting off their heads. Grimes's cabalmen meanwhile took up dolls representing the Faide warriors, inserted them into models of the depicted beast, and closed the hinged jaws, all the while projecting ideas of fear and disgust. And the Faide warriors, staring at the depicted monster, felt a sense of horror and weakness.

Inside Huss's tent, censers and braziers reeked and dolls smoked. Eyes stared, brows glistened. From time to time one of the workers gasped—signaling the entry of his projection into an enemy mind. Within the keep warriors began to mutter, to slap at burning skin, to eye each other fearfully, noting each other's symptoms. Finally one cried out, and tore at his armor. "I burn! The cursed witches burn me!" His pain aggravated the discomfort of the others; there was a growing sound throughout the keep.

Lord Ballant's oldest son, his mind penetrated by Hein Huss himself, struck his shield with his mailed fist. "They burn me! They burn us all! Better to fight than burn!"

"Fight! Fight!" came the voices of the tormented men.

Lord Ballant looked around at the twisted faces, some displaying blisters, scaldmarks. "Our own spell terrifies them; wait yet a moment!" he pleaded.

His brother called hoarsely, "It is not your belly that Hein Huss toasts in the flames, it is mine! We cannot win a battle of hoodoos; we must win a battle of arms!"

Lord Ballant cried desperately, "Wait, our own effects are working! They will flee in terror; wait, wait!"

His cousin tore off his corselet. "It's Hein Huss! I feel him! My leg's in the fire, the devil laughs at me. Next my head, he says. Fight, or I go forth to fight alone!"

"Very well," said Lord Ballant in a fateful voice. "We go forth to fight. First—the beast goes forth. Then we follow and smite them in their terror."

The gates to the keep swung suddenly wide. Out sprang what appeared to be the depicted monster; legs moving, arms waving, eyes rolling, issuing evil sounds. Normally the Faide warriors would have seen the monster for what it was; a model carried on the backs of three horses. But their minds had been influenced: they had been infected with horror; they drew back with arms hanging flaccid. From behind the monster the Ballant knights galloped, followed by the Ballant foot soldiers. The charge gathered momentum, tore into the Faide center. Lord Faide bellowed orders; discipline asserted itself. The Faide knights disengaged, divided into three platoons, and engulfed the Ballant charge, while the foot soldiers poured darts into the advancing ranks.

There was the clatter and surge of battle; Lord Ballant, seeing that his sally had failed to overwhelm the Faide forces, and thinking to conserve his own forces, ordered a retreat. In good order the Ballant warriors began to back up toward the keep. The Faide knights held close contact, hoping to win to the courtyard. Close behind came a heavily loaded wagon pushed by armored horses, to be wedged against the gate.

Lord Faide called an order; a reserve platoon of ten knights charged from the side, thrust behind the main body of Ballant horsemen, rode through the foot soldiers, fought into the keep, cut down the gate-tenders.

Lord Ballant bellowed to Anderson Grimes, "They have won inside; quick with your cursed demon! If he can help us, let him do so now!"

"Demon-possession is not a matter of an instant," muttered the jinxman. "I need time."

"You have no time! Ten minutes and we're all dead!"

"I will do my best. Everid, Everid, come swift!"

He hastened into his workroom, donned his demonmask, tossed handful after handful of incense into the brazier. Against one wall stood a great form: black, slit-eyed, noseless. Great white fangs hung from its upper palate; it stood on heavy bent legs, arms reached forward to grasp, Anderson Grimes swallowed a cup of syrup, paced slowly back and forth. A moment passed.

"Grimes!" came Ballant's call from outside. "Grimes!"

A voice spoke. "Enter without fear."

Lord Ballant, carrying his ancestral side arm, entered. He drew back with an involuntary sound. "Grimes!" he whispered.

"Grimes is not here," said the voice. "I am here. Enter."

Lord Ballant came forward stiff-legged. The room was dark except for the feeble glimmer of the brazier. Anderson Grimes crouched in a corner, head bowed under his demonmask. The shadows twisted and pulsed with shapes and faces, forms struggling to become solid. The black image seemed to vibrate with life.

"Bring in your warriors," said the voice. "Bring them in five at a time, bid them look only at the floor until commanded to raise their eyes."

Lord Ballant retreated; there was no sound in the room.

A moment passed; then five limp and exhausted warriors filed into the room, eyes low.

"Look slowly up," said the voice. "Look at the orange fire. Breathe deeply. Then look at me. I am Everid, Demon of Hate. Look at me. Who am I?"

"You are Everid, Demon of Hate," quavered the warriors.

"I stand all around you, in a dozen forms. . . . I come closer. Where am I?"

"You are close."

"Now I am you. We are together."

There was a sudden quiver of motion. The warriors stood straighter, their faces distorted.

"Go forth," said the voice. "Go quietly into the court. In a few minutes we march forth to slay."

The five stalked forth. Five more entered.

Outside the wall the Ballant knights had retreated as far as the gate; within, seven Faide knights still survived, and with their backs to the wall held the Ballant warriors away from the gate mechanism.

In the Faide camp Huss called to Commandore, "Everid is walking. Bring forth Keyril."

"Send the men," came Comandore's voice, low and harsh. "Send the men to me. I am Keyril."

Within the keep twenty warriors came marching into the courtyard. Their steps were cautious, tentative, slow. Their faces had lost individuality, they were twisted and distorted, curiously alike.

"Bewitched!" whispered the Ballant soldiers, drawing back. The seven Faide knights watched with sudden fright. But the twenty warriors, paying them no heed, marched out the gate. The Ballant knights parted; for an instant there was a lull in the fighting. The twenty sprang like tigers. Their swords glistened, twinkling in water-bright arcs. They crouched, jerked, jumped; Faide arms, legs, heads were hewed off. The twenty were cut and battered, but the blows seemed to have no effect.

The Faide attack faltered, collapsed. The knights, whose armor was no protection against the demoniac swords, retreated. The twenty possessed warriors raced out into the open toward the foot soldiers, running with great strides, slashing and rending. The Faide foot soldiers fought for a moment, then they too gave way and turned to flee.

From behind Comandore's tent appeared thirty Faide warriors, marching stiffly, slowly. Like the Ballant twenty their faces were alike—but between the Everid-possessed and the Keyril-possessed was the difference between the face of Everid and the face of Keyril.

Keyril and Everid fought, using the men as weapons, without fear, retreat, or mercy. Hack, chop, cut. Arms, legs, sundered torsos. Bodies fought headless for moments before collapsing. Only when a body was minced, hacked to bits, did the demoniac vitality depart. Presently there were no more men of Everid, and only fifteen men of Keyril. These hopped and limped and tumbled toward the keep where Faide knights still held the gate. The Ballant knights met them in despair, knowing that now was the decisive moment. Leaping, leering from chopped faces, slashing from tireless arms, the warriors cut a hole into the iron. The Faide knights, roaring victory cries, plunged after. Into the courtyard surged the battle, and now there was no longer doubt of the outcome. Ballant Keep was taken.

Back in his tent Isak Comandore took a deep breath, shuddered, flung down his demonmask. In the courtyard the twelve remaining warriors dropped in their tracks, twitched, gasped, gushed blood and died.

Lord Ballant, in the last gallant act of a gallant life, marched forth brandishing his ancestral side arm. He aimed across the bloody field at Lord Faide, pulled the trigger. The weapon spewed a brief gout of light; Lord Faide's skin prickled and hair rose from his head. The weapon crackled, turned cherry-red, and melted. Lord Ballant threw down the weapon, drew his sword, marched forth to challenge Lord Faide.

Lord Faide, disinclined to unnecessary combat, signaled to his soldiers. A flight of darts ended Lord Ballant's life, saving him the discomfort of formal execution.

There was no further resistance. The Ballant defenders threw down their arms and marched grimly out to kneel before Lord Faide, while inside the keep the Ballant women gave themselves to mourning and grief.

V

Lord Faide had no wish to linger at Ballant Keep, for he took no relish in his victories. Inevitably, a thousand decisions had to be made. Six of the closest Ballant kinsmen were summarily stabbed and the title declared defunct. Others of the clan were offered a choice: an oath of lifelong fealty together with a moderate ransom, or death. Eyes blazing hate, two chose death and were stabbed.

Lord Faide had now achieved his ambition. For over a thousand years the keep-lords had struggled for power; now one, now another gaining ascendancy. None before had ever extended his authority across the entire continent—which meant control of the planet, since all other land was either sun parched rock or eternal ice. Ballant Keep had long thwarted Lord Faide's drive to power; now—success, total and absolute. It still remained to chastise the lords of Castle Cloud and Gisborne, both of whom, seeing opportunity to overwhelm Lord Faide, had ranged themselves behind Lord Ballant. But these were matters that might well be assigned to Hein Huss.

Lord Faide, for the first time in his life, felt a trace of uncertainty. Now what? No real adversaries remained. The First Folk must be whipped back, but here was no great problem: they were numerous, but no more than savages. He knew that dissatisfaction and controversy would ultimately arise among his kinsmen and allies. Inaction and boredom would breed irritability; idle minds would calculate the pros and cons of mischief. Even the most loyal would remember the campaigns with nostalgia and long for the excitement, the release, the license, of warfare. Somehow he must find means to absorb the energy of so many active and keyed-up men. How and where, this was the problem. The construction of roads? New farmland claimed from the downs? Yearly tournaments-at-arms? Lord Faide frowned at the inadequacy of his solutions, but his imagination was impoverished by the lack of tradition. The original settlers of Pangborn had been warriors, and had brought with them a certain amount of practical rule-of-thumb knowledge, but little else. The tales they passed down the generations described the great spaceships which moved with magic speed and certainty, the miraculous weapons, the wars in the void, but told nothing of human history or civilized achievement. And so Lord Faide, full of power and success, but with no goal toward which to turn his strength, felt more morose and saturnine than ever.

He gloomily inspected the spoils from Ballant Keep. They were of no great interest to him. Ballant's ancestral car was no longer used, but displayed behind a glass case. He inspected the weapon Volcano, but this could not be moved. In any event it was useless, its magic lost forever. Lord Faide now knew that Lord Ballant had ordered it turned against the Faide car, but that it had refused to spew its vaunted fire. Lord Faide saw with disdainful amusement that Volcano had been sadly neglected. Corrosion had pitted the metal, careless cleaning had twisted the exterior tubing, undoubtedly diminishing the potency of the magic. No such neglect at Faide Keep! Jambart the weapon-tender cherished Hellmouth with absolute devotion. Elsewhere were other ancient devices, interesting but useless—the same sort of curios that cluttered shelves and cases at Faide Keep. (Peculiar, these ancient men! thought Lord Faide: at once so clever, yet so primitive and impractical. Conditions had changed: there had been enormous advances since the dark ages sixteen hundred years ago. For instance, the ancients had used intricate fetishes of metal and glass to communicate with each other. Lord Faide need merely voice his needs; Hein Huss could project his mind a hundred miles to see, to hear, to relay Lord Faide's words.) The ancients had contrived dozens of such objects, but the old magic had worn away and they never seemed to function. Lord Ballant's side arm had melted, after merely stinging Lord Faide. Imagine a troop armed thus trying to cope with a platoon of demon-possessed warriors! Slaughter of the innocents!

Among the Ballant trove Lord Faide noted a dozen old books and several reels of microfilm. The books were worthless, page after page of incomprehensible jargon; the microfilm was equally undecipherable. Again Lord Faide wondered skeptically about the ancients. Clever of course, but to look at the hard facts, they were little more advanced than the First Folk: neither had facility with telepathy or voyance or demon-command. And the magic of the ancients: might there not be a great deal of exaggeration in the legends? Volcano, for instance. A joke. Lord Faide wondered about his own Hellmouth. But no—surely Hellmouth was more trustworthy; Jambart cleaned and polished the weapon daily and washed the entire cupola with vintage wine every month. If human care could induce faithfulness, then Hellmouth was ready to defend Faide Keep!

Now there was no longer need for defense. Faide was supreme. Considering the future, Lord Faide made a decision. There should no longer be keep-lords on Pangborn; he would abolish the appellation. Habitancy of the keeps would gradually be transferred to trusted bailiffs on a yearly basis. The former lords would be moved to comfortable but indefensible manor houses, with the maintenance of private troops forbidden. Naturally they must be allowed jinxmen, but these would be made accountable to himself—perhaps through some sort of licensing provision. He must discuss the matter with Hein Huss. A matter for the future, however. Now he merely wished to settle affairs and return to Faide Keep.

There was little more to be done. The surviving Ballant kinsmen he sent to their homes after Huss had impregnated fresh dolls with their essences. Should they default on their ransoms, a twinge of fire, a few stomach cramps would more than set them right. Ballant Keep itself Lord Faide would have liked to burn—but the material of the ancients was proof to fire. But in order to discourage any new pretenders to the Ballant heritage Lord Faide ordered all the heirlooms and relics brought forth into the courtyard, and then, one at a time, in order of rank, he bade his men choose. Thus the Ballant wealth was distributed. Even the jinxmen were invited to choose, but they despised the ancient trinkets as works of witless superstition. The lesser spell-binders and apprentices rummaged through the leavings, occasionally finding an overlooked bauble or some anomalous implement. Isak Comandore was irritated to find Sam Salazar staggering under a load of the ancient books. "And what is your purpose with these?" he barked. "Why do you burden yourself with rubbish?"

Sam Salazar hung his head. "I have no definite purpose. Undoubtedly there was wisdom—or at least knowledge—among the ancients: perhaps I can use these symbols of knowledge to sharpen my own understanding."

Comandore threw up his hands in disgust. He turned to Hein Huss who stood nearby. "First he fancies himself a tree and stands in the mud; now he thinks to learn jinxmanship through a study of ancient symbols."

Huss shrugged. "They were men like ourselves, and, though limited, they were not entirely obtuse. A certain simian cleverness is required to fabricate these objects."

"Simian cleverness is no substitute for sound jinxmanship," retorted Isak Comandore. "This is a point hard to overemphasize; I have drummed it into Salazar's head a hundred times. And now, look at him."

Huss grunted noncommitally. "I fail to understand what he hopes to achieve."

Sam Salazar tried to explain, fumbling for words to express an idea that did not exist. "I thought perhaps to decipher the writing, if only to understand what the ancients thought, and perhaps to learn how to perform one or two of their tricks."

Comandore rolled up his eyes. "What enemy bewitched me when I consented to take you as apprentice? I can cast twenty hoodoos in an hour, more than any of the ancients could achieve in a lifetime."

"Nevertheless," said Sam Salazar, "I notice that Lord Faide rides in his ancestral car, and that Lord Ballant sought to kill us all with Volcano."

"I notice," said Comandore with feral softness, "that my demon Keyril conquered Lord Ballant's Volcano, and that riding on my wagon I can outdistance Lord Faide in his car."

Sam Salazar thought better of arguing further. "True, Jinxman Comandore, very true. I stand corrected."

"Then discard that rubbish and make yourself useful. We return to Faide Keep in the morning."

"As you wish, Jinxman Comandore." Sam Salazar threw the books back into the trash.

VI

The Ballant clan had been dispersed, Ballant Keep was despoiled. Lord Faide and his men banqueted somberly in the great hall, tended by silent Ballant servitors.

Ballant Keep had been built on the same splendid scale as Faide Keep. The great hall was a hundred feet long, fifty feet wide, fifty feet high, paneled in planks sawn from pale native hardwood, rubbed and waxed to a rich honey color. Enormous black beams supported the ceiling; from these hung candelabra, intricate contrivances of green, purple, and blue glass, knotted with ancient but still bright light-motes. On the far wall hung portraits of all the lords of Ballant Keep—105 grave faces in a variety of costumes. Below, a genealogical chart ten feet high detailed the descent of the Ballants and their connections with the other noble clans. Now there was a desolate air to the hall, and the 105 dead faces were meaningless and empty.

Lord Faide dined without joy, and cast dour side glances at those of his kinsmen who revelled too gladly. Lord Ballant, he thought, had conducted himself only as he himself might have done under the same circumstances; coarse exultation seemed in poor taste, almost as if it were disrespect for Lord Faide himself. His followers were quick to catch his mood, and the banquet proceeded with greater decorum.

The jinxmen sat apart in a smaller room to the side. Anderson Grimes, erstwhile Ballant Head Jinxman, sat beside Hein Huss, trying to put a good face on his defeat. After all, he had performed creditably against four powerful adversaries, and there was no cause to feel a diminution of *mana*. The five jinxmen discussed the battle, while the cabalmen and spell-binders listened respectfully. The conduct of the demon-possessed troops occasioned the most discussion. Anderson Grimes readily admitted that his conception of Everid was a force absolutely brutal and blunt, terrifying in its indomitable vigor. The other jinxmen agreed that he undoubtedly succeeded in projecting these qualities; Hein Huss however pointed out that Isak Comandore's Keyril, as cruel and vigorous as Everid, also combined a measure of crafty malice, which tended to make the possessed soldier a more effective weapon.

Anderson Grimes allowed that this might well be the case, and that in fact he had been considering such an augmentation of Everid's characteristics.

"To my mind," said Huss, "the most effective demon should be swift enough to avoid the strokes of the brute demons, such as Keyril and Everid. I cite my own Dant as example. A Dant-possessed warrior can easily destroy a Keyril or an Everid, simply through his agility. In an encounter of this sort the Keyrils and Everids presently lose their capacity to terrify, and thus half the effect is lost."

Isak Comandore pierced Huss with a hot russet glance. "You state a presumption as if it were fact. I have formulated Keyril with sufficient craft to counter any such displays of speed. I firmly believe Keyril to be the most fearsome of all demons."

"It may well be," rumbled Hein Huss thoughtfully. He beckoned to a steward, gave instructions. The steward reduced the light a trifle. "Behold," said Hein Huss. "There is Dant. He comes to join the banquet." At the side of the room loomed the tiger-striped

Dant, a creature constructed of resilient metal, with four terrible arms, and a squat black head which seemed all gaping jaw.

"Look," came the husky voice of Isak Comandore. "There is Keyril." Keyril was rather more humanoid and armed with a cutlass. Dant spied Keyril. The jaws gaped wider, it sprang to the attack.

The battle was a thing of horror; the two demons rolled, twisted, bit, frothed, uttered soundless shrieks, tore each other apart. Suddenly Dant sprang away, circled Keyril with dizzying speed, faster, faster; became a blur, a wild coruscation of colors that seemed to give off a high-pitched wailing sound, rising higher and higher in pitch. Keyril hacked brutally with his cutlass, then seemed to grow feeble and wan. The light that once had been Dant blazed white, exploded in a mental shriek; Keyril was gone and Isak Comandore lay moaning.

Hein Huss drew a deep breath, wiped his face, looked about him with a complacent grin. The entire company sat rigid as stones, staring, all except the apprentice Sam Salazar, who met Hein Huss's glance with a cheerful smile.

"So," growled Huss, panting from his exertion, "you consider yourself superior to the illusion; you sit and smirk at one of Hein Huss's best efforts."

"No, no," cried Sam Salazar, "I mean no disrespect! I want to learn, so I watched you rather than the demons. What could they teach me? Nothing!"

"Ah," said Huss, mollified. "And what did you learn?"

"Likewise, nothing," said Sam Salazar, "but at least I do not sit like a fish."

Comandore's voice came soft but crackling with wrath. "You see in me the resemblance to a fish?"

"I except you, Jinxman Comandore, naturally," Sam Salazar explained.

"Please go to my cabinet, Apprentice Salazar, and fetch me the doll that is your likeness. The steward will bring a basin of water, and we shall have some sport. With your knowledge of fish you perhaps can breathe under water. If not—you may suffocate."

"I prefer not, Jinxman Comandore," said Sam Salazar. "In fact, with your permission, I now resign your service."

Comandore motioned to one of his cabalmen. "Fetch me the Salazar doll. Since he is no longer my apprentice, it is likely indeed that he will suffocate."

"Come now, Comandore," said Hein Huss gruffly. "Do not torment the lad. He is innocent and a trifle addled. Let this be an occasion of placidity and ease."

"Certainly, Hein Huss," said Comandore. "Why not? There is ample time in which to discipline this upstart."

"Jinxman Huss," said Sam Salazar, "since I am now relieved of my duties to Jinxman Comandore, perhaps you will accept me into your service."

Hein Huss made a noise of vast distaste. "You are not my responsibility."

"There are many futures, Hein Huss," said Sam Salazar. "You have said as much yourself."

Hein Huss looked at Sam Salazar with his water-clear eyes. "Yes, there are many futures. And I think that tonight sees the full amplitude of jinxmanship. . . . I think that never again will such power and skill gather at the same table. We shall die one by one and there shall be none to fill our shoes. . . . Yes, Sam Salazar. I will take you as apprentice. Isak Comandore, do you hear? This youth is now of my company."

"I must be compensated," growled Comandore.

"You have coveted my doll of Tharon Faide, the only one in existence. It is yours."

"Ah, ha!" cried Isak Comandore leaping to his feet. "Hein Huss, I salute you! You are generous indeed! I thank you and accept!"

Hein Huss motioned to Sam Salazar. "Move your effects to my wagon. Do not show your face again tonight."

Sam Salazar bowed with dignity and departed the hall.

The banquet continued, but now something of melancholy filled the room. Presently a messenger from Lord Faide came to warn all to bed, for the party returned to Faide Keep at dawn.

VII

The victorious Faide troops gathered on the heath before Ballant Keep. As a parting gesture Lord Faide ordered the great gate torn off the hinges, so that ingress could never again be denied him. But even after sixteen hundred years the hinges were proof to all the force the horses could muster, and the gates remained in place.

Lord Faide accepted the fact with good grace and bade farewell to his cousin Renfroy, whom he had appointed bailiff. He climbed into his car, settled himself, snapped the switch. The car groaned and moved forward. Behind came the knights and the foot soldiers, then the baggage train, laden with booty, and finally the wagons of the jinxmen.

Three hours the column marched across the mossy downs. Ballant Keep dwindled behind; ahead appeared North and South Wildwood, darkening all the sweep of the western horizon. Where once the break had existed, the First Folk's new planting showed a smudge lower and less intense than the old woodlands.

Two miles from the woodlands Lord Faide called a halt and signaled up his knights. Hein Huss laboriously dismounted from his wagon, came forward.

"In the event of resistance," Lord Faide told the knights, "do not be tempted into the forest. Stay with the column and at all times be on your guard against traps."

Hein Huss spoke. "You wish me to parley with the First Folk once more?"

"No," said Lord Faide. "It is ridiculous that I must ask permission of savages to ride over my own land. We return as we came; if they interfere, so much the worse for them."

"You are rash," said Huss with simple candor.

Lord Faide glanced down at him with black eyebrows raised. "What damage can they do if we avoid their traps? Blow foam at us?"

"It is not my place to advise or to warn," said Hein Huss. "However, I point out that they exhibit a confidence which does not come from conscious weakness; also, that they carried tubes, apparently hollow grasswood shoots, which imply missiles."

Lord Faide nodded. "No doubt. However, the knights wear armor, the soldiers carry bucklers. It is not fit that I, Lord Faide of Faide Keep, choose my path to suit the whims of the First Folk. This must be made clear, even if the exercise involves a dozen or so First Folk corpses."

"Since I am not a fighting man," remarked Hein Huss, "I will keep well to the rear, and pass only when the way is secure."

"As you wish." Lord Faide pulled down the visor of his helmet. "Forward."

The column moved toward the forest, along the previous track, which showed plain across the moss. Lord Faide rode in the lead, flanked by his brother, Gethwin Faide, and his cousin, Mauve Dermont-Faide.

A half-mile passed, and another. The forest was only a mile distant. Overhead the great sun rode at zenith; brightness and heat poured down; the air carried the oily scent of thorn and tarbush. The column moved on, more slowly; the only sounds the clanking of armor, the muffled thud of hooves in the moss, the squeal of wagon wheels.

Lord Faide rose up in his car, watching for any sign of hostile preparation. A half-mile from the planting the forms of the First Folk, waiting in the shade along the forest's verge, became visible. Lord Faide ignored them, held a steady pace along the track they had traveled before.

The half-mile became a quarter-mile. Lord Faide turned to order the troops into single file and was just in time to see a hole suddenly open into the moss and his brother, Gethwin Faide, drop from sight. There was a rattle, a thud, the howling of the impaled horse; Gethwin's wild calls as the horse kicked and crushed him into the stakes. Mauve Dermont-Faide, riding beside Gethwin, could not control his own horse, which leaped aside from the pit and blundered upon a trigger. Up from the moss burst a tree trunk studded with foot-long thorns. It snapped, quick as a scorpion's tail; the thorns punctured Mauve Dermont-Faide's armor, his chest, and whisked him from his horse to carry him suspended, writhing and screaming. The tip of the scythe pounded into Lord Faide's car, splintered against the hull. The car swung groaning through the air. Lord Faide clutched at the windscreen to prevent himself from falling.

The column halted; several men ran to the pit, but Gethwin Faide lay twenty feet below, crushed under his horse. Others took Mauve Dermont-Faide down from the swaying scythe, but he, too, was dead.

Lord Faide's skin tingled with a gooseflesh of hate and rage. He looked toward the forest. The First Folk stood motionless. He beckoned to Bernard, sergeant of the foot soldiers. "Two men with lances to try out the ground ahead. All others ready with darts. At my signal spit the devils."

Two men came forward, and marching before Lord Faide's car, probed at the ground. Lord Faide settled in his seat. "Forward."

The column moved slowly toward the forest, every man tense and ready. The lances of the two men in the vanguard presently broke through the moss, to disclose a nettle trap—a pit lined with nettles, each frond ripe with globes of acid. Carefully they probed out a path to the side, and the column filed around, each man walking in the other's tracks.

At Lord Faide's side now rode his two nephews, Scolford and Edwin. "Notice," said Lord Faide in a voice harsh and tight. "These traps were laid since our last passage; an act of malice."

"But why did they guide us through before?"

Lord Faide smiled bitterly. "They were willing that we should die at Ballant Keep. But we have disappointed them."

"Notice, they carry tubes," said Scolford.

"Blowguns possibly," suggested Edwin.

Scolford disagreed. "They cannot blow through their foam-vents."

"No doubt we shall soon learn," said Lord Faide. He rose in his seat, called to the rear. "Ready with the darts!"

The soldiers raised their crossbows. The column advanced slowly, now only a hundred yards from the planting. The white shapes of the First Folk moved uneasily at the forest's edges. Several of them raised their tubes, seemed to sight along the length. They twitched their great hands.

One of the tubes was pointed toward Lord Faide. He saw a small black object leave the opening, flit forward, gathering speed. He heard a hum, waxing to a rasping, clicking flutter. He ducked behind the windscreen; the projectile swooped in pursuit, struck the windscreen like a thrown stone. It fell crippled upon the forward deck of the car—a heavy black insect like a wasp, its broken proboscis oozing ocher liquid, horny wings beating feebly, eyes like dumbbells fixed on Lord Faide. With his mailed fist, he crushed the creature.

Behind him other wasps struck knights and men; Corex Faide-Battaro took the prong through his visor into the eye, but the armor of the other knights defeated the wasps. The foot soldiers, however, lacked protection; the wasps half buried themselves in flesh. The soldiers called out in pain, clawed away the wasps, squeezed the wounds. Corex Faide-Battaro toppled from his horse, ran blindly out over the heath, and after fifty feet fell into a trap. The stricken soldiers began to twitch, then fell on the moss, thrashed, leaped up to run with flapping arms, threw themselves in wild somersaults, foaming and thrashing.

In the forest, the First Folk raised their tubes again. Lord Faide bellowed, "Spit the creatures! Bowmen, launch your darts!"

There came the twang of crossbows, darts snapped at the quiet white shapes. A few staggered and wandered aimlessly away; most, however, plucked out the darts or ignored them. They took capsules from small sacks, put them to the end of their tubes.

"Beware the wasps!" cried Lord Faide. "Strike with your bucklers! Kill the cursed things in flight!"

The rasp of horny wings came again; certain of the soldiers found courage enough to follow Lord Faide's orders, and battered down the wasps. Others struck home as before; behind came another flight. The column became a tangle of struggling, crouching men.

"Footmen, retreat!" called Lord Faide furiously. "Footmen back! Knights to me!"

The soldiers fled back along the track, taking refuge behind the baggage wagons. Thirty of their number lay dying, or dead, on the moss.

Lord Faide cried out to his knights in a voice like a bugle. "Dismount, follow slow after me! Turn your helmets, keep the wasps from your eyes! One step at a time, behind the car! Edwin, into the car beside me, test the footing with your lance. Once in the forest there are no traps! Then attack!"

The knights formed themselves into a line behind the car. Lord Faide drove slowly forward, his kinsman Edwin prodding the ground ahead. The First Folk sent out a dozen more wasps, which dashed themselves vainly against the armor. Then there was silence . . . cessation of sound, activity. The First Folk watched impassively as the knights approached, step by step.

Edwin's lance found a trap, the column moved to the side. Another trap—and the column was diverted from the planting toward the forest. Step by step, yard by yard—another trap, another detour, and now the column was only a hundred feet from the forest. A trap to the left, a trap to the right: the safe path led directly toward an enormous heavy-branched tree. Seventy feet, fifty feet, then Lord Faide drew his sword.

"Prepare to charge, kill till your arms tire!"

From the forest came a crackling sound. The branches of the great tree trembled and swayed. The knights stared, for a moment frozen into place. The tree toppled forward, the knights madly tried to flee—to the rear, to the sides. Traps opened; the knights dropped upon sharp stakes. The tree fell; boughs cracked armored bodies like nuts; there was the hoarse yelling of pinned men, screams from the traps, the crackling subsidence of breaking branches. Lord Faide had been battered down into the car, and the car had been pressed groaning into the moss. His first instinctive act was to press the switch to rest position; then he staggered erect, clambered up through the boughs. A pale unhuman face peered at him; he swung his fist, crushed the faceted eyebulge, and roaring with rage scrambled through the branches. Others of his knights were working themselves free, although almost a third were either crushed or impaled.

The First Folk came scrambling forward, armed with enormous thorns, long as swords. But now Lord Faide could reach them at close quarters. Hissing with vindictive joy he sprang into their midst, swinging his sword with both hands, as if demon-possessed. The surviving knights joined him and the ground became littered with dismembered First Folk. They drew back slowly, without excitement. Lord Faide reluctantly called back his knights. "We must succor those still pinned, as many as still are alive."

As well as possible branches were cut away, injured knights drawn forth. In some cases the soft moss had cushioned the impact of the tree. Six knights were dead, another four crushed beyond hope of recovery. To these Lord Faide himself gave the *coup de grace*. Ten minutes further hacking and chopping freed Lord Faide's car, while the First Folk watched incuriously from the forest. The knights wished to charge once more, but Lord Faide ordered retreat. Without interference they returned the way they had come, back to the baggage train.

Lord Faide ordered a muster. Of the original war party, less than two-thirds remained. Lord Faide shook his head bitterly. Galling to think how easily he had been led into a trap! He swung on his heel, strode to the rear of the column, to the wagons of the magicians. The jinxmen sat around a small fire, drinking tea. "Which of you will hoodoo these white forest vermin? I want them dead— stricken with sickness, cramps, blindness, the most painful afflictions you can contrive!"

There was general silence. The jinxmen sipped their tea.

"Well?" demanded Lord Faide. "Have you no answer? Do I not make myself plain?"

Hein Huss cleared his throat, spat into the blaze. "Your wishes are plain. Unfortunately we cannot hoodoo the First Folk."

"And why?"

"There are technical reasons."

Lord Faide knew the futility of argument. "Must we slink home around the forest? If you cannot hoodoo the First Folk, then bring out your demons! I will march on the forest and chop out a path with my sword!"

"It is not for me to suggest tactics," grumbled Hein Huss.

"Go on, speak! I will listen."

"A suggestion has been put to me, which I will pass to you. Neither I nor the other jinxmen associate ourselves with it, since it recommends the crudest of physical principles."

"I await the suggestion," said Lord Faide.

"It is merely this. One of my apprentices tampered with your car, as you may remember."

"Yes, and I will see he gets the hiding he deserves."

"By some freak he caused the car to rise high into the air. The suggestion is this: that we load the car with as much oil as the baggage train affords, that we send the car aloft and let it drift over the planting. At a suitable moment, the occupant of the car will pour the oil over the trees, then hurl down a torch. The forest will burn. The First Folk will be at least discomfited; at best a large number will be destroyed."

Lord Faide slapped his hands together. "Excellent! Quickly, to work!" He called a dozen soldiers, gave them orders; four kegs of cooking oil, three buckets of pitch, six demijohns of spirit were brought and lifted into the car. The engines grated and protested, and the car sagged almost to the moss.

Lord Faide shook his head sadly. "A rude use of the relic, but all in good purpose. Now, where is that apprentice? He must indicate which switches and which buttons he turned."

"I suggest," said Hein Huss, "that Sam Salazar be sent up with the car."

Lord Faide looked sidewise at Sam Salazar's round, bland countenance. "An efficient hand is needed, a seasoned judgment. I wonder if he can be trusted?"

"I would think so," said Hein Huss, "inasmuch as it was Sam Salazar who evolved the scheme in the first place."

"Very well. In with you, Apprentice! Treat my car with reverence! The wind blows away from us; fire this edge of the forest, in as long a strip as you can manage. The torch, where is the torch?"

The torch was brought and secured to the side of the car.

"One more matter," said Sam Salazar. "I would like to borrow the armor of some obliging knight, to protect myself from the wasps. Otherwise—"

"Armor!" bawled Lord Faide. "Bring armor!"

At last, fully accoutered and with visor down, Sam Salazar climbed into the car. He seated himself, peered intently at the buttons and switches. In truth he was not precisely certain as to which he had manipulated before. . . . He considered, reached forward, pushed, turned. The motors roared and screamed; the car shuddered, sluggishly rose into the air. Higher, higher, twenty feet, forty feet, sixty feet—a hundred, two hundred. The wind eased the car toward the forest; in the shade the First Folk watched. Several of them raised tubes, opened the shutters. The onlookers saw wasps dart through the air to dash against Sam Salazar's armor.

The car drifted over the trees; Sam Salazar began ladling out the oil. Below, the First Folk stirred uneasily. The wind carried the car too far over the forest; Sam Salazar worked the controls, succeeded in guiding himself back. One keg was empty, and another; he tossed them out, presently emptied the remaining two, and the buckets of pitch. He soaked a rag in spirit, ignited it, threw it over the side, poured the spirit after.

The flaming rag fell into leaves. A crackle; fire blazed and sprang. The car now floated at a height of five hundred feet. Salazar poured over the remaining spirits, dropped the demijohns,

guided the car back over the heath, and fumbling nervously with
the controls dropped the car in a series of swoops back to the moss.

Lord Faide sprang forward, clapped him on the shoulder. "Excellently done! The forest blazes like tinder!"

The men of Faide Keep stood back, rejoicing to see the flames
soar and lick. The First Folk scurried back from the heat, waving
their arms; foam of a peculiar purple color issued from their vents
as they ran, small useless puffs discharged as if by accident or
through excitement. The flames ate through first the forest, then
spread into the new planting, leaping through the leaves.

"Prepare to march!" called Lord Faide. "We pass directly behind
the flames, before the First Folk return."

Off in the forest the First Folk perched in the trees, blowing out
foam in great puffs and billows, building a wall of insulation. The
flames had eaten half across the new planting, leaving behind smol-
dering saplings.

"Forward! Briskly!"

The column moved ahead. Coughing in the smoke, eyes smarting,
they passed under still blazing trees and came out on the western
downs.

Slowly the column moved forward, led by a pair of soldiers prodding the moss with lances. Behind followed Lord Faide with the
knights, then came the foot soldiers, then the rumbling baggage
train, and finally the six wagons of the jinxmen.

A thump, a creak, a snap. A scythe had broken up from the moss;
the soldiers in the lead dropped flat; the scythe whipped past, a
foot from Lord Faide's face. At the same time a plaintive cry came
from the rear guard. "They pursue! The First Folk come!"

Lord Faide turned to inspect the new threat. A clot of First Folk,
two hundred or more, came across the moss, moving without haste
or urgency. Some carried wasp tubes, others thorn-rapiers.

Lord Faide looked ahead. Another hundred yards should bring
the army out upon safe ground; then he could deploy and maneuver. "Forward!"

The column proceeded, the baggage train and the jinxmen's
wagons pressing close up against the soldiers. Behind and to one
side came the First Folk, moving casually and easily.

At last Lord Faide judged they had reached secure ground. "Forward, now! Bring the wagons out, hurry now!"

The troops needed no urging; they trotted out over the heath,
the wagons trundling after. Lord Faide ordered the wagons into a
close double line, stationed the soldiers between, with the horses

behind them protected from the wasps. The knights, now dismounted, waited in front.

The First Folk came listlessly, formlessly forward. Blank white faces stared; huge hands grasped tubes and thorns; traces of the purplish foam showed at the lips of their underarm orifices.

Lord Faide walked along the line of knights. "Swords ready. Allow them as close as they care to come. Then a quick charge." He motioned to the foot soldiers. "Choose a target. . . !" A volley of darts whistled overhead, to plunge into white bodies. With chisel-bladed fingers the First Folk plucked them out, discarded them with no evidence of vexation. One or two staggered, wandered confusedly across the line of approach. Others raised their tubes, withdrew the shutter. Out flew the insects, horny wings rasping, prongs thrust forward. Across the moss they flickered, to crush themselves against the armor of the knights, to drop to the ground, to be stamped upon. The soldiers cranked their crossbows back into tension, discharged another flight of darts, caused several more First Folk casualties.

The First Folk spread into a long line, surrounding the Faide troops. Lord Faide shifted half his knights to the other side of the wagons.

The First Folk wandered closer. Lord Faide called for a charge. The knights stepped smartly forward, swords swinging. The First Folk advanced a few more steps, then stopped short. The flaps of skin at their backs swelled, pulsed; white foam gushed through their vents; clouds and billows rose up around them. The knights halted uncertainly, prodding and slashing into the foam but finding nothing. The foam piled higher, rolling in and forward, pushing the knights back toward the wagons. They looked questioningly toward Lord Faide.

Lord Faide waved his sword. "Cut through to the other side! Forward!" Slashing two-handed with his sword, he sprang into the foam. He struck something solid, hacked blindly at it, pushed forward. Then his legs were seized; he was upended and fell with a spine-rattling jar. Now he felt the grate of a thorn searching his armor. It found a crevice under his corselet and pierced him. Cursing he raised on his hands and knees, and plunged blindly forward. Enormous hard hands grasped him, heavy forms fell on his shoulders. He tried to breathe, but the foam clogged his visor; he began to smother. Staggering to his feet he half ran, half fell out into the open air, carrying two of the First Folk with him. He had lost his sword, but managed to draw his dagger. The First Folk released him and stepped back into the foam. Lord Faide sprang to his feet.

Inside the foam came the sounds of combat; some of his knights burst into the open; others called for help. Lord Faide motioned to the knights. "Back within; the devils slaughter our kinsmen! In and on to the center!"

He took a deep breath. Seizing his dagger he thrust himself back into the foam. A flurry of shapes came at him: he pounded with his fists, cut with his dagger, stumbled over a mass of living tissue. He kicked the softness, and stepped on metal. Bending, he grasped a leg but found it limp and dead. First Folk were on his back, another thorn found its mark; he groaned and thrust himself forward, and once again fell out into the open air.

A scant fifty of his knights had won back into the central clearing. Lord Faide cried out, "To the center; mount your horses!" Abandoning his car, he himself vaulted into a saddle. The foam boiled and billowed closer. Lord Faide waved his arm. "Forward, all; at a gallop! After us the wagons—out into the open!"

They charged, thrusting the frightened horses into the foam. There was white blindness, the feel of forms underneath, then the open air once again. Behind came the wagons, and the foot soldiers, running along the channel cut by the wagons. All won free—all but the knights who had fallen under the foam.

Two hundred yards from the great white clot of foam, Lord Faide halted, turned, looked back. He raised his fist, shook it in a passion. "My knights, my car, my honor! I'll burn your forests, I'll drive you into the sea, there'll be no peace till all are dead!" He swung around. "Come," he called bitterly to the remnants of his war party. "We have been defeated. We retreat to Faide Keep."

VIII

Faide Keep, like Ballant Keep, was constructed of a black, glossy substance, half metal, half stone, impervious to heat, force, and radiation. A parasol roof, designed to ward off hostile energy, rested on five squat outer towers, connected by walls almost as high as the lip of the overhanging roof.

The homecoming banquet was quiet and morose. The soldiers and knights ate lightly and drank much, but instead of becoming merry, lapsed into gloom. Lord Faide, overcome by emotion, jumped to his feet. "Everyone sits silent, aching with rage. I feel no differently. We shall take revenge. We shall put the forests to the torch. The cursed white savages will smother and burn. Drink now with good cheer; not a moment will be wasted. But we must be ready. It is no more than idiocy to attack as before. Tonight I take council with the jinxmen, and we will start a program of affliction."

The soldiers and knights rose to their feet, raised their cups and drank a somber toast. Lord Faide bowed and left the hall.

He went to his private trophy room. On the walls hung escutcheons, memorials, deathmasks, clusters of swords like many-petaled flowers; a rack of side arms, energy pistols, electric stilettos; a portrait of the original Faide, in ancient spacefarer's uniform, and a treasured, almost unique, photograph of the great ship that had brought the first Faide to Pangborn.

Lord Faide studied the ancient face for several moments, then summoned a servant. "Ask the Head Jinxman to attend me."

Hein Huss presently stumped into the room. Lord Faide turned away from the portrait, seated himself, motioned to Hein Huss to do likewise. "What of the keep-lords?" he asked. "How do they regard the setback at the hands of the First Folk?"

"There are various reactions," said Hein Huss. "At Boghoten, Candelwade, and Havve there is distress and anger."

Lord Faide nodded. "These are my kinsmen."

"At Gisborne, Graymar, Castle Cloud, and Alder there is satisfaction, veiled calculation."

"To be expected," muttered Lord Faide. "These lords must be humbled; in spite of oaths and undertakings, they still think rebellion."

"At Star Home, Julian-Douray, and Oak Hall I read surprise at the abilities of the First Folk, but in the main disinterest."

Lord Faide nodded sourly. "Well enough. There is no actual rebellion in prospect; we are free to concentrate on the First Folk. I will tell you what is in my mind. You report that new plantings are in progress between Wildwood, Old Forest, Sarrow Copse, and elsewhere—possibly with the intent of surrounding Faide Keep." He looked inquiringly at Hein Huss, but no comment was forthcoming. Lord Faide continued. "Possibly we have underestimated the cunning of the savages. They seem capable of forming plans and acting with almost human persistence. Or, I should say, more than human persistence, for it appears that after sixteen hundred years they still consider us invaders and hope to exterminate us."

"That is my own conclusion," said Hein Huss.

"We must take steps to strike first. I consider this a matter for the jinxmen. We gain no honor dodging wasps, falling into traps, or groping through foam. It is a needless waste of lives. Therefore, I want you to assemble your jinxmen, cabalmen, and spell-binders; I want you to formulate your most potent hoodoos—"

"Impossible!"

Lord Faide's black eyebrows rose high. " 'Impossible'?"

Hein Huss seemed vaguely uncomfortable. "I read the wonder in your mind. You suspect me of disinterest, irresponsibility. Not true. If the First Folk defeat you, we suffer likewise."

"Exactly," said Lord Faide drily, "You will starve."

"Nevertheless, the jinxmen cannot help you." He hoisted himself to his feet, started for the door.

"Sit," said Lord Faide. "It is necessary to pursue this matter."

Hein Huss looked around with his bland, water-clear eyes. Lord Faide met his gaze. Hein Huss sighed deeply. "I see I must ignore the precepts of my trade, break the habits of a lifetime. I must explain." He took his bulk to the wall, fingered the side arms in the rack, studied the portrait of the ancestral Faide. "These miracle workers of the old times—unfortunately we cannot use their magic! Notice the bulk of the spaceship! As heavy as Faide Keep." He turned his gaze on the table, teleported a candelabra two or three inches. "With considerably less effort they gave that spaceship enormous velocity, using ideas and forces they knew to be imaginary and irrational. We have advanced since then, of course. We no longer employ mysteries, arcane constructions, wild nonhuman forces. We are rational and practical—but we cannot achieve the effects of the ancient magicians."

Lord Faide watched Hein Huss with saturnine eyes. Hein Huss gave his deep rumbling laugh. "You think that I wish to distract you with talk? No, this is not the case. I am preparing to enlighten you." He returned to his seat, lowered his bulk with a groan. "Now I must talk at length, to which I am not accustomed. But you must be given to understand what we jinxmen can do and what we cannot do.

"First, unlike the ancient magicians, we are practical men. Naturally there is difference in our abilities. The best jinxman combines great telepathic facility, implacable personal force, and intimate knowledge of his fellow humans. He knows their acts, motives, desires, and fears; he understands the symbols that most vigorously represent these qualities. Jinxmanship in the main is drudgery—dangerous, difficult, and unromantic—with no mystery except that which we employ to confuse our enemies." Hein Huss glanced at Lord Faide to encounter the same saturnine gaze. "Ha! I still have told you nothing; I still have spent many words talking around my inability to confound the First Folk. Patience."

"Speak on," said Lord Faide.

"Listen then. What happens when I hoodoo a man? First I must enter into his mind telepathically. There are three operational levels: the conscious, the unconscious, the cellular. The most effective jinxing is done if all three levels are influenced. I feel into my victim, I learn as much as possible, supplementing my previous knowledge of him, which is part of my stock in trade. I take up his doll, which carries his traces. The doll is highly useful but not indispensable. It serves as a focus for my attention; it acts as a pattern, or a guide, as I fix upon the mind of the victim, and he is bound by his own telepathic capacity to the doll which bears his traces.

"So! Now! Man and doll are identified in my mind, and at one or more levels in the victim's mind. Whatever happens to the doll the victim feels to be happening to himself. There is no more to simple hoodooing than that, from the standpoint of the jinxmen. But naturally the victims differ greatly. Susceptibility is the key idea here. Some men are more susceptible than others. Fear and conviction breed susceptibility. As a jinxman succeeds he becomes ever more feared, and consequently the more efficacious he becomes. The process is self-generative.

"Demon-possession is a similar technique. Susceptibility is again essential; again conviction creates susceptibility. It is easiest and most dramatic when the characteristics of the demon are well known, as in the case of Comandore's Keyril. For this reason, demons can be exchanged or traded among jinxmen. The commodity actually traded is public acceptance and familiarity with the demon."

"Demons then do not actually exist?" inquired Lord Faide half-incredulously.

Hein Huss grinned vastly, showing enormous yellow teeth. "Telepathy works through a superstratum. Who knows what is created in this superstratum? Maybe the demons live on after they have been conceived; maybe they now are real. This of course is speculation, which we jinxmen shun.

"So much for demons, so much for the lesser techniques of jinxmanship. I have explained sufficient to serve as background to the present situation."

"Excellent," said Lord Faide. "Continue."

"The question, then, is: How does one cast a hoodoo into a creature of an alien race?" He looked inquiringly at Lord Faide. "Can you tell me?"

"I?" asked Lord Faide, surprised. "No."

"The method is basically the same as in the hoodooing of men. It is necessary to make the creature believe, in every cell of his being, that he suffers or dies. This is where the problems begin to arise. Does the creature think—that is to say, does he arrange the processes of his life in the same manner as men? This is a very important distinction. Certain creatures of the universe use methods other than the human nerve-node system to control their environments. We call the human system 'intelligence'—a word which properly should be restricted to human activity. Other creatures use different agencies, different systems, arriving sometimes at similar ends. To bring home these generalities, I cannot hope to merge my mind with the corresponding capacity in the First Folk. The key will not fit the lock. At least, not altogether. Once or twice when I watched the First Folk trading with men at Forest Market, I felt occasional weak significances. This implies that the First Folk mentality creates something similar to human telepathic impulses. Nevertheless, there is no real sympathy between the two races.

"This is the first and the least difficulty. If I were able to make complete telepathic contact—what then? The creatures are different from us. They have no words for 'fear,' 'hate,' 'rage,' 'pain,' 'bravery,' 'cowardice.' One may deduce that they do not feel these emotions. Undoubtedly they know other sensations, possibly as meaningful. Whatever these may be, they are unknown to me, and therefore I cannot either form or project symbols for these sensations."

Lord Faide stirred impatiently. "In short, you tell me that you cannot efficiently enter these creatures' minds; and that if you could, you do not know what influences you could plant there to do them harm."

"Succinct," agreed Hein Huss. "Substantially accurate."

Lord Faide rose to his feet. "In that case you must repair these deficiencies. You must learn to telepathize with the First Folk; you must find what influences will harm them. As quickly as possible."

Hein Huss stared reproachfully at Lord Faide. "But I have gone to great lengths to explain the difficulties involved! To hoodoo the First Folk is a monumental task! It would be necessary to enter Wildwood, to live with the First Folk, to become one of them, as my apprentice thought to become a tree. Even then an effective hoodoo is improbable! The First Folk must be susceptible to conviction! Otherwise there would be no bite to the hoodoo! I could guarantee no success. I would predict failure. No other jinxman would dare tell you this, no other would risk his *mana*. I dare because I am Hein Huss, with life behind me."

"Nevertheless we must attempt every weapon at hand," said Lord Faide in a dry voice. "I cannot risk my knights, my kinsmen, my soldiers against these pallid half-creatures. What a waste of good flesh and blood to be stuck by a poison insect! You must go to Wildwood; you must learn how to hoodoo the First Folk."

Hein Huss heaved himself erect. His great round face was stony; his eyes were like bits of water-worn glass. "It is likewise a waste to go on a fool's errand. I am no fool and I will not undertake a hoodoo which is futile from the beginning."

"In that case," said Lord Faide, "I will find someone else." He went to the door, summoned a servant. "Bring Isak Commandore here."

Hein Huss lowered his bulk into the chair. "I will remain during the interview, with your permission."

"As you wish."

Isak Comandore appeared in the doorway, tall, loosely articulated, head hanging forward. He darted a glance of swift appraisal at Lord Faide, at Hein Huss, then stepped into the room.

Lord Faide crisply explained his desires. "Hein Huss refuses to undertake the mission. Therefore I call on you."

Isak Comandore calculated. The pattern of his thinking was clear: he possibly could gain much *mana*; there was small risk of diminution, for had not Hein Huss already dodged away from the project? Comandore nodded. "Hein Huss has made clear the difficulties; only a very clever and very lucky jinxman can hope to succeed. But I accept the challenge. I will go."

"Good," said Hein Huss. "I will go, too." Isak Commandore darted him a sudden hot glance. "I wish only to observe. To Isak Comandore goes the responsibility and whatever credit may ensue."

"Very well," said Comandore presently. "I welcome your company. Tomorrow morning we leave. I go to order our wagon."

Late in the evening Apprentice Sam Salazar came to Hein Huss where he sat brooding in his workroom. "What do you wish?" growled Huss.

"I have a request to make of you, Head Jinxman Huss."

"Head Jinxman in name only," grumbled Hein Huss. "Isak Comandore is about to assume my position."

Sam Salazar blinked, laughed uncertainly. Hein Huss fixed wintry-pale eyes on him. "What do you wish?"

"I have heard that you go on an expedition to Wildwood, to study the First Folk."

"True, true. What then?"

"Surely they will now attack all men?"

"Hein Huss shrugged. "At Forest Market they trade with men. At Forest Market men have always entered the forest. Perhaps there will be change, perhaps not."

"I would go with you, if I may," said Sam Salazar.

"This is no mission for apprentices."

"An apprentice must take every opportunity to learn," said Sam

Salazar. "Also you will need extra hands to set up tents, to load and unload cabinets, to cook, to fetch water, and other such matters."

"Your argument is convincing," said Hein Huss. "We depart at dawn; be on hand."

IX

As the sun lifted over the heath the jinxmen departed Faide Keep. The high-wheeled wagon creaked north over the moss, Hein Huss and Isak Comandore riding the front seat, Sam Salazar with his legs hanging over the tail. The wagon rose and fell with the dips and mounds of the moss, wheels wobbling, and presently passed out of sight behind Skywatcher's Hill.

Five days later, an hour before sunset, the wagon reappeared. As before, Hein Huss and Isak Comandore rode the front seat, with Sam Salazar perched behind. They approached the keep, and without giving so much as a sign or a nod, drove through the gate into the courtyard.

Isak Comandore unfolded his long legs, stepped to the ground like a spider; Hein Huss lowered himself with a grunt. Both went to their quarters, while Sam Salazar led the wagon to the jinxmen's warehouse.

Somewhat later Isak Comandore presented himself to Lord Faide, who had been waiting in his trophy room, forced to a show of indifference through considerations of position, dignity, and protocol. Isak Comandore stood in the doorway, grinning like a fox. Lord Faide eyed him with sour dislike, waiting for Comandore to speak. Hein Huss might have stationed himself an entire day, eyes placidly fixed on Lord Faide, awaiting the first word; Isak Comandore lacked the absolute serenity. He came a step forward. "I have returned from Wildwood."

"With what results?"

"I believe that it is possible to hoodoo the First Folk."

Hein Huss spoke from behind Comandore. "I believe that such an undertaking, if feasible, would be useless, irresponsible, and possibly dangerous." He lumbered forward.

Isak Comandore's eyes glowed hot red-brown; he turned back to Lord Faide. "You ordered me forth on a mission; I will render a report."

"Seat yourselves. I will listen."

Isak Comandore, nominal head of the expedition, spoke. "We rode along the river bank to Forest Market. Here was no sign of disorder or of hostility. A hundred First Folk traded timber, planks, posts, and poles for knife blades, iron wire, and copper pots. When they returned to their barge we followed them aboard, wagon, horses, and all. They showed no surprise—"

"Surprise," said Hein Huss heavily, "is an emotion of which they have no knowledge."

Isak Comandore glared briefly. "We spoke to the bargetenders, explaining that we wished to visit the interior of Wildwood. We asked if the First Folk would try to kill us to prevent us from entering the forest. They professed indifference as to either our well-being or our destruction. This was by no means a guarantee of safe conduct; however, we accepted it as such, and remained aboard the barge." He spoke on with occasional emendations from Hein Huss.

They had proceeded up the river, into the forest, the First Folk poling against the slow current. Presently they put away the poles; nevertheless the barge moved as before. The mystified jinxmen discussed the possibility of teleportation, or symbological force, and wondered if the First Folk had developed jinxing techniques unknown to men. Sam Salazar, however, noticed that four enormous water beetles, each twelve feet long with oil-black carapaces and blunt heads, had risen from the river bed and pushed the barge from behind—apparently without direction or command. The First Folk stood at the bow, turning the nose of the barge this way or that to follow the winding of the river. They ignored the jinxmen and Sam Salazar as if they did not exist.

The beetles swam tirelessly; the barge moved for four hours as fast as a man could walk. Occasionally, First Folk peered from the forest shadows, but none showed interest or concern in the barge's unusual cargo. By midafternoon the river widened, broke into many channels and became a marsh; a few minutes later the barge floated out into the open water of a small lake. Along the shore, behind the first line of trees, appeared a large settlement. The jinxmen were interested and surprised. It had always been assumed that the First Folk wandered at random through the forest, as they had originally lived in the moss of the downs.

The barge grounded; the First Folk walked ashore, the men followed with the horses and wagon. Their immediate impressions were of swarming numbers, of slow but incessant activity, and they were attacked by an overpoweringly evil smell.

Ignoring the stench, the men brought the wagon in from the shore, paused to take stock of what they saw. The settlement appeared to be a center of many diverse activities. The trees had been stripped of lower branches, and supported blocks of hardened foam three hundred feet long, fifty feet high, twenty feet thick, with a space of a man's height intervening between the underside of the foam and the ground. There were a dozen of these blocks, apparently of cellular construction. Certain of the cells had broken open and seethed with small white fishlike creatures—the First Folk young.

Below the blocks masses of First Folk engaged in various occupations, in the main unfamiliar to the jinxmen. Leaving the wagon in the care of Sam Salazar, Hein Huss and Isak Comandore moved forward among the First Folk, repelled by the stench and the pressure of alien flesh, but drawn by curiosity. They were neither heeded nor halted; they wandered everywhere about the settlement. One area seemed to be an enormous zoo, divided into a number of sections. The purpose of one of these sections—a kind of range two hundred feet long—was all too clear. At one end a human corpse hung on a rope—a Faide casualty from the battle at the new planting. Certain of the wasps flew straight at the corpse; just before contact they were netted and removed. Others flew up and away or veered toward the First Folk who stood along the side of the range. These latter also were netted and killed at once.

The purpose of the business was clear enough. Examining some of the other activity in this new light, the jinxmen were able to interpret much that had hitherto puzzled them.

They saw beetles tall as dogs with heavy saw-toothed pincers attacking objects resembling horses; pens of insects even larger, long, narrow, segmented, with dozens of heavy legs and nightmare heads. All these creatures—wasps, beetles, centipedes—in smaller and less formidable form were indigenous to the forest; it was plain that the First Folk had been practicing selective breeding for many years, perhaps centuries.

Not all the activity was warlike. Moths were trained to gather nuts, worms to gnaw straight holes through timber; in another section caterpillars chewed a yellow mash, molded it into identical spheres. Much of the evil odor emanated from the zoo; the jinxmen departed without reluctance, and returned to the wagon. Sam Salazar pitched the tent and built a fire, while Hein Huss and Isak Comandore discussed the settlement.

Night came; the blocks of foam glowed with imprisoned light; the activity underneath proceeded without cessation. The jinxmen retired to the tent and slept, while Sam Salazar stood guard.

The following day Hein Huss was able to engage one of the First Folk in conversation; it was the first attention of any sort given to them.

The conversation was long; Hein Huss reported only the gist

of it to Lord Faide. (Isak Comandore turned away, ostentatiously disassociating himself from the matter.)

Hein Huss first of all had inquired as to the purpose of the sinister preparations: the wasps, beetles, centipedes, and the like.

"We intend to kill men," the creature had reported ingenuously. "We intend to return to the moss. This has been our purpose ever since men appeared on the planet."

Huss had stated that such an ambition was shortsighted, that there was ample room for both men and First Folk on Pangborn. "The First Folk," said Hein Huss, "should remove their traps and cease their efforts to surround the keeps with forest."

"No," came the response. "men are intruders. They mar the beautiful moss. All will be killed."

Isak Comandore returned to the conversation. "I noticed here a significant fact. All the First Folk within sight had ceased their work; all looked toward us, as if they, too, participated in the discussion. I reached the highly important conclusion that the First Folk are not complete individuals but components of a larger unity, joined to a greater or less extent by a telepathic phase not unlike our own."

Hein Huss continued placidly, "I remarked that if we were attacked, many of the First Folk would perish. The creature showed no concern, and in fact implied much of what Jinxman Comandore had already induced: 'There are always more in the cells to replace the elements which die. But if the community becomes sick, all suffer. We have been forced into the forests, into a strange existence. We must arm ourselves and drive away the men, and to this end we have developed the methods of men to our own purposes!' "

Isak Comandore spoke. "Needless to say, the creature referred to the ancient men, not ourselves."

"In any event," said Lord Faide, "they leave no doubt as to their intentions. We should be fools not to attack them at once, with every weapon at our disposal."

Hein Huss continued imperturbably. "The creature went on at some length. 'We have learned the value of irrationality.' 'Irrationality' of course was not his word or even his meaning. He said something like 'a series of vaguely motivated trials'—as close as I can translate. He said, 'We have learned to change our environment. We use insects and trees and plants and waterslugs. It is an enormous effort for us who would prefer a placid life in the moss. But you men have forced this life on us, and now you must suffer the consequences.' I pointed out once more that men were not helpless, that many First Folk would die. The creature seemed unworried. 'The community persists.' I asked a delicate question, 'If your purpose is to kill men, why do you allow us here?' He said,

'The entire community of men will be destroyed.' Apparently they believe the human society to be similar to their own, and therefore regard the killing of three wayfaring individuals as pointless effort."

Lord Faide laughed grimly. "To destroy us they must first win past Hellmouth, then penetrate Faide Keep. This they are unable to do."

Isak Comandore resumed his report. "At this time I was already convinced that the problem was one of hoodooing not an individual but an entire race. In theory this should be no more difficult than hoodooing one. It requires no more effort to speak to twenty than to one. With this end in view I ordered the apprentice to collect substances associated with the creatures. Skinflakes, foam, droppings, all other exudations obtainable. While he did so, I tried to put myself in rapport with the creatures. It is difficult, for their telepathy works across a different stratum from ours. Nevertheless, to a certain extent I have succeeded."

"Then you can hoodoo the First Folk?" asked Lord Faide.

"I vouchsafe nothing until I try. Certain preparations must be made."

"Go then; make your preparations."

Comandore rose to his feet and with a sly side glance for Hein Huss left the room. Huss waited, pinching his chin with heavy fingers. Lord Faide looked at him coldly. "You have something to add?"

Huss grunted, hoisted himself to his feet. "I wish that I did. But my thoughts are confused. Of the many futures, all seem troubled and angry. Perhaps our best is not good enough."

Lord Faide looked at Hein Huss with surprise; the massive Head Jinxman had never before spoken in terms so pessimistic and melancholy. "Speak then; I will listen."

Hein Huss said gruffly, "If I knew any certainties I would speak gladly. But I am merely beset by doubts. I fear that we can no longer depend on logic and careful jinxmanship. Our ancestors were miracle workers, magicians. They drove the First Folk into the forest. To put us to flight in our turn the First Folk have adopted the ancient methods: random trial and purposeless empiricism. I am dubious. Perhaps we must turn our backs on sanity and likewise return to the mysticism of our ancestors."

Lord Faide shrugged. "If Isak Comandore can hoodoo the First Folk, such a retreat may be unnecessary."

"The world changes," said Hein Huss. "Of so much I feel sure: the old days of craft and careful knowledge are gone. The future is for men of cleverness, and imagination untroubled by discipline;

the unorthodox Sam Salazar may become more effective than I. The world changes."

Lord Faide smiled his sour dyspeptic smile. "When that day comes I will appoint Sam Salazar Head Jinxman and also name him Lord Faide, and you and I will retire together to a hut on the downs."

Hein Huss made a heavy fateful gesture and departed.

X

Two days later Lord Faide, coming upon Isak Comandore, inquired as to his progress. Comandore took refuge in generalities. After another two days Lord Faide inquired again and this time insisted on particulars. Comandore grudgingly led the way to his workroom, where a dozen cabalmen, spell-binders, and apprentices worked around a large table, building a model of the First Folk settlement in Wildwood.

"Along the lakeshore," said Comandore, "I will range a great number of dolls, daubed with First Folk essences. When this is complete I will work up a hoodoo and blight the creatures."

"Good. Perform well." Lord Faide departed the workroom, mounted to the topmost pinnacle of the keep, to the cupola where the ancestral weapon Hellmouth was housed. "Jambart! Where are you?"

Weapon-tender Jambart, short, blue-jowled, red-nosed and big-bellied, appeared. "My lord?"

"I come to inspect Hellmouth. It is prepared for instant use?"

"Prepared, my lord, and ready. Oiled, greased, polished, scraped, burnished, tended—every part smooth as an egg."

Lord Faide made a scowling examination of Hellmouth—a heavy cylinder six feet in diameter, twelve feet long, studded with half-domes interconnected with tubes of polished copper. Jambart undoubtedly had been diligent. No trace of dirt or rust or corrosion showed; all was gleaming metal. The snout was covered with a heavy plate of metal and tarred canvas; the ring upon which the weapon swiveled was well greased.

Lord Faide surveyed the four horizons. To the south was fertile Faide Valley; to the west open downs; to north and east the menacing loom of Wildwood.

He turned back to Hellmouth and pretended to find a smear of grease. Jambart boiled with expostulations and protestations; Lord Faide uttered a grim warning, enjoining less laxity, then descended to the workroom of Hein Huss. He found the Head Jinxman reclining on a couch, staring at the ceiling. At a bench stood Sam Salazar surrounded by bottles, flasks, and dishes.

Lord Faide stared balefully at the confusion. "What are you doing?" he asked the apprentice.

Sam Salazar looked up guiltily. "Nothing in particular, my lord."

"If you are idle, go then and assist Isak Comandore."

"I am not idle, Lord Faide."

"Then what do you do?"

Sam Salazar gazed sulkily at the bench. "I don't know."

"Then you are idle!"

"No, I am occupied. I pour various liquids on this foam. It is First Folk foam. I wonder what will happen. Water does not dissolve it, nor spirits. Heat chars and slowly burns it, emitting a foul smoke."

Lord Faide turned away with a sneer. "You amuse yourself as a child might. Go to Isak Comandore; he can find use for you. How do you expect to become a jinxman, dabbling and prattling like a baby among pretty rocks?"

Hein Huss gave a deep sound: a mingling of sigh, snort, grunt, and clearing of the throat. "He does no harm, and Isak Comandore has hands enough. Salazar will never become a jinxman; that has been clear a long time."

Lord Faide shrugged. "He is your apprentice, and your responsibility. Well, then. What news from the keeps?"

Hein Huss, groaning and wheezing, swung his legs over the edge of the couch. "The lords share your concern, to greater or lesser extent. Your close allies will readily place troops at your disposal; the others likewise if pressure is brought to bear."

Lord Faide nodded in dour satisfaction. "For the moment there is no urgency. The First Folk hold to their forests. Faide Keep of course is impregnable, although they might ravage the valley. . . ." He paused thoughtfully. "Let Isak Comandore cast his hoodoo. Then we will see."

From the direction of the bench came a hiss, a small explosion, a whiff of acrid gas. Sam Salazar turned guiltily to look at them, his eyebrows singed. Lord Faide gave a snort of disgust and strode from the room.

"What did you do?" Hein Huss inquired in a colorless voice.

"I don't know."

Now Hein Huss likewise snorted in disgust. "Ridiculous. If you wish to work miracles, you must remember your procedures. Miracle working is not jinxmanship, with established rules and guides.

In matters so complex it is well that you take notes, so that the miracles may be repeated."

Sam Salazar nodded in agreement and turned back to the bench.

XI

Late during the day, news of new First Folk truculence reached Faide Keep. On Honeymoss Hill, not far west of Forest Market, a camp of shepherds had been visited by a wandering group of First Folk, who began to kill the sheep with thorn-swords. When the shepherds protested they, too, were attacked, and many were killed. The remainder of the sheep were massacred.

The following day came other news: four children swimming in Brastock River at Gilbert Ferry had been seized by enormous water-beetles and cut into pieces. On the other side of Wildwood, in the foothills immediately below Castle Cloud, peasants had cleared several hillsides and planted them to vines. Early in the morning they had discovered a horde of black disklike flukes devouring the vines—leaves, branches, trunks, and roots. They set about killing the flukes with spades and at once were stung to death by wasps.

Adam McAdam reported the incidents to Lord Faide, who went to Isak Comandore in a fury. "How soon before you are prepared?"

"I am prepared now. But I must rest and fortify myself. Tomorrow morning I work the hoodoo."

"The sooner the better! The creatures have left their forest; they are out killing men!"

Isak Comandore pulled his long chin. "That was to be expected; they told us as much."

Lord Faide ignored the remark. "Show me your tableau."

Isak Comandore took him into his workroom. The model was now complete, with the masses of simulated First Folk properly daubed and sensitized, each tied with a small wad of foam. Isak Comandore pointed to a pot of dark liquid. "I will explain the basis of the hoodoo. When I visited the camp I watched everywhere for powerful symbols. Undoubtedly there were many at hand, but I could not discern them. However, I remembered a circumstance from the battle at the planting; when the creatures were attacked, threatened with fire and about to die, they spewed foam of dull purple color. Evidently this purple foam is associated with death. My hoodoo will be based upon this symbol."

"Rest well, then, so that you may hoodoo to your best capacity."

The following morning Isak Comandore dressed in long robes

of black, and set a mask of the demon Nard on his head to fortify himself. He entered his workroom, closed the door.

An hour passed, two hours. Lord Faide sat at breakfast with his kin, stubbornly maintaining a pose of cynical unconcern. At last he could contain himself no longer and went out into the courtyard where Comandore's underlings stood fidgeting and uneasy. "Where is Hein Huss?" demanded Lord Faide. "Summon him here."

Hein Huss came stumping out of his quarters. Lord Faide motioned to Comandore's workshop. "What is happening? Is he succeeding?"

Hein Huss looked toward the workshop. "He is casting a powerful hoodoo. I feel confusion, anger—"

"In Comandore, or in the First Folk?"

"I am not in rapport. I think he has conveyed a message to their minds. A very difficult task, as I explained to you. In this preliminary aspect he has succeeded."

" 'Preliminary'? What else remains?"

"The two most important elements of the hoodoo: the susceptibility of the victim and the appropriateness of the symbol."

Lord Faide frowned. "You do not seem optimistic."

"I am uncertain. Isak Comandore may be right in his assumption. If so, and if the First Folk are highly susceptible, today marks a great victory, and Comandore will achieve tremendous *mana!*"

Lord Faide stared at the door to the workshop. "What now?"

Hein Huss's eyes went blank with concentration. "Isak Comandore is near death. He can hoodoo no more today."

Lord Faide turned, waved his arm to the cabalmen. "Enter the workroom! Assist your master!"

The cabalmen raced to the door, flung it open. Presently they emerged supporting the limp form of Isak Comandore, his black robe spattered with purple foam. Lord Faide pressed close. "What did you achieve? Speak!"

Isak Comandore's eyes were half closed, his mouth hung loose and wet. "I spoke to the First Folk, to the whole race. I sent the symbol into their minds—" His head fell limply sidewise.

Lord Faide moved back. "Take him to his quarters. Put him on his couch." He turned away, stood indecisively, chewing at his drooping lower lip. "Still we do not know the measure of his success."

"Ah," said Hein Huss, "but we do!"

Lord Faide jerked around. "What is this? What do you say?"

"I saw into Comandore's mind. He used the symbol of purple foam; with tremendous effort he drove it into their minds. Then he learned that purple foam means not death—purple foam means fear for the safety of the community, purple foam means desperate rage."

"In any event," said Lord Faide after a moment, "there is no harm done. The First Folk can hardly become more hostile."

Three hours later a scout rode furiously into the courtyard, threw himself off his horse, ran to Lord Faide. "The First Folk have left the forest! A tremendous number! Thousands! They are advancing on Faide Keep!"

"Let them advance!" said Lord Faide. "The more the better! Jambart, where are you?"

"Here, sir."

"Prepare Hellmouth! Hold all in readiness!"

"Hellmouth is always ready, sir!"

Lord Faide struck him across the shoulders. "Off with you! Bernard!"

The sergeant of the Faide troops came forward. "Ready, Lord Faide."

"The First Folk attack. Armor your men against wasps, feed them well. We will need all our strength."

Lord Faide turned to Hein Huss. "Send to the keeps, to the manor houses, order our kinsmen to join us, with all their troops and all their armor. Send to Bellgard Hall, to Boghoten, Camber, and Candelwade. Haste, haste, it is only hours from Wildwood."

Huss held up his hand. "I have already done so. The keeps are warned. They know your need."

"And the First Folk—can you feel their minds?"

"No."

Lord Faide walked away. Hein Huss lumbered out the main gate, walked around the keep, casting appraising glances up the black walls of the squat towers, windowless and proof even against the ancient miracle-weapons. High on top the great parasol roof Jambart the weapon-tender worked in the cupola, polishing that which already glistened, greasing surfaces already heavy with grease.

Hein Huss returned within. Lord Faide approached him, mouth hard, eyes bright. "What have you seen?"

"Only the keep, the walls, the towers, the roof, and Hellmouth."

"And what do you think?"

"I think many things."

"You are noncommittal; you know more than you say. It is best that you speak, because if Faide Keep falls to the savages you die with the rest of us."

Hein Huss's water-clear eyes met the brilliant black gaze of Lord Faide. "I know only what you know. The First Folk attack. They have proved they are not stupid. They intend to kill us. They are not jinxmen; they cannot afflict us or force us out. They cannot break in the walls. To burrow under, they must dig through solid rock. What are their plans? I do not know. Will they succeed? Again, I do not know. But the day of the jinxman and his orderly array of knowledge is past. I think that we must grope for miracles, blindly and foolishly, like Salazar pouring liquids on foam."

A troop of armored horsemen rode in through the gates: warriors from nearby Bellgard Hall. And as the hours passed contingents from other keeps came to Faide Keep, until the courtyard was dense with troops and horses.

Two hours before sunset the First Folk were sighted across the downs. They seemed a very large company, moving in an undisciplined clot with a number of stragglers, forerunners and wanderers out on the flanks.

The hotbloods from outside keeps came clamoring to Lord Faide, urging a charge to cut down the First Folk; they found no seconding voices among the veterans of the battle at the planting. Lord Faide, however, was pleased to see the dense mass of First Folk. "Let them approach only a mile more—and Hellmouth will take them! Jambart!"

"At your call, Lord Faide."

"Come, Hellmouth speaks!" He strode away with Jambart after. Up to the cupola they climbed.

"Roll forth Hellmouth, direct it against the savages!"

Jambart leaped to the glistening array of wheels and levers. He hesitated in perplexity, then tentatively twisted a wheel. Hellmouth responded by twisting slowly around on its radial track, to the groan and chatter of long-frozen bearings. Lord Faide's brows lowered into a menacing line. "I hear evidence of neglect."

"Neglect, my lord never! Find one spot of rust, a shadow of grime, you may have me whipped!"

"What is that sound?"

"That is internal and invisible—none of my responsibility."

Lord Faide said nothing. Hellmouth now pointed toward the great pale tide from Wildwood. Jambart twisted a second wheel and Hellmouth thrust forth its heavy snout. Lord Faide, in a voice harsh with anger, cried, "The cover, fool!"

"An oversight, my lord, easily repaired." Jambart crawled out along the top of Hellmouth, clinging to the protuberances for dear life, with below only the long smooth sweep of roof. With considerable difficulty he tore the covering loose, then grunting and cursing, inched himself back, jerking with his knees, rearing his buttocks.

The First Folk had slowed their pace a trifle, the main body only a half-mile distant.

"Now," said Lord Faide in high excitement, "before they disperse, we exterminate them!" He sighted through a telescopic tube, squinting through the dimness of internal films and incrustations, signaled to Jambart for the final adjustments. "Now! Fire!"

Jambart pulled the firing lever. Within the great metal barrel came a sputter of clicking sounds. Hellmouth whined, roared. Its snout glowed red, orange, white, and out poured a sudden gout of blazing purple radiation—which almost instantly died. Hellmouth's barrel quivered with heat, fumed, seethed, hissed. From within came a faint pop. Then there was silence.

A hundred yards in front of the First Folk a patch of moss burnt black where the bolt had struck. The aiming device was inaccurate. Hellmouth's bolt had killed perhaps twenty of the First Folk vanguard.

Lord Faide made feverish signals. "Quick! Raise the barrel. Now! Fire again!"

Jambart pulled the firing arm, to no avail. He tried again, with the same lack of success. "Hellmouth evidently is tired."

"Hellmouth is dead," cried Lord Faide. "You have failed me. Hellmouth is extinct."

"No, no," protested Jambart. "Hellmouth rests! I nurse it as my own child! It is polished like glass! Whenever a section wears off or breaks loose, I neatly remove the fracture, and every trace of cracked glass."

Lord Faide threw up his arms, shouted in vast, inarticulate grief, ran below. "Huss! Hein Huss!"

Hein Huss presented himself. "What is your will?"

"Hellmouth has given up its fire. Conjure me more fire for Hellmouth, and quickly!"

"Impossible."

"Impossible!" cried Lord Faide. "That is all I hear from you! Impossible, useless, impractical! You have lost your ability. I will consult Isak Comandore."

"Isak Comandore can put no more fire into Hellmouth than can I."

"What sophistry is this? He puts demons into men, surely he can put fire into Hellmouth!"

"Come, Lord Faide, you are overwrought. You know the difference between jinxmanship and miracle working."

Lord Faide motioned to a servant. "Bring Isak Comandore here to me!"

Isak Comandore, face haggard, skin waxy, limped into the courtyard. Lord Faide waved preemptorily. "I need your skill. You must restore fire to Hellmouth."

Comandore darted a quick glance at Hein Huss, who stood solid and cold. Comandore decided against dramatic promises that could not be fulfilled. "I cannot do this, my lord."

"What! You tell me this, too?"

"Remark the difference, Lord Faide, between man and metal. A man's normal state is something near madness; he is at all times balanced on a knife-edge between hysteria and apathy. His senses tell him far less of the world than he thinks they do. It is a simple trick to deceive a man, to possess him with a demon, to drive him out of his mind, to kill him. But metal is insensible; metal reacts only as its shape and condition dictates, or by the working of miracles."

"Then you must work miracles!"

"Impossible."

Lord Faide drew a deep breath, collected himself. He walked swiftly across the court. "My armor, my horse. We attack."

The column formed, Lord Faide at the head. He led the knights through the portals, with armored footmen behind.

"Beware the foam!" called Lord Faide. "Attack, strike, cut, draw back. Keep your visors drawn against the wasps! Each man must kill a hundred! Attack!"

The troop rode forth against the horde of First Folk, knights in the lead. The hooves of the horses pounded softly over the thick moss; in the west the large pale sun hung close to the horizon.

Two hundred yards from the First Folk the knights touched the club-headed horses into a lope. They raised their swords, and shouting, plunged forward, each man seeking to be first. The clotted mass of First Folk separated: black beetles darted forth and after them long segmented centipede creatures. They dashed among the horses, mandibles clicking, snouts slashing. Horses screamed, reared, fell over backwards; beetles cut open armored knights as a dog cracks a bone. Lord Faide's horse threw him and ran away; he picked himself up, hacked at a nearby beetle, lopped off its front leg. It darted forward, he lopped off the leg opposite; the heavy head dipped, tore up the moss. Lord Faide cut off the remaining legs, and it lay helpless.

"Retreat," he bellowed. "Retreat!"

The knights moved back, slashing and hacking at beetles and centipedes, killing or disabling all which attacked.

"Form into a double line, knights and men. Advance slowly, supporting each other!"

The men advanced. The First Folk dispersed to meet them, armed with their thorn-swords and carrying pouches. Ten yards from the men they reached into the pouches, brought forth dark balls which they threw at the men. The balls broke and spattered on the armor.

"Charge!" bawled Lord Faide. The men sprang forward into the mass of First Folk, cutting, slashing, killing. "Kill!" called Lord Faide in exultation. "Leave not one alive!"

A pang struck him, a sting inside his armor, followed by another and another. Small things crawled inside the metal, stinging, biting, crawling. He looked about: on all sides were harrassed expressions, faces working in anguish. Sword arms fell limp as hands beat on the metal, futilely trying to scratch, rub. Two men suddenly began to tear off their armor.

"Retreat," cried Lord Faide. "Back to the keep!"

The retreat was a rout, the soldiers shedding articles of armor as they ran. After them came a flight of wasps—a dozen or more, and half as many men cried out as the poison prongs struck into their backs.

Inside the keep stormed the disorganized company, casting aside the last of their armor, slapping their skin, scratching, rubbing, crushing the ferocious red mites that infested them.

"Close the gates," roared Lord Faide.

The gates slid shut. Faide Keep was besieged.

XII

During the night the First Folk surrounded the keep, forming a ring fifty yards from the walls. All night there was motion, ghostly shapes coming and going in the starlight.

Lord Faide watched from a parapet until midnight, with Hein Huss at his side. Repeatedly, he asked, "What of the other keeps? Do they send further reinforcements?" to which Hein Huss each time gave the same reply: "There is confusion and doubt. The keep-lords are anxious to help but do not care to throw themselves away. At this moment they consider and take stock of the situation."

Lord Faide at last left the parapet, signaling Hein Huss to follow. He went to his trophy room, threw himself into a chair, motioned Hein Huss to be seated. For a moment he fixed the jinxman with a cool, calculating stare. Hein Huss bore the appraisal without discomfort.

"You are Head Jinxman," said Lord Faide finally. "For twenty years you have worked spells, cast hoodoos, performed auguries—more effectively than any other jinxman of Pangborn. But now I find you inept and listless. Why is this?"

"I am neither inept nor listless. I am unable to achieve beyond my abilities. I do not know how to work miracles. For this you must consult my apprentice Sam Salazar, who does not know either, but who earnestly tries every possibility and many impossibilities."

"You believe in this nonsense yourself! Before my very eyes you become a mystic!"

Hein Huss shrugged. "There are limitations to my knowledge. Miracles occur—that we know. The relics of our ancestors lie everywhere. Their methods were supernatural, repellent to our own mental processes—but think! Using these same methods the First Folk threaten to destroy us. In the place of metal they use living flesh—but the result is similar. The men of Pangborn, if they assemble and accept casualties, can drive the First Folk back to Wildwood—but for how long? A year? Ten years? The First Folk plant new trees, dig more traps—and presently come forth again, with more terrible weapons: flying beetles, large as a horse; wasps strong enough to pierce armor, lizards to scale the walls of Faide Keep."

Lord Faide pulled at his chin. "And the jinxmen are helpless?"

"You saw for yourself. Isak Comandore intruded enough into their consciousness to anger them, no more."

"So then—what must we do?"

Hein Huss held out his hands. "I do not know. I am Hein Huss, jinxman. I watch Sam Salazar with fascination. He learns nothing, but he is either too stupid or too intelligent to be discouraged. If this is the way to work miracles, he will work them."

Lord Faide rose to his feet. "I am deathly tired. I cannot think, I must sleep. Tomorrow we will know more."

Hein Huss left the trophy room, returned to the parapet. The ring of First Folk seemed closer to the walls, almost within dart-range. Behind them and across the moors stretched a long pale column of marching First Folk. A little back from the keep a pile of white material began to grow, larger and larger as the night proceeded.

Hours passed, the sky lightened; the sun rose in the east. The First Folk tramped the downs like ants, bringing long bars of hardened foam down from the north, dropping them into piles around the keep, returning into the north once more.

Lord Faide came up on the parapet, haggard and unshaven. "What is this? What do they do?"

Bernard the sergeant responded. "They puzzle us all, my lord."

"Hein Huss! What of the other keeps?"

"They have armed and mounted; they approach cautiously."

"Can you communicate our urgency?"

"I can, and I have done so. I have only accentuated their caution."

"Bah!" cried Lord Faide in disgust. "Warriors they call themselves! Loyal and faithful allies!"

"They know of your bitter experience," said Hein Huss. "They ask themselves, reasonably enough, what they can accomplish which you who are already here cannot do first."

Lord Faide laughed sourly. "I have no answer for them. In the meantime we must protect ourselves against the wasps. Armor is useless; they drive us mad with mites. . . . Bernard!"

"Yes, Lord Faide."

"Have each of your men construct a frame two-feet square, fixed with a short handle. To these frames should be sewed a net of heavy mesh. When these frames are built we will sally forth, two soldiers to guard one half-armored knight on foot."

"In the meantime," said Hein Huss, "the First Folk proceed with their plans."

Lord Faide turned to watch. The First Folk came close up under the walls carrying rods of hardened foam. "Bernard! Put your archers to work! Aim for the heads!"

Along the walls bowmen cocked their weapons. Darts spun down into the First Folk. A few were affected, turned and staggered away; others plucked away the bolts without concern. Another flight of bolts, a few more First Folk were disabled. The others planted the rods in the moss, exuded foam in great gushes, their back-flaps vigorously pumping air. Other First Folk brought more rods, pushed them into the foam. Entirely around the keep, close under the walls, extended the mound of foam. The ring of First Folk now came close and all gushed foam; it bulked up swiftly. More rods were brought, thrust into the foam, reinforcing and stiffening the mass.

"More darts!" barked Lord Faide. "Aim for the heads! Bernard—your men, have they prepared the wasp nets?"

"Not yet, Lord Faide. The project requires some little time."

Lord Faide became silent. The foam, now ten feet high, rapidly piled higher. Lord Faide turned to Hein Huss. "What do they hope to achieve?"

Hein Huss shook his head. "For the moment I am uncertain."

The first layer of foam had hardened; on top of this the First Folk spewed another layer, reinforcing again with the rods, criss-crossing, horizontal and vertical. Fifteen minutes later, when the second layer was hard the First Folk emplaced and mounted rude ladders to raise a third layer. Surrounding the keep now was a ring of foam thirty feet high and forty feet thick at the base.

"Look," said Hein Huss. He pointed up. The parasol roof over-hanging the walls ended only thirty feet above the foam. "A few more layers and they will reach the roof."

"So then?" asked Lord Faide. "The roof is as strong as the walls."

"And we will be sealed within."

Lord Faide studied the foam in the light of this new thought. Already the First Folk, climbing laboriously up ladders along the outside face of their wall of foam, were preparing to lay on a fourth layer. First—rods, stiff and dry, then great gushes of white. Only twenty feet remained between roof and foam.

Lord Faide turned to the sergeant. "Prepare the men to sally forth."

"What of the wasp nets, sir?"

"Are they almost finished?"

"Another ten minutes, sir."

"Another ten minutes will see us smothering. We must force a passage through the foam."

Ten minutes passed, and fifteen. The First Folk created ramps behind their wall: first, dozens of the rods, then foam, and on top, to distribute the weight, reed mats.

Bernard the sergeant reported to Lord Faide. "We are ready."

"Good." Lord Faide descended into the courtyard. He faced the men, gave then their orders. "Move quickly, but stay together; we must not lose ourselves in the foam. As we proceed, slash ahead and to the sides. The First Folk see through the foam; they have the advantage of us. When we break through, we use the wasp nets. Two foot soldiers must guard each knight. Remember, quickly through the foam, that we do not smother. Open the gates."

The gates slid back, the troops marched forth. They faced an unbroken blank wall of foam. No enemy could be seen.

Lord Faide waved his sword. "Into the foam." He strode forward, pushed into the white mass, now crisp and brittle and harder than he had bargained for. It resisted him; he cut and hacked. His troops joined him, carving a way into the foam. First Folk appeared above them, crawling carefully on the mats. Their back flaps puffed, pumped; foam issued from their vents, falling in a cascade over the troops.

Hein Huss sighed. He spoke to Apprentice Sam Salazar. "Now they must retreat, otherwise they smother. If they fail to win through, we all smother."

Even as he spoke the foam, piling up swiftly, in places reached the roof. Below, bellowing and cursing, Lord Faide backed out from under, wiped his face clear. Once again, in desperation, he charged forward, trying at a new spot.

The foam was friable and cut easily, but the chunks detached still blocked the opening. And again down tumbled a cascade of foam, covering the soldiers.

Lord Faide retreated, waved his men back into the keep. At the same moment First Folk crawling on mats on the same level as the parapet over the gate laid rods up from the foam to rest against the projecting edge of the roof. They gushed foam; the view of the sky was slowly blocked from the view of Hein Huss and Sam Salazar.

"In an hour, perhaps two, we will die," said Hein Huss. "They have now sealed us in. There are many men here in the keep, and all will now breathe deeply."

Sam Salazar said nervously, "There is a possibility we might be able to survive—or at least not smother."

"Ah?" inquired Hein Huss with heavy sarcasm. "You plan to work a miracle?"

"If a miracle, the most trivial sort. I observed that water has no effect on the foam, nor a number of other liquids: milk, spirits, wine, or caustic. Vinegar, however, instantly dissolves the foam."

"Aha," said Hein Huss. "We must inform Lord Faide."

"Better that you do so," said Sam Salazar. "He will pay me no heed."

XIII

Half an hour passed. Light filtered into Faide Keep only as a dim gray gloom. Air tasted flat, damp, and heavy. Out from the gates sallied the troops. Each carried a crock, a jug, a skin, or a pan containing strong vinegar.

"Quickly now," called Lord Faide, "but careful! Spare the vinegar, don't throw it wildly. In close formation now—forward."

The soldiers approached the wall, threw ladles of vinegar ahead. The foam crackled, melted.

"Waste no vinegar," shouted Lord Faide, "Forward, quickly now; bring forward the vinegar!"

Minutes later they burst out upon the downs. The First Folk stared at them, blinking.

"Charge," croaked Lord Faide, his throat thick with fumes, "Mind now, wasp nets! Two soldiers to each knight! Charge, double-quick. Kill the white beasts."

The men dashed ahead. Wasp tubes were leveled. "Halt!" yelled Lord Faide. "Wasps!"

The wasps came, wings rasping. Nets rose up; wasps struck with a thud. Down went the nets; hard feet crushed the insects. The beetles and the lizard-centipedes appeared, not so many as of the last evening, for a great number had been killed. They darted forward, and a score of men died, but the insects were soon hacked into chunks of reeking brown flesh. Wasps flew, and some struck home; the agonies of the dying men were unnerving. Presently the wasps likewise decreased in number, and soon there were no more.

The men faced the First Folk, armored only with thorn-swords and their foam, which now came purple with rage.

Lord Faide waved his sword: the men advanced and began to kill the First Folk, by dozens, by hundreds.

Hein Huss came forth and approached Lord Faide. "Call a halt."

"A halt? Why? Now we kill these bestial things."

"Far better not. Neither need kill the other. Now is the time to show great wisdom."

"They have besieged us, caught us in their traps, stung us with their wasps! And you say halt?"

"They nourish a grudge sixteen hundred years old. Best not to add another one."

Lord Faide stared at Hein Huss. "What do you propose?"

"Peace between the two races, peace and cooperation."

"Very well. No more traps, no more plantings, no more breeding of deadly insects."

"Call back your men. I will try."

Lord Faide cried out, "Men, fall back. Disengage."

Reluctantly the troops drew back. Hein Huss approached the huddled mass of purple-foaming First Folk. He waited a moment. They watched him intently. He spoke in their language.

"You have attacked Faide Keep; you have been defeated. You planned well, but we have proved stronger. At this moment we can kill you. Then we can go on to fire the forest, starting a hundred blazes. Some of the fires you can control. Others not. We can destroy Wildwood. Some First Folk may survive, to hide in the thickets and breed new plans to kill men. This we do not want. Lord Faide has agreed to peace, if you likewise agree. This means no more death traps. Men will freely approach and pass through the forests. In your turn you may freely come out on the moss. Neither race shall molest the other. Which do you choose? Extinction—or peace?"

The purple foam no longer dribbled from the vents of the First Folk. "We choose peace."

"There must be no more wasps, beetles. The death traps must be disarmed and never replaced."

"We agree. In our turn we must be allowed freedom of the moss."

"Agreed. Remove your dead and wounded, haul away the foam rods."

Hein Huss returned to Lord Faide. "They have chosen peace."

Lord Faide nodded. "Very well. It is for the best." He called to his men. "Sheathe your weapons. We have won a great victory." He ruefully surveyed Faide Keep, swathed in foam and invisible except for the parasol roof. "A hundred barrels of vinegar will not be enough."

Hein Huss looked off into the sky. "Your allies approach quickly. Their jinxmen have told them of your victory."

Lord Faide laughed his sour laugh. "To my allies will fall the task of removing the foam from Faide Keep."

XIV

In the hall of Faide Keep, during the victory banquet, Lord Faide called jovially across to Hein Huss. "Now, Head Jinxman, we must deal with your apprentice, the idler and the waster Sam Salazar."

"He is here, Lord Faide. Rise, Sam Salazar, take cognizance of the honor being done you."

Sam Salazar rose to his feet, bowed.

Lord Faide proffered him a cup. "Drink, Sam Salazar, enjoy yourself. I freely admit that your idiotic tinkerings saved the lives of us all. Sam Salazar, we salute you, and thank you. Now, I trust that you will put frivolity aside, apply yourself to your work, and learn honest jinxmanship. When the time comes, I promise that you shall find a lifetime of employment at Faide Keep."

"Thank you," said Sam Salazar modestly. "However, I doubt if I will become a jinxman."

"No? You have other plans?"

Sam Salazar stuttered, grew faintly pink in the face, then straightened himself, and spoke as clearly and distinctly as he could. "I prefer to continue what you call my frivolity. I hope I can persuade others to join me."

"Frivolity is always attractive," said Lord Faide. "No doubt you can find other idlers and wasters, runaway farm boys and the like."

Sam Salazar said staunchly, "This frivolity might become serious. Undoubtedly the ancients were barbarians. They used symbols to control entities they were unable to understand. We are methodical and rational; why can't we systematize and comprehend the ancient miracles?"

"Well, why can't we?" asked Lord Faide. "Does anyone have an answer?"

No one responded, although Isak Comandore hissed between his teeth and shook his head.

"I personally may never be able to work miracles; I suspect it is more complicated than it seems," said Sam Salazar. "However, I hope that you will arrange for a workshop where I and others who might share my views can make a beginning. In this matter I have the encouragement and the support of Head Jinxman Hein Huss."

Lord Faide lifted his goblet. "Very well, Apprentice Sam Salazar. Tonight I can refuse you nothing. You shall have exactly what you wish, and good luck to you. Perhaps you will produce a miracle during my lifetime."

Isak Comandore said huskily to Hein Huss, "This is a sad event! It signalizes intellectual anarchy, the degradation of jinxmanship, the prostitution of logic. Novelty has a way of attracting youth; already I see apprentices and spell-binders whispering in excitement. The jinxmen of the future will be sorry affairs. How will they go about demon-possession? With a cog, a gear, and a push-button. How will they cast a hoodoo? They will find it easier to strike their victim with an axe."

"Times change," said Hein Huss. "There is now the one rule of Faide on Pangborn, and the keeps no longer need to employ us. Perhaps I will join Sam Salazar in his workshop."

"You depict a depressing future," said Isak Comandore with a sniff of disgust.

"There are many futures, some of which are undoubtedly depressing."

Lord Faide raised his glass. "To the best of your many futures, Hein Huss. Who knows? Sam Salazar may conjure a spaceship to lead us back to home planet."

"Who knows?" said Hein Huss. He raised his goblet. "To the best of the futures!"

POUL ANDERSON
The Longest Voyage

One of the best-known writers in science fiction, Poul Anderson made his first sale in 1947, while he was still in college, and over the course of forty-seven years he has published almost a hundred books (in several different fields, as Anderson has written historical novels, fantasies, and mysteries, in addition to SF), sold hundreds of short pieces to every conceivable market, and won seven Hugo Awards, three Nebula Awards, and the Gandalf (Grand Master) Award for life achievement.

Anderson had trained to be a scientist, taking a degree in physics from the University of Minnesota, but the writing life proved to be more seductive, and he never did get around to working in his original field of choice. Instead, the sales mounted steadily, until by the late fifties and early sixties he was one of the most prolific writers in the genre.

In spite of his high output of fiction, he managed somehow to maintain an amazingly high standard of literary quality as well, and by the mid-sixties was also on his way to becoming one of the most honored and respected writers in the genre. At one point during this period (in addition to nonrelated work, and lesser series such as the "Hoka" stories he was writing in collaboration with Gordon R. Dickson), Anderson was running three of the most popular and prestigious series in science fiction *all at the same time:* the "Technic History" series detailing the exploits of the wily trader Nicholas van Rijn (which includes novels such as *The Man Who Counts, Satan's World, Mirkheim, The People of the Wind,* and collections such as *Trader to the Stars, The Trouble Twisters,* and *The Earth Book of Stormgate*); the extremely popular series relating the adventures of interstellar secret agent Dominic Flandry, probably the most successful attempt to cross SF with the spy thriller, next to Jack Vance's

"Demon Princes" novels (the Flandry series includes novels such as *A Circus of Hells*, *The Rebel Worlds*, *The Day of Their Return*, *Flandry of Terra*, *A Knight of Ghosts and Shadows*, *A Stone in Heaven*, and *The Game of Empire*, and collections such as *Agent of the Terran Empire*); and, my own personal favorite, a series that took us along on assignment with the agents of the Time Patrol (including the collections *The Guardians of Time*, *Time Patrolman*, and later, *The Shield of Time* and *The Time Patrol*).

It's hard to convey a sense of how astonishing this was, especially in the somewhat more limited compress of the science fiction world of the day. It's as if you should find out that the most popular and high-selling series on the B. Dalton's best-seller list, Isaac Asimov's *Robot* novels, say, and Orson Scott Card's *Ender* series, and Anne McCaffrey's *Dragonrider* books, were actually all being written by the *same person*.

The effect was staggering—and when you add to it the impact of the best of Anderson's nonseries novels, work such as *Brain Wave*, *Three Hearts and Three Lions*, *The Night Face*, *The Enemy Stars*, and *The High Crusade*, all of which was being published in *addition* to the series books, it becomes clear that Anderson dominated the late fifties and the pre–New Wave sixties in a way that only Robert A. Heinlein, Isaac Asimov, and Arthur C. Clarke could rival. And, like them, he remained an active and dominant figure right through the seventies and eighties as well, and is still turning up on best-seller lists into the decade of the nineties.

The Longest Voyage may be Anderson's single best piece of short fiction, although it would have some stiff competition to overcome for that title. It won him a Hugo Award in 1960, and for its lyricism, compassion, subtlety, thoughtfulness, and, above all, the relish it takes in the bristling strangeness and *wonder* of the world, it still goes nearly unmatched in the field.

Anderson's other books (among *many* others) include: *The Broken Sword*, *Tau Zero*, *A Midsummer Tempest*, *Orion Shall Rise*, and *The Boat of a Million Years*. His short work has been collected in *The Queen of Air and Darkness and Other Stories*. *Fantasy*, *The Unicorn Trade* (with Karen Anderson), *Past Times*, *The Best of Poul Anderson*, and *Explorations*. His most recent book is a new novel, *Harvest of Stars*. Anderson lives in Orinda, California, with his wife (and fellow writer)

Karen—and their daughter Astrid is married to another prolific science fiction writer, Greg Bear.

When first we heard of the Sky Ship, we were on an island whose name, as nearly as Montalirian tongues can wrap themselves about so barbarous a noise, was Yarzik. That was almost a year after the *Golden Leaper* sailed from Lavre Town, and we judged we had come halfway round the world. So befouled was our poor caravel with weeds and shells that all sail could scarce drag her across the sea. What drinking water remained in the butts was turned green and evil, the biscuit was full of worms, and the first signs of scurvy had appeared on certain crewmen.

"Hazard or no," decreed Captain Rovic, "we must land some-where." A gleam I remembered appeared in his eyes. He stroked his red beard and murmured, "Besides, it's long since we asked for the Aureate Cities. Perhaps this time they'll have intelligence of the place."

Steering by that ogre planet which climbed daily higher as we bore westward, we crossed such an emptiness that mutinous talk broke out afresh. In my heart I could not blame the crew. Imagine, my lords. Day upon day upon day when we saw naught but blue waters, white foam, high clouds in a tropic sky; heard only the wind, *whoosh* of waves, creak of timbers, sometimes at night the huge sucking and rushing as a sea monster breached. These were terrible enough to common sailors, unlettered men who still thought the world must be flat. But then to have Tambur hang forever above the bowsprit, and climb, so we could see we must eventually pass directly beneath the brooding thing . . . and what upbore it? the crew mumbled in the forecastle. Would an angered God not let it fall down on us?

At last a deputation waited on Captain Rovic. Very timid and respectful they were, those rough burly men, as they asked him to turn about. But their comrades massed below, muscled sun-blackened bodies taut in the ragged kilts, daggers and belaying pins ready to hand. We officers on the quarterdeck had swords and pistols, true. But we numbered a mere six, including that frightened boy who was myself, and aged Froad the astrologue, whose robe and white beard were reverend to see but of small use in a fight.

Rovic stood mute for a long while after the spokesman had voiced this demand. The stillness grew, until the empty shriek of wind in our shrouds, the empty glitter of ocean out to the world's rim, became all there was. Most splendid our master looked, for he had donned scarlet hose and bell-tipped shoon when he knew the deputation was coming, as well as helmet and corselet polished to mirror brightness. The plumes blew around that blinding steel head and the diamonds on his fingers flashed against the rubies in his sword hilt. Yet when he spoke, it was not as a knight of the Queen's court, but in the broad Anday of his fisher boyhood.

"So 'tis back ye'd wend, lads? Wi' a fair wind an' a warm sun, liefer ye'd come about an' beat half round the globe? How ye're changed from yere fathers! Ken ye nay the legend, that once everything did as man commanded, an' 'twas an Andayman's lazy fault that now we must work? For see ye, 'twas nay too much that he told his ax to cut down a tree for him, an' told the faggots to walk home, but when he told 'em to carry him, then God was wroth an' took the power away. Though to be sure, as recompense God gave Andaymen sea-luck, dice-luck, an' love-luck. What more d'ye ask for, lads?"

Bewildered at this response, the spokesman wrung his hands, flushed, looked at the deck, and stammered that we'd perish miserably . . . starve, or thirst, or drown, or be crushed under that horrible moon, or sail off the world's edge . . . the *Golden Leaper* had come farther than ship had sailed since the Fall of Man, and if we returned at once, our fame would live forever—

"But can ye eat fame, Etien?" asked Rovic, still mild and smiling. "We've had fights an' storms, aye, an' merry carouses too; but devil an Aureate City we've seen, though well ye ken they lie out here someplace, stuffed wi' treasure for the first bold gang who'll come plunder 'em. What ails yere gutworks, lad? Is't nay an easy cruise? What would the foreigners say? How will yon arrogant cavaliers o' Sathayn, yon grubby chapmen o' Wondland, laugh—nay alone at us, but at all Montalir—did we turn back!"

Thus he jollied them. Only once did he touch his sword, half drawing it, as if absentmindedly, when he recalled how we had weathered the hurricane off Xingu. But they remembered the mutiny that followed then, and how that same sword had pierced three armed sailors who attacked him together. His dialect told them he would let bygones lie forgotten, if they would. His bawdy promises of sport among lascivious heathen tribes yet to be discovered, his recital of treasure legends, his appeal to their pride as seamen and Montalirians, soothed fear. And then in the end, when he saw them malleable, he dropped the provincial speech. He stood forth on the quarterdeck in burning casque and tossing plumes, and the flag of Montalir blew its sea-faded colors above him, and he said as the knights of the Queen say:

"Now you know I do not propose to turn back until the great globe has been rounded and we bring to Her Majesty that gift which is most peculiarly ours to give. The which is not gold or slaves, nor even that lore of far places that she and her most excellent Company of Merchant Adventures desire. No, what we shall lift in our hands to give her, on that day when again we lie by the long docks of Lavre, shall be our achievement: that we did this thing which no men have dared in all the world ere now, and did it to her glory."

A while longer he stood, through a silence full of the sea's noise. Then he said quietly, "Dismissed," turned on his heel and went back into his cabin.

So we continued for some days more, the men subdued but not uncheerful, the officers taking care to hide their doubts. I found myself busied, less with the clerical duties for which I was paid or the study of captaincy for which I was apprenticed—both these amounting to little by now—than with assisting Froad the astrologue. In these balmy airs he could carry on his work even on shipboard. To him it scarce mattered whether we sank or swam; he had lived more than a common span of years already. But the knowledge of the heavens to be gained here, that was something else. At night, standing on the foredeck amidst quadrant, astrolabe, and telescope, drenched in the radiance from above, he resembled some frosty-bearded saint in the windows of Provien Minster.

"See there, Zhean." His thin hand pointed above waves that glowed and rippled with light, past the purple sky and the few stars still daring to show themselves, toward Tambur. Huge it was in full phase at midnight, sprawling over seven degrees of sky, a shield or barry of soft vert and azure, splotched with angry sable that could be seen to move across its face. The firefly moon we had named Siett twinkled near the hazy edge of the giant. Balant, espied rarely and low on the horizon in our part of the world, here stood high: a crescent, but the dark part of its disk tinged by luminous Tambur.

"Observe," declared Froad, "there's no doubt left; one can *see* how the globe rotates on an axis, and how storms boil up in its air. Tambur is no longer the dimmest of frightened legends, nor a dreadful apparition seen to rise as we entered unknown waters; Tambur is real. A world like our own. Immensely bigger, certes, but still a spheroid in space, around which our own world moves, always turning the same hemisphere to her monarch. The conjectures of the ancients are triumphantly confirmed. Not merely that our world is round—*pouf*, that's obvious to anyone—but that we move about a greater center, which in turn has an annual path about the sun. But, then, how big is the sun?"

"Siett and Balant are inner satellites of Tambur," I rehearsed, struggling for comprehension. "Vieng, Darou, and the other moons commonly seen at home have paths outside our own world's. Aye. But what holds it all up?"

"That I don't know. Mayhap the crystal sphere containing the stars exerts an inward pressure. The same pressure, maybe, that hurled mankind down onto the earth, at the time of the Fall From Heaven."

The night was warm, but I shivered, as if those had been winter stars. "Then," I breathed, "there may also be men on . . . Siett, Balant, Vieng . . . even on Tambur?"

"Who knows? We'll need many lifetimes to find out. And what lifetimes they'll be! Thank the good God, Zhean, that you were born in this dawn of the coming age."

Froad returned to making measurements. A dull business, the other officers thought; but by now I had learned enough of the mathematic arts to understand that from these endless tabulations might come the true size of the earth, of Tambur, of sun and moons and stars, the paths they took through space and the direction of Paradise. So the common sailors, who muttered and made signs against evil as they passed our instruments, were closer to fact than Rovic's gentlemen, for indeed Froad practiced a most potent gramarye.

At length we saw weeds floating on the sea, birds, towering cloud masses, the signs of land. Three days later we raised an island. It was an intense green under those calm skies. Surf, still more violent than in our hemisphere, flung against high cliffs, burst in a smother of foam and roared back down again. We coasted carefully, the palomers aloft to seek an approach, the gunners standing by our cannon with lighted matches. For not only were there unknown currents and shoals—familiar hazards—but we had had brushes with canoe-sailing cannibals in the past. Especially did we fear the eclipses. My lords can visualize how in that hemisphere the sun each day must go behind Tambur. In our longitude the occurrence was about midafternoon and lasted nearly ten minutes. An awesome sight: the primary planet—for so Froad now called it, a planet akin to Diell or Coint, with our own world humbled to a mere satellite thereof!—became a black disk bordured red, up in a sky suddenly full of stars. A cold wind blew across the sea, and even the breakers seemed hushed. Yet so impudent is the soul of man that we continued about our duties, stopping only for the briefest prayer as the sun disappeared, thinking more about the chance of shipwreck in the gloom than of God's Majesty.

So bright is Tambur that we continued to work our way around the island at night. From sunup to sunup, twelve mortal hours, we kept the *Golden Leaper* slowly moving. Toward the second noon, Captain Rovic's persistence was rewarded. An opening in the cliffs revealed a long fjord. Swampy shores overgrown with saltwater trees told us that while the tides rose high in that bay, it was not one of those bores dreaded by mariners. The wind being against us, we furled sail and lowered the boats, towing in our caravel by the power of oars. This was a vulnerable moment, especially since we had perceived a village within the fjord. "Should we not stand out, master, and let them come first to us?" I ventured.

Rovic spat over the rail. "I've found it best never to show doubt," said he. "If a canoe fleet should assail us, we'll give 'em a whiff of grapeshot and trust to break their nerve. But I think, thus showing ourselves fearless of them from the very first, we're less likely to meet treacherous ambuscade later."

He proved right.

In the course of time, we learned we had come upon the eastern end of a large archipelago. The inhabitants were mighty seafarers, considering that they had only outrigger dugouts to travel in. These, though, were often a hundred feet long. With forty paddles, or with three bast-sailed masts, such a vessel could almost match our best speed, and was more maneuverable. However, the small cargo space limited their range of travel.

Albeit they lived in houses of wood and thatch, possessing only stone tools, the natives were cultivated folk. They farmed as well as fished; their priests had an alphabet. Tall and vigorous, somewhat darker and less hairy than we, they were impressive to behold, whether nude, as was common, or in full panoply of cloth and feathers and shell ornaments. They had formed a loose empire throughout the archipelago, raided islands lying farther north, and carried on a brisk trade within their own borders. Their whole nation they called the Hisagazi, and the island on which we had chanced was Yarzik.

This we learned slowly, as we mastered somewhat their tongue. For we were several weeks at that town. The duke of the island, Guzan, made us welcome, supplying us food, shelter, and helpers as we required. For our part, we pleased them with glassware, bolts of Wondish cloth, and suchlike trade goods. Nonetheless we encountered many difficulties. The shore above highwater mark being too swampy for beaching a vessel as heavy as ours, we must build a drydock before we could careen. Numerous of us took a flux from some disease, though all recovered in time, and this slowed us further.

"Yet I think our troubles will prove a blessing," Rovic told me one night. As had become his habit, once he learned I was a discreet amanuensis, he confided certain thoughts in me. The captain is ever a lonely man; and Rovic, fisher lad, freebooter, self-taught navigator, victor over the Grand Fleet of Sathayn and ennobled by the Queen herself, must have found the keeping of that necessary aloofness harder than would a gentleman born.

I waited silent, there in the grass hut they had given him. A soapstone lamp threw wavering light and enormous shadows over us; something rustled the thatch. Outside, the damp ground sloped past houses on stilts and murmurous fronded trees, to the fjord where it shimmered under Tambur. Faintly I heard drums throb, a chant and stamping of feet around a sacrificial fire. Indeed, the cool hills of Montalir seemed far.

Rovic leaned back his muscular form, y-clad a mere seaman's kilt in this heat. He had had them fetch him a civilized chair from the ship. "For see you, young fellow," he continued, "at other times we'd have established just enough communication to ask about gold. Well, we might also try to get a few sailing directions. But all in all, we'd hear little except the old story—'aye, foreign lord, indeed there's a kingdom where the very streets are paved with gold . . . a hundred miles west'—anything to get rid of us, eh? But in this prolonged stay, I've asked out the duke and the idolater priests more subtly. I've been so coy about whence we came and what we already know, that they've let slip a gobbet of knowledge they'd not otherwise have disgorged on the rack itself."

"The Aureate Cities?" I cried.

"Hush! I'd not have the crew get excited and out of hand. Not yet."

His leathery, hook-nosed face turned strange with thought. "I've always believed those cities an old wives' tale," he said. My shock must have been mirrored to his gaze, for he grinned and went on, "A useful one. Like a lodestone on a stick, it's dragging us around the world." His mirth faded. Again he got that look, which was not unlike the look of Froad considering the heavens. "Aye, of course I want gold, too. But if we find none on this voyage, I'll not care. I'll capture a few ships of Eralia or Sathayn when we're back in home waters, and pay for the voyage thus. I spoke God's truth that day on the quarterdeck. Zhean, that this journey was its own goal, until I can give it to Queen Odela, who once gave me the kiss of ennoblement."

He shook himself out of his reverie and said in a brisk tone: "Having led him to believe I already knew the most of it, I teased from Duke Guzan the admission that on the main island of this Hisagazi empire is something I scarce dare think about. A ship of the gods, he says, and an actual live god who came from the stars therein. Any of the natives will tell you that much. The secret reserved to the noble folk is that this is no legend or mummery, but sober fact. Or so Guzan claims. I know not what to think. But . . . he took me to a holy cave and showed me an object from that ship. It was some kind of clockwork mechanism, I believe. What, I know not. But of a shining silvery metal such as I've never seen before. The priest challenged me to break it. The metal was not heavy, must have been thin. But it blunted my sword, splintered a rock I pounded with, and my diamond ring would not scratch it."

I made signs against evil. A chill went along me, spine and skin and scalp, until I prickled all over. For the drums were muttering in a jungle dark, and the waters lay like quicksilver beneath gibbous Tambur, and each afternoon that planet ate the sun. Oh, the bells of Provien, heard across windswept Anday downs!

When the *Golden Leaper* was seaworthy again, Rovic had no trouble gaining permission to visit the Hisagazian emperor on the main island. He would, indeed, have found difficulty in not doing so. By now the canoes had borne word of us from one end of the realm to another, and the great lords were agog to see these blue-eyed strangers. Sleek and content once more, we disentangled ourselves from the arms of tawny wenches and embarked. Up anchor, up sail, chanties whose echoes sent sea birds whirling above the steeps, and we stood out to sea. This time we were escorted. Guzan himself was our pilot, a big middle-aged man whose handsomeness was not much injured by the livid green tattoos his folk affected on face and body. Several of his sons spread their pallets on our decks, while a swarm of warriors paddled alongside.

Rovic summoned Etien the boatswain to him in his cabin. "You're a man of some wit," he said. "I give you charge of keeping our crew alert, weapons ready, however peaceful this may look."

"Why, master!" The scarred brown face sagged with near dismay. "Think you the natives plot a treachery?"

"Who can tell?" answered Rovic. "Now, say naught to the crew. They've no skill in dissembling. Did greed or fear rise among 'em, the natives would sense as much, and grow uneasy—which would worsen the attitude of our own men, until none but God's Daughter could tell what'd happen. Only see to it, as casually as you're able, that our arms are ever close by and that our folk stay together."

Etien collected himself, bowed, and left the cabin. I made bold to ask what Rovic had in mind.

"Nothing, yet," said he. "However, I did hold in these fists a piece of clockwork such as the Grand Ban of Giair never imagined; and yarns were spun me of a Ship which flew down from heaven, bearing a god or a prophet. Guzan thinks I know more than I do, and hopes we'll be a new, disturbing element in the balance of things, by which he may further his private ambitions. He did not take those many fighting men along by accident. As for me . . . I intend to learn more about this."

He sat awhile at his table, staring at a sunbeam which sickled up and down the wainscot as the ship rocked. Finally: "Scripture tells us man dwelt beyond the stars before the Fall. The astrologues of the past generation or two have told us the planets are corporeal bodies like this earth. A traveler from Paradise—"

I left with my head in a roar.

We made an easy passage among scores of islands. After several days we raised the main one, Ulas-Erkila. It is about a hundred miles long, forty miles across at the widest, rising steep and green toward central mountains dominated by a volcanic cone. The Hisagazi worship two sorts of gods, watery and fiery, and believe this Mount Ulas houses the latter. When I saw that snowpeak afloat in the sky above emerald ridges, staining the blue with smoke, I could feel what the pagans did. The holiest act a man can perform among them is to cast himself into the burning crater of Ulas, and often an aged warrior is carried up the mountain that he may do so. Women are not allowed on the slopes.

Nikum, the royal seat, is situated at the head of a fjord, like the village where we had been staying. But Nikum is rich and extensive, being about the size of Roann. Many houses are made from timber rather than thatch; there is also a massive basalt temple atop a cliff, overlooking the city, with orchards, jungle, and mountains at its back. So great are the tree trunks available to them for pilings, the Hisagazi have built here a regular set of docks like those at Lavre— instead of moorings and floats that can rise or fall with the tides, such as most harbors use throughout the world. We were offered a berth of honor at the central wharf, but Rovic made the excuse that our ship was awkward to handle and got us tied at the far end.

"In the middle, we'd have the watchtower straight above us," he muttered to me. "And they may not have discovered the bow here, but their javelin throwers are good. Furthermore, they'd have an easy approach to our ship, plus a clutter of moored canoes between us and the bay mouth. Here, though, a few of us could hold the pier whilst the others ready for quick departure."

"But have we anything to fear, master?" I asked.

He gnawed his mustache. "I know not. Much depends on what they really believe about this god-ship of theirs . . . as well as what the truth is. But come all death and hell against us, we'll not return without that truth for Queen Odela."

* * *

Drums rolled and feathered spearmen leaped as our officers disembarked. A royal catwalk stretched above highwater level. (Common townsfolk in this realm swim from house to house when the tide laps their thresholds, or take a coracle if they have burdens to carry.) Across the graceful span of vines and canes lay the palace, which was a long building made from logs, the roof pillars carved into fantastic god-shapes.

Iskilip, Priest-Emperor of the Hisagazi, was an old and corpulent man. A soaring headdress of plumes, a feather robe, a wooden scepter topped with a human skull, his facial tattoos, his motionlessness, all made him seem unhuman. He sat on a dais, under sweet-smelling torches. His sons sat crosslegged at his feet, his courtiers on either side. Down the long walls were ranged his guardsmen. They had not our custom of standing to attention; but they were big, supple young men, bearing shields and corselets of scaly sea-monster leather, flint axes and obsidian spears that could kill as easily as iron. Their heads were shaven, which made them look the fiercer.

Iskilip greeted us well, called for refreshment, bade us be seated on a bench little lower than his dais. He asked many perceptive questions. Wide ranging, the Hisagazi knew of islands far beyond their own chain. They could even point the direction and tell us roughly the distance of a many-castled country they named Yuraka-dak, though none of them had traveled that far himself. Judging by their third-hand description, what could this be but Giair, which the Wondish adventurer Hanas Tolasson had reached overland? It blazed in me that we were indeed rounding the world. Only after that glory had faded a little did I again heed the talk.

"As I told Guzan," Rovic was saying, "another thing which drew us hither was the tale that you were blessed with a Ship from Heaven. And he showed me this was true."

A hissing went down the hall. The princes grew stiff, the courtiers blanked their countenances, the guardsmen stirred and muttered. Remotely through the walls I heard the rumbling, nearing tide. When Iskilip spoke, through the mask of himself, his voice had gone whetted: "Have you forgotten that these things are not for the uninitiate to see, Guzan?"

"No, Holy One," said the duke. Sweat sprang forth among the devils on his face, though not the sweat of fear. "However, this captain knew. His people also . . . as nearly as I could learn . . . he still has trouble speaking so I can understand . . . his people are initiate too. The claim seems reasonable, Holy One. Look at the marvels they brought. The hard, shining stone-which-is-not-stone, as in this long knife I was given—is that not like the stuff of which the Ship is built? The tubes which make distant things look close at hand, such as he has given you, Holy One—is this not akin to the far-seer the Messenger possesses?"

Iskilip leaned forward, toward Rovic. His scepter hand trembled till the pegged jaws of the skull clattered together. "Did the Star People themselves teach you to make all this?" he cried. "I never imagined. . . . The Messenger never spoke of any others—"

Rovic held up both palms. "Not so fast, Holy One, I pray you," said he. "We are poorly versed in your tongue. I couldn't recognize a word just now."

This was his deceit. His officers had been ordered to feign a knowledge of Hisagazi less than they really possessed. (We had improved our command of it by secret practicing with each other.) Thus he had an unimpeachable device for equivocation.

"Best we talk in private, Holy One," suggested Guzan, with a glance at the courtiers. They returned him a jealous glare.

Iskilip slouched in his gorgeous regalia. His words fell blunt, but in the weak tone of an old, uncertain man. "I know not. If these strangers are already initiate, certes we can show them what we have. But otherwise—if profane ears heard the Messenger's own tale—"

Guzan raised a dominator's hand. Bold and ambitious, long thwarted in his petty province, he had taken fire today. "Holy One," he said, "why has the full story been withheld these many years? In part to keep the commoners obedient, aye. But also, did you and your councillors not fear the whole world might swarm hither, greedy for knowledge, if it knew, and we then be overwhelmed? Well, if we let the blue-eyed men go home with curiosity unsatisfied, I think they are sure to return in strength. Thus we have naught to lose by revealing the truth to them. If they have never had a Messenger of their own, if they can be of no real use to us, time enough to kill them. But if they have indeed been visited like us, what might we and they not do together!"

This was spoken fast and softly, lest we Montalirians understand. And, indeed, our gentlemen failed to. I, having young ears, got the gist; and Rovic preserved such a fatuous smile of incomprehension that I knew he was seizing every word.

In the end they decided to take our leader—and my insignificant self, for no Hisagazian magnate goes anywhere quite unattended— to the temple. Iskilip led the way in person, Guzan and two brawny princes behind. A dozen spearmen brought up the rear. I thought Rovic's blade would be scant use if trouble came, but set my lips firmly together and made myself walk beside him. He looked as eager as a child on Thanksday Morning, teeth agleam in the pointed beard, a plumed bonnet slanted rakish over his brow. None would have thought him aware of any peril.

We left about sundown; in Tambur's hemisphere, folk make less distinction between day and night than our people must. Having observed Siett and Balant in high tide position, I was not surprised that Nikum lay nearly drowned. And yet, as we climbed the cliff trail toward the temple, methought I had never seen a view more alien.

Below us lay a sheet of water, on which the long grass roofs of the city appeared to float; the crowded docks, where our own ship's masts and spars raked above heathen figureheads; the fjord, winding between precipices toward its mouth, where the surf broke white and terrible on the skerries. The heights above us seemed altogether black, against a fire-colored sunset that filled nigh half the sky and bloodied the waters. Wan through those clouds I glimpsed the thick crescent of Tambur, banded in a heraldry no man could read. A basalt column chipped into the shape of a head loomed in outline athwart the planet. Right and left of the path grew sawtoothed turf, summer dry. The sky was pale at the zenith, dark purple in the east, where the first few stars had appeared. Tonight I found no comfort in the stars. We walked silent. The bare native feet made no noise. My shoes went pad-pad and the bells on Rovic's toes raised a tiny jingle.

The temple was a bold piece of work. Within a quadrangle of basalt walls guarded by tall stone heads lay several buildings of the same material. Only the fresh-cut fronds that roofed them were alive. Iskilip leading us, we brushed past acolytes and priests to a wooden cabin behind the sanctum. Two guardsmen stood watch at its door. They knelt for him. The emperor rapped with his curious scepter.

My mouth was dry and my heart thunderous. I expected almost any being hideous or radiant to stand in the doorway as it was opened. Astonishing, then, to see just a man, and of no great stature. By lamplight within I discerned his room, clean, austere, but not uncomfortable; this could have been an ordinary Hisagazian dwelling. He himself wore a simple bast skirt. The legs beneath were bent and thin, old man's shanks. His body was likewise thin, but still erect, the white head proudly carried. In complexion he was darker than a Montalirian, lighter than a Hisagazian, with brown eyes and sparse beard. His visage differed subtly, in nose and lips and slope of jaw, from any other race I had ever encountered. But he was human.

Naught else.

We entered the cabin, shutting out the spearmen. Iskilip doddered through a half-religious ceremony of introduction. I saw Guzan and the princes shift their stance, restless and unawed. Their class had long been party to this. Rovic's face was unreadable. He bowed in courtly wise to Val Nira, Messenger of Heaven, and explained our presence in a few words. But as he spoke, their eyes met and I saw him take the star man's measure.

"Aye, this is my home," said Val Nira. Habit spoke for him; he had given the same account to so many young nobles that the edges were worn off it. As yet he had not observed our metallic instruments, or else had not grasped their significance to him. "For . . . forty-three years, is that right, Iskilip? I have been treated as well as might be. If at times I was near screaming from loneliness, that is what an oracle must expect."

The emperor stirred, uneasy in his robe. "His demon left him," he explained. "Now he is simple human flesh. That's the real secret we keep. It was not ever thus. I remember when he first came. He prophesied immense things, and the people wailed and went on their faces. But sithence his demon has gone back to the stars, and the once-potent weapon he bore has equally been emptied of its force. The people would not believe this, however, so we still pretend otherwise, or there would be unrest among them."

"Affecting your own privileges," said Val Nira. His tone was tired and sardonic. "Iskilip was young then," he added to Rovic, "and the imperial succession was in doubt. I gave him my influence. He promised in return to do certain things for me."

"I tried, Messenger," said the monarch. "Ask all the sunken canoes and drowned men if I did not try. But the will of the gods was otherwise."

"Evidently." Val Nira shrugged. "These islands have few ores, Captain Rovic, and no person capable of recognizing those I required. It's too far to the mainland for Hisagazian canoes. But I don't deny you tried, Iskilip . . . then." He cocked an eyebrow back at us. "This is the first time foreigners have been taken deeply into the imperial confidence, my friends. Are you certain you can get back out again, alive?"

"Why, why, why, they're our guests!" blustered Iskilip and Guzan, almost in each other's mouths.

"Besides," smiled Rovic, "I had most of the secret already. My country has secrets of its own, to set against this. Yes, I think we might well do business, Holy One."

The emperor trembled. His voice cracked across. "Have you indeed a Messenger too?"

"What?" For a numbed moment Val Nira stared at us. Red and

white pursued each other across his countenance. Then he sat down on the bench and began to weep.

"Well, not precisely." Rovic laid a hand on the shaking shoulder. "I confess no heavenly vessel has docked at Montalir. But we've certain other secrets, belike equally valuable." Only I, who knew his moods somewhat, could sense the tautness in him. He locked eyes with Guzan and stared the duke down as a wild animal tamer does. And meanwhile, motherly gentle, he spoke with Val Nira. "I take it, friend, your Ship was wrecked on these shores, but could be repaired if you had certain materials?"

"Yes . . . yes . . . listen—" Stammering and gulping at the thought he might see his home again ere he died, Val Nira tried to explain.

The doctrinal implications of what he said are so astounding, even dangerous, that I feel sure my lords would not wish me to repeat much. However, I do not believe they are false. If the stars are indeed suns like our own, each attended by planets like our own, this demolishes the crystal-sphere theory. But Froad, when he was told later, did not think that matters to the true religion. Scriptures have never said that Paradise lies directly above the birthplace of God's Daughter; this was merely assumed, during those centuries when the earth was believed to be flat. Why should Paradise not be those planets of distant suns, where men dwell in magnificence, who possess the ancient arts and flit from star to star as casually as we might go from Lavre to West Alayn?

Val Nira believed our ancestors had been cast away on this world, several thousand years ago. They must have been fleeing the consequences of some crime or heresy, to come so far from any human domain. Somehow their ship was wrecked, the survivors went back to savagery, and only by degrees have their descendants regained a little knowledge. I cannot see where this explanation contradicts the dogma of the Fall. Rather, it amplifies it. The Fall was not the portion of all mankind but only a few—our own tainted blood— while the others continued to dwell prosperous and content in the heavens.

Our world still lies far off the trade lanes of the Paradise folk. Very few of them nowadays have any interest in seeking new realms. Val Nira, though, was such a one. He traveled at hazard for months until he chanced upon our earth. Then the curse seized him, too. Something went wrong. He descended upon Ulas-Erkila, and the Ship would fly no more.

"I know what the damage is," he said ardently. "I've not forgotten. How could I? No day has passed throughout these years that I didn't recite to myself what must be done. A certain subtle engine in the Ship requires quicksilver." (He and Rovic must spend some time talking ere they deduced this must be what he meant by the word he used.) "When the engine failed, I landed so hard that its tanks burst. All the quicksilver, what I had in reserve as well as what I was employing, poured forth. That much, in a hot enclosed space, would have poisoned me. I fled outside, forgetting to close the doorway. The deck being canted, the quicksilver ran after me. By the time I had recovered from blind panic, a tropical rainstorm had carried off the fluid metal. A series of unlikely accidents, yes, that's what's condemned me to a life's exile. It really would have made more sense to perish outright!"

He clutched Rovic's hand, staring up from his seat at the captain who stood over him. "Can you actually get quicksilver?" he begged. "I need no more than the volume of a man's head. Only that, and a few repairs easily made with tools in the Ship. When this cult grew up around me, I must needs release certain things I possessed, that each provincial temple might have a relic. But I took care never to give away anything important. Whatever I need is waiting there. A gallon of quicksilver, and—oh, God, my wife may even be alive, on Terra!"

Guzan, at least, had begun to understand the situation. He gestured to the princes, who hefted their axes and stepped a little closer. The door was shut on the cabin. Rovic looked from Val Nira to Guzan, whose face was grown ugly with tension. My captain laid hand on hilt. In no other way did he seem to feel any nearness of trouble.

"I take it, milord," he said lightly, "you're willing that the Heaven Ship be made to fly again."

Guzan was jarred. He had never expected this. "Why, of course," he exclaimed. "Why not?"

"Your tame god would depart you. What then becomes of your power in Hisagazia?"

"I—I'd not thought of that," Iskilip stuttered.

Val Nira's eyes shuttled among us, as if watching a game of paddleball. His thin body shook. "No," he whispered. "You can't. You can't keep me!"

Guzan nodded. "In a few more years," he said, not unkindly, "you would depart in death's canoe anyhow. If meanwhile we held you against your will, you might not speak the right oracles for us. Nay, be at ease; we'll get your flowing stone." With a slitted glance at Rovic: "Who shall fetch it?"

"My folk," said the knight. "Our ship can readily reach Giair, where there are civilized nations who surely have the quicksilver. We could return within a year, I think."

"Accompanied by a fleet of adventurers, to help you seize the sacred vessel?" asked Guzan bluntly. "Or, once out of our islands, you might not proceed to Yurakadak at all. You might continue the whole way home, and tell your Queen, and return with the power she commands."

Rovic lounged against a roof post, like a big pouncecat at its ease in ruffles and hose and scarlet cape. His right hand continued to rest on his sword pommel. "None save Val Nira could make that Ship go, I suppose," he drawled. "Does it matter who aids him in making repairs? Surely you don't think either of our nations could conquer Paradise!"

"The ship is very easy to operate," chattered Val Nira. "Anyone can fly it in air. I showed many nobles what levers to use. It's navigating among the stars which is more difficult. No nation on this world could even reach my people unaided—let alone fight them—but why should you think of fighting? I've told you a thousand times, Iskilip, the dwellers in the Milky Way are dangerous to nobody. They have so much wealth they're hard put to find a use for most of it. Gladly would they spend large amounts to help the peoples of this world become civilized again." With an anxious, half-hysterical look at Rovic: "Fully civilized, I mean. We'll teach you our arts. We'll give you engines, automata, homunculi, that do all the toilsome work; and boats that fly through the air; and regular passenger service on those ships that ply between the stars—"

"These things you have promised for forty years," said Iskilip. "We've naught but your word."

"And, finally, a chance to confirm his word," I blurted.

Guzan said with calculated grimness: "Matters are not that simple, Holy One. I've watched these men from across the ocean for weeks, while they lived on Yarzik. Even on their best behavior, they're a fierce and greedy lot. I trust them no further than my eyes reach. This very night I see how they've befooled us. They know our language better than they ever admitted. And they misled us to believe they might have some inkling of a Messenger. If the Ship were indeed made to fly again, them in possession, who knows what they might choose to do?"

Rovic's tone softened still further. "What do you propose, Guzan?"

"We can discuss that another time."

I saw knuckles tighten around stone axes. For a moment, only Val Nira's unsteady breathing was heard. Guzan stood heavy in the lamplight, rubbing his chin, the small black eyes turned downward in thoughtfulness. At last he shook himself. "Perhaps," he said crisply, "a crew mainly Hisagazian could sail your ship, Rovic, and fetch the flowing stone. A few of your men could go along to instruct ours. The rest could remain here as hostages."

My captain made no reply. Val Nira groaned, "You don't understand! You're squabbling over nothing! When my people come here, there'll be no more war, no more oppression. They'll cure you of every disease. They'll show friendship to all and favor to none. I beg you—"

"Enough," said Iskilip. His own words fell ragged. "We shall sleep on this. If anyone can sleep after so much strangeness."

Rovic looked past the emperor's plumes, into the face of Guzan. "Before we decide anything . . ." His fingers tightened on the sword hilt till the nails turned white. Some thought had sprung up within him. But he kept his tone even. "First I want to see that Ship. Can we go there tomorrow?"

Iskilip was the Holy One, but he stood huddled in his feather robe. Guzan nodded agreement.

We bade our good-nights and went forth under Tambur. The planet was waxing toward full, flooding the courtyard with cold luminance, but the hut was shadowed by the temple. It remained a black outline, a narrow lamplight rectangle of doorway in the middle. There was etched the frail body of Val Nira, who had come from the stars. He watched us till we had gone out of sight.

On the way down the path, Guzan and Rovic bargained in curt words. The Ship lay two days' march inland, on the slopes of Mount Ulas. We would go in a joint party to inspect it, but a mere dozen Montalirians were allowed. Afterward we would debate our course of action.

Lanthorns glowed yellow at our caravel's poop. Refusing Iskilip's hospitality, Rovic and I returned thither for the night. A pikeman on guard at the gangway inquired what I had learned. "Ask me tomorrow," I said feebly. "My head's in too much of a whirl."

"Come into my cabin, lad, for a stoup ere we retire," the captain invited me.

God knows I needed wine. We entered the low room, crowded with nautical instruments, books, and printed charts that looked quaint to me now I had seen a little of those spaces where the cartographer drew mermaids and windsprites. Rovic sat down behind his table, gestured me to a chair opposite, and poured from a carafe into two goblets of Quaynish crystal. Then I knew he had momentous thoughts in his head—far more than the problem of saving our lives.

We sipped a while, unspeaking. I heard the lap-lap of wavelets

on our hull, the tramp of men on watch, the rustle of distant surf—
otherwise nothing. At last Rovic leaned back, staring at the ruby
wine on the table. I could not read his expression.

"Well, lad," said he, "what do you think?"

"I know not what to think, master."

"You and Froad are a trifle prepared for this idea that the stars
are other suns. You're educated. As for me, I've seen sufficient
eldritch in my day that this seems quite believable. The rest of our
people, though . . ."

"An irony that barbarians like Guzan should long have been
familiar with the concept, having had the old man from the sky to
preach it privily to their class for more than forty years. Is he indeed
a prophet, master?"

"He denies it. He plays prophet because he must, but it's evident
that the dukes and earls of this realm know it's a trick. Iskilip is
senile, more than half converted to his own artificial creed. He
was mumbling about prophecies Val Nira made long ago, true
prophecies. Bah! Tricks of memory and wishfulness. Val Nira is as
human and fallible as I am. We Montalirians are the same flesh as
these Hisagazi, even if we have learned the use of metal before they
did. Val Nira's people know more in turn than us; they're still
mortals, by Heaven. I must remember that they are."

"Guzan remembers."

"Bravo, lad!" Rovic's mouth bent upward, one-sidedly. "He's a
clever one, and bold. When he came, he saw his chance to stop
stagnating as the petty lord on an outlying island. He'll not let that
chance slip without a fight. Like many a double-dealer before him,
he accuses us of plotting the very things he hopes to do."

"But what does he hope for?"

"My guess would be, he wants the Ship for himself. Val Nira said
it was easy to fly. Navigation between the stars would be too difficult
for anyone save him; nor could any man in his right mind hope to
play pirate along the Milky Way. However . . . if the Ship stayed
right here, on this earth, rising no higher than a mile above ground
. . . the warlord who used it might conquer more widely than Lame
Darveth himself."

I was aghast. "Do you mean Guzan would not even try to seek
out Paradise?"

Rovic scowled so blackly at his wine that I saw he wanted solitude.
I stole off to my bunk in the poop.

The captain was awake before dawn, readying our folk. Plainly he
had reached some decision, and it was not pleasant. But once he

set a course, he seldom veered. He was long in conference with Etien, who came out of the cabin looking frightened As if to reassure himself, the boatswain ordered the men about harshly.

Our allowed dozen were to be Rovic, Froad, myself, Etien, and eight crewmen. We were issued helmets and corselets, muskets and edged weapons. Since Guzan had told us there was a beaten path to the Ship, we assembled a supply cart on the dock. Etien supervised its landing. I was astonished to see that nearly all it carried, till the axles groaned, was barrels of gunpowder. "But we're not taking cannon!" I protested.

"Skipper's orders," rapped Etien. He turned his back on me. After a glance at Rovic's face, nobody ventured to ask him the reason. I remembered we would be going up a mountainside. A wagonful of powder, with lit fuse, set rolling down toward a hostile army, might win a battle. But did Rovic anticipate open conflict?

Certes his orders to the men and officers remaining behind suggested as much. They were to stay aboard the *Golden Leaper*, holding her ready for instant fight or flight.

As the sun rose, we said our morning prayers to God's Daughter and marched down the docks. The wood banged hollow under our boots. A few thin mists drifted on the bay; Tambur's crescent hung wan above. Nikum town lay hushed as we passed through.

Guzan met us at the temple. A son of Iskilip was supposedly in charge, but the duke ignored that youth as much as we did. They had a hundred guardsmen along, scaly-coated, shaven-headed, tattooed with storms and dragons. The early sunlight gleamed off obsidian spearheads. Our approach was watched in silence. But when we halted before those disorderly ranks, Guzan trod forth. He was also y-clad leather, and carried the sword Rovic had given him on Yarzik. The dew shimmered on his feather cloak. "What have you in that wagon?" he demanded.

"Supplies," Rovic answered.

"For four days?"

"Send home all but ten of your men," said Rovic coolly, "and I'll send back this cart."

Their eyes clashed, until Guzan turned and gave his orders. We started off, a few Montalirians surrounded by pagan warriors. The jungle lay ahead of us, a deep and burning green, rising halfway up the slope of Ulas. Then the mountain became naked black, to the snow that edged its smoking crater.

Val Nira walked between Rovic and Guzan. Strange, I thought, that the instrument of God's will for us was so shriveled. He ought to have walked tall and haughty, a star on his brow.

During the day, at night when we made camp, and again the next day, Rovic and Froad questioned him eagerly about his home. Of course, their talk was in fragments. Nor did I hear everything, since I must take my turn at pulling our wagon along that narrow, steep, damnable trail. The Hisagazi have no draft animals, therefore they make slight use of the wheel and have no proper roads. But what I did hear kept me long awake.

Ah, greater marvels than the poets have imagined for Elf Land! Entire cities built in a single tower half a mile high. The sky made to glow so that there is no true darkness after sunset. Food not grown in the earth, but manufactured in alchemical elaboratories. The lowest peasant owning a score of machines which serve him more subtly and humbly than might a thousand slaves; owning an aerial carriage which can fly him around his world in less than a day; owning a crystal window on which theatrical images appear, to beguile his abundant leisure. Argosies between suns, stuffed with the wealth of a thousand planets; yet every ship unarmed and unescorted, for there are no pirates and this realm is on such good terms with the other starfaring nations that war has also ceased. (These foreign countries, it seems, are more akin to the supernatural than Val Nira's, in that the races composing them are not human, though able to speak and reason.) In this happy land is little crime. When it does occur, the criminal is soon captured by the arts of the provost corps; yet he is not hanged, nor even transported overseas. Instead, his mind is cured of the wish to violate any law. He returns home to live as an especially honored citizen, since folk know he is now completely trustworthy. As for the government— but here I lost the thread of discourse. I believe it is in form a republic, but in practice a devoted fellowship of men, chosen by examination, who see to the welfare of everyone else.

Surely, I thought, this was Paradise!

Our sailors listened agape. Rovic's mien was reserved, but he gnawed his mustaches incessantly. Guzan, to whom this was an old tale, grew rough of manner. Plain to see, he disliked our intimacy with Val Nira, and the ease wherewith we grasped ideas that were spoken.

But, then, we came of a nation which has long encouraged natural philosophy and improvement of the mechanic arts. I myself, in my short lifetime, had witnessed the replacement of the waterwheel in regions where there are few streams by the modern form of windmill. The pendulum clock was invented the year before I was born. I had read many romances about the flying machines which no few men have tried to devise. Living at such a dizzy pace of progress, we Montalirians were all prepared to entertain still vaster concepts.

At night, sitting with Froad and Etien around a campfire, I spoke somewhat of this to the savant. "Ah," he crooned, "today Truth stood unveiled before me. Did you hear what the starman said? The three laws of planetary motion about a sun, and the one great law of attraction which explains them? Dear saints, that law can be put in a single short sentence, and yet the development will keep mathematicians busy for three hundred years!"

He stared past the flames, and the other fires around which the heathen slept, and jungle gloom, and angry volcanic glow in heaven. I started to query him. "Leave be, lad," grunted Etien. "Can ye nay tell when a man's in love?"

I shifted a little closer to the boatswain's stolid, comforting bulk. "What do you think of this?" I asked, softly, for the jungle whispered and croaked on every side.

"Me, I stopped thinking a while back," he said. "After yon day on the quarterdeck, when the skipper jested us into sailing wi' him though we went off the world's edge an' tumbled down in foam amongst the nether stars . . . well, I'm but a poor sailor man, an' my one chance o' regaining home is to follow the skipper."

"Even beyond the sky?"

"Less hazard to that, maybe, than sailing on around the world. The little man swore his vessel was safe, an' no storms blow between the suns."

"Can you trust his word?"

"Oh, aye. Even a knocked-about old palomer like me has seen enough o' men to ken when a one's too timid an' eagersome to stand by a lie. I fear not the folk in Paradise, nor does the skipper. Except in some way . . ." Etien rubbed his bearded jaw, scowling. "In some way I can nay wholly grasp, they affright Rovic. He fears nay they'll come hither wi' torch an' sword; but there's somewhat else about 'em that frets him."

I felt the ground shudder the least bit. Ulas had cleared his throat. "It does seem we'd be daring God's anger—"

"That's nay what gnaws on the skipper's mind. He was never an over-pious man." Etien scratched himself, yawned, and climbed to his feet. "Glad I am to be nay the skipper. Let him think over what's best to do. Time ye an' me was asleep."

But I slept little that night.

Rovic, I think, rested well. Yet as the next day wore on, I could see haggardness on him. I wondered why. Did he think the Hisagazi would turn on us? If so, why had he come? As the slope steepened, the wagon grew so toilsome to push and drag that my fears died for lack of breath.

Yet when we came upon the Ship, toward evening, I forgot my

weariness. And after an amazed volley of oaths, our mariners rested silent on their pikes. The Hisagazi, never talkative, crouched low in token of awe. Only Guzan remained erect among them. I glimpsed his expression as he stared at the marvel. It was a look of lust.

Wild was that place. We had gone above timberline. The land was a green sea below us, edged with silvery ocean. Here we stood among tumbled black boulders, cinders and spongy tufa underfoot. The mountain rose in steeps and scarps and ravines, on to snows and smoke, which rose another mile into a pale chilly sky. And here stood the Ship.

And the Ship was beauty.

I remember. In length—height, rather, since it stood on its tail—it was about equal to our caravel, in form not unlike a lance head, in color a shining white, untarnished after forty years. That was all. But words are paltry, my lords. What can they show of clean soaring curves, of iridescence on burnished metal, of a thing which was proud and lovely and in its very shape aquiver to be off? How can I conjure back the glamour which hazed that Ship whose keel had cloven starlight?

We stood there a long time. My vision blurred. I wiped my eyes, angry to be seen thus affected, until I noticed a tear glisten in Rovic's red beard. But the captain's visage was quite blank. When he spoke, he said merely, in a flat voice, "Come, let's make camp."

The Hisagazian guardsmen dared approach no closer than these several hundred yards to as potent an idol as the Ship had become. Our mariners were glad to maintain the same distance. But after dark, when everything else was in order, Val Nira led Rovic, Froad, Guzan, and myself to the vessel.

As we approached, a double door in the side swung noiselessly open and a metal gangplank descended therefrom. Glowing in Tambur's light, and in the dull clotted red reflected off the smoke clouds, the Ship was already as strange as I could endure. When it thus beckoned me, as if a ghost stood guard, I whimpered and fled. The cinders crunched beneath my boots; I caught a whiff of sulfurous air.

But at the edge of camp I rallied myself enough to look again. The dark ground blotted up light, so that the Ship appeared alone with its grandeur. Presently I went back.

The interior was lit by luminous panels, cool to the touch. Val Nira explained that the great engine which drove it—as if the troll of folklore were put on a treadmill—was intact, and would furnish power at the flick of a lever. As nearly as I could understand what he said, this was done by changing the metallic part of salt into light

. . . thus I do not understand after all. The quicksilver was required for a part of the controls, which channeled power from the engine into another mechanism that hurtled the Ship skyward. We inspected the broken container. Enormous indeed had been the impact of landing, to twist and bend that thick alloy. And yet Val Nira had been shielded by invisible forces, and the rest of the Ship had not suffered important damage. He fetched some tools, which flamed and hummed and whirled, and demonstrated a few repair operations on the broken part. Obviously he would have no trouble completing the work—and then he need only pour in a gallon of quicksilver, to bring his vessel alive again.

Much else did he show us that night. I shall say naught of it, for I cannot even remember such strangeness very clearly, let alone find words. Suffice that Rovic, Froad, and Zhean spent a few hours in Elf Hill.

So, too, did Guzan. Though he had been taken here before, as part of his initiation, he had never been shown this much ere now. Watching him, however, I saw less marveling in him than greed.

No doubt Rovic observed the same. There was little which Rovic did not observe. When we departed the Ship, his silence was not stunned like Froad's or mine. At the time, I thought in a vague fashion that he fretted over the trouble Guzan was certain to make. Now, looking back, I believe his mood was sadness.

Sure it is that long after we others were in our bedrolls, he stood by himself, looking at the planet-lit Ship.

Early in a cold dawn, Etien shook me awake. "Up, lad, we've work to do. Load yere pistols an' belt on yere dirk."

"What? What's to happen?" I fumbled with a hoarfrosted blanket. Last night seemed a dream.

"The skipper's nay said, but plainly he awaits a fight. Report to the wagon an' help us move into yon flying tower." Etien's thick form heelsquatted a moment longer beside me. Then, slowly: "Methinks Guzan has some idea o' murdering us here on the mountain. One officer an' a few crewmen can be made to sail the *Golden Leaper* for him, to Giair an' back. The rest o' us would be less trouble to him wi' our weasands slit."

I crawled forth, teeth clattering in my head. After arming myself, I snatched some food from the common store. The Hisagazi on the march carry dried fish and a sort of bread made from a powdered weed. The saints alone knew when I'd next get a chance to eat. I was the last to join Rovic at the cart. The natives were drifting sullenly toward us, unsure what we intended.

"Let's go, lads," said Rovic. He gave his orders. Four men started manhandling the wagon across the rocky trail toward the Ship, where this gleamed among mists. We others stood by, weapons ready. Guzan hastened toward us, Val Nira toiled in his wake.

Anger darkened his countenance. "What are you doing?" he barked.

Rovic gave him a calm stare. "Why, milord, as we may be here for some time, inspecting the wonders aboard the Ship—"

"What?" exclaimed Guzan. "What do you mean? Have you not seen ample for a first visit? We must get home again, and prepare to sail after the flowing stone."

"Go if you wish," said Rovic. "I choose to linger. And since you don't trust me, I reciprocate the feeling. My folk will stay in the Ship, which can be defended if necessary."

Guzan stormed and raged, but Rovic ignored him. Our men continued hauling the cart over the uneven ground. Guzan signaled his spearmen, who approached in a disordered but alert mass. Etien spoke a command. We fell into line. Pikes slanted forward, muskets took aim.

Guzan stepped back. We had demonstrated firearms for him at his home island. Doubtless he could overwhelm us with sheer numbers, were he determined, but the cost would be heavy. "No reason to fight, is there?" purred Rovic. "I am only taking a sensible precaution. The Ship is a most valuable prize. It could bring Paradise for all . . . or dominion over this earth for a few. There are those who'd prefer the latter. I've not accused you of being among them. However, in prudence I'd liefer keep the Ship for my hostage and my fortress, as long as it pleases me to remain here."

I think then I was convinced of Guzan's real intentions, not as a surmise of ours but as plain fact. Had he truly wished to attain the stars, his single concern would have been to keep the Ship safe. He would not have reached out, snatched little Val Nira in his powerful hands, and dragged the starman backward like a shield against our fire. Not that his intent matters, save to my own conscience. Wrath distorted his patterned visage. He screamed at us, "Then I'll keep a hostage too! And much good may your shelter do you!"

The Hisagazi milled about, muttering, hefting their spears and axes, but not prepared to follow us. We grunted our way across the black mountainside. The sun strengthened. Froad twisted his beard. "Dear me, master captain," he said, "think you they'll lay siege to us?"

"I'd not advise anyone to venture forth alone," said Rovic dryly.

"But without Val Nira to explain things, what use for us to stay at the Ship? Best we go back. I've mathematic texts to consult. My head's aspin with the law that binds the turning planets. I must ask the man from Paradise what he knows of—"

Rovic interrupted with a gruff order to three men, that they help lift a wheel wedged between two stones. He was in a savage temper. I confess his action seemed mad to me. If Guzan intended treachery, we had gained little by immobilizing ourselves in the Ship, where he could starve us. Better to let him attack in the open, where we would have a chance of fighting our way through. And if Guzan did not plan to fall on us in the jungle—or any other time—then this was senseless provocation on our part. But I dared not question.

When we had brought our wagon to the Ship, its gangplank again descended for us. The sailors started and cursed. Rovic forced himself out of his bitterness, to speak soothing words. "Easy, lads. I've been aboard already, ye ken. Naught harmful within. Now we must tote our powder thither, an' stow it as I've planned."

Being slight of frame, I was not set to carrying the heavy casks, but put at the foot of the gangplank to watch the Hisagazi. Although we were too far away to distinguish words, I saw how Guzan stood on a boulder and harangued them. They shook their weapons at us and whooped. They did not venture to attack. I wondered wretchedly what this was all about. If Rovic had foreseen us besieged, that would explain why he brought the powder along. . . . No, it would not, for there was more than a dozen men could shoot off in weeks of musketry, even if we had enough bullets . . . and we had almost no food! I looked past the poisonous volcano clouds, to Tambur where storms raged that could engulf our whole earth, and wondered what demons lurked here to possess men.

I sprang to alertness at an indignant shout from within. Froad! Almost, I ran up the gangway, then remembered my duty. I heard Rovic roar him down and order the crewfolk to carry on. Froad and Rovic must have gone by themselves into the pilot's compartment and talked for an hour or more. When the old man emerged, he protested no longer. But as he walked down the gangway, he wept.

Rovic followed, grimmer of countenance than I had ever seen ere now. The sailors filed after, some looking appalled, some relieved, but chiefly watching the Hisagazian camp. They were simply mariners; the Ship was little to them save a weird and disquieting object. Last came Etien, walking backward down the metal plank as he uncoiled a long string.

"Form square!" barked Rovic. The men snapped into position. "Get at the middle, Zhean and Froad," said the captain. "You can better carry extra ammunition than fight." He placed himself in the van.

I tugged Froad's sleeve. "Please, I beg you, master, what's happening?" He sobbed too much to answer.

Etien crouched, flint and steel in his hands. He heard me—for otherwise we were deathly silent—and said in a hard voice: "We placed casks o' powder throughout this hull, lad, wi' powder trains to join 'em. Here's the fuse to the whole."

I could not speak, could not even think, so monstrous was this. As if from immensely far away, I heard the click of stone on metal in Etien's fingers, heard him blow on the spark and add: "A good idea, methinks. I said t'other eventide, I'd follow the skipper wi'out fear o' God's curse—but let's not tempt Him overmuch."

"Forward march!" Rovic's sword blazed clear of the scabbard.

Our feet scrunched loud and horrible on the mountain as we quick-stepped away. I did not look back. I could not. I was still fumbling in a nightmare. Since Guzan would have moved to intercept us anyhow, we proceeded straight toward his band. He stepped forth as we halted at the camp's edge. Val Nira slunk shivering after him. I heard the words dimly.

"Well, Rovic, what now? Are you ready to go home?"

"Yes," said the captain. His voice was dull. "All the way home."

Guzan squinted in rising suspiciousness. "Why did you abandon your wagon? What did you leave behind?"

"Supplies. Come, let's march."

Val Nira stared at the cruel shapes of our pikes. He must wet his lips a few times ere he could quaver, "What are you talking about? There's no reason to leave food there. It would spoil in the time until . . . until—" He faltered as he looked into Rovic's eyes. The blood drained from him.

"What have you done?" he whispered.

Suddenly Rovic's free hand arose, to cover his face. "What I must," he said thickly. "Daughter of God, forgive me."

The starman regarded us an instant more. Then he turned and ran. Past the astonished warriors he burst, out onto the cindery slope, toward his Ship.

"Come back!" bellowed Rovic. "You fool, you'll never—"

He swallowed hard. As he looked after that small, stumbling, lonely shape, hurrying across a fire mountain toward the Beautiful One, the sword sank in his grasp. "Perhaps it's best," he said, like a benediction.

Guzan raised his own sword. In scaly coat and blowing feathers, he was a figure as impressive as steel-clad Rovic. "Tell me what you've done," he snarled, "or I'll kill you this moment!"

He paid our muskets no heed. He, too, had had dreams. He, too, saw them end, when the Ship exploded.

Even that adamantine hull could not withstand a wagonload of carefully placed gunpowder, set off at the same time. A crash knocked me to my knees, and the hull cracked open. White-hot chunks of metal screamed across the slopes. I saw one of them strike a boulder and split it in twain. Val Nira vanished, destroyed too quickly to have seen what happened; thus, in the ultimate, God was merciful to him. Through the flames and smokes and doomsday noise which followed, I saw the Ship fall. It rolled down the slope, strewing its mangled guts behind. Then the mountainside grumbled and slid in pursuit, and buried it, and dust hid the sky.

More than this, I have no heart to remember.

The Hisagazi shrieked and fled. They must have thought hell was come to earth. Guzan stood his ground. As the dust enveloped us, hiding the grave of the Ship and the white volcano crater, turning the sun red, he sprang at Rovic. A musketeer raised his weapon. Etien slapped it down. We stood and watched those two men fight, up and over the shaken cinder land, and knew in our private darkness that this was their right. Sparks flew where the blades clamored together. At last Rovic's skill prevailed. He took his foe in the throat.

We gave Guzan decent burial and went down through the jungle.

That night the guardsmen rallied their courage to attack us. We were aided by our muskets, but must chiefly use sword and pike. We hewed our way through them because we had no place else to go than the sea.

They retreated, but carried word ahead of us. When we reached Nikum, all the forces Iskilip could raise were besieging the *Golden Leaper* and waiting to oppose Rovic's entry. We formed a square again, and no matter how many thousands they had, only a score or so could reach us at any time. Nonetheless, we left six good men in the crimsoned mud of those streets. When our people on the caravel realized Rovic was coming back, they bombarded the town. This ignited the thatch roofs and distracted the enemy enough that a sortie from the ship was able to effect a juncture with us. We chopped our way to the pier, got aboard, and manned the capstan.

Outraged and very brave, the Hisagazi paddled their canoes up to our hull, where our cannon could not be brought to bear. They stood on each other's shoulders to reach our rail. One band forced itself aboard, and the fight was fierce which cleared them from the decks. That was when I got the shattered collarbone which plagues me to this day.

But in the end, we came out of the fjord. A fresh east wind was blowing. Sail aloft, we outran the foe. We counted our dead, bound our wounds, and slept.

Next dawning, awakened by the pain of my wound and the worse pain within, I mounted the quarterdeck. The sky was overcast. The wind had stiffened; the sea ran cold and green, whitecaps out to a cloudy-gray horizon. Timbers groaned and rigging thrummed. I stood an hour facing aft, into the chill wind that numbs pain.

When I heard boots behind me, I did not turn around. I knew they were Rovic's. He stood beside me a long while, bareheaded. I noticed that he was starting to turn gray.

Finally, not yet regarding me, still squinting into the air that lashed tears from our eyes, he said: "I had a chance to talk Froad over, that day. He was grieved, but owned I was right. Has he spoken to you about it?"

"No," I said.

"None of us are ever likely to speak of it much," said Rovic.

After another time: "I was not afraid Guzan or anyone else would seize the Ship and try to turn conqueror. We men of Montalir should well be able to deal with any such rogues. Nor was I afraid of the Paradise dwellers. That poor little man could only have been telling truth. They would never have harmed us . . . willingly. They would have brought precious gifts, and taught us their esoteric arts, and let us visit their stars."

"Then why?" I got out.

"Someday Froad's successors will solve the riddles of the universe," he said. "Someday our descendants will build their own Ship, and go forth to whatever destiny they wish."

Spume blew around us until our hair was wet. I tasted the salt on my lips.

"Meanwhile," said Rovic, "we'll sail the seas of this earth, and walk its mountains, and chart and subdue and come to understand it. Do you see, Zhean? That is what the Ship would have taken from us."

Then I was also made able to weep. He laid his hand on my uninjured shoulder and stood with me while the *Golden Leaper*, all sail set, proceeded westward.

CORDWAINER SMITH
On the Storm Planet

The late Cordwainer Smith—in "real" life Dr. Paul M. A. Linebarger, scholar, statesman, godson of Sun Yat Sen, and author of the definitive text (still taught from today) on the art of psychological warfare—was a writer of enormous talents who, from 1948 until his untimely death in 1966, produced a double-handful of some of the best short fiction this genre has ever seen—"Alpha Ralpha Boulevard," "A Planet Named Shayol," "The Ballad of Lost C'Mell," "The Dead Lady of Clown Town," "The Game of Rat and Dragon," "Drunkboat," "The Lady Who Sailed *The Soul*," "Under Old Earth," and "Scanners Live in Vain"—as well as a large number of lesser, but still fascinating, stories, all twisted and blended and woven into an interrelated tapestry of incredible lushness and intricacy. Smith created a baroque cosmology unrivaled even today for its scope and complexity: a millennia-spanning Future History, logically outlandish and elegantly strange, set against a vivid, richly colored, mythically intense universe where animals assume the shape of man, vast planoform ships whisper through multidimensional space, immense sick sheep are the most valuable objects in the universe, immortality can be bought, and the mysterious Lords of the Instrumentality rule a hunted Earth too old for history. . . .

It is a cosmology that looks as evocative and bizarre today in the 1990s as it did in the 1960s—certainly for sheer sweep and daring of conceptualization, in its vision of how different and *strange* the future will be, it rivals any contemporary vision conjured up by Young Turks such as Bruce Sterling and Greg Bear, and I suspect that it is timeless.

The landmark novella that follows, *On the Storm Planet*, gives us an almost complete cross section of Smith's fabulous private universe. All the threads are here: the Instrumentality, the underpeople, the childlike robots, forgetties, the Old North Australians, stroon, personality imprinting, plano-forming, Go Captains and Stop Captains, pinlighting, battle hypnotism, Space Three, the Rediscovery of Man, the Old Strong Religion of the God Nailed High. And at the heart of it, as at the heart of all fiction, are his people, with all their frailties and strengths, their quirks, their holiness, and carnal-ity: the driven exile Casher, and the serene turtle-girl T'ruth, a millennium old, with only another eighty-nine thousand years left to watch and wait. . . .

Cordwainer Smith's books include the novel *Norstrilia* and the collections *Space Lords*, *The Best of Cordwainer Smith*, *Quest of the Three Worlds*, *Stardreamer*, *You Will Never Be the Same*, and *The Instrumentality of Mankind*. As Felix C. Forrest, he wrote two mainstream novels, *Ria* and *Carola*, and as Carmi-chael Smith he wrote the thriller *Atomsk*.

His most recent book is the posthumous collection *The Rediscovery of Man: The Complete Short Science Fiction of Cord-wainer Smith*, an immense book (672 pages) that will certainly stand as one of the very best collections of the decade, and a book that belongs in every complete science fiction collection.

"At two seventy-five in the morning," said the Administrator to Casher O'Neill, "you will kill this girl with a knife. At two seventy-seven, a fast groundcar will pick you up and bring you back here. Then the power cruiser will be yours. Is that a deal?"

He held out his hand as if he wanted Casher O'Neill to shake it then and there, making some kind of an oath or bargain.

Casher did not slight the man, so he picked up his glass and said, "Let's drink to the deal first!"

The Administrator's quick, restless, darting eyes looked Casher up and down very suspiciously. The warm sea-wet air blew through the room. The Administrator seemed wary, suspicious, alert, but under-neath his slight hostility there was another emotion, of which Casher could perceive just the edge. Fatigue with its roots in bottomless despair: despair set deep in irrecoverable fatigue?

That other emotion, which Casher could barely discern, was very strange indeed. On all his voyages back and forth through the inhab-ited worlds, Casher had met many odd types of men and women. He had never seen anything like this Administrator before—brilliant, erratic, boastful. His title was "Mr. Commissioner" and he was an ex-Lord of the Instrumentality on this planet of Henriada, where the population had dropped from six hundred million persons down to some forty thousand. Indeed, local government had disappeared into limbo, and this odd man, with the title of Administrator, was the only law and civil authority which the planet knew.

Nevertheless, he had a surplus power cruiser and Casher O'Neill was determined to get that cruiser as a part of his long plot to return to his home planet of Mizzer and to unseat the usurper, Colonel Wedder.

The Administrator stared sharply, wearily at Casher and then he too lifted his glass. The green twilight colored his liquor and made it seem like some strange poison. It was only Earth byegarr, though a little on the strong side.

With a sip, only a sip, the older man relaxed a little. "You may be out to trick me, young man. You may think that I am an old fool running an abandoned planet. You may even be thinking that killing this girl is some kind of a crime. It is not a crime at all. I am the Administrator of Henriada and I have ordered that girl killed every year for the last eighty years. She isn't even a girl, to start with. Just an underperson. Some kind of an animal turned into a domestic servant. I can even appoint you a deputy sheriff. Or chief of detectives. That might be better. I haven't had a chief of detectives for a hundred years and more. You are my chief of detectives. Go in tomorrow. The house is not hard to find. It's the biggest and best house left on this planet. Go in tomorrow morning. Ask for her master and be sure that you use the correct title: The Mister and Owner Murray Madigan. The robots will tell you to keep out. If you persist, she will come to the door. That's when you will stab her through the heart, right there in the doorway. My groundcar will race up one metric minute later. You jump in and come back here. We've been through this before. Why don't you agree? Don't you know who I am?"

"I know perfectly well"—Casher O'Neill smiled—"who you are, Mr. Commissioner and Administrator. You are the honorable Rankin Meiklejohn, once of Earth Two. After all, the Instrumentality itself gave me a permit to land on this planet on private business. They knew who *I* was too, and what I wanted. There's something funny about all this. Why should you give me a power cruiser—the best ship, you yourself say, in your whole fleet—just for killing one modified animal which looks and talks like a girl? Why me? Why the visitor? Why the man from off-world? Why should you care whether this particular underperson is killed or not? If you've given the order for her death eighty times in eighty years, why hasn't it been carried out long ago? Mind you, Mr. Administrator, I'm not saying no. I want that cruiser. I want it very much indeed. But what's the deal? What's the trick? Is it the house you want?"

"Beauregard? No, I don't want Beauregard. Old Madigan can

rot in it for all that I care. It's between Ambiloxi and Mottile, on the Gulf of Esperanza. You can't miss it. The road is good. You could drive yourself there."

"What is it, then?" Casher's voice had an edge of persistence to it.

The Administrator's response was singular indeed. He filled his huge inhaler glass with the potent byegarr. He stared over the full glass at Casher O'Neill as if he were an enemy. He drained the glass. Casher knew that that much liquor, taken suddenly, could kill the normal human being.

The Administrator did not fall over dead.

He did not even become noticeably more drunk.

His face turned red and his eyes almost popped out, as the harsh 160-proof liquor took effect, but he still did not say anything. He just stared at Casher. Casher, who had learned in his long exile to play many games, just stared back.

The Administrator broke first.

He leaned forward and burst into a birdlike shriek of laughter. The laughter went on and on until it seemed that the man had hogged all the merriment in the galaxy. Casher snorted a little laugh along with the man, more out of nervous reflex than anything else, but he waited for the Administrator to stop laughing.

The Administrator finally got control of himself. With a broad grin and a wink at Casher, he poured himself four fingers more of the byegarr into his glass, drank it down as if he had had a sip of cream, and then—only very slightly unsteady—stood up, came over and patted Casher on the shoulder.

"You're a smart boy, my lad. I'm cheating you. I don't care whether the power cruiser is there or not. I'm giving you something which has no value at all to me. Who's ever going to take a power cruiser off this planet? It's ruined. It's abandoned. And so am I. Go ahead. You can have the cruiser. For nothing. Just take it. Free. Unconditionally."

This time it was Casher who leaped to his feet and stared down into the face of the feverish, wanton little man.

"Thank you, Mr. Administrator!" he cried, trying to catch the hand of the administrator so as to seal the deal.

Rankin Meiklejohn looked awfully sober for a man with that much liquor in him. He held his right hand behind his back and would not shake.

"You can have the cruiser, all right. No terms. No conditions. No deal. It's yours. *But kill that girl first*! Just as a favor to me. I've been a good host. I like you. I want to do you a favor. Do me one. Kill that girl. At two seventy-five in the morning. Tomorrow."

"Why?" asked Casher, his voice loud and cold, trying to wring some sense out of the chattering man.

"Just—just—just because I *say so* . . ." stammered the Administrator.

"Why?" asked Casher, cold and loud again.

The liquor suddenly took over inside the Administrator. He groped back for the arm of his chair, sat down suddenly and then looked up at Casher. He was very drunk indeed. The strange emotion, the elusive fatigue-despair, had vanished from his face. He spoke straightforwardly. Only the excessive care of his articulation would have shown a passerby that he was drunk.

"Because, you fool," said Meiklejohn, "those people, more than eighty in eighty years, that I have sent to Beauregard with orders to kill the girl . . . Those people—" he repeated, and stopped speaking, clamping his lips together.

"What happened to them?" asked Casher calmly and persuasively.

The Administrator grinned again and seemed to be on the edge of one of his wild laughs.

"What happened?" shouted Casher at him.

"I don't know," said the Administrator. "For the life of me, I don't know. Not one of them ever came back."

"What happened to them? Did she kill them?" cried Casher.

"How would I know?" said the drunken man, getting visibly more sleepy.

"Why didn't you report it?"

This seemed to rouse the Administrator. "Report that one little girl had stopped me, the planetary Administrator? Just one little girl, and not even a human being! They would have sent help, and laughed at me. By the Bell, young man, I've been laughed at enough! I need no help from outside. You're going in there tomorrow morning. At two seventy-five, with a knife. And a groundcar waiting."

He stared fixedly at Casher and then suddenly fell asleep in his chair. Casher called to the robots to show him to his room; they tended to the master as well.

II

The next morning at two seventy-five sharp, nothing happened. Casher walked down the baroque corridor, looking into beautiful barren rooms. All the doors were open.

Through one door he heard a sick deep bubbling snore.

It was the Administrator, sure enough. He lay twisted in his bed. A small nursing machine was beside him, her white-enameled body only slightly rusty. She held up a mechanical hand for silence and somehow managed to make the gesture seem light, delicate and pretty, even from a machine.

Casher walked lightly back to his own room, where he ordered hotcakes, bacon and coffee. He studied a tornado through the armored glass of his window, while the robots prepared his food. The elastic trees clung to the earth with a fury which matched the fury of the wind. The trunk of the tornado reached like the nose of a mad elephant down into the gardens, but the flora fought back. A few animals whipped upward and out of sight. The tornado then came straight for the house, but did not damage it outside of making a lot of noise.

"We have two or three hundred of those a day," said a butler robot. "That is why we store all spacecraft underground and have no weather machines. It would cost more, the people said, to make this planet livable than the planet could possibly yield. The radio and news are in the library, sir. I do not think that the honorable Rankin Meiklejohn will wake until evening, say seven-fifty or eight o'clock."

"Can I go out?"

"Why not, sir? You are a true man. You do what you wish."

"I mean is it safe for me to go out?"

"Oh, no, sir! The wind would tear you apart or carry you away."

"Don't people ever go out?"

"Yes, sir. With groundcars or with automatic body armor. I have been told that if it weighs fifty tons or better, the person inside is safe. I would not know, sir. As you see, I am a robot. I was made here, though my brain was formed on Earth Two, and I have never been outside this house."

Casher looked at the robot. This one seemed unusually talkative. He chanced the opportunity of getting some more information.

"Have you ever heard of Beauregard?"

"Yes, sir. It is the best house on this planet. I have heard people say that it is the most solid building on Henriada. It belongs to the Mister and Owner Murray Madigan. He is an Old North Australian, a renunciant who left his home planet and came here when Henriada was a busy world. He brought all his wealth with him. The underpeople and robots say that it is a wonderful place on the inside."

"Have you seen it?"

"Oh, no, sir. I have never left this building."

"Does the man Madigan ever come here?"

The robot seemed to be trying to laugh, but did not succeed. He answered, very unevenly, "Oh, no, sir. He never goes anywhere."

"Can you tell me anything about the female who lives with him?"

"No sir," said the robot.

"Do you know anything about her?"

"Sir, it is not that. I know a great deal about her."

"Why can't you talk about her, then?"

"I have been commanded not to, sir."

"I am," said Casher O'Neill, "a true human being. I herewith countermand those orders. Tell me about her."

The robot's voice became formal and cold. "The orders cannot be countermanded, sir."

"Why not?" snapped Casher. "Are they the Administrator's?"

"No, sir."

"Whose, then?"

"Hers," said the robot softly, and left the room.

III

Casher O'Neill spent the rest of the day trying to get information; he obtained very little.

The Deputy Administrator was a young man who hated his chief.

When Casher, who dined with him—the two of them having a poorly cooked state luncheon in a dining room which would have seated five hundred people—tried to come to the point by asking bluntly, "What do you know about Murray Madigan?" he got an answer which was blunt to the point of incivility.

"Nothing."

"You never heard of him?" cried Casher.

"Keep your troubles to yourself, mister visitor," said the Deputy Administrator. "I've got to stay on this planet long enough to get promoted off. You can leave. You shouldn't have come."

"I have," said Casher, "an all-world pass from the Instrumentality."

"All right," said the young man. "That shows that you are more important than I am. Let's not discuss the matter. Do you like your lunch?"

Casher had learned diplomacy in his childhood, when he was the heir apparent to the dictatorship of Mizzer. When his horrible uncle, Kuraf, lost the rulership, Casher had approved of the coup by the Colonels Wedder and Gibna; but now Wedder was supreme and enforcing a period of terror and virtue. Casher thus knew courts and ceremony, big talk and small talk, and on this occasion he let the small talk do. The young Deputy Administrator had only one ambition, to get off the planet Henriada and never to see or hear of Rankin Meiklejohn again.

Casher could understand the point.

Only one curious thing happened during dinner.

Toward the end, Casher slipped in the question, very informally: "Can underpeople give orders to robots?"

"Of course," said the young man. "That's one of the reasons we use underpeople. They have more initiative. They amplify our orders to robots on many occasions."

Casher smiled. "I didn't mean it quite that way. Could an underperson give an order to a robot which a real human being could not then countermand?"

The young man started to answer, even though his mouth was full of food. He was not a very polished young man. Suddenly he stopped chewing and his eyes grew wide. Then, with his mouth half full, he said, "You are trying to talk about this planet, I guess. You can't help it. You're on the track. Stay on the track, then. Maybe you will get out of it alive. I refuse to get mixed up with it, with you, with him and his hateful schemes. All I want to do is to leave when my time comes."

The young man resumed chewing, his eyes fixed steadfastly on his plate.

Before Casher could pass off the matter by making some casual remark, the butler robot stopped behind him and leaned over.

"Honorable sir, I heard your question. May I answer it?"

"Of course," said Casher softly.

"The answer, sir," said the butler robot, softly but clearly, "to your question is *no, no, never*. That is the general rule of the civilized worlds. But on this planet of Henriada, sir, the answer is *yes*."

"Why?" asked Casher.

"It is my duty, sir," said the robot butler, "to recommend to you this dish of fresh artichokes. I am not authorized to deal with other matters."

"Thank you," said Casher, straining a little to keep himself looking imperturbable.

Nothing much happened that night, except that Meiklejohn got up long enough to get drunk all over again. Though he invited Casher to come and drink with him, he never seriously discussed the girl except for one outburst.

"Leave it till tomorrow. Fair and square. Open and aboveboard. Frank and honest. That's me. I'll take you around Beauregard myself. You'll see it's easy. A knife, eh? A traveled young man like you would know what to do with a knife. And a little girl too. Not very big. Easy job. Don't give it another thought. Would you like some apple juice in your byegarr?"

Casher had taken three contraintoxicant pills before going to drink with the ex-Lord, but even at that he could not keep up with Meiklejohn. He accepted the dilution of apple juice gravely, gracefully and gratefully.

The little tornadoes stamped around the house. Meiklejohn, now launched into some drunken story of ancient injustices which had been done to him on other worlds, paid no attention to them. In the middle of the night, past nine-fifty in the evening, Casher woke alone in his chair, very stiff and uncomfortable. The robots must have had standing instructions concerning the Administrator, and had apparently taken him off to bed. Casher walked wearily to his own room, cursed the thundering ceiling and went to sleep again.

IV

The next day was very different indeed.

The Administrator was as sober, brisk and charming as if he had never taken a drink in his life.

He had the robots call Casher to join him at breakfast and said, by way of greeting, "I'll wager you thought I was drunk last night."

"Well . . ." said Casher.

"Planet fever. That's what it was. Planet fever. A bit of alcohol keeps it from developing too far. Let's see. It's three-sixty now. Could you be ready to leave by four?"

Casher frowned at his watch, which had the conventional twenty-four hours.

The Administrator saw the glance and apologized. "Sorry! My fault, a thousand times. I'll get you a metric watch right away. Ten hours a day, a hundred minutes an hour. We're very progressive here on Henriada."

He clapped his hands and ordered that a watch be taken to Casher's room, along with the watch-repairing robot to adjust it to Casher's body rhythms.

"Four, then," he said, rising briskly from the table. "Dress for a trip by groundcar. The servants will show you how."

There was a man already waiting in Casher's room. He looked like a plump, wise ancient Hindu, as shown in the archaeology books. He bowed pleasantly and said, "My name is Gosigo. I am a forgetty, settled on this planet, but for this day I am your guide and driver from this place to the mansion of Beauregard."

Forgetties were barely above underpeople in status. They were persons convicted of various major crimes, to whom the courts of the worlds, or the Instrumentality, had allowed total amnesia instead of death or some punishment worse than death, such as the planet Shayol.

Casher looked at him curiously. The man did not carry with him the permanent air of bewilderment which Casher had noticed in many forgetties. Gosigo saw the glance and interpreted it.

"I'm well enough now, sir. And I am strong enough to break your back if I had the orders to do it."

"You mean damage my spine? What a hostile, unpleasant thing to do!" said Casher. "Anyhow, I rather think I could kill you first if you tried it. Whatever gave you such an idea?"

"The Administrator is always threatening people that he will have me do it to them."

"Have you ever really broken anybody's back?" asked Casher, looking Gosigo over very carefully and rejudging him. The man, though shorter than Casher, was luxuriously muscled; like many plump men, he looked pleasant on the outside but could be very formidable to an enemy.

Gosigo smiled briefly, almost happily. "Well, no, not exactly."

"Why haven't you? Does the Administrator always countermand his own orders? I should think that he would sometimes be too drunk to remember to do it."

"It's not that," said Gosigo.

"Why don't you, then?"

"I have other orders," said Gosigo, rather hesitantly. "Like the orders I have today. One set from the Administrator, one set from the Deputy Administrator, and a third set from an outside source."

"Who's the outside source?"

"She has told me not to explain just yet."

Casher stood stock still. "Do you mean who I think you mean?"

Gosigo nodded very slowly, pointing at the ventilator as though it might have a microphone in it.

"Can you tell me what your orders are?"

"Oh, certainly. The Administrator has told me to drive both himself and you to Beauregard, to take you to the door, to watch you stab the undergirl, and to call the second groundcar to your rescue. The Deputy Administrator has told me to take you to Beauregard and to let you do as you please, bringing you back here by way of Ambiloxi if you happen to come out of Mr. Murray's house alive."

"And the other orders?"

"To close the door upon you when you enter and to think of you no more in this life, because you will be very happy."

"Are you crazy?" cried Casher.

"I am a forgetty," said Gosigo, with some dignity, "but I am not insane."

"Whose orders are you going to obey, then?"

Gosigo smiled a warmly human smile at him. "Doesn't that depend on you, sir, and not on me? Do I look like a man who is going to kill you soon?"

"No, you don't," said Casher.

"Do you know what you look like to me?" went on Gosigo, with a purr. "Do you really think that I would help you if I thought that you would kill a small girl?"

"You know it!" cried Casher, feeling his face go white.

"Who doesn't?" said Gosigo. "What else have we got to talk about, here on Henriada? Let me help you on with these clothes, so that you will at least survive the ride." With this he handed shoulder padding and padded helmet to Casher, who began to put on the garments, very clumsily.

Gosigo helped him.

When Casher was fully dressed, he thought that he had never dressed this elaborately for space itself. The world of Henriada must be a tumultuous place if people needed this kind of clothing to make a short trip.

Gosigo had put on the same kind of clothes.

He looked at Casher in a friendly manner, with an arch smile which came close to humor. "Look at me, honorable visitor. Do I remind you of anybody?"

Casher looked honestly and carefully, and then said, "No, you don't."

The man's face fell. "It's a game," he said. "I can't help trying to find out who I really am. Am I a Lord of the Instrumentality who has betrayed his trust? Am I a scientist who twisted knowledge into unimaginable wrong? Am I a dictator so foul that even the Instrumentality, which usually leaves things alone, had to step in and wipe me out? Here I am, healthy, wise, alert. I have the name Gosigo on this planet. Perhaps I am a mere native of this planet, who has committed a local crime. I am triggered. If anyone ever did tell me my true name or my actual past, I have been conditioned to shriek loud, fall unconscious and forget anything which might be said on such an occasion. People told me that I must have chosen this instead of death. Maybe. Death sometimes looks tidy to a forgetty."

"Have you ever screamed and fainted?"

"I don't even know *that*," said Gosigo, "no more than you know where you are going this very day."

Casher was tied to the man's mystifications, so he did not let himself be provoked into a useless show of curiosity. Inquisitive about the forgetty himself, he asked:

"Does it hurt—does it hurt to be a forgetty?"

"No," said Gosigo, "it doesn't hurt, no more than you will."

Gosigo stared suddenly at Casher. His voice changed tone and became at least one octave higher. He clapped his hands to his face and panted through his hands as if he would never speak again.

"But—oh! The fear—the eerie, dreary fear of *being me!*"

He still stared at Casher.

Quieting down at last, he pulled his hands away from his face, as if by sheer force, and said in an almost normal voice, "Shall we get on with our trip?"

Gosigo led the way out into the bare bleak corridor. A perceptible wind was blowing through it, though there was no sign of an open window or door. They followed a majestic staircase; with steps so broad that Casher had to keep changing pace on them, all the way down to the bottom of the building. This must, at some time, have been a formal reception hall. Now it was full of cars.

Curious cars.

Land vehicles of a kind which Casher had never seen before. They looked a little bit like the ancient "fighting tanks" which he had seen in pictures. They also looked a little like submarines of a singularly short and ugly shape. They had high spiked wheels, but their most complicated feature was a set of giant corkscrews, four on each side, attached to the car by intricate yet operational apparatus. Since Casher had been landed right into the palace by plano-form, he had never had occasion to go outside among the tornadoes of Henriada.

The Administrator was waiting, wearing a coverall on which was stenciled his insignia of rank.

Casher gave him a polite bow. He glanced down at the handsome metric wristwatch which Gosigo had strapped on his wrist, outside the coverall. It read 3:95.

Casher bowed to Rankin Meiklejohn and said, "I'm ready, sir, if you are."

"Watch him!" whispered Gosigo, half a step behind Casher.

The Administrator said, "Might as well be going." The man's voice trembled.

Casher stood polite, alert, immobile. Was this danger? Was this foolishness? Could the Administrator already be drunk again?

Casher watched the Administrator carefully but quietly, waiting for the older man to precede him into the nearest groundcar, which had its door standing open.

Nothing happened, except that the Administrator began to turn pale.

There must have been six or eight people present. The others must have seen the same sort of thing before, because they showed no sign of curiosity or bewilderment. The Administrator began to tremble. Casher could see it, even through the bulk of the travelwear. The man's hands shook.

The Administrator said, in a high nervous voice, "Your knife. You have it with you?"

Casher nodded.

"Let me see it," said the Administrator.

Casher reached down to his boot and brought out the beautiful, superbly balanced knife. Before he could stand erect, he felt the clamp of Gosigo's heavy fingers on his shoulder.

"Master," said Gosigo to Meiklejohn, "tell your visitor to put his weapon away. It is not allowed for any of us to show weapons in your presence."

Casher tried to squirm out of the heavy grip without losing his balance or his dignity. He found that Gosigo was knowledgeable about karate too. The forgetty held ground, even when the two men waged an immobile, invisible sort of wrestling match, the leverage of Casher's shoulder working its way hither and yon against the strong grip of Gosigo's powerful hand.

The Administrator ended it. He said, "Put away your knife . . ." in that high funny voice of his.

The watch had almost reached 4:00, but no one had yet got into the car.

Gosigo spoke again, and when he did there was a contemptuous laugh from the Deputy Administrator, who had stood by in ordinary indoor clothes.

"Master, isn't it time for 'one for the road'?"

"Of course, of course," chattered the Administrator. He began breathing almost normally again.

"Join me," he said to Casher. "It's a local custom."

Casher had let his knife slip back into his bootsheath. When the knife dropped out of sight, Gosigo released his shoulder; he now stood facing the Administrator and rubbed his bruised shoulder. He said nothing, but shook his head gently, showing that he did not want a drink.

One of the robots brought the Administrator a glass, which appeared to contain at least a liter and a half of water. The Administrator said, very politely, "Sure you won't share it?"

This close, Casher could smell the reek of it. It was pure byegarr, and at least 160 proof. He shook his head again, firmly but also politely.

The Administrator lifted the glass.

Casher could see the muscles of the man's throat work as the liquid went down. He could hear the man breathing heavily between swallows. The white liquid went lower and lower in the gigantic glass.

At last it was all gone.

The Administrator cocked his head sidewise and said to Casher in a parrotlike voice, "Well, toodle-oo!"

"What do you mean, sir?" asked Casher.

The Administrator had a pleasant glow on his face. Casher was surprised that the man was not dead after that big and sudden a drink.

"I just mean g'bye. I'm—not—feeling—well."

With that he fell straight forward, as stiff as a rock tower. One of the servants, perhaps another forgetty, caught him before he hit the ground.

"Does he always do this?" asked Casher of the miserable and contemptuous Deputy Administrator.

"Oh, no," said the Deputy. "Only at times like these."

"What do you mean, 'like these'?"

"When he sends one more armed man against the girl at Beauregard. They never come back. You won't come back, either. You could have left earlier, but you can't now. Go along and try to kill the girl. I'll see you here about five twenty-five if you succeed. As a matter of fact, if you come back at all, I'll try to wake *him* up. But you won't come back. Good luck. I suppose that's what you need. Good luck."

Casher shook hands with the man without removing his gloves. Gosigo had already climbed into the driver's seat of the machine and was testing the electric engines. The big corkscrews began to plunge down, but before they touched the floor, Gosigo had reversed them and thrown them back into the up position.

The people in the room ran for cover as Casher entered the machine, though there was no immediate danger in sight. Two of the human servants dragged the Administrator up the stairs, the Deputy Administrator following them rapidly.

"Seat belt," said Gosigo.

Casher found it and snapped it closed.

"Head belt," said Gosigo.

Casher stared at him. He had never heard of a head belt.

"Pull it down from the roof, sir. Put the net under your chin."

Casher glanced up.

There was a net fitted snugly against the roof of the vehicle, just above his head. He started to pull it down, but it did not yield. Angrily, he pulled harder, and it moved slowly downward. *By the Bell and Bank, do they want to hang me in this*! he thought to himself as he dragged the net down. There was a strong fiber belt attached to each end of the net, while the net itself was only fifteen to twenty centimeters wide. He ended up in a foolish position, holding the head belt with both hands lest it snap back into the ceiling and not knowing what to do with it. Gosigo leaned over and, half impatiently, helped him adjust the web under his chin. It pinched for a moment and Casher felt as though his head were being dragged by a heavy weight.

"Don't fight it," said Gosigo. "Relax."

Casher did. His head was lifted several centimeters into a foam pocket, which he had not previously noticed, in the back of the seat. After a second or two, he realized that the position was odd but comfortable.

Gosigo had adjusted his own head belt and had turned on the lights of the vehicle. They blazed so bright that Casher almost thought they might be a laser, capable of charring the inner doors of the big room.

The lights must have keyed the door.

V

Two panels slid open and a wild uproar of wind and vegetation rushed in. It was rough and stormy but far below hurricane velocity.

The machine rolled forward clumsily and was out of the house and on the road very quickly.

The sky was brown, bright luminous brown, shot through with streaks of yellow. Casher had never seen a sky of that color on any other world he had visited, and in his long exile he had seen many planets.

Gosigo, staring straight ahead, was preoccupied with keeping the vehicle right in the middle of the black, soft, tarry road.

"Watch it!" said a voice speaking right into his head.

It was Gosigo, using an intercom which must have been built into the helmets.

Casher watched, though there was nothing to see except for the rush of mad wind. Suddenly the groundcar turned dark, spun upside down, and was violently shaken. An oily, pungent stench of pure fetor immediately drenched the whole car.

Gosigo pulled out a panel with a console of buttons. Light and fire, intolerably bright, burned in on them through the windshield and the portholes on the side.

The battle was over before it began.

The groundcar lay in a sort of swamp. The road was visible thirty or thirty-five meters away.

There was a grinding sound inside the machine and the groundcar righted itself. A singular sucking noise followed, then the grinding sound stopped. Casher could glimpse the big corkscrews on the side of the car eating their way into the ground.

At last the machine was steady, pelted only by branches, leaves and what seemed like kelp.

A small tornado was passing over them.

Gosigo took time to twist his head sidewise and to talk to Casher.

"An air whale swallowed us and I had to burn our way out."

"A what?" cried Casher.

"An air whale," repeated Gosigo calmly on the intercom. "There are no indigenous forms of life on this planet, but the imported Earth forms have changed wildly since we brought them in. The tornadoes lifted the whales around enough so that some of them got adapted to flying. They were the meat-eating kind, so they like to crack our groundcars open and eat the goodies inside. We're safe enough from them for the time being, provided we can make it back to the road. There are a few wild men who live in the wind, but they would not become dangerous to us unless we found ourselves really helpless. Pretty soon I can unscrew us from the ground and try to get back on the road. It's not really too far from here to Ambiloxi."

The trip to the road was a long one, even though they could see the road itself all the time that they tried various approaches.

The first time, the groundcar tipped ominously forward. Red lights showed on the panel and buzzers buzzed. The great spiked wheels spun in vain as they chewed their way into a bottomless quagmire.

Gosigo, calling back to his passenger, cried, "Hold steady! We're going to have to shoot ourselves out of this one backward!"

Casher did not know how he could be any steadier, belted, hooded and strapped as he was, but he clutched the arms of his seat.

The world went red with fire as the front of the car spat flame in rocketlike quantities. The swamp ahead of them boiled into steam, so that they could see nothing. Gosigo changed the windshield over from visual to radar, and even with radar there was not much to be seen—nothing but a gray swirl of formless wraiths, and the weird lurching sensation as the machine fought its way back to solid ground. The console suddenly showed green and Gosigo cut the controls. They were back where they had been, with the repulsive burnt entrails of the air whale scattered among the coral trees.

"Try again," said Gosigo, as though Casher had something to do with the matter.

He fiddled with the controls and the groundcar rose several feet. The spikes on the wheels had been hydraulically extended until they were each at least one hundred fifty centimeters long. The car felt like a large enclosed bicycle as it teetered on its big wheels. The wind was strong and capricious but there was no tornado in sight.

"Here we go," said Gosigo redundantly. The groundcar pressed forward in a mad rush, hastening obliquely through the vegetation and making for the highway on Casher's right.

A bone-jarring crash told them that they had not made it. For a moment Casher was too dizzy to see where they were.

He was glad of his helmet and happy about the web brace which held his neck. That crash would have killed him if he had not had full protection.

Gosigo seemed to think the trip normal. His classic Hindu features relaxed in a wise smile as he said, "Hit a boulder. Fell on our side. Try again."

Casher managed to gasp, "Is the machine unbreakable?"

There was a laugh in Gosigo's voice when he answered, "Almost. We're the most vulnerable items in it."

Again fire spat at the ground, this time from the side of the groundcar. It balanced itself precariously on the four high wheels. Gosigo turned on the radar screen to look through the steam which their own jets had called up.

There the road was, plain and near.

"Try again!" he shouted, as the machine lunged forward and then performed a veritable ballet on the surface of the marsh. It rushed, slowed, turned around on a hummock, gave itself an assist with the jets and then scrambled through the water.

Casher saw the inverted cone of a tornado, half a kilometer or less away, veering toward them.

Gosigo sensed his unspoken thought, because he answered, "Problem: who gets to the road first, that or we?"

The machine bucked, lurched, twisted, spun.

Casher could see nothing anymore from the windshield in front, but it was obvious that Gosigo knew what he was doing.

There was the sickening, stomach-wrenching twist of a big drop and then a new sound was heard—a grinding as of knives.

Gosigo, unworried, took his head out of the headnet and looked over at Casher with a smile. "The twister will probably hit us in a minute or two, but it doesn't matter now. We're on the road and I've bolted us to the surface."

"Bolted?" gasped Casher.

"You know, those big screws on the outside of the car. They were made to go right into the road. All the roads here are neo-asphaltum and self-repairing. There will be traces of them here when the last known person on the last known planet is dead. These are *good* roads." He stopped for the sudden hush. "Storm's going over us—"

It began again before he could finish his sentence. Wild raving winds tore at the machine, which sat so solid that it seemed bedded in permastone.

Gosigo pushed two buttons and calibrated a dial. He squinted at his instruments, then pressed a button mounted on the edge of his navigator's seat. There was a sharp explosion, like a blasting of rock by chemical methods.

Casher started to speak but Gosigo held out a warning hand for silence.

He tuned his dials quickly. The windshield faded out, radar came on and then went off, and at last a bright map—bright red in background with sharp gold lines—appeared across the whole width of the screen. There were a dozen or more bright points on the map. Gosigo watched these intently.

The map blurred, faded, dissolved into red chaos.

Gosigo pushed another button and then could see out of the front glass screen again.

"What was that?" asked Casher.

"Miniaturized radar rocket. I sent it up twelve kilometers for a look around. It transmitted a map of what it saw and I put it on our radar screen. The tornadoes are heavier than usual, but I think we can make it. Did you notice the top right of the map?"

"The top right?" asked Casher.

"Yes, the top right. Did you see what was there?"

"Why, nothing," said Casher. "Nothing was there."

"You're utterly right," said Gosigo. "What does that mean to you?"

"I don't understand you," said Casher. "I suppose it means that there is nothing there."

"Right again. But let me tell you something. There never is."

"Never is what?"

"Anything," said Gosigo. "There never is anything on the maps at that point. That's east of Ambiloxi. That's Beauregard. It never shows on the maps. Nothing happens there."

"No bad weather—ever?" asked Casher.

"Never," said Gosigo.

"Why not?" asked Casher.

"*She* will not permit it," said Gosigo firmly, as though his words made sense.

"You mean her weather machines work?" said Casher, grasping for the only rational explanation possible.

"Yes," said Gosigo.

"Why?"

"She pays for them."

"How can she?" exclaimed Casher. "Your whole world of Henri-ada is bankrupt!"

"Her part isn't."

"Stop mystifying me," said Casher. "Tell me who she is and what this is all about."

"Put your head in the net," said Gosigo. "I'm not making puzzles because I want to do so. I have been commanded not to talk."

"Because you are a forgetty?"

"What's that got to do with it? Don't talk to me that way. Remember, I am not an animal or an underperson. I may be your servant for a few hours, but I am a *man*. You'll find out, soon enough. *Hold tight!*"

The groundcar came to a panic stop, the spiked teeth eating into the resilient firm neo-asphaltum of the road. At the instant they stopped, the outside corkscrews began chewing their way into the ground. First Casher felt as though his eyes were popping out, because of the suddenness of the deceleration; now he felt like holding the arms of his seat as the tornado reached directly for their car, plucking at it again and again. The enormous outside screws held and he could feel the car straining to meet the gigantic suction of the storm.

"Don't worry," shouted Gosigo over the noise of the storm. "I always pin us down a little bit more by firing the quickrockets straight up. These cars don't often go off the road."

Casher tried to relax.

The funnel of the tornado, which seemed almost like a living being, plucked after them once or twice more and then was gone.

This time Casher had seen no sign of the air whales which rode the storms. He had seen nothing but rain and wind and desolation.

The tornado was gone in a moment. Ghostlike shapes trailed after it in enormous prancing leaps.

"Wind men," said Gosigo glancing at them incuriously. "Wild people who have learned to live on Henriada. They aren't much more than animals. We are close to the territory of the lady. They would not dare attack us here."

Casher O'Neill was too stunned to query the man or to challenge him.

Once more the car picked itself up and coursed along the smooth, narrow, winding neo-asphaltum road, almost as though the machine itself were glad to function and to function well.

VI

Casher could never quite remember when they went from the howling wildness of Henriada into the stillness and beauty of the domains of Mr. Murray Madigan. He could recall the feeling but not the facts.

The town of Ambiloxi eluded him completely. It was so normal a town, so old-fashioned a little town that he could not think of it very much. Old people sat on the wooden boardwalk taking their afternoon look at the strangers who passed through. Horses were tethered in a row along the main street, between the parked machines. It looked like a peaceful picture from the ancient ages.

Of tornadoes there was no sign, nor of the hurt and ruin which showed around the house of Rankin Meiklejohn. There were few underpeople or robots about, unless they were so cleverly contrived as to look almost exactly like real people. How can you remember something which is pleasant and nonmemorable? Even the buildings did not show signs of being fortified against the frightful storms which had brought the prosperous planet of Henriada to a condition of abandonment and ruin.

Gosigo, who had a remarkable talent for stating the obvious, said tonelessly, "The weather machines are working here. There is no need for special precaution."

But he did not stop in the town for rest, refreshments, conversation, or fuel. He went through deftly and quietly, the gigantic armored groundcar looking out of place among the peaceful and defenseless vehicles. He went as though he had been on the same route many times before, and knew the routine well.

Once beyond Ambiloxi he speeded up, though at a moderate pace compared to the frantic elusive action he had taken against storms in the earlier part of the trip. The landscape was earthlike, wet, and most of the ground was covered with vegetation.

Old radar countermissile towers stood along the road. Casher could not imagine their possible use, even though he was sure, from the looks of them, that they were long obsolete.

"What's the countermissile radar for?" he asked, speaking comfortably now that his head was out of the headnet.

Gosigo turned around and gave him a tortured glance in which pain and bewilderment were mixed. "Countermissile radar? Countermissile radar? I don't know that word, though it seems as though I should. . . ."

"Radar is what you were using to see with, back in the storm, when the ceiling and visibility were zero."

Gosigo turned back to his driving, narrowly missing a tree. "That? That's just artificial vision. Why did you use the term 'countermissile radar'? There isn't any of that stuff here except what we have on our machine, though the mistress may be watching us if her set is on."

"Those towers," said Casher. "They look like countermissile towers from the ancient times."

"Towers. There aren't any towers here," snapped Gosigo.

"Look," cried Casher. "Here are two more of them."

"No man made those. They aren't buildings. It's just air coral. Some of the coral which people brought from earth mutated and got so it could live in the air. People used to plant it for windbreaks, before they decided to give up Henriada and move out. They didn't do much good, but they are pretty to look at."

They rode along a few minutes without asking questions. Tall trees had Spanish moss trailing over them. They were close to a sea. Small marshes appeared to the right and left of the road; here, where the endless tornadoes were kept out, everything had a parklike effect. The domains of the estate of Beauregard were unlike anything else on Henriada—an area of peaceful wildness in a world which was rushing otherwise toward uninhabitability and ruin. Even Gosigo seemed more relaxed, more cheerful as he steered the groundcar along the pleasant elevated road.

Gosigo sighed, leaned forward, managed the controls and brought the car to a stop.

He turned around calmly and looked full face at Casher O'Neill. "You have your knife?"

Casher automatically felt for it. It was there, safe enough in his bootsheath. He simply nodded.

"You have your orders."

"You mean, killing the girl?"

"Yes," said Gosigo. "Killing the girl."

"I remember that. You didn't have to stop the car to tell me that."

"I'm telling you now," said Gosigo, his wise Hindu face showing neither humor nor outrage. "Do it."

"You mean kill her? Right at first sight?"

"Do it," said Gosigo. "You have your orders."

"I'm the judge of that," said Casher. "It will be on my conscience. Are you watching me for the Administrator?"

"That drunken fool?" said Gosigo. "I don't care about him, except that I am a forgetty and I belong to him. We're in *her* territory now. You are going to do whatever she wants. You have orders to kill her. All right. Kill her."

"You mean—she wants to be murdered?"

"Of course not!" said Gosigo, with the irritation of an adult who has to explain too many things to an inquisitive child.

"Then how can I kill her without finding out what this is all about?"

"She knows. She knows herself. She knows her master. She knows this planet. She knows me and she knows something about you. Go ahead and kill her, since those are your orders. If she wants to die, that's not for you or me to decide. It's her business. If she does not want to die, you will not succeed."

"I'd like to see the person," said Casher, "who could stop me in a sudden knife attack. Have *you* told her that I am coming?"

"I've told her nothing, but she knows we are coming and she is pretty sure what you have been sent for. Don't think about it. Just do what you are told. Jump for her with the knife. She will take care of the matter."

"But—" cried Casher.

"Stop asking questions," said Gosigo. "Just follow orders and remember that she will take care of you. Even you." He started up the groundcar.

Within less than a kilometer they had crossed a low ridge of land and there before them lay Beauregard—the mansion at the edge of the waters, its white pillars shining, its pergolas glistening in the bright air, its yards and palmettos tidy.

Casher was a brave man, but he felt the palms of his hands go wet when he realized that in a minute or two he would have to commit a murder.

VII

The groundcar swung up the drive. It stopped. Without a word, Gosigo activated the door. The air smelled calm, sea-wet, salt and yet coolly fresh.

Casher jumped out and ran to the door.

He was surprised to feel that his legs trembled as he ran.

He had killed before, real men in real quarrels. Why should a mere animal matter to him?

The door stopped him.

Without thinking, he tried to wrench it open.

The knob did not yield and there was no automatic control in sight. This was indeed a very antique sort of house. He struck the door with his hands. The thuds sounded around him. He could not tell whether they resounded in the house. No sound or echo came from beyond the door.

He began rehearsing the phrase "I want to see the Mister and Owner Madigan. . . ."

The door did open.

A little girl stood there.

He knew her. He had always known her. She was his sweetheart, come back out of his childhood. She was the sister he had never had. She was his own mother, when young. She was at the marvelous age, somewhere between ten and thirteen, where the child—as the phrase goes—"becomes an old child and not a raw grownup." She was kind, calm, intelligent, expectant, quiet, inviting, unafraid. She felt like someone he had never left behind; yet, at the same moment, he knew he had never seen her before.

He heard his voice asking for the Mister and Owner Madigan while he wondered, at the back of his mind, who the girl might be. Madigan's daughter? Neither Rankin Meiklejohn nor the deputy had said anything about a human family.

The child looked at him levelly.

He must have finished braying his question at her.

"Mister and Owner Madigan," said the child, "sees no one this day, but you are seeing me." She looked at him levelly and calmly. There was an odd hint of humor, of fearlessness in her stance.

"Who are you?" he blurted out.

"I am the housekeeper of this house."

"You?" he cried, wild alarm beginning in his throat.

"My name," she said, "is T'ruth."

His knife was in his hand before he knew how it had got there. He remembered the advice of the Administrator: *plunge, plunge, stab, stab, run!*

She saw the knife but her eyes did not waver from his face.

He looked at her uncertainly.

If this was an underperson, it was the most remarkable one he had ever seen. But even Gosigo had told him to do his duty, to stab, to kill the woman named T'ruth. Here she was. He could not do it.

He spun the knife in the air, caught it by its tip and held it out to her, handle first.

"I was sent to kill you," he said, "but I find I cannot do it. I have lost a cruiser."

"Kill me if you wish," she said, "because I have no fear of you."

Her calm words were so far outside his experience that he took the knife in his left hand and lifted his arm as if to stab toward her.

He dropped his arm.

"I cannot do it," he whined. "What have you done to me?"

"I have done nothing to you. You do not wish to kill a child and I look to you like a child. Besides, I think you love me. If this is so, it must be very uncomfortable for you."

Casher heard his knife clatter to the floor as he dropped it. He had never dropped it before.

"Who are you," he gasped, "that you should do this to me?"

"I am me," she said, her voice as tranquil and happy as that of any girl, provided that the girl was caught at a moment of great happiness and poise. "I am the housekeeper of this house." She smiled almost impishly and added, "It seems that I must almost be the ruler of this planet as well." Her voice turned serious. *"Man,"* she said, "can't you see it, man? I am an animal, a turtle. I am incapable of disobeying the word of man. When I was little I was trained and I was given orders. I shall carry out those orders as long as I live. When I look at you, I feel strange. You look as though you loved me already, but you do not know what to do. Wait a moment. I must let Gosigo go."

The shining knife on the floor of the doorway she saw; she stepped over it.

Gosigo had got out of the groundcar and was giving her a formal, low bow.

"Tell me," she cried, "what have you just seen!" There was friendliness in her call, as though the routine were an old game.

"I saw Casher O'Neill bound up the steps. You yourself opened the door. He thrust his dagger into your throat and the blood spat out in a big stream, rich and dark and red. You died in the doorway. For some reason Casher O'Neill went on into the house without saying anything to me. I became frightened and I fled."

He did not look frightened at all.

"If I am dead," she said, "how can I be talking to you?"

"Don't ask me," cried Gosigo. "I am just a forgetty. I always go back to the Honorable Rankin Meiklejohn, each time that you are murdered, and I tell him the truth of what I saw. Then he gives me the medicine and I tell him something else. At that point he will get drunk and gloomy again, the way that he always does."

"It's a pity," said the child. "I wish I could help him, but I can't. He won't come to Beauregard."

"Him?" Gosigo laughed. "Oh, no, not him! Never! He just sends other people to kill you."

"And he's never satisfied," said the child sadly, "no matter how many times he kills me!"

"Never," said Gosigo cheerfully, climbing back into the groundcar. " 'Bye now."

"Wait a moment," she called. "Wouldn't you like something to eat or drink before you drive back? There's a bad clutch of storms on the road."

"Not me," said Gosigo. "He might punish me and make me a forgetty all over again. Say, maybe that's already happened. Maybe I'm a forgetty who's been put through it several times, not just once." Hope surged into his voice. "T'ruth! T'ruth! Can *you* tell me?"

"Suppose I did tell you," said she. "What would happen?"

His face became sad, "I'd have a convulsion and forget what I told you. Well, good-bye anyhow. I'll take a chance on the storms. If you ever see that Casher O'Neill again," called Gosigo, looking right through Casher O'Neill, "tell him I liked him but that we'll never meet again."

"I'll tell him," said the girl gently. She watched as the heavy brown man climbed nimbly into the car. The top crammed shut with no sound. The wheels turned and in a moment the car had disappeared behind the palmettos in the drive.

While she had talked to Gosigo in her clear warm high girlish voice, Casher had watched her. He could see the thin shape of her shoulders under the light blue shift that she wore. There was the suggestion of a pair of panties under the dress, so light was the material. Her hips had not begun to fill. When he glanced at her in one-quarter profile, he could see that her cheek was smooth, her hair well-combed, her little breasts just beginning to bud on her chest. Who was this child who acted like an empress?

She turned back to him and gave him a warm, apologetic smile.

"Gosigo and I always talk over the story together. Then he goes back and Meiklejohn does not believe it and spends unhappy months planning my murder all over again. I suppose, since I am just an animal, that I should not call it a murder when somebody tries to kill me, but I resist, of course. I do not care about me, but I have orders, strong orders, to keep my master and his house safe from harm."

"How old are you?" asked Casher. He added, "If you can tell the truth."

"I can tell nothing but the truth. I am conditioned. I am nine hundred and six Earth years old."

"Nine hundred?" he cried. "But you look like a child . . ."

"I am a child," said the girl, "and not a child. I am an earth turtle, changed into human form by the convenience of man. My life expectancy was increased three hundred times when I was modified. They tell me that my normal life span should have been three hundred years. Now it is ninety thousand years, and sometimes I am afraid. You will be dead of happy old age, Casher O'Neill, while I am still opening the drapes in this house to let the sunlight in. But let's not stand in the door and talk. Come on in and get some refreshments. You're not going anywhere, you know."

Casher followed her into the house but he put his worry into words. "You mean I am your prisoner."

"Not my prisoner, Casher. Yours. How could you cross that ground which you traveled in the groundcar? You could get to the ends of my estate all right, but then the storms would pick you up and whirl you away to a death which nobody would even see."

She turned into a big old room, bright with light-colored wooden furniture.

Casher stood there awkwardly. He had returned his knife to its bootsheath when they left the vestibule. Now he felt very odd, sitting with his victim on a sun porch.

T'ruth was untroubled. She rang a brass bell which stood on an old-fashioned round table. Feminine footsteps clattered in the hall. A female servant entered the room, dressed in a black dress with a white apron. Casher had seen such servants in the old drama cubes, but he had never expected to meet one in the flesh.

"We'll have high tea," said T'ruth. "Which do you prefer, tea or coffee, Casher? Or I have beer and wines. Even two bottles of whiskey brought all the way from Earth."

"Coffee would be fine for me," said Casher.

"And you know what I want, Eunice," said T'ruth to the servant.

"Yes, *ma'am*," said the maid, disappearing.

Casher leaned forward.

"That servant—is she human?"

"Certainly," said T'ruth.

"Then why is she working for an underperson like you? I mean—I don't mean to be unpleasant or anything—but I mean—that's against all laws."

"Not here, on Henriada, it isn't."

"And why not?" persisted Casher.

"Because, on Henriada, I am myself the law."

"But the government?"

"It's gone."

"The Instrumentality?"

T'ruth frowned. She looked like a wise, puzzled child. "Maybe you know that part better than I do. They leave an Administrator here, probably because they do not have any other place to put him and because he needs some kind of work to keep him alive. Yet they do not give him enough real power to arrest my master or to kill me. They ignore me. It seems to me that if I do not challenge them, they leave me alone."

"But their rules?" insisted Casher.

"They don't enforce them, neither here in Beauregard nor over in the town of Ambiloxi. They leave it up to me to keep these places going. I do the best I can."

"That servant, then? Did they lease her to you?"

"Oh, no," laughed the girl-woman. "She came to kill me twenty years ago, but she was a forgetty and she had no place else to go, so I trained her as a maid. She has a contract with my master, and her wages are paid every month into the satellite above the planet. She can leave if she ever wants to. I don't think she will."

Casher sighed. "This is all too hard to believe. You are a child but you are almost a thousand years old. You're an underperson, but you command a whole planet—"

"Only when I need to!" she interrupted him.

"You are wiser than most of the people I have ever known and yet you look young. How old do you feel?"

"I feel like a child," she said, "a child one thousand years old. And I have had the education and the memory and the experience of a wise lady stamped right into my brain."

"Who was the lady?" asked Casher.

"The Owner and Citizen Agatha Madigan. The wife of my master. As she was dying they transcribed her brain on mine. That's why I speak so well and know so much."

"But that's illegal!" cried Casher.

"I suppose it was," said T'ruth, "but my master had it done, anyhow."

Casher leaned forward in his chair. He looked earnestly at the person. One part of him still loved her for the wonderful little girl whom he had thought she was, but another part was in awe of a being more powerful than anyone he had seen before. She returned his gaze with that composed half smile which was wholly feminine and completely self-possessed; she looked tenderly upon him as their faces were reflected by the yellow morning light of Henriada. "I begin to understand," he said, "that you are what you have to be. It is very strange, here in this forgotten world."

"Henriada is strange," she said, "and I suppose that I must seem strange to you. You are right, though, about each of us being what she has to be. Isn't that liberty itself? If we each one *must* be something, isn't liberty the business of finding it out and then doing it—that one job, that uttermost mission compatible with our natures? How terrible it would be, to be something and never know what!"

"Like who?" said Casher.

"Like Gosigo, perhaps. He was a great king and he was a good king, on some faraway world where they still need kings. But he committed an intolerable mistake and the Instrumentality made him into a forgetty and sent him here."

"So that's the mystery!" said Casher. "And what am I?"

She looked at him calmly and steadfastly before she answered. "You are a killer too. It must make your life very hard in many ways. You keep having to justify yourself."

This was so close to the truth—so close to Casher's long worries as to whether justice might not just be a cover name for revenge— that it was his turn to gasp and be silent.

"And I have work for you," added the amazing child.

"Work? Here?"

"Yes. Something much worse than killing. And you must do it, Casher, if you want to go away from here before I die, eighty-nine thousand years from now." She looked around. "Hush!" she added. "Eunice is coming and I do not want to frighten her by letting her know the terrible things that you are going to have to do."

"Here?" he whispered urgently. "Right here, in this house?"

"Right here in this house," she said in a normal voice, as Eunice entered the room bearing a huge tray covered with plates of food and two pots of beverage.

Casher stared at the human woman who worked so cheerfully for an animal; but neither Eunice, who was busy setting things out on the table, nor T'ruth, who, turtle and woman that she was, could not help rearranging the dishes with gentle peremptories, paid the least attention to him.

The words rang in his head. "In this house . . . something worse than killing." They made no sense. Neither did it make sense to have high tea before five hours, decimal time.

He sighed and they both glanced at him, Eunice with amused curiosity, T'ruth with affectionate concern.

"He's taking it better than most of them do, ma'am," said Eunice. "Most of them who come here to kill you are very upset when they find out that they cannot do it."

"He's a killer, Eunice, a real killer, so I think he wasn't too bothered."

Eunice turned to him very pleasantly and said, "A killer, sir. It's a pleasure to have you here. Most of them are terrible amateurs and then the lady has to heal them before we can find something for them to do."

Casher couldn't resist a spot inquiry. "Are all the other would-be killers still here?"

"Most of them, sir. The ones that nothing happened to. Like me. Where else would we go? Back to the Administrator, Rankin Meiklejohn?" She said the last with heavy scorn indeed, curtsied to him, bowed deeply to the woman-girl T'ruth and left the room.

T'ruth looked friendlily at Casher O'Neill. "I can tell that you will not digest your food if you sit here waiting for bad news. When I said you had to do something worse than killing, I suppose I was speaking from a woman's point of view. We have a homicidal maniac in the house. He is a house guest and he is covered by Old North Australian law. That means we cannot kill him or expel him, though he is almost as immortal as I am. I hope that you and I can frighten him away from molesting my master. I cannot cure him or love him. He is too crazy to be reached through his emotions. Pure, utter, awful fright might do it, and it takes a man for that job. If you do this, I will reward you richly."

"And if I don't?" said Casher.

Again she stared at him as though she were trying to see through his eyes all the way down to the bottom of his soul; again he felt for her that tremor of compassion, ever so slightly tinged with male desire, which he had experienced when he first met her in the doorway of Beauregard.

Their locked glances broke apart.

T'ruth looked at the floor. "I cannot lie," she said, as though it were a handicap. "If you do not help me I shall have to do the things which it is in my power to do. The chief thing is nothing. To let you live here, to let you sleep and eat in this house until you get bored and ask me for some kind of routine work around the estate. I could make you work," she went on, looking up at him and blushing all the way to the top of her bodice, "by having you fall in love with me, but that would not be kind. I will not do it that way. Either you make a deal with me or you do not. It's up to you. Anyhow, let's eat first. I've been up since dawn, expecting one more killer. I even wondered if you might be the one who would succeed. That would be terrible, to leave my master all alone!"

"But you—wouldn't you yourself mind being killed!"

"Me? When I've already lived a thousand years and have eighty-nine thousand more to go! It couldn't matter less to me. Have some coffee."

And she poured his coffee.

VIII

Two or three times Casher tried to get the conversation back to the work at hand, but T'ruth diverted him with trivialities. She even made him walk to the enormous window, where they could see far across the marshes and the bay. The sky in the remote distance was dark and full of worms. Those were tornadoes, beyond the reach of her weather machines, which coursed around the rest of Henriada but stopped short at the boundaries of Ambiloxi and Beauregard. She made him admire the weird coral castles which had built themselves up from the bay bottom, hundreds of feet into the air. She tried to make him see a family of wild wind people who were slyly and gently stealing apples from her orchard, but either his eyes were not used to the landscape or T'ruth could see much farther than he could.

This was a world rich in water. If it had not been located within a series of bad pockets of space, the water itself could have become an export. Mankind had done the best it could, raising kelp to provide the iron and phosphorus so often lacking in offworld diets, controlling the weather at great expense. Finally the Instrumentality recommended that they give up. The exports of Henriada never quite balanced the imports. The subsidies had gone far beyond the usual times. The earth life had adapted with a vigor which was much too great. Ordinary forms rapidly found new shapes, challenged by the winds, the rains, the novel chemistry and the odd radiation patterns of Henriada. Killer whales became airborne, coral took to the air, human babies lost in the wind sometimes survived to become subhuman and wild, jellyfish became sky sweepers. The former inhabitants of Henriada had chosen a planet at a reasonable price—not cheap, but reasonable—from the owner who had in turn bought it from a post-Soviet settling cooperative. They had leased the new planet, had worked out an ecology, had emigrated and were now doing well.

Henriada kept the wild weather, the lost hopes, and the ruins.

And of these ruins, the greatest was Murray Madigan.

Once a prime landholder and host, a gentleman among gentlemen, the richest man on the whole world, Madigan had become old, senile, weak. He faced death or catalepsis. The death of his wife made him fear his own death and with his turtle-girl, T'ruth, he had chosen catalepsis. Most of the time he was frozen in a trance, his heartbeat imperceptible, his metabolism very slow. Then, for a few hours or days, he was normal. Sometimes the sleeps were for weeks, sometimes for years. The Instrumentality doctors had looked him over—more out of scientific curiosity than from any judicial right—and had decided that though this was an odd way to live, it was a legal one. They went away and left him alone. He had had the whole personality of his dying wife, Agatha Madigan, impressed on the turtle-child, though this was illegal; the doctor had, quite simply, been bribed.

All this was told by T'ruth to Casher as they ate and drank their way slowly through an immense repast.

An archaic wood fire roared in a real fireplace.

While she talked, Casher watched the gentle movement of her shoulder blades when she moved forward, the loose movement of her light dress as she moved, the childish face which was so tender, so appealing and yet so wise.

Knowing as little as he did about the planet of Henriada, Casher tried desperately to fit his own thinking together and to make sense out of the predicament in which he found himself. Even if the girl *was* attractive, this told him nothing of the real challenges which he still faced inside this very house. No longer was his preoccupation with getting the power cruiser his main job on Henriada; no evidence was at hand to show that the drunken, deranged Administrator, Rankin Meiklejohn, would give him anything at all unless he, Casher, killed the girl.

Even that had become a forgotten mission. Despite the fact that he had come to the estate of Beauregard for the purpose of killing her, he was now on a journey without a destination. Years of sad experience had taught him that when a project went completely to pieces, he still had the mission of personal survival, if his life was to mean anything to his home planet, Mizzer, and if his return, in any way or any fashion, could bring real liberty back to the Twelve Niles.

So he looked at the girl with a new kind of unconcern. How could she help his plans? Or hinder them? The promises she made were too vague to be of any real use in the sad, complicated world of politics.

He just tried to enjoy her company and the strange place in which he found himself.

The Gulf of Esperanza lay just within his vision. At the far horizon he could see the helpless tornadoes trying to writhe their way past the weather machines which still functioned, at the expense of Beauregard, all along the coast from Ambiloxi to Mottile. He could see the shoreline choked with kelp, which had once been a cash crop and was now a nuisance. Ruined buildings in the distance were probably the leftovers of processing plants; the artificial-looking coral castles obscured his view of them.

And this house—how much sense did this house make?

An undergirl, eerily wise, who herself admitted that she had obtained an unlawful amount of conditioning; a master who was a living corpse; a threat which could not even be mentioned freely within the house; a household which seemed to have displaced the planetary government; a planetary government which the Instrumentality, for unfathomable reasons of its own, had let fall into ruin. Why? Why? And why again?

The turtle-girl was looking at him. If he had been an art student, he would have said that she was giving him the tender, feminine and irrecoverably remote smile of a Madonna, but he did not know the motifs of the ancient pictures; he just knew that it was a smile characteristic of T'ruth herself.

"You are wondering . . . ?" she said.

He nodded, suddenly feeling miserable that mere words had come between them.

"You are wondering why the Instrumentality let you come here?"

He nodded again.

"I don't know either," she said, reaching out and taking his right hand. His hand felt and looked like the hairy paw of a giant as she held it with her two pretty, well-kept little-girl hands; but the strength of her eyes and the steadfastness of her voice showed that it was she who was giving the reassurance, not he.

The child was helping *him*!

The idea was outrageous, impossible, true.

It was enough to alarm him, to make him begin to pull back his hand. She clutched him with tender softness, with weak strength, and he could not resist her. Again he had the feeling, which had gripped him so strongly when he first met her at the door of Beauregard and failed to kill her, that he had always known her and had always loved her. (Was there not some planet on which eccentric people believed a weird cult, thinking that human beings were endlessly reborn with fragmentary recollections of their own previous human lives? It was almost like that. Here. Now. He did not know the girl but he had always known her. He did not love the girl and yet had loved her from the beginning of time.)

She said, so softly that it was almost a whisper, "Wait. . . . Wait. . . . Your death may come through that door pretty soon and I will tell you how to meet it. But before that, even, I have to show you the most beautiful thing in the world."

Despite her little hand lying tenderly and firmly on his, Casher spoke irritably: "I'm tired of talking riddles here on Henriada. The Administrator gives me the mission of killing you and I fail in it. Then you promise me a battle and give me a good meal instead. Now you talk about the battle and start off with some other irrelevance. You're going to make me angry if you keep on and—and—and—" He stammered out at last: "I get pretty useless if I'm angry. If you want me to do a fight for you, let me know the fight and let me go do it now. I'm willing enough.

Her remote, kind half smile did not waver. "Casher," she said, "what I am going to show you is your most important weapon in the fight."

With her free left hand she tugged at the fine chain of a thin gold necklace. A piece of jewelry came out of the top of her shift dress, under which she had kept it hidden. It was the image of two pieces of wood with a man nailed to them.

Casher stared and then he burst into hysterical laughter.

"Now you've done it, ma'am," he cried. "I'm no use to you or to anybody else. I know what that is, and up to now I've just suspected it. It's what the robot, rat and Copt agreed on when they went exploring back in Space three. It's the Old Strong Religion. You've put it in my mind and now the next person who meets me will peep it and will wipe it out. Me too, probably, along with it. That's no weapon. That's a defeat. You've done me in. I knew the sign of the Fish a long time ago, but I had a chance of getting away with just that little bit."

"Casher!" she cried. "Casher! Get hold of yourself. You will know nothing about this before you leave Beauregard. You will forget. You will be safe."

He stood on his feet, not knowing whether to run away, to laugh out loud, or to sit down and weep at the silly sad misfortune which had befallen him. To think that he himself had become brain-branded as a fanatic—forever denied travel between the stars—just because an undergirl had shown him an odd piece of jewelry!

"It's not as bad as you think," said the little girl, and stood up too. Her face peered lovingly at Casher's. "Do you think, Casher, that I am afraid?"

"No," he admitted.

"You will not remember this, Casher. Not when you leave. I am not just the turtle-girl T'ruth. I am also the imprint of the citizen Agatha. Have you ever heard of her?"

"Agatha Madigan?" He shook his head slowly. "No. I don't see how . . . No, I'm sure that I never heard of her."

"Didn't you ever hear the story of the Hechizera of Gonfalon?"

Casher looked surprised. "Sure I saw it. It's a play. A drama. It is said to be based on some legend out of immemorial time. The 'space witch' they called her, and she conjured fleets out of nothing by sheer hypnosis. It's an old story."

"Eleven hundred years isn't so long," said the girl. "Eleven hundred years, fourteen local months come next tonight."

"You weren't alive eleven hundred years ago," said Casher accusingly.

He stood up from the remains of their meal and wandered over toward the window. That terrible piece of religious jewelry made him uncomfortable. He knew that it was against all laws to ship religion from world to world. What would he do, what could he do, now that he had actually beheld an image of the God Nailed High? That was exactly the kind of contraband which the police and customs robots of hundreds of worlds were looking for.

The Instrumentality was easy about most things, but the transplanting of religion was one of its hostile obsessions. Religions leaked from world to world anyhow. It was said that sometimes even the underpeople and robots carried bits of religion through space, though this seemed improbable. The Instrumentality left religion alone when it had a settled place on a single planet, but the Lords of the Instrumentality themselves shunned other people's devotional lives and simply took good care that fanaticisms did not once more flare up between the stars, bringing wild hope and great death to all the mankinds again.

And now, thought Casher, *the Instrumentality has been good to me in its big impersonal collective way, but what will it do when my brain is on fire with forbidden knowledge?*

The girl's voice called him back to himself.

"I have the answer to your problem, Casher," said she, "if you would only listen to me. I *am* the Hechizera of Gonfalon, at least I am as much as any one person can be printed on another."

His jaw dropped as he turned back to her. "You mean that you, child, really are imprinted with this woman Agatha Madigan? Really imprinted?

"I have all her skills, Casher," said the girl quietly, "and a few more which I have learned on my own."

"But I thought it was just a story . . ." said Casher. "If you're that terrible woman from Gonfalon, you don't need me. I'm quitting. Now."

Casher walked toward the door. Disgusted, finished, through. She might be a child, she might be charming, she might need help, but if she came from that terrible old story, she did not need him.

"Oh, no, you don't," she said.

IX

Unexpectedly, she took her place in the doorway, barring it.

In her hand was the image of the man on the two pieces of wood.

Ordinarily Casher would not have pushed a lady. Such was his haste that he did so this time. When he touched her, it was like welded steel; neither her gown nor her body yielded a thousandth of a millimeter to his strong hand and heavy push.

"And now what?" she asked gently.

Looking back, he saw that the real T'ruth, the smiling girl-woman, still stood soft and real in the window.

Deep within, he began to give up; he had heard of hypnotists who could project, but he had never met one as strong as this.

She was doing it. How was she doing it? Or was she doing it? The operation could be subvolitional. There might be some art carried over from her animal past which even her re-formed mind could not explain. Operations too subtle, too primordial for analysis. Or skills which she used without understanding.

"I project," she said.

"I see you do," he replied glumly and flatly.

"I do kinesthetics," she said. His knife whipped out of his boot-sheath and floated in the air in front of him.

He snatched it out of the air instinctively. It wormed a little in his grasp, but the force on the knife was nothing more than he had felt when passing big magnetic engines.

"I blind," she said. The room went totally dark for him.

"I hear," he said, and prowled at her like a beast, going by his memory of the room and by the very soft sound of her breathing. He had noticed by now that the simulacrum of herself which she had put in the doorway did not make any sound at all, not even that of breathing.

He knew that he was near her. His fingertips reached out for her shoulder or her throat. He did not mean to hurt her, merely to show her that two could play at tricks.

"I stun," she said, and her voice came at him from all directions. It echoed from the ceiling, came from all five walls of the old odd room, from the open windows, from both the doors. He felt as though he were being lifted into space and turned slowly in a condition of weightlessness. He tried to retain self-control, to listen for the one true sound among the many false sounds, to trap the girl by some outside chance.

"I make you remember," said her multiple echoing voice.

For an instant he did not see how this could be a weapon, even if the turtle-girl had learned all the ugly tricks of the Hechizera of Gonfalon.

But then he knew.

He saw his uncle, Kuraf, again. He saw his old apartments vividly around himself. Kuraf was there. The old man was pitiable, hateful, drunk, horrible; the girl on Kuraf's lap laughed at him, Casher O'Neill, and she laughed at Kuraf too. Casher had once had a teen-ager's passionate concern with sex and at the same time had had a teen-ager's dreadful fear of all the unstated, invisible implications of what the man-woman relationship, gone sour, gone wrong, gone bad, might be. The present-moment Casher remembered the long-ago Casher and as he spun in the web of T'ruth's hypnotic powers he found himself back with the ugliest memory he had.

The killings in the palace at Mizzer.

The colonels had taken Kaheer itself, and they ultimately let Kuraf run away to the pleasure planet of Ttiolle.

But Kuraf's companions, who had debauched the old republic of the Twelve Niles, those people! They did not go. The soldiers, stung to fury, had cut them down with knives. Casher thought of the blood, blood sticky on the floors, blood gushing purple into the carpets, blood bright red and leaping like a fountain when a white throat ended its last gurgle, blood turning brown where handprints, themselves bloody, had left it on marble tables. The warm palace, long ago, had got the sweet sick stench of blood all the way through it. The young Casher had never known that people had so much blood inside them, or that so much could pour out on the perfumed sheets, the tables still set with food and drink, or that blood could creep across the floor in growing pools as the bodies of the dead yielded up their last few nasty sounds and their terminal muscular spasms.

Before that day of butchery had ended, one thousand, three hundred and eleven human bodies, ranging in age from two months to eighty-nine years, had been carried out of the palaces once occupied by Kuraf. Kuraf, under sedation, was waiting for a starship to take him to perpetual exile and Casher—Casher himself O'Neill!—was shaking the hand of Colonel Wedder, whose orders had caused all the blood. The hand was washed and the nails pared and cleaned, but the cuff of the sleeve was still rimmed with the dry blood of some other human being. Colonel Wedder either did not notice his own cuff, or he did not care.

"Touch and yield!" said the girl-voice out of nowhere.

Casher found himself on all fours in the room, his sight suddenly back again, the room unchanged, and T'ruth smiling.

"I fought you," she said.

He nodded. He did not trust himself to speak.

He reached for his water glass, looking at it closely to see if there was any blood on it.

Of course not. Not here. Not this time, not this place.

He pulled himself to his feet.

The girl had sense enough not to help him.

She stood there in her thin modest shift, looking very much like a wise female child, while he stood up and drank thirstily. He refilled the glass and drank again.

Then, only then, did he turn to her and speak:

"Do you do all that?"

She nodded.

"Alone? Without drugs or machinery?"

She nodded again.

"Child," he cried out, "you're not a person! You're a whole weapons system all by yourself. What are you, really? *Who* are you?"

"I am the turtle-child T'ruth," she said, "and I am the loyal property and loving servant of my good master, the Mister and Owner Murray Madigan."

"Madam," said Casher, "you are almost a thousand years old. I am at your service. I do hope you will let me go free later on. And especially that you will take that religious picture out of my mind."

As Casher spoke, she picked a locket from the table. He had not noticed it. It was an ancient watch or a little round box, swinging on a thin gold chain.

"Watch this," said the child, "if you trust me, and repeat what I then say."

(Nothing at all happened: nothing—anywhere.)

Casher said to her, "You're making me dizzy, swinging that ornament. Put it back on. Isn't that the one you were wearing?"

"No, Casher, it isn't."

"What were we talking about?" demanded Casher.

"Something," said she. "Don't you remember?"

"No," said Casher brusquely. "Sorry, but I'm hungry again." He wolfed down a sweet roll encrusted with sugar and decorated with fruits. His mouth full, he washed the food down with water. At last he spoke to her. "Now what?"

She had watched with timeless grace.

"There's no hurry, Casher. Minutes or hours, they don't matter."

"Didn't you want me to fight somebody after Gosigo left me here?"

"That's right," she said, with terrible quiet.

"I seem to have had a fight right here in this room." He stared around stupidly.

She looked around the room, very cool. "It doesn't look as though anybody's been fighting here, does it?"

"There's no blood here, no blood at all. Everything is clean," he said.

"Pretty much so."

"Then why," said Casher, "should I think I had a fight?"

"This wild weather on Henriada sometimes upsets off-worlders until they get used to it," said T'ruth mildly.

"If I didn't have a fight in the past, am I going to get into one in the future?"

The old room with the golden-oak furniture swam around him. The world outside was strange, with the sunlit marshes and wide bayous trailing off to the forever-thundering storm, just over the horizon, which lay beyond the weather machines. Casher shrugged and shivered. He looked straight at the girl. She stood erect and looked at him with the even regard of a reigning empress. Her young budding breasts barely showed through the thinness of her shift; she wore golden flat-heeled shoes. Around her neck there was a thin gold chain, but the object on the chain hung down inside her dress. It excited him a little to think of her flat chest barely budding into womanhood. He had never been a man who had an improper taste for children, but there was something about this person which was not childlike at all.

"You are a girl and not a girl. . . ." he said in bewilderment.

She nodded gravely.

"You are that woman in the story, the Hechizera of Gonfalon. You are reborn."

She shook her head, equally seriously. "No, I am not reborn. I am a turtle-child, an underperson with very long life, and I have been imprinted with the personality of the citizen Agatha. That is all."

"You stun," he said, "but I do not know how you do it."

"I stun," she said flatly, and around the edge of his mind there flickered up hot little torments of memory.

"Now I remember," he cried. "You have me here to kill somebody. You are sending me into a fight."

"You are going to a fight, Casher. I wish I could send somebody else, not you, but you are the only person here strong enough to do the job."

Impulsively he took her hand. The moment he touched her, she ceased to be a child or an underperson. She felt tender and exciting, like the most desirable and important person he had ever known.

His sister? But he had no sister. He felt that he was himself terribly, unendurably important to her. He did not want to let her hand go, but she withdrew from his touch with an authority which no decent man could resist.

"You must fight to the death now, Casher," she said, looking at him as evenly as might a troop commander examining a special soldier selected for a risky mission.

He nodded. He was tired of having his mind confused. He knew something had happened to him after the forgetty, Gosigo, had left him at the front door, but he was not at all sure of what it was. They seemed to have had a sort of meal together in this room. He felt himself in love with the child. He knew that she was not even a human being. He remembered something about her living ninety thousand years and he remembered something else about her having gotten the name and the skills of the greatest battle hypnotist of all history, the Hechizera of Gonfalon. There was something strange, something frightening about that chain around her neck: there were things he hoped he would never have to know.

He strained at the thought and it broke like a bubble.

"I'm a fighter," he said. "Give me my fight and let me know."

"*He* can kill you. I hope not. You must not kill him. He is immortal and insane. But in the law of Old North Australia, from which my master, the Mister and Owner Murray Madigan, is an exile, we must not hurt a house guest, nor may we turn him away in a time of great need."

"What do I *do*?" snapped Casher impatiently.

"You fight him. You frighten him. You make his poor crazy mind fearful that he will meet you again."

"I'm supposed to do this."

"You can," she said very seriously. "I've already tested you. That's where you have the little spot of amnesia about this room."

"But *why*? Why bother? Why not get some of your human servants and have them tie him up or put him in a padded room?"

"They can't deal with him. He is too strong, too big, too clever, even though insane. Besides, they don't dare follow him."

"Where does he go?" said Casher sharply.

"Into the control room," replied T'ruth, as if it were the saddest phrase ever uttered.

"What's wrong with that? Even a place as fine as Beauregard can't have too much of a control room. Put locks on the control."

"It's not that kind of a control room."

Almost angry, he shouted, "What is it, then?"

"The control room," she answered, "is for a planoform ship. This house. These counties, all the way to Mottile on the one side and to Ambiloxi on the other. The sea itself, way out into the Gulf of Esperanza. All this is one ship."

Casher's professional interest took over. "If it's turned off, he can't do any harm."

"It's not turned off," she said. "My master leaves it on a very little bit. That way, he can keep the weather machines going and make this edge of Henriada a very pleasant place."

"You mean," said Casher, "that you'd risk letting a lunatic fly all these estates off into space."

"He doesn't even fly," said T'ruth gloomily.

"What does he *do*, then?" yelled Casher.

"When he gets at the controls, he just hovers."

"He hovers? By the Bell, girl, don't try to fool me. If you hover a place as big as this, you could wipe out the whole planet any moment. There have been only two or three pilots in the history of space who would be able to hover a machine like this one."

"He can, though," insisted the little girl.

"Who is he, anyhow?"

"I thought you knew. Or had heard somewhere about it. His name is John Joy Tree."

"Tree the go captain?" Casher shivered in the warm room. "He died a long time ago after he made that record flight."

"He did not die. He bought immortality and went mad. He came here and he lives under my master's protection."

"Oh," said Casher. There was nothing else he could say. John Joy Tree, the great Norstrilian who took the first of the Long Plunges outside the galaxy: he was like Magno Taliano of ages ago, who could fly space on his living brain alone.

But fight him? How could anybody fight him?

Pilots are for piloting; killers are for killing; women are for loving or forgetting. When you mix up the purposes, everything goes wrong.

Casher sat down abruptly. "Do you have any more of that coffee?"

"You don't need coffee," she said.

He looked up inquiringly.

"You're a fighter. You need a war. That's it," she said, pointing with her girlish hand to a small doorway which looked like the entrance to a closet. "Just go in there. He's in there now. Tinkering with the machines again. Making me wait for my master to get blown to bits at any minute! And I've put up with it for over a hundred years."

"Go yourself," he said.

"You've been in a ship's control room," she declared.

"Yes." He nodded.

"You know how people go all naked and frightened inside. You know how much training it takes to make a go captain. What do you think happens to me?" At last, long last, her voice was shrill, angry, excited, childish.

"What happens?" said Casher dully, not caring very much; he felt weary in every bone. Useless battles, murder he had to try, dead people arguing after their ballads had already grown out of fashion. Why didn't the Hechizera of Gonfalon do her own work?

Catching his thought, she screeched at him, "Because I *can't!*"

"All right," said Casher. "Why not?"

"Because I turn into me."

"You what?" said Casher, a little startled.

"I'm a turtle-child. My shape is human. My brain is big. But I'm a *turtle*. No matter how much my master needs me, I'm just a turtle."

"What's that got to do with it?"

"What do turtles do when they're faced with danger? Not under-people-turtles, but real turtles, little animals. You must have heard of them somewhere."

"I've even seen them," said Casher, "on some world or other. They pull into their shells."

"That's what I do"—she wept—"when I should be defending my master. I can meet most things. I am not a coward. But in that control room, I forget, forget, forget!"

"Send a robot, then!"

She almost screamed at him. "A robot against John Joy Tree? Are you mad too?"

Casher admitted, in a mumble, that on second thought it wouldn't do much good to send a robot against the greatest go captain of them all. He concluded, lamely, "I'll go, if you want me to."

"Go now," she shouted, "go right in!"

She pulled at his arm, half dragging and half leading him to the little brightened door which looked so innocent.

"But—" he said.

"Keep going," she pleaded. "This is all we ask of you. Don't kill him, but frighten him, fight him, wound him if you must. You can do it. I can't." She sobbed as she tugged at him. "I'd just be *me*."

Before he knew quite what had happened she had opened the door. The light beyond was clear and bright and tinged with blue, the way the skies of Manhome, Mother Earth, were shown in all the viewers.

He let her push him in.

He heard the door click behind him.

Before he even took in the details of the room or noticed the man in the go captain's chair, the flavor and meaning of the room struck him like a blow against his throat.

This room, he thought, *is Hell*.

He wasn't even sure that he remembered where he had learned the word *Hell*. It denoted all good turned to evil, all hope to anxiety, all wishes to greed.

Somehow, this room was it.

And then . . .

X

And then the chief occupant of Hell turned and looked squarely at him.

If this was John Joy Tree, he did not look insane.

He was a handsome, chubby man with a red complexion, bright eyes, dancing-blue in color, and a mouth which was as mobile as the mouth of a temptress.

"Good day," said John Joy Tree.

"How do you do," said Casher inanely.

"I do not know your name," said the ruddy brisk man, speaking in a tone of voice which was not the least bit insane.

"I am Casher O'Neill, from the city of Kaheer on the planet Mizzer."

"Mizzer?" John Joy Tree laughed. "I spent a night there, long, long ago. The entertainment was most unusual. But we have other things to talk about. You have come here to kill the undergirl T'ruth. You received your orders from the honorable Rankin Meiklejohn, may he soak in drink! The child has caught you and now she wants you to kill me, but she does not dare utter those words."

John Joy Tree, as he spoke, shifted the spaceship controls to standby, and got ready to get out of his captain's seat.

Casher protested, "She said nothing about killing you. She said you might kill me."

"I might, at that." The immortal pilot stood on the floor. He was a full head shorter than Casher but he was a strong and formidable man. The blue light of the room made him look clear, sharp, distinct.

The whole flavor of the situation tickled the fear nerves inside Casher's body. He suddenly felt that he wanted very much to go to a bathroom, but he felt—quite surely—that if he turned his back on this man, in this place, he would die like a felled ox in a stockyard. He *had* to face John Joy Tree.

"Go ahead," said the pilot. "Fight me."

"I didn't say that I would fight you," said Casher. "I am supposed to frighten you and I do not know how to do it."

"This isn't getting us anywhere," said John Joy Tree. "Shall we go into the outer room and let poor little T'ruth give us a drink? You can just tell her that you failed."

"I think," said Casher, "that I am more afraid of her than I am of you."

John Joy Tree flung himself into a comfortable passenger's chair. "All right, then. Do something. Do you want to box? Gloves? Bare fists? Or would you like swords? Or wirepoints? There are some over there in the closet. Or we can each take a pilot ship and have a ship duel out in space."

"That wouldn't make much sense," said Casher, "me fighting a ship against the greatest go captain of them all. . . ."

John Joy Tree greeted this with an ugly underlaugh, a barely audible sound which made Casher feel that the whole situation was ridiculous.

"But I do have one advantage," said Casher. "I know who you are and you do not know who I am."

"How could I tell," said John Joy Tree, "when people keep on getting born all over the place?"

He gave Casher a scornful, comfortable grin. There was charm in the man's poise. Keeping his eyes focused directly on Casher, he felt for a carafe and poured himself a drink.

He gave Casher an ironic toast and Casher took it, standing frightened and alone. More alone than he had ever been before in his life.

Suddenly John Joy Tree sprang lightly to his feet and stared with a complete change of expression past Casher. Casher did not dare look around. This was some old fight trick.

Tree spat out the words, "*You've* done it, then. This time you will violate all the laws and kill me. This fashionable oaf is not just one more trick."

A voice behind Casher called very softly, "I don't know." It was a man's voice, old, slow and tired.

Casher had heard no one come in.

Casher's years of training stood him in good stead. He skipped sidewise in four or five steps, never taking his eyes off John Joy Tree, until the other man had come into his field of vision.

The man who stood there was tall, thin, yellow-skinned and yellow-haired. His eyes were an old sick blue. He glanced at Casher and said, "I'm Madigan."

Was this the master? thought Casher. *Was this the being whom that lovely child had been imprinted to adore?*

He had no more time for thought.

Madigan whispered, as if to no one in particular, "You find me waking. You find him sane. Watch out."

Madigan lunged for the pilot's controls, but his tall, thin old body could not move very fast.

John Joy Tree jumped out of his chair and ran for the controls too.

Casher tripped him.

Tree fell, rolled over and got halfway up, one knee and one foot on the floor. In his hand there shimmered a knife very much like Casher's own.

Casher felt the flame of his body as some unknown force flung him against the wall. He stared, wild with fear.

Madigan had climbed into the pilot's seat and was fiddling with the controls as though he might blow Henriada out of space at any second. John Joy Tree glanced at his old host and then turned his attention to the man in front of him.

There was another man there.

Casher knew him.

He looked familiar.

It was himself, rising and leaping like a snake, left arm weaving the knife for the neck of John Joy Tree.

The image Casher hit Tree with a thud that resounded through the room.

Tree's bright blue eyes had turned crazy-mad. His knife caught the image Casher in the abdomen, thrust hard and deep, and left the young man gasping on the floor, trying to push the bleeding entrails back into his belly. The blood poured from the image Casher all over the rug.

Blood!

Casher suddenly knew what he had to do and how he could do it—all without anybody telling him.

He created a third Casher on the far side of the room and gave him iron gloves. There was himself, unheeded against the wall; there was the dying Casher on the floor; there was the third, stalking toward John Joy Tree.

"Death is here," screamed the third Casher, with a voice which Casher recognized as a fierce crazy simulacrum of his own.

Tree whirled around. "You're not real," he said.

The image Casher stepped around the console and hit Tree with an iron glove. The pilot jumped away, a hand reaching up to his bleeding face.

John Joy Tree screamed at Madigan, who was playing with the dials without even putting on the pinlighter helmet.

"You got her in here," he screamed, "you got her in here with this young man! Get her out!"

"Who?" said Madigan softly and absentmindedly.

"T'ruth. That witch of yours. I claim guest-right by all the ancient laws. *Get her out.*"

The real Casher, standing at the wall, did not know how he controlled the image Casher with the iron gloves, but control him he did. He made him speak, in a voice as frantic as Tree's own voice:

"John Joy Tree, I do not bring you death. I bring you blood. My iron hands will pulp your eyes. Blind sockets will stare in your face. My iron hands will split your teeth and break your jaw a thousand times, so that no doctor, no machine will ever fix you. My iron hands will crush your arms, turn your hands into living rags. My iron hands will break your legs. Look at the blood, John Joy Tree. . . . There will be a lot more blood. You have killed me once. See that young man on the floor."

They both glanced at the first image Casher, who had finally shuddered into death in the great rug. A pool of blood lay in front of the body of the youth.

John Joy Tree turned to the image Casher and said to him, "You're the Hechizera of Gonfalon. You can't scare me. You're a turtle-girl and can't really hurt me."

"Look at me," said the real Casher.

John Joy Tree glanced back and forth between the duplicates. Fright began to show.

Both the Cashers now shouted, in crazy voices which came from the depths of Casher's own mind:

"Blood you shall have! Blood and ruin. But we will not kill you. You will live in ruin, blind, emasculated, armless, legless. You will be fed through tubes. You cannot die and you will weep for death but no one will hear you."

"Why?" screamed Tree. "Why? What have I done to you?"

"You remind me," howled Casher, "of my home. You remind me of the blood poured by Colonel Wedder when the poor useless victims of my uncle's lust paid with their blood for his revenge. You remind me of myself, John Joy Tree, and I am going to punish you as I myself might be punished."

Lost in the mists of lunacy, John Joy Tree was still a brave man.

He flung his knife unexpectedly at the real Casher. The image Casher, in a tremendous bound, leaped across the room and caught the knife on an iron glove. It clattered against the glove and then fell silent onto the rug.

Casher saw what he had to see.

He saw the palace of Kaheer, covered with death, with the intimate sticky silliness of sudden death—the dead men holding little packages they had tried to save, the girls, with their throats cut, lying in their own blood but with the lipstick still even and the eyebrow pencil still pretty on their dead faces. He saw a dead child, ripped open from groin upward to chest, holding a broken doll while the child itself, now dead, looked like a broken doll itself. He saw these things and he made John Joy Tree see them too.

"You're a bad man," said John Joy Tree.

"I am very bad," said Casher.

"Will you let me go if I never enter this room again?"

The image Casher snapped off, both the body on the floor and the fighter with the iron gloves. Casher did not know how T'ruth had taught him the lost art of fighter replication, but he had certainly done it well.

"The lady told me you could go."

"But who are you going to use," said John Joy Tree, calm, sad and logical, "for your dreams of blood if you don't use me?"

"I don't know," said Casher. "I follow my fate. Go now, if you do not want my iron gloves to crush you."

John Joy Tree trotted out of the room, beaten.

Only then did Casher, exhausted, grab a curtain to hold himself upright and look around the room freely.

The evil atmosphere had gone.

Madigan, old though he was, had locked all the controls on standby.

He walked over to Casher and spoke. "Thank you. She did not invent you. She found you and put you to my service."

Casher coughed out, "The girl. Yes."

"*My* girl," corrected Madigan.

"Your girl," said Casher, remembering the sight of that slight feminine body, those budding breasts, the sensitive lips, the tender eyes.

"She could not have thought you up. She is my dead wife over again. The citizeness Agatha might have done it. But not T'ruth."

Casher looked at the man as he talked. The host wore the bottoms of some very cheap yellow pajamas and a washable bathrobe which had once been stripes of purple, lavender and white. Now it was faded, like its wearer. Casher also saw the white clean plastic surgical implants on the man's arms, where the machines and tubes hooked in to keep him alive.

"I sleep a lot," said Murray Madigan, "but I am still the master of Beauregard. I am grateful to you."

The hand was frail, withered, dry, without strength.

The old voice whispered, "Tell her to reward you. You can have anything on my estate. Or you can have anything on Henriada. She manages it all for me." Then the old blue eyes opened wide and sharp and Murray Madigan was once again the man, just momentarily, that he had been hundreds of years ago—a Norstrilian trader, sharp, shrewd, wise and not unkind. He added sharply, "Enjoy her company. She is a good child. But do not take her. Do not try to take her."

"Why not?" said Casher, surprised at his own bluntness.

"Because if you do, she will die. She is *mine*. Imprinted to me. I had her made and she is mine. Without me she would die in a few days. Do not take her."

Casher saw the old man leave the room by a secret door. He left himself, the way he had come in. He did not see Madigan again for two days, and by that time the old man had gone far back into his cataleptic sleep.

XI

Two days later T'ruth took Casher to visit the sleeping Madigan.

"You can't go in there," said Eunice in a shocked voice. "*Nobody* goes in there. That's the master's room."

"I'm taking him in," said T'ruth calmly.

She had pulled a cloth-of-gold curtain aside and she was spinning the combination locks on a massive steel door. It was set in Daimoni material.

The maid went on protesting. "But even you, little ma'am, can't take him in there!"

"Who says I can't?" said T'ruth calmly and challengingly.

The awfulness of the situation sank in on Eunice.

In a small voice she muttered, "If you're taking him in, you're taking him in. But it's never been done before."

"Of course it hasn't, Eunice, not in your time. But Casher O'Neill has already met the Mister and Owner. He has fought for the Mister and Owner. Do you think I would take a stray or random guest in to look at the master, just like that?"

"Oh, not at all, no," said Eunice.

"Then go away, woman," said the lady-child. "You don't want to see this door open, do you?"

"Oh, no," shrieked Eunice and fled, putting her hands over her ears as though that would shut out the sight of the door.

When the maid had disappeared, T'ruth pulled with her whole

weight against the handle of the heavy door. Casher expected the mustiness of the tomb or the medicinality of a hospital; he was astonished when fresh air and warm sunlight poured out from that heavy, mysterious door. The actual opening was so narrow, so low, that Casher had to step sidewise as he followed T'ruth into the room.

The master's room was enormous. The windows were flooded with perpetual sunlight. The landscape outside must have been the way Henriada looked in its prime, when Mottile was a resort for the carefree millions of vacationers, and Ambiloxi a port feeding worlds halfway across the galaxy. There was no sign of the ugly snaky storms which worried and pestered Henriada in these later years. Everything was landscape, order, neatness, the triumph of man, as though Poussin had painted it.

The room itself, like the other great living rooms of the estate of Beauregard, was exuberant neo-baroque in which the architect, himself half mad, had been given wild license to work out his fantasies in steel, plastic, plaster, wood and stone. The ceiling was not flat, but vaulted. Each of the four corners of the room was an alcove, cutting deep into each of the four sides, so that the room was, in effect, an octagon. The propriety and prettiness of the room had been a little diminished by the shoving of the furniture to one side, sofas, upholstered armchairs, marble tables and knickknack stands all in an indescribable mélange to the left; while the right-hand part of the room—facing the master window with the illusory landscape—was equipped like a surgery with an operating table, hydraulic lifts, bottles of clear and colored fluid hanging from chrome stands and two large devices which (Casher later surmised) must have been heart-lung and kidney machines. The alcoves, in their turn, were wilder. One was an archaic funeral parlor with an immense coffin, draped in black velvet, resting on a heavy teak stand. The next was a spaceship control cabin of the old kind, with the levers, switches and controls all in plain sight—the meters actually read the galactically stable location of this very place, and to do so they had to whirl mightily—as well as a pilot's chair with the usual choice of helmets and the straps and shock absorbers. The third alcove was a simple bedroom done in very old-fashioned taste, the walls a Wedgwood blue with deep wine-colored drapes, coverlets and pillowcases marking a sharp but tolerable contrast. The fourth alcove was the copy of a fortress: it might even have been a fortress: the door was heavy and the walls looked as though they might be Daimoni material, indestructible by any imaginable means. Cases of emergency food and water were stacked against the walls. Weapons which looked oiled and primed stood in their racks, together with three different calibers of wirepoint, each with its own fresh-looking battery.

The alcoves had no people in them.

The parlor was deserted.

The Mister and Owner Murray Madigan lay naked on the operating table. Two or three wires led to gauges attached to his body. Casher thought that he could see a faint motion of the chest, as the cataleptic man breathed at a rate one-tenth normal or less.

The girl-lady, T'ruth, was not the least embarrassed.

"I check him four or five times a day. I never let people in here. But you're special, Casher. He's talked with you and fought beside you and he knows that he owes you his life. You're the first human person ever to get into this room."

"I'll wager," said Casher, "that the Administrator of Henriada, the Honorable Rankin Meiklejohn, would give up some of his 'honorable' just to get in here and have one look around. He wonders what Madigan is doing when Madigan is doing nothing. . . ."

"He's not just doing nothing," said T'ruth sharply. "He's sleeping. It's not everybody who can sleep for forty or fifty or sixty thousand years and can wake up a few times a month, just to see how things are going."

Casher started to whistle and then stopped himself, as though he feared to waken the unconscious, naked old man on the table. "So that's why he chose *you*."

T'ruth corrected him as she washed her hands vigorously in a washbasin. "That's why he had me made. Turtle stock, three hundred years. Multiply that with intensive stroon treatments, three hundred times. Ninety thousand years. Then he had me printed to love him and adore him. He's not my master, you know. He's my god."

"Your what?"

"You heard me. Don't get upset. I'm not going to give you any illegal memories. I worship him. That's what I was printed for, when my little turtle eyes opened and they put me back in the tank to enlarge my brain and to make a woman out of me. That's why they printed every memory of the citizeness Agatha Madigan right into my brain. I'm what he wanted. Just what he wanted. I'm the most wanted being on any planet. No wife, no sweetheart, no mother has ever been wanted as much as he wants me now, when he wakes up and knows that I am still here. You're a smart man. Would you trust any machine—any machine at all—for ninety thousand years?"

"It would be hard," said Casher, "to get batteries of monitors long enough for them to repair each other over that long a time. But that means you have ninety thousand years of it. Four times, five times a day. I can't even multiply the numbers. Don't you ever get tired of it?"

"He's my love, he's my joy, he's my darling little boy," she caroled, as she lifted his eyelids and put colorless drops in each eye. Absentmindedly, she explained. "With his slow metabolism there's always some danger that his eyelids will stick to his eyeballs. This is part of the checkup."

She tilted the sleeping man's head, looked earnestly into each eye. She then stepped a few paces aside and put her face close to the dial of a gently humming machine. There was the sound of a shot. Casher almost reached for his gun, which he did not have.

The child turned back to him with a free mischievous smile. "Sorry, I should have warned you. That's my noisemaker. I watch the encephalograph to make sure his brain keeps a little auditory intake. It showed up with the noise. He's asleep, very deeply asleep, but he's not drifting downward into death."

Back at the table she pushed Madigan's chin upward so that the head leaned far back on its neck. Deftly holding the forehead, she took a retractor, opened his mouth with her fingers, depressed the tongue and looked down into the throat.

"No accumulation there," she muttered, as if to herself.

She pushed the head back into a comfortable position. She seemed on the edge of another set of operations when it was obvious that an idea occurred to her. "Go wash your hands, thoroughly, over there, at the basin. Then push the timer down and be sure you hold your hands under the sterilizer until the timer goes off. You can help me turn him over. I don't have help here. You're the first visitor."

Casher obeyed and while he washed his hands, he saw the girl drench her hands with some flower-scented unguent. She began to massage the unconscious body with professional expertness, even with a degree of roughness. As he stood with his hands under the sterilizer-dryer, Casher marveled at the strength of those girlish arms and those little hands. Indefatigably they stroked, rubbed, pummeled, pulled, stretched and poked the old body. The sleeping man seemed to be utterly unaware of it, but Casher thought that he could see a better skin color and muscle tone appearing.

He walked back to the table and stood facing T'ruth.

A huge peacock walked across the imaginary lawn outside the window, his tail shimmering in a paroxysm of colors.

T'ruth saw the direction of Casher's glance.

"Oh, I program that too. He likes it when he wakes up. Don't

you think he was clever, before he went into catalepsis—to have
me made, to have me created to love him and to care for him? It
helps that I'm a girl. I can't ever love anybody but him, and it's easy
for me to remember that this is the man I love. And it's safer for
him. Any man might get bored with these responsibilities. I don't."

"Yet—" said Casher.

"Shh," she said, "wait a bit. This takes care." Her strong little
fingers were now plowing deep into the abdomen of the naked old
man. She closed her eyes so that she could concentrate all her senses
on the one act of tactile impression. She took her hands away and
stood erect. "All clear," she said. "I've got to find out what's going
on inside him. But I don't dare use X rays on him. Think of the
radiation he'd build up in a hundred years or so. He defecates
about twice a month while he's sleeping. I've got to be ready for
that. I also have to prime his bladder every week or so. Otherwise
he would poison himself just with his own body wastes. Here, now,
you can help me turn him over. But watch the wires. Those are the
monitor controls. They report his physiological processes, radio a
message to me if anything goes wrong, and meanwhile supply the
missing neurophysical impulses if any part of the automatic nervous
system began to fade out or just simply went off."

"Has that ever happened?"

"Never," she said, "not yet. But I'm ready. Watch that wire.
You're turning him too fast. There now, that's right. You can stand
back while I massage him on the back."

She went back to her job of being a masseuse. Starting at the
muscles joining the skull to the neck, she worked her way down the
body, pouring ointment on her hands from time to time. When she
got to his legs, she seemed to work particularly hard. She lifted the
feet, bent the knees, slapped the calves.

Then she put on a rubber glove, dipped her hand into another
jar—one which opened automatically as her hand approached—
and came out with her hand greasy. She thrust her fingers into his
rectum, probing, thrusting, groping, her brow furrowed.

Her face cleared as she dropped the rubber glove in a disposal
can and wiped the sleeping man with a soft linen towel, which also
went into a disposal can. "He's all right. He'll get along well for the
next two hours. I'll have to give him a little sugar then. All he's
getting now is normal saline."

She stood facing him. There was a faint glow in her cheeks from
the violent exercise in which she had been indulging, but she still
looked both the child and the lady—the child irrecoverably remote,
hidden in her own wisdom from the muddled world of adults, and

the lady, mistress in her own home, her own estates, her own planet, serving her master with almost immortal love and zeal.

"I was going to ask you, back there—" said Casher, and then stopped.

"You were going to ask me?"

He spoke heavily. "I was going to ask you, what happens to you when he dies? Either at the right time or possibly before his time. What happens to *you*?"

"I couldn't care less," her voice sang out. He could see by the open, honest smile on her face that she meant it. "I'm *his*. I belong to *him*. That's what I'm *for*. They may have programmed something into me, in case he dies. Or they may have forgotten. What matters is his life, not mine. He's going to get every possible hour of life that I can help him get. Don't you think I'm doing a good job?"

"A good job, yes," said Casher. "A strange one too."

"We can go now," she said.

"What are those alcoves for?"

"Oh, those—they're his make-believes. He picks one of them to go to sleep in—his coffin, his fort, his ship or his bedroom. It doesn't matter which. I always get him up with the hoist and put him back on his table, where the machines and I can take proper care of him. He doesn't really mind waking up on the table. He has usually forgotten which room he went to sleep in. We can go now."

They walked toward the door.

Suddenly she stopped. "I forgot something. I never forget things, but this is the first time I ever let anybody come in here with me. You were such a *good* friend to him. He'll talk about you for thousands of years. Long, long after you're dead," she added somewhat unnecessarily. Casher looked at her sharply to see if she might be mocking or deprecating him. There was nothing but the little-girl solemnity, the womanly devotion to an established domestic routine.

"Turn your back," she commanded peremptorily.

"Why?" he asked. "Why—when you have trusted me with all the other secrets."

"He wouldn't want you to see this."

"See what?"

"What I'm going to do. When I was the citizeness Agatha—or when I seemed to be her—I found that men are awfully fussy about some things. This is one of them."

Casher obeyed and stood facing the door.

A different odor filled the room—a strong wild scent, like a geranium pomade. He could hear T'ruth breathing heavily as she worked beside the sleeping man.

She called to him: "You can turn around now."

She was putting away a tube of ointment, standing high to get it into its exact position on a tile shelf.

Casher looked quickly at the body of Madigan. It was still asleep, still breathing very lightly and very slowly.

"What on earth did you *do*?"

T'ruth stopped in midstep. "You're going to get nosy."

Casher stammered mere sounds.

"You can't help it," she said. "People are inquisitive."

"I suppose they are," he said, flushing at the accusation.

"I gave him his bit of fun. He never remembers it when he wakes up, but the cardiograph sometimes shows increased activity. Nothing happened this time. That was my own idea. I read books and decided that it would be good for his body tone. Sometimes he sleeps through a whole Earth year, but usually he wakes up several times a month."

She passed Casher, almost pulled herself clear of the floor tugging on the inside levers of the main door.

She gestured him past. He stooped and stepped through.

"Turn away again," she said. "All I'm going to do is to spin the dials, but they're cued to give any viewer a bad headache so he will forget the combination. Even robots. I'm the only person tuned to these doors."

He heard the dials spinning but did not look around.

She murmured, almost under her breath, "I'm the only one. The only one."

"The only one for what?" asked Casher.

"To love my master, to care for him, to support his planet, to guard his weather. But isn't he beautiful? Isn't he wise? Doesn't his smile win your heart?"

Casher thought of the faded old wreck of a man with the yellow pajama bottoms. Tactfully, he said nothing.

T'ruth babbled on, quite cheerfully. "He is my father, my husband, my baby son, my master, my owner. Think of that, Casher, he owns me! Isn't he lucky—to have me? And aren't I lucky—to belong to him?"

"But what for?" asked Casher a little crossly, thinking that he was falling in and out of love with this remarkable girl himself.

"For life!" she cried, "In any form, in any way. I am made for ninety thousand years and he will sleep and wake and dream and sleep again, a large part of that."

"What's the use of it?" insisted Casher.

"The use," she said, "the use? What's the use of the little turtle egg they took and modified in its memory chains, right down to the molecular level? What's the use of turning me into an undergirl, so that even you have to love me off and on? What's the use of little me, meeting my master for the first time, when I had been manufactured to love him? I can tell you, man, what the use is. Love."

"What did you say?" said Casher.

"I said the use was love. Love is the only end of things. Love on the one side, and death on the other. If you are strong enough to use a real weapon, I can give you a weapon which will put all Mizzer at your mercy. Your cruiser and your laser would just be toys against the weapon of love. You can't fight love. You can't fight me."

They had proceeded down a corridor, forgotten pictures hanging on the walls, unremembered luxuries left untouched by centuries of neglect.

The bright yellow light of Henriada poured in through an open doorway on their right.

From the room came snatches of a man singing while playing a stringed instrument. Later, Casher found that this was a verse of the Henriada Song, the one which went:

> *Don't put your ship in the Boom Lagoon,*
> *Look up north for the raving wave.*
> *Henriada's boiled away*
> *But Ambiloxi's a saving grave.*

They entered the room.

A gentleman stood up to greet them.

It was the great go-pilot, John Joy Tree. His ruddy face smiled, his bright blue eyes lit up, a little condescendingly, as he greeted his small hostess, but then his glance took in Casher O'Neill.

The effect was sudden, and evil.

John Joy Tree looked away from both of them. The phrase which he had started to use stuck in his throat.

He said, in a different voice, very "away" and deeply troubled, "There is blood all over this place. There is a man of blood right here. Excuse me. I am going to be sick."

He trotted past them and out the door which they had entered.

"You have passed a test," said T'ruth. "Your help to my master has solved the problem of the captain and honorable John Joy Tree. He will not go near that control room if he thinks that you are there."

"Do you have more tests for me? Still more? By now you ought to know me well enough not to need tests."

"I am not a person," she said, "but just a built-up copy of one. I am getting ready to give you your weapon. This is a communications room as well as a music room. Would you like something to eat or drink?"

"Just water," he said.

"At your hand," said T'ruth.

A rock crystal carafe had been standing on the table beside him, unnoticed. Or had she transported it into the room with one of the tricks of the Hechizera, the dreaded Agatha herself? It didn't matter. He drank. Trouble was coming.

XII

T'ruth had swung open a polished cabinet panel. The communicator was the kind they mount in planoforming ships right beside the pilot. The rental on one of them was enough to make any planetary government reconsider its annual budget.

"That's *yours*?" cried Casher.

"Why not?" said the little-girl lady. "I have four or five of them."

"But you're *rich*!"

"I'm not. My master is. I belong to my master too."

"But things like this. . . . He can't handle them. How does he manage?"

"You mean money and things?" The girlish part of her came out. She looked pleased, happy and mischievous. "I manage them for him. He was the richest man on Henriada when I came here. He had credits of stroon. Now he is about forty times richer."

"He's a Rod McBan!" exclaimed Casher.

"Not even near. Mr. McBan had a lot more money than we. But he's rich. Where do you think all the people from Henriada went?"

"I don't know," said Casher.

"To four new planets. They belong to my master and he charges the new settlers a very small land rent."

"You bought them?" Casher asked.

"For him." T'ruth smiled. "Haven't you heard of planet brokers?"

"But that's a gambler's business!" said Casher.

"I gambled," she said, "and I won. Now keep quiet and watch me."

She pressed a button. "Instant message."

"Instant message," repeated the machine. "What priority?"

"War news, double A one, subspace penalty."

"Confirmed," said the machine.

"The planet Mizzer. Now. War and peace information. Will fighting end soon?"

The machine clucked to itself.

Casher, knowing the prices of this kind of communication, almost felt that he could see the arterial spurt of money go out of Henriada's budget as the machines reached across the galaxy, found Mizzer and came back with the answer.

"Skirmishing. Seventh Nile. Ends three local days."

"Close message," said T'ruth.

The machine went off.

T'ruth turned to him. "You're going home soon, Casher, if you can pass a few little tests."

He stared at her.

He blurted, "I need my weapons, my cruiser and my laser."

"You'll have weapons. Better ones than those. Right now I want you to go to the front door. When you have opened the door, you will not let anybody in. Close the door. Then please come back to me here, dear Casher, and if you are still alive, I will have some other things for you to do."

Casher turned in bewilderment. It did not occur to him to contradict her. He could end up a forgetty, like the maidservant Eunice or the Administrator's brown man, Gosigo.

Down the halls he walked. He met no one except for a few shy cleaning robots, who bowed their heads politely as he passed.

He found the front door. It stopped him. It looked like wood on the outside, but it was actually a Daimoni door, made of near-indestructible material. There was no sign of a key or dials or controls. Acting like a man in a dream, he took a chance that the door might be keyed to himself. He put his right palm firmly against it, at the left or opening edge.

The door swung in.

Meiklejohn was there. Gosigo held the Administrator upright. It must have been a rough trip. The Administrator's face was bruised and blood trickled from the corner of his mouth. His eyes focused on Casher.

"You're alive. She caught you too?"

Quite formally Casher asked, "What do you want in this house?"

"I have come," said the Administrator, "to see her."

"To see whom?" insisted Casher.

The Administrator hung almost slack in Gosigo's arms. By his own standard and in his own way, he was a very brave man indeed. His eyes looked clear, even though his body was collapsing.

"To see T'ruth, if she will see me," said Rankin Meiklejohn.

"She cannot," said Casher, "see you now. Gosigo!"

The forgetty turned to Casher and gave him a bow.

"You will forget me. You have not seen me."

"I have not seen you, lord. Give my greetings to your lady. Anything else?"

"Yes. Take you master home, as safely and swiftly as you can."

"My lord!" cried Gosigo, though this was an improper title for Casher. Casher turned around.

"My lord, tell her to extend the weather machines for just a few more kilometers and I will have him home safe in ten minutes. At top speed."

"I can tell her," said Casher, "but I cannot promise she will do it."

"Of course," said Gosigo. He picked up the Administrator and began putting him into the groundcar. Rankin Meiklejohn bawled once, like a man crying in pain. It sounded like a blurred version of the name *Murray Madigan*. No one heard it but Gosigo and Casher; Gosigo busy closing the groundcar, Casher pushing on the big house door.

The door clicked.

There was silence.

The opening of the door was remembered only by the warm sweet salty stink of seaweed, which had disturbed the odor pattern of the changeless, musty old house.

Casher hurried back with the message about the weather machines.

T'ruth received the message gravely. Without looking at the console, she reached out and controlled it with her extended right hand, not taking her eyes off Casher for a moment. The machine clicked its agreement. T'ruth exhaled.

"Thank you, Casher. Now the Instrumentality and the forgetty are gone."

She stared at him, almost sadly and inquiringly. He wanted to pick her up, to crush her to his chest, to rain his kisses on her face. But he stood stock still. He did not move. This was not just the forever-loving turtle-child; this was the real mistress of Henriada. This was the Hechizera of Gonfalon, whom he had formerly thought about only in terms of a wild, melodic grand opera.

"I think you are seeing me, Casher. It is hard to see people, even when you look at them every day. I think I can see you too, Casher. It is almost time for us both to do the things which we have to do."

"Which we have to do?" He whispered, hoping she might say something else.

"For me, my work here on Henriada. For you, your fate on your homeland of Mizzer. That's what life is, isn't it? Doing what you have to do in the first place. We're lucky people if we find it out. You are ready, Casher. I am about to give you weapons which will make bombs and cruisers and lasers seem like nothing at all."

"By the Bell, girl! Can't you tell me what those weapons are?"

Truth stood in her innocently revealing sheath, the yellow light of the old music room pouring like a halo around her.

"Yes," she said, "I can tell you now. Me."

"You?"

Casher felt a wild surge of erotic attraction for the innocently voluptuous child. He remembered his first insane impulse to crush her with kisses, to sweep her up with hugs, to exhaust her with all the excitement which his masculinity could bring to both of them.

He stared at her.

She stood there, calm.

That sort of idea did not ring right.

He was going to get her, but he was going to get something far from fun or folly—something, indeed, which he might not even like.

When at last he spoke, it was out of the deep bewilderment of his own thoughts, "What do you mean, you're going to give me yourself? It doesn't sound very romantic to me, nor the tone in which you said it."

The child stepped close to him, reaching up and patting his forehead.

"You're not going to get me for a night's romance, and if you did you would be sorry. I am the property of my master and of no other man. But I can do something with you which I have never done to anyone else. I can get myself imprinted on you. The technicians are already coming. You will be the turtle-child. You will be the citizeness Agatha Madigan, the Hechizera of Gonfalon herself. You will be many other people. And yourself. You will then win. Accidents may kill you, Casher, but no one will be able to kill you on purpose. Not when you're me. Poor man! Do you know what you will be giving up?"

"What?" he croaked, at the edge of a great fright. He had seen danger before, but never before had danger loomed up from within himself.

"You will not fear death, ever again, Casher. You will have to lead your life minute by minute, second by second, and you will not have the alibi that you are going to die anyhow. You will know that's not special."

He nodded, understanding her words and scrabbling around his mind for a meaning.

"I'm a girl, Casher. . . ."

He looked at her and his eyes widened. She was a girl—a beautiful, wonderful girl. But she was something more. She was the mistress of Henriada. She was the first of the underpeople really and truly to surpass humanity. To think that he had wanted to grab her poor little body. The body—ah, that was sweet!—but the power within it was the kind of thing that empires and religions are made of.

". . . and if you take the print of me, Casher, you will never lie with a woman without realizing that you know more about her than she does. You will be a seeing man among blind multitudes, a hearing person in the world of the deaf. I don't know how much fun romantic love is going to be to you after this."

Gloomily he said, "If I can free my home planet of Mizzer, it will be worth it. Whatever it is."

"You're not going to turn into a woman!" She laughed. "Nothing that easy. But you are going to get wisdom. And I will tell you the whole story of the Sign of the Fish before you leave here."

"Not that, please," he begged. "That's a religion and the Instrumentality would never let me travel again."

"I'm going to have you scrambled, Casher, so that nobody can read you for a year or two. And the Instrumentality is not going to send you back. *I am.* Through Space Three."

"It'll cost you a fine, big ship to do it."

"My master will approve when I tell him, Casher. Now give me that kiss you have been wanting to give me. Perhaps you will remember something of it when you come out of scramble."

She stood there. He did nothing.

"Kiss me!" she commanded.

He put his arm around her. She felt like a big little girl. She lifted her face. She thrust her lips up toward his. She stood on tiptoe.

He kissed her the way a man might kiss a picture or a religious object. The heat and fierceness had gone out of his hopes. He had not kissed a girl, but power—tremendous power and wisdom put into a single slight form.

"Is that the way your master kisses you?"

She gave him a quick smile. "How clever of you! Yes, sometimes. Come along now. We have to shoot some children before the technicians are ready. It will give you a good last chance of seeing what you can do, when you have become what I am. Come along. The guns are in the hall."

XIII

They went down an enormous light-oak staircase to a floor which Casher had never seen before. It must have been the entertainment and hospitality center of Beauregard long ago, when the Mister and Owner Murray Madigan was himself young.

The robots did a good job of keeping away the dust and the mildew. Casher saw inconspicuous little air-dryers placed at strategic places, so that the rich tooled leather on the walls would not spoil, so that the velvet bar stools would not become slimy with mold, so that the pool tables would not warp nor the golf clubs go out of shape with age and damp. *By the Bell*, he thought, *that man Madigan could have entertained a thousand people at one time in a place this size.*

The gun cabinet, now, that was functional. The glass shone. The velvet of oil showed on the steel and walnut of the guns. They were old Earth models, very rare and very special. For actual fighting, people used the cheap artillery of the present time or wirepoints for close work. Only the richest and rarest of connoisseurs had the old Earth weapons or could use them.

T'ruth touched the guard robot and waked him. The robot saluted, looked at her face and without further inquiry opened the cabinet.

"Do you know guns?" said T'ruth to Casher.

"Wirepoints," he said. "Never touched a gun in my life."

"Do you mind using a learning helmet, then? I could teach you hypnotically with the special rules of the Hechizera, but they might give you a headache or upset you emotionally. The helmet is neuroelectric and it has filters."

Casher nodded and saw his reflection nodding in the polished glass doors of the gun cabinet. He was surprised to see how helpless and lugubrious he looked.

But it was true. Never before in his life had he felt that a situation swept over him, washed him along like a great wave, left him with no choice and no responsibility. Things were her choice now, not his, and yet he felt that her power was benign, self-limited, restricted by factors at which he could no more than guess. He had come for one weapon—the cruiser which he had hoped to get from the Administrator Rankin Meiklejohn. She was offering him something else—psychological weapons in which he had neither experience nor confidence.

She watched him attentively for a long moment and then turned to the gun-watching robot.

"You're little Harry Hadrian, aren't you? The gun-watcher."

"Yes, ma'am," said the silver robot brightly, "and I'm owl-brained too. That makes me very bright."

"Watch this," she said, extending her arms the width of the gun cabinet and then dropping them after a queer flutter of her hands. "Do you know what that means?"

"Yes, ma'am," said the little robot quickly, the emotion showing in his toneless voice by the speed with which he spoke, not by the intonation. "It-means-you-have-taken-over-and-I-am-off-duty! Can-I-go-sit-in-the-garden-and-look-at-the-live-things?"

"Not quite yet, little Harry Hadrian. There are some wind people out there now and they might hurt you. I have another errand for you first. Do you remember where the teaching helmets are?"

"Silver hats on the third floor in an open closet with a wire running to each hat. Yes."

"Bring one of those as fast as you can. Pull it loose very carefully from its electrical connection."

The little robot disappeared in a sudden fast, gentle clatter up the stairs.

T'ruth turned back to Casher. "I have decided what to do with you. I am helping you. You don't have to look so gloomy about it."

"I'm not gloomy. The Administrator sent me here on a crazy errand, killing an unknown underperson. I find out that the person is really a little girl. Then I find out that she is not an underperson, but a frightening old dead woman, still walking around alive. My life gets turned upside down. All my plans are set aside. You propose to send me hope to fulfill my life's work on Mizzer. I've struggled for this, so many years! Now you're making it all come through, even though you are going to cook me through Space Three to do it, and throw in a lot of illegal religion and hypnotic tricks that I'm not sure I can handle. You tell me now to come along—to shoot children with guns. I've never done anything like that in my life and yet I find myself obeying you. I'm tired out, girl, tired out. If you have put me in your power, I don't even know it. I don't even want to know it."

"Here you are, Casher, on the ruined wet world of Henriada. In less than a week you will be recovering among the military casualties of Colonel Wedder's army. You will be under the clear sky of Mizzer, and the Seventh Nile will be near you, and you will be ready at long last to do what you have to do. You will have bits and pieces of memories of me—not enough to make you find your way back here or to tell people all the secrets of Beauregard, but enough for you to remember that you have been loved. You may even"—and she smiled very gently, with a tender wry humor on her face—

"marry some Mizzer girl because her body or her face or her manner reminds you of me."

"In a week?" he gasped.

"Less than that."

"Who are you," he cried out, "that you, an underperson, should run real people and should manipulate their lives?"

"I didn't look for power, Casher. Power doesn't usually work if you look for it. I have eighty-nine thousand years to live, Casher, and as long as my master lives I shall love him and take care of him. Isn't he handsome? Isn't he wise? Isn't he the most perfect master you ever saw?"

Casher thought of the old ruined-looking body with the plastic knobs set into it; he thought of the faded pajama bottoms; he said nothing.

"You don't have to agree," said T'ruth. "I know I have a special way of looking at him. But they took my turtle brain and raised the IQ to above normal human level. They took me when I was a happy little girl, enchanted by the voice and the glance and the touch of my master—they took me to where this real woman lay dying and they put me into a machine and they put her into one too. When they were through, they picked me up. I had on a pink dress with pastel blue socks and pink shoes. They carried me out into the corridor, on a rug. They had finished with me. They knew that I wouldn't die. I was healthy. Can't you see it, Casher? I cried myself to sleep, nine hundred years ago."

Casher could not really answer. He nodded sympathetically.

"I was a girl, Casher. Maybe I was a turtle once, but I don't remember that, any more than you remember your mother's womb or your laboratory bottle. In that one hour I was never to be a girl again. I did not need to go to school. I had *her* education, and it was a good one. She spoke twenty or more languages. She was a psychologist and a hypnotist and a strategist. She was also the tyrannical mistress of this house. I cried because my childhood was finished, because I knew what I would have to do. I cried because I knew that I could do it. I *loved* my master so, but I was no longer to be the pretty little servant who brought him his tablets or his sweetmeats or his beer. Now I saw the truth—as she died I had myself become Henriada. The planet was mine to care for, to manage—to protect my master. If I come along and I protect and help you, is that so much for a woman who will just be growing up when your grandchildren will all be dead of old age?"

"No, no," stammered Casher O'Neill. "But your own life? A family, perhaps?"

Anger lashed across her pretty face. Her features were the features of the delicious girl-child T'ruth, but her expression was that of the citizeness Agatha Madigan, perhaps, a worldly woman reborn to the endless worldliness of her own wisdom.

"Should I order a husband from the turtle bank, perhaps? Should I hire out a piece of my master's estate, to be sold to somebody because I'm an underperson, or perhaps put to work somewhere in an industrial ship? I'm *me*. I may be an animal, but I have more civilization in me than all the wind people on this planet. Poor things! What kind of people are they, if they are only happy when they catch a big mutated duck and tear it to pieces, eating it raw? I'm not going to lose, Casher. I'm going to win. My master will live longer than any person has ever lived before. He gave me that mission when he was strong and wise and well in the prime of his life. I'm going to do what I was made for, Casher, and you're going to go back to Mizzer and make it free, whether you like it or not!"

They both heard a happy scurrying on the staircase.

The small silver robot, little Harry Hadrian, burst upon them; he carried a teaching helmet.

T'ruth said, "Resume your post. You are a good boy, little Harry, and you can have time to sit in the garden later on, when it is safe."

"Can I sit in a tree?" the little robot asked.

"Yes, if it is safe."

Little Harry Hadrian resumed his post by the gun cabinet. He kept the key in his hand. It was a very strange key, sharp at the end and as long as an awl. Casher supposed that it must be one of the straight magnetic keys, cued to its lock by a series of magnetized patterns.

"Sit on the floor for a minute," said T'ruth to Casher; "you're too tall for me." She slipped the helmet on his head, adjusted the levers on each side so that the helmet sat tight and true upon his skull.

With a touching gesture of intimacy, for which she gave him a sympathetic apologetic little smile, she moistened the two small electrodes with her own spit, touching her finger to her tongue and then to the electrode. These went to his temples.

She adjusted the verniered dials on the helmet itself, lifted the rear wire and applied it to her forehead.

Casher heard the click of a switch.

"That did it," he heard T'ruth's voice saying, very far away.

He was too busy looking into the gun cabinet. He knew them all and loved some of them. He knew the feel of their stocks on his shoulder, the glimpse of their barrels in front of his eyes, the dance of the target on their various sights, the welcome heavy weight of the gun on his supporting arm, the rewarding thrust of the stock against his shoulder when he fired. He knew all this, and did not know how he knew it.

"The Hechizera, Agatha herself, was a very accomplished sportswoman," murmured T'ruth to him. "I thought her knowledge would take a second printing when I passed it along to you. Let's take these."

She gestured to little Harry Hadrian, who unlocked the cabinet and took out two enormous guns, which looked like the long muskets mankind had had on earth even before the age of space began.

"If you're going to shoot children," said Casher with his newfound expertness, "these won't do. They'll tear the bodies completely to pieces."

T'ruth reached into the little bag which hung from her belt. She took out three shotgun shells. "I have three more," she said. "Six children is all we need."

Casher looked at the slug projecting slightly from the shotgun casing. It did not look like any shell he had ever seen before. The workmanship was unbelievably fine and precise.

"What are they? I never saw these before."

"Proximity stunners," she said. "Shoot ten centimeters above the head of any living thing and the stunner knocks it out."

"You want the children alive?"

"Alive, of course. And unconscious. They are a part of your final test."

Two hours later, after an exciting hike to the edge of the weather controls, they had the six children stretched out on the floor of the great hall. Four were little boys, two girls; they were fine-boned, soft-haired people, very thin, but they did not look too far from Earth normal.

T'ruth called up a doctor underman from among her servants. There must have been a crowd of fifty or sixty undermen and robots standing around. Far up the staircase, John Joy Tree stood hidden, half in shadow. Casher suspected that he was as inquisitive as the others but afraid of himself, Casher, "the man of blood."

T'ruth spoke quietly but firmly to the doctor. "Can you give them a strong euphoric before you waken them? We don't want to have to pluck them out of all the curtains in the house, if they go wild when they wake up."

"Nothing simpler," said the doctor underman. He seemed to be of dog origin, but Casher could not tell.

He took a glass tube and touched it to the nape of each little neck. The necks were all streaked with dirt. These children had never been washed in their lives, except by the rain.

"Wake them," said T'ruth.

The doctor stepped back to a rolling table. It gleamed with equipment. He must have preset his devices, because all he did was to press a button and the children stirred into life.

The first reaction was wildness. They got ready to bolt. The biggest of the boys, who by earth standards would have been about ten, got three steps before he stopped and began laughing.

T'ruth spoke the Old Common Tongue to them, very slowly and with long spaces between the words:

"Wind—children—do—you—know—where—you—are?"

The biggest girl twittered back to her so fast that Casher could not understand it.

T'ruth turned to Casher and said, "The girl said that she is in the Dead Place, where the air never moves and where the Old Dead Ones move around on their own business. She means us." To the wind children she spoke again.

"What—would—you—like—most?"

The biggest girl went from child to child. They nodded agreement vigorously. They formed a circle and began a little chant. By the second repetition around, Casher could make it out.

Shig—shag—shuggery,
  shuck shuck shuck!
What all of us need is
  an all-around duck.
Shig—shag—shuggery,
  shuck shuck shuck!

At the fourth or fifth repetition they all stopped and looked at T'ruth, who was so plainly the mistress of the house.

She in turn spoke to Casher O'Neill. "They think that they want a tribal feast of raw duck. What they are going to get is inoculations against the worst diseases of this planet, several duck meals and their freedom again. But they need something else beyond all measure. *You know what that is, Casher, if you can only find it.*"

The whole crowd turned its eyes on Casher, the human eyes of the people and underpeople, the milky lenses of the robots.

Casher stood aghast.

"Is this a test?" he asked softly.

"You could call it that,' said T'ruth, looking away from him.

Casher thought furiously and rapidly. It wouldn't do any good to make them into forgetties. The household had enough of them. T'ruth had announced a plan to let them loose again. The Mister and Owner Murray Madigan must have told her, sometime or other, to "do something" about the wind people. She was trying to do it. The whole crowd watched him. What might T'ruth expect?

The answer came to him in a flash.

If she were asking *him*, it must be something to do with himself, something which he—uniquely among these people, underpeople and robots—had brought to the storm-sieged mansion of Beauregard.

Suddenly he saw it.

"Use me, my lady Ruth," said he, deliberately giving her the wrong title, "to print on them nothing from my intellectual knowledge, but everything from my emotional makeup. It wouldn't do them any good to know about Mizzer, where the Twelve Niles work their way down across the Intervening Sands. Nor about Pontoppidan, the Gem Planet. Nor about Olympia, where the blind brokers promenade under numbered clouds. Knowing things would not help these children. But *wanting*—"

Wanting things was different.

He was unique. He had wanted to return to Mizzer. He had wanted return beyond all dreams of blood and revenge. He had wanted things fiercely, wildly, so that even if he could not get them, he zigzagged the galaxy in search of them.

T'ruth was speaking to him again, urgently and softly, but not in so low a voice that the others in the room could not hear.

"And what, Casher O'Neill, should I give them from you?"

"My emotional structure. My determination. My desire. Nothing else. Give them that and throw them back into the winds. Perhaps if they want something fiercely enough, they will grow up to find out what it is."

There was a soft murmur of approval around the room.

T'ruth hesitated a moment and then nodded. "You answered, Casher. You answered quickly and perceptively. Bring seven helmets, Eunice. Stay here, doctor."

Eunice, the forgetty, left, taking two robots with her.

"A chair," said T'ruth to no one in particular. "For him."

A large, powerful underman pushed his way through the crowd and dragged a chair to the end of the room.

T'ruth gestured that Casher should sit in it.

She stood in front of him. *Strange*, thought Casher, *that she should be a great lady and still a little girl.* How would he ever find a girl like her? He was not even afraid of the mystery of the Fish, or the image of the man on two pieces of wood. He no longer dreaded Space Three, where so many travelers had gone in and so few had come out. He felt safe, comforted by her wisdom and authority. He felt that he would never see the likes of this again—a child running a planet and doing it well; a half-dead man surviving through the

endless devotion of his maidservant; a fierce woman hypnotist living on with all the anxieties and angers of humanity gone, but
with the skill and obstinacy of turtle genes to sustain her in her
reimprinted form.

"I can guess what you are thinking," said T'ruth, "but we have
already said the things that we had to say. I've peeped your mind
a dozen times and I know that you want to go back to Mizzer so
bad that Space Three will spit you out right at the ruined fort where
the big turn of the Seventh Nile begins. In my own way I love you,
Casher, but I could not keep you here without turning you into a
forgetty and making you a servant to my master. You know what
always comes first with me, and always will."

"Madigan."

"Madigan," she answered, and with her voice the name itself was
a prayer.

Eunice came back with the helmets.

"When we are through with these, Casher, I'll have them take
you to the conditioning room. Good-bye, my might-have-been!"

In front of everyone, she kissed him full on the lips.

He sat in the chair, full of patience and contentment. Even as his
vision blacked out, he could see the thin light sheath of a smock on
the girlish figure, he could remember the tender laughter lurking
in her smile.

In the last instant of his consciousness, he saw that another figure
had joined the crowd—the tall old man with the worn bathrobe, the
faded blue eyes, the thin yellow hair. Murray Madigan had risen from
his private life-in-death and had come to see the last of Casher O'Neill.
He did not look weak, nor foolish. He looked like a great man, wise
and strange in ways beyond Casher's understanding.

There was the touch of T'ruth's little hand on his arm and everything became a velvety cluttered dark quiet inside his own mind.

XIV

When he awoke, he lay naked and sunburned under the hot sky of
Mizzer. Two soldiers with medical patches were rolling him onto a
canvas litter.

"Mizzer!" he cried to himself. His throat was too dry to make a
sound. "I'm home."

Suddenly the memories came to him and he scrabbled and
snatched at them, seeing them dissolve within his mind before he
could get paper to write them down.

Memory: there was the front hall, himself getting ready to sleep in the chair, with the old giant of Murray Madigan at the edge of the crowd and the tender light touch of T'ruth—his girl, his girl, now uncountable light years away—putting her hand on his arm.

Memory: there was another room, with stained-glass pictures and incense, and the weepworthy scenes of a great life shown in frescoes around the wall. There were the two pieces of wood and the man in pain nailed to them. But Casher knew that scattered and coded through his mind there was the ultimate and undefeatable wisdom of the Sign of the Fish. He knew he could never fear fear again.

Memory: there was a gaming table in a bright room, with the wealth of a thousand worlds being raked toward him. He was a woman, strong, big-busted, bejeweled and proud. He was Agatha Madigan, winning at the games. (*That must have come*, he thought, *when they printed me with T'ruth.*) And in that mind of the Hechizera, which was now his own mind too, there was clear sure knowledge of how he could win men and women, officers and soldiers, even underpeople and robots, to his cause without a drop of blood or a word of anger.

The men, lifting him on the litter, made red waves of heat and pain roll over him.

He heard one of them say, "Bad case of burn. Wonder how he lost his clothes."

The words were matter-of-fact; the comment was nothing special; but the cadence, that special cadence, was the true speech of Mizzer.

As they carried him away, he remembered the face of Rankin Meiklejohn, enormous eyes staring with inward despair over the brim of a big glass. That was the Administrator. On Henriada. That was the man who sent me past Ambiloxi to Beauregard at two seventy-five in the morning. The litter jolted a little.

He thought of the wet marshes of Henriada and knew that soon he would never remember them again. The worms of the tornadoes creeping up to the edge of the estate. The mad wise face of John Joy Tree.

Space three? Space three? Already, even now, he could not remember how they had put him into Space three.

And Space three itself—

All the nightmares which mankind has ever had pushed into Casher's mind. He twisted once in agony, just as the litter reached a medical military cart. He saw a girl's face—what *was* her name?—and then he slept.

XV

Fourteen Mizzer days later, the first test came.

A doctor colonel and an intelligence colonel, both in the workaday uniform of Colonel Wedder's Special Forces, stood by his bed.

"Your name is Casher O'Neill and we do not know how your body fell among the skirmishers," the doctor was saying, roughly and emphatically. Casher O'Neill turned his head on the pillow and looked at the man.

"Say something more!" he whispered to the doctor.

The doctor said, "You are a political intruder and we do not know how you got mixed up among our troops. We do not even know how you got back among the people of this planet. We found you on the Seventh Nile."

The intelligence colonel standing beside him nodded agreement.

"Do you think the same thing, Colonel?" whispered Casher O'Neill to the intelligence colonel.

"I ask questions. I don't answer them," said the man gruffly.

Casher felt himself reaching for their minds with a kind of fingertip which he did not know he had. It was hard to put into ordinary words, but it felt as though someone had said to him, Casher: "That one is vulnerable at the left forefront area of his consciousness, but the other one is well armored and must be reached through the midbrain." Casher was not afraid of revealing anything by his expression. He was too badly burned and in too much pain to show nuances of meaning on his face. (Somewhere he had heard of the wild story of the Hechizera of Gonfalon! Somewhere endless storms boiled across ruined marshes under a cloudy yellow sky! But where, when, what was that? . . . He could not take time off for memory. He had to fight for his life.)

"Peace be with you," he whispered to both of them.

"Peace be with you," they responded in unison, with some surprise.

"Lean over me, please," said Casher, "so that I do not have to shout."

They stood stock straight.

Somewhere in the resources of his own memory and intelligence, Casher found the right note of pleading which could ride his voice like a carrier wave and make them do as he wished.

"This is Mizzer," he whispered.

"Of course this is Mizzer," snapped the intelligence colonel, "and you are Casher O'Neill. What are you doing here?"

"Lean over, gentlemen," he said softly, lowering his voice so that they could barely hear him.

This time they did lean over.

His burned hands reached for their hands. The officers noticed it, but since he was sick and unarmed, they let him touch them.

Suddenly he felt their minds glowing in his as brightly as if he had swallowed their gleaming, thinking brains at a single gulp.

He spoke no longer.

He *thought* at them—torrential, irresistible thought.

I am not Casher O'Neill. You will find his body in a room four doors down. I am the civilian Bindaoud.

The two colonels stared, breathing heavily.

Neither said a word.

Casher went on: *Our fingerprints and records have gotten mixed. Give me the fingerprints and papers of the dead Casher O'Neill. Bury him then, quickly, but with honor. Once he loved your leader and there is no point in stirring up wild rumors about returns from out of space. I am Bindaoud. You will find my records in your front office. I am not a soldier. I am a civilian technician doing studies on the salt in blood chemistry under field conditions. You have heard me, gentlemen. You hear me now. You will hear me always. But you will not remember this, gentlemen, when you awaken. I am sick. You can give me water and a sedative.*

They still stood, enraptured by the touch of his tight burned hands.

Casher O'Neill said, "Awaken."

Casher O'Neill let go their hands.

The medical colonel blinked and said amiably, "You'll be better, Mister and Doctor Bindaoud. I'll have the orderly bring you water and a sedative."

To the other officer he said, "I have an interesting corpse four doors down. I think you had better see it."

Casher O'Neill tried to think of the recent past, but the blue light of Mizzer was all around him, the sand smell, the sound of horses galloping. For a moment, he thought of a big child's blue dress and he did not know why he almost wept.

SAMUEL R. DELANY
The Star Pit

Samuel R. Delany's first novel, *The Jewels of Aptor*, was published in 1962, went almost totally unnoticed, and was followed throughout the early years of the sixties by a string of other novels such as *The Ballad of Beta-2*, *Empire Star*, *Captives of the Flame*, *The Towers of Toron*, and *City of a Thousand Suns* (these last three reissued some years later in one volume as the much more sedately titled *The Fall of the Towers*) . . . all of which were completely ignored as well. On the surface, they looked just like any of a hundred other Ace Doubles: same garish and ugly pulp covers, same florid and melodramatic pulp titles, same overheated pulp blurbs ("Between the distant stars lay terror!" "He warped time and space to deliver a message to eternity!") . . . and yet, with each Delany book I read, the more impressed I became with their power and originality, and the greater my conviction grew that here, all unnoticed, a true Master of the Form was being born.

It was a conviction shared by just about no one else in those days, perhaps because Delany's books *were* published, with maximum obscurity, as garish and pulpy looking Ace Doubles, the bottom of the novel market, and perhaps because a hurried and unsympathetic look at the plot-synopsis teasers on the inside page—or even a dip inside, if your glance happened to fall on, for instance, a character named "Comet Jo"—would lead you to assume that this was standard, lowest-common-denominator space opera of the most fundamental kind.

Well, it *was* space opera—and it wasn't. That was one of the things I loved about Delany, his ability to mix the most outrageous of space opera *shticks* (including some as wild and cosmic as anything seen since the "superscience" era of the thirties) with the most subtle of philosophies and metaphysics; as his talent grew throughout the first half of the decade, so did my admiration for the intensity and clotted eloquence of his prose, for his psychologically complex characterizations, for his radical insight into the workings of social systems, and also for the feeling I got from him—growing more powerful with every book—that here was the authentic view from *the other side*, a perspective from beyond the confining provincial world against whose boundaries and sharply limited vistas I chafed. (By the mid sixties, Delany's talent had deepened so that I imagined him to be some white-bearded sage—perhaps even forty!—steeped in years and wisdom; when I found out instead that he was only a few years older than I was—for he started selling novels when he was nineteen—the shock was considerable.)

So I went around for a few years pushing copies of Delany novels on friends who pushed them away with indifference, until he hit big with 1966's *Babel-17*, and everyone else went galloping retrospectively back through his earlier work, while I stood by smiling smugly. (I had the identical experience, at just about the same time, with Le Guin's work—it frequently pays to keep your eye on what's happening on the bottom of the heap.)

Delany went on to become one of the two most critically acclaimed new American SF writers of the sixties (the other being Roger Zelazny). He won the Nebula Award in 1966 for *Babel-17*, won two more Nebulas in 1967 for *The Einstein Intersection* and for his first short story, "Aye, and Gomorrah . . ." and won both the Nebula and the Hugo Award for his 1968 novella *Time Considered as a Helix of Semi-Precious Stones*. His monumental novel *Nova* was, in my opinion, one of the best SF novels of the sixties, and its appearance prompted critic Algis Budrys to hail him as "the best science fiction writer in the world"—an opinion it would have been possible to find a great deal of support for by the end of the decade, at least on the American side of the Atlantic.

Delany only wrote a handful of short stories—unlike Zelazny, he made his biggest impact on the field with his novels—but they deserve to be numbered among the best short work of the sixties. Aside from the stories already named and the one that follows they include "Driftglass," the ornately titled "We, in Some Strange Power's Employ, Move on a Rigorous Line," "Corona," and "Dog in a Fisherman's Net." Almost all of his short fiction was assembled in the landmark collection *Driftglass*.

Even in this august company, though, the marvelous novella that follows, *The Star Pit*, is a standout, an engrossing tale of poetry, pain, and wonder, set against an ornate and intricately detailed future . . . and a story that also suggests that no matter how wide you set your limits, they still remain, after all, *limits*.

After *Nova*, Delany fell silent for seven years, and when he did return, it was with work that no longer had as broad an appeal within the genre, like the immense, surreal *Dhalgren* . . . which did, however, become a best-seller outside of the usual genre boundaries, and helped gain him wide new audiences. Although he continued to publish a series of ornate and somewhat abstract intellectual fantasy novels throughout the rest of the seventies and the eighties, his most direct subsequent impact on SF has probably been as a critic, although it is evident that his sixties work was one of the most powerful direct influences on the Cyberpunk movement of the mid-eighties. (Delany once told me that as a young writer he was trying "to do Bester for the sixties, to write a book that would be as exciting to a twenty-five-year-old as Bester's *The Stars My Destination* had been to me when I was fourteen"—and William Gibson once admitted to me that at least part of what *he* was trying to accomplish with his work was "to do Delany for the eighties.") Delany's other works include the novels *Triton*, *Stars in My Pocket Like Grains of Sand*, *Flight from Nevèrÿon*, *The Bridge of Lost Desire*, *Tales of Nevèrÿon*, and the critical works *The Jewel-Hinged Jaw*, *Starboard Wine*, *The Straits of Messina*, and *The American Shore*. His most recent work is the short novel *They Fly at Çiron*. Upcoming is a new expanded edition of *Driftglass*, which will include some later stories, and he is at work on a new novel.

Two glass panes with dirt between and little tunnels from cell to cell: when I was a kid I had an ant colony.

But once some of our four-to-six-year-olds built an ecologarium with six-foot plastic panels and grooved aluminum bars to hold corners and top down. They put it out on the sand.

There was a mud puddle against one wall so you could see what was going on underwater. Sometimes segment worms crawling through the reddish earth hit the side so their tunnels were visible for a few inches. In hot weather the inside of the plastic got coated with mist and droplets. The small round leaves on the litmus vines changed from blue to pink, blue to pink as clouds coursed the sky and the pH of the photosensitive soil shifted slightly.

The kids would run out before dawn and belly down naked in the cool sand with their chins on the backs of their hands and stare in the half-dark till the red mill wheel of Sigma lifted over the bloody sea. The sand was maroon then, and the flowers of the crystal plants looked like rubies in the dim light of the giant sun. Up the beach the jungle would begin to whisper while somewhere an ani-wort would start warbling. The kids would giggle and poke each other and crowd closer.

Then Sigma-prime, the second member of the binary, would flare like thermite on the water, and crimson clouds would bleach from coral, through peach, to foam. The kids, half on top of each other now, lay like a pile of copper ingots with sun streaks in their hair—even on little Antoni, my oldest, whose hair was black and curly like bubbling oil (like his mother's), the down on the small of his two-year-old back was a white haze across the copper if you looked that close to see.

More children came to squat and lean on their knees, or kneel with their noses an inch from the walls, to watch, like young magicians, as things were born, grew, matured, and other things were born. Enchanted at their own construction, they stared at the miracles in their live museum.

A small, red seed lay camouflaged in the silt by the lake/puddle. One evening as white Sigma-prime left the sky violet, it broke open into a brown larva as long and of the same color as the first joint of Antoni's thumb. It flipped and swirled in the mud a couple of days, then crawled to the first branch of the nearest crystal plant to hang exhausted, head down, from the tip. The brown flesh hardened, thickened, grew black, shiny. Then one morning the children saw the onyx chrysalis crack, and by second dawn there was an emerald-eyed flying lizard buzzing at the plastic panels.

"Oh, look, Da!" they called to me. "It's trying to get out!"

The speed-hazed creature butted at the corner for a few days, then settled at last to crawling around the broad leaves of the miniature shade palms.

When the season grew cool and there was the annual debate over whether the kids should put tunics on—they never stayed in them more than twenty minutes anyway—the jewels of the crystal plant misted, their facets coarsened, and they fell like gravel.

There were little four-cupped sloths, too, big as a six-year-old's fist. Most of the time they pressed their velvety bodies against the walls and stared longingly across the sand with their retractable eye-clusters. Then two of them swelled for about three weeks. We thought at first it was some bloating infection. But one evening there were a couple of litters of white velvet balls half hidden by the low leaves of the shade palms. The parents were occupied now and didn't pine to get out.

There was a rock half in and half out of the puddle, I remember, covered with what I'd always called mustard-moss when I saw it in the wild. Once it put out a brush of white hairs. And one afternoon the children ran to collect all the adults they could drag over. "Look, oh Da, Da, Ma, look!" The hairs had detached themselves and were walking around the water's edge, turning end over end along the soft soil.

I had to leave for work in a few minutes and haul some spare drive parts out to Tau Ceti. But when I got back five days later, the hairs had taken root, thickened, and were already putting out the small round leaves of litmus vines. Among the new shoots, lying on her back, claws curled over her wrinkled belly, eyes cataracted like the foggy jewels of the crystal plant—she'd dropped her wings like cellophane days ago—was the flying lizard. Her pearl throat still pulsed, but as I watched, it stopped. Before she died, however, she had managed to deposit, nearly camouflaged in the silt by the puddle, a scattering of red seeds.

I remember getting home from another job where I'd been doing the maintenance on the shuttle-boats for a crew putting up a ring station to circle a planet itself circling Aldebaran. I was gone a long time on that one. When I left the landing complex and wandered out toward the tall weeds at the edge of the beach, I still didn't see anybody.

Which was just as well because the night before I'd put on a real winner with the crew to celebrate the completion of the station. That morning I'd taken a couple more drinks at the landing bar to undo last night's damage. Never works.

The swish of frond on frond was like clashed rasps. Sun on the sand reached out fingers of pure glare and tried to gouge my eyes. I was glad the home-compound was deserted because the kids would have asked questions I didn't want to answer; the adults wouldn't ask anything, which was even harder to answer.

Then, down by the ecologarium, a child screeched. And screeched again. Then Antoni came hurtling toward me, half running, half on all fours, and flung himself on my leg. "Oh, Da! Da! Why, oh why, Da?"

I'd kicked my boots off and shrugged my shirt back at the compound porch, but I still had my overalls on. Antoni had two fists full of my pants leg and wouldn't let go. "Hey, kid-boy, what's the matter?"

When I finally got him on my shoulder he butted his blubber wet face against my collarbone. "Oh, Da! Da! It's crazy, it's all cra*aaa*zy!" His voice rose to lose itself in sobs.

"What's crazy, kid-boy? Tell Da."

Antoni held my ear and cried while I walked down to the plastic enclosure.

They'd put a small door in one wall with a two-number combination lock that was supposed to keep this sort of thing from happening. I guess Antoni learned the combination from watching the older kids, or maybe he just figured it out.

One of the young sloths had climbed out and wandered across the sand about three feet.

"See, Da! It crazy, it bit me. Bit me, Da!" Sobs became sniffles as he showed me a puffy, bluish place on his wrist centered on which was a tiny crescent of pinpricks. Then he pointed jerkily to the creature.

It was shivering, and bloody froth spluttered from its lip flaps. All the while it was digging futilely at the sand with its clumsy cups, eyes retracted. Now it fell over, kicked, tried to right itself, breath going like a flutter valve. "It can't take the heat," I explained, reaching down to pick it up.

It snapped at me, and I jerked back. "Sunstroke, kid-boy. Yeah, it is crazy."

Suddenly it opened its mouth wide, let out all its air, and didn't take in any more. "It's all right now," I said.

Two more of the baby sloths were at the door, front cups over the sill, staring with bright, black eyes. I pushed them back with a piece of seashell and closed the door. Antoni kept looking at the white fur ball on the sand. "Not crazy now?"

"It's dead," I told him.

"Dead because it went outside, Da?"

I nodded.

"And crazy?" He made a fist and ground something already soft and wet around his upper lip.

I decided to change the subject, which was already too close to something I didn't like to think about. "Who's been taking care of you, anyway?" I asked. "You're a mess, kid-boy. Let's go and fix up that arm. They shouldn't leave a fellow your age all by himself." We started back to the compound. Those bites infect easily, and this one was swelling.

"Why it go crazy? Why it die when it go outside, Da?"

"Can't take the light," I said as we reached the jungle. "They're animals that live in shadow most of the time. The plastic cuts out the ultraviolet rays, just like the leaves that shade them when they run loose in the jungle. Sigma-prime's high on ultraviolet. That's why you're so good-looking, kid-boy. I think your ma told me their nervous systems are on the surface, all that fuzz. Under the ultraviolet, the enzymes break down so quickly that—does this mean anything to you at all?"

"Uh-uh." Antoni shook his head. Then he came out with, "Wouldn't it be nice, Da—" he admired his bite while we walked "—if some of them could go outside, just a few?"

That stopped me. There were sunspots on his blue-black hair. Fronds reflected faint green on his brown cheek. He was grinning, little, and wonderful. Something that had been anger in me a lot of times momentarily melted to raging tenderness, whirling about him like the dust in the light striking down at my shoulders, raging to protect my son. "I don't know about that, kid-boy."

"Why not?"

"It might be pretty bad for the ones who had to stay inside," I told him. "I mean after a while."

"Why?"

I started walking again. "Come on, let's fix your arm and get you cleaned up."

I washed the wet stuff off his face, and scraped the dry stuff from beneath it which had been there at least two days. Then I got some antibiotic into him.

"You smell funny, Da."

"Never mind how I smell. Let's go outside again." I put down a cup of black coffee too fast, and it and my hangover had a fight in my stomach. I tried to ignore it and do a little looking around. But I still couldn't find anybody. That got me mad. I mean he's independent, sure: he's mine. But he's only two.

Back on the beach we buried the dead sloth in sand; then I pointed out the new, glittering stalks of the tiny crystal plants. At the bottom of the pond, in the jellied mass of ani-wort eggs, you could see the tadpole forms quivering already. An orange-fringed shelf fungus had sprouted nearly eight inches since it had been just a few black spores on a pile of dead leaves two weeks back.

"Grow up," Antoni chirped with nose and fists against the plastic. "Everything grow up, and up."

"That's right."

He grinned at me. "I grow!"

"You sure as hell do."

"You grow?" Then he shook his head, twice: once to say no, and the second time because he got a kick from shaking his hair around—there was a lot of it. "You don't grow. You don't get any bigger. Why don't you grow?"

"I do too," I said indignantly. "Just very slowly."

Antoni turned around, leaned on the plastic and moved one toe at a time in the sand—I can't do that—watching me.

"You have to grow all the time," I said. "Not necessarily get bigger. But inside your head you have to grow, kid-boy. For us human-type people that's what's important. And that kind of growing never stops. At least it shouldn't. You can grow, kid-boy, or you can die. That's the choice you've got, and it goes on all of your life."

He looked back over his shoulder. "Grow up, all the time, even if they can't get out."

"Yeah," I said. And was uncomfortable all over again. I started pulling off my overalls for something to do. "Even—" The zipper got stuck. "God *damn* it!—if you can't get out." *Rnrnrnrnrnrn*—it came loose.

The rest got back that evening. They'd been on a group trip around the foot of the mountain. I did a little shouting to make sure my point got across about leaving Antoni alone. Didn't do much good. You know how family arguments go:

He didn't want to come. We weren't going to force—

So what. He's got to learn to do things he doesn't want—

Like some other people I could mention!

Now look—

It's a healthy group. Don't you want him to grow up a healthy—

I'll be happy if he just grows up period. No food, no medical—

But the server was chock full of food. He knows how to use it—

Look, when I got home the kid's arm was swollen all the way up to his elbow!

And so on and so forth, with Antoni sitting in the middle, looking confused. When he got confused enough, he ended it all by announcing matter-of-factly: "Da smell funny when he came home."

Everyone got quiet. Then someone said, "Oh, Vyme, you didn't come home that way again! I mean, in front of the children . . ."

I said a couple of things I was sorry for later and stalked off down the beach—on a four-mile hike.

Times I got home from work? The ecologarium? I guess I'm just leading up to this one.

The particular job had taken me a hectic week to get. It was putting back together a battleship that was gutted somewhere off Aurigae. Only when I got there, I found I'd already been laid off. That particular war was over—they're real quick now. So I scraped and lied and browned my way into a repair gang that was servicing

a traveling replacement station, generally had to humiliate myself
to get the job because every other drive mechanic from the battleship fiasco was after it too. Then I got canned the first day because
I came to work smelling funny. It took me another week to hitch a
ride back to Sigma. Didn't even have enough to pay passage, but I
made a deal with the pilot I'd do half the driving for him.

We were an hour out, and I was at the controls when something
I'd never heard of happening, happened. We came *this* close to
ramming another ship. Consider how much empty space there is;
the chances are infinitesimal. And on top of that, every ship should
be broadcasting an identification beam at all times.

But this big, bulbous keeler-intergalactic slid by so close I could
see her through the front viewport. Our inertia system went nuts.
We jerked around in the stasis whirl from the keeler. I slammed
on the video-intercom and shouted, "You great big stupid . . . *stupid*
. . ." so mad and scared I couldn't say anything else.

The golden piloting the ship stared at me from the view-screen
with mildly surprised annoyance. I remember his face was just
slightly more Negroid than mine.

Our little Serpentina couldn't hurt him. But had we been even a
hundred meters closer we might have ionized. The other pilot came
bellowing from behind the sleeper curtain and started cursing me
out.

"Damn it," I shouted, "it was one of those . . ." and lost all the
profanity I know to my rage, ". . . golden . . ."

"This far into galactic center? Come off it. They should be hanging out around the Star-pit!"

"It was a keeler drive," I insisted. "It came right in front of us."
I stopped because the control stick was shaking in my hand. You
know the Serpentina colophon? They have it in the corner of the
view-screen and raised in plastic on the head of the control knobs.
Well, it got pressed into the ham of my thumb so you could make
it out for an hour, I was squeezing the control rod that tight.

When he set me down, I went straight to the bar to cool off. And
got in a fight. When I reached the beach I was broke, I had a bloody
nose, I was sick, and furious.

It was just after first sunset, and the kids were squealing around
the ecologarium. Then one little girl I didn't even recognize ran
up to me and jerked my arm. "Da, oh, Da! Come look! The ani-
worts are just about to—"

I pushed her, and she sat down, surprised, on the sand.

I just wanted to get to the water and splash something cold on
my face, because every minute or so it would start to burn.

Another bunch of kids grabbed me, shouting, "Da, Da, the ani-worts, Da!" and tried to pull me over.

First I took two steps with them. Then I just swung my arms out. I didn't make a sound. But I put my head down and barreled against the plastic wall. Kids screamed. Aluminum snapped; the plastic cracked and went down. My boots were still on, and I kicked and kicked at red earth and sand. Shade palms went down and the leaves tore under my feet. Crystal plants broke like glass rods beneath a piece of plastic. A swarm of lizards flittered up around my head. Some of the red was Sigma, some was what burned behind my face.

I remember I was still shaking and watching water run out of the broken lake over the sand, then soak in so that the wet tongue of sand expanded a little, raised just a trifle around the edge. Then I looked up to see the kids coming back down the beach, crying, shouting, afraid and clustered around Antoni's ma. She walked steadily toward me—steady because she was a woman and they were children. But I saw the same fear in her face. Antoni was on her shoulder. Other grown-ups were coming behind her.

Antoni's ma was a biologist, and I think she had suggested the ecologarium to the kids in the first place. When she looked up from the ruin I'd made, I knew I'd broken something of hers too.

An odd expression got caught in the features of her—I remember it oh so beautiful—face, with compassion alongside the anger, contempt alongside the fear. "Oh, for pity's sake, Vyme," she cried, not loudly at all. "Won't you ever grow up?"

I opened my mouth, but everything I wanted to say was too big and stayed wedged in my throat.

"Grow up?" Antoni repeated and reached for a lizard that buzzed his head. "Everything stop growing up, now." He looked down again at the wreck I'd made. "All broken. Everything get out."

"He didn't mean to break it," she said to the others for me, then knifed my gratitude with a look. "We'll put it back together."

She put Antoni on the sand and picked up one of the walls.

After they got started, they let me help. A lot of the plants were broken. And only the ani-worts who'd completed metamorphosis could be saved. The flying lizards were too curious to get far away, so we—they netted them and got them back inside. I guess I didn't help that much. And I wouldn't say I was sorry.

They got just about everything back except the sloths.

We couldn't find them. We searched for a long time, too.

The sun was down so they should have been all right. They can't negotiate the sand with any speed so couldn't have reached the jungle. But there were no tracks, no nothing. We even dug in the sand to see if they'd buried themselves. It wasn't till more than a dozen years later I discovered where they went.

For the present I accepted Antoni's mildly adequate, "They just must of got out again."

Not too long after that I left the procreation group. Went off to work one day, didn't come back. But like I said to Antoni, you either grow or die. I didn't die.

Once I considered returning. But there was another war, and suddenly there wasn't anything to return to. Some of the group got out alive. Antoni and his ma didn't. I mean there wasn't even any water left on the planet.

When I finally came to the Star-pit, myself, I hadn't had a drink in years. But working there out on the galaxy's edge did something to me—something to the part that grows I'd once talked about on the beach with Antoni.

If it did it to me, it's not surprising it did it to Ratlit and the rest.

(And I remember a black-eyed creature pressed against the plastic wall, staring across impassable sands.)

Perhaps it was knowing this was as far as you could go.

Perhaps it was the golden.

Golden? I hadn't even joined the group yet when I first heard the word. I was sixteen and a sophomore at Luna Vocational. I was born in a city called New York on a planet called Earth. Luna is its one satellite. You've heard of the system, I'm sure; that's where we all came from. A few other things about it are well known. Unless you're an anthropologist, though, I doubt you've ever been there. It's way the hell off the main trading routes and pretty primitive. I was a drive-mechanics major, on scholarship, living in and studying hard. All morning in Practical Theory (a ridiculous name for a ridiculous class, I thought then) we'd been putting together a model keeler-intergalactic drive. Throughout those dozens of helical inserts and superinertia organus sensitives, I had been silently cursing my teacher, thinking, about like everyone else in the class, "So what if they can fly these jalopies from one galaxy to another. Nobody will ever be able to ride in them. Not with the Psychic and Physiologic shells hanging around this cluster of the universe."

Back in the dormitory I was lying on my bed, scraping graphite lubricant from my nails with the end of my slide rule and half reading at a folded-back copy of *The Young Mechanic* when I saw the article and the pictures.

Through some freakish accident, two people had been discovered who didn't crack up at twenty thousand light-years off the galactic rim, who didn't die at twenty-five thousand.

They were both psychological freaks with some incredible hormone imbalance in their systems. One was a little Oriental girl; the other was an older man, blond and big-boned, from a cold planet circling Cygnus-beta: golden. They looked sullen as hell, both of them.

Then there were more articles, more pictures, in the economic journals, the sociology student-letters, the legal bulletins, as various fields began acknowledging the impact that the golden and the sudden birth of intergalactic trade were having on them. The head of some commission summed it up with the statement: "Though interstellar travel has been with us for three centuries, intergalactic trade has been an impossibility, not because of mechanical limitations, but rather because of barriers that till now we have not even been able to define. Some psychic shock causes insanity in any human—or for that matter, any intelligent species or perceptual machine or computer—that goes more than twenty thousand light-years from the galactic rim; then complete physiological death, as well as recording breakdown in computers that might replace human crews. Complex explanations have been offered, none completely satisfactory, but the base of the problem seems to be this: as the nature of space and time are relative to the concentration of matter in a given area of the continuum, the nature of reality itself operates by the same, or similar, laws. The averaged mass of all the stars in our galaxy controls the 'reality' of our microsector of the universe. But as a ship leaves the galactic rim, 'reality' breaks down and causes insanity and eventual death for any crew, even though certain mechanical laws—though not all—appear to remain, for reasons we don't understand, relatively constant. Save for a few barbaric experiments done with psychedelics at the dawn of spatial travel, we have not even developed a vocabulary that can deal with 'reality' apart from its measurable, physical expression. Yet, just when we had to face the black limit of intergalactic space, bright resources glittered within. Some few of us whose sense of reality has been shattered by infantile, childhood, or prenatal trauma, whose physiological orientation makes life in our interstellar society painful or impossible—not all, but a few of these golden . . ." at which point there was static, or the gentleman coughed, ". . . can make the crossing and return."

The name golden, sans noun, stuck.

Few was the understatement of the millennium. Slightly less than one human being in thirty-four thousand is a golden. A couple of people had pictures of emptying all mental institutions by just shaking them out over the galactic rim. Didn't work like that. The particular psychosis and endocrine setup was remarkably specialized. Still, back then there was excitement, wonder, anticipation, hope, admiration in the word: admiration for the ones who could get out.

"Golden?" Ratlit said when I asked him. He was working as a grease monkey out here in the Star-pit over a Poloscki's. "Born with the word. Grew up with it. Weren't no first time with me. Though I remember when I was about six, right after the last of my parents was killed, and I was hiding out with a bunch of other lice in a broke-open packing crate in an abandoned freight yard near the ruins of Helios on Creton VII—that's where I was born, I think. Most of the city had been starved out by then, but somebody was getting food to us. There was this old crookback character who was hiding too. He used to sit on the top of the packing crate and bang his heels on the aluminum slats and tell us stories about the stars. Had a couple of rags held with twists of wire for clothes, missing two fingers off one hand; he kept plucking the loose skin under his chin with those grimy talons. And he talked about them. So I asked, 'Golden what, sir?' He leaned forward so that his face was like a mahogany bruise on the sky, and croaked, "They've been *out*, I tell you, seen more than even you or I. Human and inhuman, kid-boy, mothered by women and fathered by men, still they live by their own laws and walk their own ways!'" Ratlit and I were sitting under a street lamp with our feet over the Edge where the fence had broken. His hair was like breathing flame in the wind, his single earring glittered. Star-flecked infinity dropped away below our boot soles, and the wind created by the stasis field that held our atmosphere down—we call it the "world-wind" out here because it's never cold and never hot and like nothing on any world—whipped his black shirt back from his bony chest as we gazed on galactic night between our knees. "I guess that was back during the second Kyber war," he concluded.

"Kyber war?" I asked. "Which one was that?"

He shrugged. "I just know it was fought over possession of a couple of tons of di-allium, that's the polarized element the golden brought back from Lupe-galaxy. They used y-adna ships to fight it—that's why it was such a bad war. I mean worse than usual."

"Y-adna? That's a drive I don't know anything about."

"Some golden saw the plans for them in a civilization in Magellanic-9."

"Oh," I said. "And what was Kyber?"

"It was a weapon, a sort of fungus the golden brought back from

some overrun planet on the rim of Andromeda. It's deadly. Only
they were too stupid to bring back the antitoxin."

"That's golden for you."

"Yeah. You ever notice about golden, Vyme? I mean just the
word. I found out all about it from my publisher, once. It's semanti-
cally unsettling."

"Really?" I said. "So are they. Unsettling I mean."

I'd just finished a rough, rough day installing a rebuilt keeler in
a quantum transport hull that just wasn't big enough. The golden
having the job done stood over my shoulder the whole time, and
every hour he'd come out with the sort of added instruction that
would make the next sixty-one minutes miserable. But I did it. The
golden paid me in cash and without a word climbed into the lift,
and two minutes later, while I was still washing the grease off, the
damn five-hundred-ton hulk began to whistle for takeoff.

Sandy, a young fellow who'd come looking for a temporary mechanic's job three months back, but hadn't given me cause to fire
him yet, barely had time to pull the big waldoes out of the way and
go scooting into the shock chamber when the three-hundred-meter
doofus tore loose from the grapplers. And Sandy, who, like a lot
of these youngsters drifting around from job to job, is usually sort
of quiet and vague, got loud and specific. ". . . two thousand pounds
of non-shockproof equipment out there . . . ruin it all if he could
. . . *I'm* not expendable, I don't care what a . . . these golden out
here . . ." while the ship hove off where only the golden go. I just
flipped on the "no-open" sign, left the rest of the grease where it
was, left the hangar, and hunted up Ratlit.

So there we were, under that street lamp, sitting on the Edge, in
the world-wind.

"Golden," Ratlit said under the roar. "It would be much easier
to take if it were grammatically connected to something: golden
ones, golden people. Or even one gold, two golden."

"Male golden, female goldene?"

"Something like that. It's not an adjective, it's not a noun. My
publisher told me that for a while it was written with a dash after
it that stood for whatever it might modify."

I remembered the dash. It was an uneasy joke, a fill-in for that
cough. Golden *what*? People had already started to feel uncomfortable. Then it went past joking and back to just "golden."

"Think about that, Vyme. Just golden: one, two, or three of
them."

"That's something to think about, kid-boy," I said.

Ratlit had been six during the Kyber war. Square that and add
it once again for my age now. Ratlit's? Double six and add one. I

like kids, and they like me. But that may be because my childhood
left me a lot younger at forty-two than I should be. Ratlit's had left
him a lot older than any thirteen-year-old has a right to be.

"No golden took part in the war," Ratlit said.

"They never do." I watched his thin fingers get all tangled together.

After two divorces, my mother ran off with a salesman and left
me and four siblings with an alcoholic aunt for a year. Yeah, they
still have divorces, monogamous marriages and stuff like that where
I was born. Like I say, it's pretty primitive. I left home at fifteen,
made it through vocational school on my own, and learned enough
about what makes things fly to end up—after that disastrous marriage I told you about earlier—with my own repair hangar on the
Star-pit.

Compared with Ratlit I had a stable childhood.

That's right, he lost the last parent he remembered when he was
six. At seven he was convicted of his first felony—after escaping
from Creton VII. But part of his treatment at hospital *cum* reform
school *cum* prison was to have the details lifted from his memory.
"Did something to my head back there. That's why I never could
learn to read, I think." For the next couple of years he ran away
from one foster group after the other. When he was eleven, some
guy took him home from Play Planet where he'd been existing
under the boardwalk on discarded hot dogs, souvlakia, and falafel.
"Fat, smoked perfumed cigarettes; name was Vivian?" Turned out
to be the publisher. Ratlit stayed for three months, during which
time he dictated a novel to Vivian. "Protecting my honor," Ratlit
explained. "I had to do *something* to keep him busy."

The book sold a few hundred thousand copies as a precocious
curiosity among many. But Ratlit had split. The next years he was
involved as a shill in some illegality I never understood. He didn't
either. "But I bet I made a million, Vyme! I earned at least a
million." It's possible. At thirteen he still couldn't read or write, but
his travels had gained him fair fluency in three languages. A couple
of weeks ago he'd wandered off a stellar tramp, dirty and broke,
here at the Star-pit. And I'd gotten him a job as grease monkey
over at Poloscki's.

He leaned his elbows on his knees, his chin in his hands. "Vyme,
it's a shame."

"What's a shame, kid-boy?"

"To be washed up at my age. A has-been! To have to grapple
with the fact that this—" he spat at a star "—is it."

He was talking about golden again.

"You still have a chance." I shrugged. "Most of the time it doesn't come out till puberty."

He cocked his head up at me. "I've been pubescent since I was nine, buster."

"Ex*cuse* me."

"I feel cramped in, Vyme. There's all that night out there to grow up in, to explore."

"There was a time," I mused, "when the whole species was confined to the surface, give or take a few feet up or down, of a single planet. You've got the whole galaxy to run around in. You've seen a lot of it, yeah. But not all."

"But there are billions of galaxies out there. I want to see them. In all the stars around here there hasn't been one life form discovered that's based on anything but silicon or carbon. I overheard two golden in a bar once, talking: there's something in some galaxy out there that's big as a star, neither dead nor alive, and sings. I want to hear it, Vyme!"

"Ratlit, you can't fight reality."

"Oh, go to sleep, grandpa!" He closed his eyes and bent his head back until the cords of his neck quivered. "What is it that makes a golden? A combination of physiological and psychological . . . what?"

"It's primarily some sort of hormonal imbalance as well as an environmentally conditioned thalamic/personality response—"

"Yeah. Yeah." His head came down. "And that X-chromosome heredity nonsense they just connected up with it a few years back. But all I know is *they* can take the stasis shift from galaxy to galaxy, where you and I, Vyme, if we get more than twenty thousand light-years off the rim, we're dead."

"Insane at twenty thousand," I corrected. "Dead at twenty-five."

"Same difference." He opened his eyes. They were large, green, and mostly pupil. "You know, I stole a golden belt once? Rolled it off a staggering slob about a week ago who came out of a bar and collapsed on the corner. I went across the Pit to Calle-J where nobody knows me and wore it around for a few hours, just to see if I felt different."

"You did?" Ratlit had lengths of gut that astounded me about once a day.

"I didn't. But people walking around me did. Wearing that two-inch band of yellow metal around my waist, nobody in the worlds could tell I wasn't a golden, just walking by on the street, without talking to me awhile, or making hormone tests. And wearing that belt, I learned just how much I hated golden. Because I could suddenly see, in almost everybody who came by, how much they hated me while I had that metal belt on. I threw it over the Edge." Suddenly he grinned. "Maybe I'll steal another one."

"You really hate them, Ratlit?"

He narrowed his eyes at me and looked superior.

"Sure, I talk about them," I told him. "Sometimes they're a pain to work for. But it's not their fault we can't take the reality shift."

"I'm just a child," he said evenly, "incapable of such fine reasoning. I hate them." He looked back at the night. "How can you stand to be trapped by anything, Vyme?"

Three memories crowded into my head when he said that.

First: I was standing at the railing of the East River—runs past this New York I was telling you about—at midnight, looking at the illuminated dragon of the Manhattan Bridge that spanned the water, then at the industrial fires flickering in bright, smoky Brooklyn, and then at the template of mercury street lamps behind me bleaching out the playground and most of Houston Street; then, at the reflections in the water, here like crinkled foil, there like glistening rubber; at last, looked up at the midnight sky itself. It wasn't black but dead pink, without a star. This glittering world made the sky a roof that pressed down on me so I almost screamed. . . . That time the next night I was twenty-seven light-years away from Sol on my first star-run.

Second: I was visiting my mother after my first few years out. I was looking in the closet for something when this contraption of plastic straps and buckles fell on my head.

"What's this, Ma?"

And she smiled with a look of idiot nostalgia and crooned, "Why that's your little harness, Vymey. Your first father and I would take you on picnics up at Bear Mountain and put you in that and tie you to a tree with about ten feet of cord so you wouldn't get—" I didn't hear the rest because of the horror that suddenly flooded me, thinking of myself tied up in that thing. Okay, I was twenty and had just joined that beautiful procreation group a year back on Sigma and was the proud father of three and expecting two more. The hundred and sixty-three of us had the whole beach and nine miles of jungle and half a mountain to ourselves; maybe I was seeing Antoni caught up in that thing, trying to catch a bird or a beetle or a wave—with only ten feet of cord. I hadn't worn clothes for anything but work in a twelvemonth, and I was chomping to get away from that incredible place I had grown up in called an apartment and back to wives, husbands, kids and civilizations. Anyway, it was pretty terrible.

The third? After I had left the proke-group—fled them, I suppose, guilty and embarrassed over something I couldn't name, still having nightmares once a month that woke me screaming about what was going to happen to the kids, even though I knew one point of group marriage was to prevent the loss of one, two, or three parents of being traumatic—still wondering if I wasn't making the same mistakes my parents made, hoping my brood wouldn't turn out like me, or worse like the kids you sometimes read about in the paper (like Ratlit, though I hadn't met him yet), horribly suspicious that no matter how different I tried to be from my sires, it was just the same thing all over again. . . . Anyway, I was on the ship bringing me to the Star-pit for the first time. I'd gotten talking to a golden who, as golden go, was a pretty regular gal. We'd been discussing inter- and intra-galactic drives. She was impressed I knew so much. I was impressed that she could use them and know so little. She was digging in a very girl-way the six-foot-four, two-hundred-and-ten-pound drive mechanic with mildly grimy fingernails that was me. I was digging in a very boy-way the slim, amber-eyed young lady who had seen it *all*. From the view deck we watched the immense, artificial disk of the Star-pit approach, when she turned to me and said, in a voice that didn't sound cruel at all, "This is as far as you go, isn't it?" And I was frightened all over again, because I knew that on about nine different levels she was right.

Ratlit said: "I know what you're thinking." A couple of times when he'd felt like being quiet and I'd felt like talking I may have told him more than I should. "Well, cube that for me, dad. That's how trapped I feel!"

I laughed, and Ratlit looked very young again "Come on," I said. "Let's take a walk."

"Yeah." He stood. The wind fingered at our hair. "I want to go see Alegra."

"I'll walk you as far as Calle-G," I told him. "Then I'm going to go to bed."

"I wonder what Alegra thinks about this business? I always find Alegra a very good person to talk to," he said sagely. "Not to put you down, but her experiences are a little more up to date than yours. You have to admit she has a modern point of view. Plus the fact that she's older." Than Ratlit, anyway. She was fifteen.

"I don't think being 'trapped' ever really bothered her," I said. "Which may be a place to take a lesson from."

By Ratlit's standards Alegra had a few things over me. In my youth kids took to dope in their teens, twenties. Alegra was born with a three-hundred-milligram-a-day habit on a bizarre narcotic that combined the psychedelic qualities of the most powerful hallucinogens with the addictiveness of the strongest depressants. I can sympathize. Alegra's mother was addicted, and the tolerance was passed with the blood plasma through the placental wall. Ordinarily a couple of complete transfusions at birth would have gotten the newborn child straight. But Alegra was also a highly projective telepath. She projected the horrors of birth, the glories of her infantile hallucinated world on befuddled doctors; she was given her drug. Without too much difficulty she managed to be given her drug every day since.

Once I asked Alegra when she'd first heard of golden, and she came back with this horror story. A lot were coming back from Tiber-44 cluster with psychic shock—the mental condition of golden is pretty delicate, and sometimes very minor conflicts nearly ruin them. Anyway, the government that was sponsoring the importation of micro-micro surgical equipment from some tiny planet in that galaxy, to protect its interests, hired Alegra, age eight, as a psychiatric therapist. "I'd concretize their fantasies and make them work 'em through. In just a couple of hours I'd have 'em back to their old, mean, stupid selves again. Some of them were pretty nice when they came to me." But there was a lot of work for her; projective telepaths are rare. So they started withholding her drug to force her to work harder, then rewarding her with increased dosage. "Up till then," she told me, "I might have kicked it. But when I came away, they had me on double what I used to take. They pushed me past the point where withdrawal would be fatal. But I *could* have kicked it, up till then, Vyme." That's right. Age eight.

Oh yeah. The drug was imported by golden from Cancer-9, and most of it goes through the Star-pit. Alegra came here because illegal imports are easier to come by, and you can get it for just about nothing—if you want it. Golden don't use it.

The wind lessened as Ratlit and I started back. Ratlit began to whistle. In Calle-K the first night lamp had broken so that the level street was a tunnel of black.

"Ratlit?" I asked. "Where do you think you'll be, oh, in say five years?"

"Quiet," he said. "I'm trying to get to the end of the street without bumping into the walls, tripping on something, or some other catastrophe. If we get through the next five minutes all right, I'll worry about the next five years." He began whistling again.

"Trip? Bump the walls?"

"I'm listening for echoes." Again he commenced the little jets of music.

I put my hands in my overall pouch and went on quietly while

Ratlit did the bat bit. Then there was a catastrophe. Though I didn't realize it at the time.

Into the circle of light from the remaining lamp at the other end of the street walked a golden.

His hands went up to his face, and he was laughing. The sound skittered in the street. His belt was low on his belly the way the really down and broke—

I just thought of a better way to describe him; the resemblance struck me immediately. He looked like Sandy, my mechanic, who is short, twenty-four years old, muscled like an ape, and wears his worn-out work clothes even when he's off duty. ("I just want this job for a while, boss. I'm not staying out here at the Star-pit. As soon as I save up a little, I'm gonna make it back in toward galactic center. It's funny out here, like dead." He gazes up through the opening in the hangar roof where there are no clouds and no stars either. "Yeah. I'm just gonna be here for a little while.")

("Fine with me, kid-boy.")

(That was three months back, like I say. He's still with me. He works hard too, which puts him a cut above a lot of characters out here. Still, there was something about Sandy . . .) On the other hand Sandy's face is also hacked up with acne. His hair is always nap short over his wide head, but in these aspects, the golden was exactly Sandy's opposite, come to think of it. Still, there was something about the golden . . .

He staggered, went down on his knees still laughing, then collapsed. By the time we reached him, he was silent. With the toe of his boot Ratlit nudged the hand from the belt buckle.

It flopped, palm up, on the pavement. The little fingernail was three quarters of an inch long, the way a lot of the golden wear it. (Like his face, the tips of Sandy's fingers are all masticated wrecks. Still, something . . .)

"Now isn't that something." Ratlit shook his head. "What do you want to do with him, Vyme?"

"Nothing," I said. "Let him sleep it off."

"Leave him so somebody can come along and steal his belt?" Ratlit grinned. "I'm not that nasty."

"Weren't you just telling me how much you hated golden?"

"I'd be nasty to whoever stole the belt and wore it. Nobody but a golden should be hated that much."

"Ratlit, let's go."

But he had already kneeled down and was shaking the golden's shoulder. "Let's get him to Alegra's and find out what's the matter with him."

"He's just drunk."

"Nope," Ratlit said. "'Cause he don't smell funny."

"Look. Get back." I hoisted the golden up and laid him across my neck, fireman's carry. "Start moving," I told Ratlit. "I think you're crazy."

Ratlit grinned. "Thanks. Maybe he'll be grateful and lay some lepta on me for taking him in off the street."

"You don't know golden," I said. "But if he does, split it with me."

"Sure."

Two blocks later we reached Alegra's place. (But like I say, Sandy, though well built, is little; so I didn't have much trouble carrying him.) Halfway up the tilting stairs Ratlit said, "She's in a good mood."

"I guess she is." The weight across my shoulders was becoming pleasant.

I can't describe Alegra's place. I can describe a lot of places like it; and I can describe it before she moved in because I knew a derelict named Drunk-roach who slept on that floor before she did. You know what never-wear plastics look like when they wear out? What nonrust metals look like when they rust through? It was a shabby, crack-walled cubicle with dirt in the corners and scars on the windowpane when Drunk-roach had his pile of blankets in the corner. But since the hallucinating projective telepath took it over, who knows what it had become.

Ratlit opened the door on an explosion of classical beauty.

"Come in," she said, accompanied by symphonic arrangement scored on twenty-four staves, with full chorus. "What's that you're carrying, Vyme? Oh, it's a golden!" And before me, dizzying tides of yellow.

"Put him down, put him down quick and let's see what's wrong!" Hundreds of eyes, spotlights, glittering lenses; I lowered him to the mattress in the corner. "Ohhh . . ." breathed Alegra.

And the golden lay on orange silk pillows in a teak barge drawn by swans, accompanied by flutes and drums.

"Where did you find him?" she hissed, circling against the ivory moon on her broom. We watched the glowing barge, hundreds of feet below, sliding down the silvered waters between the crags.

"We just picked him up off the street," Ratlit said. "Vyme thought he was drunk. But he don't smell."

"Was he laughing?" Alegra asked. Laughter rolled and broke on the rocks.

"Yeah," Ratlit said. "Just before he collapsed."

"Then he must be from the Un-dok expedition that just got back." Mosquitoes darted at us through wet fronds. The insects reeled among the leaves, upsetting droplets that fell like glass as, barely visible beyond the palms, the barge drifted on the bright, sweltering river.

"That's right," I said, backpaddling frantically to avoid a hippopotamus that threatened to upset my kayak. "I'd forgotten they'd just come in."

"Okay," Ratlit's breath clouded his lips. "I'm out of it. Let me in. Where did they come back from?" The snow hissed beneath the runners, as we looked after the barge, nearly at the white horizon.

"Un-dok, of course," Alegra said. The barking grew fainter. "Where did you think?"

White eclipsed to black, and the barge was a spot gleaming in galactic night, flown on by laboring comets.

"Un-dok is the furthest galaxy reached yet," I told Ratlit. "They just got back last week."

"Sick," Alegra added.

I dug my fingers against my abdomen to grab the pain.

"They all came back sick—"

Fever heated blood-bubbles in my eyes: I slipped to the ground, my mouth wide, my tongue like paper on my lips. . . .

Ratlit coughed. "All *right*, Alegra. Cut it out! You don't have to be so dramatic!"

"Oh, I'm dreadfully sorry Ratty, Vyme." Coolth, water. Nausea swept away as solicitous nurses hastily put the pieces back together until everything was beautiful, or so austerely horrible it could be appreciated as beauty. "Anyway," she went on, "they came back with some sort of disease they picked up out there. Apparently it's not contagious, but they're stuck with it for the rest of their lives. Every few days they suddenly have a blackout. It's preceded by a fit of hysterics. It's just one of those stupid things they can't do anything about yet. It doesn't hurt their being golden."

Ratlit began to laugh. Suddenly he asked, "How long are they passed out for?"

"Only a few hours," Alegra said. "It must be terribly annoying."

And I began to feel mildly itchy in all sorts of unscratchable places, my shoulder blades, somewhere down my ear, the roof of my mouth. Have you ever tried to scratch the roof of your mouth?

"Well," Ratlit said, "let's sit down and wait it out."

"We can talk," Alegra said, patly. "That way it won't seem like such a long . . ." and hundreds of years later she finished ". . . time."

"Good," Ratlit said. "I wanted to talk to you. That's why I came up here in the first place."

"Oh, fine!" Alegra said. "I love to talk. I want to talk about love. Loving someone" (an incredible yearning twisted my stomach, rose to block my throat) "I mean really loving someone" (the yearning brushed the edge of agony) "means you are willing to admit the person you love is not what you first fell in love with, not the image you first had; and you must be able to like them still for being as close to that image as they are, and avoid disliking them for being so far away."

And through the tenderness that suddenly obliterated all hurt, Ratlit's voice came from the jeweled mosaics shielding him: "Alegra, I want to talk about loneliness."

"I'm on my way home, kids," I said. "Tell me what happens with Prince Charming when he wakes up." They kept on talking while I went through the difficulties of finding my way out without Alegra's help. When my head cleared, halfway down the stairs, I couldn't tell you if I'd been there five minutes or five years.

When I got to the hangar next morning Sandy was filing the eight-foot prongs on the conveyer. "You got a job coming in about twenty minutes," he called down from the scaffold.

"I hope it's not another of those rebuilt jobs."

"Yep."

"Hell," I said. "I don't want to see another one for six weeks."

"All he wants is a general tune-up. Maybe two hours."

"Depends on where it's been," I said. "Where has it been?"

"Just back from—"

"Never mind." I started toward the office cubicle. "I think I'll put the books in order for the last six months. Can't let it go forever."

"Boss!" Sandy protested. "That'll take all day!"

"Then I better get started." I leaned back out the door. "Don't disturb me."

Of course as soon as the shadow of the hull fell over the office window I came out in my coveralls, after giving Sandy five minutes to get it grappled and himself worried. I took the lift up to the one-fifty catwalk. When I stepped out, Sandy threw me a grateful smile from his scar-ugly face. The golden had already started his instructions. When I reached them and coughed, the golden turned to me and continued talking, not bothering to fill me in on what he had said before, figuring Sandy and I would put it together. You could tell this golden had made his pile. He wore an immaculate blue tunic, with bronze codpiece, bracelets and earrings. His hair was the same bronze, his skin was burned red black, and his blue-gray eyes and tight-muscled mouth were proud, proud, proud. While I finished getting instructions, Sandy quietly got started unwelding the eight-foot seal of the organum so we could get to the checkout circuits.

Finally the golden stopped talking—that's the only way you could tell he was finished—and leaned his angular six and a half feet against the railing, clicking his glossy, manicured nails against the pipe a few times. He had that same sword-length pinky nail, all white against his skin. I climbed out on the rigging to help Sandy.

We had been at work ten minutes when a kid, maybe eighteen or nineteen, barefoot and brown, black hair hacked off shoulder length, a rag that didn't fit tucked around under his belt, and dirty, came wandering down the catwalk. His thumbs were hooked under the metal links: golden.

First I thought he'd come from the ship. Then I realized he'd just stalked into the hangar from outside and come up on the lift.

"Hey, brother!" The kid who was golden hooked his thumbs in his belt, as Sandy and I watched the dialogue from the rigging on the side of the hull. "I'm getting tired of hanging around this Starpit. Just about broke as well. Where you running to?"

The man who was golden clicked his nails again. "Go away, distant cousin."

"Come on, brother, give me a berth on your lifeboat out of this dungheap to someplace worthwhile."

"Go away, or I'll kill you."

"Now, brother, I'm just a youngster adrift in this forsaken quarter of the sky. Come on, now—"

Suddenly the blond man whirled from the railing, grabbed up a four-foot length of pipe leaning beside him, and swung it so hard it hissed. The black-haired ragamuffin leapt back and from under his rag snatched something black that, with a flick of that long nail, grew seven inches of blade. The bar swung again, caught the shoulder of the boy, then clattered against the hull. He shrieked and came straight forward. The two bodies locked, turned, fell. A gurgle, and the man's hands slipped from the neck of the ragamuffin. The boy scrambled back to his feet. Blood bubbled and popped on the hot blade.

A last spasm caught the man; he flipped over, smearing the catwalk, rolled once more, this time under the rail, and dropped, two hundred and fifty feet to the cement flooring.

Flick. Off went the power in the knife. The golden wiped powdered blood on his thigh, spat over the rail and said softly, "No relative of mine." Flick. The blade itself disappeared. He started down the catwalk.

"Hey!" Sandy called, when he got his voice back up into his

throat, "what about . . . I mean you . . . well, your ship!" There are no familial inheritance laws among golden—only rights of plunder.

The golden glanced back. "I give it to you," he sneered. His shoulder must have been killing him, but he stepped into the lift like he was walking into a phone booth. That's a golden for you.

Sandy was horrified and bewildered. Behind his pitted ugliness there was that particularly wretched amazement only the totally vulnerable get when hurt.

"That's the first time you've ever seen an incident like that?" I felt sorry for him.

"Well, I wandered into Gerg's Bar a couple of hours after they had that massacre. But the ones who started it were drunk."

"Drunk or sober," I said. "Believe me, it doesn't mean that much difference to the way a man acts." I shook my head. "I keep forgetting you've only been here three months."

Sandy, upset, looked down at the body on the flooring. "What about him? And the ship, boss?"

"I'll call the wagon to come scrape him up. The ship is yours."

"Huh?"

"He gave it to you. It'll stand up in court. It just takes one witness. Me."

"What am I gonna do with it? I mean I would have to haul it to a junk station to get the salvage. Look, boss, I'm gonna give it to you. Sell it or something. I'd feel sort of funny with it anyway."

"I don't want it. Besides, then I'd be involved in the transaction and couldn't be a witness."

"I'll be a witness." Ratlit stepped from the lift. "I caught the whole bit when I came in the door. Great acoustics in this place." He whistled again. The echo came back. Ratlit closed his eyes for a moment. "Ceiling is . . . a hundred and twenty feet overhead, more or less. How's that, huh?"

"Hundred and twenty-seven," I said.

Ratlit shrugged. "I need more practice. Come on, Sandy, you give it to him, and I'll be a witness."

"You're a minor," Sandy said. Sandy didn't like Ratlit. I used to think it was because Ratlit was violent and flamboyant where Sandy was stolid and ugly. Even though Sandy kept protesting the temporariness of his job to me, I remember, when I first got to the Starpit, those long-dying thoughts I'd had about leaving. It was a little too easy to see Sandy a mechanic here thirty years from now. I wasn't the only one it had happened to. Ratlit had been a grease monkey here three weeks. You tell me where he was going to be in three more. "Aren't you supposed to be working at Poloscki's?" Sandy said, turning back to the organum.

"Coffee break," Ratlit said. "If you're going to give it away, Sandy, can I have it?"

"So you can claim salvage? Hell, no!"

"I don't want it for salvage. I want it for a present." Sandy looked up again. "Yeah. To give to someone else. Finish the tune-up and give it to me, okay?"

"You're nuts, kid-boy," Sandy said. "Even if I gave you the ship, what you gonna pay for the work with?"

"Aw, it'll only take a couple of hours. You're half done anyway. I figured you'd throw in the tune-up along with it. If you really want the money, I'll get it to you a little at a time. Vyme, what sort of professional discount will you give me? I'm just a grease monkey, but I'm still in the business."

I whacked the back of his red head between a-little-too-playfully and not-too-hard. "Come on, kid-boy," I said. "Help me take care of puddles downstairs. Sandy, finish it up, huh?"

Sandy grunted and plunged both hands back into the organum.

As soon as the lift door closed, Ratlit demanded, "You gonna give it to me, Vyme?"

"It's Sandy's ship," I said.

"You tell him, and he will."

I laughed. "You tell me how your golden turned out when he came to. I assume that's who you want the ship for. What sort of fellow was he?"

Ratlit hooked his fingers in the mesh wall of the lift cage and leaned back. "They're only two types of golden." He began to swing from side to side. "Mean ones and stupid ones." He was repeating a standard line around the Star-pit.

"I hope yours is stupid," I said, thinking of the two who'd just ruined Sandy's day and upset mine.

"Which is worse?" Ratlit shrugged. That is the rest of the line. When a golden isn't being outright mean, he exhibits the sort of nonthinkingness that gets other people hurt—you remember the one that nearly rammed my ship, or the ones who didn't bother to bring back the Kyber antitoxin? "But this one—" Ratlit stood up "—is unbelievably stupid."

"Yesterday you hated them. Today you want to give one a ship?"

"He doesn't have one," Ratlit explained calmly, as though that warranted all change of attitude. "And because he's sick, it'll be hard for him to find work unless he has one of his own."

"I see." We bounced on the silicon cushion. I pushed open the door and started for the office. "What all went on after I left? I must have missed the best part of the evening."

"You did. Will I really need that much more sleep when I pass thirty-five?"

"Cut the cracks and tell me what happened."

"Well—" Ratlit leaned against the office door jamb while I dialed necrotics. "Alegra and I talked a little after you left, till finally we realized the golden was awake and listening. Then he told us we were beautiful."

I raised an eyebrow. "Mmmm?"

"That's what he said. And he said it again, that watching us talk and think and build was one of the most beautiful things he'd ever seen. 'What have you seen?' we asked him. And he began to tell us." Ratlit stopped breathing, something built up, then, at once, it came out. "Oh, Vyme, the places he's been! The things he's done! The landscapes he's starved in, the hells where he's had to lie down and go to sleep he was that tired, or the heavens he's soared through screaming! Oh, the things he told us about! And Alegra made them almost real so we could all be there again, just like she used to do when she was a psychiatrist! The stories, the places, the things . . ."

"Sounds like it was really something."

"It was nothing!" he came back vehemently. "It was all in the tears that wash your eyes, in the humming in your ears, in the taste of your own saliva. It was just a hallucination, Vyme! It wasn't real." Here his voice started cracking between the two octaves that were after it. "But that thing I told you about . . . huge . . . alive and dead at the same time, like a star . . . way in another galaxy. Well, he's seen it. And last night, but it wasn't real of course, but . . . I almost heard it . . . sing!" His eyes were huge and green and bright. I felt envious of anyone who could pull this reaction from kids like Alegra and Ratlit.

"So, we decided—" his voice fixed itself on the proper side of middle C "—after he went back to sleep, and we lay awake talking a while longer, that we'd try and help him get back out there. Because it's . . . wonderful!"

"That's fascinating." When I finished my call, I stood up from the desk. I'd been sitting on the corner. "After work I'll buy you dinner and you can tell me all about the things he showed you."

"He's still there, at Alegra's," Ratlit said—helplessly, I realized after a moment. "I'm going back there right after work."

"Oh," I said. I didn't seem to be invited.

"It's just a shame," Ratlit said when we came out of the office, "that he's so stupid." He glanced at the mess staining the concrete that had been a golden and shook his head.

I'd gone back to the books when Sandy stepped in. "All finished. What say we knock off for a beer or something, huh, boss?"

"All right," I said, surprised. Sandy was usually as social as he was handsome. "Want to talk about something?"

"Yeah." He looked relieved.

"That business this morning got to your head, huh?"

"Yeah," he repeated.

"There is a reason," I said as I made ready to go. "It's got something to do with the psychological part of being a golden. Meanness and stupidity, like everyone says. But however it makes them act here, it protects them from complete insanity at the twenty thousand light-year limit."

"Yeah. I know, I know." Sandy had started stepping uncomfortably from one boot to the other. "But that's not what I wanted to talk about."

"It isn't?"

"Um-um."

"Well?" I asked after a moment.

"It's that kid, the one you're gonna give the ship to."

"Ratlit?"

"Yeah."

"I haven't made up my mind about giving him the ship," I lied. "Besides, legally it's yours."

"You'll give it to him," Sandy said. "And I don't care, I mean not about the ship. But, boss, I gotta talk to you about that kid-boy."

Something about Sandy . . .

I'd never realized he'd thought of Ratlit as more than a general nuisance. Also, he seemed sincerely worried about me. I was curious. It took him all the way to the bar and through two beers—while I drank hot milk with honey—before he tongued and chewed what he wanted to say into shape.

"Boss, understand, I'm nearer Ratlit than you. Not only my age. My life's been more like his than yours has. You look at him like a son. To me, he's a younger brother: I taught him all the tricks. I don't understand him completely, but I see him clearer than you do. He's had a hard time, but not as hard as you think. He's gonna take you—and I don't mean money—for everything he can."

Where the hell that came from I didn't know and didn't like. "He won't take anything I don't want to give."

"Boss?" Sandy suddenly asked. "You got kids of your own?"

"Nine," I said. "Did have. I don't see the ones who're left now, for which their parents have always been just as happy—except one. And she was sensible enough to go along with the rest, while she was alive."

"Oh." Sandy got quiet again. Suddenly he went scrambling in his overall pouch and pulled out a three-inch porta-pix. Those great, greasy hands that I was teaching to pick up an eggshell through a five-hundred-to-one-ratio waldo were clumsily fumbling at the push-pull levers. "I got kids," he said. "See. Seven of them."

And on the porta-pix screen was a milling, giggling group of little apes that couldn't have been anybody else's. All the younger ones lacked was acne. They even shuffled back and forth from one foot to the other. They began to wave, and the speaker in the back chirped: "Hi, Da! Hello, Da! Da, Mommy says to say we love you! Da, Da, come home soon!"

"I'm not with them now," he said throatily. "But I'm going back soon as I get enough money so I can take them all out of that hell-hole they're in now and get the whole family with a decent-sized proke-group. They're only twenty-three adults there now, and things were beginning to rub. That's why I left in the first place. It was getting so nobody could talk to anyone else. That's pretty rough on all our kids, thirty-two when I left. But soon I'll be able to fix that."

"On the salary I'm paying you?" This was the first I'd heard of any of this; that was my first reaction. My second, which I didn't voice, was: Then why the hell don't you take that ship and sell it somehow! Over forty and self-employed, the most romantic become monetarily practical.

Sandy's fist came down hard on the bar. "That's what I'm trying to say to you, boss! About you, about Ratlit. You've all got it in your heads that this, out here, is it! The end! Sure, you gotta accept limitations, but the right ones. Sure, you have to admit there are certain directions in which you can not go. But once you do that, you find there are others where you can go as far as you want. Look, I'm not gonna hang around the Star-pit all my life! And if I make my way back toward galactic center, make enough money so I can go home, raise my family the way I want, that's going forward, forward even from here. Not back."

"All right," I said. Quiet Sandy surprised me. I still wondered why he wasn't breaking his tail to get salvage on that ship that had just fallen into his hands, if getting back home with money in his pocket was that important. "I'm glad you told me about yourself. Now how does it all tie up with Ratlit?"

"Yeah. Ratlit." He put the porta-pix back in his overall pouch.

"Boss, Ratlit is the kid your own could be. You want to give him the advice, friendship, and concern he's never had, that you couldn't give yours. But Ratlit is also the kid I was about ten years ago, started no place, with no destination, and no values to help figure out the way, mixed up in all the wrong things, mainly because he's not sure where the right ones are."

"I don't think you're that much like Ratlit," I told him. "I think you may wish you were. You've done a lot of the things Ratlit's done? Ever write a novel?"

"I tried to write a trilogy," Sandy said. "It was lousy. But it pushed some things off my chest. So I got something out of it, even if nobody else did, which is what's important. Because now I'm a better mechanic for it, boss. Until I admit to myself what I can't do, it's pretty hard to work on what I can. Same goes for Ratlit. You too. That's growing up. And one thing you can't do is help Ratlit by giving him a ship he can't fly."

Growing up brought back the picture. "Sandy, did you ever build an ecologarium when you were a kid?"

"No." The word had the puzzled inflection that means, "Don't-even-know-what-one-is."

"I didn't either," I told him. Then I grinned and punched him on the shoulder. "Maybe you're a little like me, too? Let's get back to work."

"Another thing," Sandy said, not looking very happy as he got off the stool. "Boss, that kid's gonna hurt you. I don't know how, but it's gonna seem like he hunted for how to make it hurt most, too. *That's* what I wanted to tell you, boss."

I was going to urge him to take the ship, but he handed me the keys back in the hangar before I could say anything, and walked away. When people who should be clearing up their own problems start giving you advice . . . well, there was something about Sandy I didn't like.

If I can't take long walks at night with company, I take them by myself. I was strolling by the Edge, the world-wind was low, and the Stellarplex, the huge heat-gathering mirror that's hung nine thousand miles off the Pit, was out. It looks vaguely like the moon used to look from Earth, only twice as big, perfectly silver, and during the three and a half days it faces us it's always full.

Then, up ahead where the fence was broken, I saw Ratlit kicking gravel over the Edge. He was leaning against a lamppost, his shirt ballooning and collapsing at his back.

"Hey, kid-boy! Isn't the golden still at Alegra's?"

Ratlit saw me and shrugged.

"What's the matter?" I asked when I reached him. "Ate dinner yet?"

He shrugged again. His body had the sort of ravenous metabolism that shows twenty-four hours without food. "Come on. I promised you a meal. Why so glum?"

"Make it something to drink."

"I know about your phony I.D." I told him. "But we're going to eat. You can have milk, just like me."

No protests, no dissertation on the injustice of liquor laws. He started walking with me.

"Come on, kid-boy, talk to gramps. Don't you want your ship any more?"

Suddenly he clutched my forearm with white, bony fingers. My forearm is pretty thick, and he couldn't get his hands around it. "Vyme, you've got to make Sandy give it to me now! You've got to!"

"Kid-boy, talk to me."

"Alegra." He let go. "And the golden. Hate golden, Vyme. Always hate them. Because if you start to like one, and then start hating again, it's worse."

"What's going on? What are they doing?"

"He's talking. She's hallucinating. And neither one pays any attention to me."

"I see."

"You don't see. You don't understand about Alegra and me."

Then I was the only one who'd met the both of them who didn't. "I know you're very fond of each other." More could be said.

Ratlit said more. "We don't even like each other that much, Vyme. But we need each other. Since she's been here, I get her medicine for her. She's too sick to go out much now. And when I have bad changes, or sometimes bright recognitions, it doesn't matter, I bring them to her, and she builds pictures of them for me, and we explore them together and . . . learn about things. When she was a psychiatrist for the government, she learned an awful lot about how people tick. And she's got an awful lot to teach me, things I've got to know." Fifteen-year-old ex-psychiatrist drug addicts? Same sort of precocity that produces thirteen-year-old novelists. Get used to it. "I need her now almost as much as she needs her . . . medicine."

"Have you told the golden you've got him a ship?"

"You didn't say I could have it yet."

"Well, I say so right now. Why don't we go back there and tell him he can be on his way? If we put it a little more politely, don't you think that'll do the trick?"

He didn't say anything. His face just got back a lot of its life.

"We'll go right after we eat. What the hell, I'll buy you a drink. I may even have one with you."

Alegra's was blinding when we arrived. "Ratlit, oh, you're back! Hello, Vyme! I'm so glad you're both here! Everything is beautiful tonight!"

"The golden," Ratlit said. "Where's the golden?"

"He's not here." A momentary throb of sadness dispelled with tortuous joy. "But he's coming back!"

"Oh," Ratlit said. His voice echoed through the long corridors of golden absence winding the room. " 'Cause I got a ship for him. All his. Just had a tune-up. He can leave any time he wants to."

"Here're the keys," I said, taking them from my pouch for dramatic effect. "Happen to have them right here."

As I handed them to Ratlit there were fireworks, applause, a fanfare of brasses. "Oh, that's wonderful. Wonderful! Because guess what, Ratlit? Guess what, Vyme?"

"I don't know," Ratlit said. "What?"

"I'm a golden too!" Alegra cried from the shoulders of the cheering crowd that pushed its way through more admiring thousands.

"Huh?"

"I, me, myself am actually an honest to goodness golden. I just found out today."

"You can't be," Ratlit said. "You're too old for it just to show up now."

"Something about my medicine," Alegra explained. "It's dreadfully complicated." The walls were papered with anatomical charts, music by Stockhausen. "Something in my medicine kept it from coming out until now, until a golden could come to me, drawing it up and out of the depths of me, till it burst out, beautiful and wonderful and . . . golden! Right now he's gone off to Carlson Labs with a urine sample for a final hormone check. They'll let him know in an hour, and he'll bring back my golden belt. But he's sure already. And when he comes back with it, I'm going to go with him to the galaxies, as his apprentice. We're going to find a cure for his sickness and something that will make it so I won't need my medicine any more. He says if you have all the universe to roam around in, you can find anything you look for. But you need it *all*—not just a cramped little cluster of a few billion stars off in a corner by itself. Oh, I'm free, Ratlit, like you always wanted to be! While you were gone, he . . . well, did something to me that was . . . *golden!* It triggered my hormonal imbalance." The image came in through all five senses. Breaking the melodious ecstasy came the clatter of keys as Ratlit hurled them at the wall.

I left feeling pretty odd. Ratlit had started to go too, but Alegra called him back. "Oh, now don't go on like that, Ratty! Act your age. Won't you stay and do me one little last favor?"

So he stayed. When I untangled myself from the place and was walking home, I kept on remembering what Alegra had said about love.

Work next day went surprisingly smoothly. Poloscki called me up about ten and asked if I knew where Ratlit was because he hadn't been at work that day. "You're sure the kid isn't sick?"

I said I'd seen him last night and that he was probably all right. Poloscki made a disgusted sound and hung up.

Sandy left a few minutes early, as he'd been doing all week, to run over to the post office before it closed. He was expecting a letter from his group, he said. I felt strange about having given the ship away out from under him. It was sort of an immature thing to do. But he hadn't said anything about wanting it, and Ratlit was still doing Alegra favors, so maybe it would all work out for the best.

I thought about visiting Alegra that evening. But there was the last six months' paper work, still not finished. I went into the office, plugged in the computer and got ready to work late.

I was still at it sometime after eleven when the entrance light blinked, which meant somebody had opened the hangar door. I'd locked it. Sandy had the keys so he could come in early. So it was Sandy. I was ready for a break and all set to jaw with him awhile. He was always coming back to do a little work at odd hours. I waited for him to come into the office. But he didn't.

Then the needle on the power gauge, which had been hovering near zero with only the drain of the little office computer, swung up to seven. One of the big pieces of equipment had been cut in.

There was some cleanup work to do, but nothing for a piece that size. Frowning, I switched off the computer and stepped out of the office. The first great opening in the hangar roof was mostly blocked with the bulk of Ratlit's/Sandy's/my ship. Stellarplex light curved smoothly over one side, then snarled in the fine webbing of lifts, catwalks, haul-lines, and grappler rigging. The other two openings were empty, and thirty-meter circles of silver dropped through assembly riggings to the concrete floor. Then I saw Sandy.

He stood just inside the light from the last opening, staring up at the Stellarplex, its glare lost in his ruined face. As he raised his left hand—when it started to move I thought it looked too big— light caught on the silver joints of the master-gauntlet he was wearing. I knew where the power was going.

As his hand went above his head, a shadow fell over him as a fifteen-foot slave talon swung from the darkness, its movement aping the master-glove. He dropped his hand in front of his face, fingers curved. Metal claws lowered about him, beginning to quiver. Something about . . . he was trying to kill himself!

I started running toward those hesitant, gaping claws, leaped into the grip, and reached over his shoulder to slap my forearm into the control glove, just as he squeezed. Like I said, my forearm is big, but when those claws came together, it was a tight fit. Sandy was crying.

"You stupid," I shouted, "inconsiderate, bird-brained, infantile—" at last I got the glove off "—puerile . . ." Then I said, "What the hell is the matter with you?"

Sandy was sitting on the floor now, his head hung between his shoulders. He stank.

"Look," I said, maneuvering the talon back into place with the gross-motion controls on the gauntlet's wrist, "if you want to go jump off the Edge, that's fine with me. Half the gate's down anyway. But don't come here and mess up my tools. You can squeeze your own head up a little, but you're not going to bust up my glove here. You're fired. Now tell me what's wrong."

"I knew it wasn't going to work. Wasn't even worth trying. I knew . . ." His voice was getting all mixed up with the sobs. "But I thought maybe . . ." Beside his left hand was the porta-pix, its screen cracked. And a crumpled piece of paper.

I turned off the glove, and the talons stopped humming twenty feet overhead. I picked up the paper and smoothed it out. I didn't mean to read it all the way through.

Dear Sanford,
   Things have been difficult since you left but not too hard and I guess a lot of pressure is off everybody since you went away and the kids are getting used to your not being here though Bobbi-D cried a lot at first. She doesn't now. We got your letter and were glad to hear things had begun to settle down for you though Hank said you should have written before this and was very mad though Mary tried to calm him down but he just said, "When he married you all he married me too, damn it, and I've got just as much right to be angry at him as you have," which is true, Sanford, but I tell you what he said because it's a quote and I think you should know exactly what's being said, especially since it expresses something we all feel on one level or another. You said you might be able to send us a little money, if we wanted you home, which I think would be very good, the money I mean, though Laura said if I put that in

the letter she would divorce us, but she won't, and like Hank I've got a right to say what I feel which is, Yes I think you should send money, especially after that unpleasant business just before you left. But we are all agreed we do not want you to come back. And would rather not have the money if that's what it meant.

That is hard but true. As you can gather your letter caused quite an upset here. I would like—which makes me different from the others but is why they wanted me to write this letter—to hear from you again and keep track of what you are doing because I used to love you very much and I never could hate you. But like Bobbi-D, I have stopped crying.

Sincerely—

The letter was signed "Joseph." In the lower corner were the names of the rest of the men and women of the group.

"Sandy?"

"I knew they wouldn't take me back. I didn't even really try, did I? But—"

"Sandy, get up."

"But the *children*," he whispered. "What's gonna happen to the children?"

And there was a sound from the other end of the hangar. Three stories up the side of the ship in the open hatchway, silvered by Stellarplex light, stood the golden, the one Ratlit and I had found on the street.

You remember what he looked like.

He and Alegra must have sneaked in while Sandy and I were struggling with the waldo. Probably they wanted to get away as soon as possible before Ratlit made real trouble, or before I changed my mind and got the keys back. All this ship-giving had been done without witnesses. The sound was the lift rising toward the hatchway. "The children . . ." Sandy whispered again.

The door opened, and a figure stepped out in the white light. Only it was Ratlit! It was Ratlit's red hair, his gold earring, his bouncy run as he started for the hatch. And there were links of yellow metal around his waist.

Baffled, I heard the golden call: "Everything checks out inside, brother. She'll fly us anywhere."

And Ratlit cried, "I got the grapples all released, brother. Let's go!" Their voices echoed down through the hangar. Sandy raised his head, squinting.

As Ratlit leapt into the hatch, the golden caught his arm around the boy's shoulder. They stood a moment, gazing at one another, then Ratlit turned to look down into the hangar, back on the world he was about to leave. I couldn't tell if he knew we were there or not. Even as the hatch swung closed, the ship began to whistle.

I hauled Sandy back into the shock chamber. I hadn't even locked the door when the thunder came and my ears nearly split. I think the noise surprised Sandy out of himself. It broke something up in my head, but the pieces were falling wrong.

"Sandy," I said, "we've got to get going!"

"Huh?" He was fighting the drunkenness and probably his stomach too.

"I don't wanna go nowhere."

"You're going anyway. I'm sure as hell not going to leave you alone."

When we were halfway up the stairs I figured she wasn't there. I felt just the same. Was she with them in the ship?

"My medicine. Please can't you get my medicine? I've got to have my medicine, please, please . . . please." I could just hear the small, high voice when I reached the door. I pushed it open.

Alegra lay on the mattress, pink eyes wide, white hair frizzled around her balding skull. She was incredibly scrawny, her uncut nails black as Sandy's nubs without the excuse of hours in a graphite-lubricated gauntlet. The translucency of her pigmentless skin under how-many-days of dirt made my flesh crawl. Her face drew in around her lips like the flesh about a scar. "My medicine. Vyme, is that you? You'll get my medicine for me, Vyme? Won't you get my medicine?" Her mouth wasn't moving, but the voice came on. She was too weak to project on any but the aural level. It was the first time I'd seen Alegra without her cloak of hallucination, and it brought me up short.

"Alegra," I said when I got hold of myself. "Ratlit and the golden went off on the ship!"

"Ratlit. Oh, nasty Ratty, awful little boy! He wouldn't get my medicine. But you'll get it for me, won't you, Vyme? I'm going to die in about ten minutes, Vyme. I don't want to die. Not like this. The world is so ugly and painful now. I don't want to die here."

"Don't you have any?" I stared around the room I hadn't seen since Drunk-roach lived there. It was a lot worse. Dried garbage, piled first in one corner, now covered half the floor. The rest was littered with papers, broken glass, and a spilled can of something unrecognizable for the mold.

"No. None here. Ratlit gets it from a man who hangs out in Gerg's over on Calle-X. Oh, Ratlit used to get it for me every day, such a nice little boy, every day he would bring me my lovely medicine, and I never had to leave my room at all. You go get it for me, Vyme!"

"It's the middle of the night, Alegra! Gerg's is closed, and Calle-X is all the way across the Pit anyway. Couldn't even get there in ten minutes, much less find this character and come back!"

"If I were well, Vyme, I'd fly you there in a cloud of light pulled by peacocks and porpoises, and you'd come back to hautboys and tambourines, bringing my beautiful medicine to me, in less than an eye's blink. But I'm sick now. And I'm going to die."

There was a twitch in the crinkled lid of one pink eye.

"Alegra, what happened!"

"Ratlit's insane!" she projected with shocking viciousness. I heard Sandy behind me catch his breath. "Insane at twenty thousand lightyears, dead at twenty-five."

"But his golden belt . . ."

"It was mine! It was my belt and he stole it. And he wouldn't get my medicine. Ratlit's not a golden. I'm a golden, Vyme! I can go anywhere, anywhere at all! I'm a golden golden golden . . . But I'm sick now. I'm so sick."

"But didn't the golden know the belt was yours?"

"Him? Oh, he's so incredibly stupid! He would believe anything. The golden went to check some papers and get provisions and was gone all day, to get my belt. But you were here that night. I asked Ratlit to go get my medicine and take another sample to Carlson's for me. But neither of them came back till I was very sick, very weak. Ratlit found the golden, you see, told him that I'd changed my mind about going, and that he, Ratlit, was a golden as well, that he'd just been to Carlson's. So the golden gave him my belt and off they went."

"But how in the world would he believe a kid with a story like that?"

"You know how stupid a golden can be, Vyme. As stupid as they can be mean. Besides, it doesn't matter to him if Ratlit dies. He doesn't care if Ratlit was telling the truth or not. The golden will live. When Ratlit starts drooling, throwing up blood, goes deaf first and blind last and dies, the golden won't even be sad. He's too stupid to feel sad. That's the way golden are. But I'm sad, Vyme, because no one will bring me my medicine."

My frustration had to lash at something; she was there. "You mean you didn't know what you were doing to Ratlit by leaving, Alegra? You mean you didn't know how much he wanted to get out, and how much he needed you at the same time? You couldn't see what it would do to him if you deprived him of the thing he needed and rubbed his nose in the thing he hated both at once? You couldn't guess that he'd pull something crazy? Oh, kid-girl, you talk about golden. You're the stupid one!"

"Not stupid," she projected quietly. "*Mean*, Vyme. I knew he'd try to do something. I just didn't think he'd succeed. Ratlit is really such a child."

The frustration, spent, became rolling sadness. "Couldn't you have waited just a little longer, Alegra? Couldn't you have worked out the leaving some other way, not hurt him so much?"

"I wanted to get out, Vyme, to keep going and not be trapped, to be free. Like Ratlit wanted, like you want, like Sandy wants, like golden. Only I was cruel. I had the chance to do it and I took it. Why is that bad, Vyme? Unless, of course, that's what being free means."

A twitch in the eyelid again. It closed. The other stayed open. "Alegra—"

"I'm a golden, Vyme. A golden. And that's how golden are. But don't be mad at me, Vyme. Don't. Ratlit was mean too, not to give me my medi—"

The other eye closed. I closed mine too and tried to cry, but my tongue was pushing too hard on the roof of my mouth.

Sandy came to work the next day, and I didn't mention his being fired. The teletapes got hold of it, and the leadlines tried to make the thing as sordid as possible:

X-CON TEEN-AGER (they didn't mention his novel)
SLAYS JUNKY SWEETHEART! DIES HORRIBLY!

They didn't mention the golden either. They never do.

Reporters pried around the hangar awhile, trying to get us to say the ship was stolen. Sandy came through pretty well. "It was his ship," he grunted, putting lubricant in the gauntlets. "I gave it to him."

"What are you gonna give a kid like that a ship for? Maybe you loaned it to him. 'Dies horrible death in borrowed ship.' That sounds okay."

"Gave it to him. Ask the boss." He turned back toward the scaffolding. "He witnessed."

"Look, even if you liked the kid, you're not saving him anything by covering up."

"I didn't like him," Sandy said. "But I gave him the ship."

"Thanks," I told Sandy when they left, not sure what I was thanking him for, but still feeling very grateful. "I'll do you a favor back."

A week later Sandy came in and said, "Boss, I want my favor."

I narrowed my eyes against his belligerent tone. "So you're gonna quit at last. Can you finish out the week?"

He looked embarrassed, and his hands started moving around in his overall pouch. "Well, yeah. I am gonna leave. But not right away, boss. It is getting a little hard for me to take, out here."

"You'll get used to it," I said. "You know there's something about you that's, well, a lot like me. I learned. You will too."

Sandy shook his head. "I don't think I want to." His hand came out of his pocket. "See, I got a ticket." In his dirty fingers was a metal-banded card. "In four weeks I'm going back in from the Starpit. Only I didn't want to tell you just now, because, well, I did want this favor, boss."

I was really surprised. "You're not going back to your group," I said. "What are you going to do?"

He shrugged. "Get a job, I don't know. There're other groups. Maybe I've grown up a little bit." His fists went way down into his pouch, and he started to shift his weight back and forth on his feet. "About that favor, boss."

"What is it?"

"I got to talking to this kid outside. He's really had it rough, Vyme." That was the first and last time Sandy ever called me by name, though I'd asked him to enough times before. "And he could use a job."

A laugh got all set to come out of me. But it didn't, because the look on his ugly face, behind the belligerence, was so vulnerable and intense. Vulnerable? But Sandy had his ticket; Sandy was going on.

"Send him to Poloscki's," I said. "Probably needs an extra grease monkey. Now let me get back to work, huh?"

"Could you take him over there?" Sandy said very quickly. "That's the favor, boss."

"Sandy, I'm awfully busy." I looked at him again. "Oh, all right."

"Hey, boss," Sandy said as I slid from behind the desk, "remember that thing you asked me if I ever had when I was a kid?"

It took a moment to come back to me. "You mean an ecologarium?"

"Yeah. That's the word." He grinned. "The kid-boy's got one. He's right outside, waiting for you."

"He's got it with him?"

Sandy nodded.

I walked toward the hangar door picturing some kid lugging around a six-by-six plastic cage.

Outside the boy was sitting on a fuel hydrant. I'd put a few trees

there, and the "day"-light from the illumination tubes arcing the
street dappled the gravel around him.

He was about fourteen, with copper skin and curly black hair. I
saw why Sandy wanted me to go with him about the job. Around
his waist, as he sat hunched over on the hydrant with his toes spread
on the metal base-flange, was a wide-linked, yellow belt: golden.

He was looking through an odd jewel-and-brass thing that hung
from a chain around his neck.

"Hey."

He looked up. There were spots of light on his blue-black hair.

"You need a job?"

He blinked.

"My name's Vyme. What's yours?"

"You call me An." The voice was even, detached, with an inflection that is golden.

I frowned. "Nickname?"

He nodded.

"And really?"

"Androcles."

"Oh." My oldest kid is dead. I know it because I have all sorts of
official papers saying so. But sometimes it's hard to remember. And
it doesn't matter whether the hair is black, white, or red. "Well, let's
see if we can put you to work somewhere. Come on." An stood up,
eyes fixed on me, suspicion hiding behind high glitter. "What's the
thing around your neck?"

His eyes struck it and bounced back to my face. "Cousin?" he
asked.

"Huh?" Then I remembered the golden slang. "Oh, sure. First
cousins. Brothers if you want."

"Brother," An said. Then a smile came tumbling out of his face,
silent and volcanic. He began loping beside me as we started off
toward Poloscki's. "This—" he held up the thing on the chain "—
is an ecologarium. Want to see?" His diction was clipped, precise,
and detached. But when an expression caught on his face, it was
unsettlingly intense.

"Oh, a little one. With microorganisms?"

An nodded.

"Sure. Let's have a look."

The hair on the back of his neck pawed the chain as he bent to
remove it.

I held it up to see.

Some blue liquid, a fairly large air bubble, and a glob of black-
speckled jell in a transparent globe, the size of an eyeball; it was set
in two rings, one within the other, pivoted so the globe turned in

all directions. Mounted on the outside ring was a curved tongue of
metal at the top of which was a small tube with a pin-sized lens.
The tube was threaded into a bushing, and I guess you used it to
look at what was going on in the sphere.

"Self-contained," explained An. "The only thing needed to keep
the whole thing going is light. Just about any frequency will do,
except way up on the blue end. And the shell cuts that out."

I looked through the brass eyepiece.

I'd swear there were over a hundred life forms with a five to fifty
stages each: spores, zygotes, seeds, eggs, growing and developing
through larvae, pupae, buds, reproducing through sex, syzygy,
fission. And the whole ecological cycle took about two minutes.

Spongy masses like red lotuses clung to the air bubble. Every few
seconds one would expel a cloud of black things like wrinkled bits
of carbon paper into the gas where they were attacked by tiny motes
I could hardly see even with the lens. Black became silver. It fell
back to the liquid like globules of mercury, and coursed toward the
jelly that was emitting a froth of bubbles. Something in the froth
made the silver beads reverse direction. They reddened, sent out
threads and alveoli, until they reached the main bubble again as
lotuses.

The reason the lotuses didn't crowd each other out was because
every eight or nine seconds a swarm of green paramecia devoured
most of them. I couldn't tell where they came from; I never saw
one of them split or get eaten, but they must have had something
to do with the thorn-balls—if only because there were either thorn-
balls or paramecia floating in the liquid, but never both at once.

A black spore in the jelly wiggled, then burst the surface as a
white worm. Exhausted, it laid a couple of eggs, rested until it
developed fins and a tail, then swam to the bubble where it laid
more eggs among the lotuses. Its fins grew larger, its tail shriveled,
splotches of orange and blue appeared, till it took off like a weird
butterfly to sail around the inside of the bubble. The motes that
silvered the black offspring of the lotus must have eaten the parti-
colored fan because it just grew thinner and frailer till it disappeared. The eggs by the lotus would hatch into bloated fish forms
that swam back through the froth to vomit a glob of jelly on the
mass at the bottom, then collapse. The first eggs didn't do much
except turn into black spores when they were covered with enough
jelly.

All this was going on amidst a kaleidoscope of frail, wilting flowers and blooming jeweled webs, vines and worms, warts and jellyfish, symbiotes and saprophytes, while rainbow herds of algae
careened back and forth like glittering confetti. One rough-rinded

galoot, so big you could see him without the eyepiece, squatted on the wall, feeding on jelly, batting his eye-spots while the tide surged through quivering tears of gills.

I blinked as I took it from my eye.

"That looks complicated." I handed it back to him.

"Not really." He slipped it around his neck. "Took me two weeks with a notebook to get the whole thing figured out. You saw the big fellow?"

"The one who winked?"

"Yes. Its reproductive cycle is about two hours, which trips you up at first. Everything else goes so fast. But once you see him mate with the thing that looks like a spider web with sequins—same creature, different sex—and watch the offspring aggregate into paramecia, then dissolve again, the whole thing falls into—"

"One creature!" I said. "The whole thing is a single creature!"

An nodded vigorously. "Has to be to stay self-contained." The grin on his face whipped away like a snapped windowshade. A very serious look was underneath. "Even after I saw the big fellow mate, it took me a week to understand it was all one."

"But if goofus and the fishnet have paramecia—" I began. It seemed logical when I made the guess.

"You've seen one before."

I shook my head. "Not like that one, anyway. I once saw something similar, but it was much bigger, about six feet across."

An's seriousness was replaced by horror. I mean he really started to shake. "How could you . . . *ever* even *see* all the . . . stuff inside, much less *catalogue* it? You say . . . *this* is complicated?"

"Hey, relax. Relax!" I said. He did. Like that. "It was much simpler," I explained and went on to describe the one our kids had made so many years ago as best I remembered.

"Oh," An said at last, his face set in its original impassivity. "It wasn't microorganisms. Simple. Yes." He looked at the pavement. "Very simple." When he looked up, another expression had scrambled his features. It took a moment to identify. "I don't see the point at all."

There was surprising physical surety in the boy's movement; his nervousness was a cat's, not a human's. But it was one of the psychological qualities of golden.

"Well," I said, "it showed the kids a picture of the way the cycles of life progress."

An rattled his chain. "That is why they gave us these things. But everything in the one you had was so primitive. It wasn't a very good picture."

"Don't knock it," I told him. "When I was a kid, all I had was an

ant colony. I got my infantile *Weltanschauung* watching a bunch of
bugs running around between two plates of glass. I think I would
have been better prepared by a couple of hungry rats on a treadmill.
Or maybe a torus-shaped fish tank alternating sharks with schools
of piranhas: Get them all chasing around after each other real
fast—"

"Ecology wouldn't balance," An said. "You'd need snails to get
rid of the waste. Then a lot of plants to reoxygenate the water, and
some sort of herbivore to keep down the plants because they'd tend
to choke out everything since neither the sharks nor the piranhas
would eat them." Kids and their damn literal minds. "If the herbi-
vores had some way to keep the sharks off, then you might do it."

"What's wrong with the first one I described?"

The explanation worked around the muscles of his face. "The
lizards, the segment worms, the plants, worts, all their cycles were
completely circular. They were born, grew up, reproduced, maybe
took care of the kids awhile, then died. Their only function was
reproduction. That's a pretty awful picture." He made an unintelligible face.

There was something about this wise-alecky kid who was golden,
younger than Alegra, older than Ratlit, I liked.

"There are stages in here," An tapped his globe with his pinky
nail, "that don't get started on their most important functions till
after they've reproduced and grown up through a couple more
metamorphoses as well. Those little green worms are a sterile end
stage of the blue feathery things. But they put out free phosphates
that the algae live on. Everything else, just about, lives on the
algae—except the thorn-balls. They eat the worms when they die.
There're phagocytes in there that injest the dust-things when they
get out of the bubble and start infecting the liquid." All at once he
got very excited. "Each of us in the class got one of these! They
made us figure them out! Then we had to prepare these recordings
on whether the reproductive process was the primary function in
life or an adjunctive one." Something white frothed the corners of
his mouth. "I think grown-ups should just *leave* their kids the hell
alone, go on and do something *else*, stop bothering us! That's what
I said! That's what I *told* them!" He stopped, his tongue flicked the
foam at the cusp of his lips; he seemed all right again.

"Sometimes," I said evenly, "if you leave them alone and forget
about them, you end up with monsters who aren't kids any more.
If you'd been left alone, you wouldn't have had a chance to put
your two cents in in the first place, and you wouldn't have that
thing around your neck." And he was really trying to follow what

I was saying. A moment past his rage, his face was as open and receptive as a two-year-old's. God, I want to stop thinking about Antoni!

"That's not what I mean." He wrapped his arms around his shoulders and bit on his forearm pensively.

"An—you're not stupid, kid-boy. You're cocky, but I don't think you're mean. You're golden." There was all my resentment, out now, Ratlit. There it is, Alegra. I didn't grow up with the word, so it meant something different to me. An looked up to ingest my meaning. The toothmarks were white on his skin, then red around that. "How long have you been one?"

He watched me, arms still folded. "They found out when I was seven."

"That long ago?"

"Yes." He turned and started walking again. "I was very precocious."

"Oh." I nodded. "Just about half your life then. How's it been, little brother, being a golden?"

An dropped his arms. "They take you away from your group a lot of times." He shrugged. "Special classes. Training programs. I'm psychotic."

"I never would have guessed." What would you call Ratlit? What would you call Alegra?

"I know it shows. But it gets us through the psychic pressures at the reality breakdown at twenty thousand light-years. It really does. For the past few years, though, they've been planting the psychosis artificially, pretty far down in the preconscious, so it doesn't affect our ordinary behavior as much as it does the older ones. They can use this process on anybody whose hormone system is even close to golden. They can get a lot more and a lot better quality golden that way than just waiting for us to pop up by accident."

As I laughed, something else struck me. "Just what do you need a job out here for, though? Why not hitch out with some cousin or get a job on one of the intergalactics as an apprentice?"

"I have a job in another galaxy. There'll be a ship stopping for me in two months to take me out. A whole lot of Star-pits have been established in galaxies halfway to Un-dok. I'll be going back and forth, managing roboi-equipment, doing managerial work. I thought it would be a good idea to get some practical experience out here before I left."

"Precocious," I nodded. "Look, even with roboi-equipment you have to know one hell of a lot about the inside of how many different kinds of keeler drives. You're not going to get that kind of experience in two months as a grease monkey. And roboi-equipment? I don't even have any in my place. Poloscki's got some, but I don't think you'll get your hands on it."

"I know a good deal already," An said with strained modesty.

"Yeah?" I asked him a not too difficult question and got an adequate answer. Made me feel better that he didn't come back with something really brilliant. I did know more than he did. "Where'd you learn?"

"They gave me the information the same way they implanted my psychosis."

"You're pretty good for your age." Dear old Luna Vocational! Well, maybe educational methods have improved. "Come to think of it, I was just as old as you when I started playing around with those keeler models. Dozens and dozens of helical inserts—"

"And those oily organum sensitives in all that graphite? Yes, brother! But I've never even had my hands in a waldo."

I frowned. "Hell, when I was younger than you, I could—" I stopped. "Of course, with roboi-equipment, you don't need them. But it's not a bad thing to know how they work, just in case."

"That's why I want a job." He hooked one finger on his chain. "Brother-in-law Sandy and I got to talking, so I asked him about working here. He said you might help me get in someplace."

"I'm glad he did. My place only handles big ships, and it's all waldo. Me and an assistant can do the whole thing. Poloscki's place is smaller, but handles both inter- and intra-galactic jobs, so you get more variety and a bigger crew. You find Poloscki, say I sent you, tell what you can do and why you're out here. Belt or no, you'll probably get something better than a monkey."

"Thanks, brother."

We turned off Calle-D. Poloscki's hangar was ahead. Dull thunder sounded over the roof as a ship departed.

"As soon as I despair of the younger generation," I told him, "one of you kids comes by and I start to think there's hope. Granted you're a psychopath, you're a lot better than some of your older, distant relations."

An looked up at me, apprehensive.

"You've never had a run-in with some of your cousins out here. But don't be surprised if you're dead tomorrow and your job's been inherited by some character who decided to split your head open to check on what's inside. I try to get used to you, behaving like something that isn't even savage. But, boy-kid, can your kind really mess up a guy's picture of the universe."

"And what the hell do you expect us to act like?" An shot back.

Spittle glittered on his lips again. "What would *you* do if you were trapped like *us?*"

"Huh?" I said questioningly. "*You,* trapped?"

"Look." A spasm passed over his shoulders. "The psycho-technician who made sure I was properly psychotic *wasn't* a golden, *brother!* You *pay* us to bring back the weapons, dad! We don't fight your damn wars, *grampa!* You're the ones who take us away from our groups, say we're *too* valuable to submit to *your* laws, then deny us our heredity because we don't *breed* true, no-relative-of *mine!*"

"Now, wait a minute!"

An snatched the chain from around his neck and held it taut in front of him. His voice ground to a whisper, his eyes glittered. "I strangled one of my classmates with this chain, the one I've got in my hands now." One by one, his features blanked all expression. "They took it away from me for a week, as punishment for killing that little girl."

The whisper stopped decibels above silence, then went on evenly. "Out here, nobody will punish me. And my reflexes are faster than yours."

Fear lashed my anger as I followed the insanity flickering in his eyes.

"Now!" He made a quick motion with his hands; I ducked. "I give it to you!" He flung the chain toward me. Reflexively I caught it. An turned away instantly and stalked into Poloscki's.

When I burst through the rattling hangar door at my place, the lift was coming down. Sandy yelled through the mesh walls, "Did he get the job?"

"Probably," I yelled back, going toward the office.

I heard the cage settle on the silicon cushion. Sandy was at my side a moment later, grinning. "So how do you like my brother-in-law, Androcles?"

"Brother-in-law?" I remembered An using the phrase, but I'd thought it was part of the slang golden. Something about the way Sandy said it though. "He's your *real* brother-in-law?"

"He's Joey's kid brother. I didn't want to say anything until after you met him." Sandy came along with me toward the office door. "Joey wrote me again and said since An was coming out here he'd tell him to stop by and see me and maybe I could help him out."

"Now how the hell am I supposed to know who Joey is?" I pushed open the door. It banged the wall.

"He's one of my husbands, the one who wrote me that letter you told me you'd read."

"Oh, yeah. Him." I started stacking papers.

"I thought it was pretty nice of him after all that to tell An to look me up when he got out here. It means that there's still somebody left who doesn't think I'm a complete waste. So what do you think of Androcles?"

"He's quite a boy." I scooped up the mail that had come in after lunch, started to go through it but put it down to hunt for my coveralls.

"An used to come visit us when he got his one weekend a month off from his training program as golden," Sandy was going on. "Joey's and An's parents lived in the reeds near the estuary. But we lived back up the canyon by Chroma Falls. An and Joey were pretty close, even though Joey's my age and An was only eight or nine back then. I guess Joey was the only one who really knew what An was going through, since they were both golden."

Surprised and shocked, I turned back to the desk. "You were married with a golden?" One of the letters on the top of the pile was addressed to Alegra from Carlson's Labs. I had a carton of the kids' junk in the locker and had gotten the mail—there wasn't much—sent to the hangar, as though I were waiting for somebody to come for it.

"Yeah," Sandy said, surprised at my surprise. "Joey."

So I wouldn't stand there gaping, I picked up Alegra's letter.

"Since the traits that are golden are polychromazoic, it dies out if they only breed with each other. There's a big campaign back in galactic center to encourage them to join heterogeneous proke-groups."

"Like bluepoint Siamese cats, huh?" I ran my blackened thumbnail through the seal.

"That's right. But they're *not* animals, boss. I remember what they put that kid-boy through for psychotic reinforcement of the factors that were golden to make sure they stuck. It tore me up to hear him talk about it when he'd visit us."

I pulled a porta-pix out of Alegra's envelope. Carlson's tries to personalize its messages.

"I'm sure glad they can erase the conscious memory from the kids' minds when they have to do that sort of stuff."

"Small blessings and all that." I flipped the porta-pix on.

Personalized but mass produced: ". . . blessed addit . . ." the little speaker echoed me. Poloscki and I had used Carlson's a couple of times, I know. I guess every other mechanic up here had too. The porta-pix had started in the middle. Now it hummed back to the beginning.

"You know," Sandy went on, "Joey was different, yeah, sort of dense about some things . . ."

"Alegra," beamed the chic, grandmotherly type Carlson's always uses for messages of this sort, "we were so glad to receive the urine sample you sent us by Mr. Ratlit last Thursday . . ."

". . . even so, Joey was one of the sweetest men or women I've ever known. He was the easiest person in the group to live with. Maybe it was because he was away a lot . . ."

". . . and now, just a week later—remember, Carlson's gives results immediately and confirms them by personalized porta-pix in seven days—we are happy to tell you that there will be a blessed addition to your group. However . . ."

". . . All right, he was different, reacted funny to a lot of things. But nothing like this rank, destructive stupidity you find out here at the Star-pit . . ."

". . . the paternity is not Mr. Ratlit's. If you are interested, for your eugenic records, in further information, please send us other possible urine samples from the men in your group, and we will be glad to confirm paternity . . ."

". . . I can't understand the way people act out here, boss. And that's why I'm pushing on."

". . . Thank you so much for letting us give you this wonderful news. Remember, when in doubt, call Carlson's."

I said to Sandy, "You were married with—you loved a golden?"

Unbidden, the porta-pix began again. I flipped it off without looking.

"Sandy," I said, "you were hired because you were a fair mechanic and you kept off my back. Do what you're paid for. Get out of here!"

"Oh. Sure, boss." He backed quickly from the office.

I sat down.

Maybe I'm old-fashioned, but when someone runs off and abandons a sick girl like that, it gets me. That was the trip to Carlson's, the one last little favor Ratlit never came back from. On-the-spot results, and formal confirmation in seven days. In her physical condition, pregnancy would have been as fatal as the withdrawal. And she was too ill for any abortive method I know of not to kill her. On-the-spot results. Ratlit must have known all that too when he got the results back, the results that Alegra was probably afraid of, the results she sent him to find. Ratlit knew Alegra was going to die anyway. And so he stole a golden belt. "Loving someone, I mean really loving someone—" Alegra had said. When someone runs off and leaves a sick girl like that, there's got to be a reason. It came together for me like two fissionables. The explosion cut some moorings in my head I thought were pretty solidly fixed.

I pulled out the books, plugged in the computer, unplugged it, put the books away, and stared into the ecologarium in my fist.

Among the swimming, flying, crawling things, mating, giving birth, growing, changing, busy at whatever their business was, I picked out those dead-end, green worms. I hadn't noticed them before because they were at the very edge of things, bumping against the wall. After they released their free phosphates and got tired of butting at the shell, they turned on each other and tore themselves to pieces.

Fear and anger is a bad combination in me.

I came close to being killed by a golden once, through that meanness and stupidity.

The same meanness and stupidity that killed Alegra and Ratlit.

And now when this damn kid threatens to—I mean at first I had thought he was threatening to—

I reached Gerg's a few minutes after the day-lights went out and the street lamps came on. But I'd stopped in nearly a dozen places on the way. I remember trying to explain to a sailor from a star-shuttle who was just stopping over at the Star-pit for the first time and was all upset because one woman golden had just attacked another with a broken glass; I remember saying to the three-headed bulge of his shoulder, ". . . an ant colony! You know what it is, two pieces of glass with dirt between them, and you can see all the little ants make tunnels and hatch eggs and stuff. When I was a kid, I had an ant colony. . . ." I started to shake my hand in his face. The chain from the ecologarium was tangled up in my fingers.

"Look." He caught my wrist and put it down on the counter. "It's all right now, pal. Just relax."

"You look," I said as he turned away. "When I was a kid, all I had was an *ant* colony!"

He turned back and leaned his rusty elbow on the bar. "Okay," he said affably. Then he made the most stupid and frustrating mistake he possibly could have just then. "What about your aunt?"

"My mother—"

"I thought you were telling me about your aunt?"

"Naw," I said. "My aunt, she drank too much. This is about my mother."

"All right. Your mother then."

"My mother, see, she always worried about me, getting sick and things. I got sick a lot when I was a little kid. She made me mad! Used to go down and watch the ships take off from the place they called the Brooklyn Navy Yards. They were ships that went to the stars."

The sailor's Oriental face grinned. "Yeah, me too. Used to watch 'em when I was a kid."

"But it was raining, and she wouldn't let me go."

"Aw, that's too bad. Little rain never hurt a kid. Why didn't she call up and have it turned off so you could go out? Too busy to pay attention to you, huh? One of my old men was like that."

"Both of mine were," I said. "But not my ma. She was all over me all the time when she was there. But she made me mad!"

He nodded with real concern. "Wouldn't turn off the rain."

"Naw, couldn't. You didn't grow up where I did, narrow-minded, dark-side world. No modern conveniences."

"Off the main trading routes, huh?"

"Way off. She wouldn't let me go out, and that made me mad."

He was still nodding.

"So I broke it!" My fist came down hard on the counter, and the plastic globe in its brass cage clacked on the wood. "Broke it! Sand, glass all over the rug, on the windowsill!"

"What'd you break?"

"Smashed it, stamped on it, threw sand whenever she tried to make me stop!"

"Sand? You lived on a beach? We had a beach when I was a kid. A beach is nice for kids. What'd you break?"

"Let all the damn bugs out. Bugs in everything for days. Let 'em all out."

"Didn't have no bugs on our beach. But you said you were off the main trading routes."

"Let 'em *out*!" I banged my fist again. "Let *every*body out, whether they like it or not! It's their problem whether they make it, not mine! Don't care, I don't—" I was laughing now.

"She let you go out, and you didn't care?"

My hand came down on top of the metal cage, hard. I caught my breath at the pain. "On our beach," I said, turning my palm up to look. There were red marks across it. "There weren't any bugs on our beach." Then I started shaking.

"You mean you were just putting me on, before, about the bugs. Hey, are you all right?"

". . . broke it," I whispered. Then I smashed fist and globe and chain into the side of the counter. "Let 'em *out*!" I whirled away, clutching my bruised hand against my stomach.

"*Watch* it, kid-boy!"

"I'm not a kid-boy!" I shouted. "You think I'm some stupid, half-crazy kid!"

"So you're older than me. Okay?"

"I'm not a kid any more!"

"So you're ten years older than Sirius, all right? Quiet down, or they'll kick us out."

I bulled out of Gerg's. A couple of people came after me because I didn't watch where I was going. I don't know who won, but I remember somebody yelling, "Get out! Get out!" It may have been me.

I remember later, staggering under the mercury street lamp, the world-wind slapping my face, stars swarming back and forth below me, gravel sliding under my boots, the toes inches over the Edge. The gravel clicked down the metal siding, the sound terribly clear as I reeled in the loud wind, shaking my arm against the night.

As I brought my hand back, the wind lashed the cold chain across my cheek and the bridge of my nose. I lurched back, trying to claw it away. But it stayed all tangled on my fingers while the globe swung, gleaming in the street light. The wind roared. Gravel chattered down the siding.

Later, I remember the hangar door ajar, and stumbling into the darkness, so that in a moment I was held from plummeting into nothing only by my own footsteps as black swerved around me. I stopped when my hip hit a workbench. I pawed around under the lip of the table till I found a switch. In the dim orange light, racked along the back of the bench in their plastic shock-cases, were the row of master-gauntlets. I slipped one out and slid my hand into it.

"Who's over there?"

"Go 'way, Sandy." I turned from the bench, switched up the power on the wrist controls. Somewhere in the dark above, a fifteen-foot slave-hand hummed to life.

"Sorry, buster. This isn't Sandy. Put that down and get away from there."

I squinted as the figure approached in the orange light, hand extended. I saw the vibra-gun and didn't bother to look at the face.

Then the gun went down. "Vyme, baby? That you? What the hell are you doing here this hour of the night?"

"Poloscki?"

"Who'd you think it was?"

"Is this your—?" I looked around, shook my head. "But I thought it was my—" I shook my head again.

Poloscki sniffed. "Hey, have you been a naughty kid-boy tonight!"

I swung my hand, and the slave-hand overhead careened twenty feet.

The gun jumped. "Look, you mess up my waldo and I will kill you, don't care who you are! Take that thing off."

"Very funny." I brought the talon down where I could see it clawing shadow.

"Come on, Vyme. I'm serious. Turn it off and put it down. You're a mess now and you don't know what you're doing."

"That kid, the golden. Did you give him a job?"

"Sure. He said you sent him. Smart little so-and-so. He rehulled a little yacht with the roboi-anamechaniakatasthy-sizer, just to show me what he could do. If I knew a few more people who could handle them that well, I'd go all roboi. He's not worth a damn with a waldo, but as long as he's got that little green light in front of him, he's fine."

I brought the talons down another ten feet so that the spider hung between us. "Well, I happen to be very handy with a waldo, Poloscki."

"Vyme, you're gonna get *hurrrt* . . ."

"Poloscki," I said, "will you stop coming on like an overprotective aunt? I don't need another one."

"You're very drunk, Vyme."

"Yeah. But I'm no clumsy kid-boy who is going to mess up your equipment."

"If you do, you'll be——"

"Shut up and watch." I pulled the chaim out of my pouch and tossed it onto the concrete floor. In the orange light you couldn't tell whether the cage was brass or silver.

"What's that?"

The claws came down, and the fine-point tips, millimeters above the floor, closed on the ecologarium.

"Oh, hey! I haven't seen one of those since I was ten. What are you going to do with it? Those are five-hundred-to-one strength, you know. You're gonna break it."

"That's right. Break this one too."

"Aw, come on. Let me see it first."

I lifted the globe. "Could be an eggshell," I said. "Drunk or sober I can handle this damn equipment, Poloscki."

"I haven't seen one for years. Used to have one."

"You mean it wasn't spirited back from some distant galaxy by golden, from some technology beyond our limited ken?"

"Product of the home spiral. Been around since the fifties."

I raised it over Poloscki's extended hand.

"They're supposed to be very educational. What do you want to break it for?"

"I never saw one."

"You came from someplace off the routes, didn't you? They weren't that common. Don't break it."

"I want to."

"Why, Vyme?"

Something got wedged in my throat. "Because I want to get out, and if it's not that globe, it's gonna be somebody's head." Inside the gauntlet my hand began to quiver. The talons jerked. Poloscki caught the globe and jumped back.

"Vyme!"

"I'm hanging, here at the Edge." My voice kept getting caught on the things in my throat. "I'm useless, with a bunch of monsters and fools!" The talons swung, contracted, clashed on each other. "And then when the children . . . when the *children* get so bad you can't even reach them . . ." The claw opened, reached for Poloscki who jumped back in the half-dark.

"Damn it, Vyme—"

". . . can't even reach the children any more." The talon stopped shaking, came slowly back, knotting. "I want to break something and get out. Very childishly, yes. Because nobody is paying any attention to *me*." The claw jumped. "Even when I'm trying to help. I *don't* want to hurt anybody any *more*. I *swear* it, so help me, I swear—"

"Vyme, take off the glove and listen!"

I raised the slave-hand because it was about to scrape the cement.

"Vyme, I want to pay some attention to you." Slowly Poloscki walked back into the orange light. "You've been sending me kids for five years now, coming around and checking up on them, helping them out of the stupid scrapes they get in. They haven't all been Ratlits. I like kids too. That's why I take them on. I think what you do is pretty great. Part of me loves kids. Another part of me loves you."

"Aw, Poloscki . . ." I shook my head. Somewhere disgust began.

"It doesn't embarrass me. I love you a little and wouldn't mind loving you a lot. More than once I've thought about asking you to start a group."

"*Please*, Poloscki. I've had too many weird things happen to me this week. Not tonight, huh?" I then turned the power off in the glove.

"Love shouldn't frighten you, no matter when or how it comes, Vyme. Don't run from it. A marriage between us? Yeah, it would be a little hard for somebody like you, at first. But you'd get used to it before long. Then when kids came around, there'd be two—"

"I'll send Sandy over," I said. "He's the big-hearted, marrying kind. Maybe he's about ready to try again." I pulled off the glove.

"Vyme, don't go out like that. Stay for just a minute!"

"Poloscki," I said, "I'm just not that God damn drunk!" I threw the glove on the table.

"Please, Vyme."

"You're gonna use your gun to keep me here?"

"Don't be like—"

"I hope the kids I send over here appreciate you more than I do right now. I'm sorry I busted in here. Good-night!"

I turned from the table.

Nine thousand miles away the Stellarplex turned too. Circles of silver dropped through the roof. Behind the metal cage of the relaxed slave-claw I saw Poloscki's large, injured eyes, circles of crushed turquoise, glistening now.

And nine feet away someone said, "Ma'am?"

Poloscki glanced over her shoulder. "An, you awake?"

An stepped into the silver light, rubbing his neck. "That office chair is pretty hard, sister."

"He's here?" I asked.

"Sure," Poloscki said. "He didn't have any place to stay so I let him sleep in the office while I finished up some work in the back. Vyme, I meant what I said. Leave if you want, but not like this. Untwist."

"Poloscki," I said, "you're very sweet, you're fun in bed, and a good mechanic too. But I've been there before. Asking me to join a group is like asking me to do something obscene. I know what I'm worth."

"I'm also a good businesswoman. Don't think that didn't enter my head when I thought about marrying you." An came and stood beside her. He was breathing hard, the way an animal does when you wake it all of a sudden.

"Poloscki, you said it, I didn't: I'm a mess. That's why I'm not with my own group now."

"You're not always like this. I've never seen you touch a drop before."

"For a while," I said, "it happened with disgusting frequency. Why do you think my group dropped me?"

"Must have been awhile ago. I've known you a long time. So you've grown up since then. Now it only happens every half dozen years or so. Congratulations. Come have some coffee. An, run into the office and plug in the pot. I showed you where it was." An turned like something blown by the world-wind and was gone in shadow. "Come on," Poloscki said. She took my arm, and I came with her. Before we left the light, I saw my reflection in the polished steel tool-cabinet.

"Aw, no." I pulled away from her. "No, I better go home now."

"Why? An's making coffee."

"The kid. I don't want the kid to see me like this."

"He already has. Won't hurt him. Come on."

When I walked into Poloscki's office, I felt I didn't have a damn thing left. No. I had one. I decided to give it away.

When An turned to me with the cup, I put my hands on his shoulders. He jumped, but not enough to spill the coffee. "First and last bit of alcoholic advice for the evening, kid-boy. Even if you are crazy, don't go around telling people who are not golden how they've trapped you. That's like going to Earth and complimenting a nigger on how well he sings and dances and his great sense of rhythm. He may be able to tap seven with one hand against thirteen with the other while whistling a tone row. It still shows a remarkable naïveté about the way things are." That's one of the other things known throughout the galaxy about the world I come from. When I say primitive, I mean primitive.

An ducked from under my hands, put the coffee on the desk, and turned back. "I didn't say you trapped us."

"You said we treated you lousy and exploited you, which we may, and that this trapped you—"

"I said you exploited us, which you do, *and* that we were trapped. I *didn't* say by what."

Poloscki sat down on the desk, picked up my coffee and sipped it.

I raised my head. "All right. Tell me how you're trapped."

"Oh, I'm sorry," Poloscki said. "I started drinking your coffee—"

"Shut up. How are you trapped, An?"

He moved his shoulders around as though he was trying to get them comfortable. "It started in Tyber-44 cluster. Golden were coming back with really bad psychic shock."

"Yes. I heard about it. That was a few years back."

An's face started to twitch; the muscles around his eyes twisted below the skin. "*Something* out there . . ."

I put my hand on the back of his neck, my thumb in the soft spot behind his ear and began to stroke, the way you get a cat to calm down. "Take it easy. Just tell me."

"Thanks," An said and bent his head forward. "We found them first in Tiber-44, but then they turned up all *over*, on half the planets in every galaxy that could support any life, and a lot more that shouldn't have been able to at all." His breathing grew coarser. I kept rubbing, and it slowed again. "I guess we have such a funny psychology that working with them, studying them, even thinking about them too much . . . there was something about them that changes our sense of reality. The shock was bad."

"An," I said, "to be trapped, there has to be somewhere you can't go. For it to bug you, there has to be something else around that can."

He nodded under my hand, then straightened up. "I'm all right now. Just tired. You want to know where and what?"

Poloscki had put down the coffee now and was dangling the chain. An whirled to stare.

"Where?" he said. "Other universes."

"Galaxies farther out?" asked Poloscki.

"No. Completely different matrices of time and space." Staring at the swinging ball seemed to calm him even more. "No physical or temporal connection to this one at all."

"A sort of parallel—"

"Parallel? Hell!" It was almost a drawl. "There's nothing parallel about them. Out of the billions-to-the-billionth of them, most are hundreds of times the size of ours and empty. There are a few, though, whose entire spatial extent is even smaller than this galaxy. Some of them are completely dense to us, because even though there seems to be matter in them, distributed more or less as in this universe, there's no electromagnetic activity at all. No radio waves, no heat, no light." The globe swung; the voice was a whisper.

I closed my fist around the globe and took it from Poloscki. "How do you know about them? Who brings back the information? Who is it who can get out?"

Blinking, An looked back at me.

When he told me, I began to laugh. To accommodate the shifting reality tensions, the psychotic personality that is golden is totally labile. An laughed with me, not knowing why. He explained through his torrential hysteria how with the micro-micro surgical techniques from Tiber-44 they had read much of the information from a direct examination of the creature's nervous system, which covered its surface like velvet. It could take intense cold or heat, a range of pressure from vacuum to hundreds of pounds per square millimeter; but a fairly small amount of ultraviolet destroyed the neural synapses, and it died. They were small and deceptively organic because in an organic environment they appeared to breathe and eat. They had four sexes, two of which carried the young. They had clusters of retractable sense organs that first appeared to be eyes, but were sensitive to twelve distinct senses, stimulation for three of which didn't even exist in our continuum. They traveled around on four suction cups when using kinetic motion for ordinary traversal of space, were small, and looked furry. The only way to make them jump universes was to scare the life out of them. At which point they just disappeared.

An kneaded his stomach under his belt to ease the pain from so much laughter. "Working with them at Tiber-44 just cracked up a whole bunch of golden." He leaned against the desk, panting and grinning. "They had to be sent home for therapy. We still can't think about them directly, but it's easier for us to control what we think about than for you; that's part of being golden. I even had one of them for a pet, up until yesterday. The damn creatures are either totally apathetic, or vicious. Mine was a baby, all white and soft." He held out his arms. "Yesterday it bit me and disappeared." On his wrist there was a bluish place centered on which was a crescent of pinpricks. "Lucky it was a baby. The bites infect easily."

Poloscki started drinking from my cup again as An and I started laughing all over.

As I walked back that night, black coffee slopped in my belly.

There are certain directions in which you cannot go. Choose one in which you can move as far as you want. Sandy said that? He did. And there was something about Sandy, very much like someone golden. It doesn't matter how, he's going on.

Under a street lamp I stopped and lifted up the ecologarium. The reproductive function, was it primary or adjunctive? If, I thought with the whiskey lucidity always suspect at dawn, you consider the whole ecological balance a single organism, it's adjunctive, a vital reparative process along with sleeping and eating, to the primary process which is living, working, growing. I put the chain around my neck.

I was still half soused, and it felt bad. But I howled. Androcles, is drunken laughter appropriate to mourn all my dead children? Perhaps not. But tell me, Ratlit; tell me Alegra: what better way to launch my live ones who are golden into night? I don't know. I know I laughed. Then I put my fists into my overall pouch and crunched homeward along the Edge while on my left the world-wind roared.

BRIAN W. ALDISS
Total Environment

In many ways, Brian W. Aldiss was the *enfant terrible* of the late fifties, exploding into the science fiction world and shaking it up with the ferocious verve and pyrotechnic verbal brilliance of stories like "Poor Little Warrior," "Outside," "The New Father Christmas," "But Who Can Replace a Man?," "A Kind of Artistry," and "Old Hundredth," and with the somber beauty and unsettling poetic vision—in the main, of a world where Mankind signally has *not* triumphantly conquered the universe, as the Campbellian dogma of the time insisted that he would—of his classic novels *Starship* and *The Long Afternoon of Earth* (*Non-Stop* and *Hothouse*, respectively, in Britain). All this made him one of the most controversial writers of the day . . . and, some years later, he became one of the most controversial figures of the New Wave era as well, shaking up the SF world of the mid-sixties in an even more dramatic and drastic fashion with the ferociously Joycean "acidhead war" stories that were later melded into *Barefoot in the Head*, with the irreverent *Cryptozoic!*, and with his surrealistic anti-novel *Report on Probability A*.

But Aldiss has never been willing to work any one patch of ground for very long. By 1976, he had worked his way through two controversial British mainstream best-sellers—*The Hand-Reared Boy* and *A Soldier Erect*—and the strange, transmuted Gothic of *Frankenstein Unbound*, and gone on to produce a lyrical masterpiece of science fantasy, *The Malacia Tapestry*, perhaps his best book, and certainly one of the best novels of the seventies. Ahead, in the decade of the eighties, was the monumental accomplishment of his *Helliconia* trilogy—*Helliconia Spring*, *Helliconia Summer*, and *Helliconia Winter*—and by the end of that decade only the grumpiest of reactionary critics could deny that Aldiss was one of the true giants of the field, a figure of artistic complexity and amazing vigor, as much on the Cutting Edge in the nineties as he had been in the fifties.

As is clearly demonstrated by the compelling novella that follows, *Total Environment*, a story that was decades ahead of its time when it was first published in 1968, and a story whose conceptual audaciousness, razor-sharp irony, and somber intensity of vision would put it on the Cutting Edge even today, a fascinating and oddly unsettling look at an attempt to create a wholly new *kind* of human being. . . .

The Long Afternoon of Earth won a Hugo Award in 1962. "The Saliva Tree" won a Nebula Award in 1965, and Aldiss's novel *Starship* won the Prix Jules Verne in 1977. He took another Hugo Award in 1987 for his critical study of science fiction, *Trillion Year Spree*, written with David Wingrove. His other books include *An Island Called Moreau*, *Greybeard*, *Enemies of the System*, *A Rude Awakening*, *Life in the West*, *Forgotten Life*, and *Dracula Unbound*. His short fiction has been collected in *Space, Time, and Nathaniel*, *Who Can Replace a Man?*, *New Arrivals, Old Encounters*, *Galaxies Like Grains of Sand*, and *Seasons in Flight*. His many anthologies include *Space Opera*, *Space Odysseys*, *Evil Earths*, *The Penguin Science Fiction Omnibus*, and, with Harry Harrison, *Decade: the 1940s*, *Decade: the 1950s*, and *Decade: the 1960s*. His latest books include the collection *A Tupolev Too Far* and the novel *Remembrance Day*, and *Bury My Heart at W. H. Smith's*, a memoir. Upcoming is a new novel, *Burnell's Travels*, and a collection of poems, *Home Life With Cats*. He lives with his family in Oxford.

I

"What's that poem about 'caverns measureless to man'?" Thomas Dixit asked. His voice echoed away among the caverns, the question unanswered. Peter Crawley, walking a pace or two behind him, said nothing, lost in a reverie of his own.

It was over a year since Dixit had been imprisoned here. He had taken time off from the resettlement area to come and have a last look round before everything was finally demolished. In these great concrete workings, men still moved—Indian technicians mostly, carrying instruments, often with their own headlights. Cables trailed everywhere; but the desolation was mainly an effect of the constant abrasion all surfaces had undergone. People had flowed here like water in a subterranean cave; and their corporate life had flowed similarly, hidden, forgotten.

Dixit was powerfully moved by the thought of all that life. He, almost alone, was the man who had plunged into it and survived.

Old angers stirring in him, he turned and spoke directly to his companion. "What a monument to human suffering! They should leave this place standing as an everlasting memorial to what happened."

The white man said, "The Delhi government refuses to entertain any such suggestion. I see their point of view, but I also see that it would make a great tourist attraction!"

"Tourist attraction, man! Is that all it means to you?"

Crawley laughed. "As ever, you're too touchy, Thomas. I take this whole matter much less lightly than you suppose. Tourism just happens to attract me more than human suffering."

They walked on side by side. They were never able to agree.

The battered faces of flats and houses—now empty, once choked with humanity—stood on either side, doors gaping open like old men's mouths in sleep. The spaces seemed enormous; the shadows and echoes that belonged to those spaces seemed to continue indefinitely. Yet before . . . there had scarcely been room to breathe here.

"I remember what your buddy, Senator Byrnes, said," Crawley remarked. "He showed how both East and West have learned from this experiment. Of course, the social scientists are still working over their findings; some startling formulae for social groups are emerging already. But the people who lived and died here were fighting their way towards control of the universe of the ultra-small, and that's where the biggest advances have come. They were already developing power over their own genetic material. Another generation, and they might have produced the ultimate in automatic human population control: anoestrus, where too close proximity to other members of the species leads to reabsorption of the embryonic material in the female. Our scientists have been able to help them there, and geneticists predict that in another decade—"

"Yes, yes, all that I grant you. Progress is wonderful." He knew he was being impolite. These things were important, of revolutionary importance to a crowded Earth. But he wished he walked these eroded passageways alone.

Undeniably, India had learned too, just as Peter Crawley claimed. For Hinduism had been put to the test here and had shown its terrifying strengths and weaknesses. In these mazes, people had not broken under deadly conditions—nor had they thought to break away from their destiny. *Dharma*—duty—had been stronger than humanity. And this revelation was already changing the thought and fate of one-sixth of the human race.

He said, "Progress is wonderful. But what took place here was essentially a religious experience."

Crawley's brief laugh drifted away into the shadows of a great gaunt stairwell. "I'll bet you didn't feel that way when we sent you in here a year ago!"

What had he felt then? He stopped and gazed up at the gloom of the stairs. All that came to him was the memory of that appalling flood of life and of the people who had been a part of it, whose brief years had evaporated in these caverns, whose feet has endlessly trodden these warren-ways, these lugubrious decks, these crumbling flights. . . .

II

The concrete steps climbed up into darkness. The steps were wide, and countless children sat on them, listless, resting against each other. This was an hour when activity was low and even small children hushed their cries for a while. Yet there was no silence on the steps; silence was never complete there. Always, in the background, the noise of voices. Voices and more voices. Never silence.

Shamim was aged, so she preferred to run her errands at this time of day, when the crowds thronging Total Environment were less. She dawdled by a sleepy seller of life-objects at the bottom of the stairs, picking over the little artifacts and exclaiming now and again. The hawker knew her, knew she was too poor to buy, did not even press her to buy. Shamim's oldest daughter, Malti, waited for her mother by the bottom step.

Malti and her mother were watched from the top of the steps.

A light burned at the top of the steps. It had burned there for twenty-five years, safe from breakage behind a strong mesh. But dung and mud had recently been thrown at it, covering it almost entirely and so making the top of the stairway dark. A furtive man called Narayan Farhad crouched there and watched, a shadow in the shadows.

A month ago, Shamim had had an illegal operation in one of the pokey rooms off Grand Balcony on her deck. The effects of the operation were still with her; under her plain cotton sari, her thin dark old body was bent. Her share of life stood lower than it had been.

Malti was her second oldest daughter, a meek girl who had not been conceived when the Total Environment experiment began.

Even meekness had its limits. Seeing her mother dawdle so need-
lessly, Malti muttered impatiently and went on ahead, climbing the
infested steps, anxious to be home.

Extracts from Thomas Dixit's report to Senator Jacob
Byrnes, back in America: *To lend variety to the habitat, the
Environment has been divided into ten decks, each deck five stories
high, which allows for an occasional pocket-sized open space. The
architecture has been varied somewhat on each deck. On one deck,
a sort of blown-up Indian village is presented; on another, the
houses are large and appear separate, although sandwiched between decks—I need not add they are hopelessly overcrowded now.
On most decks, the available space is packed solid with flats. Despite
this attempt at variety, a general bowdlerization of both Eastern
and Western architectural styles, and the fact that everything has
been constructed out of concrete or a parastyrene for economy's
sake, has led to a dreadful sameness. I cannot imagine anywhere
more hostile to the spiritual values of life.*

The shadow in the shadows moved. He glanced anxiously up at the
light, which also housed a spy-eye; there would be a warning out,
and sprays would soon squirt away the muck he had thrown at the
fitting; but, for the moment, he could work unobserved.

Narayan bared his old teeth as Malti came up the steps towards
him, treading among the sprawling children. She was too old to
fetch a really good price on the slave market, but she was still
strong; there would be no trouble in getting rid of her at once. Of
course he knew something of her history, even though she lived on
a different deck from him. Malti! He called her name at the last
moment as he jumped out on her. Old though he was, Narayan
was quick. He wore only his dhoti, arms flashing, interlocking
round hers, one good powerful wrench to get her off her feet—
now running fast, fearful, up the rest of the steps, moving even as
he clamped one hand over her mouth to cut off her cry of fear.
Clever old Narayan!

*The stairs mount up and up in the four corners of the Total
Environment, linking deck with deck. They are now crude things
of concrete and metal, since the plastic covers have long been
stripped from them.*

*These stairways are the weak points of the tiny empires, transient
and brutal, that form on every deck. They are always guarded,
though guards can be bribed. Sometimes gangs or "unions" take
over a stairway, either by agreement or bloodshed.*

Shamim screamed, responding to her daughter's cry. She began to hobble up the stairs as fast as she could, tripping over infant feet, drawing a dagger out from under her sari. It was a plastic dagger, shaped out of a piece of the Environment.

She called Malti, called for help as she went. When she reached the landing, she was on the top floor of her deck, the Ninth, where she lived. Many people were here, standing, squatting, thronging together. They looked away from Shamim, people with blind faces. She had so often acted similarly herself when others were in trouble.

Gasping, she stopped and stared up at the roof of the deck, blue-dyed to simulate sky, cracks running irregularly across it. The steps went on up there, up to the Top Deck. She saw legs, yellow soles of feet disappearing, faces staring down at her, hostile. As she ran toward the bottom of the stairs, the watchers above threw things at her. A shard hit Shamim's cheek and cut it open. With blood running down her face, she began to wail. Then she turned and ran through the crowds to her family room.

> *I've been a month just reading through the microfiles. Sometimes a whole deck becomes unified under a strong leader. On Deck Nine, for instance, unification was achieved under a man called Ullhas. He was a strong man, and a great show-off. That was a while ago, when conditions were not as desperate as they are now. Ullhas could never last the course today. Leaders become more despotic as Environment decays.*
>
> *The dynamics of unity are such that it is always insufficient for a deck simply to stay unified; the young men always need to have their aggressions directed outwards. So the leader of a strong deck always sets out to tyrannize the deck below or above, whichever seems to be the weaker. It is a miserable state of affairs. The time generally comes when, in the midst of a raid, a counter-raid is launched by one of the other decks. Then the raiders return to carnage and defeat. And another paltry empire tumbles.*
>
> *It is up to me to stop this continual degradation of human life.*

As usual, the family room was crowded. Although none of Shamim's own children were here, there were grandchildren—including the lame granddaughter, Shirin—and six great-grand-children, none of them more than three years old. Shamim's third husband, Gita, was not in. Safe in the homely squalor of the room, Shamim burst into tears, while Shirin comforted her and endeavored to keep the little ones off.

"Gita is getting food. I will go and fetch him," Shirin said.

*When UHDRE—Ultra-High Density Research Establishment—
became operative, twenty-five years ago, all the couples selected for
living in the Total Environment had to be under twenty years of
age. Before being sealed in, they were innoculated against all
diseases. There was plenty of room for each couple then; they had
whole suites to themselves, and the best of food; plus no means of
birth control. That's always been the main pivot of the UHDRE
experiment. Now that first generation has aged severely. They are
old people pushing forty-five. The whole life cycle has speeded up—
early puberty, early senescence. The second and third generations
have shown remarkable powers of adaptation; a fourth generation
is already toddling. Those toddlers will be reproducing before their
years attain double figures, if present trends continue. Are allowed
to continue.*

Gita was younger than Shamim, a small wiry man who knew his
way around. No hero, he nevertheless had a certain style about
him. His life-object hung boldly round his neck on a chain, instead
of being hidden, as were most people's life-objects. He stood in the
line for food, chattering with friends. Gita was good at making
alliances. With a bunch of his friends, he had formed a little union
to see that they got their food back safely to their homes; so they
generally met with no incident in the crowded walkways of Deck
Nine.

The balance of power on the deck was very complex at the moment. As a result, comparative peace reigned, and might continue
for several weeks if the strong man on Top Deck did not interfere.

*Food delivery grills are fixed in the walls of every floor of every
deck. Two gongs sound before each delivery. After the second one,
hatches open and steaming food pours from the grills. Hills of rice
tumble forward, flavored with meat and spices. Chappattis fall
from a separate slot. As the men run forward with their containers,
holy men are generally there to sanctify the food.*

*Great supply elevators roar up and down in the heart of the vast
tower, tumbling out rations at all levels. Alcohol also was supplied
in the early years. It was discontinued when it led to trouble; which
is not to say that it is not secretly brewed inside the Environment.
The UHDRE food ration has been generous from the start and
has always been maintained at the same level per head of population
although, as you know, the food is now ninety-five percent factory-
made. Nobody would ever have starved, had it been shared out
equably inside the tower. On some of the decks, some of the time it
is still shared out fairly.*

One of Gita's sons, Jamsu, had seen the kidnapper Narayan making off to Top Deck with the struggling Malti. His eyes gleaming with excitement, he sidled his way into the queue where Gita stood and clasped his father's arm. Jamsu had something of his father in him, always lurked where numbers made him safe, rather than run off as his brothers and sisters had run off, to marry and struggle for a room or a space of their own.

He was telling his father what had happened when Shirin limped up and delivered her news.

Nodding grimly, Gita said, "Stay with us, Shirin, while I get the food."

He scooped his share into the family pail. Jamsu grabbed a handful of rice for himself.

"It was a dirty wizened man from Top Deck called Narayan Farhad," Jamsu said, gobbling. "He is one of the crooks who hangs about the shirt tails of . . ." He let his voice die.

"You did not go to Malti's rescue, shame on you!" Shirin said.

"Jamsu might have been killed," Gita said, as they pushed through the crowd and moved towards the family room.

"They're getting so strong on Top Deck," Jamsu said. "I hear all about it! We mustn't provoke them or they may attack. They say a regular army is forming round . . ."

Shirin snorted impatiently. "You great babe! Go ahead and name the man! It's Prahlad Patel whose very name you dare not mention, isn't it? Is he a god or something, for Siva's sake? You're afraid of him even from this distance, eh, aren't you?"

"Don't bully the lad," Gita said. Keeping the peace in his huge mixed family was a great responsibility, almost more than he could manage. As he turned into the family room, he said quietly to Jamsu and Shirin, "Malti was a favorite daughter of Shamim's, and now is gone from her. We will get our revenge against this Narayan Farhad. You and I will go this evening, Jamsu, to the holy man Vazifdar. He will even up matters for us, and then perhaps the great Patel will also be warned."

He looked thoughtfully down at his life-object. Tonight, he told himself, I must venture forth alone, and put my life in jeopardy for Shamim's sake.

Prahlad Patel's union has flourished and grown until now he rules all the Top Deck. His name is known and dreaded, we believe, three or four decks down. He is the strongest—yet in some ways curiously the most moderate—ruler in Total Environment at present.

Although he can be brutal, Patel seems inclined for peace. Of

*course, the bugging does not reveal everything; he may have plans
which he keeps secret, since he is fully aware that the bugging exists.
But we believe his interests lie in other directions than conquest.
He is only about nineteen, as we reckon years, but already gray-
haired, and the sight of him is said to freeze the muscles to silence
in the lips of his followers. I have watched him over the bugging
for many hours since I agreed to undertake this task.*

*Patel has one great advantage in Total Environment. He lives
on the Tenth Deck, at the top of the building. He can therefore be
invaded only from below and the Ninth Deck offers no strong
threats at present, being mainly oriented round an influential body
of holy men, of whom the most illustrious is one Vazifdar.*

*The staircases between decks are always trouble spots. No deck-
ruler was ever strong enough to withstand attack from above and
below. The staircases are also used by single troublemakers, thieves,
political fugitives, prostitutes, escaping slaves, hostages. Guards
can always be bribed, or favor their multitudinous relations, or
join the enemy for one reason or another. Patel, being on the Top
Deck, has only four weak points to watch for, rather than eight.*

Vazifdar was amazingly holy and amazingly influential. It was whispered that his life-object was the most intricate in all Environment,
but there was nobody who would lay claim to having set eyes upon
it. Because of his reputation, many people on Gita's deck—yes, and
from farther away—sought Vazifdar's help. A stream of men and
women moved always through his room, even when he was locked
in private meditation and far away from this world.

The holy man had a flat with a balcony that looked out onto mid-
deck. Many relations and disciples lived there with him, so that the
rooms had been elaborately and flimsily divided by screens. All day,
the youngest disciples twittered like birds upon the balconies as
Vazifdar held court, discussing among themselves the immense
wisdom of his sayings.

All the disciples, all the relations, loved Vazifdar. There had been
relations who did not love Vazifdar, but they had passed away in
their sleep. Gita himself was a distant relation of Vazifdar's and
came into the holy man's presence now with gifts of fresh water
and a long piece of synthetic cloth, enough to make a robe.

Vazifdar's brow and cheeks were painted with white to denote
his high caste. He received the gifts of cloth and water graciously,
smiling at Gita in such a way that Gita—and, behind him, Jamsu—
took heart.

Vazifdar was thirteen years old as the outside measured years.
He was sleekly fat, from eating much and moving little. His brown

body shone with oils; every morning, young women massaged and manipulated him.

He spoke very softly, husbanding his voice, so that he could scarcely be heard for the noise in the room.

"It is a sorrow to me that this woe has befallen your stepchild Malti," he said. "She was a good woman, although infertile."

"She was raped at a very early age, disrupting her womb, dear Vazifdar. You will know of the event. Her parents feared she would die. She could never bear issue. The evil shadowed her life. Now this second woe befalls her."

"I perceive that Malti's role in the world was merely to be a companion to her mother. Not all can afford to purchase who visit the bazaar."

> *There are bazaars on every floor, crowding down the corridors and balconies, and a chief one on every deck. The menfolk choose such places to meet and chatter even when they have nothing to trade. Like everywhere else, the bazaars are crowded with humanity, down to the smallest who can walk—and sometimes even those carry naked smaller brothers clamped tight to their backs.*
>
> *The bazaars are great centers for scandal. Here also are our largest screens. They glow behind their safety grills, beaming in special programs from outside; our outside world that must seem to have but faint reality as it dashes against the thick securing walls of Environment and percolates through to the screens. Below the screens, uncheckable and fecund life goes teeming on, with all its injury.*

Humbly, Gita on his knees said, "If you could restore Malti to her mother Shamim, who mourns her, you would reap all our gratitude, dear Vazifdar. Malti is too old for a man's bed, and on Top Deck all sorts of humiliations must await her."

Vazifdar shook his head with great dignity. "You know I cannot restore Malti, my kinsman. How many deeds can be ever undone? As long as we have slavery, so long must we bear to have the ones we love enslaved. You must cultivate a mystical and resigned view of life and beseech Shamim always to do the same."

"Shamim is more mystical in her ways than I, never asking much, always working, working, praying, praying. That is why she deserves better than this misery."

Nodding in approval of Shamim's behavior as thus revealed, Vazifdar said, "That is well. I know she is a good woman. In the future lie other events which may recompense her for this sad event."

Jamsu, who had managed to keep quiet behind his father until now, suddenly burst out, "Uncle Vazifdar, can you not punish Narayan Farhad for his sin in stealing poor Malti on the steps? Is he to be allowed to escape to Patel's deck, there to live with Malti and enjoy?"

"Sssh, son!" Gita looked in agitation to see if Jamsu's outburst had annoyed Vazifdar; but Vazifdar was smiling blandly.

"You must know, Jamsu, that we are all creatures of the Lord Siya, and without power. No, no, do not pout! I also am without power in his hands. To own one room is not to possess the whole mansion. But . . ."

It was a long, and heavy *but*. When Vazifdar's thick eyelids closed over his eyes, Gita trembled, for he recalled how, on previous occasions when he had visited his powerful kinsman, Vazifdar's eyelids had descended in this fashion while he deigned to think on a problem, as if he shut out all the external world with his own potent flesh.

"Narayan Farhad shall be troubled by more than his conscience." As he spoke, the pupils of his eyes appeared again, violet and black. They were looking beyond Gita, beyond the confines of his immediate surroundings. "Tonight he shall be troubled by evil dreams."

"The night-visions!" Gita and Jamsu exclaimed, in fear and excitement.

Now Vazifdar swiveled his magnificent head and looked directly at Gita, looked deep into his eyes. Gita was a small man; he saw himself as a small man within. He shrank still further under that irresistible scrutiny.

"Yes, the night-visions," the holy man said. "You know what that entails, Gita. You must go up to Top Deck and procure Narayan's life-object. Bring it back to me, and I promise Narayan shall suffer the night-visions tonight. Though he is sick, he shall be cured."

III

The women never cease their chatter as the lines of supplicants come and go before the holy men. Their marvelous resignation in that hateful prison! If they ever complain about more than the small circumstances of their lives, if they ever complain about the monstrous evil that has overtaken them all, I never heard of it. There is always the harmless talk, talk that relieves petty nervous anxieties, talk that relieves the almost noticed pressures on the brain. The women's talk practically drowns the noise of their children. But

*most of the time it is clear that Total Environment consists mainly
of children. That's why I want to see the experiment closed down;
the children would adapt to our world.*

*It is mainly on this fourth generation that the effects of the
population glut show. Whoever rules the decks, it is the babes, the
endless babes, tottering, laughing, staring, piddling, tumbling,
running, the endless babes to whom the Environment really belongs. And their mothers, for the most part, are women who—at
the same age and in a more favored part of the globe—would still
be virginally at school, many only just entering their teens.*

Narayan Farhad wrapped a blanket round himself and huddled in
his corner of the crowded room. Since it was almost time to sleep,
he had to take up his hired space before one of the loathed Dasguptas stole it. Narayan hated the Dasgupta family, its lickspittle men,
its shrill women, its turbulent children—the endless babes who
crawled, the bigger ones with nervous diseases who thieved and ran
and jeered at him. It was the vilest family on Top Deck, according to
Narayan's oft-repeated claims; he tolerated it only because he felt
himself to be vile.

He succeeded at nothing to which he turned his hand. Only an
hour ago, pushing through the crowds, he had lost his life-object
from his pocket—or else it had been stolen; but he dared not even
consider that possibility!

Even his desultory kidnapping business was a failure. This bitch
he had caught this morning—Malti. He had intended to rape her
before selling her, but had become too nervous once he had
dragged her in here, with a pair of young Dasguptas laughing at
him. Nor had he sold the woman well. Patel had beaten down his
price, and Narayan had not the guts to argue. Maybe he should
leave this deck and move down to one of the more chaotic ones.
The middle decks were always more chaotic. Six was having a slow
three-sided war even now, which should make Five a fruitful place,
with hordes of refugees to batten on.

. . . And what a fool to snatch so old a girl—practically an old
woman!

Through narrowed eyes, Narayan squatted in his corner, acid
flavors burning his mouth. Even if his mind would rest and allow
him to sleep, the Dasgupta mob was still too lively for any real
relaxation. That old Dasgupta, now—he was like a rat, totally without self-restraint, not a proper Hindu at all, doing the act openly
with his own daughters. There were many men like that in Total
Environment, men who had nothing else in life. Dirty swine! Lucky

dogs! Narayan's daughters had thrown him out many months ago when he tried it!

Over and over, his mind ran on his grievances. But he sat collectedly, prodding off with one bare foot the nasty little brats who crawled at him, and staring at the screen flickering on the wall behind its protective mesh.

He liked the screens, enjoyed viewing the madness of outside. What a world it was out there! All that heat, and the necessity for work, and the complication of life! The sheer bigness of the world—he couldn't stand that, would not want it under any circumstances.

He did not understand half he saw. After all, he was born here. His father might have been born outside, whoever his father was; but no legends from outside had come down to him: only the distortions in the general gossip, and the stuff on the screens. Now that he came to reflect, people didn't pay much attention to the screens any more. Even he didn't.

But he could not sleep. Blearily, he looked at images of cattle ploughing fields, fields cut into dice by the dirty grills before the screens. He had already gathered vaguely that this feature was about changes in the world today.

". . . are giving way to this . . ." said the commentator above the rumpus in the Dasgupta room. The children lived here like birds. Racks were stacked against the walls, and on these rickety contraptions the many little Dasguptas roosted.

". . . food factories automated against danger of infection . . ." Yak yak yak, then.

"Beef-tissue culture growing straight into plastic distribution packs . . ." Shots of some great interior place somewhere, with meat growing out of pipes, extruding itself into square packs, dripping with liquid, looking rather ugly. Was that the shape of cows now or something? Outside must be a hell of a scaring place, then! ". . . as new factory food at last spells hope for India's future in the . . ." Yak yak yak from the kids. Once, their sleep racks had been built across the screen; but one night the whole shaky edifice collapsed, and three children were injured. None killed, worse luck!

Patel should have paid more for that girl. Nothing was as good as it had been. Why, once on a time, they used to show sex films on the screens—really filthy stuff that got even Narayan excited. He was younger then. Really filthy stuff, he remembered, and pretty girls doing it. But it must be—oh, a long time since that was stopped. The screens were dull now. People gave up watching. Uneasily, Narayan slept, propped in the corner under his scruffy blanket. Eventually, the whole scruffy room slept.

> *The documentaries and other features piped into Environment*
> *are no longer specially made by UHDRE teams for internal con-*
> *sumption. When the U.N. made a major cut in UHDRE's annual*
> *subsidy, eight years ago, the private TV studio was one of the frills*
> *that had to be axed. Now we pipe in old programs bought off major*
> *networks. The hope is that they will keep the wretched prisoners in*
> *Environment in touch with the outside world, but this is clearly*
> *not happening. The degree of comprehension between inside and*
> *outside grows markedly less on both sides, on an exponential curve.*
> *As I see it, a great gulf of isolation is widening between the two*
> *environments, just as if they were sailing away from each other*
> *into different space-time continua. I wish I could think that the*
> *people in charge here—Crawley especially—not only grasped this*
> *fact but understood that it should be rectified immediately.*

Shamim could not sleep for grief.

Gita could not sleep for apprehension.

Jamsu could not sleep for excitement.

Vazifdar did not sleep.

Vazifdar shut his sacred self away in a cupboard, brought his lids
down over his eyes and began to construct, within the vast spaces
of his mind, a thought pattern corresponding to the matrix represented by Narayan Farhad's stolen life-object. When it was fully
conceived, Vazifdar began gently to inset a little evil into one edge
of the thought-pattern. . . .

Narayan slept. What roused him was the silence. It was the first
time total silence had ever come to Total Environment.

At first, he thought he would enjoy total silence. But it took on
such weight and substance. . . .

Clutching his blanket, he sat up. The room was empty, the screen
dark. Neither thing had ever happened before, could not happen!
And the silence! Dear Siva, some terrible monkey god had hammered that silence out in darkness and thrown it out like a shield
into the world, rolling over all things! There was a ringing quality
in the silence—a gong! No, no, not a gong! Footsteps!

It was footsteps, O Lord Siva, do not let it be footsteps!

Total Environment was empty. The legend was fulfilled that said
Total Environment would empty one day. All had departed except
for poor Narayan. And this thing of the footsteps was coming to
visit him in his defenseless corner. . . .

It was climbing up through the cellars of his existence. Soon it
would emerge.

Trembling convulsively, Narayan stood up, clutching the corner
of the blanket to his throat. He did not wish to face the thing.

Wildly, he thought, could he bear it best if it looked like a man or if it looked nothing like a man? It was Death for sure—but how would it look? Only Death—his heart fluttered!—only Death could arrive this way. . . .

His helplessness . . . Nowhere to hide! He opened his mouth, could not scream, clutched the blanket, felt that he was wetting himself as if he were a child again. Swiftly came the image—the infantile, round-bellied, cringing, puny, his mother black with fury, her great white teeth gritting as she smacked his face with all her might, spitting. . . . It was gone, and he faced the gong—like death again, alone in the great dark tower. In the arid air, vibrations of its presence.

He was shouting to it, demanding that it did not come.

But it came. It came with majestic sloth, like the heartbeats of a foetid slumber, came in the door, pushing darkness before it. It was like a human, but too big to be human.

And it wore Malti's face, that sickeningly innocent smile with which she had run up the steps. No! No, that was not it—oh, he fell down onto the wet floor; it was nothing like that woman, nothing at all. Cease, impossibilities! It was a man, his ebony skull shining, terrible and magnificent, stretching out, grasping, confident. Narayan struck out of his extremity and fell forward. Death was another indelible smack in the face.

One of the roosting Dasguptas blubbered and moaned as the man kicked him, woke for a moment, saw the screen still flickering meaninglessly and reassuringly, saw Narayan tremble under his blanket, tumbled back into sleep.

It was not till morning that they found it had been Narayan's last tremble.

I know I am supposed to be a detached observer. No emotions, no feelings. But scientific detachment is the attitude that has led to much of the inhumanity inherent in Environment. How do we, for all the bugging devices, hope to know what ghastly secret nightmares they undergo in there? Anyhow, I am relieved to hear you are flying over.

It is tomorrow I am due to go into Environment myself.

IV

The central offices of UHDRE were large and repulsive. At the time when they and the Total Environment tower had been built, the Indian Government would not have stood for anything else.

Poured cement and rough edges was what they wanted to see and what they got.

From a window in the office building, Thomas Dixit could see the indeterminate land in one direction, and the gigantic TE tower in the other, together with the shantytown that had grown between the foot of the tower and the other UHDRE buildings.

For a moment, he chose to ignore the Project Organizer behind him and gaze out at what he could see of the table-flat lands of the great Ganges delta.

He thought, It's as good a place as any for man to project his power fantasies. But you are a fool to get mixed up in all this, Thomas!

Even to himself, he was never just Tom.

I am being paid, well paid to do a specific job. Now I am letting wooly humanitarian ideas get in the way of action. Essentially, I am a very empty man. No center. Father Bengali, mother English, and live all my life in the States. I have excuses. . . . Other people accept them; why can't I?

Sighing, he dwelt on his own unsatisfactoriness. He did not really belong to the West, despite his long years there, and he certainly did not belong to India; in fact, he thought he rather disliked India. Maybe the best place for him was indeed the inside of the Environment tower.

He turned impatiently and said, "I'm ready to get going now, Peter."

Peter Crawley, the Special Project Organizer of UHDRE, was a rather austere Bostonian. He removed the horn-rimmed glasses from his nose and said, "Right! Although we have been through the drill many times, Thomas, I have to tell you this once again before we move. The entire—"

"Yes, yes, I know, Peter! You don't have to cover yourself. This entire organization might be closed down if I make a wrong move. Please take it as read."

Without indignation, Crawley said, "I was going to say that we are all rooting for you. We appreciate the risks you are taking. We shall be checking you everywhere you go in there through the bugging system."

"And whatever you see, you can't do a thing."

"Be fair; we have made arrangements to help!"

"I'm sorry, Peter." He liked Crawley and Crawley's decent reserve.

Crawley folded his spectacles with a snap, inserted them in a leather slipcase and stood up.

"The U.N., not to mention subsidiary organizations like the

WHO and the Indian government, have their knife into us, Thomas. They want to close us down and empty Environment. They will do so unless you can provide evidence that forms of extra-sensory perception are developing inside the Environment. Don't get yourself killed in there. The previous men we sent in behaved foolishly and never came out again." He raised an eyebrow and added dryly, "That sort of thing gets us a bad name, you know."

"Just as the blue movies did a while ago."

Crawley put his hands behind his back. "My predecessor here decided that immoral movies piped into Environment would help boost the birth rate there. Whether he was right or wrong, world opinion has changed since then as the specter of world famine has faded. We stopped the movies eight years ago, but they have long memories at the U.N., I fear. They allow emotionalism to impede scientific research."

"Do you never feel any sympathy for the thousands of people doomed to live out their brief lives in the tower?"

They looked speculatively at each other.

"You aren't on our side any more, Thomas, are you? You'd like your findings to be negative, wouldn't you, and have the U.N. close us down?"

Dixit uttered a laugh. "I'm not on anyone's *side*, Peter. I'm neutral. I'm going into Environment to look for the evidence of ESP that only direct contact may turn up. What else direct contact will turn up, neither of us can say as yet."

"But you think it will be misery. And you will emphasize that at the inquiry after your return."

"Peter—let's get on with it, shall we?" Momentarily, Dixit was granted a clear picture of the two of them standing in this room; he saw how their bodily attitudes contrasted. His attitudes were rather slovenly; he held himself rather slump-shouldered, he gesticulated to some extent (too much?); he was dressed in threadbare tunic and shorts, ready to pass muster as an inhabitant of Environment. Crawley, on the other hand, was very upright, stiff and smart in his movements, hardly ever gestured as he spoke; his dress was faultless.

And there was no need to be awed by or envious of Crawley. Crawley was encased in inhibition, afraid to feel, signaling his aridity to anyone who cared to look out from their own self-preoccupation. Crawley, moreover, feared for his job.

"Let's get on with it, as you say." He came from behind his desk. "But I'd be grateful if you would remember, Thomas, that the people in the tower are volunteers, or the descendants of volunteers.

"When UHDRE began, a quarter-century ago, back in the mid-nineteen-seventies, only volunteers were admitted to the Total Environment. Five hundred young married Indian couples were admitted, plus whatever children they had. The tower was a refuge then, free from famine, immune from all disease. They were glad, heartily glad, to get in, glad of all that Environment provided and still provides. Those who didn't qualify rioted. We have to remember that.

"India was a different place in 1975. It had lost hope. One crisis after another, one famine after another, crops dying, people starving, and yet the population spiraling up by a million every month.

"But today, thank God, that picture has largely changed. Synthetic foods have licked the problem; we don't need the grudging land any more. And at last the Hindus and Muslims have got the birth control idea into their heads. It's only *now*, when a little humanity is seeping back into this death-bowl of a subcontinent, that the UN dares complain about the inhumanity of UHDRE."

Dixit said nothing. He felt that this potted history was simply angled towards Crawley's self-justification; the ideas it represented were real enough, heaven knew, but they had meaning for Crawley only in terms of his own existence. Dixit felt pity and impatience as Crawley went on with his narration.

"Our aim here must be unswervingly the same as it was from the start. We have evidence that nervous disorders of a special kind produce extra-sensory perceptions—telepathy and the rest, and maybe kinds of ESP we do not yet recognize. High-density populations with reasonable nutritional standards develop particular nervous instabilities which may be akin to ESP spectra.

"The Ultra-High Density Research Establishment was set up to intensify the likelihood of ESP developing. Don't forget that. The people in Environment are supposed to have some ESP; that's the whole point of the operation, right? Sure, it is not humanitarian. We know that. But that is not your concern. You have to go in and find evidence of ESP, something that doesn't show over the bugging. Then UHDRE will be able to continue."

Dixit prepared to leave. "If it hasn't shown up in quarter of a century—"

"It's in there! I know it's in there! The failure's in the bugging system. I feel it coming through the screens at me—some mystery we need to get our hands on! If only I could prove it! If only I could get in there myself!"

Interesting, Dixit thought. You'd have to be some sort of a voyeur to hold Crawley's job, forever spying on the wretched people.

"Too bad you have a white skin, eh?" he said lightly. He walked towards the door. It swung open, and he passed into the corridor. Crawley ran after him and thrust out a hand. "I know how you feel, Thomas. I'm not just a stuffed shirt, you know, not entirely void of sympathy. Sorry if I was needling you. I didn't intend to do so."

Dixit dropped his gaze. "I should be the one to apologize, Peter. If there's anything unusual going on in the tower, I'll find it, never worry!"

They shook hands, without wholly being able to meet each other's eyes.

V

Leaving the office block, Dixit walked alone through the sunshine toward the looming tower that housed Total Environment. The concrete walk was hot and dusty underfoot. The sun was the one good thing that India had, he thought: that burning beautiful sun, the real ruler of India, whatever petty tyrants came and went.

The sun blazed down on the tower; only inside did it not shine.

The uncompromising outlines of the tower were blurred by pipes, ducts and shafts that ran up and down its exterior. It was a building built for looking into, not out of. Some time ago, in the bad years, the welter of visual records gleaned from Environment used to be edited and beamed out on global networks every evening; but all that had been stopped as conditions inside Environment deteriorated, and public opinion in the democracies, who were subsidizing the grandiose experiment, turned against the exploitation of human material.

A monitoring station stood by the tower walls. From here, a constant survey on the interior was kept. Facing the station were the jumbles of merchants' stalls, springing up to cater for tourists, who persisted even now that the tourist trade was discouraged. Two security guards stepped forward and escorted Dixit to the base of the tower. With ceremony, he entered the shade of the entry elevator. As he closed the door, germicides sprayed him, insuring that he entered Environment without harboring dangerous micro-organisms.

The elevator carried him up to the top deck; this plan had been settled some while ago. The elevator was equipped with double steel doors. As it came to rest, a circuit opened, and a screen showed him what was happening on the other side of the doors. He emerged from a dummy air-conditioning unit, behind a wide pillar. He was in Patel's domain.

The awful weight of human overcrowding hit Dixit with its full stink and noise. He sat down at the base of the pillar and let his senses adjust. And he thought, I was the wrong one to send; I've always had this inner core of pity for the sufferings of humanity; I could never be impartial; I've got to see that this terrible experiment is stopped.

He was at one end of a long balcony onto which many doors opened; a ramp led down at the other end. All the doorways gaped, although some were covered by rugs. Most of the doors had been taken off their hinges to serve as partitions along the balcony itself, partitioning off overspill families. Children ran everywhere, their tinkling voices and cries the dominant note in the hubbub. Glancing over the balcony, Dixit took in a dreadful scene of swarming multitudes, the anonymity of congestion; to sorrow for humanity was not to love its prodigality. Dixit had seen this panorama many times over the bugging system; he knew all the staggering figures—1,500 people in here to begin with, and by now some 75,000 people, a large proportion of them under four years of age. But pictures and figures were pale abstracts beside the reality they were intended to represent.

The kids drove him into action at last by playfully hurling dirt at him. Dixit moved slowly along, carrying himself tight and cringing in the manner of the crowd about him, features rigid, elbows tucked in to the ribs. *Mutatis mutandis*, it was Crawley's inhibited attitude. Even the children ran between the legs of their elders in that guarded way. As soon as he had left the shelter of his pillar, he was caught in a stream of chattering people, all jostling between the rooms and the stalls of the balcony. They moved very slowly.

Among the crowd were hawkers, and salesmen pressed their wares from the pitiful balcony hovels. Dixit tried to conceal his curiosity. Over the bugging he had had only distant views of the merchandise offered for sale. Here were the strange models that had caught his attention when he was first appointed to the UH-DRE project. A man with orange goat eyes, in fact probably no more than thirteen years of age, but here a hardened veteran, was at Dixit's elbow. As Dixit stared at him, momentarily suspicious he was being watched, the goat-eyed man merged into the crowd; and, to hide his face, Dixit turned to the nearest salesman.

In only a moment, he was eagerly examining the wares, forgetting how vulnerable was his situation.

All the strange models were extremely small. This Dixit attributed to shortage of materials—wrongly, as it later transpired. The biggest model the salesman possessed stood no more than two inches high. It was made, nevertheless, of a diversity of materials, in which many sorts of plastics featured. Some models were simple, and appeared to be little more than an elaborate *tughra* or monogram, which might have been intended for an elaborate piece of costume jewelry; others, as one peered among their interstices, seemed to afford a glimpse of another dimension; all possessed eye-teasing properties.

The merchant was pressing Dixit to buy. He referred to the elaborate models as "life-objects." Noticing that one in particular attracted his potential customer, he lifted it delicately and held it up, a miracle of craftsmanship, perplexing, *outre*, giving Dixit somehow as much pain as pleasure. He named the price.

Although Dixit was primed with money, he automatically shook his head. "Too expensive."

"See, master, I show you how this life-object works!" The man fished beneath his scrap of loincloth and produced a small perforated silver box. Flipping it open, he produced a live wood-louse and slipped it under a hinged part of the model. The insect, in its struggles, activated a tiny wheel; the interior of the model began to rotate, some sets of minute planes turning in counterpoint to others.

"This life-object belonged to a very religious man, master."

In his fascination, Dixit said, "Are they all powered?"

"No, master, only special ones. This was perfect model from Dalcush Bancholi, last generation master all the way from Third Deck, very very fine and masterful workmanship of first quality. I have also still better one worked by a body louse, if you care to see."

By reflex, Dixit said, "Your prices are too high."

He absolved himself from the argument that brewed, slipping away through the crowd with the merchant calling after him. Other merchants shouted to him, sensing his interest in their wares. He saw some beautiful work, all on the tiniest scale and not only life-objects but amazing little watches with millisecond hands as well as second hands; in some cases, the millisecond was the largest hand; in some, the hour hand was missing or was supplemented by a day hand; and the watches took many extraordinary shapes, tetrakishexahedrons and other elaborate forms, until their format merged with that of the life-objects.

Dixit thought approvingly: the clock and watch industry fulfills a human need for exercising elaborate skill and accuracy, while at the same time requiring a minimum of materials. These people of Total Environment are the world's greatest craftsmen. Bent over

one curious watch that involved a color change, he became suddenly
aware of danger. Glancing over his shoulder, he saw the man with
the unpleasant orange eyes about to strike him. Dixit dodged without being able to avoid the blow. As it caught him on the side of
his neck, he stumbled and fell under the milling feet.

VI

Afterwards, Dixit could hardly say that he had been totally unconscious. He was aware of hands dragging him, of being partly carried, of the sound of many voices, of the name "Patel" repeated. . . .
And when he came fully to his senses, he was lying in a cramped
room, with a guard in a scruffy turban standing by the door. His
first hazy thought was that the room was no more than a small
ship's cabin; then he realized that, by indigenous standards, this
was a large room for only one person.

He was a prisoner in Total Environment.

A kind of self-mocking fear entered him; he had almost expected
the blow, he realized; and he looked eagerly about for the bug-eye
that would reassure him his UHDRE friends outside were aware
of his predicament. There was no sign of the bug-eye. He was not
long in working out why; this room had been partitioned out of a
larger one, and the bugging system was evidently shut in the other
half—whether deliberately or accidentally, he had no way of knowing.

The guard had bobbed out of sight. Sounds of whispering came
from beyond the doorway. Dixit felt the pressure of many people
there. Then a woman came in and closed the door. She walked
cringingly and carried a brass cup of water.

Although her face was lined, it was possible to see that she had
once been beautiful and perhaps proud. Now her whole attitude
expressed the defeat of her life. And this woman might be no more
than eighteen! One of the terrifying features of Environment was
the way, right from the start, confinement had speeded life-pro-
cesses and abridged life.

Involuntarily, Dixit flinched away from the woman.

She almost smiled. "Do not fear me, sir. I am almost as much a
prisoner as you are. Equally, do not think that by knocking me
down you can escape. I promise you, there are fifty people outside
the door, all eager to impress Prahlad Patel by catching you, should
you try to get away."

So I'm in Patel's clutches, he thought. Aloud he said, "I will offer you no harm. I want to see Patel. If you are captive, tell me your name, and perhaps I can help you."

As she offered him the cup and he drank, she said, shyly, "I do not complain, for my fate might have been much worse than it is. Please do not agitate Patel about me, or he may throw me out of his household. My name is Malti."

"Perhaps I may be able to help you, and all your tribe, soon. You are all in a form of captivity here, the great Patel included, and it is from that I hope to deliver you."

Then he saw fear in her eyes.

"You really are a spy from outside!" she breathed. "But we do not want our poor little world invaded! You have so much—leave us our little!" She shrank away and slipped through the door, leaving Dixit with a melancholy impression of her eyes, so burdened in their shrunken gaze.

The babel continued outside the door. Although he still felt sick, he propped himself up and let his thoughts run on. "You have so much—leave us our little. . . ." All their values had been perverted. Poor things, they could know neither the smallness of their own world nor the magnitude of the world outside. This—this dung-heap had become to them all there was of beauty and value.

Two guards came for him, mere boys. He could have knocked their heads together, but compassion moved him. They led him through a room full of excited people; beyond their glaring faces, the screen flickered pallidly behind its mesh; Dixit saw how faint the image of outside was.

He was taken into another partitioned room. Two men were talking.

The scene struck Dixit with peculiar force, and not merely because he was at a disadvantage.

It was an alien scene. The impoverishment of even the richest furnishings, the clipped and bastardized variety of Hindi that was being talked, reinforced the impression of strangeness. And the charge of Patel's character filled the room.

There could be no doubt who was Patel. The plump cringing fellow, wringing his hands and protesting, was not Patel. Patel was the stocky white-haired man with the heavy lower lip and high forehead. Dixit had seen him in this very room over the bugging system. But to stand captive awaiting his attention was an experience of an entirely different order. Dixit tried to analyze the first fresh impact Patel had on him, but it was elusive.

It was difficult to realize that, as the outside measured years,

Patel could not be much more than nineteen or twenty years of age. Time was impacted here, jellified under the psychic pressures of Total Environment. Like the hieroglyphics of that new relativity, detailed plans of the Environment hung large on one wall of this room, while figures and names were chalked over the others. The room was the nerve center of Top Deck.

He knew something about Patel from the UHDRE records. Patel had come up here from the Seventh Deck. By guile as well as force, he had become ruler of Top Deck at an early age. He had surprised UHDRE observers by abstaining from the usual forays of conquest into other floors.

Patel was saying to the cringing man, "Be silent! You try to obscure the truth with argument. You have heard the witnesses against you. During your period of watch on the stairs, you were bribed by a man from Ninth Deck and you let him through here."

"Only for a mere seventeen minutes, Sir Patel!!"

"I am aware that such things happen every day, wretched Raital. But this fellow you let through stole the life-object belonging to Narayan Farhad and, in consequence, Narayan Farhad died in his sleep last night. Narayan was no more important than you are, but he was useful to me, and it is in order that he be revenged."

"Anything that you say, Sir Patel!"

"Be silent, wretched Raital!" Patel watched Raital with interest as he spoke. And he spoke in a firm reflective voice that impressed Dixit more than shouting would have done.

"You shall revenge Narayan, Raital, because you caused his death. You will leave here now. You will not be punished. You will go, and you will steal the life-object belonging to that fellow from whom you accepted the bribe. You will bring that life-object to me. You have one day to do so. Otherwise, my assassins will find you wherever you hide, be it even down on Deck One."

"Oh, yes, indeed, Sir Patel, all men know—" Raital was bent almost double as he uttered some face-saving formula. He turned and scurried away as Patel dismissed him.

Strength, thought Dixit. Strength, and also cunning. That is what Patel radiates. An elaborate and cutting subtlety. The phrase pleased him, seeming to represent something actual that he had detected in Patel's makeup. An elaborate and cutting subtlety.

Clearly, it was part of Patel's design that Dixit should witness this demonstration of his methods.

Patel turned away, folded his arms, and contemplated a blank piece of wall at close range. He stood motionless. The guards held Dixit still, but not so still as Patel held himself.

This tableau was maintained for several minutes. Dixit found himself losing track of the normal passage of time. Patel's habit of turning to stare at the wall—and it did not belong to Patel alone—was an uncanny one that Dixit had watched several times over the bugging system. It was that habit, he thought, which might have given Crawley the notion that ESP was rampant in the tower.

It was curious to think of Crawley here. Although Crawley might at this moment be surveying Dixit's face on a monitor, Crawley was now no more than an hypothesis.

Malti broke the tableau. She entered the room with a damp cloth on a tray, to stand waiting patiently for Patel to notice her. He broke away at last from his motionless survey of the wall, gesturing abruptly to the guards to leave. He took no notice of Dixit, sitting in a chair, letting Malti drape the damp cloth round his neck; the cloth had a fragrant smell to it.

"The towel is not cool enough, Malti, or damp enough. You will attend me properly at my morning session, or you will lose this easy job."

He swung his gaze, which was suddenly black and searching, onto Dixit to say, "Well, spy, you know I am Lord here. Do you wonder why I tolerate old women like this about me when I could have girls young and lovely to fawn on me?"

Dixit said nothing, and the self-styled Lord continued, "Young girls would merely remind me by contrast of my advanced years. But this old bag—whom I bought only yesterday—this old bag is only just my junior and makes me look good in contrast. You see, we are masters of philosophy in here, in this prison-universe; we cannot be masters of material wealth like you people outside!"

Again Dixit said nothing, disgusted by the man's implied attitude to women.

A swinging blow caught him unprepared in the stomach. He cried and dropped suddenly to the floor.

"Get up, spy!" Patel said. He had moved extraordinarily fast. He sat back again in his chair, letting Malti massage his neck muscles.

VII

As Dixit staggered to his feet, Patel said, "You don't deny you are from outside?"

"I did not attempt to deny it. I came from outside to speak to you."

"You say nothing here until you are ordered to speak. Your people—you outsiders—you have sent in several spies to us in the last few months. Why?"

Still feeling sick from the blow, Dixit said, "You should realize that we are your friends rather than your enemies, and our men emissaries rather than spies."

"Pah! You are a breed of spies! Don't you sit and spy on us from every room? You live in a funny little dull world out there, don't you? So interested in us that you can think of nothing else! Keep working, Malti! Little spy, you know what happened to all the other spies your spying people sent in?"

"They died," Dixit said.

"Exactly. They died. But you are the first to be sent to Patel's deck. What different thing to death do you expect here?"

"Another death will make my superiors very tired, Patel. You may have the power of life and death over me; they have the same over you, and over all in this world of yours. Do you want a demonstration?"

Rising, flinging the towel off, Patel said, "Give me your demonstration!"

Must do, Dixit thought. Staring in Patel's eyes, he raised his right hand above his head and gestured with his thumb. Pray they are watching—and thank God this bit of partitioned room is the bit with the bugging system!

Tensely, Patel stared, balanced on his toes. Behind his shoulder, Malti also stared. Nothing happened.

Then a sort of shudder ran through Environment. It became slowly audible as a mixture of groan and cry. Its cause became apparent in this less crowded room when the air began to grow hot and foul. So Dixit's signal had got through; Crawley had him under survey, and the air-conditioning plant was pumping in hot carbon-dioxide through the respiratory system.

"You see? We control the very air you breathe!" Dixit said. He dropped his arm, and slowly the air returned to normal, although it was at least an hour before the fright died down in the passages.

Whatever the demonstration had done to Patel, he showed nothing. Instead, he said, "You control the air. Very well. But you do not control the will to turn it off permanently—and so you do not control the air. Your threat is an empty one, spy! For some reason, you need us to live. We have a mystery, don't we?"

"There is no reason why I should be anything but honest with you, Patel. Your special environment must have bred special talents in you. We are interested in those talents; but no more than interested."

Patel came closer and inspected Dixit's face minutely, rather as he had recently inspected the blank wall. Strange angers churned inside him; his neck and throat turned a dark mottled color. Finally he spoke.

"We are the center of your outside world, aren't we? We know that you watch us all the time. We know that you are much more than 'interested'! For you, we here are somehow a matter of life and death, aren't we?"

This was more than Dixit had expected.

"Four generations, Patel, four generations have been incarcerated in Environment." His voice trembled. "Four generations, and, despite our best intentions, you are losing touch with reality. You live in one relatively small building on a sizeable planet. Clearly, you can only be of limited interest to the world at large."

"Malti!" Patel turned to the slave girl. "Which is the greater, the outer world or ours?"

She looked confused, hesitated by the door as if longing to escape. "The outside world was great, master, but then it gave birth to us, and we have grown and are growing and are gaining strength. The child now is almost the size of the father. So my step-father's son Jamsu says, and he is a clever one."

Patel turned to stare at Dixit, a haughty expression on his face. He made no comment, as if the words of an ignorant girl were sufficient to prove his point.

"All that you and the girl say only emphasizes to me how much you need help, Patel. The world outside is a great and thriving place; you must allow it to give you assistance through me. We are not your enemies."

Again the choleric anger was there, powering Patel's every word.

"What else are you, spy? Your life is so vile and pointless out there, is it not? You envy us because we are superseding you! Our people—we may be poor, you may think of us as in your power, but we rule our own universe. And that universe is expanding and falling under our control more every day. Why, our explorers have gone into the world of the ultrasmall. We discover new environments, new ways of living. By your terms, we are scientific peasants, perhaps, but I fancy we have ways of knowing the trade routes of the blood and the eternities of cell-change that you cannot comprehend. You think of us all as captives, eh? Yet you are captive to the necessity of supplying our air and our food and water; we are free. We are poor, yet you covet our riches. We are spied on all the time, yet we are secret. You need to understand us, yet we have no need to understand you. You are in *our* power, spy!"

"Certainly not in one vital respect, Patel. Both you and we are ruled by historical necessity. This Environment was set up twenty-five of our years ago. Changes have taken place not only in here but outside as well. The nations of the world are no longer prepared to finance this project. It is going to be closed down entirely, and you are going to have to live outside. Or, if you don't want that, you'd better cooperate with us and persuade the leaders of the other decks to cooperate."

Would threats work with Patel? His hooded and oblique gaze bit into Dixit like a hook.

After a deadly pause, he clapped his hands once. Two guards immediately appeared.

"Take the spy away," said Patel. Then he turned his back.

A clever man, Dixit thought. He sat alone in the cell and meditated.

It seemed as if a battle of wits might develop between him and Patel. Well, he was prepared. He trusted to his first impression, that Patel was a man of cutting subtlety. He could not be taken to mean all that he said.

Dixit's mind worked back over their conversation. The mystery of the life-objects had been dangled before him. And Patel had taken care to belittle the outside world: "funny dull little world," he had called it. He had made Malti advance her primitive view that Environment was growing, and that had fitted in very well with his brand of boasting. Which led to the deduction that he had known her views beforehand; yet he had bought her only yesterday. Why should a busy man, a leader, bother to question an ignorant slave about her views of the outside world unless he were starved for information of that world, obsessed with it.

Yes, Dixit nodded to himself. Patel was obsessed with outside and tried to hide that obsession; but several small contradictions in his talk had revealed it.

Of course, it might be that Malti was so generally representative of the thousands in Environment that her misinformed ideas could be taken for granted. It was as well, as yet, not to be too certain that he was beginning to understand Patel.

Part of Patel's speech made sense even superficially. These poor devils were exploring the world of the ultra-small. It was the only landscape left for them to map. They were human, and still burning inside them was that unquenchable human urge to open new frontiers.

So they knew some inward things. Quite, possibly, as Crawley anticipated, they possessed a system of ESP upon which some reliance might be placed, unlike the wildly fluctuating telepathic radiations which circulated in the outside world.

He felt confident, fully engaged. There was much to understand here. The bugging system, elaborate and over-used, was shown to be a complete failure; the watchers had stayed external to their problem; it remained their problem, not their life. What was needed was a whole team to come and live here, perhaps a team on every deck, anthropologists and so on. Since that was impossible, then clearly the people of Environment must be released from their captivity; those that were unwilling to go far afield should be settled in new villages on the Ganges plain, under the wide sky. And there, as they adapted to the real world, observers could live among them, learning with humility of the gifts that had been acquired at such cost within the thick walls of the Total Environment tower.

As Dixit sat in meditation, a guard brought a meal in to him. He ate thankfully and renewed his thinking.

From the little he had already experienced—the ghastly pressures on living space, the slavery, the aberrant modes of thought into which the people were being forced, the harshness of the petty rulers—he was confirmed in his view that this experiment in anything like its present form must be closed down at once. The U.N. needed the excuse of his adverse report before they moved; they should have it when he got out. And if he worded the report carefully, stressing that these people had many talents to offer, then he might also satisfy Crawley and his like. He had it in his power to satisfy all parties, when he got out. All he had to do was get out.

The guard came back to collect his empty bowl.

"When is Patel going to speak with me again?"

The guard said, "When he sends for you to have you silenced for ever."

Dixit stopped composing his report and thought about that instead.

VIII

Much time elapsed before Dixit was visited again, and then it was only the self-effacing Malti who appeared, bringing him a cup of water.

"I want to talk to you," Dixit said urgently.

"No, no, I cannot talk! He will beat me. It is the time when we sleep, when the old die. You should sleep now, and Patel will see you in the morning."

He tried to touch her hand, but she withdrew.

"You are a kind girl, Malti. You suffer in Patel's household."

"He has many women, many servants. I am not alone."

"Can you not escape back to your family?"

She looked at the floor evasively. "It would bring trouble to my family. Slavery is the lot of many women. It is the way of the world."

"It is not the way of the world I come from!"

Her eyes flashed. "Your world is of no interest to us!

Dixit thought after she had gone, She is afraid of our world. Rightly.

He slept little during the night. Even barricaded inside Patel's fortress, he could still hear the noises of Environment: not only the voices, almost never silent, but the gurgle and sob of pipes in the walls. In the morning, he was taken into a larger room where Patel was issuing commands for the day to a succession of subordinates.

Confined to a corner, Dixit followed everything with interest. His interest grew when the unfortunate guard Raital appeared. He bounded in and waited for Patel to strike him. Instead, Patel kicked him.

"You have performed as I ordered yesterday?"

Raital began at once to cry and wring his hands. "Sir Patel, I have performed as well as and better than you demanded, incurring great suffering and having myself beaten downstairs where the people of Ninth Deck discovered me marauding. You must invade them, Sir, and teach them a lesson that in their insolence they so dare to mock your faithful guards who only do those things—"

"Silence, you dog-devourer! Do you bring back that item which I demanded of you yesterday?"

The wretched guard brought from the pocket of his tattered tunic a small object, which he held out to Patel.

"Of course I obey, Sir Patel. To keep this object safe when the people caught me, I swallow it whole, sir, into the stomach for safe keeping, so that they would not know what I am about. Then my wife gives me sharp medicine so that I vomit it safely again to deliver to you."

"Put the filthy thing down on that shelf there! You think I wish to touch it when it has been in your worm-infested belly, slave?"

The guard did as he was bid and abased himself.

"You are sure it is the life-object of the man who stole Narayan Farhad's life-object, and nobody else's?"

"Oh, indeed, Sir Patel! It belongs to a man called Gita the very very same who stole Narayan's life object, and tonight you will see he will die of night-visions!"

"Get out!" Patel managed to catch Raital's buttocks with a swift kick as the guard scampered from the room

A queue of people stood waiting to speak with him, to supplicate and advise. Patel sat and interviewed them, in the main showing a better humor than he had shown his luckless guard. For Dixit, this scene had a curious interest; he had watched Patel's morning audience more than once, standing by Crawley's side in the UHDRE monitoring station; now he was a prisoner waiting uncomfortably in the corner of the room, and the whole atmosphere was changed. He felt the extraordinary intensity of these people's lives, the emotions compressed, everything vivid. Patel himself wept several times as some tale of hardship was unfolded to him. There was no privacy. Everyone stood round him, listening to everything. Short the lives might be; but those annihilating spaces that stretch through ordinary lives, the spaces through which one glimpses uncomfortable glooms and larger poverties, if not presences more sour and sinister, seemed here to have been eradicated. The Total Environment had brought its peoples total involvement. Whatever befell them, they were united, as were bees in a hive.

Finally, a break was called. The unfortunates who had not gained Patel's ear were turned away; Malti was summoned and administered the damp-towel treatment to Patel. Later, he sent her off and ate a frugal meal. Only when he had finished it and sat momentarily in meditation, did he turn his brooding attention to Dixit.

He indicated that Dixit was to fetch down the object Raital had placed on a shelf. Dixit did so and put the object before Patel. Staring at it with interest, he saw it was an elaborate little model, similar to the ones for sale on the balcony.

"Observe it well," Patel said. "It is the life-object of a man. You have these"—he gestured vaguely—"outside?"

"No."

"You know what they are?"

"No."

"In this world of ours, Mr. Dixit, we have many holy men. I have a holy man here under my protection. On the deck below is one very famous holy man, Vazifdariji. These men have many powers. Tonight, I shall give my holy man this life-object, and with it he will be able to enter the being of the man to whom it belongs, for good or ill, and in this case for ill, to revenge a death with a death."

Dixit stared at the little object, a three-dimensional maze constructed of silver and plastic strands, trying to comprehend what Patel was saying.

"This is a sort of key to its owner's mind?"

"No, no, not a key, and not to his mind. It is a—well, we do not have a scientific word for it, and our word would mean nothing to you, so I cannot say what. It is, let us say, a replica, a substitute for the man's being. Not his mind, his being. In this case, a man called Gita. You are very interested, aren't you?"

"Everyone here has one of these?"

"Down to the very poorest and even the older children. A sage works in conjunction with a smith to produce each individual life-object."

"But they can be stolen and then an ill-intentioned holy man can use them to kill the owner. So why make them? I don't understand."

Smiling, Patel made a small movement of impatience. "What you discover of yourself, you record. That is how these things are made. They are not trinkets; they are a man's record of his discovery of himself."

Dixit shook his head. "If they are so personal, why are so many sold by street traders as trinkets?"

"Men die. Then their life-objects have no value, except as trinkets. They are also popularly believed to bestow . . . well, personality-value. There also exist large numbers of forgeries, which people buy because they like to have them, simply as decorations."

After a moment, Dixit said, "So they are innocent things, but you take them and use them for evil ends."

"I use them to keep a power balance. A man of mine called Narayan was silenced by Gita of Ninth Deck. Never mind why. So tonight I silence Gita to keep the balance."

He stopped and looked closely at Dixit, so that the latter received a blast of that enigmatic personality. He opened his hand and said, still observing Dixit, "Death sits in my palm, Mr. Dixit. Tonight I shall have you silenced also, by what you may consider more ordinary methods."

Clenching his hands tightly together, Dixit said. "You tell me about the life-objects, and yet you claim you are going to kill me."

Patel pointed up to one corner of his room. "There are eyes and ears there, while your ever-hungry spying friends suck up the facts of this world. You see, I can tell them—I can tell them so much and they can never comprehend our life. All the important things can never be said, so they can never learn. But they can see you die tonight, and that they will comprehend. Perhaps then they will cease to send spies in here."

He clapped his hands once for the guards. They came forward and led Dixit away. As he went back to his cell, he heard Patel shouting for Malti.

IX

The hours passed in steady gloom. The U.N., the UHDRE, would not rescue him; the Environment charter permitted intervention by only one outsider at a time. Dixit could hear, feel, the vast throbbing life of the place going on about him and was shaken by it.

He tried to think about the life-objects. Presumably Crawley had overheard the last conversation, and would know that the holy men, as Patel called them, had the power to kill at a distance. There was the ESP evidence Crawley sought: telecide, or whatever you called it. And the knowledge helped nobody, as Patel himself observed. It had long been known that African witch doctors possessed similar talents, to lay a spell on a man and kill him at a distance; but how they did it had never been established; nor, indeed, had the fact ever been properly assimilated by the West, eager though the West was for new methods of killing. There were things one civilization could not learn from another; the whole business of life-objects, Dixit perceived, was going to be such a matter: endlessly fascinating, entirely insoluble. . . .

He thought, returning to his cell, and told himself: Patel still puzzles me. But it is no use hanging about here being puzzled. Here I sit, waiting for a knife in the guts. It must be night now. I've got to get out of here.

There was no way out of the room. He paced restlessly up and down. They brought him no meal, which was ominous.

A long while later, the door was unlocked and opened.

It was Malti. She lifted one finger as a caution to silence, and closed the door behind her.

"It's time for me . . . ?" Dixit asked.

She came quickly over to him, not touching him, staring at him.

Though she was an ugly and despondent woman, beauty lay in her time-haunted eyes.

"I can help you escape, Dixit. Patel sleeps now, and I have an understanding with the guards here. Understandings have been reached to smuggle you down to my own deck, where perhaps you can get back to the outside where you belong. This place is full of arrangements. But you must be quick. Are you ready?"

"He'll kill you when he finds out!"

She shrugged. "He may not. I think perhaps he likes me. Prahlad Patel is not inhuman, whatever you think of him."

"No? But he plans to murder someone else tonight. He has acquired some poor fellow's life-object and plans to have his holy man kill him with night-visions, whatever they are."

She said, "People have to die. You are going to be lucky. You will not die, not this night."

"If you take that fatalistic view, why help me?"

He saw a flash of defiance in her eyes. "Because you must take a message outside for me."

"Outside? To whom?"

"To everyone there, everyone who greedily spies on us here and would spoil this world. Tell them to go away and leave us and let us make our own world. Forget us! That is my message! Take it! Deliver it with all the strength you have! This is our world—not yours!"

Her vehemence, her ignorance, silenced him. She led him from the room. There were guards on the outer door. They stood rigid with their eyes closed, seeing no evil, and she slid between them, leading Dixit, and opening the door. They hurried outside, onto the balcony, which was still as crowded as ever, people sprawling everywhere in the disconsolate gestures of public sleep. With the noise and chaos and animation of daytime fled, Total Environment stood fully revealed for the echoing prison it was.

As Malti turned to go, Dixit grasped her wrist.

"I must return," she said. "Get quickly to the steps down to Ninth Deck, the near steps. That's three flights to go down, the inter-deck flight guarded. They will let you through; they expect you."

"Malti, I must try to help this other man who is to die. Do you happen to know someone called Gita?"

She gasped and clung to him. "Gita?"

"Gita of the Ninth Deck. Patel has Gita's life-object, and he is to die tonight."

"Gita is my step-father, my mother's third husband. A good man! Oh, he must not die, for my mother's sake!"

"He's to die tonight. Malti, I can help you and Gita. I appreciate how you feel about outside, but you are mistaken. You would be free in a way you cannot understand! Take me to Gita, and we'll all three get out together."

Conflicting emotions chased all over her face. "You are sure Gita is to die?"

"Come and check with him to see if his life-object has gone!"

Without waiting for her to make a decision—in fact she looked as if she were just about to bolt back into Patel's quarters—Dixit took hold of her and forced her along the balcony, picking his way through the piles of sleepers.

Ramps ran down from balcony to balcony in long zigzags. For all its multitudes of people—even the ramps had been taken up as dosses by whole swarms of urchins—Total Environment seemed much larger than it had when one looked in from the monitoring room. He kept peering back to see if they were being followed; it seemed to him unlikely that he would be able to get away.

But they had now reached the stairs leading down to Deck Nine. Oh, well, he thought, corruption he could believe in; it was the universal oriental system whereby the small man contrived to live under oppression. As soon as the guards saw him and Malti, they all stood and closed their eyes. Among them was the wretched Raital, who hurriedly clapped palms over eyes as they approached.

"I must go back to Patel," Malti gasped.

"Why? You know he will kill you," Dixit said. He kept tight hold of her thin wrist. "All these witnesses to the way you led me to safety—you can't believe he will not discover what you are doing. Let's get to Gita quickly."

He hustled her down the stairs. There were Deck Nine guards at the bottom. They smiled and saluted Malti and let her by. As if resigned now to doing what Dixit wished, she led him forward, and they picked their way down a ramp to a lower floor. The squalor and confusion were greater here than they had been above, the slumbers more broken. This was a deck without a strong leader, and it showed.

He must have seen just such a picture as this over the bugging, in the air-conditioned comfort of the UHDRE offices, and remained comparatively unmoved. You had to be among it to feel it. Then you caught also the aroma of Environment. It was pungent in the extreme.

As they moved slowly down among the huddled figures abased by fatigue, he saw that a corpse burned slowly on a wood pile. It was the corpse of a child. Smoke rose from it in a leisurely coil until it was sucked into a wall vent. A mother squatted by the body, her face shielded by one skeletal hand. "It is the time when the old die," Malti had said of the previous night; and the young had to answer that same call.

This was the Indian way of facing the inhumanity of Environment: with their age-old acceptance of suffering. Had one of the white races been shut in here to breed to intolerable numbers, they would have met the situation with a general massacre. Dixit, a half-caste, would not permit himself to judge which response he most respected.

Malti kept her gaze fixed on the worn concrete underfoot as they moved down the ramp past the corpse. At the bottom, she led him forward again without a word.

They pushed through the sleazy ways, arriving at last at a battered doorway. With a glance at Dixit, Malti slipped in and rejoined her family. Her mother, not sleeping, crouched over a wash bowl, gave a cry and fell into Malti's arms. Brothers and sisters and half-brothers and half-sisters and cousins and nephews woke up, squealing. Dixit was utterly brushed aside. He stood nervously, waiting, hoping, in the corridor.

It was many minutes before Malti came out and led him to the crowded little cabin. She introduced him to Shamim, her mother, who curtsied and rapidly disappeared, and to her step-father, Gita.

The little wiry man shooed everyone out of one corner of the room and moved Dixit into it. A cup of wine was produced and offered politely to the visitor. As he sipped it, he said, "If your step-daughter has explained the situation, Gita, I'd like to get you and Malti out of here, because otherwise your lives are worth very little. I can guarantee you will be extremely kindly treated outside."

With dignity, Gita said, "Sir, all this very unpleasant business has been explained to me by my step-daughter. You are most good to take this trouble, but we cannot help you."

"You, or rather Malti, have helped me. Now it is my turn to help you. I want to take you out of here to a safe place. You realize you are both under the threat of death? You hardly need telling that Prahlad Patel is a ruthless man."

"He is very very ruthless, sir," Gita said unhappily. "But we cannot leave here. I cannot leave here—look at all these little people who are dependent on me! Who would look after them if I left?"

"But if your hours are numbered?"

"If I have only one minute to go before I die, still I cannot desert those who depend on me."

Dixit turned to Malti. "You, Malti—you have less responsibility. Patel will have his revenge on you. Come with me and be safe!"

She shook her head. "If I came, I would sicken with worry for what was happening here and so I would die that way."

He looked about him hopelessly. The blind interdependence bred by this crowded environment had beaten him—almost. He still had one card to play.

"When I go out of here, as go I must, I have to report to my superiors. They are the people who—the people who really order everything that happens here. They supply your light, your food, your air. They are like gods to you with the power of death over every one on every deck—which perhaps is why you can hardly believe in them. They already feel that Total Environment is wrong, a crime against your humanity. I have to take my verdict to them. My verdict, I can tell you now, is that the lives of all you people are as precious as lives outside these walls. The experiment must be stopped; you all must go free.

"You may not understand entirely what I mean, but perhaps the wall screens have helped you grasp something. You will all be looked after and rehabilitated. Everyone will be released from the decks very soon. So, you can both come with me and save your lives; and then, in perhaps only a week, you will be reunited with your family. Patel will have no power then. Now, think over your decision again, for the good of your dependents, and come with me to life and freedom."

Malti and Gita looked anxiously at each other and went into a huddle. Shamim joined in, and Jamsu, and lame Shirin, and more and more of the tribe, and a great jangle of excited talk swelled up. Dixit fretted nervously.

Finally, silence fell. Gita said. "Sir, your intentions are plainly kind. But you have forgotten that Malti charged you to take a message to outside. Her message was to tell the people there to go away and let us make our own world. Perhaps you do not understand such a message and so cannot deliver it. Then I will give you my message, and you can take it to your superiors."

Dixit bowed his head.

"Tell them, your superiors and everyone outside who insists on watching us and meddling in our affairs, tell them that we are shaping our own lives. We know what is to come, and the many problems of having such a plenty of young people. But we have faith in our next generation. We believe they will have many new talents we do not possess, as we have talents our fathers did not possess.

"We know you will continue to send in food and air, because that is something you cannot escape from. We also know that in your hidden minds you wish to see us all fail and die. You wish to see us break, to see what will happen when we do. You do not have love for us. You have fear and puzzlement and hate. We shall not break. We are building a new sort of world, we are getting clever. We would die if you took us out of here. Go and tell that to your superiors and to everyone who spies on us. Please leave us to our own lives, over which we have our own commands."

There seemed nothing Dixit could say in answer. He looked at Malti, but could see she was unyielding, frail and pale and unyielding. This was what UHDRE had bred: complete lack of understanding. He turned and went.

He had his key. He knew the secret place on each deck where he could slip away into one of the escape elevators. As he pushed through the grimy crowds, he could hardly see his way for tears.

X

It was all very informal. Dixit made his report to a board of six members of the UHDRE administration, including the Special Project Organizer, Peter Crawley. Two observers were allowed to sit in, a grand lady who represented the Indian Government, and Dixit's old friend, Senator Jacob Byrnes, representing the United Nations.

Dixit delivered his report on what he had found and added a recommendation that a rehabilitation village be set up immediately and the Environment wound down.

Crawley rose to his feet and stood rigid as he said, "By your own words, you admit that these people of Environment cling desperately to what little they have. However terrible, however miserable that little may seem to you. They are acclimatized to what they have. They have turned their backs to the outside world and don't *want* to come out."

Dixit said, "We shall rehabilitate them, re-educate them, find them local homes where the intricate family patterns to which they are used can still be maintained, where they can be helped back to normality."

"But by what you say, they would receive a paralyzing shock if confronted with the outside world and its gigantic scale."

"Not if Patel still led them."

A mutter ran along the board; its members clearly thought this an absurd statement. Crawley gestured despairingly, as if his case were made, and sat down saying, "He's the sort of tyrant who causes the misery in Environment."

"The one thing they need when they emerge to freedom is a strong leader they know. Gentlemen, Patel is our good hope. His great asset is that he is oriented towards outside already."

"Just what does that mean?" one of the board asked.

"It means this. Patel is a clever man. My belief is that he arranged that Malti should help me escape from his cell. He never had any intention of killing me; that was a bluff to get me on my way. Little, oppressed Malti was just not the woman to take any initiative. What Patel probably did not bargain for was that I should mention Gita by name to her, or that Gita should be closely related to her. But because of their fatalism, his plan was in no way upset."

"Why should Patel want you to escape?"

"Implicit in much that he did and said, though he tried to hide it, was a burning curiosity about outside. He exhibited facets of his culture to me to ascertain my reactions—testing for approval or disapproval, I'd guess, like a child. Nor does he attempt to attack other decks—the time-honored sport of Environment tyrants; his attention is directed inwardly on us.

"Patel is intelligent enough to know that we have real power. He has never lost the true picture of reality, unlike his minions. So *he wants to get out.*

"He calculated that if I got back to you, seemingly having escaped death, I would report strongly enough to persuade you to start demolishing Total Environment immediately."

"Which you are doing," Crawley said.

"Which I am doing. Not for Patel's reasons, but for human reasons. And for utilitarian reasons also—which will perhaps appeal more to Mr. Crawley. Gentlemen, you were right. There are mental disciplines in Environment the world could use, of which perhaps the least attractive is telecide. UHDRE has cost the public millions on millions of dollars. We have to recoup by these new advances. We can only use these new advances by studying them in an atmosphere not laden with hatred and envy of us—in other words, by opening that black tower."

The meeting broke up. Of course, he could not expect anything more decisive than that for a day or two.

Senator Byrnes came over.

"Not only did you make out a good case, Thomas; history is with you. The world's emerging from a bad period and that dark tower, as you call it, is a symbol of the bad times, and so it has to go."

Inwardly, Dixit had his qualifications to that remark. But they walked together to the window of the boardroom and looked across at the great rough bulk of the Environment building.

"It's more than a symbol. It's as full of suffering and hope as our own world. But it's a manmade monster—it must go."

Byrnes nodded. "Don't worry. It'll go. I feel sure that the historical process, that blind evolutionary thing, has already decided that UHDRE's day is done. Stick around. In a few weeks, you'll be able to help Malti's family rehabilitate. And now I'm off to put in my two cents' worth with the chairman of that board."

He clapped Dixit on the back and walked off. Inside he knew lights would be burning and those thronging feet padding across the only world they knew. Inside there, babies would be born this night and men die of old age and night-visions. . . .

Outside, monsoon rain began to fall on the wide Indian land.

FREDERIK POHL
The Merchants of Venus

Frederik Pohl broke into the professional SF world in 1939 as the nineteen-year-old editor of two SF magazines (*Astonishing Stories* and *Super Science Stories*), and ever since has been one of the genre's major shaping forces, as writer, editor, agent, and anthologist.

On the editorial side of the slate, Pohl founded SF's first continuing original anthology series (the famous *Star* series, which lasted from 1953 to 1960), was the editor of the *Galaxy* group of magazines from 1960 to 1969 (during which time he won three consecutive Best Professional Magazine Hugos for *Worlds of If*, *Galaxy*'s sister magazine), and served throughout the mid-seventies as a consulting SF editor for Bantam, where he was responsible for the buying of such novels as Delany's *Dhalgren* and Russ's *The Female Man*.

He was science fiction's first important literary agent, and, as such, played a vital role in encouraging publishing houses such as Ballantine to develop the first category science fiction book lines in the early fifties.

As a writer, Pohl first came to prominence with a series of novels written in collaboration with the late C. M. Kornbluth, including *The Space Merchants* (one of the most famous SF novels of the fifties), *Gladiator-at-Law* (a book that comes to seem less and less like a satire every time you turn on your television set), *Search the Sky*, and *Wolfbane* (perhaps the best of the Pohl/Kornbluth novels, and decades ahead of its time in its depiction of humans forced to function as plug-in component parts in an organic alien computer). Pohl was relatively quiet as a writer throughout the last half of the sixties, but came strongly out of his slump in the early seventies, producing work a quantum jump better than most of his previous solo work. The effect of the sudden appearance of such powerful Pohl stories as "The Gold at the Starbow's End," "The Merchants of Venus," *Man Plus* (for which he won a Nebula Award), and, most especially, *Gateway* (for which he won both the Nebula and the Hugo, and which is widely regarded as one of the best novels of the seventies) was almost to make it appear as if a totally *new* writer had made a dramatic debut. Pohl, whose solo work had tended to be somewhat undervalued until then (he was widely—and unfairly—considered to be the junior partner in the Pohl/Kornbluth collaborations, and had even been accused of riding on Kornbluth's coattails), was suddenly doing work that placed him at the very forefront of the SF writers of the day . . . and that's where he's stayed, ever since. In 1992, for instance, not content to rest on his laurels, he published two of his most powerful novellas to date, *Outnumbering the Dead* and *Stopping at Slowyear*, and *Stopping at Slowyear* is on the 1993 Final Hugo Ballot.

The brilliant novella that follows, *The Merchants of Venus*, marked the first appearance of Pohl's enigmatic alien race, the "Heechee," who later became central to *Gateway* and its several sequels. An expanded and reworked version of the novella appears in the final book in the series, *The Gateway Trip*, but I think that it stands excellently on its own as an individual piece as well. Although it's a landmark, the story which (to me, anyway) announced the appearance of the New Pohl, it's no mere historical artifact, but instead a story that is still passionately *alive*, and one which, even when viewed from the unforgiving perspective of the nineties, has lost none of its power, intelligence, anger, and fierce ingenuity.

In addition to his editing Hugos (he is the only person ever to have won the Hugo both as writer and as editor), Frederik Pohl also won a Hugo for a story called "The Meeting" (completed by Pohl from an incomplete Kornbluth draft after Kornbluth's death) and another for "Fermi and Frost," the American Book Award, and the French Prix Apollo, and in 1993 was honored with the prestigious Grandmaster Nebula for Lifetime Achievement. His many other books include the novels *A Plaque of Pythons*, *Slave Ship*, *JEM*, *Beyond the Blue Event Horizon*, *Heechee Rendezvous*, *The Coming of the Quantum Cats*, *The World at the End of Time*, and *The Gateway Trip*, the collections *The Best of Frederik Pohl*, *The Gold at the Starbow's End*, *The*

Years of the City, *Critical Mass* (in collaboration with Korn-bluth), *In the Problem Pit*, and *Pohlstars*, and an autobiography, *The Way the Future Was*. His most recent books are a nonfiction book in collaboration with the late Isaac Asimov, *Our Angry Earth*, and a new novel, *Mining the Oort*.

I

My name, Audee Walthers. My job, airbody driver. My home, on Venus, in a Heechee hut most of the time; wherever I happen to be when I feel sleepy otherwise.

Until I was twenty-five I lived on Earth, in Amarillo Central mostly. My father, a Deputy Governor of Texas. He died when I was still in college, but he left me enough dependency benefits to finish school, get a master's in business administration, and pass the journeyman examination for clerk-typist. So I was set up for life.

But, after I tried it for a few years, I discovered I didn't like the life I was set up for. Not so much for the conventional reasons; I don't mind smog suits, can get along with neighbors even when there are 800 of them to the square mile, tolerate noise, can defend myself against the hood kids. It wasn't Earth itself I didn't like, it was what I was doing on Earth I didn't like, and so I sold my UOPWA journeyman's card, mortgaged my pension accrual, and bought a one-way ticket to Venus. Nothing strange about that. What every kid tells himself he's going to do, really. But I did it.

I suppose it would have been all different if I'd had a chance at Real Money. If my father had been Full Governor instead of a civil-service client. If the dependency benefits had included Unlimited Medicare. If I'd been at the top instead of in the middle, squeezed both ways. It didn't happen that way, so I opted out by the pioneer route and wound up hunting Terry marks at the Spindle.

Everybody has seen pictures of the Spindle, the Colosseum and Niagara Falls. Like everything worth looking at on Venus, the Spindle was a Heechee leftover. Nobody had ever figured out what the Heechee wanted with an underground chamber three hundred meters long and spindle-shaped, but it was there, so we used it; it was the closest thing Venus had to a Times Square or a Champs Elysées. All Terry tourists head for it first. That's where we fleece them.

My airbody-rental business is reasonably legitimate—not counting the fact that there really isn't much worth seeing on Venus that wasn't left there, below the surface, by the Heechee. The other tourist traps in the Spindle are reasonably crooked. Terries don't mind, although they must know they're being taken; they all load up on Heechee prayer fans and doll-heads, and those paperweights of transparent plastic in which a contoured globe of Venus swims in a kind of orange-brown snowstorm of make-believe fly ash, blood-diamonds, and fire-pearls. None of them are worth the price of their mass-charge back to Earth, but to a tourist who can get up the price of passage in the first place I don't suppose that matters.

To people like me, who can't get the price of anything, the tourist traps matter a lot. We live on them. I don't mean we draw our disposable income from them; I mean that they are how we get the price of what to eat and where to sleep, and if we don't have the price we die. There aren't too many ways of earning money on Venus. The ones that might produce Real Money—oh, winning a lottery; striking it rich in the Heechee diggings; blundering into a well-paying job; that kind of thing—are all real long-shots. For bread and butter everybody on Venus depends on Terry tourists, and if we don't milk them dry we've had it.

Of course, there are tourists and tourists. They come in three varieties. The difference between them is celestial mechanics.

There's the quick-and-dirty kind. On Earth, they're just well-to-do; they come every twenty-six months at Hohmann-orbit time, riding the minimum-energy circuit from Earth. Because of the critical times of a Hohmann orbit, they never can stay more than three weeks on Venus. So they come on the guided tours, determined to get the most out of the quarter-million-dollar minimum cabin fare their rich grandparents had given them for a graduation present, or they'd saved up for a second honeymoon, or whatever. The bad thing about them is that they don't have much money, since they'd spent it all on fares. The nice thing about them is that there are a lot of them. While they're on Venus, all the rental rooms are filled. Sometimes they'd have six couples sharing a single partitioned cubicle, two pairs at a time, hot-bedding eight-hour shifts around the clock. Then people like me would hold up in Heechee huts on the surface and rent out our own below-ground rooms, and maybe make enough money to live a few months.

But you couldn't make enough money to live until the next Hohmann-orbit time, so when the Class II tourists came along we cut each other's throats over them.

They were medium-rich. What you might call the poor million-aires: the ones whose annual income was barely in seven figures. They could afford to come in powered orbits, taking a hundred days or so for the run, instead of the long, slow Hohmann drift.

The price ran a million dollars and up, so there weren't nearly as many of them; but they came every month or so at the times of reasonably favorable orbital conjunctions. They also had more money to spend. So did the other medium-rich ones who hit us four or five times in a decade, when the ballistics of the planets had sorted themselves out into a low-energy configuration that allowed three planets to come into an orbit that didn't have much higher energy cost than the straight Earth-Venus run. They'd hit us first, if we were lucky, then go on to Mars. If it was the other way around, we got the leavings. The leavings were never very much.

But the very rich—ah, the very rich! They came as they liked, in orbital season or out.

When my tipper on the landing pad reported the *Yuri Gagarin*, under private charter, my money nose began to quiver. It was out of season for everybody except the very rich; the only question on my mind was how many of my competitors would be trying to cut my throat for its passengers while I was cutting theirs.

Airbody rental takes a lot more capital than opening a prayer-fan booth. I'd been lucky in buying my airbody cheap when the fellow I worked for died; I didn't have too many competitors, and a couple of them were U/S for repairs, a couple more had kited off on Heechee diggings of their own.

So, actually, I had the Gagarin's passengers, whoever they were, pretty much to myself. Assuming they could be interested in taking a trip outside the Heechee tunnels.

I had to assume they would be interested, because I needed the money very much. I had this little liver condition, you see. It was getting pretty close to total failure. The way the doctors explained it to me, I had like three choices: I could go back to Earth and linger a while on external prostheses; or I could get up the money for a transplant. Or I could die.

II

The name of the fellow who had chartered the *Gagarin* was Boyce Cochenour. Age, apparently forty. Height, two meters. Ancestry, Irish-American-French.

He was the kind of fellow who was used to command. I watched him come into the Spindle as though it belonged to him and he was getting ready to sell it. He sat down in Sub Vastra's imitation Paris Boulevard-Heechee sidewalk cafe. "Scotch," he said, and Vastra hurried to pour John Begg over super-cooled ice and hand it to him, all crackling with cold and numbing to the lips. "Smoke," he said, and the girl who was traveling with him instantly lit a cigarette and passed it to him. "Crummy looking joint," he said, and Vastra fell all over himself to agree.

I sat down next to them—well, not at the same table, I mean; I didn't even look at them. But I could hear what they said. Vastra didn't look at me, either, but of course he had seen me come in and knew I had my eye on them. But I had to let his number-three wife take my order, because Vastra wasn't going to waste any time on me when he had a charter-ship Terry at his table. "The usual," I said to her, meaning straight-alk in a tumbler of soft drink. "And a copy of your briefing," I added, more softly. Her eyes twinkled at me over her flirtation veil. Cute little vixen. I patted her hand in a friendly way, and left a rolled-up bill in it; then she left.

The Terry was inspecting his surroundings, including me. I looked back at him, polite but distant, and he gave me a sort of quarter-nod and turned back to Subhash Vastra. "Since I'm here," he said, "I might as well go along with whatever action there is. What's to do here?"

Sub grinned widely, like a tall, skinny frog. "Ah, whatever you wish, sah! Entertainment? In our private rooms we have the finest artists of three planets, nautch dancers, music, fine comedians—"

"We've got plenty of that in Cincinnati. I didn't come to Venus for a night club act." He wouldn't have known it, of course, but that was a good move; Sub's private rooms were way down the list of night spots on Venus, and the top of the list wasn't much.

"Of course, sah! Then perhaps you would like to consider a tour?"

"Aw." Cochenour shook his head. "What's the point? Does any of it look any different than the space-pad we came in on, right over our heads?"

Vastra hesitated; I could see him calculating second-order consequences in his head, measuring the chance of the Terry going for a surface tour against what he might get from me as commission. He didn't look my way. Honesty won out—that is, honesty reinforced by a quick appraisal of Cochenour's gullibility. "Not much different, no, sah," he admitted. "All pretty hot and dry on the surface, at least for the next thousand kilometers. But I wasn't thinking of the surface."

"What then?"

"Ah, the Heechee warrens, sah! There are many miles just below this settlement. A guide could be found—"

"Not interested," Cochenour growled. "Not in anything that close."

"Sah?"

"If a guide can lead us through them," Cochenour explained, "that means they've all been explored. Which means they've been looted. What's the fun of that?"

"Of course," said Vastra immediately. "I see what you're driving at, sah." He looked noticeably happier, and I could feel his radar reaching out to make sure I was listening, though he didn't look in my direction at all. "To be sure," he said, "there is always the chance of finding new digs, sah, provided one knows where to look. Am I correct in assuming that this would interest you?"

The third of Vastra's house brought me my drink and a thin powder-faxed slip of paper. "Thirty percent," I whispered to her. "Tell Sub. Only no bargaining, no getting anybody else to bid—" She nodded and winked; she'd been listening too, and she was as sure as I that this Terry was firmly on the hook. It had been my intention to nurse the drink as long as I could, but prosperity loomed before me; I was ready to celebrate; I took a long happy swallow.

But the hook didn't have a barb. Unaccountably the Terry shrugged. "Waste of time, I bet," he grumbled. "I mean, really. If you knew where to look, why wouldn't you have looked there already, right?"

"Ah, mister," cried Subhash Vastra, "but there are hundreds of tunnels not explored! Thousands! And in them, who knows, treasures beyond price!"

Cochenour shook his head. "Skip it" he said. "Bring us another drink. And see if you can't get the ice *cold* this time."

Somewhat shaken, I put down my drink, half-turned away to hide my hand from the Terries, and looked at the facsimile copy of Sub's report on them to see if it could tell me why Cochenour had lost interest.

It couldn't. It did tell me a lot, though. The girl with Cochenour was named Dorotha Keefer. She had been traveling with him for a couple of years now, this being their first time off Earth; there was no indication of any marriage, or any intention of it, at least on his part. She was in her early twenties—real age, not simulated by drugs and transplants. Cochenour himself was well over ninety.

He did not, of course, look anywhere near that. I'd watched him come over to the table, and he moved lightly and easily, for a big man. His money came from land and petro-foods; according to the synoptic on him, he had been one of the first oil millionaires to switch over from selling oil as fuel for cars and heating plants to food production, growing algae in the crude that came out of his wells and selling the algae in processed form for human consumption. So he'd stopped being a mere millionaire and turned into something much bigger.

And that accounted for the way he looked. He'd been on Full Medical, with extras. The report said his heart was titanium and plastic. His lungs had been transplanted from a twenty-year-old killed in a copter crash. His skin, muscles and fats—not to mention his various glandular systems—were sustained by hormones and cell-builders at what had to be a cost of well over a thousand dollars a day. To judge by the way he stroked the girl sitting next to him, he was getting his money's worth. He looked and acted no more than forty, at most—except perhaps for the look of his pale-blue, diamond-bright, weary and disillusioned eyes.

What a lovely mark! I swallowed the rest of my drink, and nodded to the third for another. There had to be a way to get him to charter my airbody.

All I had to do was find it.

Outside the rail of Vastra's cafe, of course, half the Spindle was thinking exactly the same thoughts. This was the worst of the low season, the Hohmann crowd were still three months in the future; all of us were beginning to run low on money. My liver transplant was just a little extra incentive; of the hundred maze-runners I could see out of the corner of my eye, ninety-nine needed to cut in on this rich tourist's money as much as I did, just for the sake of staying alive.

We couldn't all do it. Two of us, three, maybe even half a dozen could score enough to make a real difference. No more than that. And I had to be one of these few.

I took a deep swallow of my second drink, tipped Vastra's third lavishly—and conspicuously—and turned idly around until I was facing the Terries dead on.

The girl was talking with a knot of souvenir vendors, looking interested and uncertain. "Boyce?" she said over her shoulder.

"Yeah?"

"What's this thing for?"

He bent over the rail and peered. "Looks like a fan," he said.

"Heechee prayer fan, right," cried the dealer; I knew him, Booker Allemang, an old timer in the Spindle. "Found it myself, miss! It'll grant your every wish, letters every day from people reporting miraculous results—"

"Sucker bait," grumbled Cochenour. "Buy it if you want."

"But what does it do?"

He laughed raucously. "What any fan does. It cools you down." And he looked at me, grinning.

*   *   *

I finished my drink, nodded, stood up and walked over to the table. "Welcome to Venus," I said. "May I help you?"

The girl looked at Cochenour for approval before she said, "I thought this was very pretty."

"Very pretty," I agreed. "Are you familiar with the story of the Heechees?"

Cochenour pointed to a chair. I sat and went on. "They built these tunnels about a quarter of a million years ago. They lived here for a couple of centuries, give or take a lot. Then they went away again. They left a lot of junk behind, and some things that weren't junk; among other things they left a lot of these fans. Some local con-man like BeeGee here got the idea of calling them 'prayer fans' and selling them to tourists to make wishes with."

Allemang had been hanging on my every word trying to guess where I was going. "You know it's right," he said.

"But you two are too smart for that kind of come on," I added. "Still, look at the things. They're pretty enough to be worth having even without the story."

"Absolutely!" cried Allemang. "See how this one sparkles, miss! And the black and gray crystal, how nice it looks with your fair hair!"

The girl unfurled the crystalline one. It came rolled like a diploma, only cone-shaped. It took just the slightest pressure of the thumb to keep it open, and it really was very pretty as she waved it gently. Like all the Heechee fans, it weighed only about 10 grams, and its crystalline lattice caught the lights from the luminous Heechee walls, as well as the fluorescents and gas tubes we maze-runners had installed, and tossed them all back in iridescent sparks.

"This fellow's name is Booker Garey Allemang," I said. "He'll sell you the same goods as any of the others, but he won't cheat you as much as most of them."

Cochenour looked at me dourly, then beckoned Sub Vastra for another round of drinks. "All right," he said. "If we buy, we'll buy from you, Booker Garey Allemang. But not now."

He turned to me. "And what do you want to sell me?"

"Myself and my airbody, if you want to go looking for new tunnels. We're both as good as you can get."

"How much?"

"One million dollars," I said immediately. "All found."

He didn't answer at once, though it gave me some pleasure to notice that the price didn't seem to scare him. He looked as pleasant, or anyway as unangrily bored, as ever. "Drink up," he said, as Vastra and his third served us, and gestured with his glass to the Spindle. "Know what this was for?" he asked.

"You mean why the Heechees built it? No. They were pretty small, so it wasn't for headroom. And it was entirely empty when it was found."

He gazed tolerantly at the busy scene, balconies cut into the sloping sides of the Spindle with eating and drinking places like Vastra's, rows of souvenir booths, most of them empty at this idle season. But there were still a couple of hundred maze-rats around, and the number had been quietly growing all the time Cochenour and the girl had been sitting there.

He said, "It's not much to see, is it? A hole in the ground, and a lot of people trying to take my money away from me."

I shrugged.

He grinned again. "So why did I come, eh? Well, that's a good question, but since you didn't ask it I don't have to answer it. You want a million dollars. Let's see. A hundred K to charter an airbody. A hundred and eighty or so to rent equipment, per week. Ten days minimum, three weeks a safer guess. Food, supplies, permits, another fifty K. So we're up to close to seven hundred thousand, not counting your own salary and what you give our host here as his cut for not throwing you off the premises. Right, Walthers?"

I had a little difficulty in swallowing the drink I had been holding to my mouth, but I managed to say, "Close enough, Mr. Cochenour." I didn't see any point in telling him that I already owned the equipment, as well as the airbody, although I wouldn't have been surprised to find out that he knew that too.

"You've got a deal, then. And I want to leave as soon as possible, which should be, um, about this time tomorrow."

"Fair enough," I said, and got up, avoiding Sub Vastra's thunder-stricken expression. I had some work to do, and a little thinking. He'd caught me off base, which is a bad place to be when you can't afford to make a mistake. I knew he hadn't missed my calling him by name. That was all right; he'd known that I had checked him out immediately. But it was a little surprising that he had known mine.

III

The first thing I had to do was double-check my equipment; the second was go to the local, validate a contract, and settle up with Sub Vastra; the third was see my doctor. The liver hadn't been giving me much trouble for a while, but then I hadn't been drinking grain alcohol for a while.

It took about an hour to make sure that everything we would

need for the expedition was i.s., with all the spare parts I might reasonably fear needing. The Quackery was on my way to the union office, so I stopped in there first. It didn't take long. The news was no worse than I had been ready for; Dr. Morius studied the read-out from his instruments carefully. It turned out to be a hundred and fifty dollars' worth of carefully, and expressed the guarded hope that I would survive three weeks away from his office, pro-vided I took all the stuff he gave me and wandered no more than usual from his dietary restrictions. "And when I get back?" I asked.

"About the same, Audee," he said cheerily. "Total collapse in, ah, oh, maybe ninety more days."

He patted his fingertips. "I hear you've got a live one," he added. "Want me to book you for a transplant?"

"How live did you hear he was?" I asked.

"Oh, the price is the same in any case," he told me good-hu-moredly. "Two hundred K, plus the hospital, anesthesiologist, pre-op psychiatrist, pharmaceuticals—you've already got the figures."

I did, and I knew that with what I might make from Cochenour, plus what I had put away, plus a small loan on the airbody, I could just about meet it. Leaving me broke when it was over but, of course, alive.

"Go ahead," I said. "Three weeks from tomorrow." And I left him looking mildly pleased, like a Burmese hydro-rice man watching another crop being harvested. Dear daddy. Why hadn't he sent me through medical school instead of giving me an education?

It would have been nice if the Heechee had been the same size as human beings, instead of being about 40 percent shorter. In the smaller tunnels, like the one that led to the Local 88 office, I had to half-crouch all the way.

The deputy organizer was waiting for me. He had one of the few good jobs that didn't depend on the tourists, or at least not directly. He said, "Subhash Vastra's been on the line. He says you agreed to 30 percent, and besides you forgot to pay your bar bill to the third of his house."

"Admitted, both ways."

"And you owe me a little too, Audee. Three hundred for a powderfax copy of my report on your pigeon. A hundred for validating your contract with Vastra. And if you want guide's pa-pers, sixteen hundred for that."

I gave him my credit card and he checked the total out of my account into the local's. Then I signed and card-stamped the con-tract he'd drawn up. Vastra's 30 percent would not be on the whole million-dollar gross, but on my net; even so, he might make as much out of it as I would, at least in liquid cash, because I'd have to pay off all the outstanding balances on equipment and loans. The factors would carry a man until he scored, but then they wanted to get paid. They knew how long it might be until he scored again.

"Thanks, Audee," said the deputy, nodding over the signed contract. "Anything else I can do for you?"

"Not at your prices," I told him.

"Ah, you're putting me on. 'Boyce Cochenour and Dorotha Keefer, Earth-Ohio, traveling *S. V. Yuri Gagarin*, Odessa registry, chartered. No other passengers.' No other passengers," he repeated, quoting from the synoptic report he'd furnished. "Why, you'll be a rich man, Audee, if you work this pigeon right."

"That's more than I ask," I told him. "All I want is to be a living one."

But it wasn't entirely true. I did have some little hope—not much, not enough to talk about, and in fact I'd never said a word about it to anyone—that I might be coming out of this rather better than merely alive.

There was, however, a problem.

See, in the standard guide's contract and airbody leasing terms, I get my money and that's all I get. If we take a mark like Cochenour on a hunt for new Heechee tunnels and he finds something valuable—marks have, you know; not often, but enough to keep them hopeful—then it's his. We just work for him.

On the other hand, I could have gone out by myself any time and prospected; and then anything I found would be all mine.

Obviously, anybody with any sense would go by himself if he thought he was really going to find anything. But in my case, that wasn't such a good idea. If I staked myself to a trip and lost, I hadn't just wasted time and maybe fifty K in supplies and wear and tear. If I lost, I was dead.

I needed what I would make out of Cochenour to stay alive. Whether we found anything interesting or not, my fee would take care of that.

Unfortunately for my peace of mind, I had a notion that I knew where something very interesting might be found; and my problem was that, as long as I had an all-rights contract with Cochenour, I couldn't afford to find it.

The last stop I made was in my sleeping room. Under the bed, keystoned into the rock, was a guaranteed break-proof safe that held some papers I wanted to have in my pocket from then on.

When I came down onto Venus for the first time, it wasn't scenery that interested me. I wanted to make my fortune.

I didn't see much of the surface of Venus then, or for nearly two years after that. You don't see much in the kind of spacecraft that can land on Venus; a 20,000-millibar surface pressure means you need something a little more rugged than the bubble-ships that go to the Moon or Mars or farther out, and there's not much tolerance in the design for putting unnecessary windows into the hull. It didn't matter much, because anywhere except near the poles there's not much you can see. Everything worth seeing on Venus is *in* Venus, and all of it once belonged to the Heechees.

Not that we know much about the Heechees. We don't even rightly know their name—"heechee" is how somebody once wrote down the sound that a fire-pearl makes when you stroke it, and as that's the only sound anybody knows that's connected with them, it got to be a name.

The hesperologists don't know where the Heechees came from, although there are some markings on scraps of stuff that the Heechees used for paper that seem to be a star chart—faded, incomplete, pretty much unrecognizable; if we know the exact position of every star in the galaxy 250,000 years ago, we might be able to locate them from that, I suppose. Assuming they came from this galaxy. There are no traces of them anywhere else in the solar system, except maybe in Phobos; the experts still fight about whether the honeycomb cells inside the Martian moon are natural or artifacts, and if they're artifacts they're no doubt Heechee. But they don't look much like ours.

I wonder sometimes what they wanted. Escaping a dying planet? Political refugees? Tourists that had a breakdown between somewhere and somewhere, and hung around just long enough to make whatever they had to make to get themselves going again? I used to think that they'd maybe come by to watch human beings evolving on Earth, sort of stepfathers beaming over the growing young race; but we couldn't have been much to watch at that time, halfway between the Australopithecines and the Cro-Magnards.

But, though they packed up nearly everything when they left, leaving behind only empty tunnels and chambers, there were a few scraps here and there that either weren't worth taking along or were overlooked: all those "prayer fans," enough empty containers of one kind or another to look like a picnic ground at the end of a hard summer, some trinkets and trifles. I guess the best known of the "trifles" is the anisokinetic punch, the carbon crystal that transmits a blow at a ninety-degree angle; that made somebody a few billion just by being lucky enough to find one, and smart enough to analyze and duplicate it. But all we've ever found is junk. There must have been good stuff worth a million times as much as those sweepings.

Did they take all the good stuff with them?

Nobody knew. I didn't know, either, but I did think I knew something that had a bearing on it.

I thought I knew where the last Heechee ship had taken off from; and it wasn't near any of the explored diggings.

I didn't kid myself. I knew that wasn't a guarantee of anything.

But it was something to go on. *Maybe* when that last ship left they were getting impatient, and maybe not as thorough in cleaning up behind themselves.

And that was what being on Venus was all about. What other possible reason was there for being there? The life of a maze-rat was marginal at best. It took fifty thousand a year to stay alive. If you had less than that you couldn't pay air tax, capitation tax, water assessment, or even a subsistence-level bill for food. If you wanted to eat meat more than once a week, and demanded a cubicle of your own to sleep in, it cost more than that.

Guide's papers cost a week's life; when any of us bought them, we were gambling that week's cost-of-living against the chance of a big enough strike, either from the Terry tourists or from what we might find, to make it possible to get back to Earth—where no one starved, no one died for lack of air, no one was thrust out into the high-pressure incinerator that was Venus's atmosphere. Not *just* to get back to Earth. To get back in the style every maze-rat had set himself as a goal when he headed sunward in the first place: with money enough to live the full life of a human being on Full Medical.

That was what I wanted. The big score.

IV

Not by accident, the last thing I did that night was to visit the Hall of Discoveries.

The third of Vastra's house winked at me over her flirtation veil and turned to her companion, who looked around and nodded.

I joined them. "Hello, Mr. Walthers," she said.

"I thought I might find you here," I said, which was no more than the truth, since Vastra's third had promised to guide her this way. I didn't know what to call her. "Miss Keefer" was accurate, "Mrs. Cochenour" was diplomatic; I got around it by saying, "Since we'll be seeing a lot of each other, how about getting on to first names?"

"Audee, is it?"

I gave her a twelve-tooth smile. "Swede on my mother's side, old Texan on my father's. Name's been in his family a long time, I guess."

The Hall of Discoveries is meant to get Terry prospects hotted up; there's a little of everything in it, from charts of the worked diggings and a full-scale Mercator map of Venus to samples of all the principal finds. I showed her the copy of the anisokinetic punch, and the original solid-state piezophone that had made its discoverer almost as permanently rich as the guy who found the punch. There were about a dozen fire-pearls, quarter-inch jobbies, behind armor glass, on cushions, blazing away with their cold milky light.

"They're pretty," she said. "But why all the protection? I saw bigger ones lying on a counter in the Spindle without anybody even watching them."

"That's a little different, Dorotha," I told her. "These are real."

She laughed out loud. It was a very nice laugh. No girl looks beautiful when she's laughing hard, and girls who worry about looking beautiful don't do it. Dorotha Keefer looked like a healthy, pretty girl having a good time, which when you come down to it is about the best way for a girl to look.

She did not, however, look good enough to come between me and a new liver, so I took my mind off that aspect of her and put it on business. "The little red marbles over there are blood-diamonds," I told her. "They're radioactive and stay warm. Which is one way you can tell the real one from a fake: Anything over about three centimeters is a fake. A real one that big generates too much heat—square-cube law, you know—and melts."

"So the ones your friend was trying to sell me—"

"—are fakes. Right."

She nodded, still smiling. "What about what you were trying to sell us, Audee? Real or fake?"

The third of Vastra's house had discreetly vanished, and there was nobody else in the Hall of Discoveries but me and the girl. I took a deep breath and told her the truth. Not the whole truth, maybe; but nothing but the truth.

"All this stuff," I said, "is what came out of a hundred years of digging. And it's not much. The punch, the piezophone, and two or three other gadgets that we can make work; a few busted pieces of things that they're still studying; and some trinkets. That's all."

She said, "That's the way I heard it. And one more thing. None of the discovery dates on these things is less than fifty years old."

She was smart and better informed than I had expected. "And

the conclusion," I agreed, "is that the planet has been mined dry.
You're right, on the evidence. The first diggers found everything
there was to be found . . . so far."

"You think there's more?"

"I *hope* there's more. Look. Item. The tunnels. You see they're
all alike—the blue walls, perfectly smooth: the light coming from
them that never varies; the hardness. How do you suppose they
were made?"

"Why, I don't know—"

"Neither do I. Or anybody else. But every Heechee tunnel is the
same, and if you dig into them from the outside you find the basic
substrate rock, then a boundary layer that's sort of half wall-stuff
and half substrate, then the wall. Conclusion: The Heechees didn't
dig the tunnels and then line them, they had something that crawled
around underground like an earthworm, leaving these tunnels behind. And one other thing: They overdug. That's to say they dug
tunnels they didn't need, lots of them, going nowhere, never used
for anything. Does that suggest anything to you?"

"It must have been cheap and easy?" she guessed.

I nodded. "So it was probably a machine, and there really ought
to be at least one of them, somewhere on this planet, to find. Next
item. The air: They breathed oxygen like we do, and they must
have got it from somewhere. Where?"

"Why, there's oxygen in the atmosphere—"

"Sure. About a half of one percent. And better than 95 percent
carbon dioxide; and somehow they managed to get that half of one
percent out of the mixture, cheaply and easily—remember those
extra tunnels they filled!—along with enough nitrogen or some
other inert gas—and they're present in only trace amounts—to
make a breathing mixture. How? Why, I don't know, but if there's
a machine that did it, I'd like to find that machine. Next item:
Aircraft. The Heechee flew around the surface of Venus at will."

"So do you, Audee! Aren't you a pilot?"

"Sure, but look at what it takes. Surface temperature of two-
seventy C, and not enough oxygen to keep a cigarette going. So my
airbody has two fuel tanks, one for hydrocarbons, one for oxidants.
And—did you ever hear of a fellow named Carnot?"

"Old-time scientist, was he? The Carnot cycle?"

"Right again." That was the third time she'd surprised me, I
noted cautiously. "The Carnot efficiency of an engine is expressed
by its maximum temperature—the heat of combustion, let's say—
over the temperature of its exhaust. Well, but the temperature of
the exhaust can't be less than the temperature of what it flows
into—otherwise you're not running an engine, you're running a

refrigerator. And you've got that two-seventy ambient air temperature; so you have basically a lousy engine. *Any* heat engine on
Venus is lousy. Did you ever wonder why there are so few airbodies
around? I don't mind; it helps to have something close to a monop-
oly. But the reason is they're so damn expensive to run."

"And the Heechees did it better?"

"I *think* they did."

She laughed again, unexpectedly and once more very attractively.
"Why, you poor fellow," she said in good humor, "you're hooked
on the stuff you sell, aren't you? You think that some day you're
going to find the mother tunnel and pick up all this stuff."

Well, I wasn't too pleased with the way things were going; I'd
arranged with Vastra's third to bring the girl here, away from her
boy friend, so I could pick her brains in private. It hadn't worked
out that way. The way it was working out, she was making me aware
of her as a person, which was a bad development in itself, and
worse than that, making me take a good look at myself.

I said after a minute, "You may be right. But I'm sure going to
give it a good try."

"You're angry, aren't you?"

"No," I said, lying, "but maybe a little tired. And we've got a long
trip tomorrow, so I'd better take you home. Miss Keefer."

V

My airbody lay by the spacepad and was reached the same way the
spacepad was reached. Elevator to the surface lock, a tractor-cab to
carry us across the dry, tortured surface of Venus, peeling under
the three hundred kilometer an hour wind. Normally I kept it
under a foam housing, of course. You don't leave anything free
and exposed on the surface of Venus if you want to keep it intact,
not even if it's made of chrome steel. I'd had the foam stripped
free when I checked it out and loaded supplies that morning. Now
it was ready. I could see it from the bull's-eye ports of the crawler,
through the green-yellow murk outside. Cochenour and the girl
could have seen it too, if they'd known where to look, but they
might not have recognized it.

Cochenour screamed in my ear, "You and Dorrie have a fight?"

"No fight," I screamed back.

"Don't care if you did. You don't have to like each other, just do
what I want you to do." He was silent a moment, resting his throat.
"Jesus. What a wind."

"Zephyr," I told him. I didn't say any more, he would find out for himself. The area around the spacepad is a sort of natural calm area, by Venusian standards. Orographic lift throws the meanest winds up over the pad and all we get is a sort of confused back eddy. The good part is that taking off and landing are relatively easy. The bad part is that some of the heavy metal compounds in the atmosphere settle out on the pad. What passes for air on Venus has layers of red mercuric sulfide and mercurous chloride in the lower reaches, and when you get above them to those pretty fluffy clouds you find some of them are hydrochloric and hydrofluoric acid.

But there are tricks to that, too. Navigation over Venus is 3-D. It's easy enough to proceed from point to point; your transponders will link you to the radio-range and map your position continuously onto the charts. What's hard is to find the right altitude, and that's why my airbody and I were worth a million dollars to Cochenour.

We were at the airbody, and the telescoping snout from the crawler was poking out to its lock. Cochenour was staring out the bull's eye. "No wings!" he shouted, as though I was cheating him.

"No sails or snow chains, either," I shouted back. "Get aboard if you want to talk! It's easier in the airbody."

We climbed through the little snout, I unlocked the entrance, and we got aboard without much trouble.

We didn't even have the kind of trouble that I might have made myself. You see, an airbody is a big thing on Venus. I was damn lucky to have been able to acquire it and, well, I won't beat around the bush, you could say I loved it. Mine could have held ten people, without equipment. With what Sub Vastra's purchasing department had sold us and Local 88 had certified as essential aboard, it was crowded with just the three of us. I was prepared for sarcasm, at least. But Cochenour merely looked around long enough to find the best bunk, strode over to it and declared it his. The girl was a good sport, and there I was, left with my glands all charged up for an argument and no argument.

It was a lot quieter inside the airbody. You could hear the noise of the wind right enough, but it was only annoying. I passed out earplugs, and with them in place the noise was hardly even annoying.

"Sit down and strap up," I ordered, and when they were stowed away I took off.

At twenty thousand millibars wings aren't just useless, they're poison. My airbody had all the lift it needed built into the seashell-shaped hull. I fed the double fuels into the thermojets, we bounced across the reasonably flat ground around the spacepad (it was bull-dozed once a week, which is how come it stayed reasonably flat) and we were zooming off into the wild yellow-green yonder, a moment later the wild brown-gray yonder, after a run of no more than fifty meters.

Cochenour had fastened his harness loosely for comfort. I enjoyed hearing him yell as he was thrown about. It didn't last. At the thousand-meter level I found Venus's semi-permanent atmospheric inversion, and the turbulence dropped to where I could take off my belt and stand.

I took the plugs out of my ears and motioned to Cochenour and the girl to do the same.

He was rubbing his head where he'd bounced into an overhead chart rack, but grinning a little. "Pretty exciting," he admitted, fumbling in his pocket. Then he remembered to ask. "Is it all right if I smoke?"

"They're your lungs."

He grinned more widely. "They are now," he agreed, and lit up. "Say. Why didn't you give us those plugs while we were in the tractor?"

There is, as you might say, a tide in the affairs of guides, where you either let them flood you with questions and spend the whole time explaining what that funny little dial means or you go on to do your work and make your fortune. What it came down to was, was I going to come out of this liking Cochenour and his girl friend or not?

If I was, I should try to be civil to them. More than civil. Living, the three of us, for three weeks in a space about as big as an apartment kitchenette meant everybody would have to work real hard at being nice to everybody else, and as I was the one who was being paid to be nice, I should be the one to set an example. On the other hand, the Cochenours of the worlds are sometimes just not likeable. If that was going to be the case, the less talk the better; I should slide questions like that off with something like "I forgot."

But he hadn't actually been unpleasant, and the girl friend had actually tried to be friendly. I said, "Well, that's an interesting thing. You see, you hear by differences in pressure. While we were taking off, the plugs filtered out part of the sound—the pressure waves— but when I yelled at you to belt up, the plugs passed the overpressure of my voice, and you understood it. However, there's a limit. Past about a hundred and twenty decibels—that's a unit of sound—"

Cochenour growled, "I know what a decibel is."

"Right. Past a hundred and twenty the eardrum just doesn't respond anymore. So in the crawler it was too loud; with the plugs, you wouldn't have heard anything."

Dorotha had been listening while she repaired her eye makeup. "What was to hear?"

"Oh," I said, "nothing, really. Except, well—" Then I voted to think of them as friends, at least for the time being. "Except in the case of an accident. If we'd had a gust, you know, that crawler could have flipped right over. Or sometimes solid objects come flying over the hills and into you before you know it. Or—"

She was shaking her head. "I understand. Lovely place we're visiting, Boyce."

"Yeah. Look," he said. "Who's flying this thing?"

I got up and activated the virtual globe. "That's what I was just coming to. Right now it's on autopilot, heading in the general direction of this quadrant down here. We have to pick out a specific destination."

"That's Venus?" the girl asked. "It doesn't look like much."

"Those lines are just radio-range markers; you won't see them looking out the window. Venus doesn't have any oceans, and it isn't cut up into nations, so making a map of it isn't quite like what you'd expect on Earth. That bright spot is us. Now look." I overlaid the radio-range grid and the contour colors with mascon markings. "Those blobby circles are mascons. You know what a mascon is?"

"A concentration of mass. A lump of heavy stuff," offered the girl.

"Fine. Now look at the known Heechee digs." I phased them in as golden patterns.

"They're all in the mascons," Dorotha said at once. Cochenour gave her a look of tolerant approval.

"Not all. Look over here; this little one isn't, and this one. But damn near all. Why? I don't know. Nobody knows. The mass concentrations are mostly older, denser rock—basalt and so on—and maybe the Heechee found it easier to dig in. Or maybe they just liked it." In my correspondence with Professor Hegramet back on Earth, in the days when I didn't have a dying liver in my gut and took an interest in abstract knowledge, we had kicked around the possibility that the Heechee digging machines would only work in dense rock, or rock of a certain chemical composition. But I wasn't prepared to discuss that with them.

"See over here, where we are now"—I rotated the virtual globe slightly by turning a dial—"that's the big digging we just came out of. You can see the shape of the Spindle. It's a common shape, by the way. You can see it in some of the others if you look, and there are digs where it doesn't show on these tracings but it's there if you're on the spot. That particular mascon where the Spindle is

is called Serendip; it was discovered by accident by a hesperological—"

"Hesperological?"

"—a geological team operating on Venus, which makes it a
hesperological team. They were drilling out core samples and hit
the Heechee digs. Now these other digs in the northern high-
latitudes you see are all in one bunch of associated mascons. They
connect through interventions of less dense rock, but only where
absolutely necessary."

Cochenour said sharply, "They're north and we're going south.
Why?"

It was interesting that he could read the navigation instruments,
but I didn't say so. I only said, "They're no good. They've been
probed."

"They look even bigger than the Spindle."

"Hell of a lot bigger, right. But there's nothing much in them, or
anyway not much chance that anything in them is in good enough
shape to bother with. Subsurface fluids filled them up a hundred
thousand years ago, maybe more. A lot of good men have gone
broke trying to pump and excavate them, without finding anything.
Ask me. I was one of them."

"I didn't know there was any liquid water on Venus or under it,"
Cochenour objected.

"I didn't say water, did I? But as a matter of fact some of it was,
or anyway a sort of oozy mud. Apparently water cooks out of the
rocks and has a transit time to the surface of some thousands of
years before it seeps out, boils off, and cracks to hydrogen and
oxygen and gets lost. In case you didn't know it, there's some under
the Spindle. It's what you were drinking, and what you were breathing."

The girl said, "Boyce, this is all very interesting, but I'm hot and
dirty. Can I change the subject for a minute?"

Cochenour barked; it wasn't really a laugh. "Subliminal prompt-
ing, Walthers, you agree? And a little old-fashioned prudery, too,
I expect. What she really wants to do is go to the bathroom."

Given a little encouragement from the girl, I would have been
mildly embarrassed for her, but she only said, "If we're going to
live in this thing for three weeks, I'd like to know what it offers."

I said, "Certainly, Miss Keefer."

"Dorotha. Dorrie, if you like it better."

"Sure, Dorrie. Well, you see what we've got. Five bunks; they
partition to sleep ten if wanted, but we don't want. Two shower
stalls. They don't look big enough to soap yourself in, but they are
if you work at it. Three chemical toilets. Kitchen over there—well.

Pick the bunk you like, Dorrie. There's a screen arrangement that comes down when you want it for changing clothes and so on, or just if you don't want to look at the rest of us for a while."

Cochenour said, "Go on, Dorrie, do what you want to do. I want Walthers to show me how to fly this thing anyway."

It wasn't a bad start. I've had some real traumatic times, parties that came aboard drunk and steadily got drunker, couples that fought every waking minute and got together only to hassle me. This one didn't look bad at all, apart from the fact that it was going to save my life for me.

There's not much to flying an airbody, at least as far as making it move the way you want it to is concerned. In Venus's atmosphere there's lift to spare. You don't worry about things like stalling out; and anyway the autonomic controls do most of your thinking for you.

Cochenour learned fast. It turned out he had flown everything that moved on Earth and operated one-man submersibles as well. He understood as soon as I mentioned it to him that the hard part of pilotage was selecting the right flying level and anticipating when you'd have to change it, but he also understood that he wasn't going to learn that in one day. Or even in three weeks. "What the hell, Walthers," he said cheerfully enough. "At least I can make it go where I have to, in case you get caught in a tunnel or shot by a jealous husband."

I gave him the smile his pleasantry was worth, which wasn't much. "The other thing I can do," he said, "is cook. Unless you're really good at it? No, I thought not. Well, I paid too much for this stomach to fill it with hash, so I'll make the meals. That's a little skill Dorrie never got around to learning. Same with her grandmother. Most beautiful woman in the world, but had the idea that was all there was to it."

I put that aside to sort out later; he was full of little unexpected things, this ninety-year-old young athlete. He said, "All right, now while Dorrie's using up all the water in the shower—"

"Not to worry; it all recycles."

"Anyway. While she's cleaning up, finish your little lecture on where we're going."

"Right." I spun the virtual globe a little. The bright spot that was us had moved a dozen degrees already. "See that cluster where our track intersects those grid marks?"

"Yeah. Five big mascons close together, and no diggings indicated. Is that where we're going?"

"In a general sense, yes."

"Why in a general sense?"

"Well," I said, "there's one little thing I didn't tell you. I'm assuming you won't jump salty over it, because then I'll have to get salty too and tell you you should have taken the trouble to learn more about Venus before you decided to explore it."

He studied me appraisingly for a moment. Dorrie came quietly out of the shower in a long robe, her hair in a towel, and stood near him, watching. "It depends on what you didn't tell me," he said.

"There's a no-trespassing sign on most of those mascons," I said. I activated the pilotage chart overlay, and bright cherry-red warning lines sprang up all around the cluster.

"That's the south polar security area," I said. "That's where the Defense boys keep the missile range and the biggest part of their weapons development areas. And we're not allowed to enter."

He said harshly, "But there's only a little piece of one mascon that isn't off limits."

"And that's where we're going," I said.

VI

For a man more than ninety years old, Boyce Cochenour was spry. I don't mean just healthy looking. Full Medical will do that for you, because you just replace whatever wears out or begins to look shopworn and tatty. You cannot, however, very well replace the brain, so what you usually see in the very rich old ones is a bronzed, strong body that shakes and hesitates and drops things and stumbles. About that Cochenour had been very lucky.

He was going to be wearing company for three weeks. He'd insisted I show him how to pilot the airbody. When I decided to use a little flight time to give the cooling system a somewhat premature thousand-hour check, he helped me pull the covers, check the refrigerant levels and clean the filters. Then he decided to cook us lunch.

The girl took over as my helper while I restowed some of the supplies to get the autosonic probes out. At the steady noise level of the inside of an airbody our normal conversational voices wouldn't carry to Cochenour, less than three meters away, and I thought of pumping her about him. I decided against it. What I didn't know was just curiosity. I knew he was paying me the price of a new liver already. I didn't need to know what he and the girl thought about when they thought about each other.

So our conversation was along the lines of how the probes would fire charges and time the echoes, and what the chances were of finding something really good ("Well, what are the chances of winning a sweepstakes? Bad for any individual who buys a ticket—but there's always one winner somewhere!"), and what had made me come to Venus in the first place. I mentioned my father's name, but she'd never heard of him. Too young, for one thing, no doubt. And she was born and bred in Southern Ohio, where Cochenour had worked as a kid and to which he'd returned as a billionaire. He'd been building a new processing center there and it had been a lot of headaches—trouble with the unions, trouble with the banks, trouble, bad trouble, with the government—so he'd decided to take a few months off and loaf. I looked over to where he was stirring up a sauce and said, "He loafs harder than anybody else I ever saw."

"He's a work addict. I imagine that's how he got rich in the first place." The airbody lurched, and I dropped everything to jump for the controls. I heard Cochenour howl behind me, but I was busy locating the right transit level. By the time I had climbed a thousand meters and reset the autopilot, he was rubbing his wrist and glowering at me.

"Sorry," I said.

He said dourly, "I don't mind your scalding the skin off my arm, I can always buy more skin, but you nearly made me spill the gravy."

I checked the virtual globe. The bright marker was two-thirds of the way to our destination. "Is it about ready?" I asked. "We'll be there in an hour."

For the first time he looked startled. "So soon? I thought you said this thing was subsonic."

"I did. You're on Venus, Mr. Cochenour. At this level the speed of sound is maybe five thousand kilometers an hour."

He looked thoughtful, but all he said was, "Well, we can eat any minute." Later he said, while we were finishing up, "I think maybe I don't know as much about this planet as I might. If you want to give us the usual guide's lecture, we'll listen."

I said, "Well, you pretty much know the outlines. Say, you're a great cook, Mr. Cochenour. I packed all these provisions, but I don't even know what this is I'm eating."

"If you come to my office in Cincinnati," he said, "you can ask for Mr. Cochenour, but while we're living in each other's armpits you might as well call me Boyce. And if you like it, why aren't you eating it?"

The answer was, because it might kill me, but I didn't want to get into a discussion that might lead to why I needed his fee so badly. I said, "Doctor's orders, have to lay off the fats pretty much for a while. I think he thinks I'm putting on too much weight."

Cochenour looked at me appraisingly, but only said, "The lecture?"

"Well, let's start with the most important part," I said, carefully pouring coffee. "While we're in the airbody you can do what you like, walk around, eat, drink, smoke if you got 'em, whatever. The cooling system is built for more than three times as many people, plus their cooking and appliance loads, with a safety factor of two. Air and water, more than we'd need for two months. Fuel, enough for three round trips and some maneuvering. If anything went wrong we'd yell for help and somebody would come and get us in a couple of hours at most—probably it would be the Defense boys, and they have *super*sonic bodies. The worst thing would be if the hull breached and the whole Venusian atmosphere tried to come in. If it happened fast we'd be dead. It never happens fast, though. We'd have time to get in the suits, and we can live in them for thirty hours. Long before that we'd be picked up."

"Assuming, of course, that nothing went wrong with the radio at the same time," said Cochenour.

"Right. You can get killed anywhere, if enough accidents happen at once."

He poured himself another cup of coffee, tipped a little brandy into it and said, "Go on."

"Well, outside the airbody it's a little more tricky. You've only got the suit, and its useful life, as I say, is only thirty hours. It's a question of refrigeration. You can carry all the air and water you want, and you don't have to worry about food, but it takes a lot of compact energy to get rid of the diffuse energy all around you. It takes fuel for the cooling systems, and when that's gone you better be back in the airbody. Heat isn't the worst way to die. You pass out before you begin to hurt. But the end result is you're dead.

"The other thing is, you want to check your suit every time you put it on. Pressure it up and watch the gauge for leaks. I'll check it too, but *don't rely on me*. It's your life. And the faceplates are pretty strong; you can drive nails with them without breaking them, but they can be broken if hit hard enough against a hard enough surface. That way you're dead too."

Dorrie said quietly, "One question. Have you ever lost a tourist?"

"No." But then I added, "Others have. Five or six get killed every year."

"I don't mind odds like that," said Cochenour. "Actually, that wasn't the lecture I was asking for, Audee. I mean, I certainly want to hear how to stay alive, but I assume you would have told us all this before we left the ship anyway. What I really wanted to know was how come you picked this particular mascon to prospect."

This old geezer with the muscle-beach body was beginning to bother me. He had a disturbing habit of asking the questions I didn't want to answer. There was a reason why I had picked this site; it had to do with about five years of study, a lot of digging, and about a quarter of a million dollars' worth of correspondence, at space-mail rates, with people like Professor Hegramet back on Earth.

But I didn't want to tell him all of my reasons. There were about a dozen sites that I really wanted to explore. If this happened to be one of the payoff places, he would come out of it richer than I would—that's what the contracts you sign say: 40 percent to the charterer, 25 percent to the guide, the rest to the government—and that should be enough for him. If it happened not to pay off, I didn't want him taking some other guide to one of the others I'd marked.

So I only said, "Call it an informed guess. I promised you a good shot at a tunnel that's never been opened, and I hope to keep my promise. And now let's get the food put away; we're within ten minutes of where we're going."

With everything strapped down and ourselves belted up, we dropped out of the relatively calm layers into the big winds again.

We were over the big south-central massif, about the same elevation as the lands surrounding the Spindle. That's the elevation where most of the action is on Venus. Down in the lowlands and the deep rift valleys the pressures run fifty thousand millibars and up. My airbody wouldn't take any of that for very long, and neither would anybody else's, except for a few of the special research and military types. Fortunately, the Heechee didn't care for the lowlands either. Nothing of theirs has ever been located much below twenty-bar. Doesn't mean it isn't there, of course.

Anyway, I verified our position on the virtual globe and on the detail charts, and deployed the autosonic probes. The winds threw them all over the place as soon as they dropped free. It doesn't much matter where they go, within broad limits, which is a good thing. They dropped like javelins at first, then flew around like straws until the little rockets cut in and the ground-seeking controls fired them to the ground.

Every one embedded itself properly. You aren't always that lucky, so it was a good start.

I verified their position on the detail charts; it was close enough to an equilateral triangle, which is about how you want them. Then I opened the scanning range and began circling around.

"Now what?" bellowed Cochenour. I noticed the girl had put the earplugs back, but he wasn't willing to miss a thing.

"Now we wait for the probes to feel around for Heechee tunnels. It'll take a couple of hours." While I was talking I brought the airbody down through the surface layers. Now we were being thrown around. The buffeting got pretty bad, and so did the noise.

But I found what I was looking for, a surface formation like a blind arroyo, and tucked us into it with only one or two bad moments. Cochenour was watching very carefully, and I grinned to myself. That was where pilotage counted, not en route or at the prepared pads around the Spindle. When he could do that he could get along without somebody like me.

Our position looked all right, so I fired four hold-downs, tethered stakes with explosive heads that opened out in the ground. I winched them tight and all of them held.

That was also a good sign. Reasonably pleased with myself, I opened the belt catches and stood up. "We're here for at least a day or two," I said. "More if we're lucky. How did you like the ride?"

The girl was taking the earplugs out, now that the protecting walls of the arroyo had cut the thundering down to a mere constant scream. "I'm glad I don't get airsick," she said.

Cochenour was thinking, not talking. He was studying the control board while he lit another cigarette.

Dorotha said, "One question, Audee. Why couldn't we stay up where it's quieter?"

"Fuel. I carry about thirty hours, full thrust, but that's it. Is the noise bothering you?"

She made a face.

"You'll get used to it. It's like living next to a spaceport. At first you wonder how anybody stands the noise for a single hour. After you've been there a week you miss it if it stops."

She moved over to the bull's-eye and gazed pensively out at the landscape. We'd crossed into the night portion, and there wasn't much to see but dust and small objects whirling through our external light beams. "It's that first week that I'm worried about," she said.

I flicked on the probe read-out. The little percussive heads were firing their slap-charges and measuring each other's sounds, but it was too early to see anything. The screen was barely beginning to build up a shadowy pattern, more holes than detail.

Cochenour finally spoke. "How long until you can make some sense out of that?" he demanded. Another point: He didn't ask what it was.

"Depends on how close and how big anything is. You can make

a guess in an hour or so, but I like all the data I can get. Six or eight hours, I'd say. There's no hurry."

He growled, "*I'm* in a hurry, Walthers. Keep that in mind."

The girl cut in. "What should we do, Audee? Play three-handed bridge?"

"Whatever you want, but I'd advise some sleep. I've got pills if you want them. If we do find anything—and remember, if we hit on the first try it's just hundred-to-one luck—we'll want to be wide awake for a while."

"All right," said Dorotha, reaching out for the spansules, but Cochenour demanded:

"What about you?"

"Pretty soon. I'm waiting for something." He didn't ask what. Probably, I thought, because he already knew. I decided that when I did hit my bunk I wouldn't take a sleepy pill right away. This Cochenour was not only the richest tourist I had ever guided, he was one of the best informed, and I wanted to think about that for a while.

What I was waiting for took almost an hour to come. The boys were getting a little sloppy; they should have been after us before this.

The radio buzzed and then blared: "Unidentified vessel at one three five, zero seven, four eight and seven two, five one, five four! Please identify yourself and state your purpose!"

Cochenour looked up inquiringly from his gin game with the girl. I smiled reassuringly. "As long as they're saying 'please' there's no problem," I told him, and opened the transmitter.

"This is Pilot Audee Walthers, airbody Poppa Tare Nine One, out of the Spindle. We are licensed and have filed approved flight plans. I have two Terry tourists aboard, purpose recreational exploration."

"Acknowledge. Please wait," blared the radio. The military always broadcasts at maximum gain. Hangover from drill-sergeant days, no doubt.

I turned off the microphone and told my passengers, "They're checking our flight plan. Not to worry about."

In a moment the Defense communicator came back, loud as ever. "You are eleven point four kilometers bearing one eight three degrees from terminator of a restricted area. Proceed with caution. Under Military Regulations One Seven and One Eight, Sections—"

I cut in, "I know the drill. I have my guide's license and have explained the restrictions to the passengers."

"Acknowledged," blared the radio. "We will keep you under surveillance. If you observe vessels or parties on the surface, they are our perimeter teams. Do not interfere with them in any way. Respond at once to any request for identification or information." The carrier buzz cut off.

Cochenour said, "They act nervous."

"No. They're used to seeing us around. They've got nothing else to do, that's all."

Dorrie said hesitantly, "Audee, you told them you'd explained the restrictions to us. I don't remember that part."

"Oh, I explained them all right. We stay out of the restricted area, because if we don't they'll start shooting. That is the Whole of the Law."

VII

I set a wake-up for four hours, and the others heard me moving around and got up too. Dorrie fetched us coffee from the warmer, and we stood drinking it and looking at the patterns the computer had traced.

I took several minutes to study them, although it was clear enough at first look. There were eight major anomalies that could have been Heechee warrens. One was almost right outside our door. We wouldn't even have to move the airbody to dig for it.

I showed them the anomalies, one by one. Cochenour just looked at them thoughtfully. Dorotha asked after a moment, "You mean all of these are unexplored tunnels?"

"No. Wish they were. But, one: Any or all of them could have been explored by someone who didn't go to the trouble of recording it. Two: They don't have to be tunnels. They might be fracture faults, or dikes, or little rivers of some kind of molten material that ran out of somewhere and hardened and got covered over a billion years ago. The only thing we know for sure so far is that there probably aren't any unexplored tunnels in this area *except* in those eight places."

"So what do we do?"

"We dig. And then we see what we've got."

Cochenour said, "Where do we dig?"

I pointed right next to the bright delta of our airbody. "Right here."

"Because it's the best bet?"

"Well, not necessarily." I considered what to tell him, and decided the truth was the best. "There are three that look like better bets than the others—here, I'll mark them." I keyed the chart controls, and the best looking traces immediately displayed letters: A, B and C. "A runs right under the arroyo here, so we'll dig it first."

"Those three because they're the brightest?"

I nodded, somewhat annoyed at his quickness, although it was obvious enough.

"But C over here is the brightest of the lot. Why don't we dig that first?"

I chose my words carefully. "Because we'd have to move the airbody. And because it's on the outside perimeter of the survey area; that means the results aren't as reliable as they are for this one right under us. But those aren't the most important reasons. The most important reason is that C is on the edge of the line our itchy-fingered friends are telling us to stay away from."

Cochenour laughed incredulously. "You mean you're telling me that if you find a real untouched Heechee tunnel you'll stay out of it just because some soldier tells you it's a no-no?"

I said, "The problem doesn't arise just yet; we have seven anomalies to look at that are legal. Also, the military will be checking us from time to time, particularly in the next day or two."

Cochenour insisted, "All right, suppose we check them and find nothing. What do we do then?"

I shook my head. "I never borrow trouble. Let's check the legal ones."

"But suppose."

"Damn it, Boyce! How do I know?"

He gave it up then, but winked at Dorrie and chuckled. "What did I tell you, honey? He's a bigger bandit than I am."

For the next couple of hours we didn't have much time to talk about theoretical possibilities, because we were too busy with concrete facts.

The biggest fact was an awful lot of hot high-speed gas that we had to keep from killing us. My own hotsuit was custom made, of course, and only needed the fittings and tanks to be checked. Boyce and the girl had rental units. They'd paid top dollar for them, and they were good, but good isn't perfect. I had them in and out of them a dozen times, checking the fit and varying tensions until they were as right as I could get them. There's a lot of heat and pressure to keep out when you go about the surface of Venus. The suits were laminated twelve-ply, with nine degrees of freedom at the essential joints. They wouldn't fail; that wasn't what I was worried about. What I was worried about was comfort, because a very small itch or rub can get serious when there's no way to stop it.

But finally they were good enough for a first trial, and we all huddled in the lock and exited onto the surface of Venus.

We were still darkside, but there's so much scatter from the sun that it doesn't get really dark more than a quarter of the time. I let them practice walking around the airbody, leaning into the wind, bracing themselves against the hold-downs and the side of the ship, while I got ready to dig.

I hauled out our first instant igloo, dragged it into position, and ignited it. As it smoldered it puffed up like the children's toy that used to be called a Pharaoh's Serpent, producing a light, tough ash that grew up around the digging site and joined in a seamless dome at the top. I'd already emplaced the digging torch and the crawl-through lock; as the ash grew I manhandled the lock to get a close union, and got a perfect join first time.

Dorrie and Cochenour stayed out of the way when they caught sight of my waving arm, but hung together, watching through their triple-vision plugs. I keyed on the radio. "You want to come in and watch me start it up?" I shouted.

Inside the helmets, they both nodded their heads. "Come on, then," I yelled, and wiggled through the crawl lock. I signed for them to leave it open as they followed me in.

With the three of us and the digging equipment in it, the igloo was even more crowded than the airbody. They backed away as far as they could get, bent against the arc of the igloo wall, while I started up the augers, checked they were vertical, and watched the first castings spiral out.

The foam igloo absorbs more sound than it reflects. Even so, the din inside the igloo was a lot worse than in the howling winds outside. When I thought they'd seen enough to satisfy them for the moment, I waved them out of the crawl-through, followed, sealed it behind us, and led them back into the airbody.

"So far, so good," I said, twisting off the helmet and loosening the suit. "We've got about forty meters to go, I think. Might as well wait in here as out there."

"How long is that?"

"Maybe an hour. You can do what you like; what I'm going to do is take a shower. Then we'll see how far we've got."

That was one of the nice things about having only three people aboard: We didn't have to worry about water discipline very much. It's astonishing how a quick wet-down revives you after coming out of a hotsuit. When I'd finished mine I felt ready for anything.

I was even prepared to eat some of Boyce Cochenour's gourmet cookery, but fortunately it wasn't necessary. The girl had taken over the kitchen, and what she laid out was simple, light, and reasonably non-toxic. On cooking like hers I might be able to survive long enough to collect my charter fee. It crossed my mind for a moment to wonder what made her do it; and then I thought, of course, she'd had a lot of practice. With all the spare parts in Cochenour, no doubt he had dietary problems far worse than mine.

Well, not "worse," exactly, in the sense that I didn't think he was quite as likely to die of them.

According to the autosonic probes, the highest point of the tunnel I had marked "A," or of whatever it was that had seemed like tunnels to their shock waves, was close to the little blind valley in which I'd tied down.

That was very lucky. It meant that we might very possibly be right over the Heechee's own entrance.

The reason that was lucky was not that we would be able to use it the way the Heechee had used it. There wasn't much chance that its mechanisms would have survived a quarter of a million years, much of it exposed to surface wind, ablation, and chemical corrosion. The good part was that if the tunnel had surfaced here it would be relatively easy to bore down to it. Even a quarter of a million years doesn't produce really hard rock, especially without surface water to dissolve out solids and produce compact sediments.

Up to a point, it turned out pretty much the way I had hoped. What was on the surface was little more than ashy sand, and the augers chewed it out very rapidly. Too rapidly; when I went back into the igloo it was filled almost solid with castings, and I had a devil of a job getting to the machines to switch the auger over to pumping the castings out through the crawl lock.

It was a dull, dirty part of the job, but it didn't take long.

I didn't bother to go back into the airbody. I reported what was happening over the radio to Boyce and the girl, staring out the ports at me. I told them I thought we were getting close.

But I didn't tell them exactly how close. Actually, we were only a meter or two from the indicated depth of the anomaly, so close that I didn't bother to pump out all of the castings. I just made enough room to maneuver around, then re-directed the augers; and in five minutes the castings were beginning to come up with the pale blue glimmer that was the sign of a Heechee tunnel.

VIII

About ten minutes after that I keyed on my helmet transmitter and shouted: "Boyce! Dorrie! We've hit a tunnel!"

Either they were sitting around in their suits or they dressed faster than any maze-rat. I unsealed the crawl-through and wiggled out to help them, and they were already coming out of the airbody, staggering against the wind over to me.

They were both yelling questions and congratulations, but I stopped them. "Inside," I ordered. "See for yourself." As a matter of fact, they didn't have to go that far. They could see the color as soon as they knelt to enter the crawl-through.

I followed, and sealed the lock behind me. The reason for that is simple enough. As long as the tunnel isn't breached, it doesn't matter what you do. But the interior of a Heechee tunnel that has remained inviolate is at a pressure only slightly above Earth-normal. Without the sealed dome, the minute you crack the casing you let the whole 20,000-millibar atmosphere of Venus pour in, heat and ablation and all. If the tunnel is empty, or if what's in it is simple, sturdy stuff, there might not be any harm. But if you hit the jackpot you can destroy in half a second what has waited for a quarter of a million years.

We gathered around the shaft and I pointed down. The augers had left a clean shaft, about seventy centimeters by a little over a hundred, with rounded ends. At the bottom you could see the cold blue glow of the outside of the tunnel, only pocked and blotched by the loose castings I hadn't bothered to get out.

"Now what?" demanded Boyce. His voice was hoarse with excitement, which was, I guessed, natural enough.

"Now we burn our way in."

I backed my clients away as far as they could get, pressed against the remaining heap of castings, and unlimbered the fire-jets. I'd already hung sheer-legs over the shaft, and they went right down on their cable with no trouble until they were a few centimeters above the round of the tunnel. Then I fired them up.

You wouldn't think that anything a human being might do would change the temperature of the surface of Venus, but those fire-drills were something special. In the small space of the igloo the heat flamed up and around us, and our hotsuit cooling systems were overloaded in seconds.

Dorrie gasped, "Oh! I—I think I'm going to—"

Cochenour grabbed her. "Faint if you want to," he said fiercely, "but don't get sick. Walthers! How long does this go on?"

It was as hard for me as it was for them; practice doesn't get you used to something like standing in front of a blast furnace with the doors off the hinges. "Maybe a minute," I gasped. "Hold on—it's all right."

It actually took a little more than that, maybe ninety seconds; my suit telltales were shouting alarm for more than half of the time. But they were built for these overloads, and as long as we didn't cook, the suits wouldn't take any permanent harm.

Then we were through. A half-meter circular section sagged, fell at one side and hung there.

I turned off the firejets, and we all breathed hard for a couple of minutes, while the suit coolers gradually caught up with the load.

"Wow," said Dorotha. "That was pretty rough."

I looked at Cochenour. In the light that splashed up out of the shaft I could see he was frowning. I didn't say anything. I just gave the jets another five-second burn to cut away the rest of the circular section, and it fell free into the tunnel. We could hear it clatter against the floor.

Then I turned on my helmet radio. "There's no pressure differential," I said.

The frown didn't change, nor did he speak.

"Which means this one has been breached," I went on. "Let's go back to the airbody and take a break before we do anything else."

Dorotha shrieked, "Audee! What's the matter with you? I want to go down there and see what's inside!"

Cochenour said bitterly, "Shut up, Dorrie. Don't you hear what he's saying? This one's a dud."

Well, there's always the chance that a breached tunnel opened up to a seismological invasion, not a maze-rat with a cutting torch, and if so, there might be something worthwhile in it anyway. And I didn't have the heart to kill all Dorotha's enthusiasm with one blow.

So we did swing down the cable, one by one, into the Heechee dig, and look around.

It was wholly bare, as most of them are, as far as we could see. That wasn't actually very far, for the other thing wrong with a breached tunnel is that you need pretty good equipment to explore it. With the overloads they'd already had, our suits were all right for a couple hours but not much more than that, and when we tramped about half a mile down the tunnel without finding a thing, they were both willing to tramp back and return to the airbody.

We cleaned up and made ourselves something to drink. Even squandering more of the water reserves on showers didn't do much for our spirits.

We had to eat, but Cochenour didn't bother with his gourmet exhibition. Silently, Dorotha threw tabs into the radar oven, and we fed gloomily on emergency rations.

"Well, that's only the first one," she said at last, determined to be sunny about it. "And it's only our second day."

Cochenour said, "Shut up, Dorrie; the one thing I'm not is a good loser." He was staring at the probe trace. "Walthers, how many tunnels are unmarked but empty, like this one?"

"How can I answer a question like that? If they're unmarked, there's no record of them."

"So those traces don't mean anything. We might dig one a day for the next three weeks and find every one a dud."

I nodded. "We surely might, Boyce."

He looked at me alertly. "And?"

"And that's not the worst part of it. I've taken parties out to dig who would've gone mad with joy to open even a breached tunnel. It's perfectly possible to dig every day for weeks and never hit a real Heechee tunnel at all. Don't knock it; at least you got some action for your money."

"I told you, Walthers, I'm not a loser. Second place is no good." He thought for a minute, then barked: "You picked this spot. Did you know what you were doing?"

Did I? The only way to answer that question would be to find a live one, of course. I could have told him about the months of studying records from the first landings on. I could have mentioned how much trouble I went to, and how many regulations I broke, to get the military survey reports, or how far I'd traveled to talk to the Defense crews who'd been on those early digs. I might have let him know how hard it had been to locate old Jorolemon Hegramet, now teaching exotic archeology back in Tennessee, and how many times we'd corresponded; but all I said was, "The fact that we found one tunnel shows I knew my business as a guide. That's all you paid for. It's up to you if we keep looking or not."

He looked at his thumbnail, considering.

The girl said cheerfully, "Buck up, Boyce. Look at all the other chances we've got—and even if we miss, it'll still be fun telling everybody about it back in Cincinnati."

He didn't even look at her, just said, "Isn't there any way to tell whether a tunnel has been breached or not without going inside?"

"Sure," I said. "You can tell by tapping the outside shell. You can hear the difference in the sound."

"But you have to dig down to it first?"

"Right."

We left it at that, and I got back into my hotsuit to strip away the now useless igloo so that we could move the drills.

I didn't really want to discuss it anymore, because I didn't want him to ask a question that I might want to lie about. I try the best I can to tell the truth, because it's easier to remember what you've said that way.

On the other hand, I'm not fanatic about it, and I don't see that it's any of my business to correct a mistaken impression. For instance, obviously Cochenour and the girl had the impression that I hadn't bothered to sound the tunnel casing because we'd already dug down to it and it was just as easy to cut in.

But, of course, I had tested it. That was the first thing I did as soon as the drill got down that far. And when I heard the high-pressure *thunk* it broke my heart. I had to wait a couple of minutes before I could call them to tell them that we'd reached the outer casing.

At that time, I had not quite faced up to the question of just what I would have done if it had turned out that the tunnel had not been breached.

IX

Cochenour and Dorrie Keefer were maybe the fiftieth or sixtieth party I'd taken on a Heechee dig, and I wasn't surprised that they were willing to work like coolies. I don't care how lazy and bored they start out, by the time they actually come close to finding something that belonged to an almost completely unknown alien race, left there when the closest thing to a human being on Earth was a slope-browed furry little beast killing other beasts with antelope bones, they begin to burn with exploration fever.

So they worked hard, and drove me hard, and I was as eager as they. Maybe more so, as the days went past and I found myself rubbing my right side, just under the short ribs, more and more of the time.

The military boys overflew us half a dozen times in the first few days. They didn't say much, just formal requests for identification, which they already well knew, then away. Regulations say if you find anything you're supposed to report it right away. Over Cochenour's objections, I reported finding that first breached tunnel, which surprised them a little, I think.

And that's all we had to report.

Site B was a pegmatite dike. The other two fairly bright ones, that I called D and E, showed nothing at all when we dug, meaning that the sound reflections had probably been caused by nothing more than invisible interfaces in layers of rock or ash or gravel. I vetoed trying to dig C, the best looking of the bunch. Cochenour gave me a hell of an argument about it, but I held out. The military were still looking in on us every now and then, and I didn't want to get any closer to their perimeter than we already were. I half-promised that, if we didn't have any luck elsewhere in the mascons, we'd sneak back to C for a quick dig before returning to the Spindle, and we left it at that.

We lifted the airbody, moved to a new position, and set out a new pattern of probes.

By the end of the second week we had dug nine times and come up empty every time. We were getting low on igloos and probes. We'd run out of tolerance for each other completely.

Cochenour had turned sullen and savage. I hadn't planned on liking the man much when I first met him, but I hadn't expected him to be as bad as that. Considering that it had to be only a game with him—with all his money, the extra fortune he might pick up by discovering some new Heechee artifacts couldn't have meant anything but extra points on a score pad—he was playing for blood.

I wasn't particularly graceful myself, for that matter. The plain fact was that the pills from the Quackery weren't helping as much as they should. My mouth tasted like rats had nested in it, I was getting headaches, and I was beginning to knock things over. See, the thing about the liver is that it sort of regulates your internal diet. It filters out poisons, it converts some of the carbohydrates into other carbohydrates that you can use, it patches together amino acids into proteins. If it isn't working, you die. The doctor had been all over it with me, and I could visualize what was going on inside me, the mahogany-red cells dying and being replaced by clusters of fat and yellowish matter. It was an ugly kind of picture. The ugliest part was that there wasn't anything I could do about it. Only go on taking pills, and they wouldn't work past a matter of a few days more. Liver, by-by; hepatic failure, hello.

So we were a bad bunch. Cochenour was a bastard because it was his nature to be a bastard, and I was a bastard because I was sick and desperate. The only decent human being aboard was the girl.

She did her best, she really did. She was sometimes sweet and often even pretty, and she was always ready to meet the power people, Cochenour and me, more than halfway. It was clearly tough on her. She was only a kid. No matter how grownup she acted, she just hadn't been alive long enough to grow a defense against concentrated meanness. Add in the fact that we were all beginning to hate the sight and sound and smell of each other (and in an airbody you get to know a lot about how people smell). There wasn't much joy on Venus for Dorrie Keefer.

Or for any of us, especially after I broke the news that we were down to our last igloo.

Cochenour cleared his throat. He sounded like a fighter-plane jockey blowing the covers off his guns in preparation for combat, and Dorrie attempted to head him off with a diversion. "Audee," she said brightly, "you know what I think we could do? We could go back to that site that looked good near the military reservation."

It was the wrong diversion. I shook my head. "No."

"What the hell do you mean, 'No'?" rumbled Cochenour, revving up for battle.

"What I said. No. That's a desperation trick, and I'm not that desperate."

"Walthers," he snarled, "you'll be desperate when I tell you to be desperate. I can still stop payment on that check."

"No, you can't. The union won't let you. The regulations are very clear about that. You pay up unless I disobey a lawful directive; you can't make me do anything against the law, and going inside the military reservation is extremely against the law."

He shifted over to cold war. "No," he said softly, "you're wrong about that. It's only against the law if a court says it is, after we do it. You're only right if your lawyers are smarter than my lawyers. Honestly, Walthers, I pay my lawyers to be the smartest there are."

The difficult part was that he was even more right than he knew he was, because my liver was on his side. I couldn't spare time for arbitration because without his money and my transplant I wouldn't live that long.

Dorrie, listening with her birdlike look of friendly interest, got between us again. "Well, then, how about this? We just put down here. Why don't we wait and see what the probes show? Maybe we'll hit something even better than that Trace C—"

"There isn't going to be anything good here," he said without looking at her.

"Why, Boyce, how do you know that? We haven't even finished the soundings."

He said, "Look, Dorotha, listen close one time and then shut up. Walthers is playing games. You see where we are now?"

He brushed past me and tapped out the program for a full map display, which somewhat surprised me because I didn't know he knew how. The charts sprang up with virtual images of our position, the shafts we'd already cut, the great irregular edge of the military reservation overlaid on the plot of mascons and navigation aids.

"You see? We're not even in the high-density mass areas now. Is that true, Walthers? We've tried all the good locations and come up dry?"

I said, "You're partly right, Mr. Cochenour, but I'm not playing games. This site is a good possibility. You can see it on the map. We're not over any mascon, that's true, but we're right between two of them that are located pretty close together. Sometimes you find a dig that connects two complexes, and it has happened that the connecting passage was closer to the surface than any other part of the system. I can't guarantee we'll hit anything here, but it's not impossible."

"Just damn unlikely?"

"Well, no more unlikely than anywhere else. I told you a week ago, you got your money's worth the first day just finding any Heechee tunnel at all, even a spoiled one. There are maze-rats in the Spindle who went five years without seeing that much." I thought for a minute. "I'll make a deal with you," I said.

"I'm listening."

"We're down here, and there's at least a chance we can hit something. Let's try. We'll deploy the probes and see what they turn up. If we get a good trace we'll dig it. If we don't—then I'll think about going back to Trace C."

"*Think* about it!" he roared.

"Don't push me, Cochenour. You don't know what you're getting into. The military reservation is not to be fooled with. Those boys shoot first and ask later, and there aren't any policemen or courts on Venus to even ask them questions."

"I don't know," he said after a moment.

"No," I said, "you don't, Mr. Cochenour, and that's what you're paying me for. I do know."

"Yes," he agreed, "you probably do, but whether you're telling me the truth about what you know is another question. Hegramet never said anything about digging between mascons."

And then he looked at me with a completely opaque expression, waiting to see whether I would catch him up on what he had just said.

I didn't respond. I gave him an opaque look back. I didn't say a word; I only waited to see what would come next. I was pretty sure that it would not be any sort of explanation of how he happened to know Hegramet's name, or what dealings he had had with the greatest Earthside authority on Heechee diggings, and it wasn't.

"Put out your probes and we'll try it your way one more time," he said at last.

I plopped the probes out, got good penetration on all of them, started firing the noisemakers. I sat watching the first buildup of lines on the scan as though I expected them to carry useful information. They couldn't, of course, but it was a good excuse to think privately for a moment.

Cochenour needed to be thought about. He hadn't come to Venus just for the ride, that was clear. He had known he was going to be sinking shafts after Heechee digs before he ever left Earth. He had briefed himself on the whole bit, even to handling the instruments on the airbody. My sales talk about Heechee treasures had been wasted on a customer whose mind had been made up to buy at least half a year earlier and tens of millions of miles away.

All that I understood, but the more I understood the more I saw that I didn't understand. What I really wanted was to give Cochenour a quarter and send him to the movies for a while so I could talk privately to the girl. Unfortunately, there was nowhere to send him. I managed to force a yawn, complain about the boredom of waiting for the probe traces to build up, and suggest a nap. Not that I would have been real confident he wasn't lying there with his ears flapping, listening to us. It didn't matter. Nobody acted sleepy but me. All I got out of it was an offer from Dorrie to watch the screen and wake me if anything interesting turned up.

So I said the hell with it and went to sleep myself.

It was not a good sleep, because lying there waiting for it gave me time to notice how truly lousy I felt, and in how many ways. There was a sort of permanent taste of bile in the back of my mouth, not so much as though I wanted to throw up as it was as though I just had. My head ached, and I was beginning to see ghost images wandering fuzzily around my field of vision. When I took my pills I didn't count the ones that were left. I didn't want to know.

I'd set my private alarm for three hours, thinking maybe that would give Cochenour time to get sleepy and turn in, leaving the girl up and about and perhaps conversational. But when I woke up there was Cochenour, cooking himself an herb omelette with the last of our sterile eggs. "You were right, Walthers," he grinned, "I was sleepy. Had a nice little nap. Ready for anything now. Want some eggs?"

Actually I did want them; but of course I didn't dare eat them, so I glumly swallowed what the Quackery had allowed me to have and watched him stuff himself. It was unfair that a man of ninety could be so healthy that he didn't have to think about digestion, while I was—well, there wasn't any profit in that kind of thinking, so I offered to play some music, and Dorrie picked *Swan Lake*, and I started it up.

And then I had an idea and headed for the tool lockers. They needed checking. The auger heads were about due for replacement, and I knew we were low on spares; and the other thing about the tool lockers was that they were as far from the galley as you could get and stay inside the airbody, and I hoped Dorrie would follow me. And she did.

"Need any help, Audee?"

"Glad to have it," I said. "Here, hold these for me. Don't get the grease on your clothes." I didn't expect her to ask me why they had to be held. She didn't. She only laughed.

"Grease? I don't think I'd even notice it, dirty as I am. I guess we're all about ready to get back to civilization."

Cochenour was frowning over the probe trace and paying us no attention. I said, "Meaning which kind of civilization, the Spindle or Earth."

What I had in mind was to start her talking about Earth, but she went the other way. "Oh, the Spindle, Audee. I thought it was fascinating, and we really didn't get to see much of it. And the people. Like that Indian fellow who ran the cafe. The cashier was his wife, wasn't she?"

"One of them. She's the number-one wife; the waitress was number three, and he has another one at home with the kids. There are five of them, all three wives involved." But I wanted to go in the other direction, so I said, "It's pretty much the same as on Earth. Vastra would be running a tourist trap in Benares if he wasn't running one here, and he wouldn't be here if he hadn't shipped out with the military and terminated here. I'd be guiding in Texas, I suppose. If there's any open country left to guide in, maybe up along the Canadian River. How about you?"

All the time I was picking up the same four or five tools, studying the serial numbers and putting them back. She didn't notice.

"How do you mean?"

"Well, what did you do before you came here?"

"Oh, I worked in Boyce's office for a while."

That was encouraging; maybe she'd remember something about his connection with Professor Hegramet. "What were you, a secretary?"

"Something like that. Boyce let me handle—oh, what's that?"

That was an incoming call on the radio, that was what that was.

"So go answer," snarled Cochenour from across the airbody.

I took it on the earjack, since that is my nature; there isn't any privacy to speak of in an airbody, and I want what little crumbs of it I can find. It was the base calling, a comm sergeant I knew named Littleknees. I signed in irritably, regretting the chance to pump Dorotha about her boss.

"A private word for you, Audee," said Sergeant Littleknees. "Got your sahib around?"

Littleknees and I had exchanged radio chatter for a long time, and there was something about the cheerfulness of the tone that bothered me. I didn't look at Cochenour, but I knew he was listening—only to my side, of course, because of the earjack. "In sight but not receiving," I said. "What have you got for me?"

"Just a little news bulletin," the sergeant purred. "It came over the synsat net a couple of minutes ago. Information only. That means we don't have to do anything about it, but maybe you do, honey."

"Standing by," I said, studying the plastic housing of the radio.

The sergeant chuckled. "Your sahib's charter captain would like to have a word with him when found. It's kind of urgent, 'cause the captain is righteously kissed off."

"Yes, base," I said. "Your signals received, strength ten."

The sergeant made an amused noise again, but this time it wasn't a chuckle, it was a downright giggle. "The thing is," she said, "his check for the charter fee bounced. Want to know what the bank said? You'd never guess. 'Insufficient funds,' that's what they said."

The pain under my right lower ribs was permanent, but right then it seemed to get a lot worse. I gritted my teeth. "Ah, Sergeant Littleknees," I croaked, "can you, ah, verify that estimate?"

"Sorry, honey," she buzzed sympathetically in my ear, "but there's no doubt in the world. Captain got a credit report on him and it turned up n.g. When your customer gets back to the Spindle there'll be a makegood warrant waiting for him."

"Thank you for the synoptic report," I said hollowly. "I will verify departure time before we take off."

And I turned off the radio and gazed at my rich billionaire client.

"What the hell's the matter with you, Walthers?" he growled.

But I wasn't hearing his voice. I was hearing what the happy fellow at the Quackery had told me. The equations were unforgettable. Cash = new liver + happy survival. No cash = total hepatic failure + death. And my cash supply had just dried up.

X

When you get a really big piece of news you have to let it trickle through your system and get thoroughly absorbed before you do anything about it. It isn't a matter of seeing the implications. I saw them right away, you bet. It's a matter of letting the system reach an equilibrium state. So I puttered for a minute. I listened to Tschaikovsky. I made sure the radio switch was off so as not to waste power. I checked the synoptic plot. It would have been nice if there had been something to show, but, the way things were going, there wouldn't be, of course, and there wasn't. A few pale echoes were building up. But nothing with the shape of a Heechee dig, and nothing very bright. The data were still coming in, but there was no way for those feeble plots to turn into the mother-lode that could save us all, even broke bastard Cochenour. I even looked out at as much of the sky as I could to see how the weather was. It didn't matter, but some of the high white calomel clouds were scudding among the purples and yellows of the other mercury halides. It was beautiful and I hated it.

Cochenour had forgotten about his omelette and was watching me thoughtfully. So was Dorrie, still holding the augers in their grease-paper wrap. I grinned at her. "Pretty," I said, referring to the music. The Auckland Philharmonic was just getting to the part where the little swans come out arm in arm and do a fast, bouncy *pas de quatre* across the stage. It has always been one of my favorite parts of *Swan Lake*. "We'll listen to the rest of it later," I said, and snapped it off.

"All right," snarled Cochenour, "what's going on?"

I sat down on an igloo pack and lit a cigarette, because one of the adjustments my internal system had made was to calculate that we didn't have to worry much about coddling our oxygen supply any more. I said. "There's a question that's bothering me, Cochenour. How did you get on to Professor Hegramet?"

He grinned and relaxed. "Is that all that's on your mind? I checked the place out before I came. Why not?"

"No reason, except that you let me think you didn't know a thing."

He shrugged. "If you had any brains you'd know I didn't get rich by being stupid. You think I'd come umpty-million miles without knowing what I was coming to?"

"No, you wouldn't, but you did your best to make me think you would. No matter. So you dug up somebody who could point you to whatever was worth stealing on Venus, and somebody steered you to Hegramet. Then what? Did he tell you I was dumb enough to be your boy?"

Cochenour wasn't quite as relaxed, but he wasn't aggressive either. He said, "Hegramet told me you were the right guide to find a virgin tunnel. That's all—except briefing on the Heechee and so on. If you hadn't come to us I would have come to you; you just saved me the trouble."

I said, a little surprised, "You know, I think you're telling me the truth. Except you left out one thing: It wasn't the fun of making more money that you were after, it was just money, right? Money that you needed." I turned to Dorotha, standing frozen with the augers in her hand. "How about it, Dorrie? Did you know the old man was broke?"

Putting it that way was not too smart. I saw what she was about to do just before she did it, and jumped off the igloo. I was a little too late. She dropped the augers before I could get them from her, but fortunately they landed flat and the blades weren't chipped. I picked them up and put them away.

She had answered the question well enough.

I said, "I see you didn't know. Tough on you, doll. His check to the captain of the *Gagarin* is still bouncing, and I would imagine the one he gave me isn't going to be much better. I hope you got it in furs and jewels, and my advice to you is to hide them before the creditors want them back."

She didn't even look at me. She was only looking at Cochenour, whose expression was all the confirmation she needed.

I don't know what I expected from her, rage or reproaches or tears. What she did was whisper, "Oh, Boyce, I'm so sorry," and she went over and put her arm around him.

I turned my back on them, because I didn't like looking at him. The strapping ninety-year-old buck on Full Medical had turned into a defeated old man. For the first time, he looked all of his age and maybe a little more: the mouth half open, trembling; the straight back stooped; the bright blue eyes watering. She stroked him and crooned to him.

I looked at the synoptic web again, for lack of anything better to do. It was about as clear as it was going to get, and it was empty. We had nearly a 50 percent overlap from our previous soundings, so I could tell that the interesting-looking scratches at one edge were nothing to get excited about. We'd checked them out already. They were only ghosts.

There was no rescue there.

Curiously, I felt kind of relaxed. There is something tranquilizing about the realization that you have nothing much left to lose. It puts things in a different perspective. I don't mean to say that I had given up completely. There were still things I could do. They might not have anything to do with prolonging my life, but the taste in my mouth and the pain in my gut weren't letting me enjoy life very much anyway. I could, for instance, write Audee Walthers off; since only a miracle could keep me from dying in a matter of days, I could accept the fact that I wasn't going to be alive a week from now and use what time I had for something else. What else? Well, Dorrie was a nice kid. I could fly the airbody back to the Spindle, turn Cochenour over to the gendarmes, and spend my last day or so introducing her around. Vastra or BeeGee would help her get organized. She might not even have to go into prostitution or the rackets. The high season wasn't that far off, and she would do well with a little booth of prayer fans and Heechee lucky pieces for the Terry tourists. Maybe that wasn't much, even from her point of view, but it was something.

Or I could fling myself on the mercy of the Quackery. They might let me have the new liver on credit. The only reason I had for thinking they wouldn't was that they never had.

Or I could open the two-fuel valves and let them mix for ten minutes or so before hitting the igniter. The explosion wouldn't leave much of the airbody or us, and nothing at all of our problems.

Or—

"Oh, hell," I said. "Buck up, Cochenour. We're not dead yet."

He looked at me for a minute. He patted Dorrie's shoulder and pushed her away, gently enough. He said, "I will be, soon enough. I'm sorry about all this, Dorotha. And I'm sorry about your check, Walthers; I expect you needed the money."

"You have no idea."

He said with difficulty, "Do you want me to explain?"

"I don't see that it makes any difference, but, yes, out of curiosity I do."

I let him tell me, and he did it steadily and succinctly. I could have guessed. A man his age is either very, very rich or dead. He was only quite rich. He'd kept his industries going on what was left after he siphoned off the costs of transplant and treatment, calciphylaxis and prosthesis, protein regeneration here, cholesterol flushing there, a million for this, a hundred grand a week for that . . . oh, it went, I could see that. "You just don't know," he said, "what it takes to keep a hundred-year-old man alive until you try it."

I corrected him automatically. "Ninety, you mean."

"No, not ninety, and not even a hundred. I think it's at least a hundred and ten, and it could be more than that. Who counts? You pay the doctors and they patch you up for a month or two. You wouldn't know."

Oh, wouldn't I just, I said, but not out loud. I let him go on, telling about how the federal inspectors were closing in and he skipped Earth to make his fortune all over again on Venus.

But I wasn't listening any more; I was writing on the back of a navigation form. When I was finished, I passed it over to Cochenour. "Sign it," I said.

"What is it?"

"Does it matter? You don't have any choice, do you? But it's a release from the all-rights section of our charter agreement; you acknowledge you have no claim, that your check's rubber, and that you voluntarily waive your ownership of anything we find in my favor."

He frowned. "What's this bit at the end?"

"That's where I give you ten percent of anything we do find, *if* we do find anything."

"That's charity," he said, but he was signing. "I don't mind charity, especially since, as you point out, I don't have any choice. But I can read that web as well as you can, Walthers, and there's nothing on it to find."

"No," I said, folding the paper and putting it in my pocket, "But we're not going to dig here. That trace is bare as your bank account. What we're going to do is dig Trace C."

I lit another cigarette and thought for a minute. I was wondering how much to tell them of what I had spent five years finding out and figuring out, schooling myself not even to hint at it to anyone else. I was sure in my mind that nothing I said would make a difference, but the words didn't want to say themselves anyway.

I made myself say:

"You remember Subhash Vastra, the fellow who ran the trap where I met you. He came to Venus with the military. He was a weapons specialist. There's no civilian career for a weapons specialist so he went into the cafe business when they terminated him, but he was pretty big at it in the service."

Dorrie said, "Do you mean there are Heechee weapons on the reservation?"

"No. Nobody has ever found a Heechee weapon. But they found targets."

It was actually physically difficult for me to speak the next part, but I got it out. "Anyway, Sub Vastra says they were targets. The higher brass wasn't sure, and I think the matter has been pigeonholed on the reservation by now. But what they found was triangular pieces of Heechee wall material—that blue, light-emitting stuff they lined the tunnels with. There were dozens of them, and they all had a pattern of radiating lines; Sub said they looked like targets to him. And they had been drilled through, by something that left the holes chalky as talc. Do you know anything that would do that to Heechee wall material?"

Dorrie was about to say she didn't, but Cochenour interrupted her. "That's impossible," he said flatly.

"Right, that's what the brass said. They decided it had to be done in the process of fabrication, for some Heechee purpose we'll never know. But Vastra says not. He says they looked exactly like the paper targets from the firing range under the reservation. The holes weren't all in the same place; the lines looked like scoring markers. That's evidence he's right. Not proof. But evidence."

"And you think you can find the gun that made those holes where we marked Trace C?"

I hesitated. "I wouldn't put it that strongly. Call it a hope. But there is one more thing.

"These targets were turned up by a prospector nearly forty years ago. He turned them in, reported his find, went out looking for more and got killed. That happened a lot in those days. No one paid much

attention until some military types got a look at them; and that's how
come the reservation is where it is. They spotted the site where he'd
reported finding them, staked out everything for a thousand kilometers around and labeled it all off limits. And they dug and dug, turned
up about a dozen Heechee tunnels, but most of them bare and the
rest cracked and spoiled."

"Then there's nothing there," growled Cochenour, looking per-
plexed.

"There's nothing they found," I corrected him. "But in those
days prospectors lied a lot. He reported the wrong location for the
find. At the time, he was shacked up with a young lady who later
married a man named Allemang, and her son is a friend of mine.
He had a map. The right location, as near as I can figure—the
navigation marks weren't what they are now—is right about where
we are now, give or take some. I saw digging marks a couple of
times and I think they were his." I slipped the little private magne-
tofiche out of my pocket and put it into the virtual map display; it
showed a single mark, an orange X. "That's where I think we might
find the weapon, somewhere near that X. And as you can see, the
only undug indication there is good old Trace C."

Silence for a minute. I listened to the distant outside howl of the
winds, waiting for them to say something.

Dorrie was looking troubled. "I don't know if I like trying to find
a new weapon," she said. "It's—it's like bringing back the bad old
days again."

I shrugged. Cochenour, beginning to look more like himself
again, said, "The point isn't whether we really want to find a
weapon, is it? The point is that we want to find an untapped
Heechee dig for whatever is in it—but the soldiers think there *might*
be a weapon somewhere around, so they aren't going to let us dig,
right? They'll shoot us first and ask questions later. Wasn't that
what you said?"

"That's what I said."

"So how do you propose to get around that little problem?" he
asked.

If I were a truthful man I would have said I wasn't sure I could.
Looked at honestly, the odds were we would get caught and very
likely shot; but we had so little to lose, Cochenour and I, that I
didn't think that important enough to mention. I said:

"We try to fool them. We send the airbody off, and you and I
stay behind to do the digging. If they think we're gone, they won't
be keeping us under surveillance, and all we have to worry about
is being picked up on a routine perimeter search."

"Audee!" cried the girl. "If you and Boyce stay here—But that means I have to take the airbody, and *I* can't fly this thing."

"No, you can't. But you can let it fly itself." I rushed on: "Oh, you'll waste fuel and you'll get bounced around a lot. But you'll get there on autopilot. It'll even land you at the Spindle." Not necessarily easily or well; I closed my mind to the thought of what an automatic landing might do to my one and only airbody. She would survive it, though, ninety-nine chances out of a hundred.

"Then what?" Cochenour demanded.

There were big holes in the plan at this point, but I closed my mind to them, too. "Dorrie looks up my friend BeeGee Allemang. I'll give you a note to give him with all the coordinates and so on, and he'll come and pick us up. With extra tanks, we'll have air and power for maybe forty-eight hours after you leave. That's plenty of time for you to get there, find BeeGee and give him the message, and for him to get back. If he's late, of course, we're in trouble. If we don't find anything, we've wasted our time. But if we do—"

I shrugged. "I didn't say it was a guarantee," I added, "I only said it gave us a chance."

Dorrie was quite a nice person, considering her age and her circumstances, but one of the things she lacked was self-confidence. She had not been trained to it; she had been getting it as a prosthesis, from Cochenour most recently, I suppose before that from whoever preceded Cochenour in her life—at her age, maybe her father.

That was the biggest problem, persuading Dorrie she could do her part. "It won't work," she kept saying. "I'm sorry. It isn't that I don't want to help. I do, but I can't. It just won't work."

Well, it would have.

Or at least I think it would have.

In any event, we never got to try it. Between us, Cochenour and I did get Dorrie to agree to give it a try. We packed up what little gear we'd put outside, flew back to the ravine, landed and began to set up for the dig. But I was feeling poorly, thick, headachy, clumsy, and I suppose Cochenour had his own problems. Between the two of us we managed to catch the casing of the drill in the exit port while we were offloading it, and while I was jockeying it one way from above, Cochenour pulled the other way from beneath and the whole thing came down on top of him. It didn't kill him. But it gouged his suit and broke his leg, and that took care of my idea of digging Trace C with him.

XI

The suit leg had been ruptured through eight or ten plies, but there was enough left to keep the air out, if not the pressure.

The first thing I did was check the drill to make sure it wasn't damaged. It wasn't. The second thing was to fight Cochenour back into the lock. That took about everything I had, with the combined weight of our suits and bodies, getting the drill out of the way, and my general physical condition. But I managed it.

Dorrie was great. No hysterics, no foolish questions. We got him out of his suit and looked him over. He was unconscious. The leg was compounded, with bone showing through; he was bleeding from the mouth and nose, and he had vomited inside his helmet. All in all he was about the worst-looking hundred-and-some-year-old man you'll ever see—live one, anyway. But he hadn't taken enough heat to cook his brain, his heart was still going—well, whoever's heart it had been in the first place, I mean; it was a good investment, because it pumped right along. The bleeding stopped by itself, except from the nasty business on the leg.

Dorrie called the military reservation for me, got Eve Littleknees, was put right through to the Base Surgeon. He told me what to do. At first he wanted me to pack up and bring Cochenour right over, but I vetoed that—said I wasn't in shape to fly and it would be too rough a ride. Then he gave me step-by-steps and I followed it easily enough: reduced the fracture, packed the gash, closed the wound with surgical Velcro and meat glue, sprayed a bandage all around and poured on a cast. It took about an hour, and Cochenour would have come to while we were doing it except I gave him a sleepy needle.

So then it was just a matter of taking pulse and respiration and blood-pressure readings to satisfy the surgeon, and promising to get him back to the Spindle shortly. When the surgeon was through, still annoyed at me for not bringing Cochenour over, Sergeant Littleknees came back on. I could tell what was on her mind. "Uh, honey? How did it happen?"

"A great big Heechee came up out of the ground and bit him," I said. "I know what you're thinking and you've got an evil mind. It was just an accident."

"Sure," she said. "Okay. I just wanted you to know I don't blame you a bit." And she signed off.

Dorrie was cleaning Cochenour up as best she could—pretty profligate with the water reserves, I thought. I left her to it while I made myself some coffee, lit a cigarette, and sat and thought.

By the time Dorrie had done what she could for Cochenour, then cleaned up the worst of the mess and begun to do such important tasks as repairing her eye makeup, I had thought up a dandy.

I gave Cochenour a wake-up needle, and Dorrie patted him and talked to him while he got his bearings. She was not a girl who carried a grudge. I did, a little. I got him up to try out his muscles faster than he really wanted to. His expression told me that they all ached. They worked all right, though.

He was able to grin. "Old bones," he said. "I knew I should have gone for the recalciphylaxis. That's what happens when you try to save a buck."

He sat down heavily, the leg stuck out in front of him. He wrinkled his nose. "Sorry to have messed up your nice clean airbody," he added.

"You want to clean yourself up?"

He looked surprised. "Well, I think I'd better, pretty soon—"

"Do it now. I want to talk to you both."

He didn't argue, just held out his hand, and Dorrie took it. He stumped, half-hopped toward the clean-up. Actually Dorrie had done the worst of it, but he splashed a little water on his face and swished some around in his mouth. He was pretty well recovered when he turned around to look at me.

"All right, what is it? Are we giving up?"

I said. "No. We'll do it a different way."

Dorrie cried, "He can't, Audee! Look at him. And the condition his suit's in, he couldn't last outside an hour, much less help you dig."

"I know that, so we'll have to change the plan. I'll dig by myself. The two of you will slope off in the airbody."

"Oh, brave man," said Cochenour flatly. "Who are you kidding? It's a two-man job."

I hesitated. "Not necessarily. Lone prospectors have done it before, although the problems were a little different. I admit it'll be a tough 48 for me, but we'll have to try it. One reason. We don't have any alternative."

"Wrong," said Cochenour. He patted Dorrie's rump. "Solid muscle, that girl. She isn't big, but she's healthy. Takes after her grandmother. Don't argue, Walthers. Just think a little bit. It's as safe for Dorrie as it is for you; and with the two of you, there's a chance we might luck in. By yourself, no chance at all."

For some reason, his attitude put me in a bad temper. "You talk as though she didn't have anything to say about it."

"Well," said Dorrie, sweetly enough, "come to that, so do you. I appreciate your wanting to make things easy for me, Audee, but, honestly, I think I could help. I've learned a lot. And if you want the truth, you look a lot worse than I do."

I said with all the sneer I could get into my voice, "Forget it. You can both help me for an hour or so, while I get set up. Then we'll do it my way. No arguments. Let's get going."

That made two mistakes. The first was that we didn't get set up in an hour; it took more than two, and I was sweating sick oily sweat before we finished. I really felt bad. I was past hurting or worrying about it; I just thought it a little surprising every time my heart beat. Dorrie did more muscle work than I did, strong and willing as promised, and Cochenour checked over the instruments, and asked a couple of questions when he had to to make sure he could handle his part of the job, flying the airbody. I took two cups of coffee heavily laced with my private supply of gin and smoked my last cigarette for a while, meanwhile checking out with the military reservation. Eve Littleknees was flirtatious but a little puzzled.

Then Dorrie and I tumbled out of the lock and closed it behind us, leaving Cochenour strapped in the pilot's seat.

Dorrie stood there for a moment, looking forlorn; but then she grabbed my hand and the two of us lumbered to the shelter of the igloo we'd already ignited. I had impressed on her the importance of being out of the wash of the twin-fuel jets. She was good about it; flung herself flat and didn't move.

I was less cautious. As soon as I could judge from the flare that the jets were angled away from us, I stuck my head up and watched Cochenour take off in a sleet of heavy-metal ash. It wasn't a bad takeoff. In circumstances like that I define "bad" as total demolition of the airbody and the death or maiming of one or more persons. He avoided that, but the airbody skittered and slid wildly as the gusts caught it. It would be a rough ride for him, going just the few hundred kilometers north that would take him out of detection range.

I touched Dorrie with my toe and she struggled up. I slipped the talk cord into the jack on her helmet—radio was out, because of possible perimeter patrols that we wouldn't be able to see.

"Change your mind yet?" I asked.

It was a fairly obnoxious question, but she took it nicely. She giggled. I could tell that because we were faceplate to faceplate and I could see her face shadowed inside the helmet. But I couldn't hear what she was saying until she remembered to nudge the voice switch, and then what I heard was:

"—romantic, just the two of us."

Well, we didn't have time for that kind of chitchat. I said irritably, "Let's quit wasting time. Remember what I told you. We have air, water and power for 48 hours. Don't count on any margin. One or two of them might hold out a little longer, but you need all three to stay alive. Try not to work too hard; the less you metabolize, the less your waste system has to handle. If we find a tunnel and get in, maybe we can eat some of those emergency rations over there—provided it's unbreached and hasn't heated up too much in a quarter of a million years. Otherwise don't even think about food. As for sleeping, forget—"

"Now who's wasting time? You told me all this before." But she was still cheery.

So we climbed into the igloo and started work.

The first thing we had to do was clear out some of the tailings that had already begun to accumulate where we left the drill going. The usual way, of course, is to reverse and redirect the augers. We couldn't do that. It would have meant taking them away from cutting the shaft. We had to do it the hard way, namely manually.

It was hard, all right. Hotsuits are uncomfortable to begin with. When you have to work in them, they're miserable. When the work is both very hard physically and complicated by the cramped space inside an igloo that already contains two people and a working drill, it's next to impossible.

We did it anyhow, having no choice.

Cochenour hadn't lied; Dorrie was as good as a man. The question was whether that was going to be good enough. The other question, which was bothering me more and more every minute, was whether I was as good as a man. The headache was really pounding at me, and I found myself blacking out when I moved suddenly. The Quackery had promised me three weeks before acute hepatic failure, but that hadn't been meant to include this kind of work. I had to figure I was on plus time already. That is a disconcerting way to figure.

Especially when ten hours went by and I realized that we were down lower than the soundings had shown the tunnel to be, and no luminous blue tailings were in sight.

We were drilling a dry hole.

Now, if we had had the airbody close by, this would have been an annoyance. Maybe a big annoyance, but not a disaster. What I would have done was get back in the airbody, clean up, get a good night's sleep, eat a meal, and recheck the trace. We were digging in the wrong place. All right, next step is to dig in the right place. Study the terrain, pick a spot, ignite another igloo, start up the drills and try, try again.

That's what we *would* have done. But we didn't have any of those advantages. We didn't have the airbody. We had no chance for sleep or food. We were out of igloos. We didn't have the trace to look at. And I was feeling lousier every minute.

I crawled out of the igloo, sat down in the next thing there was to the lee of the wind, and stared at the scudding yellow-green sky.

There ought to be something to do, if I could only think of it. I ordered myself to think.

Well, let's see. Could I maybe uproot the igloo and move it to another spot?

No. I could break it loose all right with the augers, but the minute it was free the winds would catch it and it would be good-by, Charlie. I'd never see that igloo again. Plus there would be no way to make it gastight anyway.

Well, then, how about drilling without an igloo?

Possible, I judged. Pointless, though. Suppose we did hit lucky and hole in? Without an igloo to lock out those twenty thousand millibars of hot gas, we'd destroy the contents anyway.

I felt a nudge on my shoulder, and discovered that Dorrie was sitting next to me. She didn't ask any questions, didn't try to say anything at all. I guess it was all clear enough without talking about it.

By my suit chronometer fifteen hours were gone. That left thirty-some before Cochenour would come back and get us. I didn't see any point in spending it all sitting there, but on the other hand I didn't see any point in doing anything else.

Of course, I thought, I could always go to sleep for a while . . . and then I woke up and realized that that was what I had been doing.

Dorrie was asleep beside me.

You may wonder how a person can sleep in the teeth of a south polar thermal gale. It isn't all that hard. All it takes is that you be wholly worn out, and wholly despairing. Sleeping isn't just to knit the raveled sleeve, it is a good way to shut the world off when the world is too lousy to face. As ours was.

But Venus is the last refuge of the Puritan ethic. Crazy. I knew I was as good as dead, but I felt I had to be doing something. I eased away from Dorrie, made sure her suit was belted to the hold-tight ring at the base of the igloo, and stood up. It took a great deal of concentration for me to be able to stand up, which was almost as good at keeping care out as sleep.

It occurred to me that there still might be eight or ten live Heechees in the tunnel, and maybe they'd heard us knocking and opened up the bottom of the shaft for us. So I crawled into the igloo to see.

I peered down the shaft to make sure. No. They hadn't. It was still just a blind hole that disappeared into dirty dark invisibility at the end of the light from my head lamp. I swore at the Heechees who hadn't helped us out, and kicked some tailings down the shaft on their non-existent heads.

The Puritan ethic was itching me, and I wondered what I ought to do. Die? Well, yes, but I was doing that fast enough. Something constructive?

I remembered that you always ought to leave a place the way you found it, so I hauled up the drills on the eight-to-one winch and stowed them neatly. I kicked some more tailings down the useless hole to make a place to sit, and I sat down and thought.

I mused about what we had done wrong, as you might think about a chess puzzle.

I could still see the trace in my mind. It was bright and clear, so there was definitely something there. It was just tough that we'd lucked out and missed it.

How had we missed it?

After some time, I thought I knew the answer to that.

People like Dorrie and Cochenour have an idea that a seismic trace is like one of those underground maps of downtown Dallas, with all the sewers and utility conduits and water pipes marked, so you just dig where it says and you find what you want.

It isn't exactly like that. The trace comes out as a sort of hazy approximation. It is built up, hour by hour, by measuring the echoes from the pinger. It looks like a band of spiderweb shadows, much wider than an actual tunnel and very fuzzy at the edges. When you look at it you know that somewhere in the shadows there's something that makes them. Maybe it's a rock interface or a pocket of gravel. Hopefully it's a Heechee dig. Whatever it is, it's there somewhere, but you don't just know where, exactly. If a tunnel is twenty meters wide, which is a fair average for a Heechee connecting link, the shadow trace is sure to look like fifty, and maybe a hundred.

So where do you dig?

That's where the art of prospecting comes in. You have to make an informed guess.

Maybe you dig in the exact geometrical center—as far as it is given you to see where the center is. That's the easiest way. Maybe you dig where the shadows are densest, which is the way the half-smart prospectors do, and that works almost half the time. Or maybe you do what I did, and try to think like a Heechee. You look at the trace as a whole and try to see what points they might have been trying to connect. Then you plot an imaginary course between them, where you would have put the tunnel if you had been the Heechee engineer in charge, and you dig somewhere along there.

That's what I had done, but evidently I had done wrong.

In a fuzzy-brained sort of way, I began to think I saw what I'd done.

I visualized the trace. The right place to dig was where I had set the airbody down, but of course I couldn't set up the igloo there

because the airbody was in the way. So I'd set up about ten yards
upslope.

I was convinced that ten yards was what made us miss.

I was pleased with myself for figuring it out, although I couldn't
see that it made a lot of practical difference. If I'd had another igloo
I would have been glad to try again, assuming I could hold out that
long. But that didn't mean much, because I didn't have another igloo.

So I sat on the edge of the dark shaft, nodding sagaciously over
the way I had solved the problem, dangling my legs and now and
then sweeping tailings in. I think that was part of a kind of death
wish, because I know I thought, now and then, that the nicest thing
to do would be to jump in and pull the tailings down over me.

But the Puritan ethic didn't want me to do that. Anyway, it would
have solved only my own personal problem. It wouldn't have done
anything for old Dorrie Keefer, snoring away outside in the thermal
hurricane.

I then began to wonder why I was worrying about Dorrie. It was a
pleasant enough subject to be thinking about, but sort of sad.

I went back to thinking about the tunnel.

The bottom of the shaft couldn't be more than a few yards away
from where we had bottomed out empty. I thought of jumping down
and scraping away with my bare gloves. It seemed like a good idea.
I'm not sure how much was whimsy and how much the fantasy of a
sick man, but I kept thinking how nice it would be if there were
Heechees still in there, and when I scratched into the blue wall material I could just knock politely and they'd open up and let me in. I
even had a picture of what they looked like: sort of friendly and
godlike. It would have been very pleasant to meet a Heechee, a live
one that could speak English. "Heechee, what did you really use those
things we call prayer fans for?" I could ask him. Or, "Heechee, have
you got anything that will keep me from dying in your medicine
chest?" Or, "Heechee, I'm sorry we messed up your front yard and
I'll try to clean it up for you."

I pushed more of the tailings back into the shaft. I had nothing
better to do, and who could tell, maybe they'd appreciate it. After a
while I had it half full and I'd run out of tailings, except for the ones
that were pushed outside the igloo, and I didn't have the strength to
go after them. I looked for something else to do. I reset the augers,
replaced the dull blades with the last sharp ones we had, pointed them
in the general direction of a twenty-degree offset angle downslope,
and turned them on.

It wasn't until I noticed that Dorrie was standing next to me, helping me steady the augers for the first yards of cut, that I realized I had made a plan.

Why not try an offset cut? Did we have any better chance?

We did not. We cut.

When the drills stopped bucking and settled down to chew into the rock and we could leave them, I cleared a space at the side of the igloo and shoved tailings out for a while; then we just sat there and watched the drills spit rock chips into the old shaft. It was filling up nicely. We didn't speak. Presently I fell asleep again.

I didn't wake up until Dorrie pounded on my head. We were buried in tailings, but they weren't just rock. They glowed blue, so bright they almost hurt my eyes.

The augers must have been scratching at the Heechee wall liner for hours. They had actually worn pits into it.

We looked down, and we could see the round bright blue eye of the tunnel wall staring up at us. She was a beauty, all ours.

Even then we didn't speak.

Somehow I managed to kick and wriggle my way through the drift to the crawl-through. I got the lock closed and sealed, after kicking a couple of cubic meters of rock outside. Then I began fumbling through the pile of refuse for the flame drills. Ultimately I found them. Somehow. Ultimately I managed to get them shipped and primed. I fired them, and watched the bright pot of light that bounced out of the shaft and made a pattern on the igloo roof.

Then there was a sudden short scream of gas, and a clatter as the loose fragments at the bottom of the shaft dropped free.

We had cut into the Heechee tunnel. It was unbreached and waiting for us. Our beauty was a virgin. We took her maidenhead with all love and reverence and entered into her.

XII

I must have blacked out again, and when I realized where I was I was on the floor of the tunnel. My helmet was open. So were the side-zips of my hotsuit. I was breathing stale, foul air that had to be a quarter of a million years old and smelled every minute of it. But it was air. It was denser than Earth normal and a lot more humid; but the partial pressure of oxygen was about the same. It was enough to live on, in any case. I was proving that by breathing it and not dying.

Next to me was Dorrie Keefer.

The blue Heechee wall light didn't flatter her complexion. At first I wasn't sure she was breathing. But in spite of the way she looked her pulse was going, her lungs were functioning, and when she felt me poking at her she opened her eyes.

"We made it," she said.

We sat there grinning foolishly at each other, like Hallowe'en masks in the blue Heechee glow.

To do anything more than that, just then, was quite impossible. I had my hands full just comprehending the fact that I was alive. I didn't want to endanger that odds-against precarious fact by moving around. But I wasn't comfortable, and after a moment I realized that I was very hot. I closed up my helmet to shut out some of the heat, but the smell inside was so bad that I opened it up, figuring the heat was better.

Then it occurred to me to wonder why the heat was only unpleasant, instead of instantly fatal. Energy transport through a Heechee wall-material surface is very slow, but not a quarter of a million years slow. My sad old brain ruminated that thought around for a while and came up with a conclusion: At least until quite recently, some centuries or thousands of years, maybe, this tunnel had been kept cool. Automatic machinery, of course, I thought sagely. Wow, that by itself was worth finding. Broken down or not, it would be worth a lot of fortunes . . . .

And that made me remember why we were there in the first place, and I looked up the corridor and down, to see what treasures were waiting there for us.

When I was a school kid in Amarillo Central my favorite teacher was a crippled lady named Miss Stevenson, and she used to tell us stories out of Bulfinch and Homer. She spoiled a whole weekend for me with the story of one Greek fellow who wanted to be a god. He was king of a little place in Lydia, but he wanted more, and the gods let him come to Olympus, and he had it made until he fouled up. I forget how; it had something to do with a dog, and some nasty business about tricking the gods into eating his own son. Whatever it was, they gave him solitary confinement for eternity, standing neck deep in a cool lake in hell and unable to drink. The fellow's name was Tantalus, and in that Heechee tunnel I had a lot in common with him. The treasure trove was there all right, but we couldn't reach it. We hadn't hit the main tunnel but a sort of angled, Thielly-tube detour in it, and it was blocked at both ends. We could peer past half-closed gates into the main shaft. We could see Heechee machines and irregular mounds of things that might once have been containers, now rotted, with their contents on the floor. But we hadn't the strength to get at them.

It was the suits that made us so clumsy. With them off we might have been able to slip through, but then would we have the strength to put them back on again in time to meet Cochenour? I doubted it. I stood there with my helmet pressed to the gate, feeling like Alice peering into her garden without the bottle of drink-me, and then I thought about Cochenour again and checked the time.

It was forty-six hours and some odd minutes since he had left us. He was due back any time.

And if he came back while we were here, and opened the crawl-through to look for us and was careless about the seal at both ends, twenty thousand millibars of poison gas would hammer in on us. It would kill us, of course, but besides that it would damage the virgin tunnel. The corrosive scouring of that implosion of gas might wreck everything.

"We have to go back," I told Dorrie, showing her the time. She smiled.

"Temporarily," she said, and turned and led the way.

After the cheerful blue glow of the Heechee tunnel the igloo was cramped and miserable, and what was worse was that we couldn't even stay inside it. Cochenour probably would remember to lock in and out of both ends of the crawl-through. But he might not. I couldn't take that chance. I tried to think of a way of plugging the shaft, maybe by pushing all the tailings back in again, but although my brain wasn't working very well, I could see that was stupid.

So we had to wait outside in the breezy Venusian weather, and not too much later, either. The little watch dial next to my life-support meters, all running well into the red now, showed that Cochenour should in fact have arrived by now.

I pushed Dorrie into the crawl-through, squeezed in with her, locked us both through, and we waited.

We waited a long time, Dorrie bent over the crawl-through and me leaning beside her, holding on to her and the tie-down clips. We could have talked, but I thought she was either unconscious or asleep from the way she didn't move, and anyway it seemed like an awful lot of work to plug in the phone jack.

We waited longer than that, and still Cochenour didn't come.

I tried to think things through.

There could have been a number of reasons for his being late. He could have crashed. He could have been challenged by the military. He could have got lost.

But there was another possibility that made more sense than all of them. The time dial told me he was nearly five hours late now, and the life-support meters told me we were right up against the upper maximum for power, near it for air, well past it for water. If it hadn't been for breathing the Heechee gases for a while, we would have been dead by then, and Cochenour didn't know about that.

He had said he was a bad loser. He had worked out an end-game maneuver so he wouldn't have to lose. I could see him as clearly as though I were in the airbody with him, watching his own clocks, cooking himself a light lunch and playing music while he waited for us to die.

That was no frightening thought; I was close enough to it for the difference to be pretty much a technicality, and tired enough of being trapped in that foul hotsuit to be willing to accept almost any deliverance. But the girl was involved, and the one tiny little rational thought that stayed in my half-poisoned brain was that it was unfair for Cochenour to kill us both. Me, yes. Her, no. I beat on her suit until she moved a little, and after some time managed to make her move back into the crawl-through.

There were two things Cochenour didn't know. He didn't know we'd found breathable air, and he didn't know we could tap the drill batteries for additional power.

In all the freaked-out fury of my head, I was still capable of that much consecutive thought. We could surprise him, if he didn't wait much longer. We could stay alive for a few hours yet, and then when he came to find us dead and see what prize we had won for him, he would find me waiting.

And so he did.

It must have been a terrible shock to him when he entered the igloo with the monkey-wrench in his hand and leaned over me, and found that I was still alive and able to move, where he had expected only a well-done roast of meat. The drill caught him right in the chest. I couldn't see his face, but I guess at his expression.

Then it was only a matter of doing four or five impossible things. Things like getting Dorrie up out of the tunnel and into the airbody. Like getting myself in after her, and sealing up, and setting a course. All these impossible things, and one other, that was harder than all of them, but very important to me.

I totaled the airbody when we landed, but we were strapped in and suited up, and when the ground crews came to investigate, Dorrie and I were still alive.

XIII

They had to patch me and rehydrate me for three days before they could even think about putting my new liver in. In the old days they would have kept me sedated the whole time, but, of course, they kept waking me up every couple of hours for some feedback training on monitoring my hepatic flows. I hated it, because it was all sickness and pain and nagging from Dr. Morius and the nurses and I could have wished for the old days back again, except, of course, that in the old days I would have died.

But by the fourth day I hardly hurt at all, except when I moved, and they were letting me take my fluids by mouth instead of the other way.

I realized I was going to be alive for a while, and looked upon my surroundings, and found them good.

There's no such thing as a season in the Spindle, but the Quackery is all sentimental about tradition and ties with the Mother Planet. They were playing scenes of fleecy white clouds on the wall panels, and the air from the ventilator ducts smelled of green leaves and lilac.

"Happy spring," I said to Dr. Morius.

"Shut up," he said, shifting a couple of the needles that pincushioned my abdomen and watching the telltales. "Um." He pursed his lips, pulled out a couple of needles, and said:

"Well, let's see, Walthers. We've taken out the splenovenal shunt. Your new liver is functioning well, although you're not flushing wastes through as fast as you ought to. We've got your ion levels back up to something like a human being, and most of your tissues have a little moisture in them again. Altogether," he scratched his head, "yes, in general, I would say you're alive, so presumably the operation was a success."

"Don't be a funny doctor," I said. "When do I get out of here?"

"Like right now?" he asked thoughtfully. "We could use the bed. Got a lot of paying patients coming in."

Now, one of the advantages of having blood in my brain instead of the poison soup it had been living on was that I could think reasonably clearly. So I knew right away that he was kidding me; I wouldn't have been there if I hadn't been a paying patient, one way or another, and though I couldn't imagine how, I was willing to wait a while to find out.

Anyway, I was more interested in getting out. They packed me up in wetsheets and rolled me through the Spindle to Sub Vastra's place. Dorrie was there before me, and the Third of Vastra's house fussed over us both, lamb broth and that flat hard bread they like, before tucking us in for a good long rest. There was only the one bed, but Dorrie didn't seem to mind, and anyway at that point the question was academic. Later on, not so academic. After a couple days of that I was up and as good as I ever was.

By then I had found out who paid my bill at the Quackery. For about a minute I had hoped it was me, quickly filthy rich from the spoils of our tunnel, but I knew that was impossible. We could have made money only on the sly, and we were both too near dead when we got back to the Spindle to conceal anything.

So the military had moved in and taken everything, but they had shown they had a heart. Atrophied and flinty, but a heart. They'd gone into the dig while I was still getting glucose enemas in my sleep, and had been pleased enough with what they found to decide that I was entitled to some sort of finder's fee. Not much, to be sure. But enough to save my life. It turned out to be enough to pay off the loosely secured checks I'd written to finance the expedition, and surgical fee and hospital costs, and just about enough left over to put a down payment on a Heechee hut of our own.

For a while it bothered me that they wouldn't tell me what they'd found. I even tried to get Sergeant Littleknees drunk when she was in the Spindle on furlough. But Dorrie was right there, and how drunk can you get one girl when another girl is right there watching you? Probably Eve Littleknees didn't know anyhow. Probably no one did except a few weapons specialists. But it had to be something, because of the cash award, and most of all because they didn't prosecute for trespass on the military reservation. And so we get along, the two of us. Or three of us.

Dorrie turned out to be good at selling fire pearls to the Terry tourists, especially when her pregnancy began to show. She kept us in eating money until the high season started, and by then I found I was a sort of celebrity, which I parlayed into a bank loan and a new airbody, and so we're doing well enough. I've promised that I'll marry her if our kid turns out to be a boy, but as a matter of fact I'm going to do it anyway. She was a great help, especially with my own private project back there at the dig. She couldn't have known what I wanted to bring back Cochenour's body for, but she didn't argue, and sick and wretched as she was, she helped me get it into the airbody lock.

Actually, I wanted it very much.

It's not actually a *new* liver, of course. Probably it's not even second-hand. Heaven knows where Cochenour bought it, but I'm sure it wasn't original equipment with him. But it works. And bastard though he was, I kind of liked him in a way, and I don't mind at all the fact that I've got a part of him with me always.

GENE WOLFE
The Death of Doctor Island

Gene Wolfe made his first sale in 1965. By 1970, he was a regular in Damon Knight's *Orbit* anthologies with stories such as "Trip, Trap," "The Encounter," and "Paul's Tree-house," and had published his first novel, *Operation Ares* (in retrospect, his weakest book). Little that he had done to date had attracted any attention, and there was little to indicate that a new giant of the form was about to loom above the literary horizon, someone who would be instrumental in establishing the new Cutting Edge of science fiction in the years ahead . . . and yet, that was exactly what was about to happen.

As the decade progressed, Wolfe's work seemed to undergo a quantum leap in sophistication and intensity, and he went on to produce much of the really superior short fiction of the seventies—pieces such as the extraordinary "The Fifth Head of Cerberus," "The Hero as Werewolf," "Seven American Nights," "Alien Stones," "The Eyeflash Miracles," "Tracking Song," and "The Island of Doctor Death and Other Stories," among many others, as well as one of the decade's best novels, the brilliant 1975 novel *Peace*, (which, published almost anonymously as a main-stream hardback in a plain tan dustcover, sank without arousing a single ripple). In spite of this lush outpouring of talent, Wolfe remained severely underappreciated throughout most of the decade (although he did take a Nebula Award for the story that follows, *The Death of Doctor Island*), and as late as 1978 or 1979, book editors were telling me that Wolfe had no real audience and no future as a mass-market author . . . something that would later be proven to be untrue.

Perhaps all this was because Wolfe was strongly identified with *Orbit* in the early seventies, and, as *Orbit* was the major

American recipient for the spleen of the reactionary backlash that developed early in the decade, his reputation probably suffered from the association, as would the reputations of Joanna Russ, Kate Wilhelm, R. A. Lafferty, and several other frequent *Orbit* contributors. Wolfe and Russ became bugbears to the conservatives in much the same way that Heinlein had become a bugbear to the New Wavers, and Wolfe in particular was loathed and pointed at as an example of the kind of nonrigorous, scientifically illiterate, custardheaded intellectuals that the reactionaries saw hiding under every bed. This was very ironic, since, as a professional engineer and an editor for many years of the trade publication *Plant Engineering*, Wolfe was probably more conversant with the hard sciences than many of his detractors, and much of his work shows a fine understanding of technology and a concern for the intricacies of its workings.

Wolfe finally established his reputation with his landmark *The Book of the New Sun* novel series at the beginning of a new decade, one of the true masterworks of science fiction, and there are few serious critics today who would deny that Wolfe is one of the best writers working in (or out of) the genre in the nineties.

All of which should have been as evident in 1973 as it is today, especially to anyone reading the complex, lyrical, and scary novella that follows, a child's-eye view of a strange and frightening high-tech world where the walls are full of watching eyes, and the stakes for even the simplest of actions can be life itself. . . .

Gene Wolfe was born in New York, and grew up in Houston, Texas. Individual volumes of his monumental *The Book of the New Sun* series have won the Nebula Award, the World Fantasy Award, and the John W. Campbell Memorial Award, and he also won a Nebula Award for his novella *The Death of Doctor Island*. His other books include *Peace, The Fifth Head of Cerberus, The Devil in a Forest, Soldier of the Mist, Free Live Free, Soldier of Arête, There Are Doors, Castleview, Pandora by Holly Hollander*, and *The Urth of the New Sun*. His short fiction has been collected in *The Island of Doctor Death and Other Stories, and Other Stories, Gene Wolfe's Book of Days, The Wolfe Archipelago*, the recent World Fantasy Award–winning collection *Storeys From the Old Hotel*, and *Endangered Species*. His most recent books are *Nightside the Long Sun* and *Lake of the Long Sun*, the start of a new series.

I have desired to go
  Where springs not fail,
To fields where flies no sharp and sided hail
And a few lilies blow.

And I have asked to be
  Where no storms come,
Where the green swell is in the heavens dumb,
And out of the swing of the sea.
                              —GERARD MANLEY HOPKINS

A grain of sand, teetering on the brink of the pit, trembled and fell in; the ant lion at the bottom angrily flung it out again. For a moment there was quiet. Then the entire pit, and a square meter of sand around it, shifted drunkenly while two coconut palms bent to watch. The sand rose, pivoting at one edge, and the scarred head of a boy appeared—a stubble of brown hair threatened to erase the marks of the sutures; with dilated eyes hypnotically dark he paused, his neck just where the ant lion's had been; then, as though goaded from below, he vaulted up and onto the beach, turned, and kicked sand into the dark hatchway from which he had emerged. It slammed shut. The boy was about fourteen.

For a time he squatted, pushing the sand aside and trying to find the door. A few centimeters down, his hands met a gritty, solid material which, though neither concrete nor sandstone, shared the qualities of both—a sand-filled organic plastic. On it he scraped his fingers raw, but he could not locate the edges of the hatch.

Then he stood and looked about him, his head moving continually as the heads of certain reptiles do—back and forth, with no pauses at the terminations of the movements. He did this constantly, ceaselessly—always—and for that reason it will not often be described again, just as it will not be mentioned that he breathed. He did; and as he did, his head, like a rearing snake's, turned from side to side. The boy was thin, and naked as a frog.

Ahead of him the sand sloped gently down toward sapphire water; there were coconuts on the beach, and sea shells, and a scuttling crab that played with the finger-high edge of each dying wave. Behind him there were only palms and sand for a long distance, the palms growing ever closer together as they moved away from the water until the forest of their columniated trunks seemed architectural; like some palace maze becoming as it progressed more and more draped with creepers and lianas with green, scarlet and yellow leaves, the palms interspersed with bamboo and deciduous trees dotted with flaming orchids until almost at the limit of his sight the whole ended in a spangled wall whose predominant color was black-green.

The boy walked toward the beach, then down the beach until he stood in knee-deep water as warm as blood. He dipped his fingers and tasted it—it was fresh, with no hint of the disinfectants to which he was accustomed. He waded out again and sat on the sand about five meters up from the high-water mark, and after ten minutes, during which he heard no sound but the wind and the murmuring of the surf, he threw back his head and began to scream. His screaming was high-pitched, and each breath ended in a gibbering, ululant note, after which came the hollow, iron gasp of the next indrawn breath. On one occasion he had screamed in this way, without cessation, for fourteen hours and twenty-two minutes, at the end of which a nursing nun with an exemplary record stretching back seventeen years had administered an injection without the permission of the attending physician.

After a time the boy paused—not because he was tired, but in order to listen better. There was, still, only the sound of the wind in the palm fronds and the murmuring surf, yet he felt that he had heard a voice. The boy could be quiet as well as noisy, and he was quiet now, his left hand sifting white sand as clean as salt between its fingers while his right tossed tiny pebbles like beachglass beads into the surf.

"*Hear me,*" said the surf. "*Hear me. Hear me.*"

"I hear you," the boy said.

"Good," said the surf, and it faintly echoed itself: "*Good, good, good.*"

The boy shrugged.

"What shall I call you?" asked the surf.

"My name is Nicholas Kenneth de Vore."

"Nick, *Nick . . . Nick?*"

The boy stood, and turning his back on the sea, walked inland. When he was out of sight of the water he found a coconut palm growing sloped and angled, leaning and weaving among its companions like the plume of an ascending jet blown by the wind. After feeling its rough exterior with both hands, the boy began to climb; he was inexpert and climbed slowly and a little clumsily, but his body was light and he was strong. In time he reached the top, and disturbed the little brown plush monkeys there, who fled chattering into other palms, leaving him to nestle alone among the stems of the fronds and the green coconuts. "I am here also," said a voice from the palm.

"Ah," said the boy, who was watching the tossing, sapphire sky far over his head.

"I will call you Nicholas."

The boy said, "I can see the sea."

"Do you know my name?"

The boy did not reply. Under him the long, long stem of the twisted palm swayed faintly.

"My friends all call me Dr. Island."

"I will not call you that," the boy said.

"You mean that you are not my friend."

A gull screamed.

"But you see, I take you for my friend. You may say that I am not yours, but I say that you are mine. I like you, Nicholas, and I will treat you as a friend."

"Are you a machine or a person or a committee?" the boy asked.

"I am all those things and more. I am the spirit of this island, the tutelary genius."

"Bullshit."

"Now that we have met, would you rather I leave you alone?"

Again the boy did not reply.

"You may wish to be alone with your thoughts. I would like to say that we have made much more progress today than I anticipated. I feel that we will get along together very well."

After fifteen minutes or more, the boy asked, "Where does the light come from?" There was no answer. The boy waited for a time, then climbed back down the trunk, dropping the last five meters and rolling as he hit in the soft sand.

He walked to the beach again and stood staring out at the water. Far off he could see it curving up and up, the distant combers breaking in white foam until the sea became white-flecked sky. To his left and his right the beach curved away, bending almost infinitesimally until it disappeared. He began to walk, then saw, almost at the point where perception was lost, a human figure. He broke into a run; a moment later, he halted and turned around. Far ahead another walker, almost invisible, strode the beach; Nicholas ignored him; he found a coconut and tried to open it, then threw it aside and walked on. From time to time fish jumped, and occasionally he saw a wheeling sea bird dive. The light grew dimmer. He was aware that he had not eaten for some time, but he was not in the strict sense hungry—or rather, he enjoyed his hunger now in the same way that he might, at another time, have gashed his arm to watch himself bleed. Once he said, "Dr. Island!" loudly as he passed a coconut palm, and then later began to chant "Dr.

Island, Dr. Island, Dr. Island" as he walked until the words had lost all meaning. He swam in the sea as he had been taught to swim in the great quartanary treatment tanks on Callisto to improve his coordination, and spluttered and snorted until he learned to deal with the waves. When it was so dark he could see only the white sand and the white foam of the breakers, he drank from the sea and fell asleep on the beach, the right side of his taut, ugly face relaxing first, so that it seemed asleep even while the left eye was open and staring; his head rolling from side to side; the left corner of his mouth preserving, like a death mask, his characteristic expression—angry, remote, tinged with that inhuman quality which is found nowhere but in certain human faces.

When he woke it was not yet light, but the night was fading to a gentle gray. Headless, the palms stood like tall ghosts up and down the beach, their tops lost in fog and the lingering dark. He was cold. His hands rubbed his sides; he danced on the sand and sprinted down the edge of the lapping water in an effort to get warm; ahead of him a pinpoint of red light became a fire, and he slowed.

A man who looked about twenty-five crouched over the fire. Tangled black hair hung over this man's shoulders, and he had a sparse beard; otherwise he was as naked as Nicholas himself. His eyes were dark, and large and empty, like the ends of broken pipes; he poked at his fire, and the smell of roasting fish came with the smoke. For a time Nicholas stood at a distance, watching.

Saliva ran from a corner of the man's mouth, and he wiped it away with one hand, leaving a smear of ash on his face. Nicholas edged closer until he stood on the opposite side of the fire. The fish had been wrapped in broad leaves and mud, and lay in the center of the coals. "I'm Nicholas," Nicholas said. "Who are you?" The young man did not look at him, had never looked at him.

"Hey, I'd like a piece of your fish. Not much. All right?"

The young man raised his head, looking not at Nicholas but at some point far beyond him; he dropped his eyes again. Nicholas smiled. The smile emphasized the disjointed quality of his expression, his mouth's uneven curve.

"Just a little piece? Is it about done?" Nicholas crouched, imitating the young man, and as though this were a signal, the young man sprang for him across the fire. Nicholas jumped backward, but the jump was too late—the young man's body struck his and sent him sprawling on the sand; fingers clawed for his throat. Screaming, Nicholas rolled free, into the water; the young man splashed after him; Nicholas dove.

He swam underwater, his belly almost grazing the wave-rippled sand until he found deeper water; then he surfaced, gasping for breath, and saw the young man, who saw him as well. He dove again, this time surfacing far off, in deep water. Treading water, he could see the fire on the beach, and the young man when he returned to it, stamping out of the sea in the early light. Nicholas then swam until he was five hundred meters or more down the beach, then waded in to shore and began walking back toward the fire.

The young man saw him when he was still some distance off, but he continued to sit, eating pink-tinted tidbits from his fish, watching Nicholas. "What's the matter?" Nicholas said while he was still a safe distance away. "Are you mad at me?"

From the forest, birds warned, "Be careful, Nicholas."

"I won't hurt you," the young man said. He stood up, wiping his oily hands on his chest, and gestured toward the fish at his feet. "You want some?"

Nicholas nodded, smiling his crippled smile.

"Come then."

Nicholas waited, hoping the young man would move away from the fish, but he did not; neither did he smile in return.

"Nicholas," the little waves at his feet whispered, "this is Ignacio."

"Listen," Nicholas said, "is it really all right for me to have some?"

Ignacio nodded, unsmiling.

Cautiously Nicholas came forward; as he was bending to pick up the fish, Ignacio's strong hands took him; he tried to wrench free but was thrown down, Ignacio on top of him. "Please!" he yelled. "Please!" Tears started into his eyes. He tried to yell again, but he had no breath; the tongue was being forced, thicker than his wrist, from his throat.

Then Ignacio let go and struck him in the face with his clenched fist. Nicholas had been slapped and pummeled before, had been beaten, had fought, sometimes savagely, with other boys; but he had never been struck by a man as men fight. Ignacio hit him again and his lips gushed blood.

He lay a long time on the sand beside the dying fire. Consciousness returned slowly; he blinked, drifted back into the dark, blinked again. His mouth was full of blood, and when at last he spit it out onto the sand, it seemed a soft flesh, dark and polymerized in strange shapes; his left cheek was hugely swollen, and he could scarcely see out of his left eye. After a time he crawled to the water; a long time after that, he left it and walked shakily back to the ashes of the fire. Ignacio was gone, and there was nothing left of the fish but bones.

"Ignacio is gone," Dr. Island said with lips of waves.

Nicholas sat on the sand, cross-legged.

"You handled him very well."

"You saw us fight?"

"I saw you; I see everything, Nicholas."

"This is the worst place," Nicholas said; he was talking to his lap.

"What do you mean by that?"

"I've been in bad places before—places where they hit you or squirted big hoses of ice water that knocked you down. But not where they would let someone else—"

"Another patient?" asked a wheeling gull.

"—do it."

"You were lucky, Nicholas. Ignacio is homicidal."

"You could have stopped him."

"No, I could not. All this world is my eye, Nicholas, my ear and my tongue; but I have no hands."

"I thought you did all this."

"Men did all this."

"I mean, I thought you kept it going."

"It keeps itself going, and you—all the people here—direct it."

Nicholas looked at the water. "What makes the waves?"

"The wind and the tide."

"Are we on Earth?"

"Would you feel more comfortable on Earth?"

"I've never been there; I'd like to know."

"I am more like Earth than Earth now is, Nicholas. If you were to take the best of all the best beaches of Earth, and clear them of all the poisons and all the dirt of the last three centuries, you would have me."

"But this isn't Earth?"

There was no answer. Nicholas walked around the ashes of the fire until he found Ignacio's footprints. He was no tracker, but the depressions in the soft beach sand required none; he followed them, his head swaying from side to side as he walked, like the sensor of a mine detector.

For several kilometers Ignacio's trail kept to the beach; then, abruptly, the footprints swerved, wandered among the coconut palms, and at last were lost on the firmer soil inland. Nicholas lifted his head and shouted, "Ignacio? Ignacio!" After a moment he heard a stick snap, and the sound of someone pushing aside leafy branches. He waited.

"Mum?"

A girl was coming toward him, stepping out of the thicker growth of the interior. She was pretty, though too thin, and appeared to be about nineteen; her hair was blond where it had been most exposed to sunlight, darker elsewhere. "You've scratched yourself," Nicholas said. "You're bleeding."

"I thought you were my mother," the girl said. She was a head taller than Nicholas. "Been fighting, haven't you. Have you come to get me?"

Nicholas had been in similar conversations before and normally would have preferred to ignore the remark, but he was lonely now. He said, "Do you want to go home?"

"Well, I think I should, you know."

"But do you want to?"

"My mum always says if you've got something on the stove you don't want to burn—she's quite a good cook. She really is. Do you like cabbage with bacon?"

"Have you got anything to eat?"

"Not now. I had a thing a while ago."

"What kind of thing?"

"A bird." The girl made a vague little gesture, not looking at Nicholas. "I'm a memory that has swallowed a bird."

"Do you want to walk down by the water?" They were moving in the direction of the beach already.

"I was just going to get a drink. You're a nice tot."

Nicholas did not like being called a "tot." He said, "I set fire to places."

"You won't set fire to this place; it's been nice the last couple of days, but when everyone is sad, it rains."

Nicholas was silent for a time. When they reached the sea, the girl dropped to her knees and bent forward to drink, her long hair falling over her face until the ends trailed in the water, her nipples, then half of each breast, in the water. "Not there," Nicholas said. "It's sandy, because it washes the beach so close. Come on out here." He waded out into the sea until the lapping waves nearly reached his armpits, then bent his head and drank.

"I never thought of that," the girl said. "Mum says I'm stupid. So does Dad. Do you think I'm stupid?"

Nicholas shook his head.

"What's your name?"

"Nicholas Kenneth de Vore. What's yours?"

"Diane. I'm going to call you Nicky. Do you mind?"

"I'll hurt you while you sleep," Nicholas said.

"You wouldn't."

"Yes I would. At St. John's where I used to be, it was zero G most of the time, and a girl there called me something I didn't like, and I got loose one night and came into her cubical while she was asleep

and nulled her restraints, and then she floated around until she
banged into something, and that woke her up and she tried to grab,
and then that made her bounce all around inside and she broke
two fingers and her nose and got blood all over. The attendants
came, and one told me—they didn't know then I did it—when he
came out his white suit was, like, polka-dot red all over because
wherever the blood drops had touched him they soaked right in."

The girl smiled at him, dimpling her thin face. "How did they
find out it was you?"

"I told someone and he told them."

"I bet you told them yourself."

"I bet I didn't!" Angry, he waded away, but when he had stalked
a short way up the beach he sat down on the sand, his back toward
her.

"I didn't mean to make you mad, Mr. de Vore."

"I'm not mad!"

She was not sure for a moment what he meant. She sat down
beside and a trifle behind him, and began idly piling sand in her
lap.

Dr. Island said, "I see you've met."

Nicholas turned, looking for the voice, "I thought you saw everything."

"Only the important things, and I have been busy on another
part of myself. I am happy to see that you two know one another;
do you find you interact well?"

Neither of them answered.

"You should be interacting with Ignacio; he needs you."

"We can't find him," Nicholas said.

"Down the beach to your left until you see the big stone, then
turn inland. Above five hundred meters."

Nicholas stood up, and turning to his right, began to walk away.
Diane followed him, trotting until she caught up.

"I don't like," Nicholas said, jerking a shoulder to indicate something behind him.

"Ignacio?"

"The doctor."

"Why do you move your head like that?"

"Didn't they tell you?"

"No one told me anything about you."

"They opened it up"—Nicholas touched his scars—"and took
this knife and cut all the way through my corpus . . . corpus . . ."

"Corpus callosum," muttered a dry palm frond.

"—corpus callosum," finished Nicholas. "See, your brain is like
a walnut inside. There are the two halves, and then right down in

the middle a kind of thick connection of meat from one to the other. Well, they cut that."

"You're having a bit of fun with me, aren't you?"

"No, he isn't," a monkey who had come to the water line to look for shellfish told her. "His cerebrum has been surgically divided; it's in his file." It was a young monkey, with a trusting face full of small, ugly beauties.

Nicholas snapped, "It's in my head."

Diane said, "I'd think it would kill you, or make you an idiot or something."

"They say each half of me is about as smart as both of us were together. Anyway, this half is . . . the half . . . the *me* that talks."

"There are two of you now?"

"If you cut a worm in half and both parts are still alive, that's two, isn't it? What else would you call us? We can't ever come together again."

"But I'm talking to just one of you?"

"We both can hear you."

"Which one answers?"

Nicholas touched the right side of his chest with his right hand. "Me; I do. They told me it was the left side of my brain, that one has the speech centers, but it doesn't feel that way; the nerves cross over coming out, and it's just the right side of me, I talk. Both my ears hear for both of us, but out of each eye we only see half and half—I mean, I only see what's on the right of what I'm looking at, and the other side, I guess, only sees the left, so that's why I keep moving my head. I guess it's like being a little bit blind; you get used to it."

The girl was still thinking of his divided body. She said, "If you're only half, I don't see how you can walk."

"I can move the left side a little bit, and we're not mad at each other. We're not supposed to be able to come together at all, but we do: down through the legs and at the ends of the fingers and then back up. Only I can't talk with my other side because he can't, but he understands."

"Why did they do it?"

Behind them the monkey, who had been following them, said, "He had uncontrollable seizures."

"Did you?" the girl asked. She was watching a sea bird swooping low over the water and did not seem to care.

Nicholas picked up a shell and shied it at the monkey, who skipped out of the way. After half a minute's silence he said, "I had visions."

"Ooh, did you?"

"They didn't like that. They said I would fall down and jerk around horrible, and sometimes I guess I would hurt myself when I fell, and sometimes I'd bite my tongue and it would bleed. But that wasn't what it felt like to me; I wouldn't know about any of those things until afterward. To me it was like I had gone way far ahead, and I had to come back. I didn't want to."

The wind swayed Diane's hair, and she pushed it back from her face. "Did you see things that were going to happen?" she asked.

"Sometimes."

"Really? Did you?"

"Sometimes."

"Tell me about it. When you saw what was going to happen."

"I saw myself dead. I was all black and shrunk up like the dead stuff they cut off in the pontic gardens; and I was floating and turning, like in water but it wasn't water—just floating and turning out in space, in nothing. And there were lights on both sides of me, so both sides were bright but black, and I could see my teeth because the stuff"—he pulled at his cheeks—"had fallen off there, and they were really white."

"That hasn't happened yet."

"Not here."

"Tell me something you saw that happened."

"You mean, like somebody's sister was going to get married, don't you? That's what the girls where I was mostly wanted to know. Or were they going to go home; mostly it wasn't like that."

"But sometimes it was?"

"I guess."

"Tell me one."

Nicholas shook his head. "You wouldn't like it, and anyway it wasn't like that. Mostly it was lights like I never saw anyplace else, and voices like I never heard any other time, telling me things there aren't any words for; stuff like that, only now I can't ever go back. Listen, I wanted to ask you about Ignacio."

"He isn't anybody," the girl said.

"What do you mean, he isn't anybody? Is there anybody here besides you and me and Ignacio and Dr. Island?"

"Not that we can see or touch."

The monkey called, "There are other patients, but for the present, Nicholas, for your own well-being as well as theirs, it is best for you to remain by yourselves." It was a long sentence for a monkey.

"What's that about?"

"If I tell you, will you tell me about something you saw that really happened?"

"All right."

"Tell me first."

"There was this girl where I was—her name was Maya. They had, you know, boys' and girls' dorms, but you saw everybody in the rec room and the dining hall and so on, and she was in my psychodrama group." Her hair had been black, and shiny as the lacquered furniture in Dr. Hong's rooms, her skin white like the mother-of-pearl, her eyes long and narrow (making him think of cats' eyes) and darkly blue. She was fifteen, or so Nicholas believed—maybe sixteen. *"I'm going home,"* she told him. It was psychodrama, and he was her brother, younger than she, and she was already at home; but when she said this the floating ring of light that gave them the necessary separation from the small doctor-and-patient audience, ceased, by instant agreement, to be Maya's mother's living room and became a visiting lounge. Nicholas/Jerry said: "Hey, that's great! Hey, I got a new bike—when you come home you want to ride it?"

Maureen/Maya's mother said, "Maya, don't. You'll run into something and break your teeth, and you know how much they cost."

"You don't want me to have any fun."

"We do, dear, but *nice* fun. A girl has to be so much more careful—oh, Maya, I wish I could make you understand, really, how careful a girl has to be."

Nobody said anything, so Nicholas/Jerry filled in with, "It has a three-bladed prop, and I'm going to tape streamers to them with little weights at the ends, an' when I go down old thirty-seven B passageway, look out, here comes that old coleslaw grater!"

"Like this," Maya said, and held her legs together and extended her arms, to make a three-bladed bike prop or a crucifix. She had thrown herself into a spin as she made the movement, and revolved slowly, stage center—red shorts, white blouse, red shorts, white blouse, red shorts, no shoes.

Diane asked, "And you saw that she was never going home, she was going to hospital instead, she was going to cut her wrist there, she was going to die?"

Nicholas nodded.

"Did you tell her?"

"Yes," Nicholas said. "No."

"Make up your mind. Didn't you tell her? Now, don't get mad."

"Is it telling, when the one you tell doesn't understand?"

Diane thought about that for a few steps while Nicholas dashed water on the hot bruises Ignacio had left upon his face. "If it was plain and clear and she ought to have understood—that's the trouble I have with my family."

"What is?"

"They won't say things—do you know what I mean? I just say look, just tell me, just tell me what I'm supposed to do, tell me what it is you want, but it's different all the time. My mother says, 'Diane, you ought to meet some boys, you can't go out with him, your father and I have never met him, we don't even know his family at all, Douglas, there's something I think you ought to know about Diane, she gets confused sometimes, we've had her to doctors, she's been in a hospital, try—' "

"Not to get her excited," Nicholas finished for her.

"Were you listening? I mean, are you from the Trojan Planets? Do you know my mother?"

"I only live in these places," Nicholas said, "that's for a long time. But you talk like other people."

"I feel better now that I'm with you; you're really nice. I wish you were older."

"I'm not sure I'm going to get much older."

"It's going to rain—feel it?"

Nicholas shook his head.

"Look." Diane jumped, bunnyrabbit-clumsy, three meters into the air. "See how high I can jump? That means people are sad and it's going to rain. I told you."

"No, you didn't."

"Yes, I did, Nicholas."

He waved the argument away, struck by a sudden thought. "You ever been to Callisto?"

The girl shook her head, and Nicholas said, "I have; that's where they did the operation. It's so big the gravity's mostly from natural mass, and it's all domed in, with a whole lot of air in it."

"So?"

"And when I was there it rained. There was a big trouble at one of the generating piles, and they shut it down and it got colder and colder until everybody in the hospital wore their blankets, just like Amerinds in books, and they locked the switches off on the heaters in the bathrooms, and the nurses and the comscreen told you all the time it wasn't dangerous, they were just rationing power to keep from blacking out the important stuff that was still running. And then it rained, just like on Earth. They said it got so cold the water condensed in the air, and it was like the whole hospital was right under a shower bath. Everybody on the top floor had to come down because it rained right on their beds, and for two nights I had a man in my room with me that had his arm cut off in a machine. But we couldn't jump any higher, and it got kind of dark."

"It doesn't always get dark here," Diane said. "Sometimes the rain sparkles. I think Dr. Island must do it to cheer everyone up."

"No," the waves explained, "or at least not in the way you mean, Diane."

Nicholas was hungry and started to ask them for something to eat, then turned his hunger in against itself, spat on the sand, and was still.

"It rains here when most of you are sad," the waves were saying, "because rain is a sad thing, to the human psyche. It is that, that sadness, perhaps because it recalls to unhappy people their own tears, that palliates melancholy."

Diane said, "Well, I know sometimes I feel better when it rains."

"That should help you to understand yourself. Most people are soothed when their environment is in harmony with their emotions, and anxious when it is not. An angry person becomes less angry in a red room, and unhappy people are only exasperated by sunshine and birdsong. Do you remember:

> *And, missing thee, I walk unseen*
> *On the dry smooth-shaven green*
> *To behold the wandering moon,*
> *Riding near her highest noon,*
> *Like one that had been led astray*
> *Through the heaven's wide pathless way?*

The girl shook her head.

Nicholas said, "No. Did somebody write that?" and then "You said you couldn't do anything."

The waves replied, "I can't—except talk to you."

"You make it rain."

"Your heart beats; I sense its pumping even as I speak—do you control the beating of your heart?"

"I can stop my breath."

"Can you stop your heart? Honestly, Nicholas?"

"I guess not."

"No more can I control the weather of my world, stop anyone from doing what he wishes, or feed you if you are hungry; with no need of volition on my part your emotions are monitored and averaged, and our weather responds. Calm and sunshine for tranquility, rain for melancholy, storms for rage, and so on. This is what mankind has always wanted."

Diane asked, "What is?"

"That the environment should respond to human thought. That is the core of magic and the oldest dream of mankind; and here, on me, it is fact."

"So that we'll be well?"

Nicholas said angrily, "You're not sick!"

Dr. Island said, "So that some of you, at least, can return to society."

Nicholas threw a sea shell into the water as though to strike the mouth that spoke. "Why are we talking to this thing?"

"Wait, tot, I think it's interesting."

"Lies and lies."

Dr. Island said, "How do I lie, Nicholas?"

"You said it was magic—"

"No, I said that when humankind has dreamed of magic, the wish behind that dream has been the omnipotence of thought. Have you never wanted to be a magician, Nicholas, making palaces spring up overnight, or riding an enchanted horse of ebony to battle with the demons of the air?"

"I am a magician—I have preternatural powers, and before they cut us in two—"

Diane interrupted him. "You said you averaged emotions. When you made it rain."

"Yes."

"Doesn't that mean that if one person was really, terribly sad, he'd move the average so much he could make it rain all by himself? Or whatever? That doesn't seem fair."

The waves might have smiled. "That has never happened. But if it did, Diane, if one person felt such deep emotion, think how great her need would be. Don't you think we should answer it?"

Diane looked at Nicholas, but he was walking again, his head swinging, ignoring her as well as the voice of the waves. "Wait," she called. "You said I wasn't sick; I am, you know."

"No, you're not."

She hurried after him. "Everyone says so, and sometimes I'm so confused, and other times I'm boiling inside, just boiling. Mum says if you've got something on the stove you don't want to have burn, you just have to keep one finger on the handle of the pan and it won't, but I can't, I can't always find the handle or remember."

Without looking back the boy said, "Your mother is probably sick; maybe your father too, I don't know. But you're not. If they'd just let you alone you'd be all right. Why shouldn't you get upset, having to live with two crazy people?"

"Nicholas!" She grabbed his thin shoulders. "That's not true!"

"Yes, it is."

"I am sick. Everyone says so."

"I don't; so 'everyone' just means the ones that do—isn't that right? And if you don't either, that will be two; it can't be everyone then."

The girl called, "Doctor? Dr. Island?"

Nicholas said, "You aren't going to believe that, are you?"

"Dr. Island, is it true?"

"Is what true, Diane?"

"What he said. Am I sick?"

"Sickness—even physical illness—is relative, Diane; and complete health is an idealization, an abstraction, even if the other end of the scale is not."

"You know what I mean."

"You are not physically ill." A long, blue comber curled into a line of hissing spray reaching infinitely along the sea to their left and right. "As you said yourself a moment ago, you are sometimes confused, and sometimes disturbed."

"He said if it weren't for other people, if it weren't for my mother and father, I wouldn't have to be here."

"Diane . . ."

"Well, is that true or isn't it?"

"Most emotional illness would not exist, Diane, if it were possible in every case to separate oneself—in thought as well as circumstance—if only for a time."

"Separate oneself?"

"Did you ever think of going away, at least for a time?"

The girl nodded, then as though she were not certain Dr. Island could see her, said, "Often, I suppose; leaving the school and getting my own compartment somewhere—going to Achilles. Sometimes I wanted to so badly."

"Why didn't you?"

"They would have worried. And anyway, they would have found me, and made me come home."

"Would it have done any good if I—or a human doctor—had told them not to?"

When the girl said nothing Nicholas snapped, "You could have locked them up."

"They were functioning, Nicholas. They bought and sold; they worked, and paid their taxes—"

Diane said softly, "It wouldn't have done any good anyway, Nicholas; they are inside me."

"Diane was no longer functioning: she was failing every subject at the university she attended, and her presence in her classes, when she came, disturbed the instructors and the other students. You were not functioning either, and people of your own age were afraid of you."

"That's what counts with you, then. Functioning."

"If I were different from the world, would that help you when you got back into the world?"

"You are different." Nicholas kicked the sand. "Nobody ever saw a place like this."

"You mean that reality to you is metal corridors, rooms without windows, noise."

"Yes."

"That is the unreality, Nicholas. Most people have never had to endure such things. Even now, this—my beach, my sea, my trees—is more in harmony with most human lives than your metal corridors; and here, I am your social environment—what individuals call 'they.' You see, sometimes if we take people who are troubled back to something like me, to an idealized natural setting, it helps them."

"Come on," Nicholas told the girl. He took her arm, acutely conscious of being so much shorter than she.

"A question," murmured the waves. "If Diane's parents had been taken here instead of Diane, do you think it would have helped them?"

Nicholas did not reply.

"We have treatments for disturbed persons, Nicholas. But, at least for the time being, we have no treatment for disturbing persons." Diane and the boy had turned away, and the waves' hissing and slapping ceased to be speech. Gulls wheeled overhead, and once a red-and-yellow parrot fluttered from one palm to another. A monkey running on all fours like a little dog approached them, and Nicholas chased it, but it escaped.

"I'm going to take one of those things apart someday," he said, "and pull the wires out."

"Are we going to walk all the way 'round?" Diane asked. She might have been talking to herself.

"Can you do that?"

"Oh, you can't walk all around Dr. Island; it would be too long, and you can't get there anyway. But we could walk until we get back to where we started—we're probably more than halfway now."

"Are there other islands you can't see from here?"

The girl shook her head. "I don't think so; there's just this one big island in this satellite, and all the rest is water."

"Then if there's only the one island, we're going to have to walk all around it to get back to where we started. What are you laughing at?"

"Look down the beach, as far as you can. Never mind how it slips off to the side—pretend it's straight."

"I don't see anything."

"Don't you? Watch." Diane leaped into the air, six meters or more this time, and waved her arms.

"It looks like there's somebody ahead of us, way down the beach."

"Uh-huh. Now look behind."

"Okay, there's somebody there too. Come to think of it, I saw someone on the beach when I first got here. It seemed funny to see so far, but I guess I thought they were other patients. Now I see two people."

"They're us. That was probably yourself you saw the other time, too. There are just so many of us to each strip of beach, and Dr. Island only wants certain ones to mix. So the space bends around. When we get to one end of our strip and try to step over, we'll be at the other end."

"How did you find out?"

"Dr. Island told me about it when I first came here." The girl was silent for a moment, and her smile vanished. "Listen, Nicholas, do you want to see something really funny?"

Nicholas asked, "What?" As he spoke, a drop of rain struck his face.

"You'll see. Come on, though. We have to go into the middle instead of following the beach, and it will give us a chance to get under the trees and out of the rain."

When they had left the sand and the sound of the surf, and were walking on solid ground under green-leaved trees, Nicholas said, "Maybe we can find some fruit." They were so light now that he had to be careful not to bound into the air with each step. The rain fell slowly around them, in crystal spheres.

"Maybe," the girl said doubtfully. "Wait, let's stop here." She sat down where a huge tree sent twenty-meter wooden arches over dark, mossy ground. "Want to climb up there and see if you can find us something?"

"All right," Nicholas agreed. He jumped, and easily caught hold of a branch far above the girl's head. In a moment he was climbing in a green world, with the rain pattering all around him; he followed narrowing limbs into leafy wildernesses where the cool water ran from every twig he touched, and twice found the empty nests of birds, and once a slender snake, green as any leaf with a head as long as his thumb; but there was no fruit. "Nothing," he said, when he dropped down beside the girl once more.

"That's all right, we'll find something."

He said, "I hope so," and noticed that she was looking at him oddly, then realized that his left hand had lifted itself to touch her right breast. It dropped as he looked, and he felt his face grow hot. He said, "I'm sorry."

"That's all right."

"We like you. He—over there—he can't talk, you see. I guess I can't talk either."

"I think it's just you—in two pieces. I don't care."

"Thanks." He had picked up a leaf, dead and damp, and was tearing it to shreds; first his right hand tearing while the left held the leaf, then turnabout. "Where does the rain come from?" The dirty flakes clung to the fingers of both.

"Hmm?"

"Where does the rain come from? I mean, it isn't because it's colder here now, like on Callisto; it's because the gravity's turned down some way, isn't it?"

"From the sea. Don't you know how this place is built?"

Nicholas shook his head.

"Didn't they show it to you from the ship when you came? It's beautiful. They showed it to me—I just sat there and looked at it, and I wouldn't talk to them, and the nurse thought I wasn't paying any attention, but I heard everything. I just didn't want to talk to her. It wasn't any use."

"I know how you felt."

"But they didn't show it to you?"

"No, on my ship they kept me locked up because I burned some stuff. They thought I couldn't start a fire without an igniter, but if you have electricity in the wall sockets it's easy. They had a thing on me—you know?" He clasped his arms to his body to show how he had been restrained. "I bit one of them, too—I guess I didn't tell you that yet: I bite people. They locked me up, and for a long time I had nothing to do, and then I could feel us dock with something, and they came and got me and pulled me down a regular companionway for a long time, and it just seemed like a regular place. Then they stuck me full of Tranquil-C—I guess they didn't know it doesn't hardly work on me at all—with a pneumo-gun, and lifted a kind of door thing and shoved me up."

"Didn't they make you undress?"

"I already was. When they put the ties on me I did things in my clothes and they had to take them off me. It made them mad." He grinned unevenly. "Does Tranquil-C work on you? Or any of that other stuff?"

"I suppose they would, but then I never do the sort of thing you do anyway."

"Maybe you ought to."

"Sometimes they used to give me medication that was supposed to cheer me up; then I couldn't sleep, and I walked and walked, you know, and ran into things and made a lot of trouble for everyone; but what good does it do?"

Nicholas shrugged. "Not doing it doesn't do any good either—I mean, we're both here. My way, I know I've made them jump; they shoot that stuff in me and I'm not mad anymore, but I know what it is and I just think what I would do if I *were* mad, and I do it, and when it wears off I'm glad I did."

"I think you're still angry somewhere, deep down."

Nicholas was already thinking of something else. "This island says Ignacio kills people." He paused. "What does it look like?"

"Ignacio?"

"No, I've seen him. Dr. Island."

"Oh, you mean when I was in the ship. The satellite's round of course, and all clear except where Dr. Island is, so that's a dark spot. The rest of it's temperglass, and from space you can't even see the water."

"That *is* the sea up there, isn't it?" Nicholas asked, trying to look up at it through the tree leaves and the rain. "I thought it was when I first came."

"Sure. It's like a glass ball, and we're inside, and the water's inside too, and just goes all around up the curve."

"That's why I could see so far out on the beach, isn't it? Instead of dropping down from you like on Callisto it bends up so you can see it."

The girl nodded. "And the water lets the light through, but filters out the ultraviolet. Besides, it gives us thermal mass, so we don't heat up too much when we're between the sun and the Bright Spot."

"Is that what keeps us warm? The Bright Spot?"

Diane nodded again. "We go around in ten hours, you see, and that holds us over it all the time."

"Why can't I see it, then? It ought to look like Sol does from the Belt, only bigger; but there's just a shimmer in the sky, even when it's not raining."

"The waves diffract the light and break up the image. You'd see the Focus, though, if the air weren't so clear. Do you know what the Focus is?"

Nicholas shook his head.

"We'll get to it pretty soon, after this rain stops. Then I'll tell you."

"I still don't understand about the rain."

Unexpectedly Diane giggled. "I just thought—do you know what I was supposed to be? While I was going to school?"

"Quiet," Nicholas said.

"No, silly. I mean what I was being trained to do, if I graduated and all that. I was going to be a teacher, with all those cameras on me and tots from everywhere watching and popping questions on the two-way. Jolly time. Now I'm doing it here, only there's no one but you."

"You mind?"

"No, I suppose I enjoy it." There was a black-and-blue mark on Diane's thigh, and she rubbed it pensively with one hand as she spoke. "Anyway, there are three ways to make gravity. Do you know them? Answer, clerk."

"Sure; acceleration, mass, and synthesis."

"That's right; motion and mass are both bendings of space, of course, which is why Zeno's paradox doesn't work out that way, and why masses move toward each other—what we call falling— or at least try to; and if they're held apart it produces the tension we perceive as a force and call weight and all that rot. So naturally if you bend the space direct, you synthesize a gravity effect, and that's what holds all that water up against the translucent shell— there's nothing like enough mass to do it by itself."

"You mean"—Nicholas held out his hand to catch a slow-moving globe of rain—"that this is water from the sea?"

"Right-o, up on top. Do you see, the temperature differences in the air make the winds, and the winds make the waves and surf you saw when we were walking along the shore. When the waves break they throw up these little drops, and if you watch you'll see that even when it's clear they go up a long way sometimes. Then if the gravity is less they can get away altogether, and if we were on the outside they'd fly off into space; but we aren't, we're inside, so all they can do is go across the center, more or less, until they hit the water again, or Dr. Island."

"Dr. Island said they had storms sometimes, when people got mad."

"Yes. Lots of wind, and so there's lots of rain too. Only the rain then is because the wind tears the tops off the waves, and you don't get light like you do in a normal rain."

"What makes so much wind?"

"I don't know. It happens somehow."

They sat in silence, Nicholas listening to the dripping of the leaves. He remembered then that they had spun the hospital module, finally, to get the little spheres of clotting blood out of the air; Maya's blood was building up on the grills of the purification intake ducts, spotting them black, and someone had been afraid they would decay there and smell. He had not been there when they did it, but he could imagine the droplets settling, like this, in the slow spin. The old psychodrama group had already been broken up, and when he saw Maureen or any of the others in the rec room they talked about Good Old Days. It had not seemed like Good Old Days then except that Maya had been there.

Diane said, "It's going to stop."

"It looks just as bad to me."

"No, it's going to stop—see, they're falling a little faster now, and I feel heavier."

Nicholas stood up. "You rested enough yet? You want to go on?"

"We'll get wet."

He shrugged.

"I don't want to get my hair wet, Nicholas. It'll be over in a minute."

He sat down again. "How long have you been here?"

"I'm not sure."

"Don't you count the days?"

"I lose track a lot."

"Longer than a week?"

"Nicholas, don't ask me, all right?"

"Isn't there anybody on this piece of Dr. Island except you and me and Ignacio?"

"I don't think there was anyone but Ignacio before you came."

"Who is he?"

She looked at him.

"Well, who is he? You know me—us—Nicholas Kenneth de Vore; and you're Diane who?"

"Phillips."

"And you're from the Trojan Planets, and I was from the Outer Belt, I guess, to start with. What about Ignacio? You talk to him sometimes, don't you? Who is he?"

"I don't know. He's important."

For an instant, Nicholas froze. "What does that mean?"

"Important." The girl was feeling her knees, running her hands back and forth across them.

"Maybe everybody's important."

"I know you're just a tot, Nicholas, but don't be so stupid. Come on, you wanted to go, let's go now. It's pretty well stopped." She stood, stretching her thin body, her arms over her head. "My knees are rough—you made me think of that. When I came here they were still so smooth, I think. I used to put a certain lotion on them. Because my Dad would feel them, and my hands and elbows too, and he'd say if they weren't smooth nobody'd ever want me; Mum wouldn't say anything, but she'd be cross after, and they used to come and visit, and so I kept a bottle in my room and I used to put it on. Once I drank some."

Nicholas was silent.

"Aren't you going to ask me if I died?" She stepped ahead of him, pulling aside the dripping branches. "See here, I'm sorry I said you were stupid."

"I'm just thinking," Nicholas said. "I'm not mad at you. Do you really know anything about him?"

"No, but look at it." She gestured. "Look around you; someone *built* all this."

"You mean it cost a lot."

"It's automated, of course, but still . . . well, the other places where you were before—how much space was there for each patient? Take the total volume and divide it by the number of people there."

"Okay, this is a whole lot bigger, but maybe they think we're worth it."

"Nicholas . . ." She paused. "Nicholas, Ignacio is homicidal. Didn't Dr. Island tell you?"

"Yes."

"And you're fourteen and not very big for it, and I'm a girl. Who are they worried about?"

The look on Nicholas's face startled her.

After an hour or more of walking they came to it. It was a band of withered vegetation, brown and black and tumbling, and as straight as if it had been drawn with a ruler. "I was afraid it wasn't going to be here," Diane said. "It moves around whenever there's a storm. It might not have been in our sector any more at all."

Nicholas asked, "What is it?"

"The Focus. It's been all over, but mostly the plants grow back quickly when it's gone."

"It smells funny—like the kitchen in a place where they wanted me to work in the kitchen once."

"Vegetables rotting, that's what that is. What did you do?"

"Nothing—put detergent in the stuff they were cooking. What makes this?"

"The Bright Spot. See, when it's just about overhead the curve of the sky and the water up there make a lens. It isn't a very good lens—a lot of the light scatters. But enough is focused to do this. It wouldn't fry us if it came past right now, if that's what you're wondering, because it's not that hot. I've stood right in it, but you want to get out in a minute."

"I thought it was going to be about seeing ourselves down the beach."

Diane seated herself on the trunk of a fallen tree. "It was, really.

The last time I was here it was further from the water, and I suppose it had been there a long time, because it had cleared out a lot of the dead stuff. The sides of the sector are nearer here, you see; the whole sector narrows down like a piece of pie. So you could look down the Focus either way and see yourself nearer than you could on the beach. It was almost as if you were in a big, big room, with a looking-glass on each wall, or as if you could stand behind yourself. I thought you might like it."

"I'm going to try it here," Nicholas announced, and he clambered up one of the dead trees while the girl waited below, but the dry limbs creaked and snapped beneath his feet, and he could not get high enough to see himself in either direction. When he dropped to the ground beside her again, he said, "There's nothing to eat here either, is there?"

"I haven't found anything."

"They—I mean, Dr. Island wouldn't just let us starve, would he?"

"I don't think he could do anything; that's the way this place is built. Sometimes you find things, and I've tried to catch fish, but I never could. A couple of times Ignacio gave me part of what he had, though; he's good at it. I bet you think I'm skinny, don't you? But I was a lot fatter when I came here."

"What are we going to do now?"

"Keep walking, I suppose, Nicholas. Maybe go back to the water."

"Do you think we'll find anything?"

From a decaying log, insect stridulations called, "Wait."

Nicholas asked, "Do *you* know where anything is?"

"Something for you to eat? Not at present. But I can show you something much more interesting, not far from here, than this clutter of dying trees. Would you like to see it?"

Diane said, "Don't go, Nicholas."

"What is it?"

"Diane, who calls this 'the Focus,' calls what I wish to show you 'the Point.' "

Nicholas asked Diane, "Why shouldn't I go?"

"I'm not going. I went there once anyway."

"I took her," Dr. Island said. "And I'll take you. I wouldn't take you if I didn't think it might help you."

"I don't think Diane liked it."

"Diane may not wish to be helped—help may be painful, and often people do not. But it is my business to help them if I can, whether or not they wish it."

"Suppose I don't want to go?"

"Then I cannot compel you; you know that. But you will be the

only patient in this sector who has not seen it, Nicholas, as well as
the youngest; both Diane and Ignacio have, and Ignacio goes there
often."

"Is it dangerous?"

"No. Are you afraid?"

Nicholas looked questioningly at Diane. "What is it? What will I
see?"

She had walked away while he was talking to Dr. Island, and was
now sitting cross-legged on the ground about five meters from
where Nicholas stood, staring at her hands. Nicholas repeated,
"What will I see, Diane?" He did not think she would answer.

She said, "A glass. A mirror."

"Just a mirror?"

"You know how I told you to climb the tree here? The Point is
where the edges come together. You can see yourself—like on the
beach—but closer."

Nicholas was disappointed. "I've seen myself in mirrors lots of times."

Dr. Island, whose voice was now in the sighing of the dead leaves,
whispered, "Did you have a mirror in your room, Nicholas, before
you came here?"

"A steel one."

"So that you could not break it?"

"I guess so. I threw things at it sometimes, but it just got puckers
in it." Remembering dimpled reflections, Nicholas laughed.

"You can't break this one either."

"It doesn't sound like it's worth going to see."

"I think it is."

Diane, do you still think I shouldn't go?"

There was no reply. The girl sat staring at the ground in front
of her. Nicholas walked over to look at her and found a tear had
washed a damp trail down each thin cheek, but she did not move
when he touched her. "She's catatonic, isn't she," he said.

A green limb just outside the Focus nodded. "Catatonic schizo-
phrenia."

"I had a doctor once that said those names—like that. They
didn't mean anything." (The doctor had been a therapy robot, but a
human doctor gave more status. Robots' patients sat in doorless
booths—two and a half hours a day for Nicholas: an hour and
a half in the morning, an hour in the afternoon—and talked to
something that appeared to be a small, friendly food freezer. Some
people sat every day in silence, while others talked continually, and
for such patients as these the attendants seldom troubled to turn
the machines on.)

"He meant cause and treatment. He was correct."

Nicholas stood looking down at the girl's streaked, brown-blond head. "What *is* the cause? I mean for her."

"I don't know."

"And what's the treatment?"

"You are seeing it."

"Will it help her?"

"Probably not."

"Listen, she can hear you, don't you know that? She hears everything we say."

"If my answer disturbs you, Nicholas, I can change it. It will help her if she wants to be helped; if she insists on clasping her illness to her it will not."

"We ought to go away from here," Nicholas said uneasily.

"To your left you will see a little path, a very faint one. Between the twisted tree and the bush with the yellow flowers."

Nicholas nodded and began to walk, looking back at Diane several times. The flowers were butterflies, who fled in a cloud of color when he approached them, and he wondered if Dr. Island had known. When he had gone a hundred paces and was well away from the brown and rotting vegetation, he said, "She was sitting in the Focus."

"Yes."

"Is she still there?"

"Yes."

"What will happen when the Bright Spot comes?"

"Diane will become uncomfortable and move, if she is still there."

"Once in one of the places I was in there was a man who was like that, and they said he wouldn't get anything to eat if he didn't get up and get it, they weren't going to feed him with the nose tube anymore; and they didn't, and he died. We told them about it and they wouldn't do anything and he starved to death right there, and when he was dead they rolled him off onto a stretcher and changed the bed and put somebody else there."

"I know, Nicholas. You told the doctors at St. John's about all that, and it is in your file; but think: well men have starved themselves—yes, to death—to protest what they felt were political injustices. Is it so surprising that your friend killed himself in the same way to protest what he felt as a psychic injustice?"

"He wasn't my friend. Listen, did you really mean it when you said the treatment she was getting here would help Diane if she wanted to be helped?"

"No."

Nicholas halted in mid-stride. "You didn't mean it? You don't think it's true?"

"No, I doubt that anything will help her."

"I don't think you ought to lie to us."

"Why not? If by chance you become well you will be released, and if you are released you will have to deal with your society, which will lie to you frequently. Here, where there are so few individuals, I must take the place of society. I have explained that."

"Is that what you are?"

"Society's surrogate? Of course. Who do you imagine built me? What else could I be?"

"The doctor."

"You have had many doctors, and so has she. Not one of them has benefited you much."

"I'm not sure you even want to help us."

"Do you wish to see what Diane calls 'the Point'?"

"I guess so."

"Then you must walk. You will not see it standing here."

Nicholas walked, thrusting aside leafy branches and dangling creepers wet with rain. The jungle smelled of the life of green things; there were ants on the tree trunks, and dragonflies with hot, red bodies and wings as long as his hands. "Do you want to help us?" he asked after a time.

"My feelings toward you are ambivalent. But when you wish to be helped, I wish to help you."

The ground sloped gently upward, and as it rose became somewhat more clear, the big trees a trifle farther apart, the underbrush spent in grass and fern. Occasionally there were stone outcrops to be climbed, and clearings open to the tumbling sky. Nicholas asked, "Who made this trail?"

"Ignacio. He comes here often."

"He's not afraid, then? Diane's afraid."

"Ignacio is afraid too, but he comes."

"Diane says Ignacio is important."

"Yes."

"What do you mean by that? Is he important? More important than we are?"

"Do you remember that I told you I was the surrogate of society? What do you think society wants, Nicholas?"

"Everybody to do what it says."

"You mean conformity. Yes, there must be conformity, but something else too—consciousness."

"I don't want to hear about it."

"Without consciousness, which you may call sensitivity if you are careful not to allow yourself to be confused by the term, there is no progress. A century ago, Nicholas, mankind was suffocating on

Earth; now it is suffocating again. About half of the people who have contributed substantially to the advance of humanity have shown signs of emotional disturbance."

"I told you, I don't want to hear about it. I asked you an easy question—is Ignacio more important than Diane and me—and you won't tell me. I've heard all this you're saying. I've heard it fifty, maybe a hundred times from everybody, and it's lies; it's the regular thing, and you've got it written down on a card somewhere to read out when anybody asks. Those people you talk about that went crazy, they went crazy because while they were 'advancing humanity,' or whatever you call it, people kicked them out of their rooms because they couldn't pay, and while they were getting thrown out you were making other people rich that had never done anything in their whole lives except think about how to get that way."

"Sometimes it is hard, Nicholas, to determine before the fact—or even at the time—just who should be honored."

"How do you know if you've never tried?"

"You asked if Ignacio was more important than Diane or yourself. I can only say that Ignacio seems to me to hold a brighter promise of a full recovery coupled with a substantial contribution to human progress."

"If he's so good, why did he crack up?"

"Many do, Nicholas. Even among the inner planets space is not a kind environment for mankind; and our space, trans-Martian space, is worse. Any young person here, anyone like yourself or Diane who would seem to have a better-than-average chance of adapting to the conditions we face, is precious."

"Or Ignacio."

"Yes, or Ignacio. Ignacio has a tested IQ of two hundred and ten, Nicholas. Diane's is one hundred and twenty. Your own is ninety-five."

"They never took mine."

"It's on your records, Nicholas."

"They tried to and I threw down the helmet and it broke; Sister Carmela—she was the nurse—just wrote down something on the paper and sent me back."

"I see. I will ask for a complete investigation of this, Nicholas."

"Sure."

"Don't you believe me?"

"I don't think you believed me."

"Nicholas, Nicholas . . ." The long tongues of grass now beginning to appear beneath the immense trees sighed. "Can't you see that a certain measure of trust between the two of us is essential?"

"Did you believe me?"

"Why do you ask? Suppose I were to say I did; would you believe that?"

"When you told me I had been reclassified."

"You would have to be retested, for which there are no facilities here."

"If you believed me, why did you say retested? I told you I haven't ever been tested at all—but anyway you could cross out the ninety-five."

"It is impossible for me to plan your therapy without some estimate of your intelligence, Nicholas, and I have nothing with which to replace it."

The ground was sloping up more sharply now, and in a clearing the boy halted and turned to look back at the leafy film, like algae over a pool, beneath which he had climbed, and at the sea beyond. To his right and left his view was still hemmed with foliage, and ahead of him a meadow on edge (like the square of sand through which he had come, though he did not think of that), dotted still with trees, stretched steeply toward an invisible summit. It seemed to him that under his feet the mountainside swayed ever so slightly. Abruptly he demanded of the wind, "Where's Ignacio?"

"Not here. Much closer to the beach."

"And Diane?"

"Where you left her. Do you enjoy the panorama?"

"It's pretty, but it feels like we're rocking."

"We are. I am moored to the temperglass exterior of our satellite by two hundred cables, but the tide and the currents none the less impart a slight motion to my body. Naturally this movement is magnified as you go higher."

"I thought you were fastened right onto the hull; if there's water under you, how do people get in and out?"

"I am linked to the main air lock by a communication tube. To you when you came, it probably seemed an ordinary companionway."

Nicholas nodded and turned his back on leaves and sea and began to climb again.

"You are in a beautiful spot, Nicholas; do you open your heart to beauty?" After waiting for an answer that did not come, the wind sang:

> *The mountain wooded to the peak, the lawns*
> *And winding glades high up like ways to Heaven,*
> *The slender coco's drooping crown of plumes,*
> *The lightning flash of insect and of bird,*

The lustre of the long convolvuluses
That coil'd around the stately stems, and ran
Ev'n to the limit of the land, the glows
And glories of the broad belt of the world,
All these he saw.

"Does this mean nothing to you, Nicholas?"

"You read a lot, don't you?"

"Often, when it is dark, everyone else is asleep and there is very little else for me to do."

"You talk like a woman; are you a woman?"

"How could I be a woman?"

"You know what I mean. Except, when you were talking mostly to Diane, you sounded more like a man."

"You haven't yet said you think me beautiful."

"You're an Easter egg."

"What do you mean by that, Nicholas?"

"Never mind." He saw the egg as it had hung in the air before him, shining with gold and covered with flowers.

"Eggs are dyed with pretty colors for Easter, and my colors are beautiful—is that what you mean, Nicholas?"

His mother had brought the egg on visiting day, but she could never have made it. Nicholas knew who must have made it. The gold was that very pure gold used for shielding delicate instruments; the clear flakes of crystallized carbon that dotted the egg's surface with tiny stars could only have come from a laboratory high-pressure furnace. How angry he must have been when she told him she was going to give it to him.

"It's pretty, isn't it, Nicky?"

It hung in the weightlessness between them, turning very slowly with the memory of her scented gloves.

"The flowers are meadowsweet, fraxinella, lily of the valley, and moss rose—though I wouldn't expect you to recognize them, darling." His mother had never been below the orbit of Mars, but she pretended to have spent her girlhood on Earth; each reference to the lie filled Nicholas with inexpressible fury and shame. The egg was about twenty centimeters long and it revolved, end over end, in some small fraction more than eight of the pulse beats he felt in his cheeks. Visiting time had twenty-three minutes to go.

"Aren't you going to look at it?"

"I can see it from here." He tried to make her understand. "I can see every part of it. The little red things are aluminum oxide crystals, right?"

"I mean, look *inside*, Nicky."

He saw then that there was a lens at one end, disguised as a dewdrop in the throat of an asphodel. Gently he took the egg in his hands, closed one eye, and looked. The light of the interior was not, as he had half expected, gold tinted, but brilliantly white, deriving from some concealed source. A world surely meant for Earth shone within, as though seen from below the orbit of the moon—indigo sea and emerald land. Rivers brown and clear as tea ran down long plains.

His mother said, "Isn't it pretty?"

Night hung at the corners in funereal purple, and sent long shadows like cold and lovely arms to caress the day; and while he watched and it fell, long-necked birds of so dark a pink that they were nearly red trailed stilt legs across the sky, their wings making crosses.

"They are called flamingos," Dr. Island said, following the direction of his eyes. "Isn't it a pretty word? For a pretty bird, but I don't think we'd like them as much if we called them sparrows, would we?"

His mother said, "I'm going to take it home and keep it for you. It's too nice to leave with a little boy, but if you ever come home again it will be waiting for you. On your dresser, beside your hairbrushes."

Nicholas said, "Words just mix you up."

"You shouldn't despise them, Nicholas. Besides having great beauty of their own, they are useful in reducing tension. You might benefit from that."

"You mean you talk yourself out of it."

"I mean that a person's ability to verbalize his feelings, if only to himself, may prevent them from destroying him. Evolution teaches us, Nicholas, that the original purpose of language was to ritualize men's threats and curses, his spells to compel the gods; communication came later. Words can be a safety valve."

Nicholas said, "I want to be a bomb; a bomb doesn't need a safety valve." To his mother, "Is that South America, Mama?"

"No, dear, India. The Malabar Coast on your left, the Coromandel Coast on your right, and Ceylon below." Words.

"A bomb destroys itself, Nicholas."

"A bomb doesn't care."

He was climbing resolutely now, his toes grabbing at tree roots and the soft, mossy soil; his physician was no longer the wind but a small brown monkey that followed a stone's throw behind him. "I hear someone coming," he said.

"Yes."

"Is it Ignacio?"

"No, it is Nicholas. You are close now."

"Close to the Point?"

"Yes."

He stopped and looked around him. The sounds he had heard, the naked feet padding on soft ground, stopped as well. Nothing seemed strange; the land still rose, and there were large trees, widely spaced, with moss growing in their deepest shade, grass where there was more light. "The three big trees," Nicholas said, "they're just alike. Is that how you know where we are?"

"Yes."

In his mind he called the one before him "Ceylon"; the others were "Coromandel" and "Malabar." He walked toward Ceylon, studying its massive, twisted limbs; a boy naked as himself walked out of the forest to his left, toward Malabar—this boy was not looking at Nicholas, who shouted and ran toward him.

The boy disappeared. Only Malabar, solid and real, stood before Nicholas; he ran to it, touched its rough bark with his hand, and then saw beyond it a fourth tree, similar too to the Ceylon tree, around which a boy peered with averted head. Nicholas watched him for a moment, then said, "I see."

"Do you?" the monkey chattered.

"It's like a mirror, only backwards. The light from the front of me goes out and hits the edge, and comes in the other side, only I can't see it because I'm not looking that way. What I see is the light from my back, sort of, because it comes back this way. When I ran, did I get turned around?"

"Yes, you ran out the left side of the segment, and of course returned immediately from the right."

"I'm not scared. It's kind of fun." He picked up a stick and threw it as hard as he could toward the Malabar tree. It vanished, whizzed over his head, vanished again, slapped the back of his legs. "Did this scare Diane?"

There was no answer. He strode farther, palely naked boys walking to his left and right, but always looking away from him, gradually coming closer.

"Don't go farther," Dr. Island said behind him. "It can be dangerous if you try to pass through the Point itself."

"I see it," Nicholas said. He saw three more trees, growing very close together, just ahead of him; their branches seemed strangely intertwined as they danced together in the wind, and beyond them there was nothing at all.

"You can't actually go through the Point," Dr. Island Monkey said. "The tree covers it."

"Then why did you warn me about it?" Limping and scarred, the boys to his right and left were no more than two meters away now; he had discovered that if he looked straight ahead he could sometimes glimpse their bruised profiles.

"That's far enough, Nicholas."

"I want to touch the tree."

He took another step, and another, then turned. The Malabar boy turned too, presenting his narrow back, on which the ribs and spine seemed welts. Nicholas reached out both arms and laid his hands on the thin shoulders, and as he did, felt other hands—the cool, unfeeling hands of a stranger, dry hands too small—touch his own shoulders and creep upward toward his neck.

"Nicholas!"

He jumped sidewise away from the tree and looked at his hands, his head swaying. "It wasn't me."

"Yes, it was, Nicholas," the monkey said.

"It was one of them."

"You are all of them."

In one quick motion Nicholas snatched up an arm-long section of fallen limb and hurled it at the monkey. It struck the little creature, knocking it down, but the monkey sprang up and fled on three legs. Nicholas sprinted after it.

He had nearly caught it when it darted to one side; as quickly, he turned toward the other, springing for the monkey he saw running toward him there. In an instant it was in his grip, feebly trying to bite. He slammed its head against the ground, then catching it by the ankles swung it against the Ceylon tree until at the third impact he heard the skull crack, and stopped.

He had expected wires, but there were none. Blood oozed from the battered little face, and the furry body was warm and limp in his hands. Leaves above his head said, "You haven't killed me, Nicholas. You never will."

"How does it work?" He was still searching for wires, tiny circuit cards holding micro-logic. He looked about for a sharp stone with which to open the monkey's body, but could find none.

"It is just a monkey," the leaves said. "If you had asked, I would have told you."

"How did you make him talk?" He dropped the monkey, stared at it for a moment, then kicked it. His fingers were bloodly, and he wiped them on the leaves of the tree.

"Only my mind speaks to yours, Nicholas."

"Oh," he said. And then, "I've heard of that. I didn't think it would be like this. I thought it would be in my head."

"Your record shows no auditory hallucinations, but haven't you ever known someone who had them?"

"I knew a girl once . . ." He paused.

"Yes?"

"She twisted noises—you know?"

"Yes."

"Like, it would just be a service cart out in the corridor, but she'd hear the fan, and think . . ."

"What?"

"Oh, different things. That it was somebody talking, calling her."

"Hear them?"

"What?" He sat up in his bunk. "Maya?"

"They're coming after me."

"Maya?"

Dr. Island, through the leaves, said, "When I talk to you, Nicholas, your mind makes any sound you hear the vehicle for my thoughts' content. You may hear me softly in the patter of rain, or joyfully in the singing of a bird—but if I wished I could amplify what I say until every idea and suggestion I wished to give would be driven like a nail into your consciousness. Then you would do whatever I wished you to."

"I don't believe it," Nicholas said. "If you can do that, why don't you tell Diane not to be catatonic?"

"First, because she might retreat more deeply into her disease in an effort to escape me; and second, because ending her catatonia in that way would not remove its cause."

"And thirdly?"

"I did not say 'thirdly,' Nicholas."

"I thought I heard it—when two leaves touched."

"Thirdly, Nicholas, because both you and she have been chosen for your effect on someone else; if I were to change her—or you—so abruptly, that effect would be lost." Dr. Island was a monkey again now, a new monkey that chattered from the protection of a tree twenty meters away. Nicholas threw a stick at him.

"The monkeys are only little animals, Nicholas; they like to follow people, and they chatter."

"I bet Ingacio kills them."

"No, he likes them; he only kills fish to eat."

Nicholas was suddenly aware of his hunger. He began to walk.

He found Ignacio on the beach, praying. For an hour or more, Nicholas hid behind the trunk of a palm watching him, but for a long time he could not decide to whom Ignacio prayed. He was kneeling just where the lacy edges of the breakers died, looking out toward the water; and from time to time he bowed, touching his forehead to the damp sand; then Nicholas could hear his voice, faintly, over the crashing and hissing of the waves. In general, Nicholas approved of prayer, having observed that those who prayed were usually more interesting companions than those who did not; but he had also noticed that though it made no difference what name the devotee gave the object of his devotions, it was important to discover how the god was conceived. Ignacio did not seem to be praying to Dr. Island— he would, Nicholas thought, have been facing the other way for that— and for a time he wondered if he were not praying to the waves. From his position behind him he followed Ignacio's line of vision out and out, wave upon wave into the bright, confused sky, up and up until at last it curved completely around and came to rest on Ignacio's back again; and then it occurred to him that Ignacio might be praying to himself. He left the palm trunk then and walked about halfway to the place where Ignacio knelt, and sat down. Above the sounds of the sea and the murmuring of Ignacio's voice hung a silence so immense and fragile that it seemed that at any moment the entire crystal satellite might ring like a gong.

After a time Nicholas felt his left side trembling. With his right hand he began to stroke it, running his fingers down his left arm, and from his left shoulder to the thigh. It worried him that his left side should be so frightened, and he wondered if perhaps that other half of his brain, from which he was forever severed, could hear what Ignacio was saying to the waves. He began to pray himself, so that the other (and perhaps Ignacio too) could hear, saying not quite beneath his breath, "Don't worry, don't be afraid, he's not going to hurt us, he's nice, and if he does we'll get him; we're only going to get something to eat, maybe he'll show us how to catch fish, I think he'll be nice this time." But he knew, or at least felt he knew, that Ignacio would not be nice this time.

Eventually Ingacio stood up; he did not turn to face Nicholas, but waded out to sea; then, as though he had known Nicholas was behind him all the time (though Nicholas was not sure he had been heard—perhaps, so he thought, Dr. Island had told Ignacio), he gestured to indicate that Nicholas should follow him.

The water was colder than he remembered, the sand coarse and gritty between his toes. He thought of what Dr. Island had told him—about floating—and that a part of her must be this sand, under the water, reaching out (how far?) into the sea; when she ended there would be nothing but the clear temperglass of the satellite itself, far down.

"Come," Ignacio said. "Can you swim?" Just as though he had

forgotten the night before. Nicholas said yes, he could, wondering if Ignacio would look around at him when he spoke. He did not.

"And do you know why you are here?"

"You told me to come."

"Ignacio means *here*. Does this not remind you of any place you have seen before, little one?"

Nicholas thought of the crystal gong and the Easter egg, then of the micro-thin globes of perfumed vapor that, at home, were sometimes sent floating down the corridors at Christmas to explode in clean dust and a cold smell of pine forests when the children stuck them with their hoppingcanes; but he said nothing.

Ignacio continued, "Let Ignacio tell you a story. Once there was a man—a boy, actually—on the Earth, who—"

Nicholas wondered why it was always men (most often doctors and clinical psychologists, in his experience) who wanted to tell you stories. Jesus, he recalled, was always telling everyone stories, and the Virgin Mary almost never, though a woman he had once known who thought she was the Virgin Mary had always been talking about her son. He thought Ignacio looked a little like Jesus. He tried to remember if his mother had ever told him stories when he was at home, and decided that she had not; she just turned on the comscreen to the cartoons.

"—wanted to—"

"—tell a story," Nicholas finished for him.

"How did you know?" Angry and surprised.

"It was you, wasn't it? And you want to tell one now."

"What you said was not what Ignacio would have said. He was going to tell you about a fish."

"Where is it?" Nicholas asked, thinking of the fish Ignacio had been eating the night before, and imagining another such fish, caught while he had been coming back, perhaps, from the Point, and now concealed somewhere waiting the fire. "Is it a big one?"

"It is gone now," Ignacio said, "but it was only as long as a man's hand. I caught it in the big river."

Huckleberry—"I know, the Mississippi; it was a catfish. Or a sunfish."—*Finn.*

"Possibly that is what you call them; for a time he was as the sun to a certain one." The light from nowhere danced on the water. "In any event he was kept on that table in the salon in the house where life was lived. In a tank, but not the old kind in which one sees the glass, with metal at the corner. But the new kind in which the glass is so strong, but very thin, and curved so that it does not reflect, and there are no corners, and a clever device holds the water clear." He dipped up a handful of sparkling water, still not meeting Nicholas's eyes. "As clear even as this, and there were no ripples, and so you could not see it at all. My fish floated in the center of my table above a few stones."

Nicholas asked, "Did you float on the river on a raft?"

"No, we had a little boat. Ignacio caught this fish in a net, of which he almost bit through the strands before he could be landed; he possessed wonderful teeth. There was no one in the house but him and the other, and the robots; but each morning someone would go to the pool in the patio and catch a goldfish for him. Ignacio would see this goldfish there when he came down for his breakfast, and would think, 'Brave goldfish, you have been cast to the monster, will you be the one to destroy him? Destroy him and you shall have his diamond house forever.' And then the fish, who had a little spot of red beneath his wonderful teeth, a spot like a cherry, would rush upon that young goldfish, and for an instant the water would be all clouded with blood."

"And then what?" Nicholas asked.

"And then the clever machine would make the water clear once more, and the fish would be floating above the stones as before, the fish with the wonderful teeth, and Ignacio would touch the little switch on the table, and ask for more bread, and more fruit."

"Are you hungry now?"

"No, I am tired and lazy now; if I pursue you I will not catch you, and if I catch you—through your own slowness and clumsiness—I will not kill you, and if I kill you I will not eat you."

Nicholas had begun to back away, and at the last words, realizing that they were a signal, he turned and began to run, splashing through the shallow water. Ignacio ran after him, much helped by his longer legs, his hair flying behind his dark young face, his square teeth—each white as a bone and as big as Nicholas's thumbnail— showing like spectators who lined the railings of his lips.

"Don't run, Nicholas," Dr. Island said with the voice of a wave. "It only makes him angry that you run." Nicholas did not answer, but cut to his left, up the beach and among the trunks of the palms, sprinting all the way because he had no way of knowing Ignacio was not right behind him, about to grab him by the neck. When he stopped it was in the thick jungle, among the boles of the hard-woods, where he leaned, out of breath, the thumping of his own heart the only sound in an atmosphere silent and unwaked as Earth's long, prehuman day. For a time he listened for any sound Ignacio might make searching for him; there was none. He drew a deep breath then and said, "Well, that's over," expecting Dr. Island to answer from somewhere; there was only the green hush.

The light was still bright and strong and nearly shadowless, but some interior sense told him the day was nearly over, and he noticed that such faint shades as he could see stretched long, horizontal distortions of their objects. He felt no hunger, but he had fasted before and knew on which side of hunger he stood; he was not as strong as he had been only a day past, and by this time next day he would probably be unable to outrun Ignacio. He should, he now realized, have eaten the monkey he had killed; but his stomach revolted at the thought of the raw flesh, and he did not know how he might build a fire, although Ignacio seemed to have done so the night before. Raw fish, even if he were able to catch a fish, would be as bad, or worse, than raw monkey; he remembered his effort to open a coconut—he had failed, but it was surely not impossible. His mind was hazy as to what a coconut might contain, but there had to be an edible core, because they were eaten in books. He decided to make a wide sweep through the jungle that would bring him back to the beach well away from Ignacio; he had several times seen coconuts lying in the sand under the trees.

He moved quietly, still a little afraid, trying to think of ways to open the coconut when he found it. He imagined himself standing before a large and raggedly faceted stone, holding the coconut in both hands. He raised it and smashed it down, but when it struck it was no longer a coconut but Maya's head; he heard her nose cartilage break with a distinct, rubbery snap. Her eyes, as blue as the sky above Madhya Pradesh, the sparkling blue sky of the egg, looked up at him, but he could no longer look into them, they retreated from his own, and it came to him quite suddenly that Lucifer, in falling, must have fallen up, into the fires and the coldness of space, never again to see the warm blues and browns and greens of Earth: *I was watching Satan fall as lightning from heaven.* He had heard that on tape somewhere, but he could not remember where. He had read that on Earth lightning did not come down from the clouds, but leaped up from the planetary surface toward them, never to return.

"Nicholas."

He listened, but did not hear his name again. Faintly water was babbling; had Dr. Island used that sound to speak to him? He walked toward it and found a little rill that threaded a way among the trees, and followed it. In a hundred steps it grew broader, slowed, and ended in a long blind pool under a dome of leaves. Diane was sitting on moss on the side opposite him; she looked up as she saw him, and smiled.

"Hello," he said.

"Hello, Nicholas. I thought I heard you. I wasn't mistaken after all, was I?"

"I didn't think I said anything." He tested the dark water with his foot and found that it was very cold.

"You gave a little gasp, I fancy. I heard it, and I said to myself, *that's Nicholas*, and I called you. Then I thought I might be wrong, or that it might be Ignacio."

"Ignacio was chasing me. Maybe he still is, but I think he's probably given up by now."

The girl nodded, looking into the dark waters of the pool, but did not seem to have heard him. He began to work his way around to her, climbing across the snakelike roots of the crowding trees. "Why does Ignacio want to kill me, Diane?"

"Sometimes he wants to kill me too," the girl said.

"But why?"

"I think he's a bit frightened of us. Have you ever talked to him, Nicholas?"

"Today I did a little. He told me a story about a pet fish he used to have."

"Ignacio grew up all alone; did he tell you that? On Earth. On a plantation in Brazil, way up the Amazon—Dr. Island told me."

"I thought it was crowded on Earth."

"The cities are crowded, and the countryside closest to the cities. But there are places where it's emptier than it used to be. Where Ignacio was, there would have been Red Indian hunters two or three hundred years ago; when he was there, there wasn't anyone, just the machines. Now he doesn't want to be looked at, doesn't want anyone around him."

Nicholas said slowly, "Dr. Island said lots of people wouldn't be sick if only there weren't other people around all the time. Remember that?"

"Only there are other people around all the time; that's how the world is."

"Not in Brazil, maybe," Nicholas said. He was trying to remember something about Brazil, but the only thing he could think of was a parrot singing in a straw hat from the comview cartoons; and then a turtle and a hedgehog that turned into armadillos for the love of God, Montressor. He said, "Why didn't he stay here?"

"Did I tell you about the bird, Nicholas?" She had been not-listening again.

"What bird?"

"I have a bird. Inside." She patted the flat stomach below her small breasts, and for a moment Nicholas thought she had really found food. "She sits in here. She has tangled a nest in my entrails, where she sits and tears at my breath with her beak. I look healthy to you, don't I? But inside I'm hollow and rotten and turning brown, dirt and old feathers, oozing away. Her beak will break through soon."

"Okay." Nicholas turned to go.

"I've been drinking water here, trying to drown her. I think I've swallowed so much I couldn't stand up now if I tried, but she isn't even wet, and do you know something, Nicholas? I've found out I'm not really me, I'm her."

Turning back Nicholas asked, "When was the last time you had anything to eat?"

"I don't know. Two, three days ago. Ignacio gave me something."

"I'm going to try to open a coconut. If I can I'll bring you back some."

When he reached the beach, Nicholas turned and walked slowly back in the direction of the dead fire, this time along the rim of dampened sand between the sea and the palms. He was thinking about machines.

There were hundreds of thousands, perhaps millions, of machines out beyond the belt, but few or none of the sophisticated servant robots of Earth—those were luxuries. Would Ignacio, in Brazil (whatever that was like), have had such luxuries? Nicholas thought not; those robots were almost like people, and living with them would be like living with people. Nicholas wished that he could speak Brazilian.

There had been the therapy robots at St. John's; Nicholas had not liked them, and he did not think Ignacio would have liked them either. If he had liked his therapy robot he probably would not have had to be sent here. He thought of the chipped and rusted old machine that had cleaned the corridors—Maya had called it *Corradora*, but no one else ever called it anything but *Hey!* It could not (or at least did not) speak, and Nicholas doubted that it had emotions, except possibly a sort of love of cleanness that did not extend to its own person. "You will understand," someone was saying inside his head, "that motives of all sorts can be divided into two sorts." A doctor? A therapy robot? It did not matter. "Extrinsic and intrinsic. An extrinsic motive has always some further end in view, and that end we call an intrinsic motive. Thus when we have reduced motivation to intrinsic motivation we have reduced it to its simplest parts. Take that machine over there."

What machine?

"Freud would have said that it was fixated at the latter anal stage, perhaps due to the care its builders exercised in seeing that the dirt it collects is not released again. Because of its fixation it is, as you see, obsessed with cleanliness and order; compulsive sweeping and scrubbing palliate its anxieties. It is a strength of Freud's theory, and not a weakness, that it serves to explain many of the activities of machines as well as the acts of persons."

Hello there, Corradora.

And hello, Ignacio.

My head, moving from side to side, must remind you of a radar scanner. My steps are measured, slow, and precise. I emit a scarcely audible humming as I walk, and my eyes are fixed, as I swing my head, not on you, Ignacio, but on the waves at the edge of sight, where they curve up into the sky. I stop ten meters short of you, and I stand.

You go, I follow, ten meters behind. What do I want? Nothing.

Yes, I will pick up the sticks, and I will follow—five meters behind.

"Break them, and put them on the fire. Not all of them, just a few."

Yes.

"Ignacio keeps the fire here burning all the time. Sometimes he takes the coals of fire from it to start others, but here, under the big palm log, he has a fire always. The rain does not strike it here. Always the fire. Do you know how he made it the first time? Reply to him!"

"No."

"No, *Patrão!*"

" 'No, *Patrão.*' "

"Ignacio stole it from the gods, from Poseidon. Now Poseidon is dead, lying at the bottom of the water. Which is the top. Would you like to see him?"

"If you wish it, *Patrão.*"

"It will soon be dark, and that is the time to fish; do you have a spear?"

"No, *Patrão.*"

"Then Ignacio will get you one."

Ignacio took a handful of the sticks and thrust the ends into the fire, blowing on them. After a moment Nicholas leaned over and blew too, until all the sticks were blazing.

"Now we must find you some bamboo, and there is some back here. Follow me."

The light, still nearly shadowless, was dimming now, so that it seemed to Nicholas that they walked on insubstantial soil, though he could feel it beneath his feet. Ignacio stalked ahead, holding up the burning sticks until the fire seemed about to die, then pointing the ends down, allowing it to lick upward toward his hand and come to life again. There was a gentle wind blowing out toward the sea, carrying away the sound of the surf and bringing a damp coolness; and when they had been walking for several minutes, Nicholas heard in it a faint, dry, almost rhythmic rattle.

Ignacio looked back at him and said, "The music. The big stems talking; hear it?"

They found a cane a little thinner than Nicholas's wrist and pilled the burning sticks around its base, then added more. When it fell, Ignacio burned through the upper end too, making a pole about as long as Nicholas was tall, and with the edge of a seashell scrapped the larger end to a point. "Now you are a fisherman," he said. Nicholas said, "Yes, *Patrão*," still careful not to meet his eyes.

"You are hungry?"

"Yes, *Patrão*."

"Then let me tell you something. Whatever you get is Ignacio's, you understand? And what he catches, that is his too. But when he has eaten what he wants, what is left is yours. Come on now, and Ignacio will teach you to fish or drown you."

Ignacio's own spear was buried in the sand not far from the fire; it was much bigger than the one he had made for Nicholas. With it held across his chest he went down to the water, wading until it was waist high, then swimming, not looking to see if Nicholas was following. Nicholas found that he could swim with the spear by putting all his effort into the motion of his legs, holding the spear in his left hand and stroking only occasionally with his right. "You breathe," he said softly, "and watch the spear," and after that he had only to allow his head to lift from time to time.

He had thought Ignacio would begin to look for fish as soon as they were well out from the beach, but the Brazilian continued to swim, slowly but steadily, until it seemed to Nicholas that they must be a kilometer or more from land. Suddenly, as though the lights in a room had responded to a switch, the dark sea around them became an opalescent blue. Ignacio stopped, treading water and using his spear to buoy himself.

"Here," he said. "Get them between yourself and the light."

Open-eyed, he bent his face to the water, raised it again to breathe deeply, and dove. Nicholas followed his example, floating belly-down with open eyes.

All the world of dancing glitter and dark island vanished as though he had plunged his face into a dream. Far, far below him Jupiter displayed its broad, striped disk, marred with the spreading Bright Spot where man-made silicone enzymes had stripped the hydrogen from methane for kindled fusion: a cancer and a burning infant sun. Between that sun and his eyes lay invisible a hundred thousand kilometers of space, and the temperglass shell of the satellite; hundreds of meters of illuminated water, and in it the spread body of Ignacio, dark against the light, still kicking downward, his spear a pencil line of blackness in his hand.

Involuntarily Nicholas's head came up, returning to the universe of sparkling waves, aware now that what he had called "night" was only the shadow cast by Dr. Island when Jupiter and the Bright Spot slid beneath her. That shadow line, indetectable in air, now lay sharp across the water behind him. He took breath and plunged.

Almost at once a fish darted somewhere below, and his left arm thrust the spear forward, but it was far out of reach. He swam after it, then saw another, larger, fish farther down and dove for that, passing Ignacio surfacing for air. The fish was too deep, and he had used up his oxygen; his lungs aching for air, he swam up, wanting to let go of his spear, then realizing at the last moment that he could, that it would only bob to the surface if he released it. His head broke water and he gasped, his heart thumping; water struck his face and he knew again, suddenly, as though they had ceased to exist while he was gone, the pulsebeat pounding of the waves.

Ignacio was waiting for him. He shouted, "This time you will come with Ignacio, and he will show you the dead sea god. Then we will fish."

Unable to speak, Nicholas nodded. He was allowed three more breaths; then Ignacio dove and Nicholas had to follow, kicking down until the pressure sang in his ears. Then through blue water he saw, looming at the edge of the light, a huge mass of metal anchored to the temperglass hull of the satellite itself; above it, hanging lifelessly like the stem of a great vine severed from the root, a cable twice as thick as a man's body; and on the bottom, sprawled beside the mighty anchor, a legged god that might have been a dead insect save that it was at least six meters long. Ignacio turned and looked back at Nicholas to see if he understood; he did not, but he nodded, and with the strength draining from his arms, surfaced again.

After Ignacio brought up the first fish, they took turns on the surface guarding their catch, and while the Bright Spot crept beneath the shelving rim of Dr. Island, they speared two more, one of them quite large. Then when Nicholas was so exhausted he could scarcely lift his arms, they made their way back to shore, and Ignacio showed him how to gut the fish with a thorn and the edge of a shell, and reclose them and pack them in mud and leaves to be roasted by the fire. After Ignacio had begun to eat the largest fish, Nicholas timidly drew out the smallest, and ate for the first time since coming to Dr. Island. Only when he had finished did he remember Diane.

He did not dare to take the last fish to her, but he looked covertly at Ignacio, and began edging away from the fire. The Brazilian seemed not to have noticed him. When he was well into the shadows he stood, backed a few steps, then—slowly, as his instincts warned him—walked away, not beginning to trot until the distance between them was nearly a hundred meters.

He found Diane sitting apathetic and silent at the margin of the cold pool, and had some difficulty persuading her to stand. At last he lifted her, his hands under her arms pressing against her thin ribs. Once on her feet she stood steadily enough, and followed him when he took her by the hand. He talked to her, knowing that although she gave no sign of hearing she heard him, and that the right words might wake her to response. "We went fishing—Ignacio showed me how. And he's got a fire, Diane, he got it from a kind of robot that was supposed to be fixing one of the cables that holds Dr. Island, I don't know how. Anyway, listen, we caught three big fish, and I ate one and Ignacio ate a great big one, and I don't think he'd mind if you had the other one, only say, 'Yes, *Patrão*,' and 'No, *Patrão*,' to him—he likes that, and he's only used to machines. You don't have to smile at him or anything—just look at the fire, that's what I do, just look at the fire."

To Ignacio, perhaps wisely, he at first said nothing at all, leading Diane to the place where he had been sitting himself a few minutes before and placing some scraps from his fish in her lap. When she did not eat he found a sliver of the tender, roasted flesh and thrust it into her mouth. Ignacio said, "Ignacio believed that one dead," and Nicholas answered, "No *Patrão*."

"There is another fish. Give it to her."

Nicholas did, raking the gob of baked mud from the coals to crack with the heel of his hand, and peeling the broken and steaming fillets from the skins and bones to give to her when they had cooled enough to eat; after the fish had lain in her mouth for perhaps half a minute she began to chew and swallow, and after the third mouthful she fed herself, though without looking at either of them.

"Ignacio believed that one dead," Ignacio said again.

"No, *Patrão*," Nicholas answered, and then added, "Like you can see, she's alive."

"She is a pretty creature, with the firelight on her face—no?"

"Yes, *Patrão*, very pretty."

"But too thin." Ignacio moved around the fire until he was sitting almost beside Diane, then reached for the fish Nicholas had given her. Her hands closed on it, though she still did not look at him.

"You see, she knows us after all," Ignacio said. "We are not ghosts."

Nicholas whispered urgently, "Let him have it."

Slowly Diane's fingers relaxed, but Ignacio did not take the fish. "I was only joking, little one," he said. "And I think not such good joke after all." Then when she did not reply, he turned away from her, his eyes reaching out across the dark, tossing water for something Nicholas could not see.

"She likes you, *Patrão*," Nicholas said. The words were like swallowing filth, but he thought of the bird ready to tear through Diane's skin, and Maya's blood soaking in little round dots in the white cloth, and continued. "She is only shy. It is better that way."

"You. What do you know?"

At least Ignacio was no longer looking at the sea. Nicholas said, "Isn't it true, *Patrão*?"

"Yes, it is true."

Diane was picking at the fish again, conveying tiny flakes to her mouth with delicate fingers; distinctly but almost absently she said, "Go, Nicholas."

He looked at Ignacio, but the Brazilian's eyes did not turn toward the girl, nor did he speak.

"Nicholas, go away. Please."

In a voice he hoped was pitched too low for Ignacio to hear, Nicholas said, "I'll see you in the morning. All right?"

Her head moved a fraction of a centimeter.

Once he was out of sight of the fire, one part of the beach was as good to sleep on as another; he wished he had taken a piece of wood from the fire to start one of his own and tried to cover his legs with sand to keep off the cool wind, but the sand fell away whenever he moved, and his legs and his left hand moved without volition on his part.

The surf, lapping at the rippled shore, said, "That was well done, Nicholas."

"I can feel you move," Nicholas said. "I don't think I ever could before except when I was high up."

"I doubt that you can now; my roll is less than one one-hundredth of a degree."

"Yes, I can. You wanted me to do that, didn't you? About Ignacio."

"Do you know what the Harlow effect is, Nicholas?"

Nicholas shook his head.

"About a hundred years ago Dr. Harlow experimented with monkeys who had been raised in complete isolation—no mothers, no other monkeys at all."

"Lucky monkeys."

"When the monkeys were mature he put them into cages with normal ones; they fought with any that came near them, and sometimes they killed them."

"Psychologists always put things in cages; did he ever think of turning them loose in the jungle instead?"

"No, Nicholas, though we have . . . Aren't you going to say anything?"

"I guess not."

"Dr. Harlow tried, you see, to get the isolate monkeys to breed—sex is the primary social function—but they wouldn't. Whenever another monkey of either sex approached they displayed aggressiveness, which the other monkeys returned. He cured them finally by introducing immature monkeys—monkey children—in place of the mature, socialized ones. These needed the isolate adults so badly that they kept on making approaches no matter how often or how violently they were rejected, and in the end they were accepted, and the isolates socialized. It's interesting to note that the founder of Christianity seems to have had an intuitive grasp of the principle—but it was almost two thousands years before it was demonstrated scientifically."

"I don't think it worked here," Nicholas said. "It was more complicated than that."

"Human beings are complicated monkeys, Nicholas."

"That's about the first time I ever heard you make a joke. You like not being human, don't you?"

"Of course. Wouldn't you?"

"I always thought I would, but now I'm not sure. You said that to help me, didn't you? I don't like that."

A wave higher than the others splashed chill foam over Nicholas's legs, and for a moment he wondered if this were Dr. Island's reply. Half a minute later another wave wet him, and another, and he moved farther up the beach to avoid them. The wind was stronger, but he slept despite it, and was awakened only for a moment by a flash of light from the direction from which he had come; he tried to guess what might have caused it, thought of Diane and Ignacio throwing the burning sticks into the air to see the arcs of fire, smiled—too sleepy now to be angry—and slept again.

Morning came cold and sullen; Nicholas ran up and down the beach, rubbing himself with his hands. A thin rain, or spume (it was hard to tell which), was blowing in the wind, clouding the light to gray radiance. He wondered if Diane and Ignacio would mind if he came back now and decided to wait, then thought of fishing so that he would have something to bring when he came; but the sea was very cold and the waves so high they tumbled him,

wrenching his bamboo spear from his hand. Ignacio found him
dripping with water, sitting with his back to a palm trunk and
staring out toward the lifting curve of the sea.

"Hello, you," Ignacio said.

"Good morning, *Patrão*."

Ignacio sat down. "What is your name? You told me, I think,
when we first met, but I have forgotten. I am sorry."

"Nicholas."

"Yes."

"*Patrão*, I am very cold. Would it be possible for us to go to your
fire?"

"My name is Ignacio; call me that."

Nicholas nodded, frightened.

"But we cannot go to my fire, because the fire is out."

"Can't you make another one, *Patrão*?"

"You do not trust me, do you? I do not blame you. No, I cannot
make another—you may use what I had, if you wish, and make one
after I have gone. I came only to say goodbye."

"You're leaving?"

The wind in the palm fronds said, "Ignacio is much better now.
He will be going to another place, Nicholas."

"A hospital?"

"Yes, a hospital, but I don't think he will have to stay there long."

"But . . ." Nicholas tried to think of something appropriate. At
St. John's and the other places where he had been confined, when
people left, they simply left, and usually were hardly spoken of
once it was learned that they were going and thus were already
tainted by whatever it was that froze the smiles and dried the tears
of those outside. At last he said, "Thanks for teaching me how to
fish."

"That was all right," Ignacio said. He stood up and put a hand
on Nicholas's shoulder, then turned away. Four meters to his left
the damp sand was beginning to lift and crack. While Nicholas
watched, it opened on a brightly lit companionway walled with
white. Ignacio pushed his curly black hair back from his eyes and
went down, and the sand closed with a thump.

"He won't be coming back, will he?" Nicholas said.

"No."

"He said I could use his stuff to start another fire, but I don't
even know what it is."

Dr. Island did not answer. Nicholas got up and began to walk
back to where the fire had been, thinking about Diane and wondering if she was hungry; he was hungry himself.

* * *

He found her beside the dead fire. Her chest had been burned away, and lying close by, near the hole in the sand where Ignacio must have kept it hidden, was a bulky nuclear welder. The power pack was too heavy for Nicholas to lift, but he picked up the welding gun on its short cord and touched the trigger, producing a two-meter plasma discharge which he played along the sand until Diane's body was ash. By the time he had finished the wind was whipping the palms and sending stinging rain into his eyes, but he collected a supply of wood and built another fire, bigger and bigger until it roared like a forge in the wind. "He killed her!" he shouted to the waves.

"YES." Dr. Island's voice was big and wild.

"You said he was better."

"HE IS," howled the wind. "YOU KILLED THE MONKEY THAT WANTED TO PLAY WITH YOU, NICHOLAS AS I BELIEVED IGNACIO WOULD EVENTUALLY KILL YOU, WHO ARE SO EASILY HATED, SO DIFFERENT FROM WHAT IT IS THOUGHT A BOY SHOULD BE. BUT KILLING THE MONKEY HELPED YOU, REMEMBER? MADE YOU BETTER. IGNACIO WAS FRIGHTENED BY WOMEN; NOW HE KNOWS THAT THEY ARE REALLY VERY WEAK, AND HE HAS ACTED UPON CERTAIN FANTASIES AND FINDS THEM BITTER."

"You're rocking," Nicholas said. "Am I doing that?"

"YOUR THOUGHT."

A palm snapped in the storm; instead of falling, it flew crashing among the others, its fronded head catching the wind like a sail. "I'm killing you," Nicholas said. "Destroying you." The left side of his face was so contorted with grief and rage that he could scarcely speak.

Dr. Island heaved beneath his feet. "NO."

"One of your cables is already broken—I saw that. Maybe more than one. You'll pull loose. I'm turning this world, isn't that right? The attitude rockets are tuned to my emotions, and they're spinning us around, and the slippage is the wind and the high sea, and when you come loose nothing will balance anymore."

"NO."

"What's the stress on your cables? Don't you know?"

"THEY ARE VERY STRONG."

"What kind of talk is that? You ought to say something like: 'The D-twelve cable tension is twenty-billion kilograms' force. WARNING! WARNING! Expected time to failure is ninety-seven seconds! WARNING!' *Don't you even know how a machine is supposed to talk?*" Nicholas was screaming now, and every wave reached farther up the beach than the last, so that the bases of the most seaward palms were awash.

"GET BACK, NICHOLAS. FIND HIGHER GROUND. GO INTO THE JUNGLE." It was the crashing waves themselves that spoke.

"I won't."

A long serpent of water reached for the fire, which hissed and sputtered.

"GET BACK!"

"I won't!"

A second wave came, striking Nicholas calf-high and nearly extinguishing the fire.

"ALL THIS WILL BE UNDER WATER SOON. GET BACK!"

Nicholas picked up some of the still-burning sticks and tried to carry them, but the wind blew them out as soon as he lifted them from the fire. He tugged at the welder, but it was too heavy for him to lift.

"GET BACK!"

He went into the jungle, where the trees lashed themselves to leafy rubbish in the wind and broken branches flew through the air like debris from an explosion; for a while he heard Diane's voice crying in the wind; it became Maya's, then his mother's or Sister Carmela's, and a hundred others; in time the wind grew less, and he could no longer feel the ground rocking. He felt tired. He said, "I didn't kill you after all, did I?" but there was no answer. On the beach, when he returned to it, he found the welder half buried in sand. No trace of Diane's ashes, nor of his fire. He gathered more wood and built another, lighting it with the welder.

"Now," he said. He scooped aside the sand around the welder until he reached the rough understone beneath it, and turned the flame of the welder on that; it blackened and bubbled.

"No," Dr. Island said.

"Yes." He was bending intently over the flame, both hands locked on the welder's trigger.

"Nicholas, stop that." When he did not reply, "Look behind you." There was a splashing louder than the crashing of the waves, and a groaning of metal. He whirled and saw the great, beetle-like robot Ignacio had shown him on the sea floor. Tiny shellfish clung to its metal skin, and water, faintly green, still poured from its body. Before he could turn the welding gun toward it, it shot forward hands like clamps and wrenched it from him. All up and down the beach similar machines were smoothing the sand and repairing the damage of the storm.

"That thing was dead," Nicholas said. "Ignacio killed it."

It picked up the power pack, shook it clean of sand, and turning, stalked back toward the sea.

"That is what Ignacio believed, and it was better that he believed so."

"And you said you couldn't do anything, you had no hands."

"I also told you that I would treat you as society will when you are released, that that was my nature. After that, did you still believe all I told you? Nicholas, you are upset now because Diane is dead—"

"You could have protected her!"

"—but by dying she made someone else—someone very important—well. Her prognosis was bad; she really wanted only death, and this was the death I chose for her. You could call it the death of Dr. Island, a death that would help someone else. Now you are alone, but soon there will be more patients in this segment, and you will help them, too—if you can—and perhaps they will help you. Do you understand?"

"No," Nicholas said. He flung himself down on the sand. The wind had dropped, but it was raining hard. He thought of the vision he had once had, and of describing it to Diane the day before, "This isn't ending the way I thought," he whispered. It was only a squeak of sound far down in his throat. "Nothing ever turns out right."

The waves, the wind, the rustling palm fronds and the pattering rain, the monkeys who had come down to the beach to search for food washed ashore, answered, "Go away—go back—don't move."

Nicholas pressed his scarred head against his knees, rocking back and forth.

"Don't move."

For a long time he sat still while the rain lashed his shoulders and the dripping monkeys frolicked and fought around him. When at last he lifted his face, there was in it some element of personality which had been only potentially present before, and with this an emptiness and an expression of surprise. His lips moved, and the sounds were the sounds made by a deaf-mute who tries to speak.

"Nicholas is gone," the waves said. "Nicholas, who was the right side of your body, the left half of your brain, I have forced into catatonia; for the remainder of your life he will be to you only what you once were to him—or less. Do you understand?"

The boy nodded.

"We will call you Kenneth, silent one. And if Nicholas tries to come again, Kenneth, you must drive him back—or return to what you have been."

The boy nodded a second time, and a moment afterward began to collect sticks for the dying fire. As though to themselves the waves chanted:

"Seas are wild tonight . . .
Stretching over Sado island
Silent clouds of stars."

There was no reply.

KATE WILHELM

Where Late the Sweet Birds Sang

Kate Wilhelm began publishing in 1956, and first attracted attention with her story "The Mile-Long Spaceship" in *Astounding*—a place that would later come to seem like an alien and unlikely milieu for her, considering the political and aesthetic thrust of her mature work. Wilhelm's early work was often thin and rudimentary and sometimes clumsy (her work of this period was collected in *The Mile-Long Spaceship*; her best-known story of this period was probably "The Man Without a Planet"), and didn't make much of an impact on the world of the late fifties or early sixties. In retrospect, she can more usefully be thought of as belonging to the New Wave era of the mid-sixties instead, in spite of her earlier publications, because that's when her work attained mature levels of power and sophistication, and she began to produce major work. By 1968, she had won a Nebula Award for her short story, "The Planners," and her work continued to grow in complexity, ambition, depth of characterization, and maturity of expression, until she was producing some of the best work of the early seventies, particularly at novella length: *Somerset Dreams*, *April Fool's Day Forever*, *The Infinity Box*, *The Encounter*, *The Fusion Bomb*, *The Plastic Abyss*.

Or the story that follows, 1974's complex and darkly lyrical *Where Late the Sweet Birds Sang*.

One of Wilhelm's fortes is the exploration of the shifting and elusive borderland between illusion and reality, and, of all SF writers, only Philip K. Dick can be said to have covered this territory with the kind of originality, grace, and vividness of insight that Wilhelm has brought to it. Like Dick, she is also perhaps one of the most deeply and genuinely radical of SF writers, all the more so because she doesn't seem to have any one particular political axe to grind. Her 1967 novel *The Killer Thing* is one of the earliest anti-Vietnam analogues in the field, and her short story "The Village" is still one of its strongest.

Not surprisingly, politics and illusion are two of the main concerns of the story that follows, a bittersweet and compelling novella that deals with humankind's age-old trait of seeing what they *want* to see, instead of the unpleasant and uncomfortable truths that are right under their noses. . . .

Wilhelm's early SF novels were also somewhat routine, starting in 1965 with *The Clone*, a weak collaborative effort with Ted Thomas, but she soon worked herself into more complex and original material like 1969's *Let the Fire Fall*, and by 1971 she was capable of writing the eerie and fascinating *Margaret and I*, which still strikes me as one of the most underappreciated novels of the seventies. A few years later, she took a Hugo in 1976 for the novel version of *Where Late the Sweet Birds Sang*, and added another two Nebulas to her collection in the late eighties with her stories "Forever Yours, Anna" and "The Girl Who Fell Into the Sky." By this time, she was widely regarded as one of the best of today's writers, outside the genre as well as in it, for her work has never been limited to the strict boundaries of the field, and she has published mysteries, mainstream thrillers, and comic novels as well.

Wilhelm's other books include the novels *More Bitter than Death, Fault Lines, The Clewiston Test, Juniper Time, Welcome, Chaos, Oh, Susannah!, Huysman's Pets, Crazy Time, Cambio Bay, Death Qualified,* and the Constance Leidl–Charlie Meiklejohn mystery novels *The Hamlet Trap, Smart House, Seven Kinds of Death,* and *Sweet, Sweet Poison,* as well as the collections *The Downstairs Room, Somerset Dreams, The Infinity Box, Listen, Listen, Children of the Wind,* and *And the Angels Sing.* Her most recent book is a new mystery novel, *Justice for Some.* Wilhelm and her husband, writer Damon Knight, ran the Milford Writer's Conference for many years, and both are still deeply involved in the operation of the Clarion workshop for new young writers. She lives with her family in Eugene, Oregon, and is currently at work on *The Best Defense,* a sequel to *Death Qualified.*

What David always hated most about the Sumner family dinners was the way everyone talked about him as if he were not there.

"Has he been eating enough meat lately? He looks peaked."

"You spoil him, Carrie. If he won't eat his dinner, don't let him go out and play. You were like that, you know."

"When I was his age, I was husky enough to cut down a tree with a hatchet. He couldn't cut his way out of a fog."

David would imagine himself invisible, floating unseen over their heads as they discussed him. Someone would ask if he had a girl friend yet, and they would *tsk-tsk* whether the answer was yes or no. From his vantage point he would aim a ray gun at Uncle Clarence, whom he especially disliked because he was fat, bald, and very rich. Uncle Clarence dipped his biscuits in his gravy, or in syrup, or more often in a mixture of sorghum and butter that he stirred together on his plate until it looked like baby shit.

"Is he still planning to be a biologist? He should go to med school and join Walt in his practice."

He would point his ray gun at Uncle Clarence and cut a neat plug out of his stomach and carefully ease it out, and Uncle Clarence would ooze from the opening and flow all over them.

"David." He started with alarm, then relaxed again. "David, why don't you go out and see what the other kids are up to?" His father's quiet voice, saying actually, that's enough of that. And they would turn their collective mind to one of the other offspring.

As David grew older, he learned the complex relationships that he had merely accepted as a child. Uncles, aunts, cousins, second cousins, third cousins. The honorary members: brothers and sisters and parents of those who had married into the family. There were the Sumners and Wistons and O'Gradys and Heinemans and the Meyers and Capeks and Rizzos, all part of the same river that flowed through the fertile Virginia valley.

He remembered the holidays especially. The old Sumner house was rambling, with many bedrooms upstairs and an attic that was wall-to-wall mattresses, pallets for the children, with an enormous fan in the west window. Someone was forever checking to make certain that they hadn't all suffocated in the attic. The older children were supposed to keep an eye on the younger ones, but what they did in fact was to frighten them night after night with ghost stories and inhuman sighs and groans. Eventually the noise level would rise until adult intervention was demanded. Uncle Ron would clump up the stairs heavily and there would be a scurrying, with suppressed giggles and muffled screams, until everyone found a bed again, so that by the time he turned on the hall light that illuminated the attic dimly, all the children seemed to be sleeping. He would pause briefly in the doorway, then close the door, turn off the light, and tramp back down the stairs, apparently deaf to the renewed merriment behind him.

Whenever Aunt Claudia came up, it was like an apparition. One minute pillows would be flying, someone would be crying, someone else trying to read with a flashlight, several of the boys playing cards with another flashlight, some of the girls huddled together whispering what had to be delicious secrets, judging by the way they blushed and looked desperate if an adult came upon them suddenly, and then the door would snap open, the light would fall on the disorder, and she would be standing there. Aunt Claudia was very tall and thin, her nose was too big and she was tanned to a permanent old-leather color. She would stand there, immobile and terrible, and the children would creep back into bed without a sound. She would not move until everyone was back where he or she belonged, then she would close the door soundlessly. The silence would drag on and on. The ones nearest the door would hold their breath, trying to hear breathing on the other side. Eventually someone would become brave enough to open the door a crack, and if she was truly gone, the party would resume.

The smells of holidays were fixed in David's memory. All the usual smells: fruitcakes and turkeys, the vinegar that went in the egg dyes, the greenery, and the thick, creamy smoke of bayberry candles. But what he remembered most vividly was the Fourth of July smell of gunpowder that permeated their hair, their clothes, that lasted on their hands for days and days. Their hands would be stained purple-black from berry picking, and the color and smell were one of the indelible images of his childhood. Mixed in with it was the smell of sulfur that was dusted on them liberally to confound the chiggers.

If it hadn't been for Celia, his childhood would have been perfect. Celia was his cousin, his mother's sister's daughter. She was one year younger than David and by far the prettiest of all his cousins. When they were very young they had promised to marry one day, and when they grew older and it was made abundantly clear that no cousins might ever marry in that family, they had become implacable enemies. He didn't know how they had been told. He was certain that no one ever put it in words, but they knew. When they could not avoid each other after that, they fought. She pushed him out of the hayloft and broke his arm when he was fifteen, and when he was sixteen they wrestled from the back door of the Wiston farmhouse to the fence fifty or sixty yards away. They tore the clothes off each other and he was bleeding from her fingernails down his back, she from scraping her shoulder on a rock. Then somehow in their rolling and squirming frenzy, his cheek came down on her uncovered chest, and he stopped fighting. He sud-

denly became a melting, sobbing, incoherent idiot and she hit him
on the head with a rock and ended the fight.

Up to that point the battle had been in almost total silence, broken
only by gasps for breath and whispered language that would have
shocked their parents. But when she hit him and he went limp, not
unconscious, but dazed, uncaring, inert, she screamed, abandoning
herself to anguish and terror. The family tumbled from the house
as if they had been shaken out, and their first thought must have
been that he had raped her. His father hustled him to the barn,
presumably for a thrashing. But in the barn, his father, belt in hand,
looked at him with an expression that was furious and strangely
sympathetic. He didn't touch David, and only after he had turned
and left did David realize that tears were still running down his
face.

In the family there were farmers, a few lawyers, two doctors,
insurance brokers and bankers and millers, hardware merchandis-
ers, other shopkeepers. David's father owned a large department
store that catered to the upper-middle-class clientele of the valley.
The valley was rich. David always supposed that the family, except
for a few ne'er-do-wells, was rather wealthy. Of all his relatives his
favorite was his father's brother Walt. Dr. Walt, they all called him.
He played with the children and taught them grown-up things, like
where to hit if you really meant it, where not to hit in a friendly
scrap. He seemed to know when to stop treating them as children
long before anyone else in the family did. Dr. Walt was the reason
David had decided very early to become a scientist.

David was seventeen when he went to Harvard. His birthday was
in September and he didn't go home for it. When he did return at
Thanksgiving and the clan had gathered, Grandfather Sumner
poured the ritual before-dinner martinis and handed one to him.
And Uncle Warner said to him, "What do you think we should do
about Bobbie?"

He had arrived at that mysterious crossing that is never deline-
ated clearly enough to be seen in advance. He sipped his martini,
not liking it particularly, and knew that childhood had ended, and
he felt a profound sadness and loneliness.

The Christmas that David was twenty-three seemed out of focus.
The scenario was the same, the attic full of children, the food smells,
the powdering of snow, none of that had changed, but he was
seeing it from a new position and it was not the wonderland it had
been, and he knew with regret that the enchantment had vanished
and could never be recaptured. When his parents went home he

stayed on at the Wiston farm for a day or two, waiting for Celia. She had missed the Christmas Day celebration, getting ready for her coming trip to Brazil, but she would be there, her mother had assured Grandmother Wiston, and David was waiting for her, not happily, not with any expectation of reward, but with a fury that grew and caused him to stalk the old house like a boy being punished for another's sin.

When she came home and he saw her standing with her mother and her grandmother, his anger melted. It was like seeing Celia in a time distortion, as she was and would be or had been. Her pale hair would not change much, but her bones would become more prominent, and the almost-emptiness of her face would have written on it a message of concern, of love, of giving, of being decisively herself, of a strength unsuspected in her frail body. Grandmother Wiston was a beautiful old lady, he thought in wonder, amazed that he never had seen her beauty before. Celia's mother was more beautiful than the girl. And he saw the resemblance to his own mother in the trio. Wordlessly, defeated, he turned and went to the rear of the house and put on one of his grandfather's heavy jackets because he didn't want to see her at all now, and his own outdoor clothing was in the front hall closet too near where she was still standing.

He walked a long time in the frosty afternoon, seeing very little, and shaking himself from time to time when he realized that the cold was entering his shoes or making his ears numb. And he found that he was climbing the slope to the antique forest where his grandfather had taken him once, a long time ago. He climbed and became warmer, and at dusk he was under the branches of the tiers of trees that had been there since the beginning of time. They or others that were just like them. Forever waiting for the day when they would reclaim the land and cover the continent once more. Here were the relicts his grandfather had brought him to see. Here was a silverbell grown to the stature of a large tree, while down the slopes, in the lower reaches, it remained always a shrub. Here the white basswood grew alongside the hemlock and the bitternut hickory, and the beeches and sweet buckeyes locked arms.

"David!" He stopped and listened, certain he had imagined it, but the call came again. "David, are you up here?"

He turned then and saw Celia among the massive tree trunks. Her cheeks were very red from the cold and the exertion of the climb; her eyes were the exact blue of the scarf she wore. She stopped six feet from him and started to speak again, but didn't. Instead she drew off a glove and touched the smooth trunk of a beech. "Grandfather Wiston brought me up here, too, when I was twelve. It was very important to him that we understand this place."

David nodded.

"Why did you leave like that? They all think we're going to fight again."

"We might," he said.

She smiled. "I don't think so."

"We should start down. It'll be dark in a few minutes." But he didn't move.

"David, try to make Mother see, will you? You understand that I have to go, that I have to do something, don't you? She thinks you're so clever. She'd listen to you."

He laughed. "They think I'm clever like a puppy dog."

Celia shook her head. "You're the one they'd listen to. They treat me like a child and always will."

David shook his head, smiling. "Why are you going, Celia? What are you trying to prove?"

"Damn it, David! If you don't understand, who will?" She took a deep breath. "People are starving in South America. Not just a few Indians, but millions of people. And practically no one has done any real research in tropical farming methods. It's all lateritic soil, and no one down there understands it. Well, we trained in tropical farming and we're going to start classes down there, in the field. It's what I trained for. This project will get me a doctorate."

The Wistons were farmers, had always been farmers. "Custodians of the soil," Grandfather Wiston had said once, "not its owners, just custodians." Celia reached down and moved aside some matted leaves and muck on the ground, and straightened with her hand full of black dirt. "The famines are spreading. They need so much. And I have so much to give! Can't you understand that?" she cried. She closed her hand hard, compacting the soil into a ball that crumbled again when she opened her fist. She let the soil fall from her hand and carefully pushed the protective covering of leaves back over the bared spot.

"You followed me to tell me good-bye, didn't you?" David said suddenly, and his voice was harsh. "It's really good-bye this time, isn't it?" He watched her and slowly she nodded. "There's someone in your group?"

"I'm not sure, David. Maybe." She bowed her head and started to pull her glove on again. "I thought I was sure. But when I saw you in the hall, saw the look on your face when I came in . . . I realized that I just don't know."

"Celia, you listen to me! There aren't any hereditary defects that would surface! Damn it, you know that! If there were, we simply wouldn't have children, but there's no reason. You know that, don't you?"

She nodded. "I know."

"Come with me, Celia. We don't have to get married right away, let them get used to the idea first. They will. They always do. We have a resilient family, you and me. Celia, I love you."

She turned her head and he saw that she was weeping; she wiped her cheeks with her glove, then with her bare hand, leaving dirt streaks. David pulled her to him, held her and kissed her tears, her cheeks, her lips.

She finally drew away and started back down the slope, with David following. "I can't decide anything right now. It isn't fair. I should have stayed at the house. I shouldn't have followed you up here. David, I'm committed to going in two days. I can't just say I've changed my mind. It's important to me. To the people down there. I can't just decide not to go."

He caught her arm and held her, kept her from moving ahead again. "Just tell me you love me. Say it, just once."

"I love you," she said very slowly.

"How long will you be gone?"

"Three years. I signed a contract."

He stared at her. "Change it! Make it one year. I'll be out of grad school then. You can teach here. Let their bright young students come to you."

"We have to get back, or they'll send a search party for us," she said. "I'll try to change it," she whispered then. "If I can." Two days later she left.

David spent New Year's Eve at the Sumner farm with his parents and a horde of aunts and uncles and cousins. On New Year's Day, Grandfather Sumner made an announcement. "We're building a hospital up at Bear Creek, this side of the mill."

David blinked. That was a mile from the farm, miles from anything else. "A hospital?" He looked at his uncle Walt, who nodded.

Clarence was studying his eggnog with a sour expression, and David's father, the third brother, was watching the smoke curl from his pipe.

"Why up here?" David asked finally.

"It's going to be a research hospital," Walt said. "Genetic diseases, hereditary defects, that sort of thing. Two hundred beds."

David shook his head in disbelief. "You have any idea how much something like that would cost? Who's financing it?"

His grandfather laughed nastily. "Senator Burke has graciously arranged to get federal funds," he said. His voice became more caustic. "And I cajoled a few members of the family to put a little in the kitty." David glanced at Clarence, who looked pained. "I'm giving the land," Grandfather Sumner went on. "So here and there we got support."

"But why would Burke go for it? You've never voted for him in a single campaign in his life."

"Told him we'd dig out a lot of stuff we've been sitting on, support his opposition. If he was a baboon, we'd support him, and there's a lot of family these days, David. A heap of family."

"Well, hats off," David said, still not fully believing it. "You giving up your practice to go into research?" he asked Walt. His uncle nodded. David drained his cup of eggnog.

"David," Walt said, "we want to hire you."

He looked up quickly. "Why? I'm not into medical research."

"I know what your specialty is," Walt said quietly. "We want you for a consultant, and later on to head a department of research."

"But I haven't even finished my thesis yet," David said, and he felt as if he had stumbled into a pot party.

"You'll do another year of donkey work for Selnick and eventually you'll write the thesis, a bit here, a dab there. You could write it in a month, couldn't you, if you had time?" David nodded reluctantly. "I know," Walt said, smiling faintly. "You think you're being asked to give up a lifetime career for a pipe dream."

Grandfather Sumner let out his breath explosively. He was a large man with a massive chest and great bulging biceps. His hands were big enough to grip a basketball in each. But it was his head that you remembered. It was the head of a giant, and although he had farmed for many years, and later overseen the others who did it for him, he had found time to read more extensively than anyone else David knew. And he remembered what he read. His library was better than most public libraries. Now he leaned forward and said, "You listen to me, David. You listen hard. I'm telling you what the goddam government doesn't dare admit yet. We're on the first downslope of a slide that is going to plummet the world to a depth that they never dreamed of. I know the signs, David. Pollution's catching up to us faster than anyone knows. There's more radiation in the atmosphere than there's been since Hiroshima—French tests, Chinese tests. Leaks. God knows where all it's coming from. We reached zero population growth a couple of years ago, but, David, we were trying, and other nations are getting there too, and they aren't trying. There's famine in a quarter of the world right now. The famines are here, and they're getting worse. There are more diseases than there's ever been since the good Lord sent the plagues to Egypt. And they're plagues that we don't know anything about.

There's more drought and more flooding than there's ever been. England's changing into a desert, the bogs and moors are drying up. Entire species of fish are gone, just damn gone, and in only a year or two. The anchovies are gone. The codfish industry is gone. The cods they are catching are diseased, unfit to use. There's no fishing off the west coast of the Americas, North or South. Every damn protein crop on earth has some sort of blight that gets worse and worse. We're restricting our exports of food now, and next year we'll stop them for good. We're having shortages no one ever dreamed of. Tin, copper, aluminum, paper. Chlorine, by God! And what do you think will happen in the world when we suddenly can't even purify our drinking water?"

His face was darkening as he spoke, and he was getting angrier and angrier, directing his unanswerable questions to David, who stared at him with nothing at all to say.

"And they don't know what to do about any of it," his grandfather went on. "No more than the dinosaurs knew how to stop their own extinction. We've changed the photochemical reactions of our own atmosphere, and we can't adapt to the new radiations fast enough to survive! There've been hints here and there that this is a major concern, but who listens? The damn fools will lay each and every catastrophe at the foot of a local condition and turn their backs on the fact that this is global, until it's too late to do anything."

"But, if it's what you think, what could they do?" David asked, looking to Dr. Walt for support and finding none.

"Turn off the factories, ground the airplanes, stop the mining, junk the cars. But they won't, and even if they did, it would still be a catastrophe. It's going to break wide open. Within the next couple of years, David, it's going to break. There's going to be the biggest bust since man began scratching marks on rocks, that's what! And we're getting ready for it! I'm getting ready for it! We've got the land and we've got the men to farm it, and we'll get our hospital and we'll do research on ways to keep our animals and our people alive, and when the world goes into a tailspin we'll be alive and when it starves we'll be eating."

Suddenly he stopped and studied David with his eyes narrowed. "I said you'd leave here convinced that we've all gone mad. But you'll be back, David, my boy. You'll be back before the dogwoods bloom, because you'll see the signs."

David returned to school and his thesis and the donkey work Selnick gave him to do. Celia didn't write, and he had no address for her. In response to his questions his mother admitted that no one had heard from her. In February, in retaliation for the food embargo, Japan imposed trade restrictions that made further

United States trade with her impossible. Japan and China signed a mutual aid treaty. In March, Japan seized the Philippines and their fields of rice, and China resumed its long-dormant trusteeship over the Indochina peninsula, with the rice paddies of Cambodia and Vietnam.

Cholera struck in Rome, Los Angeles, Galveston, and Savannah. Saudi Arabia, Kuwait, Jordan, and other Arab-bloc nations issued an ultimatum: the United States must guarantee a yearly ration of wheat to the Arab states and discontinue all aid to Israel, or there would be no oil for the United States or Europe. They refused to believe the United States could not meet their demands. Worldwide travel restrictions were imposed immediately, and the United States government, by presidential decree, formed a new department with Cabinet status: the Bureau of Information.

The redbuds were hazy blurs of pink against the clear, May-softened sky when David returned home. He stopped by his house only long enough to change his clothes and get rid of his boxes of college mementos before he drove out to the Sumner farm, where Walt was staying while he oversaw the construction of his hospital.

Walt had an office downstairs. It was a clutter of books, note-books, blueprints, correspondence. He greeted David as if he hadn't been away at all. "Look," he said, "this research of Semple and Ferrer, what do you know about it? The first generation of cloned mice showed no deviation, no variation in viability or potency, nor did the second or third, but with the fourth the viability decreased sharply. And there was a steady, and irreversible, slide to extinction. Why?"

David sat down hard and stared at Walt. "How did you get that?"

"Vlasic," Walt said. "We went to med school together. We've corresponded all these years. I asked him."

"You know his work?"

"Yes. His rhesus monkeys show the same decline during the fourth generation, and on to extinction."

"It isn't just like that," David said. "He had to discontinue his work last year—no funds. So we don't know the life expectancies of the later strains. But the decline starts in the third clone genera-tion, a decline of potency. He was breeding each clone generation sexually, testing the offspring for normalcy. The third clone gener-ation had only twenty-five percent potency. The sexually repro-duced offspring started with that same percentage, and, in fact, potency dropped until the fifth generation of sexually reproduced offspring, and then it started to climb back up and presumably would have reached normalcy again."

Walt was watching him closely, nodding now and then. David

went on. "That was the clone-three strain. With the clone-four strain there was a drastic change. Some abnormalities were present, and life expectancy was down seventeen percent. The abnormals were all sterile. Potency was generally down to forty-eight percent. It was downhill all the way with each sexually reproduced generation. By the fifth generation no offspring survived longer than an hour or two. So much for clone-four strain. Cloning the fours was worse. Clone-five strain had gross abnormalities, and they were all sterile. Life expectancy figures were not completed. There was no clone-six strain. None survived."

"A dead end," Walt said. He indicated a stack of magazines and extracts. "I had hoped that they were out of date, that there were newer methods, or perhaps an error had been found in their figures. It's the third generation that is the turning point, then?"

David shrugged. "My information could be out of date. I know Vlasic stopped last year, but Semple and Ferrer are still at it, or were last month. They may have something I don't know about. You're thinking of livestock?"

"Of course. You know the rumors? They're just not breeding well, no figures available, but hell, we have our own livestock. They're down by half."

"Can you get materials for the hospital?" David asked.

"For now. We're rushing it like there's no tomorrow, naturally. And we're not worrying about money right now. We'll have things that we won't know what to do with, but I thought it would be better to order everything I can think of than to find out next year that what we really need isn't available."

David went to the window and looked out at the farm. The green was well established by now, spring would give way to summer without a pause and the corn would be shiny, silky green in the fields. Just like always. "Let me have a look at your lab equipment orders, and the stuff that's been delivered already," he said. "Then let's see if we can wrangle me travel clearance, out to the coast. I'll talk to Semple; I've met him a few times. If anyone's doing anything, it's that team."

"What is Selnick working on?"

"Nothing. He lost his grant, his students were sent packing." David grinned at his uncle suddenly. "Look, up on the hill, you can see a dogwood ready to burst open, some of the blooms are already showing."

David was bone-tired, every muscle seemed to ache at once, and his head was throbbing. For nine days he had been on the go, to the coast, to Harvard, to Washington, and now he wanted nothing more than to sleep, even if the world ground to a stop while he was unaware. He had taken a train from Washington to Richmond, and there, unable to rent a car, or buy gasoline if a car had been available, he had stolen a bicycle and pedaled the rest of the way. He had never realized his legs could ache so much.

"You're sure that bunch in Washington won't be able to get a hearing?" Grandfather Sumner asked.

"No one wants to hear the Jeremiahs," David said. Selnick had been one of the group, and he had talked to David briefly. His committee was trying to force the government to admit the seriousness of the coming catastrophe and take strict measures to alleviate it. The government chose instead to paint glowing pictures of the coming upturn that would be apparent by fall. During the next six months, Selnick had warned, those with sense and money would buy everything they could to see them through, because after that period of grace there would be nothing to buy.

"Selnick says we should offer to buy his equipment. The school will jump at the chance to unload it right now. Cheap." David laughed. "Cheap. A quarter of a million, possibly."

"Make the offer," Grandfather Sumner said.

David stood up shakily and went off to bed.

People still went to work. The factories were still producing, not as much, and none of the nonessentials, but they were converting to coal as fast as possible. David thought about the darkened cities, and the fleets of trucks rusting, and the corn and wheat rotting in the fields. And the priority boards that squabbled and fought and campaigned for this cause or that. It was a long time before his twitching muscles relaxed enough for him to lie quietly, and a longer time before he could relax his mind enough to sleep.

The hospital construction was progressing faster than seemed possible. There were two shifts at work; again a case of damn-the-cost. Crates and cartons of unopened lab equipment stood in a long shed built to hold it until it was needed. David went to work in a makeshift laboratory trying to replicate Ferrer's and Semple's tests. And in early July, Harry Vlasic arrived at the farm. He was short, fat, near-sighted, and short-tempered. David regarded him with the same awe and respect that an undergraduate physics student would have felt toward Einstein.

"All right," Vlasic said. "The corn crop has failed, as predicted. Monoculture! Bah! They'll save sixty percent of the wheat, no more. This winter, hah, just wait until winter! Now where is the cave?"

They took him to the cave entrance a hundred yards from the hospital. Inside the cave they used lanterns. The cave was over a mile long in the main section and there were several branches. Deep in one of them flowed a river that was black and silent. Spring

water, good water. Vlasic nodded again and again. When they
finished the cave tour he was still nodding. "It's good," he said.
"It'll work. The laboratories go in there, underground passage
from the hospital, safe from contamination. Good."

They worked sixteen hours a day that summer and into the fall.
In October the first wave of flu swept the country, worse than the
outbreak of 1917 and 1918. In November a new illness swept the
country, and here and there it was whispered that it was plague, but
the government Bureau of Information said it was flu. Grandfather
Sumner died in November. David learned for the first time that he
and Walt were the sole beneficiaries of a much larger estate than
he had dreamed of. And the estate was in cash. Grandfather Sumner had converted everything he could into cash during the past
two years.

In December the family began to arrive, leaving the towns and
villages and cities scattered throughout the valley to take up residence in the hospital and staff buildings. Rationing, black markets,
inflation, and looting had turned the cities into battlegrounds. And
the government had frozen the assets of every business—nothing
could be bought or sold without approval. The family brought their
stocks with them. Jeremy Streit brought his hardware merchandise
in four truckloads. Eddie Beauchamp brought his dental equipment. David's father brought all that he could from his department
store. With the failure of radio and television communication, there
was no way for the government to cope with the rising panic.
Martial law was declared on December 28, six months too late.

There was no child left under eight years of age when the spring
rains came, and the original three hundred nineteen people who
had come to the upper valley had dwindled to two hundred one.
In the cities the toll had been much higher.

David studied the fetal pig he was about to dissect. It was wrinkled
and desiccated, its bones too soft, its lymph glands lumpy, hard.
Why? Why did the fourth generation decline? Harry Vlasic came
to watch briefly, then walked away, his head bowed in thought. Not
even he could come up with any answers, David thought, almost
with satisfaction.

That night David, Walt, and Vlasic met and went over it all again.
They had enough livestock to feed the two hundred people for a
long time, through cloning and breeding of the fertile animals.
They could clone up to four hundred animals at a time. Chickens,
swine, cattle. If the livestock all became sterile, as seemed likely,
then the food supply was limited.

Watching the two older men, David knew they were purposely

skirting the other question. If the people also became sterile, how long would they need a continuing supply of food? He said, "We should isolate some of the sterile mice, clone them, and test for the reemergence of fertility with each new generation of clones."

Vlasic frowned and shook his head. "If we had a dozen undergraduate students, perhaps," he said.

"We have to know," David said, feeling hot suddenly. "You're both acting like this is just a five-year emergency plan to tide us over a few bad years. What if it isn't that at all? Whatever is causing the sterility is affecting all the animals. We have to know."

Walt glanced at David and said, "We don't have the time or the facilities to do any research like that."

"That's a lie," David said. "We can generate all the electricity we can use, more than enough power. We have equipment we haven't even unloaded yet . . ."

"Because there's no one who can use it yet," Walt said patiently.

"I can. I'll do it in my free time."

"What free time?"

"I'll find it."

In June, David had his preliminary answers. "The A-four strain," he said, "has twenty-five percent fertility." Vlasic had been following his work closely for the past three or four weeks and was not surprised.

Walt stared at him in disbelief. "Are you sure?" he whispered after a moment.

"The fourth generation of cloned sterile mice showed the same degeneracy that all clones show by then," David said. "But they also had a twenty-five percent fertility factor. The offspring have shorter lives, but more fertile individuals. This trend continues to the sixth generation, where fertility is up to ninety-four percent, and life expectancy starts to climb up again, and then it's on its way to normalcy." He had it all on the charts that Walt now studied. A, A^1, A^2, A^3, A^4, and then the offspring by sexual reproduction, a, a^1, a^2 . . . There were no clone strains after A^4; none had survived to maturity.

David leaned back and closed his eyes. He thought about bed and a blanket up around his neck and black, black sleep. "Higher organisms must reproduce sexually or die out, and the ability to do so is there. Something remembers and heals itself," he said dreamily.

"You'll be a great man when you publish," Vlasic said softly, his hand on David's shoulder. He then moved to sit next to Walt, to point out some of the details that Walt might miss. "A marvelous piece of work," he said, his eyes glowing as he looked over the pages. "Marvelous." Then he glanced back at David. "Of course, you are aware of the other implications of your work."

David opened his eyes and met Vlasic's gaze. He nodded. Walt, puzzled, looked from one to the other of them. David got up and stretched. "I have to sleep," he said.

But it was a long time before he slept. He had a single room at the hospital, more fortunate than most. The hospital had more than two hundred beds, but few single rooms. The implications, he mused. He had been aware of them from the start, although he had not admitted it even to himself then, and was not ready to discuss it now. Three of the women were pregnant finally, after a year and a half. Margaret was near term, the baby well and kicking at the moment. Five more weeks, he thought. Five more weeks, and perhaps he never would have to discuss the implications of his work.

But Margaret didn't wait five weeks. In two weeks she gave birth to a stillborn child. Zelda had a miscarriage the following week, and in the next week May lost her child. That spring the rains kept them from planting anything more than a truck garden.

Walt began testing the men for fertility. He reported to David and Vlasic that no man in the valley was fertile.

"So," Vlasic said softly, "we now see the significance of David's work."

Winter came early in sheets of icy rain that went on day after day after day. The work in the laboratories increased, and David found himself blessing his grandfather for his purchase of Selnick's equipment, which had come with detailed instructions for making artificial placentas as well as nearly completed work on computer programs for chemical amniotic fluids. When David had gone to talk to Selnick about the equipment, Selnick had insisted—madly, David had thought at the time—that he take everything or nothing. "You'll see," he had said wildly. "You'll see." The following week he hanged himself, and the equipment was on its way to the Virginia valley.

They worked and slept in the lab, leaving only for meals. The winter rains gave way to spring rains, and a new softness was in the air.

David was hardly aware of the spring until one day his mother found him in the cafeteria. He hadn't seen her for weeks, and would have brushed past her with a quick hello if she hadn't stopped him. She looked strange, childlike; he turned from her to stare out the window, waiting for her to release his arm.

"Celia's coming home," she told him. "She's well, she says."

David felt frozen; he continued to stare out the window, seeing nothing. "Where is she now?" He listened to the rustle of cheap paper and when it seemed that his mother was not going to answer him, he wheeled about. *"Where is she?"*

"Miami," she said finally, after scanning the two pages. "It's post-marked Miami, I think. It's over two weeks old. Dated May twenty-eighth. She never got any of our mail."

David didn't read the letter until his mother had left the cafeteria. *I was in Colombia for a while, eight months, I think. And I got a touch of the bug that nobody wants to name.* The writing was spindly and uncertain. He looked for Walt.

"I have to go get her. She can't walk in on that gang at the Wiston place."

"You know you can't leave now."

"It isn't a question of can or can't. I have to."

Walt studied him for a moment, then shrugged. "How will you get there and back? No gas. You know we don't dare use it for anything but the harvest."

"I know," David said impatiently. "I'll take Mike and the cart. I can stay on the back roads with Mike." He knew that Walt was calculating, as he had done, the time involved, and he felt his face tightening, his hands clenching. Walt simply nodded. "I'll leave as soon as it's light in the morning." Again Walt nodded. "Thanks," David said suddenly. He meant: for not arguing with him, for not pointing out what both already knew; that there was no way of knowing how long he would have to wait for Celia, that she might never make it to the farm.

Three miles from the Wiston farm David unhitched the cart and hid it in thick underbrush. He swept the tracks where he had left the dirt road, then led Mike into the woods. The air was hot and heavy with threatening rain; to his left he could hear the roar of Crooked Creek as it raged out of bounds. The ground was spongy and he walked carefully, not wanting to sink to his knees in unsuspected mud here in the lowlands. The Wiston farm always had been flood-prone; it enriched the soil, Grandfather Wiston had claimed, not willing to damn nature for its periodic rampages. "God didn't mean for this piece of ground to have to bear year after year after year," he said. "Comes a time when the earth needs a rest, same as you and me. We'll let it be this year, give it some clover when the ground dries out." David started to climb, still leading Mike, who whinnied softly at him now and again.

"Just to the knob, boy," David said quietly. "Then you can rest and eat meadow grass until she gets here." The horse whinnied.

Grandfather Wiston had taken him to the knob once, when David was twelve. He remembered the day, hot and still, like this day, he thought, and Grandfather Wiston had been straight and strong. At the knob his grandfather had paused and touched the massive bole of a white oak tree. "This tree saw the Indians in that valley, David, and the first settlers, and my great-grandfather when he came along. It's our friend, David. It knows all the family secrets."

"Is it still your property up here, Grandfather?"

"Up to and including this tree, son. Other side's national forest land, but this tree, it's on our land. Yours too, David. One day you'll come up here and put your hand on this tree and you'll know it's your friend, just like it's been my friend all my life. God help us all if anyone ever lays an ax to it."

They had gone on that day, down the other side of the knob, then up again, farther and steeper this time until once more his grandfather had stopped and, his hand on David's shoulder, paused for a few moments. "This is how this land looked a million years ago, David." Time had shifted suddenly for the boy; a million years ago, or a hundred million, was all the same distant past, and he had imagined the tread of giant reptiles. He had imagined that he smelled the fetid breath of a tyrannosaur. It was cool and misty beneath the tall trees, and under them the saplings grew, their branches spread horizontally as if to catch any stray bit of sunlight that penetrated the high canopy, and where the sun did find a path through, it was golden and soft, the sun of another time. In even deeper shadows grew bushes and shrubs, and at the foot of it all were the mosses and lichens, liverworts and ferns. The arching, heaving roots of the trees were clothed in velvet emerald plants.

David stumbled and caught himself against the giant oak tree that was, somehow, his friend. He pressed his cheek against the rough bark, and stayed there for a few minutes. Then he pushed himself away and looked up through the luxuriant branches; he could see no sky beyond them. When it rained, the tree would protect him from the full force of the storm, but he needed shelter from the fine drops that eventually would make their way through the leaves to fall quietly on the absorbent ground.

He examined the farm through his binoculars. Behind the house there was a garden being tended by five people, impossible to tell immediately if they were male or female. Long-haired, jeans, barefoot, thin. It didn't matter. He noted that the garden was not producing yet, that the plants were sparse and frail. He studied the east field, aware that it was changed, not certain how. Then he realized that it was planted to corn. Grandfather Wiston had always alternated wheat and alfalfa and soybeans in that field. The lower fields were flooded, and the north field was grown up in grasses and weeds. He studied the people he could see and swung the glasses slowly over the buildings. He spotted seventeen of them altogether. No child younger than eight or nine. No sign of Celia, nor of any recent use of the road; it was also overgrown with weeds. No doubt the people down there were just as happy to let the road hide under weeds.

He built a leanto against the oak where he could lie down and observe the farm. He used fir branches to roof his shelter, and when the storm came half an hour later, he stayed dry. Rivulets ran among the garden rows below, and the farmyard turned silver and sparkly from this distance, although he knew that closer at hand it would simply be muddy water, inches deep. The ground was too saturated in the valley to absorb any more water. It would have to run off into Crooked Creek, which was inching higher and higher toward the north field and the vulnerable corn there.

By the third day the water had started to invade the cornfield, and he pitied the people who stood and watched helplessly. The garden was still being tended, but it would be a meager harvest. By now he had counted twenty-two people; he thought that was all of them. During the storm that lashed the valley that afternoon, he heard Mike whinny. He crawled from the leanto and stood up. Mike, down the slope of the knob, wouldn't mind the rain much, and he was protected from the wind. Still he whinnied again, and then again. Cautiously, holding his shotgun in one hand, shielding his eyes with the other, David edged around the tree. A figure stumbled up the knob haltingly, stopping with bowed head often, not looking up, probably blinded by the rain. Suddenly David threw the shotgun under the leanto and ran to meet her. "Celia!" he cried. "Celia!"

She stopped and raised her head, and the rain ran over her cheeks, plastered her hair to her forehead. She dropped the shoulder bag that had weighed her down and ran toward him, and only when he caught her and held her tight and hard did he realize that he was weeping, as she was.

Under the leanto he pulled her wet clothes off and rubbed her dry, then wrapped her in one of his shirts. Her lips were blue, her skin seemed almost translucent; it was an unearthly white.

"I knew you'd be here," she said. Her eyes were very large, deep blue, bluer than he remembered, or bluer in contrast to her pale skin. Always before she had been sunburned.

"I knew you'd come here," he said. "When did you eat?"

She shook her head. "I didn't believe it was this bad here. I thought it was propaganda. Everyone thinks it's propaganda."

He lighted the Sterno. She sat wrapped in his plaid shirt and watched him as he opened a can of stew.

"Who are those people down there?"

"Squatters. Grandmother and Grandfather Wiston died last year. That gang showed up. They gave Aunt Hilda and Uncle Eddie a choice, join them or get out. They didn't give Wanda any chance at all. They kept her."

She stared down the valley and nodded slowly. "I didn't know it was this bad. I didn't believe it." Without looking back at him she asked then, "And Mother, Father?"

"They're dead, Celia. Flu, both of them. Last winter."

"I didn't get any letters," she said. "Almost two years. They made us leave Brazil, you know. But there wasn't any transportation home. We went to Colombia. They promised to let us go home in three months. And then they came one night and said we had to get out immediately. There were riots, you know."

He nodded, although she was still staring down at the valley and couldn't see. He wanted to tell her to weep for her parents, to cry out, so that he could take her in his arms and try to comfort her. But she continued to sit motionless and speak in a dead voice.

"They were coming for us, for the Americans. They blame us for letting them starve. They really believe that everything is still all right here. I did too. No one believed any of the reports. And the mobs were coming for us. We left on a small boat, a skiff. Nineteen of us. They shot at us when we got too near Cuba."

David touched her arm, and she jerked and trembled. "Celia, turn around and eat now. Don't talk any longer. Later. You can tell us about it later."

She shook her head. "Never again. I'll never mention any of it again, David. I just wanted you to know there was nothing I could do. I wanted to come home and there wasn't any way."

The storm was over, and the night air was cool. They huddled under a blanket and sat without talking, drinking hot black coffee. When the cup began to tilt in Celia's hand, David took it from her and gently lowered her to the bed he had prepared. "I love you, Celia," he said softly. "I've always loved you."

"I love you, too, David. Always." Her eyes were closed and her lashes were very black on her white cheeks. David leaned over and kissed her forehead, pulled the blanket higher about her, and watched her sleep for a long time before he lay down beside her.

The next morning they left the oak tree and started for the Sumner farm. She rode Mike until they got to the cart; by then she was trembling with exhaustion and her lips were blue again, although the day was already hot. There wasn't room for her to lie down in the cart, so he padded the back of the wooden seat with his bedroll and blanket, and let her sit behind him where she could at least put her head back and rest, when the road wasn't too bumpy. She smiled faintly when he covered her legs with another shirt, the one he had been wearing.

"It isn't cold, you know," she said matter-of-factly. "That goddamn bug does something to the heart, I think. No one would tell us anything about it. My symptoms are all in the circulatory system."

"How bad was it? When did you get it?"

"Eighteen months ago. Just before they made us leave Brazil. It swept Rio. That's where they took us when we got sick. Not many survived it. Hardly any of the later cases. It became more virulent as time went on."

He nodded. "Same here. Something like sixty percent fatal, increasing up to eighty percent by now, I guess."

There was a long silence then, and he thought perhaps she had drifted off to sleep. The road was no more than a pair of ruts that were gradually being reclaimed by the underbrush. Already grass covered it almost totally, except where the rains had washed the dirt away and left only rocks. Mike walked deliberately, and David didn't hurry him.

"David, how many are up at the northern end of the valley?"

"About one hundred and ten now," he said. He thought, two out of three dead, but he didn't say it.

"And the hospital? Was it built?"

"It's there. Walt is running it."

"David, while you're driving, now that you can't watch me for reactions or anything, just tell me about it here. What's been happening, who's alive, who's dead. Everything."

When they stopped for lunch hours later, she said, "David, will you make love to me now, before the rains start again?"

They lay under a stand of yellow poplars and the leaves rustled incessantly with a motion that needed no appreciable wind to start. Under the susurrous trees, their own voices became whispers. She was so thin and so pale, and inside she was so warm and alive; her body rose to meet his and her breasts seemed to lift, to seek his touch. Her fingers were in his hair, on his back, digging into his flanks, strong now, then relaxed and trembling, then clenched into fists that opened spasmodically; and he felt her nails distantly, aware that his back was being clawed, but distantly, distantly. And finally there were only the susurrant leaves.

"I've loved you for more than twenty years, did you realize that?" he said.

She laughed. "Remember when I broke your arm?"

Later, in the cart again, her voice came from behind him, softly, sadly. "We're finished, aren't we, David? You, I, all of us?"

And he thought, Walt be damned, promises be damned, secrecy be damned. And he told her about the clones developing under the mountain, in the laboratory deep in the Great Bear Cave.

Celia started to work in the laboratory a week later. "It's the only way I'll ever get to see you at all," she said when David protested. "I promised Walt I would work only four hours a day to start. Okay?"

David took her through the lab the following morning. The entrance to the cave was concealed in the furnace room of the hospital basement. The door was steel, set in the limestone bedrock. As soon as they stepped through the doorway, the air was cold and David put a coat about Celia's shoulders. "We keep them here at all times," he said, taking a second coat from a wall hanger. "Twice government inspectors have come here, and it might look suspicious if we put them on to go down the cellar. They won't be back," he said. She nodded.

The passageway was dimly lighted, the floor smooth. It went four hundred feet to another steel door. This one opened into the first cave chamber, a large, high-domed room. It had been left almost as they had found it, with stalactites and stalagmites on all sides, but now there were many cots, and picnic tables and benches, and a row of cooking tables and serving tables. "Our emergency room, for the 'hot' rains," David said, hurrying her through. There was another passage, narrower and rougher than the first. At the end of this passage was the animal experiment room.

One wall had been cut through and the computer installed, looking grotesquely out of place against a wall of pale pink travertine. In the center of the room were tanks and vats and pipes, all stainless steel and glass. On either side of these were the tanks that held the animal embryos. Celia stared without moving for several moments, then turned to look at David with startled eyes. "How many tanks do you have?"

"Enough to clone six hundred animals of varying sizes," he said. "We took a lot of them out, put them in the other side, and we're not using all that we have here. We're afraid our supplies of chemicals will run out, and so far we haven't come up with alternatives that we can extract from anything at our disposal here."

Eddie Beauchamp came from the side of the tanks, jotting figures in a ledger. He grinned at David and Celia. "Slumming?" he asked. He checked his figures against a dial and adjusted it a fraction, and continued down the row checking the other dials, stopping now and again to make a minor adjustment.

Celia's eyes questioned David and he shook his head. Eddie didn't know what they were doing in the other lab. They walked past the tanks, row after row of them, all sealed, with only the needles of the meters and gauges to indicate that there was anything inside. They returned to the corridor. David led her through another doorway, another shorter passage, then unlocked a door and took her into the second laboratory.

Walt looked up as they entered, nodded, turned again to his desk. Vlasic didn't even look up. Sarah smiled and hurried past them and sat down before a computer console and began to type. Another woman in the room didn't seem to be aware that anyone had come in. Hilda. Celia's aunt. David glanced at Celia, but she was staring wide-eyed at the tanks, and in this room the tanks were glass-fronted. Each was filled with a pale liquid, a yellow so faint that the color seemed almost illusory. Floating in the liquid were sacs, no larger than small fists. Slender transparent tubes connected the sacs to the top of the tanks; each one was attached to a pipe that led back into a large stainless steel apparatus which seemed to be covered with dials.

Celia walked slowly down the aisle between the tanks, stopped midway and didn't move again for a long time. David took her arm. She was trembling slightly.

"Are you all right?"

She nodded. "I . . . it's a shock, seeing them. I . . . maybe I didn't quite believe it." There was a film of perspiration on her face.

"Better take off the coat now," David said. "We have to keep it pretty warm in here. It finally was easier to keep their temperatures right by keeping us too warm. The price we pay," he said, smiling slightly.

"All the lights? The heat? The computer? You can generate that much electricity?"

He nodded. "That'll be our tour tomorrow, or sometime. Like everything else around here, the generating system has bugs in it. We can store enough power for no longer than six hours, and we just don't let it go out for more than that."

She nodded. "Six hours is a lot. If you stop breathing for six minutes, you're dead." With her hands clasped behind her she stepped closer to the shiny control system at the end of the room. "This isn't the computer. What is it?"

"It's a computer terminal. The computer controls the input of nutrients and oxygen, and the output of toxins." He nodded toward the wall. "The animal room is on the other side. Those tanks are linked to it, too. Separate set of systems, but the same machinery."

She nodded again. They went through the nursery for the animals, and then the nursery for the human babies. There was the dissection room, several small offices where the scientists could withdraw to work, the stock rooms. In every room except the one where the human clones were being grown, people were working. "They never saw a bunsen burner or a test tube before, but they have become scientists and technicians practically overnight," David said. "And thank God for that, or it never would have worked. I don't know what they think we're doing now, but they don't ask questions. They just do their jobs."

In August, Avery Handley got through to a shortwave contact in Richmond who warned of a band of marauders working up the valley. "They're bad," he said. "They took over the Phillpotts' place, ransacked it, and then burned it to the ground."

In September they fought off the first attack. In October they learned the band was grouping for a second attack, this time with thirty to forty men. "We can't keep fighting them off," Walt said. "They must know we have food here. They'll come from all directions this time. They know we're watching for them."

"We should blow up the dam," Clarence said. "Wait until they're in the upper valley and flood them out."

The meeting was being held in the cafeteria, with everyone present. Celia's hand tightened in David's, but she didn't protest. No one protested.

"They'll try to take the mill," Clarence went on. "They'll probably think there's wheat there, or something." A dozen men volunteered to stand guard at the mill. Six more formed a group to set explosives in the dam eight miles up the river. Others would be a scouting party.

David and Celia left the meeting early. He had volunteered for everything and had been turned down. He was not one of the expendable ones. The rains had become "hot" again, and the people were all sleeping in the cave. David and Celia, Walt, Vlasic, the others who worked in the various labs, all slept there on cots. In one of the small offices David held Celia's hand and they whispered before they fell asleep. Their talk was of their childhood.

Long after Celia fell asleep David stared into the blackness, still holding her hand. She had grown even thinner, and earlier that week when he had tried to get her to leave the lab to rest, Walt had said, "Leave her be." She stirred fitfully, and he knelt by the side of her cot and held her; he could feel her heart flutter wildly for a moment. Then she was still again and slowly he released her and sat on the stone floor with his eyes closed. Later he heard Walt moving about, the creaking of his cot in the next office. David was getting stiff, and finally he returned to his own bed.

The next day the people worked to get everything up to high

ground. Nothing could be spared, and board by board they carried a barn up the hillside and stacked the pieces. Two days later the signal was given and the dam was destroyed. David and Celia stood in one of the upper hospital rooms and watched together as the wall of water roared down the valley. It was like a jet takeoff; a crowd furious with an umpire's decision; an express train out of control; a roar like nothing he had ever heard, or like everything he had ever heard, recombined to make this noise that shook the building, that vibrated in his bones. A wall of water, fifteen feet high, twenty feet high, raced down the valley, accelerating as it came, smashing, destroying everything in its path.

They walked back through the empty hospital, through the long dimly lighted passage, through the large chamber where the people were trying to find comfortable positions on the cots, on the benches, through the smaller passages and finally into the lab office.

"How many people did we kill?" she asked, stepping out of her jeans. She turned her back to lay her clothes on the foot of her cot. Her buttocks were nearly as flat as an adolescent boy's. When she faced him again, her ribs seemed to be straining against her skin. She looked at him for a moment, and then came to him and held his head tight against her chest as he sat on his cot and she stood naked before him. He could feel her tears as they fell onto his cheek.

There was a hard freeze in November, and with the valley flooded and the road and bridges gone, they knew they were safe from attack, at least until spring. The people had moved out of the cave again, and work in the lab went on at the same numbing pace. The fetuses were developing, growing, moving now with sudden motions of feet and elbows. David was working on substitutes for the chemicals that already were substituting for amniotic fluids. He worked each day until his vision blurred, or his hands refused to obey his directions, or Walt ordered him out of the lab. Celia was working longer hours now, still resting in the middle of the day for several hours, but she returned after that and stayed almost as late as David did.

David was aware of her, as he always was, even when preoccupied with his own work. He was aware that she stood up, that she didn't move for a moment, and when she said, in a tremulous voice that betrayed disbelief, "David . . . David . . ." he was already starting to his feet. He caught her as she crumpled.

Her eyes were open, her look almost quizzical, asking what he could not answer, expecting no answer. A tremor passed through her and she closed her eyes, and although her lids fluttered, she did not open them again.

*   *   *

"David, are you going to pull yourself together? You just giving up?" Walt didn't wait for a reply. He sat down on the only chair in the tiny room and leaned forward, cupping his chin, staring at the floor. "We've got to tell them. Sarah thinks there'll be trouble. So do I."

David stood at the window, looking at the bleak landscape, done in grays and blacks and mud colors. It was raining, but the rain had become clean. The river was a gray swirling monster that he could glimpse from up here, a dull reflection of the dull sky.

"They might try to storm the lab," Walt went on. "God knows what they might decide to do."

"I don't care," David said.

"You're going to care! Because those babies are going to come busting out of those sacs, and those babies are the only hope we have, and you know it. Our genes, yours, mine, Celia's, those genes are the only thing that stand between us and oblivion." He was white, his lips were pale, his eyes sunken. There was a tic in his cheek that David never had seen before.

"Why now?" David asked. "Why change the plan and tell them now, so far ahead of time?"

"Because it isn't that far ahead of time." Walt rubbed his eyes hard. "Something's going wrong, David. I don't know what it is. Something's not working. I think we're going to have our hands full with prematures."

David couldn't stop the rapid calculations he made. "It's twenty-six weeks," he said. "We can't handle that many premature babies."

"I know that." Walt put his head back and closed his eyes. "We don't have much choice," he said. "We lost one yesterday. Three today. We have to bring them out and treat them like preemies."

Slowly David nodded. "Which ones?" he asked, but he knew. Walt told him the names, and again he nodded. He had known that they were not his, not Walt's, not Celia's. "What are you planning?" he asked then, and sat down on the side of his bed.

"I have to sleep," Walt said. "Then a meeting, posted for seven. After that we prepare the nursery for a hell of a lot of preemies. As soon as we're ready, we begin getting them out. That'll be morning. We need nurses, half a dozen, more if we can get them. Sarah says Margaret would be good. I don't know."

David didn't know either. Margaret's four-year-old son had been one of the first to die of the plague, and she had lost a baby in stillbirth. He trusted Sarah's judgment, however. "Think between them they can get enough others, tell them what to do, see that they do it properly?"

Walt mumbled something, and one hand fell off the chair arm. He jerked upright.

"Okay, Walt, you get in my bed," David said, almost resentfully. "I'll go down to the lab, get things rolling there. I'll come up for you at six-thirty." Walt didn't protest, but fell onto the bed without bothering to take off his shoes. David pulled them off. Walt's socks were mostly holes, but probably they kept his ankles warm. David left them on, pulled the blanket over him, and went to the lab.

At seven the hospital cafeteria was crowded when Walt stood up to make his announcement. "There's not a person in this room hungry tonight. We don't have any more plague here. The rain is washing away the radioactivity. We have food stores that will carry us for years even if we can't plant crops in the spring. We have men capable of doing just about anything we might ever want done." He paused and looked at them again, from left to right, back again, taking his time. He had their absolute attention. "What we don't have," he said, his voice hard and flat now, "is a woman who can conceive a child, or a man who could impregnate her if she was able to bear."

There was a ripple of movement, like a collective sigh, but no one spoke. Walt said, "You know how we are getting our meat. You know the cattle are good, the chickens are good. Tomorrow, ladies and gentlemen, we will have our own babies developed the same way."

There was a moment of utter silence, of stillness, then they broke. Clarence leaped to his feet shouting at Walt. Vernon fought to get to the front of the room, but there were too many people between him and Walt. One of the women pulled on Walt's arm, almost dragging him over, screaming in his face. Walt yanked free and climbed onto a table. "Stop this! I'm going to answer any questions, but not this way."

For the next three hours they questioned, argued, prayed, formed alliances, reformed them as arguments broke out in the smaller groups. At ten Walt took his place on the table again and called out, "We will recess this discussion until tomorrow night at seven. Coffee will be served now, and I understand we have cakes and sandwiches." He jumped from the table and moved to the door too fast to let any of them catch up to him. He and David hurried to the cave entrance and went through, locking the massive door behind them.

"Clarence was ugly," Walt muttered. "Bastard."

David's father, Walt, and Clarence were brothers, David reminded himself, but he couldn't help regarding Clarence as an outsider, a stranger with a fat belly and a lot of money who expected instant obedience from the world.

"They might organize," Walt said after a moment. "We'll have to be ready for them."

David nodded. They had counted on delaying this meeting until they had live babies, human babies that laughed and gurgled and took milk from the bottle. Instead they would have a roomful of not-quite-finished preemies, certainly not human-looking, with no more human appeal than a calf born too soon.

They worked all night preparing the nursery. Sarah had enlisted Margaret, Hilda, Lucy, and half a dozen other women. They were all gowned and masked professionally. One of them dropped a basin and three others screamed in unison. David cursed under his breath. They would be all right when they had the babies, he told himself.

The bloodless births started at five forty-five, and at twelve thirty they had twenty-five infants. Four died in the first hour, another died three hours later; the rest of them thrived. The only baby left in the tanks was the fetus that would be Celia, nine weeks younger than the others.

The first visitor Walt permitted in the nursery was Clarence. After that there was no further talk of destroying the inhuman monstrosities.

There was a celebration party, and a drawing was held to select eleven female names and ten male. In the record book the babies were labeled R-1 strain: Repopulation 1. But in David's mind, as in Walt's, the babies were W-1, D-1, and soon, C-1 . . .

For the next months there was no shortage of nurses, male or female, no shortage of help doing any of the chores that so few had done before. Everyone wanted to become a doctor or a biologist, Walt grumbled, but he was sleeping more now, and the fatigue lines on his face were smoothing out. Often he would nudge David and tow him along, away from the nursery, propel him toward his own room in the hospital and see to it that he remained there for a night's sleep. One night as they walked side by side back to their rooms, Walt said, "Now you understand what I meant when I said this was all that mattered, don't you?"

David understood. Every time he looked down at the tiny, pink new Celia he understood more fully.

David watched the boys from the window in Walt's office. There was Clarence, already looking too pudgy—he'd be fat in another three or four years. And a young Walt, frowning in concentration

over a problem that he wouldn't put on paper until he had a solution. Mark, too pretty almost, but determinedly manly, always trying harder than the others to endure, to jump higher, run faster,
hit harder. And D-4, himself . . . He turned away and pondered
the future of the boys, uncles, fathers, grandfathers, all the same
age. He was starting a headache again.

"They're inhuman, aren't they?" he said bitterly to Walt. "They
come and go, and we know nothing about them. What do they
think? Why do they hang so close to each other? Why won't they
talk to us?"

"Remember that old cliché, generation gap? It's here, I reckon."
Walt was looking very old. He was tired, and seldom tried to hide
it any longer. He looked up at David and said, "Maybe they're
afraid of us."

David nodded. He had thought of that, too. "I know why Hilda
did it," he said. "I didn't at the time, but now I know." Hilda had
strangled the small girl who looked more like her every day.

"Me too." Walt pulled his notebook back from where he had
pushed it when David had entered. "It's a bit spooky to walk into
a crowd that's all you, in various stages of growth. They do cling to
their own kind." He started to write then, and David left him.

Spooky, he thought, and veered from the laboratory where he
had been heading originally. Let the damn embryos do their thing
without him. He knew he didn't want to enter because D-1 or D-2
would be there working. The D-4 strain would be the one, though,
to prove or disprove the experiment. If Four didn't make it, then
chances were that Five wouldn't either, and then what? A mistake.
Woops, wrong, sir. Sorry about that.

Behind the hospital, he climbed the ridge over the cave, and sat
down on an outcrop of limestone that felt cool and smooth. The
boys were clearing another field. They worked well together, with
little conversation and much laughter that seemed to arise sponta-
neously. A line of girls came into view from nearer the river; they
were carrying baskets of berries. Blackberries and gunpowder, he
thought suddenly, and he remembered the ancient celebrations of
the Fourth of July, with blackberry stains and fireworks, sulfur for
the chiggers. And birds. Thrushes, meadowlarks, warblers, purple
martins. Three Celias came into view, swinging easily with the
weight of the baskets, a stairway succession of Celias. He shouldn't
do that, he reminded himself harshly. They weren't Celias, none
of them had that name. They were Mary and Ann and something
else. He couldn't remember for a moment the third one's name,
and he knew it didn't matter. The one in the middle might have

pushed him from the loft just yesterday; the one on the left might have been the one who rolled in savage combat with him in the mud.

Once, three years ago, he had had a fantasy in which Celia-3 had come to him shyly and asked that he take her. And in the fantasy he had taken her; in his dreams for weeks to come, he had taken her, over and over and over again. And he had awakened weeping for his own Celia. Unable to endure it any longer, he had sought out C-3 and asked her haltingly if she would come to his room with him, and she had drawn back quickly, involuntarily, with fear written too clearly on her smooth face for her to pretend it was not there.

"David, forgive me. I was startled . . ."

They were promiscuous, indeed it was practically required of them to be free in their loving. No one could anticipate how many of them eventually would be fertile, what the percentage of boys to girls would be. Walt was able to test the males, but since the tests for female fertility required rabbits, which they did not have, he said the best test for fertility was pregnancy. The children lived together, and promiscuity was the norm. But only with one another. They all shunned the elders. David had felt his eyes burning as the girl spoke, still moving away from him.

He had turned and left abruptly, and had not spoken to her again in the intervening years. Sometimes he thought he saw her watching him warily, and each time he glared at her and hurried away.

C-1 had been like his own child. He had watched her develop, watched her learn to walk, talk, feed herself. His child, his and Celia's. C-2 had been much the same. A twin, somewhat smaller, identical nevertheless. But C-3 had been different. No, he corrected himself, his perceptions of her had been different. When he looked at her now he saw Celia, and he ached.

He had grown chilled on the ridge, and he realized that the sun had set long ago and that the lanterns had been lighted below. The scene looked pretty, like a sentimental picture titled "Rural Life." The large farmhouse with glowing windows, the blackness of the barn; closer, the hospital and staff building with the cheerful yellow lights in the windows. Stiffly he descended into the valley again. He had missed dinner, but he was not hungry.

"David!" one of the youngest boys, a Five, called to him. David didn't know whom he had been cloned from. There were many people he hadn't known when they were that young. He stopped and the boy ran to him, then past him, calling as he went, "Dr. Walt wants you."

On Walt's desk and spread over a table were the medical charts of the Four strain. "I've finished," Walt said. "You'll have to double-check, of course."

David scanned the final lines quickly, H-4 and D-4. He didn't look up, but nodded. "Have you told the two boys yet?"

"I told them all. They understand." Walt rubbed his eyes. "They have no secrets from each other," he said. "They understand about the girls' ovulation periods, about the necessity of keeping records. If any of those girls can conceive, they'll do it." His voice was almost bitter when he looked up at David. "They're taking it over completely from now on."

"What do you mean?"

"W-1 made a copy of my records for his files. He'll follow it through."

David nodded. The elders were being excluded again. The time was coming when they wouldn't be needed for anything—extra mouths to feed, nothing else. He sat down and for a long time he and Walt sat in companionable silence.

In class the following day nothing seemed different. No pair bonding, David thought cynically. They accepted being mated as casually as the cattle did. If there was any jealousy of the two fertile males, it was well hidden. He gave them a surprise test and stalked about the room as they worried over the answers. They would all pass, he knew—not only pass, but do well. They had motivation. They were learning in their teens what he hadn't grasped in his twenties. There were no educational frills, no distractions. Work in the classroom, in the fields, in the kitchens, in the laboratories. They worked interchangeably, incessantly—the first really classless society. He pulled his thoughts back when he realized that they were finishing already. He had allowed an hour, and they were finishing in forty minutes—slightly longer for the Fives, who, after all, were two years younger than the Fours.

The two oldest D's headed for the laboratory after class, and David followed them. They were talking earnestly until he drew near. He remained in the laboratory for fifteen minutes of silent work, then left. Outside the door he paused and once more could hear the murmur of quiet voices. Angrily he tramped down the hallway.

In Walt's office, he raged. "Damn it, they're up to something! I can smell it."

Walt regarded him with a detached thoughtfulness. David felt helpless. There was nothing he could point to, nothing he could attach significance to, but there was a feeling, an instinct that wouldn't be quieted.

"All right," David said, almost in desperation. "Look at how they took the test results. Why aren't the boys jealous? Why aren't the girls making passes at the two available studs?"

Walt shook his head.

"I don't even know what they're doing in the lab anymore," David said. "And Harry has been relegated to caretaker for the livestock." He paced the room in frustration. "They're taking over."

"We knew they would one day," Walt reminded him gently.

"But there are only seventeen Fives, eighteen Fours. Out of the lot there might be six or seven fertile ones. With a decreased life expectancy. With an increased chance of abnormality. Don't they know that?"

"David, relax. They know all that. They're living it. Believe me, they know." Walt stood up and put his arm about David's shoulders. "We've done it, David. Can't you understand that? We made it happen. Even if there are only three fertile girls now, they could have up to thirty babies, David. And the next generation will have more who will be fertile. We have done it, David. Let them carry it now if they want to."

By the end of summer two of the Four girls were pregnant. There was a celebration in the valley that was as frenetic as any Fourth of July holiday any of the older people could remember.

The apples were turning red on the trees when Walt became too ill to leave his room. Two more girls were pregnant; one of them was a Five. Every day David spent hours with Walt, no longer wanting to work at all in the laboratory, feeling an outsider in the classrooms, where the Ones were gradually taking over.

"You might have to deliver those babies come spring," Walt said, grinning. "Might start a class in delivery procedures. Walt-3 is ready, I guess."

"We'll manage," David said. "Don't worry about it. I expect you'll be there."

"Maybe. Maybe." Walt closed his eyes for a moment and said, "You were right about them, David. They're up to something."

David leaned forward, and involuntarily lowered his voice. "What do you know?"

Walt looked at him and shook his head. "About as much as you did when you first came to me early this summer. David, find out what they're doing in the lab. And find out what they think about the pregnant girls. Harry tells me they have devised a new immersion suspension system that doesn't require artificial placentas. They're adding them as fast as they can." He sighed. "Harry has cracked, David. Senile or crazy. W-1 can't do anything for him."

David stood up, but hesitated. "Walt, I think it's time you told me. What's wrong with you?"

"Get out of here, damn it," Walt said, but the timbre of his voice was gone, the force that should have propelled David from the room was not there.

David walked by the river for a long time. Find out. How? He hadn't been in the lab for weeks, months perhaps. No one needed him there any longer. The winters were getting colder, starting earlier, lasting longer, with more snows than he could remember from childhood. As soon as man stopped adding his megatons of filth to the atmosphere, he thought, the atmosphere had reverted to what it must have been long ago, moister weather summer and winter, more stars than he had ever seen before: the sky a clear endless blue by day, velvet blue-black at night with blazing stars that modern man had never seen.

The hospital wing where W-1 and W-2 were working now was ablaze with lights when David turned toward it. As he neared the hospital he began to hurry; there were too many lights, and he could see people moving behind the windows, too many people, elders.

Margaret met him in the lobby. She was weeping silently, oblivious of the tears that ran erratically down her cheeks. She wasn't yet fifty, but she looked older; she looked like an elder, David thought with a pang. When had they started calling themselves that? Was it because they had to differentiate somehow, and none of them had permitted himself to call the others what they were? Clones! he said to himself vehemently. Clones! Not quite human.

"What happened, Margaret?" She clutched his arm but couldn't speak, and he looked over her head at Warren, who was pale and shaking. "What happened?"

"Accident down at the mill. Jeremy and Eddie are dead. A couple of the young people were hurt. Don't know how bad. They're in there." He pointed toward the operating-room wing. "They left Clarence. Just walked away and left him. We brought him up, but I don't know." He shook his head. "They just left him there and brought up their own."

David put Margaret aside and ran down the hall toward the emergency room. Sarah was working over Clarence while several of the elders moved back and forth to keep out of her way without leaving entirely.

David breathed a sigh of relief. Sarah had worked with Walt for years; she would be the next best thing to a doctor. He flung his coat off and hurried to her. "What can I do?"

"It's his back," she said tightly. She was very pale, but her hands were steady as she swabbed a long gash on Clarence's leg and put a heavy pad over it. "This needs stitches. But I'm afraid it's his back."

"Broken?"

"I think so. Internal injuries."

"Where the hell is W-1 or W-2?"

"With their own. They have two injuries, I think." She put his hand over the pad. "Hold it tight a minute." She used her stethoscope deliberately, peered into Clarence's eyes, and finally straightened and said, "I can't do a thing for him."

"Stitch his leg. I'm going to get W-1." David strode down the hall fast, not seeing any of the elders who moved out of his way. At the door to the operating room he was stopped by three of the young men. He saw an H-3 and said to him, "We have a man who's probably dying. Where's W-2?"

"Who?" H-3 asked, almost innocently.

David couldn't think of the name immediately. He stared at the young face, and he felt his fist tighten. "You know damn well who I mean. We need a doctor, and you have one or two in there. I'm going to bring one of them out."

He became aware of movement and turned to see four more of them approaching, two girls, two boys. Interchangeable, he thought. It didn't matter which ones did what. "Tell him I want him," he said harshly. One of the newcomers was a Cl-2, he realized, and still more harshly he said, "It's Clarence. Sarah thinks his back is broken."

Cl-2 didn't change his expression. They had moved very close. They encircled him, and behind him H-3 said, "As soon as they're through in there, I'll tell them, David." And David knew there was nothing he could do, nothing at all.

He stared at their smooth young faces; so familiar, living memories every one of them, like walking through his own past, seeing his aged and aging cousins rejuvenated, but with something missing. Familiar and alien, known and unknowable. Behind H-3 the swinging door opened and W-1 came out, still in surgical gown and mask, now down about his throat.

"I'll come now," he said, and the small group opened for him. He didn't look at David after dismissing him with one glance.

David followed him to the emergency room and watched his deft hands as he felt Clarence's body, tested for reflexes, probed confidently along the spinal column. "I'll operate," he said, and that same confidence came through with the words. He motioned for S-1 and W-2 to bring Clarence, and left once more.

Sarah had moved back out of the way, and now she slowly turned

and stripped off the gloves she had put on in preparing to stitch
up the leg wound. Warren watched the two young people cover
Clarence, strap him securely, and wheel him out the door. No one
spoke. Sarah methodically started to clean up the emergency-room
equipment. Sarah finished her tasks and looked uncertainly about
for something else to do.

"Will you take Margaret home and put her to bed?" David asked.
She looked at him gratefully and nodded. When she was gone,
David turned to Warren. "Someone has to see to the bodies, clean
them up, prepare for burial."

"Sure, David," Warren said in a heavy voice. "I'll get Avery and
Sam. We'll take care of it. I'll just go get them now and we'll take
care of it. I'll . . . David, what have we done?" And his voice that
had been too heavy, too dead, became almost shrill. "What are
they?"

"What do you mean?"

"When the accident happened, I was down to the mill. Having a
bite with Avery. He was just finishing up down there. Section of
the floor caved in, you know that old part where we should have
put in a new floor last year, or year before. It gave way somehow.
And suddenly there they were, the kids, out of nowhere. No one
had time to go get them, to yell for them. Nothing, but there they
were. They got their own two out of there and up to the hospital
like their tails was on fire, David. Out of nowhere."

Several of the elders were still in the waiting room when David
went there. Lucy and Vernon were sitting near the window, staring
out at the black night. Since Clarence's wife had died, he and Lucy
had lived together, not as man and wife, but for companionship,
because as children they had been as close as brother and sister, and
now each needed someone to cling to. Sometimes sister, sometimes
mother, sometimes daughter, Lucy had fussed over him, sewed for
him, fetched and carried for him, and now, if he died, what would
she do? David went to her and took her cold hand. She was very
thin, with dark hair that hadn't started to gray, and deep blue eyes
that had twinkled with merriment once, a long, long time ago.

"Go on home, Lucy. I'll wait, and as soon as there is anything to
tell you, I promise I'll come."

She continued to stare at him. David turned toward Vernon
helplessly. Vernon's brother had been killed in the accident, but
there was nothing to say to him.

"Let her be," Vernon said. "She has to wait."

David sat down, still holding Lucy's hand. After a moment or so
she pulled it free gently and clutched it herself until both of her
hands were white-knuckled. None of the young people came near

the waiting room. David wondered where they were waiting to hear about the condition of their own. Or maybe they didn't have to wait anywhere, maybe they would just know. He pushed the thought aside angrily, not believing it, not able to be rid of it. A long time later W-1 entered and said to no one in particular, "He's resting. He'll sleep until tomorrow afternoon. Go on home now."

Lucy stood up. "Let me stay with him. In case he needs something, or there's a change."

"He won't be left alone," W-1 said. He turned toward the door, paused and glanced back, and said to Vernon, "I'm sorry about your brother." Then he left.

Lucy stood undecided until Vernon took her arm. "I'll see you home," he said, and she nodded. David watched them leave together. He turned off the light in the waiting room and walked slowly down the hall, not planning anything, not thinking about going home, or anywhere else. He found himself outside the office that W-1 used, and he knocked softly. W-1 opened the door. He looked tired, David thought, and wasn't sure that his surprise was warranted. Of course, he should be tired. Three operations. He looked like a young, tired Walt, too keyed up to go to sleep immediately, too fatigued to walk off the tension.

"Can I come in?" David asked hesitantly. W-1 nodded and moved aside, and David entered. He never had been inside this office.

"Clarence will not live," W-1 said suddenly, and his voice, behind David, because he had not yet moved from the door, was so like Walt's that David felt a thrill of something that might have been fear, or more likely, he told himself, just surprise again. "I did what I could," W-1 said. He walked around his desk and sat down.

W-1 sat quietly, with none of the nervous mannerisms that Walt exhibited, none of the finger tapping that was as much a part of Walt's conversation as his words. No pulling his ears or rubbing his nose. A Walt with something missing, David thought. They all had something missing, a dead area. Now, with fatigue drawing his face, W-1 sat unmoving, waiting patiently for David to begin, much the same way an adult might wait for a hesitant child to initiate a conversation.

"How did your people know about the accident?" David asked. "No one else knew."

W-1 shrugged. A time-consumer question, he seemed to imply. "We just knew."

"What are you doing in the lab now?" David asked, and heard a strained note in his voice. Somehow he had been made to feel like an interloper; his question sounded like idle chatter.

"Perfecting the methods," W-1 said. "The usual thing."

And something else, David thought, but he didn't press it. "The equipment should be in excellent shape for another ten years or more," he said. "And the methods, while probably not the best conceivable, are efficient enough. Why tamper now when the experiment seems to be proving itself?" For a moment he thought he saw a flicker of surprise cross W-1's face, but it was gone too swiftly and once more the smooth mask revealed nothing.

"Remember when one of your women killed one of us a long time ago, David? Hilda murdered the child of her own likeness. We all shared that death, and we realized that each of you is alone. We're not like you, David. I think you know it, but now you must accept it." He stood up. "And we won't go back to what you have."

David stood up also, and his legs felt curiously weak. He gripped the edge of the desk. "What exactly do you mean?"

"Sexual reproduction isn't the only answer. Just because the higher organisms evolved to it doesn't mean it's the best. Each time a species has died out, there has been another higher one to replace it."

"Cloning is one of the worst ways for a higher species," David said. "It stifles diversity." The weakness in his legs seemed to be climbing, and he felt his hands start to tremble. He clenched the desk harder.

"That's assuming diversity is beneficial. Perhaps it isn't," W-1 said. "You pay a high price for individuality."

"There is still the decline and the inevitable slide to extinction. Have you got around that?" David wanted suddenly to end this conversation, to hurry from the sterile office and the smooth unreadable face with the sharp eyes that seemed to know what he was feeling.

"Not yet," W-1 said slowly. "But we have the fertile members to fall back on until we do." He moved around his desk and walked toward the door. "I have to check my patients," he said, and held the door open for David.

"Before I leave," David said, "will you tell me what is the matter with Walt?"

"Don't you know?" W-1 shook his head. "I keep forgetting, you don't tell each other things, do you? He has cancer. Inoperable. It metastasized. He's dying, David. I thought you knew that."

David walked blankly for an hour or more, and finally found himself in his room, exhausted, unwilling yet to go to bed. He sat at his window until dawn, and then he went to Walt's room. When Walt woke up he reported what W-1 had told him.

"They'll use the fertile ones only to replenish their supply of clones," he said. "The humans among them will be pariahs. They'll destroy what we worked so hard to create."

"Don't let them do it, David. For God's sake, don't let them do it!" Walt's color was bad, and he was too weak to sit up. "Vlasic's mad, so he'll be of no help. You have to stop them somehow." Bitterly he said, "They want to take the easy way out, give up now when we know everything will work."

David didn't know if he was sorry or glad that he had told Walt. No more secrets, he thought. Never again. "I'll stop them somehow," he said. "I don't know how, or when. But soon."

A Four brought Walt's breakfast, and David returned to his room. He rested and slept fitfully for a few hours, then showered and went to the cave entrance, where he was stopped by a Two.

"I'm sorry, David," he said. "Jonathan says that you need a rest, that you are not to work now."

Wordlessly David turned and left. Jonathan. W-l. If they had decided to bar him from the lab, they could do it. He and Walt had planned it that way: the cave was impregnable. He thought of the elders, forty-four of them left, and two of that number terminally ill. One of the remaining elders insane. Forty-one then, twenty-nine women. Eleven able-bodied men. Ninety-four clones.

He waited for days for Harry Vlasic to appear, but no one had seen him in weeks, and Vernon thought he was living in the lab. He had all his meals there. David gave that up; he found D-l in the dining room and offered his help in the lab.

"I'm too bored doing nothing," he said. "I'm used to working twelve hours a day or more."

"You should rest now that there are others who can take the load off you," D-l said pleasantly. "Don't worry about the work, David. It is going quite well." He moved away, and David caught his arm.

"Why won't you let me in? Haven't you learned the value of an objective opinion?"

D-l pulled away, and still smiling easily, said, "You want to destroy everything, David. In the name of mankind, of course. But still, we can't let you do that."

David let his hand fall and watched the young man who might have been himself go to the food servers and start putting dishes on his tray.

"I'm working on a plan," he lied to Walt again and again in the weeks that followed. Daily Walt grew feebler, and now he was in great pain.

David's father was with Walt most of the time now. He was gray and aged but in good health. He talked of their boyhood, of the coming hunting season, of the recession he feared might reduce his profits, of his wife, who had been dead for fifteen years. He was cheerful and happy, and Walt seemed to want him there.

In March, W-1 sent for David. He was in his office. "It's about Walt," he said. "We should not let him continue to suffer. He has done nothing to deserve this."

"He is trying to last until the girls have their babies," David said. "He wants to know."

"But it doesn't matter any longer," W-1 said patiently. "And meanwhile he suffers."

David stared at him with hatred.

W-1 continued to watch him for several more moments, then said, "We will decide." The next morning it was found that Walt had died in his sleep.

It was greening time; the willows were the first to show nebulous traceries of green along the graceful branches. Forsythias and flaming bushes were in bloom, brilliant yellows and scarlets against the gray background. The river was high with spring runoffs up north and heavy March rains, but it was an expected high, not dangerous, not threatening this year. The air had a balminess that had been missing since September; the air was soft and smelled of wet woods and fertile earth. David sat on the slope overlooking the farm. There were calves in the field, and they looked the way spring calves always looked: thin legs, awkward, slightly stupid. No fields had been worked yet, but the garden was green: pale lettuce, blue-green kale, green spears of onions, dark green cabbage. The newest wing of the hospital, not yet painted, crude compared to the finished brick buildings, was being used already, and he could even see some of the young people at the windows studying. They had the best teachers, themselves, and the best students. They learned amazingly well from one another, better than they had in the early days.

They came out of the school in matched sets: four of this, three of that, two of another. He sought and found three Celias. He could no longer tell them apart; they were all grown-up Celias now, and indistinguishable. He watched them with no feeling of desire; no hatred moved him, no love. They vanished into the barn, and he looked up over the farm, into the hills on the other side of the valley. The ridges were hazy and had no sharp edges anywhere. They looked soft and welcoming. Soon, he thought. Soon. Before the dogwoods bloomed.

The night the first baby was born, there was another celebration. The elders talked among themselves, laughed at their own jokes,

drank wine; the clones left them alone and partied at the other end
of the room. When Vernon began to play his guitar and dancing
started, David slipped away. He wandered on the hospital grounds
for a few minutes, as though aimlessly, and then, when he was
certain no one had followed him out, he began to trot toward the
mill and the generator. Six hours, he thought. Six hours without
electricity would destroy everything in the lab.

David approached the mill cautiously, hoping the rushing creek
would mask any sound he might make. The building was three
stories high, very large, with windows ten feet above ground, on
the level where the offices were. The ground floor was filled with
machinery. In the back the hill rose sharply; David could reach the
windows by bracing himself on the steep incline and steadying
himself with one hand on the building. He found a window that
went up easily when he pushed it, and in a moment he was inside
a dark office. He closed the window, and then, moving slowly with
his hands outstretched to avoid any obstacle, crossed the room to
the door and opened it a crack. The mill was never left unattended,
but he hoped that those on duty tonight would be down with the
machinery. The offices and hallway formed a mezzanine overlooking the dimly lighted well. Grotesque shadows made the hallway
strange, with deep pools of darkness and places where he would
be clearly visible should anyone happen to look up at the right
moment. Suddenly David stiffened. Voices.

He slipped his shoes off and opened the door wider. The voices
were below him. Soundlessly he ran toward the control room, keeping close to the wall. He was almost to the door when the lights
came on all over the building. There was a shout, and he could
hear them running up the stairs. He made a dash for the door and
yanked it open, slammed it behind him. There was no way to lock
it. He pushed a file cabinet an inch or so, gave up, and picked up
a metal stool by its legs. He raised it and swung it hard against the
main control panel. At the same moment he felt a crushing pain in
his shoulders, and he stumbled and fell forward as the lights went
out.

He opened his eyes painfully. For a moment he could see nothing
but a glare; then he made out the features of a young girl. She was
reading a book, concentrating on it. Dorothy? She was his cousin
Dorothy. He tried to rise, and she looked up and smiled at him.

"Dorothy? What are you doing here?" He couldn't get off the
bed. On the other side of the room a door opened and Walt came
in, also very young, unlined, with his nice brown hair ruffled.

David's head began to hurt, and he reached up to find bandages that came down almost to his eyes. Slowly memory came back and he closed his eyes, willing the memory to fade away again, to let them be Dorothy and Walt.

"How do you feel?" W-1 asked. David felt the cool fingers on his wrist. "You'll be all right. A slight concussion, badly bruised, I'm afraid. You're going to be pretty sore for a while."

Without opening his eyes, David asked, "Did I do much damage?"

"Very little," W-1 said.

Two days later David was asked to attend a meeting in the cafeteria. His head was still bandaged, but with little more than a strip of adhesive now. His shoulder ached. He went to the cafeteria slowly, with two of the clones as escorts.

Most of them were in the cafeteria. D-1 stood up and offered David a chair at the front of the room. David accepted it silently and sat down to wait. D-1 remained standing.

"Do you remember our class discussions about instinct, David?" D-1 asked. "We ended up agreeing that probably there are no instincts, only conditioned responses to certain stimuli. We have changed our minds about that. We agree now that there is still the instinct to preserve one's species. Preservation of the species is a very strong instinct, a drive, if you will." He looked at David and asked, "What are we to do with you?"

"Don't be an ass," David said sharply. "You are not a separate species."

D-1 didn't reply. None of them moved. They were watching him quietly, intelligently, dispassionately. David stood up and pushed his chair back. "Then let me work. I'll give you my word of honor that I won't try to disrupt anything again."

D-1 shook his head. "We discussed that. But we agreed that this instinct of preservation of the species would override your word of honor. As it would our own."

David felt his hands clench, and he straightened his fingers, forced them to relax. "Then you have to kill me."

"We talked about that, too," D-1 said gravely. "We don't want to do it. We owe you too much. In time we will erect statues to you, Walt, Harry. We have very carefully recorded all of your efforts in our behalf. Our gratitude and affection for you won't permit us to kill you."

David looked about the room again, picking out familiar faces. Dorothy. Walt. Vernon. Margaret. Herbie. Celia. They all met his gaze without flinching. Here and there one of them smiled at him faintly.

"You tell me, then," he said finally.

"You have to go away," D-1 said. "You will be escorted for three days, downriver. There is a cart loaded with food, seeds, a few tools. The valley is fertile, the seeds will do well. It is a good time of year for starting a garden."

W-2 was one of the three who accompanied him for the first three days. They didn't speak. The boys took turns pulling the cart of supplies. David didn't offer to pull it. At the end of the third day, on the other side of the river from the Sumner farm, they left him. W-2 lingered a moment and said, "They wanted me to tell you, David. One of the girls you call Celia has conceived. One of the boys you call David impregnated her. They wanted you to know." Then he turned and joined the others. They vanished among the trees very quickly.

David slept where they had left him, and in the morning he continued south, leaving the cart behind, taking only enough food for the next few days. He stopped once to look at a maple seedling sheltered among the pines. He touched the soft green leaves very gently. On the sixth day he reached the Wiston farm; alive in his memory was the day he had waited there for Celia. The white oak tree that was his friend was the same, perhaps larger, he couldn't tell. He could not see the sky through its branches covered with new, vivid green leaves. He made a leanto and slept under the tree that night, and the next morning he told it good-bye solemnly and began to climb the slopes overlooking the farm. The house was still there, but the barn was gone, and the other outbuildings. Swept away by the flood they had made so long ago.

He reached the antique forest late in the afternoon. He watched a flying insect beat its wings almost lazily and remembered his grandfather telling him that even the insects here were primitive— slower than their more advanced cousins, less adaptable to hot weather, dry spells.

It was misty and very cool under the trees. The insect had settled on a leaf spread out horizontally to catch what sun it could. In the golden sunlight the insect was also golden. For a brief moment David thought he heard a bird's trill—a thrush. It was gone too fast to be certain, and he shook his head. Wishful thinking, no more than wishful thinking.

In the antique forest, a cove forest, the trees waited, keeping their genes intact, ready to move down the slopes when the conditions were right for them again. David stretched out on the ground under the great trees and slept, and in the cool, misty milieu of his dream saurians walked and a bird sang.

JOANNA RUSS
Souls

Like Kate Wilhelm and R. A. Lafferty, Joanna Russ began selling in the late fifties, but did not become widely known until the late sixties. Unlike Wilhelm, who served a long apprenticeship while learning her craft, even Russ's early work displayed the same kind of wit, sophistication, and elegance of style that would characterize her later work, and the best of it—stories like "My Dear Emily," "There Is Another Shore, You Know, Upon the Other Side," and "The New Men"—holds up well even today. Almost all of Russ's early work is fantasy, much of it about vampires— 1962's "My Dear Emily" remains one of the most stylish and fascinating vampire stories of modern times, and she might have established her reputation years earlier than she did if she had steadily continued to produce work like this, but her output was sparse throughout the first half of the decade, and mostly overlooked. (Even at her peak of production, Russ was never a prolific writer, even when compared to a careful craftsman like Wilhelm, let alone to the high-production sausage factories that have always been common in the genre.)

By 1967, Russ began attracting attention with her "Alyx" stories, which at first seemed to be merely better-than-usual sword & sorcery stories, featuring a tough-minded and wily female cutpurse rather than the usual male hero, sort of the Gray Mouser in drag (this may seem an obvious enough reversal now, when the fantasy genre is flooded with sword-swinging Amazons and swashbuckling women adventurers, but it was radical stuff at the time—with even Damon Knight saying that, before Russ, he would have thought that "nobody could get away with a series of heroic fantasies of prehistory in which the central character, the barbarian adventurer, is a woman"). The Alyx stories veered suddenly

into science fiction with "The Barbarian" in *Orbit 3*, in which
Alyx outwits a degenerate time-traveler, and then Alyx herself was snatched out of the past and thrown into a decadent
and fascinating future for Russ's first novel, 1968's *Picnic on
Paradise*, the work with which she made her first significant
impact on the field, and a work which even now strikes me
as one of the best novels of the late sixties.

By the early seventies, Russ had published her complex
second novel, *And Chaos Died*, by turns brilliantly effective
and opaque almost to the point of deliberate obscurity, won
a Nebula Award for her controversial feminist story "When
It Changed," and was producing work like the brilliant
"Nobody's Home," a sleek, sly, and blackly witty story that
was more sophisticated in its depiction of what the society
of the future was going to be like (and, more importantly,
what the people who *lived* in it were going to be like) than
anything else the genre would see until the best work of
Young Turks such as William Gibson and Bruce Sterling
in the mid-eighties.

By the early seventies, Russ was also, in some circles at
least, one of the most hated writers in the business. I'm not
quite sure why, since there were other writers around who
were producing work that ostensibly seemed much further
from the aesthetic center of the field. Perhaps it was her
large body of critical work—she was the regular reviewer
for *F&SF* at one point—in which she would express a lot
of unpopular opinions, although her often incisive criticism
can be shown to have had a demonstrable effect on other
writers such as Le Guin. Maybe it was just that she was an
uppity woman who wouldn't stay in her place.

Later, when she published her fierce and passionate feminist novel *The Female Man* in 1975, she became a *bête noire*
of unparalleled blackness, practically the Antichrist. Perhaps all this furor, added to the general malaise of the late
seventies, contributed to her slow drift out of the field. She
published two more books in the next three years—
including her weakest novel, 1977's *We Who Are About
To . . .*—and then fell silent for several years.

She returned to SF in 1982 with the stunning novella that
follows, the intricate, compassionate, and tough-minded
Souls, which won her a well-deserved Hugo Award.

Souls was generally received with great enthusiasm, as
were the other stories that went into making up her "novel"
Extra(ordinary) People (it's really a short-story collection, in

my opinion, in spite of the perhaps overly clever intersticial bits that are supposed to knit it into a novel, and contains one other marvelous story, "The Mystery of the Young Gentleman," that I like almost as well as *Souls*) . . . but it seems that Russ is doomed always to be a controversial author. *This* time, ironically, instead of the conservative wing, it was the young, leftist, radical new writers who fiercely attacked her, with *Souls* in particular coming in for some exceptionally fierce and sneering criticism; Russ, it seemed, was suddenly a card-carrying member of the fat and complaisant Establishment, and *proving* it by winning Hugo Awards!

Almost nothing has been heard of from Russ in SF since then, perhaps not surprisingly, but I personally miss her work, and hope that she will decide to take another tour of duty on the barricades sometime in the nineties—at her best, she was one of the best writers ever to work in the field, and one of those who helped to shape it the most profoundly.

Russ's other books include the novel *The Two of Them*, the collections *The Zanzibar Cat*, *The Adventures of Alyx*, and *The Hidden Side of the Moon*, and the critical works *Magic Mommas, Trembling Sisters, Puritans, and Perverts* and *How to Suppress Women's Writing*.

> *Deprived of other Banquet*
> *I entertained Myself—*
> —EMILY DICKINSON

This is the tale of the Abbess Radegunde and what happened when the Norsemen came. I tell it not as it was told to me but as I saw it, for I was a child then and the Abbess had made a pet and errand-boy of me, although the stern old Wardress, Cunigunt, who had outlived the previous Abbess, said I was more in the Abbey than out of it and a scandal. But the Abbess would only say mildly, "Dear Cunigunt, a scandal at the age of seven?" which was turning it off with a joke, for she knew how harsh and disliking my new step-mother was to me and my father did not care and I with no sisters or brothers. You must understand that joking and calling people "dear" and "my dear" was only her manner; she was in every way an unusual woman. The previous Abbess, Herrade, had found that Radegunde, who had been given to her to be fostered, had great gifts and so sent the child south to be taught, and that has never happened here before. The story has it that the Abbess Herrade found Radegunde seeming to read the great illuminated book in the Abbess's study; the child had somehow pulled it off its stand and was sitting on the floor with the volume in her lap, sucking her thumb and turning the pages with her other hand just as if she were reading.

"Little two-years," said the Abbess Herrade, who was a kind woman, "what are you doing?" She thought it amusing, I suppose, that Radegunde should pretend to read this great book, the largest and finest in the Abbey, which had many, many books, more than any other nunnery or monastery I have ever heard of: a full forty then, as I remember. And then little Radegunde was doing the book no harm.

"Reading, Mother," said the little girl.

"Oh, reading?" said the Abbess, smiling; "Then tell me what are you reading," and she pointed to the page.

"This," said Radegunde, "is a great *D* with flowers and other beautiful things about it, which is to show that *Dominus*, our Lord God, is the greatest thing and the most beautiful and makes everything to grow and be beautiful, and then it goes on to say *Domine nobis pacem*, which means *Give peace to us, O Lord*."

Then the Abbess began to be frightened but she said only, "Who showed you this?" thinking that Radegunde had heard someone read and tell the words or had been pestering the nuns on the sly.

"No one," said the child; "Shall I go on?" and she read page after page of the Latin, in each case telling what the words meant.

There is more to the story, but I will say only that after many prayers the Abbess Herrade sent her foster-daughter far southwards, even to Poitiers, where Saint Radegunde had ruled an Abbey before, and some say even to Rome, and in these places Radegunde was taught all learning, for all the learning there is in the world remains in these places. Radegunde came back a grown woman and nursed the Abbess through her last illness and then became Abbess in her turn. They say that the great folk of the Church down there in the south wanted to keep her because she was such a prodigy of female piety and learning, there where life is safe and comfortable and less rude than it is here, but she said that the gray skies and flooding winters of her birthplace called to her very soul. She often told me the story when I was a child: how headstrong she had been and how defiant, and how she had sickened so desperately for her native land that they had sent her back, deciding that a rude life in the mud of a northern village would be a good cure for such a rebellious soul as hers.

"And so it was," she would say, patting my cheek or tweaking my ear; "See how humble I am now?" for you understand, all this about her rebellious girlhood, twenty years back, was a kind of joke between us. "Don't you do it," she would tell me and we would laugh together, I so heartily at the very idea of my being a pious monk full of learning that I would hold my sides and be unable to speak.

She was kind to everyone. She knew all the languages, not only ours, but the Irish too and the tongues folks speak to the north and south, and Latin and Greek also, and all the other languages in the world, both to read and write. She knew how to cure sickness, both the old women's way with herbs or leeches and out of books also. And never was there a more pious woman! Some speak ill of her now she's gone and say she was too merry to be a good Abbess, but she would say, "Merriment is God's flowers," and when the winter wind blew her headdress awry and showed the gray hair—which happened once; I was there and saw the shocked faces of the Sisters with her—she merely tapped the band back into place, smiling and saying, "Impudent wind! Thou showest thou hast power which is more than our silly human power, for it is from God"—and this quite satisfied the girls with her.

No one ever saw her angry. She was impatient sometimes, but in a kindly way, as if her mind were elsewhere. It was in Heaven, I used to think, for I have seen her pray for hours or sink to her knees—right in the marsh!—to see the wild duck fly south, her hands clasped and a kind of wild joy on her face, only to rise a moment later, looking at the mud on her habit and crying half-ruefully, half in laughter, "Oh, what will Sister Laundress say to me? I am hopeless! Dear child, tell no one; I will say I fell," and then she would clap her hand to her mouth, turning red and laughing even harder, saying, "I *am* hopeless, telling lies!"

The town thought her a saint, of course. We were all happy then, or so it seems to me now, and all lucky and well, with this happiness of having her amongst us burning and blooming in our midst like a great fire around which we could all warm ourselves, even those who didn't know why life seemed so good. There was less illness; the food was better; the very weather stayed mild; and people did not quarrel as they had before her time and do again now. Nor do I think, considering what happened at the end, that all this was nothing but the fancy of a boy who's found his mother, for that's what she was to me; I brought her all the gossip and ran errands when I could and she called me Boy News in Latin; I was happier than I have ever been.

And then one day those terrible beaked prows appeared in our river.

I was with her when the warning came, in the main room of the

Abbey tower just after the first fire of the year had been lit in the great hearth; we thought ourselves safe, for they had never been seen so far south and it was too late in the year for any sensible shipman to be in our waters. The Abbey was host to three Irish priests, who turned pale when young Sister Sibihd burst in with the news, crying and wringing her hands; one of the brothers exclaimed a thing in Latin which means "God protect us!" for they had been telling us stories of the terrible sack of the monastery of Saint Columbanus and how everyone had run away with the precious manuscripts or had hidden in the woods, and that was how Father Cairbre and the two others had decided to go "walk the world," for this (the Abbess had been telling it all to me for I had no Latin) is what the Irish say when they leave their native land to travel elsewhere.

"God protects our souls, not our bodies," said the Abbess Radegunde briskly. She had been talking with the priests in their own language or in the Latin, but this she said in ours so even the women workers from the village would understand. Then she said, "Father Cairbre, take your friends and the younger Sisters to the underground passages; Sister Diemud, open the gates to the villagers; half of them will be trying to get behind the Abbey walls and the others will be fleeing to the marsh. You, Boy News, down to the cellars with the girls." But I did not go and she never saw it; she was up and looking out one of the window slits instantly. So was I. I had always thought the Norsemen's big ships came right up on land—on legs, I supposed—and was disappointed to see that after they came up our river they stayed in the water like other ships and the men were coming ashore by wading in the water, just as if they had been like all other folk. Then the Abbess repeated her order—"Quickly! Quickly!"—and before anyone knew what had happened she was gone from the room. I watched from the tower window; in the turmoil nobody bothered about me. Below, the Abbey grounds and gardens were packed with folk, all stepping on the herb plots and the Abbess's paestum roses, and great logs were being dragged to bar the door set in the stone walls round the Abbey, not high walls, to tell truth, and Radegunde was going quickly through the crowd, crying, Do this! Do that! Stay, thou! Go, thou! and like things.

Then she reached the door and motioned Sister Oddha, the doorkeeper, aside—the old Sister actually fell to her knees in entreaty—and all this, you must understand, was wonderfully pleasant to me. I had no more idea of danger than a puppy. There was some tumult by the door—I think the men with the logs were trying to get in her way—and Abbess Radegunde took out from the neck of her habit her silver crucifix, brought all the way from Rome, and shook it impatiently at those who would keep her in. So of course they let her through at once.

I settled into my corner of the window, waiting for the Abbess's crucifix to bring down God's lightning on those tall, fair men who defied Our Savior and the law and were supposed to wear animal horns on their heads, though these did not (and I found out later that's just a story; that is not what the Norse do). I did hope that the Abbess or Our Lord would wait just a little while before destroying them, for I wanted to get a good look at them before they all died, you understand. I was somewhat disappointed, as they seemed to be wearing breeches with leggings under them and tunics on top, like ordinary folk, and cloaks also, though some did carry swords and axes and there were round shields piled on the beach at one place. But the long hair they had was fine, and the bright colors of their clothes, and the monsters growing out of the heads of the ships were splendid and very frightening, even though one could see that they were only painted, like the pictures in the Abbess's books.

I decided that God had provided me with enough edification and could now strike down the impious strangers.

But He did not.

Instead the Abbess walked alone towards these fierce men, over the stony river bank, as calmly as if she were on a picnic with her girls. She was singing a little song, a pretty tune that I repeated many years later, and a well-traveled man said it was a Norse cradle-song. I didn't know that then, but only that the terrible, fair men, who had looked up in surprise at seeing one lone woman come out of the Abbey (which was barred behind her; I could see that), now began a sort of whispering astonishment among themselves. I saw the Abbess's gaze go quickly from one to the other—we often said that she could tell what was hidden in the soul from one look at the face—and then she picked the skirt of her habit up with one hand and daintily went among the rocks to one of the men—one older than the others, as it proved later, though I could not see so well at the time—and said to him, in his own language:

"Welcome, Thorvald Einarsson, and what do you, good farmer, so far from your own place, with the harvest ripe and the great autumn storms coming on over the sea?" (You may wonder how I knew what she said when I had no Norse; the truth is that Father Cairbre, who had not gone to the cellars after all, was looking out the top of the window while I was barely able to peep out the bottom, and he repeated everything that was said for the folk in the room, who all kept very quiet.)

Now you could see that the pirates were dumbfounded to hear her speak their own language and even more so that she called one by his name; some stepped backwards and made strange signs in the air and others unsheathed axes or swords and came running towards the Abbess. But this Thorvald Einarsson put up his hand for them to stop and laughed heartily.

"Think!" he said; "There's no magic here, only cleverness—what pair of ears could miss my name with the lot of you bawling out 'Thorvald Einarsson, help me with this oar'; 'Thorvald Einarsson, my leggings are wet to the knees'; 'Thorvald Einarsson, this stream is as cold as a Fimbulwinter!' "

The Abbess Radegunde nodded and smiled. Then she sat down plump on the river bank. She scratched behind one ear, as I had often seen her do when she was deep in thought. Then she said (and I am sure that this talk was carried on in a loud voice so that we in the Abbey could hear it):

"Good friend Thorvald, you are as clever as the tale I heard of you from your sister's son, Ranulf, from whom I learnt the Norse when I was in Rome, and to show you it was he, he always swore by his gray horse, Lamefoot, and he had a difficulty in his speech; he could not say the sounds as we do and so spoke of you always as 'Torvald.' Is not that so?"

I did not realize it then, being only a child, but the Abbess was—by this speech—claiming hospitality from the man, and had also picked by chance or inspiration the cleverest among these thieves and robbers, for his next words were:

"I am not the leader. There are no leaders here."

He was warning her that they were not his men to control, you see. So she scratched behind her ear again and got up. Then she began to wander, as if she did not know what to do, from one to the other of these uneasy folk—for some backed off and made signs at her still, and some took out their knives—singing her little tune again and walking slowly, more bent over and older and in-firm-looking than we had ever seen her, one helpless little woman in black before all those fierce men. One wild young pirate snatched the headdress from her as she passed, leaving her short gray hair bare to the wind; the others laughed and he that had done it cried out:

"Grandmother, are you not ashamed?"

"Why, good friend, of what?" said she mildly.

"Thou art married to thy Christ," he said, holding the headdress covering behind his back, "but this bridegroom of thine cannot even defend thee against the shame of having thy head uncovered! Now if thou wert married to me—"

There was much laughter. The Abbess Radegunde waited until
it was over. Then she scratched her bare head and made as if to
turn away, but suddenly she turned back upon him with the age
and infirmity dropping from her as if they had been a cloak, seeming taller and very grand, as if lit from within by some great fire.
She looked directly into his face. This thing she did was something
we had all seen, of course, but they had not, nor had they heard that
great, grand voice with which she sometimes read the Scriptures to
us or talked with us of the wrath of God. I think the young man
was frightened, for all his daring. And I know now what I did not
then: that the Norse admire courage above all things and that—to
be blunt—everyone likes a good story, especially if it happens right
in front of your eyes.

"Grandson!"—and her voice tolled like the great bell of God; I
think folk must have heard her all the way to the marsh!—"Little
grandchild, thinkest thou that the Creator of the World who made
the stars and the moon and the sun and our bodies, too, and the
change of the seasons and the very earth we stand on—yea, even
unto the shit in thy belly!—thinkest thou that such a being has a
big house in the sky where he keeps his wives and goes in to fuck
them as thou wouldst thyself or like the King of Turkey? Do not
dishonor the wit of the mother who bore thee! We are the servants
of God, not his wives, and if we tell our silly girls they are married
to the Christ it is to make them understand that they must not run
off and marry Otto Farmer or Ekkehard Blacksmith, but stick to
their work, as they promised. If I told them they were married to
an Idea they would not understand me, and neither dost thou."

(Here Father Cairbre, above me in the window, muttered in a
protesting way about something.)

Then the Abbess snatched the silver cross from around her neck
and put it into the boy's hand, saying: "Give this to thy mother with
my pity. She must pull out her hair over such a child."

But he let it fall to the ground. He was red in the face and
breathing hard.

"Take it up," she said more kindly, "take it up, boy; it will not
hurt thee and there's no magic in it. It's only pure silver and good
workmanship; it will make thee rich." When she saw that he would
not—his hand went to his knife—she *tched* to herself in a motherly
way (or I believe she did, for she waved one hand back and forth
as she always did when she made that sound) and got down on her
knees—with more difficulty than was truth, I think—saying loudly,
"I will stoop, then; I will stoop," and got up, holding it out to him,
saying, "Take. Two sticks tied with a cord would serve me as well."

The boy cried, his voice breaking, "My mother is dead and thou art a witch!" and in an instant he had one arm around the Abbess's neck and with the other his knife at her throat. The man Thorvald Einarsson roared "Thorfinn!" but the Abbess only said clearly, "Let him be. I have shamed this man but did not mean to. He is right to be angry."

The boy released her and turned his back. I remember wondering if these strangers could weep. Later I heard—and I swear that the Abbess must have somehow known this or felt it, for although she was no witch, she could probe at a man until she found the sore places in him and that very quickly—that this boy's mother had been known for an adulteress and that no man would own him as a son. It is one thing among those people for a man to have what the Abbess called a concubine and they do not hold the children of such in scorn as we do, but it is a different thing when a married woman has more than one man. Such was Thorfinn's case; I suppose that was what had sent him *viking*. But all this came later; what I saw then—with my nose barely above the window-slit—was that the Abbess slipped her crucifix over the hilt of the boy's sword— she really wished him to have it, you see—and then walked to a place near the walls of the Abbey but far from the Norsemen. I think she meant them to come to her. I saw her pick up her skirts like a peasant woman, sit down with legs crossed, and say in a loud voice:

"Come! Who will bargain with me?"

A few strolled over, laughing, and sat down with her.

"All!" she said, gesturing them closer.

"And why should we all come?" said one who was farthest away.

"Because you will miss a bargain," said the Abbess.

"Why should we bargain when we can take?" said another.

"Because you will only get half," said the Abbess. "The rest you will not find."

"We will ransack the Abbey," said a third.

"Half the treasure is not in the Abbey," said she.

"And where is it then?" said yet another.

She tapped her forehead. They were drifting over by twos and threes. I have heard since that the Norse love riddles and this was a sort of riddle; she was giving them good fun.

"If it is in your head," said the man Thorvald, who was standing behind the others, arms crossed, "we can get it out, can we not?" And he tapped the hilt of his knife.

"If you frighten me, I shall become confused and remember nothing," said the Abbess calmly. "Besides, do you wish to play that old game? You saw how well it worked the last time. I am surprised at you, Ranulf's mother's-brother."

"I will bargain then," said the man Thorvald, smiling.

"And the rest of you?" said Radegunde. "It must be all or none; decide for yourselves whether you wish to save yourselves trouble and danger and be rich," and she deliberately turned her back on them. The men moved down to the river's edge and began to talk among themselves, dropping their voices so that we could not hear them any more. Father Cairbre, who was old and short-sighted, cried, "I cannot hear them. What are they doing?" and I cleverly said, "I have good eyes, Father Cairbre," and he held me up to see, so it was just at the time that the Abbess Radegunde was facing the Abbey tower that I appeared in the window. She clapped one hand across her mouth. Then she walked to the gate and called (in a voice I had learned not to disregard; it had often got me a smacked bottom), "Boy News, down! Come down to me here *at once*! And bring Father Cairbre with you."

I was overjoyed. I had no idea that she might want to protect me if anything went wrong. My only thought was that I was going to see it all from wonderfully close by, so I wormed my way, half-suffocated, through the folk in the tower room, stepping on feet and skirts, and having to say every few seconds, "But I *have* to! The Abbess wants me," and meanwhile she was calling outside like an Empress, "Let that boy through! Make a place for that boy! Let the Irish priest through!" until I crept and pushed and complained my way to the very wall itself—no one was going to open the gate for us, of course—and there was a great fuss and finally someone brought a ladder. I was over at once, but the old priest took a longer time, although it was a low wall, as I've said, the builders having been somewhat of two minds about making the Abbey into a true fortress.

Once outside it was lovely, away from all that crowd, and I ran, gloriously pleased, to the Abbess, who said only, "Stay by me, whatever happens," and immediately turned her attention away from me. It had taken so long to get Father Cairbre outside the walls that the tall foreign men had finished their talking and were coming back—all twenty or thirty of them—towards the Abbey and the Abbess Radegunde, and most especially of all, me. I could see Father Cairbre tremble. They did look grim, close by, with their long, wild hair and the brightness of their strange clothes. I remember that they smelled different from us, but cannot remember how after all these years. Then the Abbess spoke to them in that outlandish language of theirs, so strangely light and lilting to hear from their bearded lips, and then she said something in Latin to Father Cairbre, and he said to us, with a shake in his voice:

"This is the priest, Father Cairbre, who will say our bargains aloud in our own tongue so that my people may hear. I cannot deal behind their backs. And this is my foster-baby, who is very dear to me and who is now having his curiosity rather too much satisfied, I think." (I was trying to stand tall like a man but had one hand secretly holding on to her skirt; so that was what the foreign men had chuckled at!) The talk went on, but I will tell it as if I had understood the Norse, for to repeat everything twice would be tedious.

The Abbess Radegunde said, "Will you bargain?"

There was a general nodding of heads, with a look of: After all, why not?

"And who will speak for you?" said she.

A man stepped forward; I recognized Thorvald Einarsson.

"Ah yes," said the Abbess dryly. "The company that has no leaders. Is this leaderless company agreed? Will it abide by its word? I want no treachery-planners, no Breakwords here!"

There was a great mutter at this. The Thorvald man (he *was* big, close up!) said mildly, "I sail with none such. Let's begin."

We all sat down.

"Now," said Thorvald Einarsson, raising his eyebrows, "according to my knowledge of this thing, you begin. And according to my knowledge you will begin by saying that you are very poor."

"But no," said the Abbess, "we are rich." Father Cairbre groaned. A groan answered him from behind the Abbey walls. Only the Abbess and Thorvald Einarsson seemed unmoved; it was as if these two were joking in some way that no one else understood. The Abbess went on, saying, "We are very rich. Within is much silver, much gold, many pearls, and much embroidered cloth, much fine-woven cloth, much carved and painted wood, and many books with gold upon their pages and jewels set into their covers. All this is yours. But we have more and better: herbs and medicines, ways to keep food from spoiling, the knowledge of how to cure the sick; all this is yours. And we have more and better even than this; we have the knowledge of Christ and the perfect understanding of the soul, which is yours, too, any time you wish; you have only to accept it."

Thorvald Einarsson held up his hand. "We will stop with the first," he said, "and perhaps a little of the second. That is more practical."

"And foolish," said the Abbess politely, "in the usual way." And again I had the odd feeling that these two were sharing a joke no one else even saw. She added, "There is one thing you may not have, and that is the most precious of all."

Thorvald Einarsson looked inquiring.

"*My people.* Their safety is dearer to me than myself. They are not to be touched, not a hair on their heads, not for any reason.

Think: you can fight your way into the Abbey easily enough, but the folk in there are very frightened of you and some of the men are armed. Even a good fighter is cumbered in a crowd. You will slip and fall upon each other without meaning to or knowing that you do so. Heed my counsel. Why play butcher when you can have treasure poured into your laps like kings, without work? And after that there will be as much again, when I lead you to the hidden place. An earl's mountain of treasure. Think of it! And to give all this up for slaves, half of whom will get sick and die before you get them home—and will need to be fed if they are to be any good. Shame on you for bad advice-takers! Imagine what you will say to your wives and families: Here are a few miserable bolts of cloth with blood spots that won't come out, here are some pearls and jewels smashed to powder in the fighting, here is a torn piece of embroidery which was whole until someone stepped on it in the battle, and I had slaves but they died of illness and I fucked a pretty young nun and meant to bring her back, but she leapt into the sea. And oh yes, there was twice as much again and all of it whole but we decided not to take that. Too much trouble, you see."

This was a lively story and the Norsemen enjoyed it. Radegunde held up her hand.

"People!" she called in German, adding, "Sea-rovers, hear what I say; I will repeat it for you in your tongue," (and so she did): *"People, if the Norsemen fight us, do not defend yourselves but smash everything! Wives, take your cooking knives and shred the valuable cloth to pieces! Men, with your axes and hammers hew the altars and the carved wood to fragments! All, grind the pearls and smash the jewels against the stone floors! Break the bottles of wine! Pound the gold and silver to shapelessness! Tear to pieces the illuminated books! Tear down the hangings and burn them!*

"But" (she added, her voice suddenly mild) "if these wise men will accept our gifts, let us heap untouched and spotless at their feet all that we have and hold nothing back, so that their kinsfolk will marvel and wonder at the shining and glistering of the wealth they bring back, though it leave us nothing but our bare stone walls."

If anyone had ever doubted that the Abbess Radegunde was inspired by God, their doubts must have vanished away, for who could resist the fiery vigor of her first speech or the beneficent unction of her second? The Norsemen sat there with their mouths open. I saw tears on Father Cairbre's cheeks. Then Thorvald Einarsson said, "Abbess—"

He stopped. He tried again but again stopped. Then he shook himself, as a man who has been under a spell, and said:

"Abbess, my men have been without women for a long time."

Radegunde looked surprised. She looked as if she could not believe what she had heard. She looked the pirate up and down, as if puzzled, and then walked around him as if taking his measure. She did this several times, looking at every part of his big body as if she were summing him up while he got redder and redder. Then she backed off and surveyed him again, and with her arms akimbo like a peasant, announced very loudly in both Norse and German:

"What! Have they lost the use of their hands?"

It was irresistible, in its way. The Norse laughed. Our people laughed. Even Thorvald laughed. I did too, though I was not sure what everyone was laughing about. The laughter would die down and then begin again behind the Abbey walls, helplessly, and again die down and again begin. The Abbess waited until the Norsemen had stopped laughing and then called for silence in German until there were only a few snickers here and there. She then said:

"These good men—Father Cairbre, tell the people—these good men will forgive my silly joke. I meant no scandal, truly, and no harm, but laughter is good; it settles the body's waters, as the physicians say. And my people know that I am not always as solemn and good as I ought to be. Indeed I am a very great sinner and scandalmaker. Thorvald Einarsson, do we do business?"

The big man—who had not been so pleased as the others, I can tell you!—looked at his men and seemed to see what he needed to know. He said: "I go in with five men to see what you have. Then we let the poor folk on the grounds go, but not those inside the Abbey. Then we search again. The gate will be locked and guarded by the rest of us; if there's any treachery, the bargain's off."

"Then I will go with you," said Radegunde. "That is very just and my presence will calm the people. To see us together will assure them that no harm is meant. You are a good man, Torvald—forgive me; I call you as your nephew did so often. Come, Boy News, hold on to me.

"Open the gate!" she called then; "All is safe!" and with the five men (one of whom was that young Thorfinn who had hated her so) we waited while the great logs were pulled back. There was little space within, but the people shrank back at the sight of those fierce warriors and opened a place for us.

I looked back and the Norsemen had come in and were standing just inside the walls, on either side the gate, with their swords out and their shields up. The crowd parted for us more slowly as we reached the main tower, with the Abbess repeating constantly, "Be calm, people, be calm. All is well," and deftly speaking by name to this one or that. It was much harder when the people gasped upon hearing the big logs pushed shut with a noise like thunder, and it was very close on the stairs; I heard her say something like an apology in the queer foreign tongue, something that probably meant, "I'm sorry that we must wait." It seemed an age until the stairs were even partly clear and I saw what the Abbess had meant by the cumbering of a crowd; a man might swing a weapon in the press of people but not very far and it was more likely he would simply fall over someone and crack his head. We gained the great room with the big crucifix of painted wood and the little one of pearls and gold, and the scarlet hangings worked in gold thread that I had played robbers behind so often before I learned what real robbers were: these tall, frightening men whose eyes glistened with greed at what I had fancied every village had. Most of the Sisters had stayed in the great room, but somehow it was not so crowded, as the folk had huddled back against the walls when the Norsemen came in. The youngest girls were all in a corner, terrified—one could smell it, as one can in people—and when that young Thorfinn went for the little gold-and-pearl cross, Sister Sibihd cried in a high, cracked voice, "It is the body of our Christ!" and leapt up, snatching it from the wall before he could get to it.

"Sibihd!" exclaimed the Abbess, in as sharp a voice as I had ever heard her use; "Put that back or you will feel the weight of my hand, I tell you!"

Now it is odd, is it not, that a young woman desperate enough not to care about death at the hands of a Norse pirate should nonetheless be frightened away at the threat of getting a few slaps from her Abbess? But folk are like that. Sister Sibihd returned the cross to its place (from whence young Thorfinn took it) and fell back among the nuns, sobbing, "He desecrates Our Lord God!"

"Foolish girl!" snapped the Abbess. "God only can consecrate or desecrate; man cannot. That is a piece of metal."

Thorvald said something sharp to Thorfinn, who slowly put the cross back on its hook with a sulky look which said, plainer than words: Nobody gives me what I want. Nothing else went wrong in the big room or the Abbess's study or the storerooms, or out in the kitchens. The Norsemen were silent and kept their hands on their swords but the Abbess kept talking in a calm way in both tongues; to our folk she said, "See? It is all right but everyone must keep still. God will protect us." Her face was steady and clear and I believed her a saint, for she had saved Sister Sibihd and the rest of us.

But this peacefulness did not last, of course. Something had to go wrong in all that press of people; to this day I do not know what. We were in a corner of the long refectory, which is the place where

the Sisters or Brothers eat in an Abbey, when something pushed
me into the wall and I fell, almost suffocated by the Abbess's lying
on top of me. My head was ringing and on all sides there was a
terrible roaring sound with curses and screams, a dreadful tumult
as if the walls had come apart and were falling on everyone. I could
hear the Abbess whispering something in Latin over and over in
my ear. There were dull, ripe sounds, worse than the rest, which I
know now to have been the noise steel makes when it is thrust into
bodies. This all seemed to go on forever and then it seemed to me
that the floor was wet. Then all became quiet. I felt the Abbess
Radegunde get off me. She said:

"So this is how you wash your floors up north." When I lifted my
head from the wet rushes and saw what she meant, I was very sick
into the corner. Then she picked me up in her arms and held my
face against her bosom so that I would not see but it was no use; I
had already seen: all the people lying about sprawled on the floor
with their bellies coming out, like heaps of dead fish, old Walafrid
with an axe-handle standing out of his chest—he was sitting up
with his eyes shut in a press of bodies that gave him no room to lie
down—and the young beekeeper, Uta, from the village, who had
been so merry, lying on her back with her long braids and her gown
all dabbled in red dye and a great stain of it on her belly. She was
breathing fast and her eyes were wide open. As we passed her, the
noise of her breathing ceased.

The Abbess said mildly, "Thy people are thorough housekeepers,
Earl Split-gut."

Thorvald Einarsson roared something at us and the Abbess replied softly, "Forgive me, good friend. You protected me and the
boy and I am grateful. But nothing betrays a man's knowledge of
the German like a word that bites, is it not so? And I had to be
sure."

It came to me then that she had called him "Torvald" and reminded him of his sister's son so that he would feel he must protect
us if anything went wrong. But now she would make him angry, I
thought, and I shut my eyes tight. Instead he laughed and said in
odd, light German, "I did no housekeeping but to stand over you
and your pet. Are you not grateful?"

"Oh very, thank you," said the Abbess with such warmth as she
might show to a Sister who had brought her a rose from the garden,
or another who copied her work well, or when I told her news, or
if Ita the cook made a good soup. But he did not know that the
warmth was for everyone and so seemed satisfied. By now we were
in the garden and the air was less foul; she put me down, although

my limbs were shaking, and I clung to her gown, crumpled, stiff, and blood-reeking though it was. She said, "Oh, my God, what a deal of washing hast Thou given us!" She started to walk towards the gate and Thorvald Einarsson took a step towards her. She said, without turning round: "Do not insist, Thorvald, there is no reason to lock me up. I am forty years old and not likely to be running away into the swamp what with my rheumatism and the pain in my knees and the folk needing me as they do."

There was a moment's silence. I could see something odd come into the big man's face. He said quietly:

"I did not speak, Abbess."

She turned, surprised. "But you did. I heard you."

He said strangely, "I did not."

Children can guess sometimes what is wrong and what to do about it without knowing how; I remember saying, very quickly, "Oh, she does that sometimes. My stepmother says old age has addled her wits," and then, "Abbess, may I go to my stepmother and my father?"

"Yes, of course," she said, "run along, Boy News—" and then stopped, looking into the air as if seeing in it something we could not. Then she said very gently, "No, my dear, you had better stay here with me," and I knew, as surely as if I had seen it with my own eyes, that I was not to go to my stepmother or my father because both were dead.

She did things like that, too, sometimes.

For a while it seemed that everyone was dead. I did not feel grieved or frightened in the least, but I think I must have been, for I had only one idea in my head: that if I let the Abbess out of my sight, I would die. So I followed her everywhere. She was let to move about and comfort people, especially the mad Sibihd, who would do nothing but rock and wail, but towards nightfall, when the Abbey had been stripped of its treasures, Thorvald Einarsson put her and me in her study, now bare of its grand furniture, on a straw pallet on the floor, and bolted the door on the outside. She said:

"Boy News, would you like to go to Constantinople, where the Emperor is and the domes of gold and all the splendid pagans? For that is where this man will take me to sell me."

"Oh yes!" said I, and then, "But will he take me, too?"

"Of course," said the Abbess, and so it was settled. Then in came Thorvald Einarsson, saying:

"Thorfinn is asking for you." I found out later that they were

waiting for him to die; none other of the Norse had been wounded
but a farmer had crushed Thorfinn's chest with an axe and he was
expected to die before morning. The Abbess said:

"Is that a good reason to go?" She added, "I mean that he hates
me; will not his anger at my presence make him worse?"

Thorvald said slowly, "The folk here say you can sit by the sick
and heal them. Can you do that?"

"To my knowledge, not at all," said the Abbess Radegunde, "but
if they believe so, perhaps that calms them and makes them better.
Christians are quite as foolish as other people, you know. I will come
if you want," and though I saw that she was pale with tiredness, she
got to her feet. I should say that she was in a plain brown gown
taken from one of the peasant women because her own was being
washed clean, but to me she had the same majesty as always. And
for him too, I think.

Thorvald said, "Will you pray for him or damn him?"

She said, "I do not pray, Thorvald, and I never damn anybody;
I merely sit." She added, "Oh let him; he'll scream your ears off if
you don't," and this meant me for I was ready to yell for my life if
they tried to keep me from her.

They had put Thorfinn in the chapel, a little stone room with
nothing left in it now but a plain wooden cross, not worth carrying
off. He was lying, his eyes closed, on the stone altar with furs under
him, and his face was gray. Every time he breathed there was a
bubbling sound, a little, thin, reedy sound, and as I crept closer I
saw why, for in the young man's chest was a great red hole with
pink things sticking out of it, all crushed, and in the hole one could
see something jump and fall, jump and fall, over and over again.
It was his heart beating. Blood kept coming from his lips in a froth.
I do not know, of course, what either said, for they spoke in the
Norse, but I saw what they did and heard much of it talked of
between the Abbess and Thorvald Einarsson later, so I will tell it
as if I knew.

The first thing the Abbess did was to stop suddenly on the thresh-
old and raise both hands to her mouth as if in horror. Then she
cried furiously to the two guards:

"Do you wish to kill your comrade with the cold and damp? Is
this how you treat one another? Get fire in here and some woollen
cloth to put over him! No, not more skins, you idiots, *wool* to mold
to his body and take up the wet. Run now!"

One said sullenly, "We don't take orders from you, Grandma."

"Oh no?" said she. "Then I shall strip this wool dress from my
old body and put it over that boy and then sit here all night in my

flabby naked skin! What will this child's soul say to God when it departs this flesh? That his friends would not give up a little of their booty so that he might fight for life? Is this your fellowship? Do it, or I will strip myself and shame you both for the rest of your lives!"

"Well, take it from his share," said the one in a low voice, and the other ran out. Soon there was a fire on the hearth and russet-colored woollen cloth—"From my own share," said one of them loudly, though it was a color the least costly, not like blue or red— and the Abbess laid it loosely over the boy, carefully putting it close to his sides but not moving him. He did not look to be in any pain, but his color got no better. But then he opened his eyes and said in such a little voice as a ghost might have, a whisper as thin and reedy and bubbling as his breath:

"You . . . old witch. But I beat you . . . in the end."

"Did you, my dear?" said the Abbess. "How?"

"Treasure," he said, "for my kinfolk. And I lived as a man at last. Fought . . . and had a woman . . . the one here with the big breasts, Sibihd . . . . Whether she liked it or not. That was good."

"Yes, Sibihd," said the Abbess mildly. "Sibihd has gone mad. She hears no one and speaks to no one. She only sits and rocks and moans and soils herself and will not feed herself, although if one puts food in her mouth with a spoon, she will swallow."

The boy tried to frown. "Stupid," he said at last. "Stupid nuns. The beasts do it."

"Do they?" said the Abbess, as if this were a new idea to her. "Now that is very odd. For never yet heard I of a gander that blacked the goose's eye or hit her over the head with a stone or stuck a knife in her entrails when he was through. When God puts it into their hearts to desire one another, she squats and he comes running. And a bitch in heat will jump through the window if you lock the door. Poor fools! Why didn't you camp three hours' down-river and wait? In a week half the young married women in the village would have been slipping away at night to see what the foreigners were like. Yes, and some unmarried ones, and some of my own girls, too. But you couldn't wait, could you?"

"No," said the boy, with the ghost of a brag. "Better . . . this way."

"This way," said she. "Oh yes, my dear, old granny knows about *this* way! Pleasure for the count of three or four and the rest of it as much joy as rolling a stone uphill."

He smiled a ghostly smile. "You're a whore, grandma."

She began to stroke his forehead. "No, grandbaby," she said, "but all Latin is not the Church Fathers, you know, great as they are.

One can find a great deal in those strange books written by the ones who died centuries before Our Lord was born. Listen," and she leaned closer to him and said quietly:

> *"Syrian dancing girl, how subtly you sway*
> *   those sensuous limbs,*
> *Half-drunk in the smoky tavern, lascivious*
> *   and wanton,*
> *Your long hair bound back in the Greek way,*
> *   clashing the castanets in your hands—"*

The boy was too weak to do anything but look astonished. Then she said this:

> *"I love you so that anyone permitted to sit near you and talk to you*
> *seems to me like a god; when I am near you my spirit is broken, my*
> *heart shakes, my voice dies, and I can't even speak. Under my skin*
> *I flame up all over and I can't see; there's thunder in my ears and*
> *I break out in a sweat, as if from fever; I turn paler than cut grass*
> *and feel that I am utterly changed; I feel that Death has come near*
> *me."*

He said, as if frightened. "Nobody feels like that."

"They do," she said.

He said, in feeble alarm, "You're trying to kill me!"

She said, "No, my dear. I simply don't want you to die a virgin."

It was odd, his saying those things and yet holding on to her hand where he had got at it through the woollen cloth; she stroked his head and he whispered, "Save me, old witch."

"I'll do my best," she said. "You shall do your best by not talking and I by not tormenting you any more, and we'll both try to sleep."

"Pray," said the boy.

"Very well," said she, "but I'll need a chair," and the guards—seeing, I suppose, that he was holding her hand—brought in one of the great wooden chairs from the Abbey, which were too plain and heavy to carry off, I think. Then the Abbess Radegunde sat in the chair and closed her eyes. Thorfinn seemed to fall asleep. I crept nearer her on the floor and must have fallen asleep myself almost at once, for the next thing I knew a gray light filled the chapel, the fire had gone out, and someone was shaking Radegunde, who still slept in her chair, her head leaning to one side. It was Thorvald Einarsson and he was shouting with excitement in his strange German, "Woman, how did you do it! How did you do it!"

"Do what?" said the Abbess thickly. "Is he dead?"

"Dead?" exclaimed the Norseman. "He is healed! Healed! The lung is whole and all is closed up about the heart and the shattered pieces of the ribs are grown together! Even the muscles of the chest are beginning to heal!"

"That's good," said the Abbess, still half asleep. "Let me be."

Thorvald shook her again. She said again, "Oh, let me sleep." This time he hauled her to her feet and she shrieked, "My back, my back! Oh, the saints, my rheumatism!" and at the same time a sick voice from under the blue woollens—a sick voice but a man's voice, not ghost's—said something in Norse.

"Yes, I hear you," said the Abbess; "you must become a follower of the White Christ right away, this very minute. But *Dominus noster*, please do You put it into these brawny heads that I must have a tub of hot water with pennyroyal in it? I am too old to sleep all night in a chair and I am one ache from head to foot."

Thorfinn got louder.

"Tell him," said the Abbess Radegunde to Thorvald in German, "that I will not baptize him and I will not shrive him until he is a different man. All that child wants is someone more powerful than your Odin god or your Thor god to pull him out of the next scrape he gets into. Ask him: Will he adopt Sibihd as his sister? Will he clean her when she soils herself and feed her and sit with his arm about her, talking to her gently and lovingly until she is well again? The Christ does not wipe out our sins only to have us commit them all over again and that is what he wants and what you all want, a God that gives and gives and gives, but God does not give; He takes and takes and takes. He takes away everything that is not God until there is nothing left but God, and none of you will understand that! There is no remission of sins; there is only change and Thorfinn must change before God will have him."

"Abbess, you are eloquent," said Thorvald, smiling, "but why do you not tell him all this yourself?"

"Because I ache so!" said Radegunde, "Oh, do get me into some hot water!" and Thorvald half led and half supported her as she hobbled out. That morning, after she had had her soak—when I cried, they let me stay just outside the door—she undertook to cure Sibihd, first by rocking her in her arms and talking to her, telling her she was safe now, and promising that the Northmen would go soon, and then when Sibihd became quieter, leading her out into the woods with Thorvald as a bodyguard to see that we did not run away, and little dark Sister Hedwic, who had stayed with Sibihd and cared for her. The Abbess would walk for a while in the mild autumn sunshine and then she would direct Sibihd's face upwards by touching her gently under the chin and say, "See? There is God's sky still," and then, "Look, there are God's trees; they have not changed," and telling her that the world was just the same and God still kindly to folk, only a few more souls had joined the Blessed and were happier waiting for us in Heaven than we could ever be, or even imagine being, on the poor earth. Sister Hedwic kept hold of Sibihd's hand. No one paid more attention to me than if I had been a dog, but every time poor Sister Sibihd saw Thorvald she would shrink away and you could see that Hedwic could not bear to look at him at all; every time he came in her sight she turned her face aside, shut her eyes hard, and bit her lower lip. It was a quiet, almost warm day, as autumn can be sometimes, and the Abbess found a few little blue late flowers growing in a sheltered place against a log and put them into Sibihd's hand, speaking of how beautifully and cunningly God had made all things. Sister Sibihd had enough wit to hold on to the flowers, but her eyes stared and she would have stumbled and fallen if Hedwic had not led her.

Sister Hedwic said timidly, "Perhaps she suffers because she has been defiled, Abbess," and then looked ashamed. For a moment the Abbess looked shrewdly at young Sister Hedwic and then at the mad Sibihd. Then she said:

"Dear daughter Sibihd and dear daughter Hedwic, I am now going to tell you something about myself that I have never told to a single living soul but my confessor. Do you know that as a young woman I studied at Avignon and from there was sent to Rome, so that I might gather much learning? Well, in Avignon I read mightily our Christian Fathers but also in the pagan poets, for as it has been said by Ermenrich of Ellwangen: As dung spread upon a field enriches it to good harvest, thus one cannot produce divine eloquence without the filthy writings of the pagan poets. This is true but perilous; only I thought not so, for I was very proud and fancied that if the pagan poems of love left me unmoved that was because I had the gift of chastity right from God Himself and I scorned sensual pleasures and those tempted by them. I had forgotten, you see, that chastity is not given once and for all like a wedding ring that is put on never to be taken off, but is a garden which each day must be weeded, watered, and trimmed anew, or soon there will be only brambles and wilderness.

"As I have said, the words of the poets did not tempt me, for words are only marks on the page with no life save what we give them. But in Rome there were not only the old books, daughters, but something much worse.

"There were statues. Now you must understand that these are not such as you can imagine from our books, like Saint John or the

Virgin; the ancients wrought so cunningly in stone that it is like magic; one stands before the marble holding one's breath, waiting for it to move and speak. They are not statues at all but beautiful naked men and women. It is a city of sea-gods pouring water, daughter Sibihd and daughter Hedwic, of athletes about to throw the discus, and runners and wrestlers and young emperors, and the favorites of kings, but they do not walk the streets like real men, for they are all of stone.

"There was one Apollo, all naked, which I knew I should not look on but which I always made some excuse to my companions to pass by, and this statue, although three miles distant from my dwelling, drew me as if by magic. Oh, he was fair to look on! Fairer than any youth alive now in Germany, or in the world, I think. And then all the old loves of the pagan poets came back to me: Dido and Aeneas, the taking of Venus and Mars, the love of the moon, Diana, for the shepherd boy—and I thought that if my statue could only come to life, he would utter honeyed love-words from the old poets and would be wise and brave, too, and what woman could resist him?"

Here she stopped and looked at Sister Sibihd but Sibihd only stared on, holding the little blue flowers. It was Sister Hedwic who cried, one hand pressed to her heart:

"Did you pray, Abbess?"

"I did," said Radegunde solemnly, "and yet my prayers kept becoming something else. I would pray to be delivered from the temptation that was in the statue and then, of course, I would have to think of the statue itself, and then I would tell myself that I must run, like the nymph Daphne, to be armored and sheltered within a laurel tree, but my feet seemed to be already rooted to the ground, and then at the last minute I would flee and be back at my prayers again. But it grew harder each time and at last the day came when I did not flee."

"Abbess, *you?*" cried Hedwic with a gasp. Thorvald, keeping his watch a little way from us, looked surprised. I was very pleased— I loved to see the Abbess astonish people; it was one of her gifts— and at seven I had no knowledge of lust except that my little thing felt good sometimes when I handled it to make water, and what had that to do with statues coming to life or women turning into laurel trees? I was more interested in mad Sibihd, the way children are; I did not know what she might do, or if I should be afraid of her, or, if I should go mad myself, what it would be like. But the Abbess was laughing gently at Hedwic's amazement.

"Why not me?" said the Abbess. "I was young and healthy and had no special grace from God any more than the hens or the cows do! Indeed I burned so with desire for that handsome young hero—for so I had made him in my mind, as a woman might do with a man she has seen a few times on the street—that thoughts of him tormented me waking and sleeping. It seemed to me that because of my vows I could not give myself to this Apollo of my own free will, so I would dream that he took me against my will, and oh, what an exquisite pleasure that was!"

Here Hedwic's blood came all to her face and she covered it with her hands. I could see Thorvald grinning, back where he watched us.

"And then," said the Abbess, as if she had not seen either of them, "a terrible fear came to my heart that God might punish me by sending a ravisher who would use me unlawfully, as I had dreamed my Apollo did, and that I would not even wish to resist him, and would feel the pleasures of a base lust, and would know myself a whore and a false nun forever after. This fear both tormented and drew me. I began to steal looks at young men in the streets, not letting the other Sisters see me do it, thinking: Will it be he? Or he? Or he?

"And then it happened. I had lingered behind the others at a melon-seller's, thinking of no Apollos or handsome heroes but only of the convent's dinner, when I saw my companions disappearing round a corner. I hastened to catch up with them—and made a wrong turning—and was suddenly lost in a narrow street—and at that very moment a young fellow took hold of my habit and threw me to the ground! You may wonder why he should do such a mad thing, but as I found out afterwards, there are prostitutes in Rome who affect our way of dress to please the appetites of certain men who are depraved enough to—Well, really, I do not know how to say it! Seeing me alone, he had thought I was one of them and would be glad of a customer and a bit of play. So there was a reason for it.

"Well, there I was on my back with this young fellow, sent as a vengeance by God, as I thought, trying to do exactly what I had dreamed, night after night, my statue should do. And do you know, it was nothing in the least like my dream! The stones at my back hurt me, for one thing. And instead of melting with delight, I was screaming my head off in terror and kicking at him as he tried to pull up my skirts, and praying to God that this insane man might not break any of my bones in his rage!

"My screams brought a crowd of people and he went running, so I got off with nothing worse than a bruised back and a sprained knee. But the strangest thing of all was that, while I was cured forever of lusting after my Apollo, instead I began to be tormented by a new fear—that I had lusted after *him*, that foolish young man with the foul breath and the one tooth missing!—and I felt strange creepings and crawlings over my body that were half like desire and half like fear and half like disgust and shame with all sorts of other things mixed in—I know that is too many halves, but it is how I felt—and nothing at all like the burning desire I had felt for my Apollo. I went to see the statue once more before I left Rome and it seemed to look at me sadly, as if to say: Don't blame me, poor girl; I'm only a piece of stone. And that was the last time I was so proud as to believe that God had singled me out for a special gift, like chastity—or a special sin, either—or that being thrown down on the ground and hurt had anything to do with any sin of mine, no matter how I mixed the two together in my mind. I dare say you did not find it a great pleasure yesterday, did you?"

Hedwic shook her head. She was crying quietly. She said, "Thank you, Abbess," and the Abbess embraced her. They both seemed happier, but then all of a sudden Sibihd muttered something, so low that one could not hear her.

"The—" she whispered and then she brought it out but still in a whisper: "The blood."

"What, dear, your blood?" said Radegunde.

"No mother," said Sibihd, beginning to tremble, "the blood. All over us. Walafrid and—and Uta—and Sister Hildegarde—and everyone broken and spilled out like a dish! And none of us had done anything but I could smell it all over me and the children screaming because they were being trampled down, and those demons come up from Hell though we had done nothing and—and—I understand, mother, about the rest, but I will never, ever forget it, oh Christ, it is all around me now, oh mother, the *blood*!"

Then Sister Sibihd dropped to her knees on the fallen leaves and began to scream, not covering her face as Sister Hedwic had done, but staring ahead with her wide eyes as if she were blind or could see something we could not. The Abbess knelt down and embraced her, rocking her back and forth, saying, "Yes, yes, dear, but we are here; we are here now; that is gone now," but Sibihd continued to scream, covering her ears as if the scream were someone else's and she could hide herself from it.

Thorvald said, looking, I thought, a little uncomfortable, "Cannot your Christ cure this?"

"No," said the Abbess. "Only by undoing the past. And that is the one thing He never does, it seems. She is in Hell now and must go back there many times before she can forget."

"She would make a bad slave," said the Norseman, with a glance at Sister Sibihd, who had fallen silent and was staring ahead of her again; "You need not fear that anyone will want her."

"God," said the Abbess Radegunde calmly, "is merciful."

Thorvald Einarsson said, "Abbess, I am not a bad man."

"For a good man," said the Abbess Radegunde, "you keep surprisingly bad company."

He said angrily, "I did not choose my shipmates. I have had bad luck!"

"Ours has," said the Abbess, "been worse, I think."

"Luck is luck," said Thorvald, clenching his fists. "It comes to some folk and not to others."

"As you came to us," said the Abbess mildly. "Yes, yes, I see, Thorvald Einarsson; one may say that luck is Thor's doing or Odin's doing, but you must know that our bad luck is your own doing and not some god's. You are our bad luck, Thorvald Einarsson. It's true that you're not as wicked as your friends, for they kill for pleasure and you do it without feeling, as a business, the way one hews down grain. Perhaps you have seen today some of the grain you have cut. If you had a man's soul, you would not have gone *viking*, luck or no luck, and if your soul were bigger still, you would have tried to stop your shipmates, just as I talk honestly to you now, despite your anger, and just as Christ Himself told the truth and was nailed on the cross. If you were a beast, you could not break God's law and if you were a man you would not, but you are neither and that makes you a kind of monster that spoils everything it touches and never knows the reason, and that is why I will never forgive you until you become a man, a true man with a true soul. As for your friends—"

Here Thorvald Einarsson struck the Abbess on the face with his open hand and knocked her down. I heard Sister Hedwic gasp in horror, and behind us Sister Sibihd began to moan. But the Abbess only sat there, rubbing her jaw and smiling a little. Then she said:

"Oh, dear, have I been at it again? I am ashamed of myself. You are quite right to be angry, Torvald; no one can stand me when I go on in that way, least of all myself; it is such a bore. Still, I cannot seem to stop it; I am too used to being the Abbess Radegunde, that is clear. I promise never to torment you again, but you, Thorvald, must never strike me again, because you will be very sorry if you do."

He took a step forward.

"No, no, my dear man," the Abbess said merrily, "I mean no threat—how could I threaten you?—I mean only that I will never tell you any jokes, my spirits will droop, and I will become as dull as any other woman. Confess it now: I am the most interesting thing that has happened to you in years and I have entertained you better, sharp tongue and all, than all the *skalds* at the Court of Norway. And I know more tales and stories than they do—more than anyone in the whole world—for I make new ones when the old ones wear out.

"Shall I tell you a story now?"

"About your Christ?" said he, the anger still in his face.

"No," said she, "about living men and women. Tell me, Torvald, what do you men want from us women?"

"To be talked to death," said he, and I could see there was some anger in him still, but he was turning it to play also.

The Abbess laughed in delight. "Very witty!" she said, springing to her feet and brushing the leaves off her skirt. "You are a very clever man, Torvald. I beg your pardon, Thorvald. I keep forgetting. But as to what men want from women, if you asked the young men, they would only wink and dig one another in the ribs, but that is only how they deceive themselves. That is only body calling to body. They themselves want something quite different and they want it so much that it frightens them. So they pretend it is anything and everything else: pleasure, comfort, a servant in the home. Do you know what it is that they want?"

"What?" said Thorvald.

"The mother," said Radegunde, "as women do, too; we all want the mother. When I walked before you on the riverbank yesterday, I was playing the mother. Now you did nothing, for you are no young fool, but I knew that sooner or later one of you, so tormented by his longing that he would hate me for it, would reveal himself. And so he did: Thorfinn, with his thoughts all mixed up between witches and grannies and whatnot. I knew I could frighten him, and through him, most of you. That was the beginning of my bargaining. You Norse have too much of the father in your country and not enough mother, with all your honoring of your women; that is why you die so well and kill other folk so well—and live so very, very badly."

"You are doing it again," said Thorvald, but I think he wanted to listen all the same.

"Your pardon, friend," said the Abbess. "You are brave men; I don't deny it. But I know your *sagas* and they are all about fighting and dying and afterwards not Heavenly happiness but the end of the world: everything, even the gods, eaten by the Fenris-wolf and the Midgard snake! What a pity, to die bravely only because life is not worth living! The Irish knew better. The pagan Irish were heroes, with their Queens leading them to battle as often as not, and Father Cairbre, God rest his soul, was complaining only two days ago that the common Irish folk were blasphemously making a goddess out of God's mother, for do they build shrines to Christ or Our Lord or pray to them? No! It is Our Lady of the Rocks and Our Lady of the Sea and Our Lady of the Grove and Our Lady of this or that from one end of the land to the other. And even here it is only the Abbey folk who speak of God the Father and of Christ. In the village if one is sick or another in trouble it is: Holy Mother, save me! and: *Mariam Virginem*, intercede for me, and: Blessed Virgin, blind my husband's eyes! and: Our Lady, preserve my crops, and so on, men and women both. We all need the mother."

"You, too?"

"More than most," said the Abbess.

"And I?"

"Oh no," said the Abbess, stopping suddenly, for we had all been walking slowly back towards the village as she spoke. "No, and that is what drew me to you at once. I saw it in you and knew you were the leader. It is followers who make leaders, you know, and your shipmates have made you leader, whether you know it or not. What you want is—how shall I say it? You are a clever man, Thorvald, perhaps the cleverest man I have ever met, more even than the scholars I knew in my youth. But your cleverness has had no food. It is a cleverness of the world and not of books. You want to travel and know about folk and their customs, and what strange places are like, and what has happened to men and women in the past. If you take me to Constantinople, it will not be to get a price for me but merely to go there; you went seafaring because this longing itched at you until you could bear it not a year more; I know that."

"Then you are a witch," said he, and he was not smiling.

"No, I only saw what was in your face when you spoke of that city," said she. "Also there is gossip that you spent much time in Göteborg as a young man, idling and dreaming and marveling at the ships and markets when you should have been at your farm."

She said, "Thorvald, I can feed that cleverness. I am the wisest woman in the world. I know everything—everything! I know more than my teachers; I make it up or it comes to me, I don't know how, but it is real—real!—and I know more than anyone. Take me from here, as your slave if you wish but as your friend also, and let us go to Constantinople and see the domes of gold, and the walls all inlaid with gold, and the people so wealthy you cannot imagine it, and the whole city so gilded it seems to be on fire, and pictures as high as a wall, set right in the wall and all made of jewels so there is nothing else like them, redder than the reddest rose, greener than the grass, and with a blue that makes the sky pale!"

"You are indeed a witch," said he, "and not the Abbess Rade-gunde."

She said slowly, "I think I am forgetting how to be the Abbess Radegunde."

"Then you will not care about them any more," said he and pointed to Sister Hedwic, who was still leading the stumbling Sister Sibihd.

The Abbess's face was still and mild. She said, "I care. Do not strike me, Thorvald, not ever again, and I will be a good friend to you. Try to control the worst of your men and leave as many of my people free as you can—I know them and will tell you which can be taken away with the least hurt to themselves or others—and I will feed that curiosity and cleverness of yours until you will not recognize this old world any more for the sheer wonder and awe of it; I swear this on my life."

"Done," said he, adding, "but with my luck, your life is some-where else, locked in a box on top of a mountain, like the troll's in the story, or you will die of old age while we are still at sea."

"Nonsense," she said, "I am a healthy mortal woman with all my teeth, and I mean to gather many wrinkles yet."

He put his hand out and she took it; then he said, shaking his head in wonder, "If I sold you in Constantinople, within a year you would become Queen of the place!"

The Abbess laughed merrily and I cried in fear, "Me, too! Take me too!" and she said, "Oh yes, we must not forget little Boy News," and lifted me into her arms. The frightening tall man, with his face close to mine, said in his strange sing-song German:

"Boy, would you like to see the whales leaping in the open sea and the seals barking on the rocks? And cliffs so high that a giant could stretch his arms up and not reach their tops? And the sun shining at midnight?"

"Yes!" said I.

"But you will be a slave," he said, "and may be illtreated and will always have to do as you are bid. Would you like that?"

"No!" I cried lustily, from the safety of the Abbess's arms; "I'll fight!"

He laughed a mighty, roaring laugh and tousled my head—rather too hard, I thought—and said, "I will not be a bad master, for I am named for Thor Red-beard and he is strong and quick to fight but good-natured, too, and so am I," and the Abbess put me down and so we walked back to the village, Thorvald and the Abbess Radegunde talking of the glories of this world and Sister Hedwic saying softly, "She is a saint, our Abbess, a saint, to sacrifice herself for the good of the people," and all the time behind us, like a memory, came the low, witless sobbing of Sister Sibihd, who was in Hell.

When we got back we found that Thorfinn was better and the Norsemen were to leave in the morning. Thorvald had a second pallet brought into the Abbess's study and slept on the floor with us that night. You might think his men would laugh at this, for the Abbess was an old woman, but I think he had been with one of the young ones before he came to us. He had that look about him. There was no bedding for the Abbess but an old brown cloak with holes in it, and she and I were wrapped in it when he came in and threw himself down, whistling, on the other pallet. Then he said:

"Tomorrow, before we sail, you will show me the old Abbess's treasure."

"No," said she. "That agreement was broken."

He had been playing with his knife and now ran his thumb along the edge of it. "I can make you do it."

"No," said she patiently, "and now I am going to sleep."

"So you make light of death?" he said. "Good! That is what a brave woman should do, as the *skalds* sing, and not move, even when the keen sword cuts off her eyelashes. But what if I put this knife here not to your throat but to your little boy's? You would tell me then quick enough!"

The Abbess turned away from him, yawning and saying, "No, Thorvald, because you would not. And if you did, I would despise you for a cowardly oathbreaker and not tell you for that reason. Good night."

He laughed and whistled again for a bit. Then he said:

"Was all that true?"

"All what?" said the Abbess. "Oh, about the statue. Yes, but there was no ravisher. I put him in the tale for poor Sister Hedwic."

Thorvald snorted, as if in disappointment. "Tale? You tell lies, Abbess!"

The Abbess drew the old brown cloak over her head and closed her eyes. "It helped her."

Then there was a silence, but the big Norseman did not seem able to lie still. He shifted this way and that, stared at the ceiling, turned over, shifted his body again as if the straw bothered him, and again turned over. He finally burst out, "But what happened!"

She sat up. Then she shut her eyes. She said, "Maybe it does not come into your man's thoughts that an old woman gets tired and that the work of dealing with folk is hard work, or even that it is work at all. Well!

"Nothing 'happened,' Thorvald. Must something happen only if this one fucks that one or one bangs in another's head? I desired my statue to the point of such foolishness that I determined to find a real, human lover, but when I raised my eyes from my fancies to the real, human men of Rome and unstopped my ears to listen to their talk, I realized that the thing was completely and eternally impossible. Oh, those younger sons with their skulking, jealous hatred of the rich, and the rich ones with their noses in the air because they thought themselves of such great consequence because of their silly money, and the timidity of the priests to their superiors, and their superiors' pride, and the artisans' hatred of the peasants, and the peasants being worked like animals from morning until night, and half the men I saw beating their wives and the other half out to cheat some poor girl of her money or her virginity or both— this was enough to put out any fire! And the women doing less harm only because they had less power to do harm, or so it seemed to me then. So I put all away, as one does with any disappointment. Men are not such bad folk when one stops expecting them to be gods, but they are not for me. If that state is chastity, then a weak stomach is temperance, I think. But whatever it is, I have it, and that's the end of the matter."

"*All* men?" said Thorvald Einarsson with his head to one side, and it came to me that he had been drinking, though he seemed sober.

"Thorvald," said the Abbess, "what you want with this middle-aged wreck of a body I cannot imagine, but if you lust after my wrinkles and flabby breasts and lean, withered flanks, do whatever you want quickly and then for Heaven's sake, let me sleep. I am tired to death."

He said in a low voice, "I need to have power over you."

She spread her hands in a helpless gesture. "Oh Thorvald, Thorvald, I am a weak little woman over forty years old! Where is the power? All I can do is talk!"

He said, "That's it. That's how you do it. You talk and talk and talk and everyone does just as you please; I have seen it!"

The Abbess said, looking sharply at him, "Very well. If you must. *But if I were you, Norseman, I would as soon bed my own mother.* Remember that as you pull my skirts up."

That stopped him. He swore under his breath, turning over on his side, away from us. Then he thrust his knife into the edge of his pallet, time after time. Then he put the knife under the rolled-up cloth he was using as a pillow. We had no pillow so I tried to make mine out of the edge of the cloak and failed. Then I thought that the Norseman was afraid of God working in Radegunde, and then I thought of Sister Hedwic's changing color and wondered why. And then I thought of the leaping whales and the seals, which must be like great dogs because of the barking, and then the seals jumped on land and ran to my pallet and lapped at me with great icy tongues of water so that I shivered and jumped and then I woke up.

The Abbess Radegunde had left the pallet—it was her warmth I had missed—and was walking about the room. She would step and pause, her skirts making a small noise as she did so. She was careful not to touch the sleeping Thorvald. There was a dim light in the room from the embers that still glowed under the ashes in the hearth, but no light came from between the shutters of the study window, now shut against the cold. I saw the Abbess kneel under the plain wooden cross which hung on the study wall and heard her say a few words in Latin; I thought she was praying. But then she said in a low voice:

" 'Do not call upon Apollo and the Muses, for they are deaf things and vain.' But so are you, Pierced Man, deaf and vain."

Then she got up and began to pace again. Thinking of it now frightens me, for it was the middle of the night and no one to hear her—except me, but she thought I was asleep—and yet she went on and on in that low, even voice as if it were broad day and she were explaining something to someone, as if things that had been in her thoughts for years must finally come out. But I did not find anything alarming in it then, for I thought that perhaps all Abbesses had to do such things, and besides she did not seem angry or hurried or afraid; she sounded as calm as if she were discussing the profits from the Abbey's bee-keeping—which I had heard her do—or the accounts for the wine cellars—which I had also heard—and there was nothing alarming in that. So I listened as she continued walking about the room in the dark. She said:

"Talk, talk, talk, and always to myself. But one can't abandon the kittens and puppies; that would be cruel. And being the Abbess Radegunde at least gives one something to do. But I am so sick of the good Abbess Radegunde; I have put on Radegunde every morning of my life as easily as I put on my smock, and then I have had to hear the stupid creature praised all day!—sainted Radegunde, just Radegunde who is never angry or greedy or jealous, kindly Radegunde who sacrifices herself for others and always the talk, talk, talk, bubbling and boiling in my head with no one to hear or understand, and no one to answer. No, not even in the south, only a line here or a line there, and all written by the dead. Did they feel as I do? That the world is a giant nursery full of squabbles over toys and the babes thinking me some kind of goddess because I'm not greedy for their dolls or bits of straw or their horses made of tied-together sticks?

"Poor people, if only they knew! It's so easy to be temperate when one enjoys nothing, so easy to be kind when one loves nothing, so easy to be fearless when one's life is no better than one's death. And so easy to scheme when the success or failure of the scheme doesn't matter.

"Would they be surprised, I wonder, to find out what my real thoughts were when Thorfinn's knife was at my throat? Curiosity! But he would not do it, of course; he does everything for show. And they would think I was twice holy, not to care about death.

"'Then why not kill yourself, impious Sister Radegunde? Is it your religion which stops you? Oh, you mean the holy wells, and the holy trees, and the blessed saints with their blessed relics, and the stupidity that shamed Sister Hedwic and the promises of safety that drove poor Sibihd mad when the blessed body of her Lord did not protect her and the blessed love of the blessed Mary turned away the sharp point of not one knife? Trash! Idle leaves and sticks, reeds and rushes, filth we sweep off our floors when it grows too thick. As if holiness had anything to do with all of that. As if every place were not as holy as every other and every thing as holy as every other, from the shit in Thorfinn's bowels to the rocks on the ground. As if all places and things were not clouds placed in front of our weak eyes, to keep us from being blinded by that glory, that eternal shining, that blazing all about us, that torrent of light that is everything and is in everything! That is what keeps me from the river, but it never speaks to me or tells me what to do, and to it good and evil are the same—no, it is something else than good or evil; it *is*, only—so it is not God. That I know.

"So, people, is your Radegunde a witch or a demon? Is she full of pride or is Radegunde abject? Perhaps she is a witch. Once, long ago, I confessed to Old Gerbertus that I could see things that were far away merely by closing my eyes, and I proved it to him, too, and he wept over me and gave me much penance, crying, 'If it come of itself it may be a gift of God, daughter, but it is more likely the work of a demon, so do not do it!' And then we prayed and I told him the power had left me, to make the poor old puppy less troubled in its mind, but that was not true, of course. I could still see Turkey as easily as I could see him, and places far beyond: the squat wild men of the plains on their ponies, and the strange tall people beyond that with their great cities and odd eyes, as if one pulled one's eyelid up on a slant, and then the seas with the great

wild lands and the cities more full of gold than Constantinople, and
then the water again until one comes back home, for the world's a
ball, as the ancients said.

"But I did stop somehow, over the years. Radegunde never had
time, I suppose. Besides, when I opened that door it was only
pictures, as in a book, and all to no purpose, and after a while I
had seen them all and no longer cared for them. It is the other
door that draws me, when it opens itself but a crack and strange
things peep through, like Ranulf sister's-son and the name of his
horse. That door is good but very heavy; it always swings back after
a little. I shall have to be on my deathbed to open it all the way, I
think.

"The fox is asleep. He is the cleverest yet; there is something in
him so that at times one can almost talk to him. But still a fox, for
the most part. Perhaps in time . . .

"But let me see; yes, he is asleep. And the Sibihd puppy is asleep,
though it will be having a bad dream soon, I think, and the Thorfinn kitten is asleep, as full of fright as when it wakes, with its claws
going in and out, in and out, lest something strangle it in its sleep."

Then the Abbess fell silent and moved to the shuttered window
as if she were looking out, so I thought that she was indeed looking
out—but not with her eyes—at all the sleeping folk, and this was
something she had done every night of her life to see if they were
safe and sound. But would she not know that *I* was awake? Should
I not try very hard to get to sleep before she caught me? Then it
seemed to me that she smiled in the dark, although I could not see
it. She said in that same low, even voice: "Sleep or wake, Boy News;
it is all one to me. Thou hast heard nothing of any importance,
only the silly Abbess talking to herself, only Radegunde saying
goodbye to Radegunde, only Radegunde going away—don't cry,
Boy News; I am still here—but there: Radegunde has gone. This
Norseman and I are alike in one way: our minds are like great
houses with many of the rooms locked shut. We crowd in a miserable huddled few, like poor folk, when we might move freely among
them all, as gracious as princes. It is fate that locked away so much
of the Norseman from the Norseman—see, Boy News, I do not say
his name, not even softly, for that wakes folks—but I wonder if the
one who bolted me in was not Radegunde herself, she and Old
Gerbertus—whom I partly believed—they and the years and years
of having to be Radegunde and do the things Radegunde did and
pretend to have the thoughts Radegunde had and the endless,
endless lies Radegunde must tell everyone, and Radegunde's utter
and unbearable loneliness."

She fell silent again. I wondered at the Abbess's talk this time:

saying she was not there when she was, and about living locked up in small rooms—for surely the Abbey was the most splendid house in all the world and the biggest—and how could she be lonely when all the folk loved her? But then she said in a voice so low that I could hardly hear it:

"Poor Radegunde! So weary of the lies she tells and the fooling of men and women with the collars round their necks and bribes of food for good behavior and a careful twitch of the leash that they do not even see or feel. And with the Norseman it will be all the same: lies and flattery and all of it work that never ends and no one ever even sees, so that finally Radegunde will lie down like an ape in a cage, weak and sick from hunger, and will never get up.

"Let her die now. There: Radegunde is dead. Radegunde is gone. Perhaps the door was heavy only because she was on the other side of it, pushing against me. Perhaps it will open all the way now. I have looked in all directions: to the east, to the north and south, and to the west, but there is one place I have never looked and now I will: away from the ball, straight up. Let us see—"

She stopped speaking all of a sudden. I had been falling asleep, but this silence woke me. Then I heard the Abbess gasp terribly, like one mortally stricken, and then she said in a whisper so keen and thrilling that it made the hair stand up on my head: *Where art thou?* The next moment she had torn the shutters open and was crying out with all her voice: *Help me! Find me! Oh come, come, come, or I die!*

This waked Thorvald. With some Norse oath he stumbled up and flung on his sword-belt, and then put his hand to his dagger; I had noticed this thing with the dagger was a thing Norsemen liked to do. The Abbess was silent. He let out his breath in an oof! and went to light the tallow dip at the live embers under the hearth-ashes; when the dip had smoked up, he put it on its shelf on the wall.

He said in German, "What the devil, woman! What has happened?"

She turned round. She looked as if she could not see us, as if she had been dazed by a joy too big to hold, like one who has looked into the sun and is still dazzled by it so that everything seems changed, and the world seems all God's and everything in it like Heaven. She said softly, with her arms around herself, hugging herself: "My people. The real people."

"What are you talking of!" said he.

She seemed to see him then, but only as Sibihd had beheld us; I do not mean in horror as Sibihd had, but beholding through something else, like someone who comes from a vision of bliss which still lingers about her. She said in the same soft voice, "They are coming for me, Thorvald. Is it not wonderful? I knew all this year that something would happen, but I did not know it would be the one thing I wanted in all the world."

He grasped his hair. "*Who* is coming?"

"My people," she said, laughing softly. "Do you not feel them? I do. We must wait three days, for they come from very far away. But then—oh, you will see!"

He said, "You've been dreaming. We sail tomorrow."

"Oh no," said the Abbess simply. "You cannot do that for it would not be right. They told me to wait; they said if I went away, they might not find me."

He said slowly, "You've gone mad. Or it's a trick."

"Oh no, Thorvald," said she. "How could I trick you? I am your friend. And you will wait these three days, will you not, because you are my friend also."

"You're mad," he said, and started for the door of the study, but she stepped in front of him and threw herself on her knees. All her cunning seemed to have deserted her, or perhaps it was Rade-gunde who had been the cunning one. This one was like a child. She clasped her hands and tears came out of her eyes; she begged him, saying:

"Such a little thing, Thorvald, only three days! And if they do not come, why then we will go anywhere you like, but if they do come you will not regret it, I promise you; they are not like the folk here and that place is like nothing here. It is what the soul craves, Thorvald!"

He said, "Get up, woman, for your God's sake!"

She said, smiling in a sly, frightened way through her blubbered face, "If you let me stay, I will show you the old Abbess's buried treasure, Thorvald."

He stepped back, the anger clear in him. "So this is the brave old witch who cares nothing for death!" he said. Then he made for the door, but she was up again, as quick as a snake, and had flung herself across it.

She said, still with that strange innocence, "Do not strike me. Do not push me. I am your friend!"

He said, "You mean that you lead me by a string round the neck, like a goose. Well, I am tired of that!"

"But I cannot do that any more," said the Abbess breathlessly, "not since the door opened. I am not able now." He raised his arm to strike her and she cowered, wailing, "Do not strike me! Do not push me! Do not, Thorvald!"

He said, "Out of my way then, old witch!"

She began to cry in sobs and gulps. She said, "One is here but another will come! One is buried but another will rise! She will come, Thorvald!" and then in a low, quick voice, "Do not push open this last door. There is one behind it who is evil and I am afraid"—but one could see that he was angry and disappointed and would not listen. He struck her for a second time and again she fell, but with a desperate cry, covering her face with her hands. He unbolted the door and stepped over her and I heard his footsteps go down the corridor. I could see the Abbess clearly—at that time I did not wonder how this could be, with the shadows from the tallow dip half hiding everything in their drunken dance—but I saw every line in her face as if it had been full day and in that light I saw Radegunde go away from us at last.

Have you ever been at some great King's court or some Earl's and heard the story-tellers? There are those so skilled in the art that they not only speak for you what the person in the tale said and did, but they also make an action with their faces and bodies as if they truly were that man or woman, so that it is a great surprise to you when the tale ceases, for you almost believe that you have seen the tale happen in front of your very eyes and it is as if a real man or woman had suddenly ceased to exist, for you forget that all this was only a teller and a tale.

So it was with the woman who had been Radegunde. She did not change; it was still Radegunde's gray hairs and wrinkled face and old body in the peasant woman's brown dress, and yet at the same time it was a stranger who stepped out of the Abbess Radegunde as out of a gown dropped to the floor. This stranger was without feeling, though Radegunde's tears still stood on her cheeks, and there was no kindness or joy in her. She got up without taking care of her dress where the dirty rushes stuck to it; it was as if the dress were an accident and did not concern her. She said in a voice I had never heard before, one with no feeling in it, as if I did not concern her or Thorvald Einarsson either, as if neither of us were worth a second glance:

"Thorvald, turn around."

Far up in the hall something stirred.

"Now come back. This way."

There were footsteps, coming closer. Then the big Norseman walked clumsily into the room—jerk! jerk! jerk! at every step as if he were being pulled by a rope. Sweat beaded his face. He said, "You—how?"

"By my nature," she said. "Put up the right arm, fox. Now the left. Now both down. Good."

"You—troll!" he said.

"That is so," she said. "Now listen to me, you. There's a man inside you but he's not worth getting at; I tried moments ago when I was new-hatched and he's buried too deep, but now I have grown beak and claws and care nothing for him. It's almost dawn and your boys are stirring; you will go out and tell them that we must stay here another three days. You are weatherwise; make up some story they will believe. And don't try to tell anyone what happened here tonight; you will find that you cannot."

"Folk—come," said he, trying to turn his head, but the effort only made him sweat.

She raised her eyebrows. "Why should they? No one has heard anything. Nothing has happened. You will go out and be as you always are and I will play Radegunde. For three days only. Then you are free."

He did not move. One could see that to remain still was very hard for him; the sweat poured and he strained until every muscle stood out. She said:

"Fox, don't hurt yourself. And don't push me; I am not fond of you. My hand is light upon you only because you still seem to me a little less unhuman than the rest; do not force me to make it heavier. To be plain: I have just broken Thorfinn's neck, for I find that the change improves him. Do not make me do the same to you."

"No worse . . . than death," Thorvald brought out.

"Ah no?" said she, and in a moment he was screaming and clawing at his eyes. She said, "Open them, open them; your sight is back," and then, "I do not wish to bother myself thinking up worse things, like worms in your guts. Or do you wish dead sons and a dead wife? Now go.

"As you always do," she added sharply, and the big man turned and walked out. One could not have told from looking at him that anything was wrong.

I had not been sorry to see such a bad man punished, one whose friends had killed our folk and would have taken them for slaves— yet I was sorry, too, in a way, because of the seals barking and the whales—and he *was* splendid, after a fashion—and yet truly I forgot all about that the moment he was gone, for I was terrified of this strange person or demon or whatever it was, for I knew that whoever was in the room with me was not the Abbess Radegunde. I knew also that it could tell where I was and what I was doing, even if I made no sound, and was in a terrible riddle as to what I ought to do when soft fingers touched my face. It was the demon, reaching swiftly and silently behind her.

And do you know, all of a sudden everything was all right! I don't mean that she was the Abbess again—I still had very serious suspicions about that—but all at once I felt light as air and nothing seemed to matter very much because my stomach was full of bubbles of happiness, just as if I had been drunk, only nicer. If the Abbess Radegunde were really a demon, what a joke that was on her people! And she did not, now that I came to think of it, seem a bad sort of demon, more the frightening kind than the killing kind, except for Thorfinn, of course, but then Thorfinn had been a very wicked man. And did not the angels of the Lord smite down the wicked? So perhaps the Abbess was an angel of the Lord and not a demon, but if she were truly an angel, why had she not smitten the Norsemen down when they first came and so saved all our folk? And then I thought that, whether angel or demon, she was no longer the Abbess and would love me no longer, and if I had not been so full of the silly happiness which kept tickling about inside me, this thought would have made me weep.

I said, "Will the bad Thorvald get free, demon?"

"No," she said. "Not even if I sleep."

I thought: *But she does not love me.*

"I love thee," said the strange voice, but it was not the Abbess Radegunde's and so was without meaning, but again those soft fingers touched me and there was some kindness in them, even if it was a stranger's kindness.

Sleep, they said.

So I did.

The next three days I had much secret mirth to see the folk bow down to the demon and kiss its hands and weep over it because it had sold itself to ransom them. That is what Sister Hedwic told them. Young Thorfinn had gone out in the night to piss and had fallen over a stone in the dark and broken his neck, which secretly rejoiced our folk, and his comrades did not seem to mind much either, save for one young fellow who had been Thorfinn's friend, I think, and so went about with a long face. Thorvald locked me up in the Abbess's study with the demon every night and went out—or so folk said—to one of the young women, but on those nights the demon was silent and I lay there with the secret tickle of merriment in my stomach, caring about nothing.

On the third morning I woke sober. The demon—or the Abbess—for in the day she was so like the Abbess Radegunde that I wondered—took my hand and walked us up to Thorvald, who was out picking the people to go aboard the Norsemen's boats at the riverbank to be slaves. Folk were standing about weeping and wringing their hands; I thought this strange, because of the Abbess's promise to pick those whose going would hurt least, but I know now that least is not none. The weather was bad, cold rain out of mist, and some of Thorvald's companions were speaking sourly to him in the Norse, but he talked them down—bluff and hearty—as if making light of the weather. The demon stood by him and said, in German, in a low voice so that none might hear: "You will say we go to find the Abbess's treasure and then you will go with us into the woods."

He spoke to his fellows in Norse and they frowned; but the end of it was that two must come with us, for the demon said it was such a treasure as three might carry. The demon had the voice and manner of the Abbess Radegunde, all smiles, so they were fooled. Thus we started out into the trees behind the village, with the rain worse and the ground beginning to soften underfoot. As soon as the village was out of sight the two Norsemen fell behind, but Thorvald did not seem to notice this; I looked back and saw the first man standing in the mud with one foot up, like a goose, and the second with his head lifted and his mouth open so that the rain fell in it. We walked on, the earth sucking at our shoes and all of us getting wet: Thorvald's hair stuck fast against his face and the demon's old brown cloak clinging to its body. Then suddenly the demon began to breathe harshly and it put its hand to its side with a cry. Its cloak fell off and it stumbled before us between the wet trees, not weeping but breathing hard. Then I saw, ahead of us through the pelting rain, a kind of shining among the bare tree-trunks, and as we came nearer the shining became more clear until it was very plain to see, not a blazing thing like a fire at night but a mild and even brightness as though the sunlight were coming through the clouds pleasantly but without strength, as it often does at the beginning of the year.

And then there were folk inside the brightness, both men and women, all dressed in white, and they held out their arms to us and the demon ran to them, crying out loudly and weeping, but paying no mind to the tree-branches which struck it across the face and body. Sometimes it fell but it quickly got up again. When it reached the strange folk they embraced it and I thought that the filth and mud of its gown would stain their white clothing, but the foulness dropped off and would not cling to those clean garments. None of the strange folk spoke a word, nor did the Abbess—I knew then that she was no demon, whatever she was—but I felt them talk to one another, as if in my mind, although I know not how this could be nor the sense of what they said. An odd thing was that as I came closer I could see they were not standing on the ground, as in the way of nature, but higher up, inside the shining, and that their

white robes were nothing at all like ours, for they clung to the body
so that one might see the people's legs all the way up to the place
where the legs joined, even the women's. And some of the folk
were like us, but most had a darker color and some looked as if
they had been smeared with soot—there are such persons in the
far parts of the world, you know, as I found out later; it is their
own natural color—and there were some with the odd eyes the
Abbess had spoken of—but the oddest thing of all I will not tell
you now. When the Abbess had embraced and kissed them all and
all had wept, she turned and looked down upon us: Thorvald
standing there as if held by a rope and I, who had lost my fear and
had crept close in pure awe, for there was such a joy about these
people, like the light about them, mild as spring light and yet as
strong as in a spring where the winter has gone forever.

"Come to me, Thorvald," said the Abbess, and one could not see
from her face if she loved or hated him. He moved closer—jerk!
jerk!—and she reached down and touched his forehead with her
fingertips, at which one side of his lip lifted, as a dog's does when
it snarls.

"As thou knowest," said the Abbess quietly, "I hate thee and
would be revenged upon thee. Thus I swore to myself three days
ago, and such vows are not lightly broken."

I saw him snarl again and he turned his eyes from her.

"I must go soon," said the Abbess, unmoved, "for I could stay
here long years only as Radegunde and Radegunde is no more;
none of us can remain here long as our proper selves or even in
our true bodies, for if we do we go mad like Sibihd or walk into the
river and drown or stop our own hearts, so miserable, wicked, and
brutish does your world seem to us. Nor may we come in large
companies, for we are few and our strength is not great and we
have much to learn and study of thy folk so that we may teach and
help without marring all in our ignorance. And ignorant or wise,
we can do naught except thy folk aid us.

"Here is my revenge," said the Abbess, and he seemed to writhe
under the touch of her fingers, for all they were so light; "Hence-
forth be not Thorvald Farmer nor yet Thorvald Seafarer but Thorvald Peacemaker, Thorvald War-hater, put into anguish by
bloodshed and agonized at cruelty. I cannot make long thy life—
that gift is beyond me—but I give thee this: to the end of thy days,
long or short, thou wilt know that it is neither good nor evil, as I
do, and this knowing will trouble and frighten thee always, as it
does me, and so about this one thing, as about many another,
Thorvald Peacemaker will never have peace.

"Now, Thorvald, go back to the village and tell thy comrades I was assumed into the company of the saints, straight up to Heaven. Thou mayst believe it, if thou wilt. That is all my revenge."

Then she took away her hand and he turned and walked from us like a man in a dream, holding out his hands as if to feel the rain and stumbling now and again, as one who wakes from a vision.

Then I began to grieve, for I knew she would be going away with the strange people and it was to me as if all the love and care and light in the world were leaving me. I crept close to her, meaning to spring secretly onto the shining place and so go away with them, but she spied me and said, "Silly Radulphus, you cannot," and that *you* hurt me more than anything else, so that I began to bawl.

"Child," said the Abbess, "come to me," and loudly weeping I leaned against her knees. I felt the shining around me, all bright and good and warm, that wiped away all grief, and then the Abbess's touch on my hair.

She said, "Remember me. And be . . . content."

I nodded, wishing I dared to look up at her face, but when I did, she had already gone with her friends. Not up into the sky, you understand, but as if they moved very swiftly backwards among the trees—although the trees were still behind them somehow—and as they moved, the shining and the people faded away into the rain until there was nothing left.

Then there was no rain. I do not mean that the clouds parted or the sun came out; I mean that one moment it was raining and cold and the next the sky was clear blue from side to side and it was splendid, sunny, breezy, bright, sailing weather. I had the oddest thought that the strange folk were not agreed about doing such a big miracle—and it was hard for them, too—but they had decided that no one would believe this more than all the other miracles folk speak of, I suppose. And it would surely make Thorvald's lot easier when he came back with wild words about saints and Heaven, as indeed it did, later.

Well, that is the tale, really. She said to me "Be content" and so I am; they call me Radulf the Happy now. I have had my share of trouble and sickness but always somewhere in me there is a little spot of warmth and joy to make it all easier, like a traveler's fire burning out in the wilderness on a cold night. When I am in real sorrow or distress I remember her fingers touching my hair and that takes part of the pain away, somehow. So perhaps I got the best gift, after all. And she said also, "Remember me," and thus I have, every little thing, although it all happened when I was the age my own grandson is now, and that is how I can tell you this tale today.

And the rest? Three days after the Norsemen left, Sibihd got back her wits and no one knew how, though I think I do! And as for Thorvald Einarsson, I have heard that after his wife died in Norway he went to England and ended his days there as a monk, but whether this story be true or not I do not know.

I know this: they may call me Happy Radulf all they like, but there is much that troubles me. Was the Abbess Radegunde a demon, as the new priest says? I cannot believe this, although he called half her sayings nonsense and the other half blasphemy when I asked him. Father Cairbre, before the Norse killed him, told us stories about the Sidhe, that is the Irish fairy people, who leave changelings in human cradles, and for a while it seemed to me that Radegunde must be a woman of the Sidhe when I remembered that she could read Latin at the age of two and was such a marvel of learning when so young, for the changelings the fairies leave are not their own children, you understand, but one of the fairy-folk themselves, who are hundreds upon hundreds of years old, and the other fairy-folk always come back for their own in the end. And yet this could not have been, for Father Cairbre said also that the Sidhe are wanton and cruel and without souls, and neither the Abbess Radegunde nor the people who came for her were one blessed bit like that, although she did break Thorfinn's neck—but then it may be that Thorfinn broke his own neck by chance, just as we all thought at the time, and she told this to Thorvald afterwards, as if she had done it herself, only to frighten him. She had more of a soul with a soul's griefs and joys than most of us, no matter what the new priest says. He never saw her or felt her sorrow and lonesomeness, or heard her talk of the blazing light all around us—and what can that be but God Himself? Even though she did call the crucifix a deaf thing and vain, she must have meant not Christ, you see, but only the piece of wood itself, for she was always telling the Sisters that Christ was in Heaven and not on the wall. And if she said the light was not good or evil, well, there is a traveling Irish scholar who told me of a holy Christian monk named Augustinus who tells us that all which is, is good, and evil is only a lack of the good, like an empty place not filled up. And if the Abbess truly said there was no God, I say it was the sin of despair, and even saints may sin, if only they repent, which I believe she did at the end.

So I tell myself and yet I know the Abbess Radegunde was no saint, for are the saints few and weak, as she said? Surely not! And then there is a thing I held back in my telling, a small thing and it will make you laugh and perhaps means nothing one way or the other but it is this:

Are the saints bald?

These folk in white had young faces but they were like eggs;

there was not a stitch of hair on their domes! Well, God may shave His saints if He pleases, I suppose.

But I know she was no saint. And then I believe that she did kill Thorfinn and the light was not God and she not even a Christian or maybe even human and I remember how Radegunde was to her only a gown to step out of at will, and how she truly hated and scorned Thorvald until she was happy and safe with her own people. Or perhaps it was like her talk about living in a house with the rooms shut up; when she stopped being Radegunde first one part of her came back and then the other—the joyful part that could not lie or plan and then the angry part—and then they were all together when she was back among her own folk. And then I give up trying to weigh this matter and go back to warm my soul at the little fire she lit in me, that one warm, bright place in the wide and windy dark.

But something troubles me even there, and will not be put to rest by the memory of the Abbess's touch on my hair. As I grow older it troubles me more and more. It was the very last thing she said to me, which I have not told you but will now. When she had given me the gift of contentment, I became so happy that I said, "Abbess, you said you would be revenged on Thorvald, but all you did was change him into a good man. That is no revenge!"

What this saying did to her astonished me, for all the color went out of her face and left it gray. She looked suddenly old, like a death's head, even standing there among her own true folk with love and joy coming from them so strongly that I myself might feel it. She said, "I did not change him. I lent him my eyes; that is all." Then she looked beyond me, as if at our village, at the Norsemen loading their boats with weeping slaves, at all the villages of Germany and England and France where the poor folk sweat from dawn to dark so that the great lords may do battle with one another, at castles under siege with the starving folk within eating mice and rats and sometimes each other, at the women carried off or raped or beaten, at the mothers wailing for their little ones, and beyond this at the great wide world itself with all its battles which I had used to think so grand, and the misery and greediness and fear and jealousy and hatred of folk one for the other, save—perhaps— for a few small bands of savages, but they were so far from us that one could scarcely see them. She said: *No revenge? Thinkest thou so, boy?* And then she said as one who believes absolutely, as one who has seen all the folk at their living and dying, not for one year but for many, not in one place but in all places, as one who knows it all over the whole wide earth:

Think again . . . .

LUCIUS SHEPARD
A Traveler's Tale

Lucius Shepard was perhaps the most popular and influential new writer of the eighties, rivaled for that title only by
William Gibson, Connie Willis, and Kim Stanley Robinson
. . . and, as he is far more prolific than any of them (especially at shorter lengths), his impact on the short fiction
market of the decade was perhaps even more profound. In
fact, pound for pound, Shepard may have produced the
most vital and consistently excellent body of short work of
the eighties, and may come to be seen as one of the best
short fiction writers ever to enter the field.

Shepard made his first sale in 1983, to Terry Carr's *Universe*. That particular story attracted little notice at the time,
but the floodgates were about to open, and the next seven
years would see a steady stream of bizarre and powerfully
compelling stories, such as the landmark novella *R & R*,
"The Jaguar Hunter," "Black Coral," "A Spanish Lesson,"
"The Man Who Painted the Dragon Griaule," "Shades,"
"Aymara," "How the Wind Spoke at Madaket," "On the
Border," "Fire Zone Emerald," and *The Scalehunter's Beautiful Daughter*, among dozens of others . . . for even Shepard's
second-rate tales are strong enough to serve as first-rate
stuff for many another writer. The field had not seen such
a concentrated outpouring of outstanding work from a
single writer since Robert Silverberg's most prolific days in
the early seventies. Nor has he slowed down much in the
new decade of the nineties, continuing to produce superior
short work such as "Beast of the Heartland," "The All-
Consuming," "Skull City," and "Sports in America." His
novella *Barnacle Bill the Spacer* won the Hugo Award in
1993, and his vampire novel *The Golden* was appearing on
nationwide best-seller lists by the end of that year.

Shepard's work is both nightmarish and hallucinatorily

beautiful, a strange and contradictory mixture of wild romance, vivid eroticism, brutal violence, intricate metaphysical structures, radical politics, and intensely concentrated
Lovecraftian horror, all peopled by lowlife bums and winos
and junkies who also turn out to be psychologically complex
and broodingly introverted characters, and who often find
themselves enmeshed in a desperate quest for personal
transcendence—all this frequently set in authentically described Third World milieus, often structured by an almost
Victorian concern with personal ethics and moral responsibility, and expressed in a mannered, cadenced, complexly
structured, formal prose that would probably be considered old-fashioned and fustian if it wasn't at the same time
so vivid and supple.

All of which is demonstrated, and *then* some, in the wild,
passionate, and almost unbelievably lush novella that follows, one that packs enough action and high concept into
its pages for many another writer's trilogy of novels, and
one of Shepard's best, *A Traveler's Tale*.

Lucius Shepard won the John W. Campbell Award in
1985 as the year's Best New Writer, and no year since has
gone by without him adorning the final ballot for one major
award or another, and often for several. In 1987 he won
the Nebula Award for *R & R*, and in 1988 he picked up
a World Fantasy Award for his monumental short-story
collection *The Jaguar Hunter*, following it in 1992 with a
second World Fantasy Award for his second collection, *The
Ends of the Earth*. His novels include *Green Eyes*, the bestsel-
ling *Life During Wartime*, and *Kalimantan*. His most recent
books are the novels *The Golden* and *The Off-Season*. He's
currently at work on a new novel, *The 'Velt*. Born in
Lynchburg, Virginia, he now lives in Seattle, Washington.

All this happened several years ago on the island of Guanoja
Menor, most of it to a young American named Ray Milliken. I
doubt you will have heard of him, not unless you have been blessed
with an exceptional memory and chanced to read the sketchy article
about his colony printed by one of the national tabloids; but in
these parts his name remains something to conjure with.

"Who were dat Yankee," a drunkard will say (the average Guanojan conversation incorporates at least one), "de one who lease de
Buryin' Ground and say he goin' to bring down de space duppies?"

"Dat were Ray Milliken," will be the reply, and this invariably will
initiate a round of stories revolving about the theme of Yankee

foolishness, as if Ray's experiences were the central expression of such a history—which they well may be.

Most Americans one meets abroad seem to fall into types. I ascribe this to the fact that when we encounter a fellow countryman, we tend to exaggerate ourselves, to adopt categorizable modes of behavior, to advertise our classifiable eccentricities and political views, anything that may later prove a bone of contention, all so we may be more readily recognizable to the other. This tendency, I believe, bears upon our reputation for being people to whom time is a precious commodity; we do not want to waste a moment of our vacations or, as in the case of expatriates like myself, our retirements, by pursuing relationships based on a mistaken affinity. My type is of a grand tradition. Fifty-eight years old, with a paunch and a salt-and-pepper beard; retired from a government accounting job to this island off the coast of Honduras; once-divorced; now sharing my days with a daughter of the island, a twenty-year-old black girl named Elizabeth, whose cooking is indifferent but whose amatory performance never lacks enthusiasm. When I tally up these truths, I feel that my life has been triangulated by the works of Maugham, Greene, and Conrad. The Ex-Civil Servant Gone To Seed In A Squalid Tropic. And I look forward to evolving into a further type, a gray eminence, the sort of degenerate emeritus figure called upon to settle disputes over some trifling point of island lore.

"Better now you ask ol' Franklin Winship 'bout dat," they'll say. "De mon been here since de big storm in 'seventy-eight."

Ray's type, however, was of a more contemporary variety; he was one of those child-men who are to be found wandering the sun-struck ends of the earth, always seeming to be headed toward some rumored paradise, a beach said to be unspoiled, where they hope to achieve . . . something, the realization of a half-formed ambition whose criteria of peace and purity are so high as to guarantee failure. Travelers, they call themselves, and in truth, travel is their only area of expertise. They know the cheapest restaurant in Belize City, how to sleep for free on Buttermilk Key, the best sandalmaker in Panajachel; they have languished in Mexican jails, contracted dysentery while hiking through the wilds of Olancho, and been run out of various towns for drug abuse or lack of funds. But despite their knowledge and experience, they are curiously empty young men, methodical and unexcitable, possessing personalities that have been carefully edited to give the least effrontery to the widest spectrum of the populace. As they enter their thirties—and this was Ray's age when I met him—they will often settle for long periods in a favorite spot, and societies of even younger travelers will accrete around them. During these periods a subtype may emerge—

crypto-Charles Mansons who use their self-assurance to wield influence over the currencies of sex and drugs. But Ray was not of this mold. It seemed to me that his wanderings had robbed him of guile, of all predilection for power-tripping, and had left him a worldly innocent. He was of medium stature, tanned, with ragged sunstreaked hair and brown eyes set in a handsome but unremarkable face; he had the look of a castaway frat boy. Faint, fine lines radiated from the corners of his eyes, like scratches in sandstone. He usually dressed in shorts and a flour-sack shirt, one of several he owned that were decorated with a line drawing of a polar bear above the name of the mill and the words HARINA BLANCA.

"That's me," he would say, pointing to the words and smiling. "White bread."

I first saw him in the town square of Meachem's Landing, sitting on a stone bench beneath the square's single tree—a blighted acacia—and tying trick knots for the amusement of a clutch of spidery black children. He grinned at me as I passed, and, surprised, being used to the hostile stares with which many young Americans generally favor their elders, I grinned back and stopped to watch. I had just arrived on the island and was snarled in red tape over the leasing of land, aggravated by dealing with a lawyer who insisted on practicing his broken English when explaining things, driven to distraction by the incompetent drunks who were building my house, transforming my neat blueprints into the reality of a Cubist nightmare. I welcomed Ray's companionship as a respite. Over a span of four months we met two or three times a week for drinks at the Salón de Carmín—a ramshackle bar collapsing on its pilings above the polluted shallows of the harbor. To avoid the noise and frequent brawls, we would sit out back on the walkway from which the proprietress tossed her slops.

We did not dig into each other's souls, Ray and I; we told stories. Mine described the vicissitudes of Washington life, while his were exotic accounts of chicleros and cursed Mayan jade; how he had sailed to Guayaquil on a rock star's yacht or paddled alone up the Río de la Pasión to the unexcavated ruin of Yaxchilán; a meeting with guerrillas in Salvador. Quite simply, he was the finest storyteller I have ever known. A real spellbinder. Each of his stories had obviously been worked and reworked until the emotional valence of their events had been woven into clear, colorful prose; yet they maintained a casual edge, and when listening to him it was easy to believe that they had sprung full-blown from his imagination. They were, he told me, his stock-in-trade. Whenever times were lean, he would find a rich American and manage to weasel a few dollars by sharing his past.

Knowing he considered me rich, I glanced at him suspiciously; but he laughed and reminded me that he had bought the last two rounds.

Though he was always the protagonist of his stories, I realized that some of them must have been secondhand, otherwise he would have been a much older, much unhealthier man; but despite this I came to understand that secondhand or not, they *were* his, that they had become part of his substance in the way a poster glued to a wall eventually merges with the surface beneath through a process of the weather. In between the stories I learned that he had grown up in Sacramento and had briefly attended Cal Tech, majoring in astronomy; but thereafter the thread of his life story unraveled into a welter of anecdote. From various sources I heard that he had rented a shanty near Punta Palmetto, sharing it with a Danish girl named Rigmor and several others, and that the police had been nosing around in response to reports of nudity and drugs; yet I never impinged on this area of his life. We were drinking companions, nothing more, and only once did I catch a glimpse of the soul buried beneath his placid exterior.

We were sitting as usual with our feet propped on the walkway railing, taking shelter in the night from the discordant reggae band inside and gazing out at the heat lightning that flashed orange above the Honduran coast. Moths batted at the necklace of light bulbs strung over the door, and the black water was lacquered with reflection. On either side, rows of yellow-lit windows marked the shanties that followed the sweep of the harbor. We had been discussing women—in particular a local woman whose husband appeared to be more concerned with holding on to her than curbing her infidelities.

"Being cuckolded seems the official penalty for marriage down here," I said. "It's as if they're paying the man back for being fool enough to marry them."

"Women are funny," said Ray; he laughed, realizing the inadequacy of the cliché. "They're into sacrifice," he said. "They'll break your heart and mean well by it." He made a gesture of frustration, unable to express what he intended, and stared gloomily down at his hands.

I had never before seen such an intense expression on his face; it was clear that he was not talking about women in the abstract. "Having trouble with Rigmor?" I asked.

"Rigmor?" He looked confused, then laughed again. "No, that's just fun and games." He went back to staring at his hands.

I was curious; I had a feeling that I had glimpsed beneath his surface, that the puzzle he presented—a bright young man wasting himself in endless wandering—might have a simple solution. I phrased my next words carefully, hoping to draw him out.

"I suppose most men have a woman in their past," I said, "one who failed to recognize the mutuality of a relationship."

Ray glanced at me sharply, but made no comment.

"Sometimes," I continued, "we use those women as justifications for our success or failure, and I guess they do deserve partial credit or blame. After all, they do sink their claws in us . . . but we let them."

He opened his mouth, and I believe he was about to tell me a story, the one story of real moment in his life; but just then old Spurgeon James, drunk, clad in tattered shirt and shorts, the tangle of his once-white beard stained a motley color by nicotine and rum, staggered out of the bar and began to urinate into the shallows. "Oh, mon!" he said. "Dis night wild!" He reeled against the wall, half-turning, the arc of his urine glistening in the yellow light and splashing near Ray's feet. When he had finished, he tried to extort money from us by relating the story that had gained him notoriety the week before—he claimed to have seen flying saucers hanging over Flower's Bay. Anxious to hear Ray's story, I thrust a *lempira* note at Spurgeon to get rid of him; but by the time he had gone back in, Ray had lost the impulse to talk about his past and was off instead on the subject of Spurgeon's UFOs.

"You don't believe him, do you?" I said. "Once Spurgeon gets a load on, he's liable to see the Pope driving a dune buggy."

"No," said Ray. "But I wish I could believe him. Back at Cal Tech I'd planned on joining one of the projects that were searching for extraterrestrial life."

"Well then," I said, fumbling out my wallet, "you'd probably be interested to know that there's been a more reliable sighting on the island. That is, if you consider a pirate reliable. Henry Meachem saw a UFO back in the 1700s—1793, I think." I pulled out a folded square of paper and handed it to Ray. "It's an excerpt from the old boy's journal. I had the clerk at the Historical Society run me off a Xerox. My youngest girl reads science fiction, and I thought she might get a laugh out of it."

Ray unfolded the paper and read the excerpt, which I reproduce below.

May 7th, 1793. I had just gone below to my Cabin after negotiating the Reef, when I heard divers Cries of astonishment and panic echoing down the Companion-way. I return'd to the Fore-Deck and there found most of the Crew gather'd along the Port-Rail, many of them pointing to the Heavens. Almost directly overhead and at an unguessable Distance, I espi'd an Object of supernal red brilliance, round, no larger than a Ha'penny. The brightness of the Object was most curious, and perhaps brightness is not the proper Term to describe its Effect. While it was, indeed, bright, it was not sufficiently so to cause me to shield my Eyes; and yet whenever I attempt'd to direct my Gaze upon it, I experienc'd a sensation of Vertigo and so was forc'd to view it obliquely. I call'd for my Glass, but before it could be bro't there was a Windy Noise—yet not a whit more Wind—and the Object began to expand, all the while maintaining its circular Forme. Initially, I thought it to be falling towards us, as did the Crew, and several Men flung themselves into the Sea to escape immolation. However, I soon realis'd that it was merely growing larger, as tho' a Hole were being burned thro' the Sky to reveal the flame-lash'd Sky of Hell behind. Suddenly a Beam of Light, so distinct as to appear a reddish-gold Wire strung between Sky and Sea, lanc'd down from the Thing and struck the Waters inside the Reef. There was no Splash, but a great hissing and venting of Steam, and after this had subsided, the Windy Noise also began to subside, and the fiery Circle above dwindled to a point and vanish'd. I consider'd putting forth a Long-Boat to discover what had fall'n, but I was loathe to waste the Southerly Wind. I mark'd the position of the Fall—a scant 3 miles from our Camp at Sandy Bay—and upon our Return there will be ample Opportunity to explore the Phenomenon . . . .

As I recall, Ray was impressed by the excerpt, saying that he had never read of a sighting quite like this one. Our conversation meandered over the topics of space colonies, quasars, and UFO nuts—whom he deprecated as having given extraterrestrial research a bad name—and though I tried to resurrect the topic of women, I never succeeded.

At the time I was frantically busy with supervising the building of my house, maneuvering along the path of bribery and collusion that would lead to my obtaining final residence papers, and I took for granted these meetings at the Salón de Carmín. If I had been asked my opinion of Ray in those days, I would have said that he was a pleasant-enough sort but rather shallow. I never considered him my friend; in fact, I looked on our relationship as being free from the responsibilities of friendship, as a safe harbor from the storms of social convention—new friends, new neighbors, new woman—that were blowing around me. And so, when he finally left the island after four months of such conversations, I was surprised to find that I missed him.

*   *   *

Islands are places of mystery. Washed by the greater mysteries of wind and sea, swept over by tides of human event, they accumulate eerie magnetisms that attract the lawless, the eccentric, and—it is said—the supernatural; they shelter oddments of civilization that evolve into involute societies, and their histories are less likely to reflect orderly patterns of culture than mosaics of bizarre circumstance. Guanoja's embodiment of the mystery had fascinated me from the beginning. It had originally been home to Caribe Indians, who had moved on when Henry Meachem's crews and their slaves established their colonies—their black descendants still spoke an English dotted with eighteenth- and nineteenth-century colloquialisms. Rum-running, gun-smuggling, and revolution had all had their moment in the island's tradition; but the largest part of this tradition involved the spirit world. Duppies (a word used to cover a variety of unusual manifestations, but generally referring to ghosts, both human and animal); the mystical rumors associated with the smoking of black coral; and then there was the idea that some of the spirits dwelling there were not the shades of dead men and women, but ancient and magical creatures, demigods left over from the days of the Caribe. John Anderson McCrae, the patriarch of the island's storytellers, once put it to me this way:

"Dis island may look like a chewed-up bone some dog have dropped in a puddle, and de soil may be no good for plantains, no good for corn. But when it come to de breedin' of spirits, dere ain't no soil better."

It was, as John Anderson McCrae pointed out, no tropic paradise. Though the barrier reef was lovely and nourished a half-dozen diving resorts, the interior consisted of low scrub-thatched hills and much of the coast was given over to mangrove. A dirt road ran partway around the island, connecting the shantytowns of Meachem's Landing, Spanish Harbor, and West End, and a second road crossed from Meachem's Landing to Sandy Bay on the northern coast—a curving stretch of beach that at one moment seemed beautiful, and the next abysmally ugly. That was the charm of the island, that you could be walking along a filthy beach, slapping at flies, stepping carefully to avoid dead fish and pig droppings; and then, as if a different filter had slid across the sun, you suddenly noticed the hummingbirds flitting in the sea grape, the hammocks of coco palms, the reef water glowing in bands of jade and turquoise and aquamarine. Sprinkled among the palms at Sandy Bay were a few dozen shanties set on pilings, their tin roofs scabbed by rust; jetties with gap-boarded outhouses at their seaward ends extended out over the shallows, looking like charcoal sketches by Picasso. It had no special point of attraction, but because Elizabeth's family lived nearby, I had built my house—three rooms of concrete block and a wooden porch—about a hundred yards from the terminus of the cross-island road.

A half-mile down the beach stood The Chicken Shack, and its presence had been a further inducement to build in Sandy Bay. Not that the food or decor was in the least appealing; the sole item on the menu was fried chicken, mostly bone and gristle, and the shanty was hardly larger than a chicken coop itself, containing three picnic tables and a kitchen. Mounted opposite each other on the walls was a pair of plates upon which a transient artist had painted crude likenesses of the proprietor, John James, and his wife; and these two black faces, their smiles so poorly rendered as to appear ferocious, always seemed to me to be locked in a magical duel, one whose stray energies caused the food to be overdone. If your taste was for a good meal, you would have done better elsewhere; but if you had an appetite for gossip, The Chicken Shack was unsurpassed in this regard; and it was there one night, after a hiatus of almost two years, that I next had word of Ray Milliken.

I had been out of circulation for a couple of weeks, repairing damage done to my house by the last norther, and since Elizabeth was grouchy with her monthlies, I decided to waste a few hours watching Hatfield Brooks tell fortunes at the Shack. He did so each Wednesday without fail. On arriving, I found him sitting at the table nearest the door—a thin young man who affected natty dreads but none of the hostility usually attendant to the hairstyle. Compared to most of the islanders, he was a saintly sort. Hardworking; charitable; a nondrinker; faithful to his wife. In front of him was what looked to be a bowling ball of marbled red plastic, but was actually a Zodiac Ball—a child's toy containing a second ball inside, and between the inner and outer shells, a film of water. There was a small window at the top, and if you shook the ball, either the word *Yes* or *No* would appear in the window, answering your question. Sitting beside Hatfield, scrunched into the corner, was his cousin Jimmy Mullins, a diminutive wiry man of thirty-five. He had fierce black eyes that glittered under the harsh light; the skin around them was puckered as if they had been surgically removed and later reembedded. He was shirtless, his genitals partly exposed by a hole in his shorts. John James, portly and white-haired, waved to me from behind the counter, and Hatfield asked, "How de night goin', Mr. Winship?"

"So-so," I replied, and ordered a bottle of Superior from John. "Not much business," I remarked to Hatfield, pressing the cold bottle against my forehead.

"Oh, dere's a trickle now and den," he said.

All this time Mullins had said not a word. He was apparently angry at something, glowering at Hatfield, shifting uncomfortably on the bench, the tip of his tongue darting in and out.

"Been hunting lately?" I asked him, taking a seat at the table by the counter.

I could tell he did not want to answer, to shift his focus from whatever had upset him; but he was a wheedler, a borrower, and he did not want to offend a potential source of small loans. In any case, hunting was his passion. He did his hunting by night, hypnotizing the island deer with beams from his flashlight; nonetheless he considered himself a great sportsman, and not even his bad mood could prevent him from boasting.

"Shot me a nice little buck Friday mornin'," he mumbled; and then, becoming animated, he said, "De minute I see he eye, podner, I know he got to crumble."

There was a clatter on the stairs, and a teenage girl wearing a man's undershirt and a print skirt pushed in through the door. Junie Elkins. She had been causing the gossip mills to run overtime due to a romance she was having with a boy from Spanish Harbor, something of which her parents disapproved. She exchanged greetings, handed a coin to Hatfield, and sat across from him. Then she looked back at me, embarrassed. I pretended to be reading the label of my beer bottle.

"What you after knowin', darlin'?" asked Hatfield.

Junie leaned over the table and whispered. Hatfield nodded, made a series of mystic passes, shook the ball, and Junie peered intently at the window in its top.

"Dere," said Hatfield. "Everything goin' to work out in de end."

Other Americans have used Hatfield's method of fortunetelling to exemplify the islanders' gullibility and ignorance, and even Hatfield would admit to an element of hoax. He did not think he had power over the ball; he had worked off-island on the steamship lines and had gained a measure of sophistication. Still he credited the ball with having some magical potential. "De thing made to tell fortunes even if it just a toy," he said to me once. He did not deny that it gave wrong answers, but suggested these might be blamed on changing conditions and imperfect manufacture. The way he explained it was so sweetly reasonable that I almost believed him; and I did believe that if the ball was going to work anywhere, it would be on this island, a place where the rudimentary underpinnings of culture were still in evidence, where simpler laws obtained.

After Junie had gone, Mullins's hostility again dominated the room and we sat in silence. John set about cleaning the kitchen, and the clatter of dishes accentuated the tension. Suddenly Mullins brought his fist down on the table.

"Damn it, mon!" he said to Hatfield. "Gimme my money!"

"Ain't your money," said Hatfield gently.

"De mon has got to pay *me* for *my* land!"

"Ain't your land."

"I got testimony dat it's mine!" Again Mullins pounded the table.

John moved up to the counter. "Dere's goin' to be no riot in dis place tonight," he said sternly.

Land disputes—as this appeared to be—were common on the island and often led to duels with conch shells or machetes. The pirates had not troubled with legal documents, and after taking over the island, the Hondurans had managed to swindle the best of the land from the blacks; though the old families had retained much of the acreage in the vicinity of Sandy Bay. But, since most of the blacks were at least marginally related, matters of ownership proved cloudy.

"What's the problem?" I asked.

Hatfield shrugged, and Mullins refused to answer; anger seemed visible above his head like heat ripples rising from a tin roof.

"Some damn fool have leased de Buryin' Ground," said John. "Now dese two feudin'."

"Who'd want that pesthole?"

"A true damn fool, dat's who," said John. "Ray Milliken."

I was startled to hear Ray's name—I had not expected to hear it again—and also by the fact that he or anyone would spend good money on the Burying Ground. It was a large acreage three miles west of Sandy Bar near Punta Palmetto, mostly mangrove swamp, and notable for its population of snakes and insects.

"It ain't de Garden of Eden, dat's true," said Hatfield. "I been over de other day watchin' dem clear stumps, and every time de blade dig down it churn up three or four snakes. *Coralitos*, yellowjaws."

"Snakes don't bother dis negro," said Mullins pompously.

His referral to himself as "dis negro" was a sure sign that he was drunk, and I realized now that he had scrunched into the corner to preserve his balance. His gestures were sluggish, and his eyes were bloodshot and rolling.

"Dat's right," he went on. "Everybody know dat if de yellowjaw bite, den you just bites de pizen back in he neck."

John made a noise of disgust.

"What's Milliken want the place for?" I asked.

"He goin' to start up a town," said Hatfield. "Least dat's what he hopin'. De lawyer say we best hold up de paperwork 'til we find out what de government think 'bout de idea."

"De fools dat goin' to live in de town already on de island," said John. "Dey stayin' over in Meachem's Landin'. Must be forty or fifty of dem. Dey go 'round smilin' all de time, sayin', 'Ain't dis nice,' and 'Ain't dat pretty.' Dey of a cult or somethin'."

"All I know," said Hatfield, "is dat de mon come to me and say, 'Hatfield, I got three thousand *lemps*, fifteen hundred dollars gold, if you give me ninety-nine years on de Buryin' Ground.' And I say, 'What for you want dat piece of perdition? My cousin Arlie he lease you a nice section of beachfront.' And den he tell me 'bout how de Caribe live dere 'cause dat's where dey get together with de space duppies . . . ."

"Aliens," said John disparagingly.

"Correct! Aliens." Hatfield stroked the Zodiac Ball. "He say de aliens talk to de Caribe 'cause de Caribe's lives is upful and just naturally 'tracts de aliens. I tell him, 'Mon, de Caribe fierce! Dey warriors!' And he say, 'Maybe so, but dey must have been doin' somethin' right or de aliens won't be comin' 'round.' And den he tell me dat dey plan to live like de Caribe and bring de aliens back to Guanoja."

"Gimme a Superior, John," said Mullins bossily.

"You got de money?" asked John, his arms folded, knowing the answer.

"No, I ain't got de money!" shouted Mullins. "Dis boog clot got my money!" He threw himself at Hatfield and tried to wrestle him to the floor; but Hatfield, being younger, stronger, and sober, caught his wrists and shoved him back into the corner. Mullins's head struck the wall with a *thwack*, and he grabbed the injured area with both hands.

"Look," I said. "Even if the government permits the town, which isn't likely, do you really believe a town can survive on the Burying Ground? Hell, they'll be straggling back to Meachem's Landing before the end of the first night."

"Dat's de gospel," said John, who had come out from back of the counter to prevent further riot.

"Has any money changed hands?" I asked.

"He give me two hundred *lemps* as security," said Hatfield. "But I 'spect he want dat back if de government disallow de town."

"Well," I said, "if there's no town, there's no argument. Why not ask the ball if there's going to be a town on the Burying Ground?"

"Sound reasonable to me," said John; he gave the ball no credence, but was willing to suspend disbelief in order to make peace.

"Lemme do it!" Mullins snatched the ball up, staring crosseyed into the red plastic. "Is dere goin' to be a town on de Buryin' Ground?" he asked solemnly; then he turned it over twice and set it down. I stood and leaned forward to see the little window.

No, it read.

"Let's have beers all around," I said to John. "And a soda for Hatfield. We'll toast the solution of a problem."

But the problem was not solved—it was only in the first stages of inception—and though the Zodiac Ball's answer eventually proved accurate, we had not asked it the right question.

This was in October, a time for every sort of inclement weather, and it rained steadily over the next few days. Fog banks moved in, transforming the sea into a mystic gray dimension, muffling the crash of waves on the reef so they sounded like bones being crunched in an enormous mouth. Not good weather for visiting the Burying Ground. But finally a sunny day dawned, and I set out to find Ray Milliken. I must admit I had been hurt by his lack of interest in renewing our acquaintance, but I had too many questions to let this stop me from hunting him up. Something about a colony built to attract aliens struck me as sinister rather than foolhardy— this being how it struck most people. I could not conceive of a person like Ray falling prey to such a crackpot notion; nor could I support the idea, one broached by Elizabeth, that he was involved in a swindle. She had heard that he had sold memberships in the colony and raised upwards of a hundred thousand dollars. The report was correct, but I doubt that Ray's original motives have much importance.

There was no road inland, only a snake-infested track, and so I borrowed a neighbor's dory and rowed along inside the reef. The tide was low, and iron-black coral heads lifted from the sea like the crenellated parapets of a drowned castle; beyond, the water was banded with sun-spattered streaks of slate and lavender. I could not help being nervous. People steered clear of the Burying Ground—it was rumored to harbor duppies . . . but then so was every other part of the island, and I suspect the actual reason for its desertion was that it had no worth to anyone, except perhaps to a herpetologist. The name of the place had come down from the Caribe; this was a puzzling fact, since all their grave sites were located high in the hills. Pottery and tools had been found in the area, but no solid evidence of burials. Two graves did exist, those belonging to Ezekiel Brooks, the son of William, a mate on Henry

Meachem's privateer, and to Ezekiel's son Carl. They had lived most of their lives on the land as hermits, and it was their solitary endurance that had ratified the Brooks family's claim to ownership.

On arriving, I tied the dory to a mangrove root and immediately became lost in a stand of scrub palmetto. I had sweated off my repellent, and mosquitoes swarmed over me; I stepped cautiously, probing the weeds with my machete to stir up any lurking snakes. After a short walk I came to a clearing about fifty yards square; it had been scraped down to the raw dirt. On the far side stood a bulldozer, and next to it was a thatched shelter beneath which a group of men were sitting. The primary colors and simple shapes—yellow bulldozer, red dirt, dark green walls of brush—made the clearing look like a test for motor skills that might be given to a gigantic child. As I crossed to the shelter, one of the men jumped up and walked toward me. It was Ray. He was shirtless, wearing boots and faded jeans, and a rosy sheen of new sunburn overlaid his tan.

"Frank," he said, pumping my hand.

I was taken aback by the religious affirmation in his voice—it was as if my name were something he had long treasured.

"I was planning to drop around in a few days," he said. "After we got set up. How are you?"

"Old and tormented," I said, slapping at a mosquito.

"Here." He gestured at the shelter. "Let's get into the shade."

"How are *you*?" I asked as we walked.

"Great, Frank," he replied. "Really great." His smile seemed the product of an absolute knowledge that things, indeed, were really great.

He introduced me to the others; I cannot recall their names, a typical sampling of Jims and Daves and Toms. They all had Ray's Krishna-conscious smile, his ultrasincerity, and they delighted in sharing with me their lunch of banana fritters and coconut. "Isn't this food beautiful?" said one. There was so much beatitude around me that I, grumpy from the heat and mosquitoes, felt like a heathen among them. Ray kept staring at me, smiling, and this was the main cause of my discomfort. I had the impression that something was shining too brightly behind his eyes, a kind of manic brilliance flaring in him the way an old light bulb flares just before it goes dark for good. He began to tell me of the improvements they were planning—wells, electronic mosquito traps, generators, schools with computers, a medical clinic for the islanders, on and on. His friends chimed in with additions to the list, and I had the feeling that I was listening to a well-rehearsed litany.

"I thought you were going to live off the land like the Caribe," I said.

"Oh, no," said Ray. "There are some things they did that we're going to do, but we'll do them better."

"Suppose the government denies your permits?"

I was targeted by a congregation of imperturbable smiles. "They came through two days ago," said Ray. "We're going to call the colony Port Ezekiel."

After lunch, Ray led me through the brush to a smaller clearing where half-a-dozen shelters were erected; hammocks were strung beneath each one. His had a fringe of snakeskins tacked to the roofpoles, at least thirty of them; they were crusted with flies, shifting horribly in the breeze. They were mostly yellowjaws—the local name for the fer-de-lance—and he said they killed ten or twelve a day. He sat cross-legged on the ground and invited me to take the hammock.

"Want to hear what I've been up to?" he asked.

"I've heard some of it."

"I bet you have." He laughed. "They think we're looney." He started as the bulldozer roared to life in the clearing behind us. "Do you remember showing me old Meachem's journal?"

"Yes."

"In a way you're responsible for all this." He waved at the dirt and the shelters. "That was my first real clue." He clasped his hands between his legs. "When I left here, I went back to the States. To school. I guess I was tired of traveling, or maybe I realized what a waste of space I'd been. I took up astronomy again. I wasn't very interested in it, but I wasn't more interested in anything else. Then one day I was going over a star chart, and I noticed something amazing. You see, while I was here I'd gotten into the Caribe culture. I used to wander around the Burying Ground looking for pottery. Found some pretty good pieces. And I'd hike up into the hills and make maps of the villages, where they'd stationed their lookouts and set their signal fires. I still had those maps, and what I'd noticed was that the pattern of the Caribe signal fires corresponded exactly to the constellation Cassiopeia. It was incredible! The size of the fires even corresponded to the magnitudes of the specific stars. I dropped out of school and headed back to the island." He gave me an apologetic look. "I tried to see you, but you were on the mainland."

"That must have been when Elizabeth's old boyfriend was giving us some trouble," I said. "We had to lie low for a while."

"I guess so." Ray reached for a pack that was propped against the wall and extracted a sheaf of 8″ by 11″ photographs; they appeared to consist chiefly of smudges and crooked lines. "I began digging through the old sites, especially here—this is the only place I found pottery with these particular designs . . . ."

From this point on I had difficulty keeping a straight face. Have you ever had a friend tell you something unbelievable, something they believed in so strongly that for you to discredit it would cause them pain? Perhaps it was a story about a transcendent drug experience or their conversion to Christianity. And did they stare at you earnestly as they spoke, watching your reactions? I mumbled affirmatively and nodded and avoided Ray's eyes. Compared to Ray's thesis, Erich von Däniken's ravings were a model of academic discipline. From the coincidental pattern of the signal fires, the incident of Meachem's UFO and some drunken tales he had solicited, from these smudges and lines that—if you exerted your imagination—bore a vague resemblance to bipeds wearing fishbowls on their heads, Ray had concocted an intricate scenario of alien visitation. It was essentially the same story as von Däniken's—the ancient star-seeding race. But where Ray's account differed was in his insistence that the aliens had had a special relationship with the Caribe, that the Caribe could call them down by lighting their fires. The landing Meachem had witnessed had been one of the last, because with the arrival of the English the Caribe had gradually retreated from the island, and the aliens no longer had a reason for visiting. Ray meant to lure them back by means of a laser display that would cast a brighter image of Cassiopeia than the Caribe could have managed; and when the aliens returned, he would entreat them to save our foundering civilization.

He had sold the idea of the colony by organizing a society to study the possibility of extraterrestrial life; he had presented slides and lectured on the Guanojan Outer Space Connection. I did not doubt his ability to make such a presentation, but I was amazed that educated people had swallowed it. He told me that his group included a doctor, an engineer, and sundry Ph.D.s, and that they all had some college background. And yet perhaps it was not so amazing. Even today there must be in America, as there were when I left it, a great many aimless and exhausted people like Ray and his friends, people damaged by some powerful trouble in their past and searching for an acceptable madness.

When Ray had finished, he looked at me soberly and said, "You think we're nuts, don't you?"

"No," I said; but I did not meet his eyes.

"We're not," he said.

"It's not important." I tried to pass it off as a joke. "Not down here, anyway."

"It's not just the evidence that convinced me," he said. "I knew it the first time I came to the Burying Ground. I could feel it."

"Do you remember what else we talked about the night I showed you Meachem's journal?" I am not sure why I wanted to challenge him; perhaps it was simply curiosity, a desire to know how fragile his calm mask really was.

"No," he said, and smiled. "We talked about a lot of things."

"We were talking about women, and then Spurgeon James interrupted us. But I think you were on the verge of telling me about a woman who had hurt you. Badly. Is all that behind you now?"

His smile dissolved, and the expression that flared briefly in its place was terrible to see—grieving, and baffled by the grief. This time it was *his* eyes that drifted away from mine. "You're wrong about me, Frank," he said. "Port Ezekiel is going to be something very special."

Shortly thereafter I made my excuses, and he walked me down to the dory. I invited him to visit me and have a meal, but I knew he would not come. I had threatened his beliefs, the beliefs he thought would shore him up, save him, and there was now a tangible barrier between us.

"Come back anytime," he called as I rowed away.

He stood watching me, not moving at all, an insignificant figure being merged by distance into the dark green gnarl of the mangrove; even when I could barely see him, he continued to stand there, as ritually attendant as his mythical Caribe hosts might have been while watching the departure of their alien guests.

Over five weeks passed before I again gave much thought to Ray and Port Ezekiel. (Port Ezekiel! That name as much as anything had persuaded me of Ray's insanity, smacking as it did of Biblical smugness, a common shelter for the deluded.) This was a studied lack of concern on my part. I felt he was lost and wanted no involvement with his tragedy. And besides, though the colony remained newsworthy, other events came to supersede it. The shrimp fleet struck against its parent American company, and riots broke out in the streets of Spanish Harbor. The old talk of independence was revived in the bars—idle talk, but it stirred the coals of anti-Americanism. Normally smiling faces frowned at me, the prices went up when I shopped in town, and once a child yelled at me, "Get off de island!" Small things, but they shook me. And since the establish-

ment of Port Ezekiel had been prelude to these events, I could not
help feeling that Ray was somehow to blame for this peculiarly
American darkness now shadowing my home.

Despite my attempt to ignore Ray's presence, I did have news of
him. I heard that he had paid Hatfield in full and that Jimmy
Mullins was on the warpath. Three thousand *lempira* must have
seemed a king's ransom to him; he lived in a tiny shanty with his
wife Hettie and two underfed children, and he had not worked for
over a year. I also heard that the shipments of modern conveniences
intended for Port Ezekiel had been waylaid by customs—someone
overlooked in the chain of bribery, no doubt—and that the colonists
had moved into the Burying Ground and were living in brushwood
shacks. And then, over a span of a couple of weeks, I learned that
they were deserting the colony. Groups of them turned up daily in
Meachem's Landing, complaining that Ray had misled them. Two
came to our door one evening, a young man and woman, both
delirious, sick with dysentery and covered with infected mosquito
bites. They were too wasted to tell us much, but after we had bedded
them down I asked the woman what was happening at the colony.

"It was awful," she said, twisting her hand in the blanket and
shivering. "Bugs and snakes . . . and . . . ." Her eyes squeezed shut.
"He just sits there with the snakes."

"You mean Ray?"

"I don't know," she said, her voice cracking into hysteria. "I don't
know."

Then, one night as Elizabeth and I were sitting on the porch, I
saw a flashlight beam weaving toward us along the beach. By the
way the light wavered, swooping up to illuminate the palm crowns,
down to shine upon a stoved-in dory, I could tell the bearer was
very drunk. Elizabeth leaned forward, peering into the dark. "Oh,
Lord," she said, holding her bathrobe closed. "It dat damn Jimmy
Mullins." She rose and went into the house, pausing at the door to
add, "If he after foolin' with me, you tell him I'm goin' to speak
with my uncle 'bout him."

Mullins stopped at the margin of the porch light to urinate, then
he staggered up onto the steps; he dropped his flashlight, and it
rolled over beside my machete, which was propped by the door.
He was wearing his town clothes—a white rayon shirt with the silk-
screened photo of a soccer star on the back, and brown slacks
spattered with urine. Threads of saliva hung from his chin.

"Mr. Frank, sir," he said with great effort. His eyes rolled up,
and for a moment I thought he was going to pass out; but he pulled
himself together, shook his head to clear the fog, and said, "De
mon have got to pay me."

I wanted no part of his feud with Hatfield. "Why don't I give you a ride home?" I said. "Hettie'll be worried."

Blearily, he focused on me, clinging to a support post. "Dat boog Yankee clot have cheated me," he said. "You talk to him, Mr. Frank. You tell him he got to pay."

"Ray Milliken? He doesn't owe you anything."

"Somebody owe me!" Mullins flailed his arm at the night. "And I ain't got de force to war with Hatfield." He adopted a clownish expression of sadness. "I born in de summer and never get no bigger den what you seein now."

So, sucked along by the feeble tide of anti-Americanism, Mullins had given up on Hatfield and shifted his aim to a more vulnerable target. I told him that Ray was crazy and would likely not respond to either threats or logic; but Mullins insisted that Ray should have checked Hatfield's claim before paying him. Finally I agreed to speak to Ray on his behalf and—somewhat mollified—he grew silent. He clung to the post, pouting; I settled back in my chair. It was a beautiful night, the phosphorescent manes of the breakers tossing high above the reef, and I wished he would leave us alone to the view.

"Damn boog Yankee!" He reeled away from the post and careened against the doorframe; his hand fell upon my machete. Before I could react, he picked it up and slashed at the air. "I cut dat bastard down to de deck!" he shouted, glaring at me.

The moment seemed endless, as if the flow of time had snagged on the point of the machete. Drunk, he might do anything. I felt weak and helpless, my stomach knotted by a chill. The blade looked to have the same drunken glitter as his eyes. God knows what might have happened, but at that moment Elizabeth—her robe belling open, eyes gleaming crazily—sneaked up behind him and smacked him on the neck with an ax handle. Her first blow sent him tottering forward, the machete still raised in a parody of attack; and the second drove him off the porch to sprawl facedown in the sand.

Later, after John James and Hettie had dragged Mullins home, as Elizabeth and I lay in bed, I confessed that I had been too afraid to move during the confrontation. "Don't vex yourself, Frank," she said. "Dere's enough trouble on de island dat sooner or later you be takin' care of some of mine." And after we had made love, she curled against me, tucked under my arm, and told me of a dream that had frightened her the previous night. I knew what she was doing—nothing about her was mysterious—and yet, as with every woman I have known, I could not escape the feeling that a stranger lay beside me, someone whose soul had been molded by a stronger gravity and under a hotter star.

                              *   *   *

I spent the next morning patching things up with Mullins, making
him a gift of vegetable seeds and listening to his complaints, and I
did not leave for the Burying Ground until midafternoon. It had
rained earlier, and gray clouds were still passing overhead, hazy
fans of sunlight breaking through now and again. The chop of the
water pulled against me, and it was getting on toward sunset by the
time I arrived—out on the horizon the sea and sky were blending
in lines of blackish squalls. I hurried through the brush, intending
to convey my warning as quickly as possible and be home before
the winds; but when I reached the first clearing, I stopped short.

The thatch and poles of the brushwood huts were strewn over
the dirt, torn apart, mixed in with charred tin cans, food wrappers,
the craters of old cooking fires, broken tools, mildewed paperbacks,
and dozens of conch shells, each with their whorled tops sliced
off—that must have been a staple of their diet. I called Ray's name,
and the only answer was an intensification in the buzzing of the
flies. It was like the aftermath of a measly war, stinking and silent.
I picked my way across the litter to the second clearing and again
was brought up short. An identical mess carpeted the dirt and
Ray's shelter remained intact, the fringe of rotting snakeskins still
hanging from the roofpoles—but that was not what had drawn my
attention.

A trench had been dug in front of the shelter and covered with
a sheet of wire mesh; large rocks held the wire in place. Within the
trench were forty or fifty snakes. *Coralitos*, yellowjaws, Tom Goffs,
cottonmouths. Their slithering, their noses scraping against the
wire as they tried to escape, created a sibilance that tuned my nerves
a notch higher. As I stepped over the trench and into the shelter,
several of them struck at me; patches of the mesh glistened with
their venom. Ray's hammock was balled up in a corner, and the
ground over which it had swung had been excavated; the hole was
nearly full of murky water—groundwater by the briny smell. I
poked a stick into it and encountered something hard at a depth
of about three feet. A boulder, probably. Aside from Ray's pack,
the only other sign of habitation was a circular area of dirt that had
been patted smooth; dozens of bits of oyster shell were scattered
across it, all worked into geometric shapes—stars, hexagons,
squares, and so forth. A primitive gameboard. I did not know what
exactly to make of these things, but I knew they were the trappings
of madness. There was an air of savagery about them, of a mind
as tattered as its surroundings, shriveled to the simplest of considerations; and I did not believe that the man who lived here would

understand any warning I might convey. Suddenly afraid, I turned to leave and was given such a shock that I nearly fell back into the water-filled pit.

Ray was standing an arm's length away, watching me. His hair was ragged, shoulder-length, and bound by a cottonmouth-skin band; his shorts were holed and filth-encrusted. The dirt smeared on his cheeks and forehead made his eyes appear round and staring. Mosquito bites speckled his chest—though not as many as had afflicted the colonists I had treated. In his right hand he carried a long stick with a twine noose at one end, and in his left hand was a burlap sack whose bottom humped and writhed.

"Ray," I said, sidling away from him.

I expected a croak or a scream of rage for an answer, but when he spoke it was in his usual voice. "I'm glad you're here," he said. He dropped the sack—it was tied at the top—beside the trench and leaned his stick against the wall of the shelter.

Still afraid, but encouraged by the normalcy of his actions, I said, "What's going on here?"

He gave me an appraising stare. "You better see her for yourself, Frank. You wouldn't believe me if I told you." He sat cross-legged beside the patch of smoothed dirt and began picking up the shell-bits. The way he picked them up fascinated me—so rapidly, pinching them up between thumb and forefinger, and funneling them back into his palm with the other three fingers, displaying an expert facility. And, I noticed, he was only picking up the hexagons.

"Sit down," he said. "We've got an hour or so to kill."

I squatted on the opposite side of the gameboard. "You can't stay here, Ray."

He finished with the hexagons, set them aside, and started on the squares. "Why not?"

I told him about Mullins, but as I had presumed he was unconcerned. All his money, he said, was tied up in investment funds; he would find a way to deal with Mullins. He was calm in the face of my arguments, and though this calm seemed to reflect a more deep-seated confidence than had been evident on my first visit, I did not trust it. To my mind the barrier between us had hardened, become as tricky to navigate as the reef around the island. I gave up arguing and sat quietly, watching him play with the shells. Night was falling, banks of dark clouds were rushing overhead, and gusts of wind shredded the thatch. Heavy seas would soon be washing over the reef, and it would be beyond my strength to row against them. But I did not want to abandon him. Under the dreary storm-light, the wreckage of Port Ezekiel looked leached of color and vitality, and I had an image of the two of us being survivors of a great disaster, stalemated in debate over the worth of restarting civilization.

"It's almost time," he said, breaking the silence. He gazed out to the swaying tops of the bushes that bounded the clearing. "This is so wild, Frank. Sometimes I can't believe it myself."

The soft astonishment in his voice brought the pathos of his situation home to me. "Jesus, Ray," I said. "Come back with me. There's nothing here."

"Tell me that when you've seen her." He stood and walked over to the water-filled pit. "You were right, Frank. I was crazy, and maybe I still am. But I was right, too. Just not in the way I expected."

"Right about what?"

He smiled. "Cassiopeia." He hunkered down by the pit. "I've got to get in the water. There has to be physical contact or else the exchange can't occur. I'll be unconscious for a while, but don't worry about it. All right?"

Without waiting for my approval, he lowered himself into the water. He seemed to be groping for something, and he shifted about until he had found a suitable position. His shoulders just cleared the surface. Then he bowed his head so that I could no longer see his face.

My thoughts were in turmoil. His references to "her," his self-baptism, and now the sight of his disembodied head and tendrils of hair floating on the water, all this had rekindled my fear. I decided that the best thing I could do for him, for both of us, would be to knock him out, to haul him back to Sandy Bay for treatment. But as I looked around for a club, I noticed something that rooted me in my tracks. The snakes had grown frantic in their efforts to escape; they were massed at the far side of the trench, pushing at the mesh with such desperation that the rocks holding it down were wobbling. And then, an instant later, I began to sense another presence in the clearing.

How did I sense this? It was similar to the feeling you have when you are alone for the first time with a woman to whom you are attracted, how it seems you could close your eyes and stopper your ears and still be aware of her every shift in position, registering these changes as thrills running along your nerves and muscles. And I knew beyond a shadow of a doubt that this presence was female. I whirled around, certain that someone was behind me. Nothing. I turned back to Ray. Tremors were passing through his shoulders, and his breath came in hoarse shudders as if he had been removed from his natural element and were having trouble with the air. Scenes from old horror movies flashed through my brain. The stranger lured to an open grave by an odd noise; the ghoul rising from the swamp, black water dripping from his talons; the maniac with the split-personality, smiling, hiding a bloody knife under his coat. And then I saw, or imagined I saw, movement on the surface of the water; it was bulging—not bubbling, but the entire surface bulging upward as if some force below were building to an explosion. Terrified, I took a backward step, and as my foot nudged the wire screen over the trench, as the snakes struck madly at the mesh, terrified themselves, I broke and ran.

I went crashing through the brush, certain that Ray was after me, possessed by some demon dredged up from his psyche . . . or by worse. I did not stop to untie the dory, but grabbed the machete from beneath the seat, hacked the rope in two, and pulled hard out into the water. Waves slopped over the bow, the dory bucked and plunged, and the noise from the reef was deafening. But even had a hurricane been raging, I would not have put back into the Burying Ground. I strained at the oars, gulping down breaths that were half salt spray, and I did not feel secure until I had passed beyond Punta Palmetto and was hidden from the view of whatever was now wandering that malarial shore.

After a night's sleep, after dosing my fears with the comforts of home, all my rational structures were re-erected. I was ashamed at having run, at having left Ray to endure his solitary hell, and I assigned everything I had seen and felt to a case of nerves or—and I did not think this impossible—to poltergeistlike powers brought on by his madness. Something had to be done for him. As soon as I had finished breakfast, I drove over to Meachem's Landing and asked the militia for their help. I explained the situation to one Sergeant Colmenares, who thanked me for my good citizenship but said he could do nothing unless the poor man had committed a crime. If I had been clearheaded, I would have invented a crime, anything to return Ray to civilization; instead, I railed at the sergeant, stumped out of the office, and drove back to Sandy Bay.

Elizabeth had asked me to buy some cooking oil, and so I stopped off at Sarah's Store, a green-painted shanty the size of a horse stall not far from The Chicken Shack. Inside, there was room for three people to stand at the counter, and behind it Sarah was enthroned on her stool. An old woman, almost ninety, with a frizzy crown of white hair and coal-black skin that took on bluish highlights under the sun. It was impossible to do business with her and not hear the latest gossip, and during our conversation she mentioned that Ray had stopped in the night before.

"He after havin' a strife wit dat Jimmy Mullins," she said. "Now

Jimmy he have followed dis tourist fella down from de Sea Breeze where dey been drinkin', and he settin' up to beg de mon fah somet'ing. You know how he gets with his lies." She did her Jimmy Mullins imitation, puffing out her chest and frowning. " 'I been in Vietnam,' he say, and show de mon dat scar from when he shot himself in de leg. 'I bleed fah Oncle Sam, and now Oncle Sam goin' to take care of dis negro.' Den in walk Ray Milliken. He did not look left or right but jus' stare at de cans of fruit juice and ax how much dey was. Talkin' wit dat duppy voice. Lord! De duppy force crawlin' all over him. Now dis tourist fella have gone 'cause de sight of Ray wit his wild look and his scrapes have made de fella leery. But Jimmy jus' stand dere, watchful. And when Ray pay fah de juice, Jimmy say, 'Gimme dat money.' Ray make no reply. He drink de juice down and den he amble out de door. Jimmy follow him and he screamin'. 'You scorn me like dat!' he say. 'You scorn me like dat!' It take no wisdom to know dere's blood in de air, so I set a Superior on de counter and call out, 'Jimmy, you come here 'fore yo' beer lose de chill.' And dat lure him back."

I asked Sarah what she meant by "duppy voice," but she would only say, "Dat's what it were—de duppy voice." I paid for my oil, and as I went out the door, she called, "God bless America!" She always said it as a farewell to her American customers; most thought she was putting them on, but knowing Sarah's compassion for waifs and strays, her conviction that material wealth was the greatest curse one could have, I believe it was heartfelt.

Sarah's story had convinced me of the need for action, and that afternoon I returned to the Burying Ground. I did not confront Ray; I stationed myself behind some bushes twenty feet to the right of the shelter. I planned to do as I should have done before—hit him and drag him back to Sandy Bay. I had with me Elizabeth's ax handle and an ample supply of bug repellent.

Ray was not at the clearing when I arrived, and he did not put in an appearance until after five o'clock. This time he was carrying a guitar, probably gleaned from the debris. He sat beside the trench and began chording, singing in a sour, puny voice that sent a chill through me despite the heat; it seemed he was giving tongue to the stink of the rotting snakeskins, amplifying the whine of the insects. The sun reflected an orange fire on the panels of the guitar.

"Cas-si-o-pee-ee-ya," he sang, country-western style, "I'll be yours tonight." He laughed—cracked, high-pitched laughter—and rocked back and forth on his haunches. "Cas-si-o-pee-ee-ya, why don't you treat me right?"

Either he was bored or else that was the whole song. He set down the guitar and for the next hour he hardly moved, scratching, looking up to the sun as if checking its decline. Sunset faded, and the evening star climbed above Alps of purple cumulus. Finally, stretching and shaking out the kinks, he stood and walked to the pit and lowered himself into the water. It was at this point that I had intended to hit him, but my curiosity got the best of me and I decided to observe him instead; I told myself that I would be better able to debunk his fantasies if I had some personal experience of them. I would hit him after he had fallen asleep.

It was over an hour before he emerged from the water, and when he did I was very glad to be hidden. Icy stars outlined the massed clouds, and the moon had risen three-quarters full, transforming the clearing into a landscape of black and silvery-gray. Everything had a shadow, even the tattered fronds lying on the ground. There was just enough wind to make the shadows tremble, and the only noise apart from the wind was the pattering of lizards across the desiccated leaves. From my vantage I could not see if the water was bulging upward, but soon the snakes began their hissing, their pushing at the mesh, and I felt again that female presence.

Then Ray leaped from the pit.

It was the most fluid entrance I have ever seen—like a dancer mounting onto stage from a sunken level. He came straight up in a shower of silver droplets and landed with his legs straddling the pit, snapping his head from side to side. He stepped out of the shelter, pacing back and forth along the trench, and as the light struck him full, I stopped thinking of him as *he*.

Even now, at a remove from the events, I have difficulty thinking of Ray as a man; the impression of femininity was so powerful that it obliterated all my previous impressions of him. Though not in the least dainty or swishy, every one of his movements had a casual female sensuality, and his walk was potently feminine in the way of a lioness. His face was leaner, sleeker of line. Aside from these changes was the force of that presence pouring over me. I had the feeling that I was involved in a scene out of prehistory—the hominid warrior with his club spying on an unknown female, scenting her, knowing her sex along the circuits of his nerves. When he . . . when she had done pacing, she squatted beside the trench, removed one of the rocks, and lifted the edge of the screen. With incredible speed, she reached in and snatched out a wriggling yellowjaw. I heard a sickening mushy crack as she crushed its head between her thumb and forefinger. She skinned it with her teeth, worrying a rip, tearing loose long peels until the blood-rilled meat gleamed in the moonlight. All this in a matter of seconds. Watching her eat, I found I was gripping the ax handle so tightly that my hand ached.

She tossed the remains of the snake into the bushes, then she stood—again, that marvelous fluidity—and turned toward the spot where I was hiding.

"Frank," she said; she barely pronounced the *a* and trilled the *r*, so that the word came out as "Frrenn-kuh."

It was like hearing one's name spoken by an idol. The ax handle slipped from my hand. I stood, weak-kneed. If her speed afoot was equal to her speed of hand, I had no chance of escape.

"I won't kill you," she said, her accent slurring the words into the rhythm of a musical phrase. She went back under the shelter and sat beside the patch of smoothed dirt.

The phrasing of her assurance did nothing to ease my fears, yet I came forward. I told myself that this was Ray, that he had created this demoness from his sick needs and imaginings; but I could not believe it. With each step I became more immersed in her, as if her soul were too large for the body and I was passing through its outer fringes. She motioned me to sit, and as I did, her strangeness lapped over me like heat from an open fire.

My throat was constricted, but I managed to say, "Cassiopeia?"

Her lips thinned and drew back from her teeth in a feral smile. "That's what Ray calls me. He can't pronounce my name. My home . . ." She glanced at the sky. "The clouds obscure it."

I gawped at her; I had so many questions, I could not frame even one. Finally I said, "Meachem's UFO. Was that your ship?"

"The ship was destroyed far from here. What Meachem saw was a ghost, or rather the opening and closing of a road traveled by one." She gestured at the pit. "It lies there, beneath the water."

I remembered the hard something I had poked with a stick; it had not felt in the least ectoplasmic, and I pointed this out.

" 'Ghost' is a translation of the word for it in my language," she said. "You touched the energy fields of a . . . a machine. It was equipped with a homing capacity, but its fields were disrupted by the accident that befell my ship. It can no longer open the roads between the worlds."

"Roads?" I said.

"I don't understand the roads, and if I could explain them it would translate as metaphysics. The islanders would probably accept the explanation, but I doubt you would." She traced a line in the dirt with her forefinger. "To enter the superluminal universe the body must die and be reanimated at journey's end. The other components of the life travel with the machine. All I know of the roads is that though journeys often last for years, they appear to be direct. When Meachem saw flame in the sky, it was because I came from flame, from the destruction of my ship."

"The machine . . ." I began.

"It's an engineered life form," she said. "You see, any life consists of a system of energy fields unified in the flesh. The machine is a partial simulation of that system, a kind of phantom life that's designed to sustain the most crucial of those fields—what you'd call the *anima*, the soul—until the body can be reanimated . . . or, if the body has been destroyed, until an artificial host has been supplied. Of course there was no such host here. So the machine attracted those whose souls were impaired, those with whom a temporary exchange could be made. Without embodiment I would have gone mad." She scooped up a handful of shell-bits. "I suppose I've gone mad in spite of it. I've rubbed souls with too many madmen."

She tossed out the shell-bits. A haphazard toss, I thought; but then I noticed that they had fallen into neat rows.

"The differences between us are too great for the exchange to be other than temporary," she went on. "If I didn't reenter the machine each morning, both I and my host—and the machine— would die."

Despite the evidence of my senses, this talk of souls and energy fields—reminding me of the occult claptrap of the sixties—had renewed my doubts. "People have been digging up the Burying Ground for years," I said. "Why hasn't someone found this machine?"

"It's a very clever machine," she said, smiling again. "It hides from those who aren't meant to find it."

"Why would it choose only impaired hosts?"

"To choose an unimpaired one would run contrary to the machine's morality. And to mine."

"How does it attract them?"

"My understanding of the machine is limited, but I assume there's a process of conditioning involved. Each time I wake in a new host, it's always the same. A clearing, a shelter, the snakes."

I started to ask another question, but she waved me off.

"You act as though I must prove something," she said. "I have no wish to prove anything. Even if I did, I'm not sure I could. Most of my memories were stripped from me at the death of my body, and those that remain are those that have stained the soul. In a sense I'm as much Ray as I am myself. Each night I inherit his memories, his abilities. It's like living in a closet filled with someone else's belongings."

I continued to ask questions, with part of my mind playing the psychiatrist, eliciting answers in order to catalog Ray's insanity; yet my doubts were fading. She could not recall the purpose of her journey or even of her life, but she said that her original body had been similar to the human form—her people, too, had a myth of an ancient star-seeding race—though it had been larger, stronger, with superior organs of perception. Her world was a place of thick jungles, and her remote ancestors had been nocturnal predators. An old Caribe man had been her first host on the island; he had wandered onto the Burying Ground six months after her arrival, maddened by pain from a cancer that riddled his stomach. His wife had been convinced that a goddess had possessed him, and she had brought the tribal elders to bear witness.

"They were afraid of me," she said. "And I was equally afraid of them. Little devil-men with ruddy skins and necklaces of jaguar teeth. They built fires around me, hemming me in, and they'd dance and screech and thrust their spears at me through the flames. It was nightmarish. I knew they might lose control of their fear at any second and try to kill me. I might have defended myself, but life was sacred to me then. They were whole, vital beings. To harm them would have been to mock what remained of me."

She had cultivated them, and they had responded by providing her with new hosts, by arranging their fires to depict the constellation Cassiopeia, hoping to call down other gods to keep her company. It had been a fruitless hope, and there were other signals that would have been more recognizable to her people, but she had been touched by their concern and had not told them.

I will not pretend that I recall exactly everything she said, yet I believe what follows captures the gist of her tale. At first I was disconcerted by its fluency and humanity; but I soon realized that not only had she had two centuries in which to practice her humanity, not only was she taking advantage of Ray's gift for storytelling, but also that she had told much of it before.

For twenty-two years [she said] I inhabited Caribe bodies, most of them terribly damaged. Cripples, people with degenerative diseases, and once a young girl with a huge dent in her skull, an injury gotten during a raid. Though my energies increased the efficiency of their muscles, I endured all their agonies. But as the Caribe retreated from the island in face of the English, even this tortured existence was denied to me. I spent four years within the machine, despairing of ever leaving it again. Then, in 1819, Ezekiel Brooks stumbled onto the Burying Ground. He was a retarded boy of seventeen and had become lost in the mangrove. When his father, William, came in search of him, he found me instead. He remembered the fiery object that had fallen from the sky and was delighted to have solved a puzzle that had baffled his captain for so many years. Thereafter he visited every week and dragged old Henry Meachem along.

Meachem was in his seventies then, fat, with a doughy, wrinkled face and long gray hair done up into ringlets; he affected foppish clothes and a lordly manner. He had the gout and had to be carried through the mangrove by his slaves. They brought with them a teakwood chair, its grips carved into lions' heads, and there he'd sit, wheezing, bellowing at the slaves to keep busy with their fly whisks, plying me with questions. He did not believe my story, and on his second visit, a night much like this one, moonstruck and lightly winded, he was accompanied by a Spanish woman, a scrawny old hag enveloped in a black shawl and skirt, who he told me was a witch.

"Sit you down with Tía Claudia," he said, prodding her forward with his cane, "and she'll have the truth of you. She'll unravel your thoughts like a ball of twine."

The old woman sat cross-legged beside the pit, pulled a lump of clouded crystal from her skirt, and set it on the ground before her. Beneath the shawl her shadowed wrinkles had the look of a pattern in tree bark, and despite her apparent frailty I could feel her presence as a chill pressure on my skin. Uneasy, I sat down on the opposite side of the pit. Her eyelids drooped, her breath grew shallow and irregular, and the force of her life flooded me, intensifying in the exercise of her power. The fracture planes inside the crystal appeared to be gleaming with more than refracted moonlight, and as I stared at them, a drowsy sensation stole over me . . . but then I was distracted by a faint rushing noise from the pit.

Hatchings of fine lines were etching the surface of the water, sending up sprays of mist. The patterns they formed resembled the fracture planes of the crystal. I glanced up at Tía Claudia. She was trembling, a horror-stricken expression on her face, and the rushing noise was issuing from her parted lips as though she had been invaded by a ghostly wind. The ligature of her neck was cabled, her hands were clawed. I looked back to the pit. Beneath the surface, shrinking and expanding in a faltering rhythm, was a point of crimson light. Tía Claudia's power, I realized, was somehow akin to that of the machine. She was healing it, restoring its homing capacity, and it was opening a road! Hope blazed in me. I eased into the pit, and the fields gripped me, stronger than ever. But as the old woman let out a shriek and slumped to the ground, they weakened; the point of light shrank to nothing, gone glimmering like my hope. It had only been a momentary restoration, a product of her mind joined to the machine's.

Two of Meachem's slaves helped Tía Claudia to her feet, but she shook them off and backed out of the shelter, her eyes fixed on the pit. She leaned against Meachem's chair for support.

"Well?" he said.

"Kill him!" she said. "He's too dangerous, too powerful."

"Him?" Meachem laughed.

Tía Claudia said that I was who I claimed to be and argued that I was a threat to him. I understood that she was really concerned with my threat to her influence over Meachem, but I was so distressed by the lapsing of the machine's power that I didn't care what they did to me. Bathed in the silvery light, stars shining around their heads, they seemed emblematic of something—perhaps of all humanity—this ludicrous old pirate in his ruffled shirt, and, shaking her knobbly finger at him, the manipulative witch who wanted to be his master.

After that night, Meachem took me under his wing. I learned that he was an exile, outlawed by the English and obsessed with the idea of returning home, and I think he was happy to have met someone even more displaced than he. Occasionally he'd invite me to his house, a gabled building of pitch-coated boards that clung to a strip of iron shore east of Sandy Bay. He'd sit me down in his study and read to me for hours from his journals; he thought that—being a member of an advanced civilization—I'd have the wit to appreciate his intellect. The study was a room that reflected his obession with England, its walls covered with Union Jacks, a riot of scarlet and blue. Sometimes, watching the flies crusting the lip of his pewter mug, his sagging face looming above them, the colors on the wall appearing to drip in the unsteady glare of the oil lamp . . . sometimes it seemed a more nightmarish environment than the Caribe's circle of fires. He'd pore over the pages, now and again saying, "Ah, here's one you'll like," and would quote the passage.

" 'Wars,' " he read to me once, " 'are the solstices of the human spirit, ushering in winter to a young man's thought and rekindling the spring of an old man's anger.' "

Every page was filled with aphorisms like that—high-sounding, yet empty of meaning except as regarded his own nature. He was the cruelest man I've ever known. A wife-beater, a tyrant to his slaves and children. Some nights he would have himself borne down to the beach, order torches lit, and watch as those who had offended him were flogged—often to the death—with stalks of withe. After witnessing one of the floggings, I considered killing him, even though such an act would have been in violation of everything I believed.

Then one night he brought another woman to the Burying Ground, a young mulatto girl named Nora Mullins.

"She be weak-minded like Ezekiel," said Meachem. "She'll make you a perfect wife."

She would have run, but his slaves herded her forward. Her eyes darted left and right, her hands fidgeted with the folds of her skirt.

"I don't need a wife," I said.

"Don't you now? Here's a chance to create your own lineage, to escape that infernal contraption of yours. Nora'll bear you a child, and if blood holds true, it'll be as witless as its parents. After Ezekiel's gone, you can take up residence in your heir." His laugh disintegrated into a hacking cough.

The idea had logic behind it, but the thought of being intimate with a member of another species, especially one whose sex might be said to approximate my own, repelled me. Further, I didn't trust his motives. "Why are you doing this?" I asked.

"I'm dyin'." The old monster worked up a tear over the prospect. "Nora's my legacy to you. I've always thought it a vast irony that a high-flyin' soul such as yourself should have been brought so low. It'll please me to think of you marooned among generations of idiots while I'm wingin' off to my reward."

"This island is your reward," I said. "Even the soul dies."

"You know that for a fact?" He was worried.

"No," I said, relenting. "No one knows that."

"Well, then I'll come back to haunt you."

But he never did.

I had intended to send Nora away after he left, but Ezekiel—though too timid to approach her sexually—found her attractive and I didn't want to deprive him of her companionship. In addition, I began to realize how lonely I had been myself. The idea of keeping her with me and fathering a child seemed more and more appealing, and a week later, using Ezekiel's memories to rouse lust, I set out to become a family man.

What a strange union that was! The moon sailing overhead, chased by ragged blue clouds; the wind and insects and frogs combining into a primitive music. Nora was terrified. She whimpered and rolled her eyes and halfheartedly tried to fight me off. I don't believe she was clear as to what was happening, but eventually her instincts took control. It would be hard to imagine two more inept virgins. I had a logical understanding of the act, at least one superior to Nora's; but this was counterbalanced by her sluggish coordination and my revulsion. Somehow we managed. I think it was mainly due to the fact that she sensed I was like her, female in a way that transcended anatomy, and this helped us to employ tenderness with one another. Over the succeeding nights an honest affection developed between us; though her speech was limited to strangled cries, we learned to communicate after a fashion, and our lovemaking grew more expert, more genuine.

Fourteen years we were together. She bore me three children, two stillborn, but the third a slow-witted boy whom we named Carl—it was a name that Nora could almost pronounce. By day she and Ezekiel were brother and sister, and by night she and I were husband and wife. Carl needed things the land couldn't provide, milk, vegetables, and these were given us by William Brooks; but when he died several years after Carl's birth, taking with him the secret of my identity, Nora began going into Sandy Bay to beg— or so I thought until I was visited by her brother Robert. I knew something must be wrong. We were the shame of the family; they had never acknowledged us in any way.

"Nora she dead," he told me. "Murdered."

He explained that two of her customers had been fighting over her, and that when she had tried to leave, one—a man named Halsey Brooks—had slit her throat. I didn't understand. Customers? Nothing Mullins said made sense.

"Don't you know she been whorin'?" he said. "Mon, you a worse fool dan I think. She been whorin' dese six, seven years."

"Carl," I said. "Where is he?"

"My woman takin' charge of him," he said. "I come for to bring you to dis Brooks. If you ain't mon enough, den I handle it myself. Family's family, no matter how crooked de tie."

What I felt then was purely human—loss, rage, guilt over the fact that Nora had been driven to such straits. "Show him to me," I said.

Hearing the murderousness in my voice, Robert Mullins smiled.

Halsey Brooks was drinking in a shanty bar, a single room lit by oil lamps whose glass tops were so sooty that the light penetrated them as baleful orange gleams. The rickety tables looked like black spiders standing at attention. Brooks was sitting against the rear wall, a big slack-bellied man with skin the color of sunbaked mud, wearing a shirt and trousers of sailcloth. Mullins stationed himself out of sight at the door, his machete at the ready in case I failed, and I went inside.

Catching sight of me, Brooks grinned and drew a knife from his boot. "Dat little squint of yours be missin' you down in hell," he said, and threw the knife.

I twisted aside, and the knife struck the wall. Brooks's eyes widened. He got to his feet, wary; the other customers headed for the door, knocking over chairs in their haste.

"You a quick little nigger," said Brooks, advancing on me. "But quick won't help you now."

He would have been no match for me; but confronted by the actual task of shedding blood, I found that I couldn't go through with it. I was nauseated by the thought that I had even considered it. I backed away, tripped over a chair, and went sprawling in the corner.

"Dat de best you got to offer?" said Brooks, chuckling.

As he reached for me, Mullins slipped up behind and slashed him across the neck and back. Brooks screamed—an incredibly girlish sound for a man so large—and sank to his knees beside me, trying to pinch together the lips of his wounds. He held a hand to his face, seemingly amazed by the redness. Then he pitched forward on top of me. The reek of his blood and sweat, just the feel of him in my hands as I started to push him away, all that drove me into a fury. One of his eyes was an inch from mine, half-closed and clouding over. He was dying, but I wanted to dig the last flicker of life out of him. I tore at his cheek with my teeth. The eye snapped open, I heard the beginning of his scream, and I remember nothing more until I threw him aside. His face was flayed to the muscle-strings, his nose was pulped, and there were brimming dark-red craters where his eyes had been.

"My God!" said Mullins, staring at the ruin of Brooks's head; he turned to me. "Go home! De thing more dan settled."

All my rage had drained and been replaced by self-loathing. Home! I *was* home. The island had eroded my spirit, transformed me into one of its violent creatures.

"Don't come 'round no more," said Mullins, wiping his blade on Brooks's trousers; he gave me a final look of disgust. "Get back to de damn Buryin' Ground where you belong."

Cassiopeia sprang to her feet and stepped out into the clearing. Her expression was grim, and I was worried that she might have worked herself into a rage by rehashing the killing. But she only walked a few paces away. Silvered by the moonlight, she looked unnaturally slim, and it seemed more than ever that I was seeing an approximation of her original form. The snakes had grown dead-still in the trench.

"You didn't really kill him," I said.

"I would have," she said. "But never again." She kicked at a pile of conch shells and sent them clattering down.

"What happened then?"

She did not answer for a moment, gazing out toward the sound of the reef. "I was sickened by the changes I'd undergone," she said. "I became a hermit, and after Ezekiel died I continued my hermitage in Carl's body. That poor soul!" She walked a little farther away. "I taught him to hide whenever men visited the Burying Ground. He lived like a wild animal, grubbing for roots, fishing with his bare hands. At the time it seemed the kindest thing I could do. I wanted to cleanse him of the taint of humanity. Of course that proved impossible . . . for both of us."

"You know," I said, "with all the technological advances these days, you might be able to contact . . . ."

"Don't you think I've considered my prospects!" she said angrily; and then, in a quieter tone, "I used to hope that human science would permit me to return home someday, but I'm not sure I want to anymore. I've been perverted by this culture. I'd be as repulsive to my people as Ezekiel was to Robert Mullins, and I doubt that I'd be comfortable among them myself."

I should have understood the finality of her loneliness—she had been detailing it in her story. But I understood now. She was a mixture of human and alien, spiritually a half-breed, gone native over a span of two centuries. She had no people, no place except this patch of sand and mangrove, no tradition except the clearing and the snakes and a game made of broken shells. "I'm sorry," I said.

"It's not your fault, Frank," she said, and smiled. "It's your American heritage that makes you tend to enshrine the obvious."

"Ray and I aren't a fair sample," I said defensively.

"I've known other Americans," she said. "They've all had that tendency. Everyone down here thought they were fools when they first came. They seemed totally unaware of the way things worked, and no one understood that their tremendous energy and capacity for deceit would compensate. But they were worse than either the pirates or the Spanish."

Without another word, she turned and walked toward the brush.

"Wait!" I said; I was eager to hear about her experiences with Americans.

"You can come back tomorrow, Frank," she said. "Though maybe you shouldn't."

"Why not?" Then, thinking that she might have some personal reason for distrusting Americans, I said, "I won't hurt you. I don't believe I'm physically capable of it."

"What a misleading way to measure security," she said. "In terms of hurt. You avoid using the word 'kill,' and yet you kill so readily. It's as though you're all pretending it's a secret."

She slipped into the brush, moving soundlessly, somehow avoiding the dry branches, the papery fronds.

I drove all over the island the next day, trying to find a tape recorder, eventually borrowing one from a tourist in Meachem's Landing. Half-baked delusions of grandeur had been roused in me. I would be the Schliemann of extraterrestrial research, uncovering the ruin of an alien beneath the waste of a human being. There would be best-sellers, talk shows, exclamations of academic awe. Of course there was no real proof. A psychiatrist would point out how conveniently pat the story was—the machine that hid itself, the loss of memory, the alien woman conjured up by a man whose disorder stemmed from a disappointment in love. He would say it was the masterwork of a gifted tale-spinner, complete with special effects. Yet I thought that whoever heard it would hear—as I had—the commonplace perfection of truth underlying its exotic detail.

I had forgotten my original purpose for visiting the Burying Ground, but that afternoon Jimmy Mullins turned up at my door, eager to learn if I had news for him. He was only moderately drunk and had his wife Hettie in tow—a slender, mahogany-skinned woman wearing a dirty blue dress. She was careworn, but still prettier than Mullins deserved. I was busy and put him off, telling him that I was exploring something with Ray that could lead to money. And, I realized, I was. Knowing his character, I had assumed Mullins was attempting to swindle Hatfield; but Nora Mullins's common-law marriage to Ezekiel Brooks gave credence to his claim. I should have explained it to him. As it was, he knew I was just getting rid of him, and Hettie had to pull him down from the porch to cut short his arguments. My news must have given him some heart, though, because a few minutes later Hatfield knocked at the door.

"What you tellin' Jimmy?" he asked. "He braggin' dat you got proof de Buryin' Ground his."

I denied the charge and told him what I had learned, but not how I had learned it.

"I never mean to cheat Jimmy," he said, scratching his head. "I just want to make sure he not cheatin' me. If he got a case . . . well, miserable as he is, he blood."

After he left, I had problems. I found I needed new batteries for the recorder and had to drive into Meachem's Landing; and when I returned home I had an argument with Elizabeth that lasted well past sunset. As a result, I did not start out for the Burying Ground until almost ten o'clock, and while I was stowing my pack in the dory, I saw Cassiopeia walking toward me along the beach.

It was a clear night, the shadows of the palms sharp on the sand, and each time she passed through a shadow, it seemed I was seeing Ray; but then, as she emerged into the light, I would undergo a peculiar dislocation and realize that it was not Ray at all.

"I was on my way out to you," I said. "You didn't have to come into town."

"I gave up being a hermit long ago, Frank," she said. "I like coming here. Sometimes it jogs my memory to be around so many others, though there's nothing really familiar about them."

"What do you remember?"

"Not much. Flashes of scenery, conversations. But once I did remember something concrete. I think it had to do with my work, my profession. I'll show you."

She squatted, smoothed a patch of sand, and began tracing a design. As with all her actions, this one was quick and complicated; she used three fingers of each hand, moving them in contrary directions, adding a squiggle here, a straight line there, until the design looked like a cross between a mandala and a printed circuit. Watching it evolve, I was overcome by a feeling of peace, not the drowsiness of hypnotism, but a powerful, enlivening sensation that alerted me to the peacefulness around me. The soughing of the palms, the lapping of the water, the stillness of the reef—it was low tide. This feeling was as potent as the effect of a strong drug, and yet it had none of the fuzziness that I associate with drugs. By the time she had finished, I was so wrapped in contentment that all my curiosity had abated—I was not even curious about the design— and I put aside for the moment the idea of recording her. We strolled eastward along the beach without talking, past Sarah's Store and The Chicken Shack, taking in the sights. The tin roofs of the shanties gleamed under the moonlight, and, their imperfections hidden by the darkness, the shanties themselves looked quaint and cozy. Shadows were dancing behind the curtains, soft reggae drifted on the breeze. Peace. When I finally broke the silence, it was not out of curiosity but in the spirit of that peace, of friendship.

"What about Ray?" I asked. "He was in pretty rough shape when I visited him the other afternoon."

"He's better off than he would be elsewhere," she said. "Calmer, steadier."

"But he can't be happy."

"Maybe not," she said. "But in a way I'm what he was always seeking, even before he began to deteriorate. He actually thinks of me in romantic terms." She laughed—a trilling note. "I'm very happy with him myself. I've never had a host with so few defects."

We were drawing near the New Byzantine Church of the Archangel, a small white-frame building set back from the shore. This being Friday, it had been turned into a movie theater. The light above the door illuminated a gaudy poster that had been inserted into the glass case normally displaying the subject of the sermon; the poster showed two bloodstained Chinese men fighting with curved knives. Several teenagers were silhouetted by the light, practicing martial-arts kicks beside the steps—like stick figures come to life—and a group of men was watching them, passing a bottle. One of the men detached himself from the group and headed toward us. Jimmy Mullins.

"Mr. Milliken!" he shouted. "Dis de owner of de Buryin' Ground wantin' to speak with you!"

Cassiopeia spun on her heel and went wading out into the water. Infuriated, Mullins ran after her, and—myself infuriated at the interruption, this breach of peace—I stuck out a foot and tripped him. I threw myself on top of him, trying for a pin, but he was stronger than I had supposed. He wrenched an arm loose, stunned me with a blow to the head, and wriggled free. I clamped my arms around his leg, and he dragged me along, yelling at Cassiopeia.

"Pay me my money, bastard!"

"*I'll* pay you!" I said out of desperation.

It might have been a magic spell that I had pronounced. He quit dragging me; I clung to his leg with one hand, and with the other I wiped a crust of mucky sand from my mouth.

"You goin' to pay me three thousand *lemps*?" he said in a tone of disbelief.

It occurred to me that he had not expected the entire amount, that he had only been hoping for a nuisance payment. But I was committed. Fifteen hundred dollars was no trifle to me, but I might be able to recoup it from Ray, and if not, well, I could make it up by foregoing my Christmas trip to the States. I pulled out my wallet and handed Mullins all the bills, about fifty or sixty *lempira*.

"That's all I've got now," I said, "but I'll get the rest in the morning. Just leave Milliken alone."

Mullins stared at the money in his hand, his little snappish eyes blinking rapidly, speechless. I stared out to sea, searching for a sign of Cassiopeia, but found none. Not at first. Then I spotted her, a slim, pale figure standing atop a coral head about fifteen yards from shore. Without taking a running start, she leaped—at that distance she looked like a white splinter being blown through the night—and landed upon another coral head some twenty, twenty-five feet away. Before I could absorb the improbability of the leap, she dived and vanished into the water beyond the reef.

"I be at your house nine o'clock sharp," said Mullins joyfully.

"And we go to de bank together. You not goin' to be havin' no more strife with dis negro!"

But Mullins did not show up the next morning, not at nine o'clock or ten or eleven. I asked around and heard that he had been drinking in Spanish Harbor; he had probably forgotten the appointment and passed out beneath some shanty. I drove to the bank, withdrew the money, and returned home. Still no Mullins. I wandered the beach, hoping to find him, and around three o'clock I ran into Hettie at Sarah's Store.

"Jimmy he never home of a Saturday," she told me ruefully.

I considered giving her the money, but I suspected that she would not tell Mullins, would use it for the children, and though this would be an admirable use, I doubted that it would please Mullins. Twilight fell, and my patience was exhausted. I left a message for Mullins with Elizabeth, stashed the money in a trunk, and headed for the Burying Ground.

After mooring the dory, I switched on the recorder and secreted it in my pack. My investigative zeal of the previous day had been reborn, and not even the desolation of Port Ezekiel could dim my spirits. I had solved the ultimate problem of the retiree; I had come up with a project that was not only time-consuming but perhaps had some importance. And now that Mullins had been taken care of, nothing would interfere.

Cassiopeia was sitting beneath the shelter when I reached the clearing, a silvery star of moonlight shifting across her face from a ragged hole in the thatch. She pointed to my pack and asked, "What's that?"

"The pack?" I said innocently.

"Inside it."

I knew she meant the recorder. I showed it to her and said, "I want to document your story."

She snatched it from me and slung it into the bushes.

"You're a stupid man, Frank," she said. "What do you suppose would happen if you played a recording of me for someone? They'd say it was an interesting form of insanity, and if they could profit, or if they were driven by misguided compassion, they'd send me away for treatment. And that would be that."

For a long while afterward she would not talk to me. Clouds were passing across the moon, gradually thinning, so that each time the light brightened it was brighter than the time before, as if the clearing were being dipped repeatedly into a stream and washed free of a grimy film. Cassiopeia sat brooding over her gameboard. Having grown somewhat accustomed to her, to that strong female presence, I was beginning to be able to detect her changes in mood. And they were rapid changes, fluctuating every few seconds between hostility and sadness. I recalled her telling me that she was probably mad; I had taken the statement to be an expression of gloom, but now I wondered if any creature whose moods shifted with such rapidity could be judged sane. Nonetheless, I was about to ask her to continue her story when I heard an outboard motor, and, moments after it had been shut off, a man's voice shouting, "Mr. Milliken!"

It was Jimmy Mullins.

A woman's voice shrilled, unintelligible, and there was a crash as if someone had fallen; a second later Mullins pushed into the clearing. Hettie was clinging to his arm, restraining him; but on seeing us, he cuffed her to the ground and staggered forward. His town clothes were matted with filth and damp. Two other men crowded up behind Hettie. They were both younger than Mullins, slouching, dressed in rags and sporting natty dreads. One held a rum bottle, and the second, the taller, carried a machete.

"You owe me three thousand *lemps*!" said Mullins to Cassiopeia; his head lolled back, and silver dots of moonlight flared in his eyes.

"Sick of dis Yankee domination," said the taller man; he giggled. "Ain't dat right, Jimmy?"

"Jimmy," I said. "We had a bargain."

Mullins said nothing, his face a mask of sodden fury; he teetered on the edge of the trench, unaware of the snakes.

"Tired of dis exploitation," said the man, and his friend, who had been taking a pull from the bottle, elbowed him gleefully and said, "Dat pretty slick, mon! Listen up." He snapped his fingers in a reggae tempo and sang in a sweet, tremulous voice:

> *"Sick of dis Yankee domination,*
> *Oh yea—aa-ay,*
> *Tired of dis exploitation . . ."*

The scenario was clear—these two had encountered the drunken Mullins in a bar, listened to the story of his windfall, and, thinking that he was being had, hoping to gain by it, they had egged him into this confrontation.

"Dis my land, and you ain't legal on it," said Mullins.

"What about our bargain, Jimmy?" I asked. "The money's back at the house."

He was tempted, but drunkenness and politics had infected his pride. "I ain't no beggar," he said. "I wants what's mine, and *dis* mon's money mine." He bent down and picked up one of the conch shells that were lying about; he curled his fingers around the inner curve of the shell—it fit over his hand like the spiked glove of a gladiator. He took a vicious swipe in our direction, and it *whooshed* through the air.

Cassiopeia let out a hissing breath.

It was very tense in the clearing. The two men were watching Mullins with new respect, new alertness, no longer joking. Even in the hands of a fool, conch shells were serious business; they had a ritual potency. Cassiopeia was deadpan, measuring Mullins. Her anger washed over me—I gauged it to be less anger than a cold disapproval, the caliber of emotion one experiences in reaction to a nasty child. But I was ready to intervene if her mood should escalate. Mullins was a coward at heart, and I thought that he would go to the brink but no further. I edged forward, halfway between them. My mouth was dry.

"I goin' to bash you simple, and you not pay me," said Mullins, crossing over the trench.

"Listen, Jimmy . . ." I said, raising the voice of reason.

Cassiopeia lunged for him. I threw my arms around her, and Mullins, panicked, seeing her disadvantage, swung the shell. She heaved me aside with a shrug and tried to slip the punch. But I had hampered her just enough. The shell glanced off her shoulder. She gave a cawing guttural screech that scraped a nail down the slate of my spine, and clutched at the wound.

"See dere," said Mullins to his friends, triumphant. "Dis negro take care of he own." He went reeling back over the trench, nearly tripping, and in righting himself, he caught sight of the snakes. It would have been impossible not to see them—they were thrusting frenziedly at the wire. Mullins's jaw fell, and he backed away. One of the rocks was dislodged from the screen. The snakes began to slither out, writing rippling black figures on the dirt and vanishing into the litter, rustling the dead fronds.

"Oh, Jimmy!" Hettie held out a hand to him. "Have a care!"

Cassiopeia gave another of those chilling screeches and lowered into a crouch. Her torso swaying, her hands hooked. The flesh of her left shoulder was torn, and blood webbed her arm, dripping from her fingertips, giving them the look of claws. She stepped across the trench after Mullins. Without warning, the taller of the two men sprinted toward her, his machete raised. Cassiopeia caught his wrist and flipped him one-handed into the trench as easily as she might have tossed away an empty bottle.

There were still snakes in the trench.

They struck at his arms, his legs, and he thrashed about wildly, crying out; but one must have hit a vein, for the cry was sheared off. His limbs beat a tattoo against the dirt, his eyes rolled up. Slivers of iris peeped beneath the lids. A tiny *coralito* hung like a tassel from his cheek, and a yellowjaw was coiling around his throat; its flat head poked from the spikes of his hair. I heard a squawk, a sharp crack, and looked to the center of the clearing. The second man was crumpled at Cassiopeia's feet, his neck broken. Dark blood poured from his mouth, puddling under his jaw.

"Mr. Milliken," said Mullins, backing, his bravado gone. "I goin' to make things right. Hettie she fix dat little scrape . . . ."

He stumbled, and as he flung out an arm for balance, Cassiopeia leaped toward him, going impossibly high. It was a gorgeous movement, as smooth as the arc of a diver but more complex. She maintained a crouch in midair, and passing close to Mullins, she plucked the conch shell from his waving hand, fitted it to her own, and spun round to face him—all before she had landed.

Hettie began to scream. Short, piercing shrieks, as if she were being stabbed over and over.

Mullins ran for the brush, but Cassiopeia darted ahead of him and blocked his path. She was smiling. Again Mullins ran, and again she cut him off, keeping low, flowing across the ground. Again and again she let him run, offering him hope and dashing it, harrying him this way and that. The wind had increased, and clouds were racing overhead, strobing the moonlight; the clearing seemed to be spinning, a carousel of glare and shadow, and Hettie's screams were keeping time with the spin. Mullins's legs grew rubbery, he weaved back and forth, his arms windmilling, and at last he collapsed in a heap of fronds. Almost instantly he scrambled to his knees, yelling and tearing loose a snake that had been hanging from his wrist.

A *coralito*, I think.

"Ah!" he said. "Ah . . . ah!"

His stare lanced into my eyes, freezing me with its hopelessness; a slant of light grazed his forehead, shining his sweat to silver beads.

Cassiopeia walked over and grabbed a handful of his shirtfront, hoisting him up until his feet were dangling. He kicked feebly and made a piteous bubbling noise. Then she drove the conch shell into his face. Once. Twice. Three times. Each blow splintered bone and sent a spray of blood flying. Hettie's scream became a wail. After the final blow, a spasm passed through Mullins's body—it looked too inconsequential to be death.

I was dimly aware that Hettie had stopped screaming, that the outboard motor had been started, but I was transfixed. Cassiopeia was still holding Mullins aloft, as if admiring her handiwork. His head glistened black in the moonlight, featureless and oddly misshapen. At least a minute went by before she dropped him. The thump of the body broke the spell that the scene had cast. I eased toward the brush.

"You can leave, Frank," she said. "I won't kill you."

I was giddy with fear, and I almost laughed. She did not turn but cocked an eye at me over her shoulder—a menacing posture. I was afraid that if I tried to leave she would hunt me through the brush.

"I won't kill you," she said again. She lowered her head, and I could feel her despair, her shame; it acted to lessen my fear.

"The soldiers will be coming," I said.

She was silent, motionless.

"You should make the exchange with Ray."

I was horrified by what she had done, but I wanted her to live. Insane or not, she was too rare to lose—a voice of mystery in all this ordinary matter.

"No more." She said it in a grim whisper. "I know it's much to ask, Frank, but will you keep me company?"

"What are you going to do?"

"Nothing. Wait for the soldiers." She inspected her wound; the blood had quit flowing. "And if they don't come before dawn, I'll watch the sunrise. I've always been curious about it."

She scarcely said a word the rest of the night. We went down to the shore and sat beside a tangle of mangrove. I tried to convince her to survive, but she warded off every argument with a slashing gesture. Toward dawn, as the first gray appeared in the east, she had a convulsion, a brief flailing of the limbs that stretched her out flat. Dawn comes swiftly on the water, and by the time she had regained consciousness, pink streaks were infiltrating the gray.

"Make the exchange," I urged her. "It's not too late, is it?"

She ignored me. Her eyes were fixed on the horizon, where the rim of the solar disc was edging up; the sea reflected a rippling path of crimson and purple leading away from it, and the bottoms of the clouds were dyed these same colors.

Ten minutes later she had a more severe convulsion. This one left a froth of bloody bubbles rimming her nostrils. She groped for my hand, and as she squeezed it, I felt my bones grinding together. My emotions were grinding together as well; my situation—like Henry Meachem's—was so similar to hers. Aliens and strangers, all of us, unable to come to grips with this melancholy island.

Shortly after her third convulsion, I heard an outboard motor. A dory was cutting toward us from the reef wall; it was not a large enough craft to be the militia, and as it drew near, I recognized

Hatfield Brooks by his silhouette hunched over the tiller, his natty dreads. He switched off the motor and let the dory drift until he was about fifty feet away; then he dropped the anchor and picked up a rifle that had been leaning against the front seat. He set the stock to his shoulder.

"Keep clear of dere, Mr. Winship!" he called. "I can't vouch for de steadiness of my aim."

Behind him, shafts of light were spearing up through balconies of cloud—a cathedral of a sky.

"Don't, Hatfield!" I stepped in front of Cassiopeia, waving my arms. "She's . . . he's dying! There's no need for it!"

"Keep clear!" he shouted. "De mon have killed Jimmy, and I come for him!"

"Just let him die!"

"He don't just let Jimmy die! Hettie been sayin' how dat crazy mon batter him!" He braced himself in the stern and took aim.

With a hoarse sigh, Cassiopeia climbed to her feet. I caught her wrist. Her skin was burning hot, her pulse drummed. Nerves twitched at the corners of her eyes, and one of the pupils was twice the size of the other. It was Ray's face I was seeing in that dawn light—hollow-cheeked, dirt-smeared, haggard; but even then I saw a sleeker shape beneath. She peeled my fingers off her wrist.

"Goodbye, Frank," she said; she pushed me away and ran toward Hatfield.

Ran!

The water was waist-deep all the way to the reef, yet she knifed through it as if it were nothing, ploughing a wake like the hull of a speedboat. It was a more disturbing sight than her destruction of Mullins had been. Thoroughly inhuman. Hatfield's first shot struck her in the chest and barely slowed her. She was twenty feet from the dory when the second shot hit, and that knocked her sideways, clawing at her stomach. The third drilled a jet of blood from her shoulder, driving her back; but she came forward again. One plodding step after another, shaking her head with pain. Four, five, six. Hatfield kept squeezing off the rounds, and I was screaming for him to finish her—each shot was a hammerblow that shivered loose a new scream. An arm's length from the dory, she sank to her knees and grabbed the keel, rocking it violently. Hatfield bounced side to side, unable to bring the rifle to bear. It discharged twice. Wild misses aimed at the sky, the trees.

And then, her head thrown back, arms upflung, Cassiopeia leaped out of the water.

Out of the world.

I am not sure whether she meant to kill Hatfield or if this was just a last expression of physicality—whatever her intent, she went so high that it was more a flight than a leap. Surrounded by a halo of fiery drops, twisting above the dory, her chest striped with blood, she seemed a creation of some visionary's imagination, bursting from a jeweled egg and being drawn gracefully into the heavens. But at the peak of the leap, she came all disjointed and fell, disappearing in a splash. Moments later, she floated up—face downward—and began to drift away. The sound of the reef faded in a steady, soothing hiss. The body spun slowly on the tide; the patch of water around it was stained gold and purple, as if the wounds were leaking the colors of sunrise.

Hatfield and I stared at each other across the distance. He did not lower the rifle. Strangely enough, I was not afraid. I had come to the same conclusion as Cassiopeia, the knowledge that the years could only decline from this point onward. I felt ready to die. The soft crush of waves building louder and louder on the reef, the body drifting leisurely toward shore, the black snaky-haired figure bobbing in his little boat against the enormous flag of the sunburst—it was a perfect medium for death. The whole world was steeped in it. But Hatfield laid the rifle down. He half raised his hand to me—an aborted salute or farewell—and held the pose a second or two; he must have recognized the futility of any gesture, for he ducked his head then and fired up the motor, leaving me to take charge of the dead.

The authorities were unable to contact Ray's family. It may be that he had none; he had never spoken of them. The local cemetery refused his remains—too many Brookses and Mullinses under the soil; and so, as was appropriate, he was laid to rest beside Ezekiel and Carl on the Burying Ground. Hatfield fled off-island and worked his passage to Miami; though he is still considered something of a hero, the tide of anti-Americanism ebbed—it was as if Ray had been a surrogate for the mercenaries and development bankers who had raped the island over the years. Once more there were friendly greetings, smiling faces, and contented shrimp-workers. As for me, I married Elizabeth. I have no illusions about the relationship; in retrospect, it seems a self-destructive move. But I was shaken, haunted. If I had not committed my stupidity with the recorder, if I had not thrown my arms around Cassiopeia, would she have been able to control her anger? Would she merely have disarmed Mullins? I needed the bitter enchantment of a marriage to ground myself in the world again, to obscure the answers to these questions, to blur the meaning of these events.

And what was their meaning?

Was this a traveler's tale like none other, a weaving together of starships and pirates, madmen and ghosts, into the history of an alien being and a sorry plot of mangrove? Or was it simply an extraordinary instance of psychosis, a labyrinthine justification for a young man's lack of inner strength?

I have no proof that would be measurable by any scientific rule, though I can offer one that is purely Guanojan and therefore open to interpretation—what was seen might have been an actual event or the shade of such an event, or it might have been the relic of a wish powerful enough to outlast the brain that conceived it. Witness the testimony of Donald Ebanks, a fisherman, who put in at night to the Burying Ground for repairs several months after Cassiopeia's death. I heard him tell the story at The Chicken Shack, and since it was only the third retelling, since he had only downed two rums, it had not changed character much from the original.

"I tinkerin' wit de fuel line," he said, "when of a sudden dere's de sound of wind, and yet dere ain't no wind to feel. I 'ware dat dis de duppy sign, but I ain't fearful 'cause my mother she take me to Escuilpas as a child and have de Black Virgin bless me. After dat no duppy can do me harm. Still, I wary. I turn and dere dey is. Two of dem, bot' shinin' pale white wit dat duppy glow dat don't 'low you to see dere trut'ful colors. One were Ray Milliken, and de other . . . God! I fall back in de boat to see it. De face ain't not'ing but teeth and eyes, and dere's a fringe 'round de head like de fringe of de anemone—snappin' and twistin'. And tall! Dis duppy mus' be two foot taller than Ray. Skinny-tall. Wearin' somet'ing dat fit tight to it frame neck-to-toe, and shine even brighter dan de glow 'round dere bodies. Now Ray he smile and come a step to me, but dis other cotch he arm and 'pear to be scoldin' him. It point behind dem, and dere, right where it pointin', some of de glow clear a spot, and de spot growin' wider and wider to a circle, and t'rough de circle I'm seein' creepers, trees . . . solid jungle like dey gots in Miskitia. Ray have a fretful look on he face, but he shrug and dey walks off into de circle. Not walkin' proper, you understand. Dey dwindlin', and de wind dwindlin' wit dem. See, dey not travelin' over de Buryin' Ground but 'pon duppy roads dat draws dem quick from de world, and dey jus' dwindlin' and dwindlin' 'til dey's not'ing but a speck of gleam and a whisper of wind. Den dey gone. Gone for good was de feelin' I got. But where, I cannot tell you."

ROBERT SILVERBERG
Sailing to Byzantium

Robert Silverberg is one of the most famous SF writers of modern times, with more than a hundred novels, anthologies, and collections to his credit, and, as both writer and editor, was one of the most influential figures of the post—New Wave era of the seventies.

Born in Brooklyn, New York, in 1935, Silverberg, like Poul Anderson before him, started a successful career as an SF writer while he was still in college. His first novel was sold in 1954, during his junior year at Columbia University; by 1955, still prior to graduation, he was earning "quite a good living" by writing, and by 1956 he had won his first Hugo Award. In order to *make* that good living, however, at the abysmally low word-rates typical of the period, Silverberg was forced to turn himself into, in his own words, "the complete writing machine," churning out such an awesome flood of "mechanical junk" that he already had more than a million words in print by 1956. When the SF boom of the fifties collapsed, and the SF magazines began disappearing in droves, Silverberg was forced to turn elsewhere to find markets for his vast annual output—more than a million words a year—writing first for confession magazines and "twenty different subliterate markets," and then going on to establish a prosperous and respectable career as the author of a long string of well-received nonfiction books (something Asimov and de Camp were also doing, and at about the same time).

Although Silverberg became one of the most prolific writers alive during this period, producing hundreds of books and thousands of magazine pieces, his SF output had fallen practically to zero, and his name meant little to the new generations of SF readers who entered the field in the mid-sixties.

In 1962, however, Frederik Pohl, then editor of *Galaxy*, had begun to coax Silverberg back into SF with the promise of absolute creative freedom, and gradually over the next few years Silverberg found himself drawn back into the genre, turning away from "more profitable work to indulge in SF out of love." By 1967, the so-called "New Silverberg" began to seize center stage once again, producing brooding and darkly powerful work like the novella *Hawksbill Station*, work that was able to compete successfully with the stuff that the Young Turks like Samuel Delany and Roger Zelazny were doing, and that fit in well with the artistic requirements of the New Wave revolution.

In the next seven years, Silverberg won a Hugo Award and four Nebula Awards, and went from relative obscurity within the field to the forefront of the genre. His fiction continued to grow in power and complexity, his prose becoming ever more stylish and sleek, his wit becoming darker and razor-sharp. By the early seventies, Silverberg was at the height of his powers, and in the first four or five years of the decade, he produced a large and remarkable body of work: the brilliant *Dying Inside*, easily one of the best books of the seventies, *Downward to the Earth*, *The Book of Skulls*, *Tower of Glass*, *The World Inside*, *The Second Trip*, *A Time of Changes*, *The Stochastic Man*, and *Shadrach in the Furnace*, as well as high-quality short work such as "Born with the Dead," "Sundance," "In Entropy's Jaws," "Breckenridge and the Continuum," "Push No More," "In the Group," "Capricorn Games," "Trips," "Schwartz Between the Galaxies," and many more. Seldom has SF witnessed such a concentrated outpouring of high-level talent, work that would be highly influential on writers such as Barry N. Malzberg and the later Gregory Benford, to name just two, and which I strongly suspect was influential on writers of subsequent generations—such as Alexander Jablokov—as well. When you add in the influence that Silverberg exerted on the field through his editorship of the *New Dimensions* original anthology series, the most important anthology series of its day, you can see that the strength of Silverberg's impact on the SF world of the seventies can hardly be overestimated.

In 1976, depressed by the general malaise that had settled over the field at the time, and perhaps exhausted from his efforts over the previous years, Silverberg publicly announced his "retirement" . . . and, indeed, did not write another word until 1980, when he suddenly came out of retirement to write his huge science fantasy novel, *Lord Valentine's Castle*. His output of new fiction was relatively low in the early years of the decade, but when a new surge of creative energy revitalized the field in the mid-eighties, Silverberg shifted into high gear once again, and would win two more Hugo Awards and another Nebula by the beginning of the nineties.

One of those things that Everyone Knows is that Silverberg's output since returning from his self-imposed exile is markedly inferior to his Good Stuff of the early seventies . . . but this is simply not true; if anything, Silverberg's work, at least at shorter lengths, has grown even *more* stylish and elegant, more self-assured and less self-conscious, more subtle and less mannered, and more deeply and complexly felt than his earlier work, and he produced some of the best work of the eighties with stories such as "The Pope of the Chimps," "Multiples," "The Palace at Midnight," "We Are for the Dark," "In Another Country," "Basileus," "The Secret Sharer," the recent Hugo-winner "Enter a Soldier. Later: Enter Another," and the story that follows, the award-winning novella *Sailing to Byzantium*.

Here he takes us to the very far future, on tour with a twentieth-century man in a world where *everyone* is a tourist, and nothing is quite what it seems. . . .

Silverberg's other books include the novels *Son of Man*, *Thorns*, *Up the Line*, *The Man in the Maze*, *Tom O'Bedlam*, *Star of Gypsies*, and *At Winter's End*. His collections include *Unfamiliar Territory*, *Capricorn Games*, *Majipoor Chronicles*, *The Best of Robert Silverberg*, *Born with the Dead*, *The Conglomeroid Cocktail Party*, and *Beyond the Safe Zone*. His reprint anthologies are far too numerous to list here, but include *The Science Fiction Hall of Fame*, *Volume One* and the distinguished *Alpha* series, among dozens of others. His most recent books are two novel-length expansions of famous Isaac Asimov stories, *Nightfall* and *The Ugly Little Boy*, the solo novels *The Face of the Waters* and *Kingdoms of the Wall*, and a massive retrospective collection *The Collected Stories of Robert Silverberg*, *Volume One: Secret Sharers*. Recently, along with his wife, writer Karen Haber, he has taken over the editing of the *Universe* anthology series. They live in Oakland, California.

At dawn he arose and stepped out onto the patio for his first look at Alexandria, the one city he had not yet seen. That year the five cities were Changan, Asgard, New Chicago, Timbuctoo, Alexandria: the usual mix of eras, cultures, realities. He and Gioia, making the long flight from Asgard in the distant north the night before, had arrived late, well after sundown, and had gone straight to bed. Now, by the gentle apricot-hued morning light, the fierce spires and battlements of Asgard seemed merely something he had dreamed.

The rumor was that Asgard's moment was finished anyway. In a little while, he had heard, they were going to tear it down and replace it, elsewhere, with Mohenjo-daro. Though there were never more than five cities, they changed constantly. He could remember a time when they had had Rome of the Caesars instead of Changan, and Rio de Janeiro rather than Alexandria. These people saw no point in keeping anything very long.

It was not easy for him to adjust to the sultry intensity of Alexandria after the frozen splendors of Asgard. The wind, coming off the water, was brisk and torrid both at once. Soft turquoise wavelets lapped at the jetties. Strong presences assailed his senses: the hot heavy sky, the stinging scent of the red lowland sand borne on the breeze, the sullen swampy aroma of the nearby sea. Everything trembled and glimmered in the early light. Their hotel was beautifully situated, high on the northern slope of the huge artificial mound known as the Paneium that was sacred to the goat-footed god. From here they had a total view of the city: the wide noble boulevards, the soaring obelisks and monuments, the palace of Hadrian just below the hill, the stately and awesome Library, the temple of Poseidon, the teeming marketplace, the royal lodge that Marc Antony had built after his defeat at Actium. And of course the Lighthouse, the wondrous many-windowed Lighthouse, the seventh wonder of the world, that immense pile of marble and limestone and reddish-purple Aswan granite rising in majesty at the end of its mile-long causeway. Black smoke from the beacon fire at its summit curled lazily into the sky. The city was awakening. Some temporaries in short white kilts appeared and began to trim the dense dark hedges that bordered the great public buildings. A few citizens wearing loose robes of vaguely Grecian style were strolling in the streets.

There were ghosts and chimeras and phantasies everywhere about. Two slim elegant centaurs, a male and a female, grazed on the hillside. A burly thick-thighed swordsman appeared on the porch of the temple of Poseidon holding a Gorgon's severed head and waved it in a wide arc, grinning broadly. In the street below the hotel gate three small pink sphinxes, no bigger than housecoats, stretched and yawned and began to prowl the curbside. A larger one, lion-sized, watched warily from an alleyway: their mother, surely. Even at this distance he could hear her loud purring.

Shading his eyes, he peered far out past the Lighthouse and across the water. He hoped to see the dim shores of Crete or Cyprus to the north, or perhaps the great dark curve of Anatolia. *Carry me toward that great Byzantium,* he thought. *Where all is ancient, singing at the oars.* But he beheld only the endless empty sea, sun-bright and blinding though the morning was just beginning. Nothing was ever where he expected it to be. The continents did not seem to be in their proper places any longer. Gioia, taking him aloft long ago in her little flitterflitter, had shown him that. The tip of South America was canted far out into the Pacific; Africa was weirdly foreshortened; a broad tongue of ocean separated Europe and Asia. Australia did not appear to exist at all. Perhaps they had dug it up and used it for other things. There was no trace of the world he once had known. This was the fiftieth century. "The fiftieth century after *what?*" he had asked several times, but no one seemed to know, or else they did not care to say.

"Is Alexandria very beautiful?" Gioia called from within.

"Come out and see."

Naked and sleepy-looking, she padded out onto the white-tiled patio and nestled up beside him. She fit neatly under his arm. "Oh, yes, yes!" she said softly. "So very beautiful, isn't it? Look, there, the palaces, the Library, the Lighthouse! Where will we go first? The Lighthouse, I think. Yes? And then the marketplace—I want to see the Egyptian magicians—and the stadium, the races—will they be having races today, do you think? Oh, Charles, I want to see everything!"

"Everything? All on the first day?"

"All on the first day, yes," she said. "Everything."

"But we have plenty of time, Gioia."

"Do we?"

He smiled and drew her tight against his side.

"Time enough," he said gently.

He loved her for her impatience, for her bright bubbling eagerness. Gioia was not much like the rest in that regard, though she seemed identical in all other ways. She was short, supple, slender, dark-eyed, olive-skinned, narrow-hipped, with wide shoulders and flat muscles. They were all like that, each one indistinguishable from the rest, like a horde of millions of brothers and sisters—a world of small lithe childlike Mediterraneans, built for juggling, for bull-dancing, for sweet white wine at midday and rough red wine at night. They had the same slim bodies, the same broad mouths, the same great glossy eyes. He had never seen anyone who appeared to be younger than twelve or older than twenty. Gioia was somehow a little different, although he did not quite know how; but he knew that it was for that imperceptible but significant difference that he loved her. And probably that was why she loved him also.

He let his gaze drift from west to east, from the Gate of the Moon down broad Canopus Street and out to the harbor, and off to the tomb of Cleopatra at the tip of long slender Cape Lochias. Everything was here and all of it perfect, the obelisks, the statues and marble colonnades, the courtyards and shrines and groves, great Alexander himself in his coffin of crystal and gold: a splendid gleaming pagan city. But there were oddities—an unmistakable mosque near the public gardens, and what seemed to be a Christian church not far from the Library. And those ships in the harbor, with all those red sails and bristling masts—surely they were medieval, and late medieval at that. He had seen such anachronisms in other places before. Doubtless these people found them amusing. Life was a game for them. They played at it unceasingly. Rome, Alexandria, Timbuctoo—why not? Create an Asgard of translucent bridges and shimmering ice-girt palaces, then grow weary of it and take it away? Replace it with Mohenjo-daro? Why not? It seemed to him a great pity to destroy those lofty Nordic feasting halls for the sake of building a squat brutal sun-baked city of brown brick; but these people did not look at things the way he did. Their cities were only temporary. Someone in Asgard had said that Timbuctoo would be the next to go, with Byzantium rising in its place. Well, why not? Why not? They could have anything they liked. This was the fiftieth century, after all. The only rule was that there could be no more than five cities at once. "Limits," Gioia had informed him solemnly when they first began to travel together, "are very important." But she did not know why, or did not care to say.

He stared out once more toward the sea.

He imagined a newborn city congealing suddenly out of mists, far across the water: shining towers, great domed palaces, golden mosaics. That would be no great effort for them. They could just summon it forth whole out of time, the Emperor on his throne and the Emperor's drunken soldiery roistering in the streets, the brazen clangor of the cathedral gong rolling through the Grand Bazaar, dolphins leaping beyond the shoreside pavilions. Why not? They had Timbuctoo. They had Alexandria. Do you crave Constantinople? Then behold Constantinople! Or Avalon, or Lyonesse, or Atlantis. They could have anything they liked. It is pure

Schopenhauer here: the world as will and imagination. Yes! These slender dark-eyed people journeying tirelessly from miracle to miracle. Why not Byzantium next? Yes! Why not? *That is no country for old men*, he thought. *The young in one another's arms, the birds in the trees*—yes! Yes! Anything they liked. They even had him. Suddenly he felt frightened. Questions he had not asked for a long time burst through into his consciousness. *Who am I? Why am I here? Who is this woman beside me?*

"You're so quiet all of a sudden, Charles," said Gioia, who could not abide silence for very long. "Will you talk to me? I want you to talk to me. Tell me what you're looking for out there."

He shrugged. "Nothing."

"Nothing?"

"Nothing in particular."

"I could see you seeing something."

"Byzantium," he said. "I was imagining that I could look straight across the water to Byzantium. I was trying to get a glimpse of the walls of Constantinople."

"Oh, but you wouldn't be able to see as far as that from here. Not really."

"I know."

"And anyway Byzantium doesn't exist."

"Not yet. But it will. Its time comes later on."

"Does it?" she said. "Do you know that for a fact?"

"On good authority. I heard it in Asgard," he told her. "But even if I hadn't, Byzantium would be inevitable, don't you think? Its time would have to come. How could we not do Byzantium, Gioia? We certainly will do Byzantium, sooner or later. I know we will. It's only a matter of time. And we have all the time in the world."

A shadow crossed her face. "Do we? Do we?"

He knew very little about himself, but he knew that he was not one of them. That he knew. He knew that his name was Charles Phillips and that before he had come to live among these people he had lived in the year 1984, when there had been such things as computers and television sets and baseball and jet planes, and the world was full of cities, not merely five but thousands of them, New York and London and Johannesburg and Paris and Liverpool and Bangkok and San Francisco and Buenos Aires and a multitude of others, all at the same time. There had been four and a half billion people in the world then; now he doubted that there were as many as four and a half million. Nearly everything had changed beyond comprehension. The moon still seemed the same, and the sun; but at night he searched in vain for familiar constellations. He had no idea how they had brought him from then to now, or why. It did no good to ask. No one had any answers for him; no one so much appeared to understand what it was that he was trying to learn. After a time he had stopped asking; after a time he had almost entirely ceased wanting to know.

He and Gioia were climbing the Lighthouse. She scampered ahead, in a hurry as always, and he came along behind her in his more stolid fashion. Scores of other tourists, mostly in groups of two or three, were making their way up the wide flagstone ramps, laughing, calling to one another. Some of them, seeing him, stopped a moment, stared, pointed. He was used to that. He was so much taller than any of them; he was plainly not one of them. When they pointed at him he smiled. Sometimes he nodded a little acknowledgment.

He could not find much of interest in the lowest level, a massive square structure two hundred feet high built of huge marble blocks: within its cool musty arcades were hundreds of small dark rooms, the offices of the Lighthouse's keepers and mechanics, the barracks of the garrison, the stables for the three hundred donkeys that carried the fuel to the lantern far above. None of that appeared inviting to him. He forged onward without halting until he emerged on the balcony that led to the next level. Here the Lighthouse grew narrower and became octagonal: its face, granite now and handsomely fluted, rose in a stunning sweep above him.

Gioia was waiting for him there. "This is for you," she said, holding out a nugget of meat on a wooden skewer. "Roast lamb. Absolutely delicious. I had one while I was waiting for you." She gave him a cup of some cool green sherbet also, and darted off to buy a pomegranate. Dozens of temporaries were roaming the balcony, selling refreshments of all kinds.

He nibbled at the meat. It was charred outside, nicely pink and moist within. While he ate, one of the temporaries came up to him and peered blandly into his face. It was a stocky swarthy male wearing nothing but a strip of red and yellow cloth about its waist. "I sell meat," it said. "Very fine roast lamb, only five drachmas."

Phillips indicated the piece he was eating. "I already have some," he said.

"It is excellent meat, very tender. It has been soaked for three days in the juices of—"

"Please," Phillips said. "I don't want to buy any meat. Do you mind moving along?"

The temporaries had confused and baffled him at first, and there was still much about them that was unclear to him. They were not machines—they looked like creatures of flesh and blood—but they did not seem to be human beings, either, and no one treated them as if they were. He supposed they were artificial constructs, products of a technology so consummate that it was invisible. Some appeared to be more intelligent than others, but all of them behaved as if they had no more autonomy than characters in a play, which was essentially what they were. There were untold numbers of them in each of the five cities, playing all manner of roles: shepherds and swineherds, street-sweepers, merchants, boatmen, vendors of grilled meats and cool drinks, hagglers in the marketplace, schoolchildren, charioteers, policemen, grooms, gladiators, monks, artisans, whores and cutpurses, sailors—whatever was needed to sustain the illusion of a thriving, populous urban center. The dark-eyed people, Gioia's people, never performed work. There were not enough of them to keep a city's functions going, and in any case they were strictly tourists, wandering with the wind, moving from city to city as the whim took them, Chang-an to New Chicago, New Chicago to Timbuctoo, Timbuctoo to Asgard, Asgard to Alexandria, onward, ever onward.

The temporary would not leave him alone. Phillips walked away and it followed him, cornering him against the balcony wall. When Gioia returned a few minutes later, lips prettily stained with pomegranate juice, the temporary was still hovering about him, trying with lunatic persistence to sell him a skewer of lamb. It stood much too close to him, almost nose to nose, great sad cowlike eyes peering intently into his as it extolled with mournful mooing urgency the quality of its wares. It seemed to him that he had had trouble like this with temporaries on one or two earlier occasions. Gioia touched the creature's elbow lightly and said, in a short sharp tone Phillips had never heard her use before, "He isn't interested. Get away from him." It went at once. To Phillips she said, "You have to be firm with them."

"I was trying. It wouldn't listen to me."

"You ordered it to go away, and it refused?"

"I asked it to go away. Politely. Too politely, maybe."

"Even so," she said. "It should have obeyed a human, regardless."

"Maybe it didn't think I was human," Phillips suggested. "Because of the way I look. My height, the color of my eyes. It might have thought I was some kind of temporary myself."

"No," Gioia said, frowning. "A temporary won't solicit another temporary. But it won't ever disobey a citizen, either. There's a very clear boundary. There isn't ever any confusion. I can't understand why it went on bothering you." He was surprised at how troubled she seemed: far more so, he thought, than the incident warranted. A stupid device, perhaps miscalibrated in some way, overenthusiastically pushing its wares—what of it? What of it? Gioia, after a moment, appeared to come to the same conclusion. Shrugging, she said, "It's defective, I suppose. Probably such things are more common than we suspect, don't you think?" There was something forced about her tone that bothered him. She smiled and handed him her pomegranate. "Here. Have a bite, Charles. It's wonderfully sweet. They used to be extinct, you know. Shall we go on upward?"

The octagonal midsection of the Lighthouse must have been several hundred feet in height, a grim claustrophobic tube almost entirely filled by the two broad spiraling ramps that wound around the huge building's central well. The ascent was slow: a donkey team was a little way ahead of them on the ramp, plodding along laden with bundles of kindling for the lantern. But at last, just as Phillips was growing winded and dizzy, he and Gioia came out onto the second balcony, the one marking the transition between the octagonal section and the Lighthouse's uppermost story, which was cylindrical and very slender.

She leaned far out over the balustrade. "Oh, Charles, look at the view! Look at it!"

It was amazing. From one side they could see the entire city, and swampy Lake Mareotis and the dusty Egyptian plain beyond it, and from the other they peered far out into the gray and choppy Mediterranean. He gestured toward the innumerable reefs and shallows that infested the waters leading to the harbor entrance. "No wonder they needed a lighthouse here," he said. "Without some kind of gigantic landmark they'd never have found their way in from the open sea."

A blast of sound, a ferocious snort, erupted just above him. He looked up, startled. Immense statues of trumpet-wielding Tritons jutted from the corners of the Lighthouse at this level; that great blurting sound had come from the nearest of them. A signal, he thought. A warning to the ships negotiating that troubled passage. The sound was produced by some kind of steam-powered mechanism, he realized, operated by teams of sweating temporaries clustered about bonfires at the base of each Triton.

Once again he found himself swept by admiration for the clever way these people carried out their reproductions of antiquity. Or *were* they reproductions, he wondered? He still did not understand how they brought their cities into being. For all he knew, this place was the authentic Alexandria itself, pulled forward out of its proper time just as he himself had been. Perhaps this was the true and original Lighthouse, and not a copy. He had no idea which was the case, nor which would be the greater miracle.

"How do we get to the top?" Gioia asked.

"Over there, I think. That doorway."

The spiraling donkey-ramps ended here. The loads of lantern fuel went higher via a dumbwaiter in the central shaft. Visitors continued by way of a cramped staircase, so narrow at its upper end that it was impossible to turn around while climbing. Gioia, tireless, sprinted ahead. He clung to the rail and labored up and up, keeping count of the tiny window slits to ease the boredom of the ascent. The count was nearing a hundred when finally he stumbled into the vestibule of the beacon chamber. A dozen or so visitors were crowded into it. Gioia was at the far side, by the wall that was open to the sea.

It seemed to him he could feel the building swaying in the winds up here. How high were they? Five hundred feet, six hundred, seven? The beacon chamber was tall and narrow, divided by a catwalk into upper and lower sections. Down below, relays of temporaries carried wood from the dumbwaiter and tossed it on the blazing fire. He felt its intense heat from where he stood, at the rim of the platform on which the giant mirror of polished metal was hung. Tongues of flame leaped upward and danced before the mirror, which hurled its dazzling beam far out to sea. Smoke rose through a vent. At the very top was a colossal statue of Poseidon, austere, ferocious, looming above the lantern.

Gioia sidled along the catwalk until she was at his side. "The guide was talking before you came," she said, pointing. "Do you see that place over there, under the mirror? Someone standing there and looking into the mirror gets a view of ships at sea that can't be seen from here by the naked eye. The mirror magnifies things."

"Do you believe that?"

She nodded toward the guide. "It said so. And it also told us that if you look in a certain way, you can see right across the water into the city of Constantinople."

She is like a child, he thought. They all are. He said, "You told me yourself this very morning that it isn't possible to see that far. Besides, Constantinople doesn't exist right now."

"It will," she replied. "*You* said that to me, this very morning. And when it does, it'll be reflected in the Lighthouse mirror. That's the truth. I'm absolutely certain of it." She swung about abruptly toward the entrance of the beacon chamber. "Oh, look, Charles! Here come Nissandra and Aramayne! And there's Hawk! There's Stengard!" Gioia laughed and waved and called out names. "Oh, everyone's here! *Everyone!*"

They came jostling into the room, so many newcomers that some of those who had been there were forced to scramble down the steps on the far side. Gioia moved among them, hugging, kissing. Phillips could scarcely tell one from another—it was hard for him even to tell which were the men and which the women, dressed as they all were in the same sort of loose robes—but he recognized some of the names. These were her special friends, her set, with whom she had journeyed from city to city on an endless round of gaiety in the old days before he had come into her life. He had met a few of them before, in Asgard, in Rio, in Rome. The beacon-chamber guide, a squat wide-shouldered old temporary wearing a laurel wreath on its bald head, reappeared and began its potted speech, but no one listened to it; they were all too busy greeting one another, embracing, giggling. Some of them edged their way over to Phillips and reached up, standing on tiptoes, to touch their fingertips to his cheek in that odd hello of theirs. "Charles," they said gravely, making two syllables out of the name, as these people often did. "So good to see you again. Such a pleasure. You and Gioia—such a handsome couple. So well suited to each other."

Was that so? He supposed it was.

The chamber hummed with chatter. The guide could not be heard at all. Stengard and Nissandra had visited New Chicago for the water-dancing—Aramayne bore tales of a feast in Chang-an that had gone on for *days*—Hawk and Hekna had been to Timbuctoo to see the arrival of the salt caravan, and were going back there soon—a final party soon to celebrate the end of Asgard that absolutely should not be missed—the plans for the new city, Mohenjo-daro—we have reservations for the opening, we wouldn't pass it up for anything—and, yes, they were definitely going to do Constantinople after that, the planners were already deep into their Byzantium research—so good to see you, you look so beautiful all the time—have you been to the Library yet? The zoo? To the temple of Serapis?—

To Phillips they said, "What do you think of our Alexandria, Charles? Of course, you must have known it well in your day. Does it look the way you remember it?" They were always asking things like that. They did not seem to comprehend that the Alexandria of the Lighthouse and the Library was long lost and legendary by the time his twentieth century had been. To them, he suspected, all the places they had brought back into existence were more or less contemporary. Rome of the Caesars, Alexandria of the Ptolemies, Venice of the Doges, Chang-an of the T'angs, Asgard of the Aesir, none any less real than the next nor any less unreal, each one simply a facet of the distant past, the fantastic immemorial past, a plum plucked from that dark backward abysm of time. They had no contexts for separating one era from another. To them all the past was one borderless timeless realm. Why, then, should he not have seen the Lighthouse before, he who had leaped into this era from the New York of 1984? He had never been able to explain it to them. Julius Caesar and Hannibal, Helen of Troy and Charlemagne, Rome of the gladiators and New York of the Yankees and Mets, Gilgamesh and Tristan and Othello and Robin Hood and George Washington and Queen Victoria—to them, all equally real and unreal, none of them any more than bright figures moving about on a painted canvas. The past, the past, the elusive and fluid past—to them it was a single place of infinite accessibility and infinite connectivity. Of course, they would think he had seen the Lighthouse before. He knew better than to try again to explain things. "No," he said simply. "This is my first time in Alexandria."

They stayed there all winter long, and possibly some of the spring. Alexandria was not a place where one was sharply aware of the change of seasons, nor did the passage of time itself make itself very evident when one was living one's entire life as a tourist.

During the day there was always something new to see. The zoological garden, for instance: a wondrous park, miraculously green and lush in this hot dry climate, where astounding animals roamed in enclosures so generous that they did not seem like enclosures at all. Here were camels, rhinoceroses, gazelles, ostriches, lions, wild asses; and here, too, casually adjacent to those familiar African beasts, were hippogriffs, unicorns, basilisks, and fire-snorting dragons with rainbow scales. Had the original zoo of Alexandria had dragons and unicorns? Phillips doubted it. But this one did; evidently it was no harder for the backstage craftsmen to manufacture mythic beasts than it was for them to turn out camels and gazelles. To Gioia and her friends all of them were equally mythical, anyway. They were just as awed by the rhinoceros as by the hippogriff. One was no more strange—or any less—than the other. So far as Phillips had been able to discover, none of the mammals or birds of his era had survived into this one except for a few cats and dogs, though many had been reconstructed.

And then the Library! All those lost treasures, reclaimed from the jaws of time! Stupendous columned marble walls, airy high-vaulted reading rooms, dark coiling stacks stretching away to infinity. The ivory handles of seven hundred thousand papyrus scrolls bristling on the shelves. Scholars and librarians gliding quietly about, smiling faint scholarly smiles but plainly preoccupied with serious matters of the mind. They were all temporaries, Phillips realized. Mere props, part of the illusion. But were the scrolls illusions, too? "Here we have the complete dramas of Sophocles," said the guide with a blithe wave of its hand, indicating shelf upon shelf of texts. Only seven of his hundred twenty-three plays had survived the successive burnings of the library in ancient times by Romans, Christians, Arabs: were the lost ones here, the *Triptolemus*, the *Nausicaa*, the *Jason*, and all the rest? And would he find here, too, miraculously restored to being, the other vanished treasures of ancient literature—the memoirs of Odysseus, Cato's history of Rome, Thucidydes' life of Pericles, the missing volumes of Livy? But when he asked if he might explore the stacks, the guide smiled apologetically and said that all the librarians were busy just now. Another time, perhaps? Perhaps, said the guide. It made no difference, Phillips decided. Even if these people somehow had brought back those lost masterpieces of antiquity, how would he read them? He knew no Greek.

The life of the city buzzed and throbbed about him. It was a dazzlingly beautiful place: the vast bay thick with sails, the great avenues running rigidly east-west, north-south, the sunlight rebounding almost audibly from the bright walls of the palaces of kings and gods. They have done this very well, Phillips thought: very well indeed. In the marketplace hard-eyed traders squabbled in half a dozen mysterious languages over the price of ebony, Arabian incense, jade, panther skins. Gioia bought a dram of pale musky Egyptian perfume in a delicate tapering glass flask. Magicians and jugglers and scribes called out stridently to passersby, begging for a few moments of attention and a handful of coins for their labor. Strapping slaves, black and tawny and some that might have been Chinese, were put up for auction, made to flex their muscles, to bare their teeth, to bare their breasts and thighs to prospective buyers. In the gymnasium naked athletes hurled javelins and discuses, and wrestled with terrifying zeal. Gioia's friend Stengard came rushing up with a gift for her, a golden necklace that would not have embarrassed Cleopatra. An hour later she had lost it, or perhaps had given it away while Phillips was looking elsewhere. She bought another, even finer, the next day. Anyone could have all the money he wanted, simply by asking: it was as easy to come by as air for these people.

Being here was much like going to the movies, Phillips told himself. A different show every day: not much plot, but the special effects were magnificent and the detail work could hardly have been surpassed. A megamovie, a vast entertainment that went on all the time and was being played out by the whole population of Earth. And it was all so effortless, so spontaneous: just as when he had gone to a movie he had never troubled to think about the

myriad technicians behind the scenes, the cameramen and the costume designers and the set builders and the electricians and the
model makers and the boom operators, so, too, here he chose not
to question the means by which Alexandria had been set before
him. It felt real. It *was* real. When he drank the strong red wine it
gave him a pleasant buzz. If he leaped from the beacon chamber
of the Lighthouse he suspected he would die, though perhaps he
would not stay dead for long: doubtless they had some way of
restoring him as often as was necessary. Death did not seem to be
a factor in these people's lives.

By day they saw sights. By night he and Gioia went to parties, in
their hotel, in seaside villas, in the palaces of the high nobility. The
usual people were there all the time, Hawk and Hekna, Aramayne,
Stengard and Shelimir, Nissandra, Asoka, Afonso, Protay. At the
parties there were five or ten temporaries for every citizen, some
as mere servants, others as entertainers or even surrogate guests,
mingling freely and a little daringly. But everyone knew, all the
time, who was a citizen and who just a temporary. Phillips began to
think his own status lay somewhere between. Certainly they treated
him with a courtesy that no one ever would give a temporary, and
yet there was a condescension to their manner that told him not
simply that he was not one of them but that he was someone or
something of an altogether different order of existence. That he
was Gioia's lover gave him some standing in their eyes, but not a
great deal: obviously he was always going to be an outsider, a
primitive, ancient and quaint. For that matter he noticed that Gioia
herself, though unquestionably a member of the set, seemed to be
regarded as something of an outsider, like a tradesman's great-
granddaughter in a gathering of Plantagenets. She did not always
find out about the best parties in time to attend; her friends did
not always reciprocate her effusive greetings with the same degree
of warmth; sometimes he noticed her straining to hear some bit of
gossip that was not quite being shared with her. Was it because she
had taken him for her lover? Or was it the other way around: that
she had chosen to be his lover precisely because she was *not* a full
member of their caste?

Being a primitive gave him, at least, something to talk about at
their parties. "Tell us about war," they said. "Tell us about elections.
About money. About disease." They wanted to know everything,
though they did not seem to pay close attention: their eyes were
quick to glaze. Still, they asked. He described traffic jams to them,
and politics, and deodorants, and vitamin pills. He told them about
cigarettes, newspapers, subways, telephone directories, credit
cards, and basketball. "Which was your city?" they asked. New York,

he told them. "And when was it? The seventh century, did you say?" The twentieth, he told them. They exchanged glances and nodded. "We will have to do it," they said. "The World Trade Center, the Empire State Building, the Citicorp Center, the Cathedral of St. John the Divine: how fascinating! Yankee Stadium. The Verrazano Bridge. We will do it all. But first must come Mohenjo-daro. And then, I think, Constantinople. Did your city have many people?" Seven million, he said. Just in the five boroughs alone. They nodded, smiling amiably, unfazed by the number. Seven million, seventy million—it was all the same to them, he sensed. They would just bring forth the temporaries in whatever quantity was required. He wondered how well they would carry the job off. He was no real judge of Alexandrias and Asgards, after all. Here they could have unicorns and hippogriffs in the zoo, and live sphinxes prowling in the gutters, and it did not trouble him. Their fanciful Alexandria was as good as history's, or better. But how sad, how disillusioning it would be, if the New York that they conjured up had Greenwich Village uptown and Times Square in the Bronx, and the New Yorkers, gentle and polite, spoke with the honeyed accents of Savannah or New Orleans. Well, that was nothing he needed to brood about just now. Very likely they were only being courteous when they spoke of doing his New York. They had all the vastness of the past to choose from: Nineveh, Memphis of the Pharaohs, the London of Victoria or Shakespeare or Richard the Third, Florence of the Medici, the Paris of Abelard and Heloise or the Paris of Louis XIV, Moctezuma's Tenochtitlan and Atahuallpa's Cuzco; Damascus, St. Petersburg, Babylon, Troy. And then there were all the cities like New Chicago, out of time that was time yet unborn to him but ancient history to them. In such richness, such an infinity of choices, even mighty New York might have to wait a long while for its turn. Would he still be among them by the time they got around to it? By then, perhaps, they might have become bored with him and returned him to his own proper era. Or possibly he would simply have grown old and died. Even here, he supposed, he would eventually die, though no one else ever seemed to. He did not know. He realized that in fact he did not know anything.

The north wind blew all day long. Vast flocks of ibises appeared over the city, fleeing the heat of the interior, and screeched across the sky with their black necks and scrawny legs extended. The sacred birds, descending by the thousands, scuttered about in every crossroad, pouncing on spiders and beetles, on mice, on the debris of the meat shops and the bakeries. They were beautiful but annoyingly ubiquitous, and they splashed their dung over the marble buildings; each morning squadrons of temporaries carefully washed it off. Gioia said little to him now. She seemed cool, withdrawn, depressed; and there was something almost intangible about her, as though she were gradually becoming transparent. He felt it would be an intrusion upon her privacy to ask her what was wrong. Perhaps it was only restlessness. She became religious, and presented costly offerings at the temples of Serapis, Isis, Poseidon, Pan. She went to the necropolis west of the city to lay wreaths on the tombs in the catacombs. In a single day she climbed the Lighthouse three times without any sign of fatigue. One afternoon he returned from a visit to the Library and found her naked on the patio; she had anointed herself all over with some aromatic green salve. Abruptly she said, "I think it's time to leave Alexandria, don't you?"

She wanted to go to Mohenjo-daro, but Mohenjo-daro was not yet ready for visitors. Instead they flew eastward to Chang-an, which they had not seen in years. It was Phillips's suggestion: he hoped that the cosmopolitan gaudiness of the old T'ang capital would lift her mood.

They were to be guests of the Emperor this time: an unusual privilege, which ordinarily had to be applied for far in advance, but Phillips had told some of Gioia's highly placed friends that she was unhappy, and they had quickly arranged everything. Three endlessly bowing functionaries in flowing yellow robes and purple sashes met them at the Gate of Brilliant Virtue in the city's south wall and conducted them to their pavilion, close by the imperial palace and the Forbidden Garden. It was a light, airy place, thin walls of plastered brick braced by graceful columns of some dark, aromatic wood. Fountains played on the roof of green and yellow tiles, creating an unending cool rainfall of recirculating water. The balustrades were of carved marble, the door fittings were of gold.

There was a suite of private rooms for him, and another for her, though they would share the handsome damask-draped bedroom at the heart of the pavilion. As soon as they arrived, Gioia announced that she must go to her rooms to bathe and dress. "There will be a formal reception for us at the palace tonight," she said. "They say the imperial receptions are splendid beyond anything you could imagine. I want to be at my best." The Emperor and all his ministers, she told him, would receive them in the Hall of the Supreme Ultimate; there would be a banquet for a thousand people; Persian dancers would perform, and the celebrated jugglers of Chung-nan. Afterward everyone would be conducted into the fantastic landscape of the Forbidden Garden to view the dragon races and the fireworks.

He went to his own rooms. Two delicate little maidservants undressed him and bathed him with fragrant sponges. The pavilion came equipped with eleven temporaries who were to be their servants: soft-voiced unobtrusive catlike Chinese, done with perfect verisimilitude, straight black hair, glowing skin, epicanthic folds. Phillips often wondered what happened to a city's temporaries when the city's time was over. Were the towering Norse heroes of Asgard being recycled at this moment into wiry dark-skinned Dravidians for Mohenjo-daro? When Timbuctoo's day was done, would its brightly robed black warriors be converted into supple Byzantines to stock the arcades of Constantinople? Or did they simply discard the old temporaries like so many excess props, stash them in warehouses somewhere, and turn out the appropriate quantities of the new model? He did not know; and once when he had asked Gioia about it she had grown uncomfortable and vague. She did not like him to probe for information, and he suspected it was because she had very little to give. These people did not seem to question the workings of their own world; his curiosities were very twentieth-century of him, he was frequently told, in that gently patronizing way of theirs. As his two little maids patted him with their sponges he thought of asking them where they had served before Chang-an. Rio? Rome? Haroun al-Raschid's Baghdad? But these fragile girls, he knew, would only giggle and retreat if he tried to question them. Interrogating temporaries was not only improper but pointless: it was like interrogating one's luggage.

When he was bathed and robed in rich red silks he wandered the pavilion for a little while, admiring the tinkling pendants of green jade dangling on the portico, the lustrous auburn pillars, the rainbow hues of the intricately interwoven girders and brackets that supported the roof. Then, wearying of his solitude, he approached the bamboo curtain at the entrance to Gioia's suite. A porter and one of the maids stood just within. They indicated that he should not enter; but he scowled at them and they melted from him like snowflakes. A trail of incense led him through the pavilion to Gioia's innermost dressing room. There he halted, just outside the door.

Gioia sat naked with her back to him at an ornate dressing table of some rare flame-colored wood inlaid with bands of orange and green porcelain. She was studying herself intently in a mirror of polished bronze held by one of her maids: picking through her scalp with her fingernails, as a woman might do who was searching out her gray hairs.

But that seemed strange. Gray hair, on Gioia? On a citizen? A temporary might display some appearance of aging, perhaps, but surely not a citizen. Citizens remained forever young. Gioia looked like a girl. Her face was smooth and unlined, her flesh was firm, her hair was dark: that was true of all of them, every citizen he had ever seen. And yet there was no mistaking what Gioia was doing. She found a hair, frowned, drew it taut, nodded, plucked it. Another. Another. She pressed the tip of her finger to her cheek as if testing it for resilience. She tugged at the skin below her eyes, pulling it downward. Such familiar little gestures of vanity; but so odd here, he thought, in this world of the perpetually young. Gioia, worried about growing old? Had he simply failed to notice the signs of age on her? Or was it that she worked hard behind his back at concealing them? Perhaps that was it. Was he wrong about the citizens, then? Did they age even as the people of less blessed eras had always done, but simply have better ways of hiding it? How old was she, anyway? Thirty? Sixty? Three hundred?

Gioia appeared satisfied now. She waved the mirror away; she rose; she beckoned for her banquet robes. Phillips, still standing unnoticed by the door, studied her with admiration: the small round buttocks, almost but not quite boyish, the elegant line of her spine, the surprising breadth of her shoulders. No, he thought, she is not aging at all. Her body is still like a girl's. She looks as young as on the day they first had met, however long ago that was—he could not say; it was hard to keep track of time here; but he was sure some years had passed since they had come together. Those gray hairs, those wrinkles and sags for which she had searched just now with such desperate intensity, must all be imaginary, mere artifacts of vanity. Even in this remote future epoch, then, vanity was not extinct. He wondered why she was so concerned with the fear of aging. An affectation? Did all these timeless people take some perverse pleasure in fretting over the possibility that they might be growing old? Or was it some private fear of Gioia's, another symptom of the mysterious depression that had come over her in Alexandria?

Not wanting her to think that he had been spying on her, when all he had really intended was to pay her a visit, he slipped silently away to dress for the evening. She came to him an hour later, gorgeously robed, swaddled from chin to ankles in a brocade of brilliant colors shot through with threads of gold, face painted, hair drawn up tightly and fastened with ivory combs: very much the lady of the court. His servants had made him splendid also, a lustrous black surplice embroidered with golden dragons over a sweeping floor-length gown of shining white silk, a necklace and pendant of red coral, a five-cornered gray felt hat that rose in tower upon tower like a ziggurat. Gioia, grinning, touched her fingertips to his cheek. "You look marvelous!" she told him. "Like a grand mandarin!"

"And you like an empress," he said. "Of some distant land: Persia, India. Here to pay a ceremonial visit on the Son of Heaven." An excess of love suffused his spirit, and, catching her lightly by the wrist, he drew her toward him, as close as he could manage it considering how elaborate their costumes were. But as he bent forward and downward, meaning to brush his lips lightly and affectionately against the tip of her nose, he perceived an unexpected strangeness, an anomaly: the coating of white paint that was her makeup seemed oddly to magnify rather than mask the contours of her skin, highlighting and revealing details he had never observed before. He saw a pattern of fine lines radiating from the corners of her eyes, and the unmistakable beginning of a quirk mark in her cheek just to the left of her mouth, and perhaps the faint indentation of frown lines in her flawless forehead. A shiver traveled along the nape of his neck. So it was not affectation, then, that had had her studying her mirror so fiercely. Age was in truth beginning to stake its claim on her, despite all that he had come to believe about these people's agelessness. But a moment later he was not so sure. Gioia turned and slid gently half a step back from him—she must have found his stare disturbing—and the lines he had thought he had seen were gone. He searched for them and saw only girlish smoothness once again. A trick of the light? A figment of an overwrought imagination? He was baffled.

"Come," she said. "We mustn't keep the Emperor waiting."

Five mustachioed warriors in armor of white quilting and seven musicians playing cymbals and pipes escorted them to the Hall of the Supreme Ultimate. There they found the full court arrayed: princes and ministers, high officials, yellow-robed monks, a swarm of imperial concubines. In a place of honor to the right of the royal thrones, which rose like gilded scaffolds high above all else, was a little group of stern-faced men in foreign costumes, the ambassadors of Rome and Byzantium, of Arabia and Syria, of Korea, Japan, Tibet, Turkestan. Incense smoldered in enameled braziers. A poet sang a delicate twanging melody, accompanying himself on a small harp. Then the Emperor and Empress entered: two tiny aged people, like waxen images, moving with infinite slowness, taking steps no greater than a child's. There was the sound of trumpets as they ascended their thrones. When the little Emperor was seated—he looked like a doll up there, ancient, faded, shrunken, yet still somehow a figure of extraordinary power—he stretched forth both his hands, and enormous gongs began to sound. It was a scene of astonishing splendor, grand and overpowering.

These are all temporaries, Phillips realized suddenly. He saw only a handful of citizens—eight, ten, possibly as many as a dozen—scattered here and there about the vast room. He knew them by their eyes, dark, liquid, knowing. They were watching not only the imperial spectacle but also Gioia and him; and Gioia, smiling secretly, nodding almost imperceptibly to them, was acknowledging their presence and their interest. But those few were the only ones in here who were autonomous living beings. All the rest—the entire splendid court, the great mandarins and paladins, the officials, the giggling concubines, the haughty and resplendent ambassadors, the aged Emperor and Empress themselves, were simply part of the scenery. Had the world ever seen entertainment on so grand a scale before? All this pomp, all this pageantry, conjured up each night for the amusement of a dozen or so viewers?

At the banquet the little group of citizens sat together at a table apart, a round onyx slab draped with translucent green silk. There turned out to be seventeen of them in all, including Gioia; Gioia appeared to know all of them, though none, so far as he could tell, was a member of her set that he had met before. She did not attempt introductions. Nor was conversation at all possible during the meal: there was a constant astounding roaring din in the room. Three orchestras played at once and there were troupes of strolling musicians also, and a steady stream of monks and their attendants marched back and forth between the tables loudly chanting sutras and waving censers to the deafening accompaniment of drums and gongs. The Emperor did not descend from his throne to join the banquet; he seemed to be asleep, though now and then he waved his hand in time to the music. Gigantic half-naked brown slaves with broad cheekbones and mouths like gaping pockets brought forth the food, peacock tongues and breast of phoenix heaped on mounds of glowing saffron-colored rice, served on frail alabaster plates. For chopsticks they were given slender rods of dark jade. The wine, served in glistening crystal beakers, was thick and sweet, with an aftertaste of raisins, and no beaker was allowed to remain empty for more than a moment. Phillips felt himself growing dizzy: when the Persian dancers emerged he could not tell whether there were five of them or fifty, and as they performed their intricate whirling routines it seemed to him that their slender muslin-veiled forms were blurring and merging one into another. He felt frightened by their proficiency, and wanted to look away, but he could not. The Chung-nan jugglers that followed them were equally skillful, equally alarming, filling the air with scythes, flaming torches, live animals, rare porcelain vases, pink jade hatchets, silver bells, gilded cups, wagon wheels, bronze vessels, and never missing a catch. The citizens applauded politely but did not seem impressed. After the jugglers, the dancers returned, performing this time on stilts; the waiters brought platters of steaming meat of a pale lavender color, unfamiliar in taste and texture: filet of camel, perhaps, or haunch of hippopotamus, or possibly some choice chop from a young dragon. There was more wine. Feebly Phillips tried to wave it away, but the servitors were implacable. This was a drier sort, greenish-gold, austere, sharp on the tongue. With it came a silver dish, chilled to a polar coldness, that held shaved ice flavored with some potent smoky-flavored brandy. The jugglers were doing a second turn, he noticed. He thought he was going to be ill. He looked helplessly toward Gioia, who seemed sober but fiercely animated, almost manic, her eyes blazing like rubies. She touched his cheek fondly. A cool draft blew through the hall: they had opened one entire wall, revealing the garden, the night, the stars. Just outside was a colossal wheel of oiled paper stretched on wooden struts. They must have erected it in the past hour: it stood a hundred fifty feet high or even more, and on it hung lanterns by the thousands, glimmering like giant fireflies. The guests began to leave the hall. Phillips let himself be swept along into the garden, where under a yellow moon strange crook-armed trees with dense black needles loomed ominously. Gioia slipped her arm through his. They went down to a lake of bubbling crimson fluid and watched scarlet flamingolike birds ten feet tall fastidiously spearing angry-eyed turquoise eels. They stood in awe before a fat-bellied Buddha of gleaming blue tilework, seventy feet high. A horse with a golden mane came prancing by, striking showers of brilliant red sparks wherever its hooves touched the ground. In a grove of lemon trees that seemed to have the power to wave their slender limbs about, Phillips came upon the Emperor, standing by himself and rocking gently back and forth. The old man seized Phillips by the hand and pressed something into his palm, closing his fingers tight about it; when he opened his fist a few moments later he found his palm full of gray irregular pearls. Gioia took them from him and cast them into the air, and they burst like exploding firecrackers, giving off splashes of colored light. A little later, Phillips realized that he was no longer wearing his surplice or his white silken undergown. Gioia was naked, too, and she drew him gently down into a carpet of moist blue moss, where they made love until dawn, fiercely at first, then slowly, languidly, dreamily. At sunrise he looked at her tenderly and saw that something was wrong.

"Gioia?" he said doubtfully.

She smiled. "Ah, no. Gioia is with Fenimon tonight. I am Belilala."

"With—Fenimon?"

"They are old friends. She had not seen him in years."

"Ah. I see. And you are—?"

"Belilala," she said again, touching her fingertips to his cheek.

It was not unusual, Belilala said. It happened all the time; the only
unusual thing was that it had not happened to him before now.
Couples formed, traveled together for a while, drifted apart, eventually reunited. It did not mean that Gioia had left him forever. It
meant only that just now she chose to be with Fenimon. Gioia would
return. In the meanwhile he would not be alone. "You and I met
in New Chicago," Belilala told him. "And then we saw each other
again in Timbuctoo. Have you forgotten? Oh, yes, I see that you
have forgotten!" She laughed prettily; she did not seem at all offended.

She looked enough like Gioia to be her sister. But, then, all the
citizens looked more or less alike to him. And apart from their
physical resemblance, so he quickly came to realize, Belilala and
Gioia were not really very similar. There was a calmness, a deep
reservoir of serenity, in Belilala, that Gioia, eager and volatile and
ever impatient, did not seem to have. Strolling the swarming streets
of Chang-an with Belilala, he did not perceive in her any of Gioia's
restless feverish need always to know what lay beyond, and beyond,
and beyond even that. When they toured the Hsing-ch'ing Palace,
Belilala did not after five minutes begin—as Gioia surely would
have done—to seek directions to the Fountain of Hsuan-tsung or
the Wild Goose Pagoda. Curiosity did not consume Belilala as it did
Gioia. Plainly she believed that there would always be enough time
for her to see everything she cared to see. There were some days
when Belilala chose not to go out at all, but was content merely to
remain at their pavilion playing a solitary game with flat porcelain
counters, or viewing the flowers of the garden.

He found, oddly, that he enjoyed the respite from Gioia's intense
world-swallowing appetites; and yet he longed for her to return.
Belilala—beautiful, gentle, tranquil, patient—was too perfect for
him. She seemed unreal in her gleaming impeccability, much like
one of those Sung celadon vases that appear too flawless to have
been thrown and glazed by human hands. There was something a
little soulless about her: an immaculate finish outside, emptiness
within. Belilala might almost have been a temporary, he thought,
though he knew she was not. He could explore the pavilions and
palaces of Chang-an with her, he could make graceful conversation

with her while they dined, he could certainly enjoy coupling with her; but he could not love her or even contemplate the possibility. It was hard to imagine Belilala worriedly studying herself in a mirror for wrinkles and gray hairs. Belilala would never be any older than she was at this moment; nor could Belilala ever have been any younger. Perfection does not move along an axis of time. But the perfection of Belilala's glossy surface made her inner being impenetrable to him. Gioia was more vulnerable, more obviously flawed—her restlessness, her moodiness, her vanity, her fears—and therefore she was more accessible to his own highly imperfect twentieth-century sensibility.

Occasionally he saw Gioia as he roamed the city, or thought he did. He had a glimpse of her among the miracle-vendors in the Persian Bazaar, and outside the Zoroastrian temple, and again by the goldfish pond in the Serpentine Park. But he was never quite sure that the woman he saw was really Gioia, and he never could get close enough to her to be certain: she had a way of vanishing as he approached, like some mysterious Lorelei luring him onward and onward in a hopeless chase. After a while he came to realize that he was not going to find her until she was ready to be found.

He lost track of time. Weeks, months, years? He had no idea. In this city of exotic luxury, mystery, and magic all was in constant flux and transition and the days had a fitful, unstable quality. Buildings and even whole streets were torn down of an afternoon and reerected, within days, far away. Grand new pagodas sprouted like toadstools in the night. Citizens came in from Asgard, Alexandria, Timbuctoo, New Chicago, stayed for a time, disappeared, returned. There was a constant round of court receptions, banquets, theatrical events, each one much like the one before. The festivals in honor of past emperors and empresses might have given some form to the year, but they seemed to occur in a random way, the ceremony marking the death of T'ai Tsung coming around twice the same year, so it seemed to him, once in a season of snow and again in high summer, and the one honoring the ascension of the Empress Wu being held twice in a single season. Perhaps he had misunderstood something. But he knew it was no use asking anyone.

One day Belilala said unexpectedly, "Shall we go to Mohenjo-daro?"

"I didn't know it was ready for visitors," he replied.

"Oh, yes. For quite some time now."

He hesitated. This had caught him unprepared. Cautiously he said, "Gioia and I were going to go there together, you know."

Belilala smiled amiably, as though the topic under discussion were nothing more than the choice of that evening's restaurant.

"Were you?" she asked.

"It was all arranged while we were still in Alexandria. To go with you instead—I don't know what to tell you, Belilala." Phillips sensed that he was growing terribly flustered. "You know that I'd like to go. With you. But on the other hand I can't help feeling that I shouldn't go there until I'm back with Gioia again. If I ever am." How foolish this sounds, he thought. How clumsy, how adolescent. He found that he was having trouble looking straight at her. Uneasily he said, with a kind of desperation in his voice, "I did promise her—there was a commitment, you understand—a firm agreement that we would go to Mohenjo-daro together—"

"Oh, but Gioia's already there!" said Belilala in the most casual way.

He gaped as though she had punched him.

"What?"

"She was one of the first to go, after it opened. Months and months ago. You didn't know?" she asked, sounding surprised, but not very. "You really didn't know?"

That astonished him. He felt bewildered, betrayed, furious. His cheeks grew hot, his mouth gaped. He shook his head again and again, trying to clear it of confusion. It was a moment before he could speak. "Already there?" he said at last. "Without waiting for me? After we had talked about going there together—after we had agreed—"

Belilala laughed. "But how could she resist seeing the newest city? You know how impatient Gioia is!"

"Yes. Yes."

He was stunned. He could barely think.

"Just like all short-timers," Belilala said. "She rushes here, she rushes there. She must have it all, now, now, right away, at once, instantly. You ought never expect her to wait for you for anything for very long: the fit seizes her, and off she goes. Surely you must know that about her by now."

"A short-timer?" He had not heard that term before.

"Yes. You knew that. You must have known that." Belilala flashed her sweetest smile. She showed no sign of comprehending his distress. With a brisk wave of her hand she said, "Well, then, shall we go, you and I? To Mohenjo-daro?"

"Of course," Phillips said bleakly.

"When would you like to leave?"

"Tonight," he said. He paused a moment. "What's a short-timer, Belilala?"

Color came to her cheeks. "Isn't it obvious?" she asked.

* * *

Had there ever been a more hideous place on the face of the earth
than the city of Mohenjo-daro? Phillips found it difficult to imagine
one. Nor could he understand why, out of all the cities that had
ever been, these people had chosen to restore this one to existence.
More than ever they seemed alien to him, unfathomable, incomprehensible.

From the terrace atop the many-towered citadel he peered down
into grim claustrophobic Mohenjo-daro and shivered. The stark,
bleak city looked like nothing so much as some prehistoric prison
colony. In the manner of an uneasy tortoise it huddled, squat and
compact, against the gray monotonous Indus River plain: miles of
dark burnt-brick walls enclosing miles of terrifyingly orderly
streets, laid out in an awesome, monstrous gridiron pattern of
maniacal rigidity. The houses themselves were dismal and forbid-
ding too, clusters of brick cells gathered about small airless courtyards. There were no windows, only small doors that opened not
onto the main boulevards but onto the tiny mysterious lanes that
ran between the buildings. Who had designed this horrifying me-
tropolis? What harsh sour souls they must have had, these frightening and frightened folk, creating for themselves in the lush fertile
plains of India such a Supreme Soviet of a city!

"How lovely it is," Belilala murmured. "How fascinating!"

He stared at her in amazement.

"Fascinating? Yes," he said. "I suppose so. The same way that the
smile of a cobra is fascinating."

"What's a cobra?"

"Poisonous predatory serpent," Phillips told her. "Probably extinct. Or formerly extinct, more likely. It wouldn't surprise me if
you people had re-created a few and turned them loose in Mohenjo
to make things livelier."

"You sound angry, Charles."

"Do I? That's not how I feel."

"How do you feel, then?"

"I don't know," he said after a long moment's pause. He
shrugged. "Lost, I suppose. Very far from home."

"Poor Charles."

"Standing here in this ghastly barracks of a city, listening to you
tell me how beautiful it is, I've never felt more alone in my life."

"You miss Gioia very much, don't you?"

He gave her another startled look.

"Gioia has nothing to do with it. She's probably been having
ecstasies over the loveliness of Mohenjo just like you. Just like all

of you. I suppose I'm the only one who can't find the beauty, the charm. I'm the only one who looks out there and sees only horror, and then wonders why nobody else sees it, why in fact people would set up a place like this for *entertainment,* for *pleasure*—"

Her eyes were gleaming. "Oh, you are angry! You really are!"

"Does that fascinate you, too?" he snapped. "A demonstration of genuine primitive emotion? A typical quaint twentieth-century outburst?" He paced the rampart in short quick anguished steps. "Ah. Ah. I think I understand it now, Belilala. Of course: I'm part of your circus, the star of the sideshow. I'm the first experiment in setting up the next stage of it, in fact." Her eyes were wide. The sudden harshness and violence in his voice seemed to be alarming and exciting her at the same time. That angered him even more. Fiercely he went on, "Bringing whole cities back out of time was fun for a while, but it lacks a certain authenticity, eh? For some reason you couldn't bring the inhabitants, too; you couldn't just grab a few million prehistorics out of Egypt or Greece or India and dump them down in this era, I suppose because you might have too much trouble controlling them, or because you'd have the problem of disposing of them once you were bored with them. So you had to settle for creating temporaries to populate your ancient cities. But now you've got me. I'm something more real than a temporary, and that's a terrific novelty for you, and novelty is the thing you people crave more than anything else: maybe the *only* thing you crave. And here I am, complicated, unpredictable, edgy, capable of anger, fear, sadness, love, and all those other formerly extinct things. Why settle for picturesque architecture when you can observe picturesque emotion, too? What fun I must be for all of you! And if you decide that I was really interesting, maybe you'll ship me back where I came from and check out a few other ancient types—a Roman gladiator, maybe, or a Renaissance pope, or even a Neanderthal or two—"

"Charles," she said tenderly. "Oh, Charles, Charles, Charles, how lonely you must be, how lost, how troubled! Will you ever forgive me? Will you ever forgive us all?"

Once more he was astounded by her. She sounded entirely sincere, altogether sympathetic. Was she? Was she, really? He was not sure he had ever had a sign of genuine caring from any of them before, not even Gioia. Nor could he bring himself to trust Belilala now. He was afraid of her, afraid of all of them, of their brittleness, their slyness, their elegance. He wished he could go to her and have her take him in her arms; but he felt too much the shaggy prehistoric just now to be able to risk asking that comfort of her.

He turned away and began to walk around the rim of the citadel's massive wall.

"Charles?"

"Let me alone for a little while," he said.

He walked on. His forehead throbbed and there was a pounding in his chest. All stress systems going full blast, he thought: secret glands dumping gallons of inflammatory substances into his blood-stream. The heat, the inner confusion, the repellent look of this place—

Try to understand, he thought. Relax. Look about you. Try to enjoy your holiday in Mohenjo-daro.

He leaned warily outward, over the edge of the wall. He had never seen a wall like this; it must be forty feet thick at the base, he guessed, perhaps even more, and every brick perfectly shaped, meticulously set. Beyond the great rampart, marshes ran almost to the edge of the city, although close by the wall the swamps had been dammed and drained for agriculture. He saw lithe brown farmers down there, busy with their wheat and barley and peas. Cattle and buffaloes grazed a little farther out. The air was heavy, dank, humid. All was still. From somewhere close at hand came the sound of a droning, whining stringed instrument and a steady insistent chanting.

Gradually a sort of peace pervaded him. His anger subsided. He felt himself beginning to grow calm again. He looked back at the city, the rigid interlocking streets, the maze of inner lanes, the millions of courses of precise brickwork.

It is a miracle, he told himself, that this city is here in this place and at this time. And it is a miracle that I am here to see it.

Caught for a moment by the magic within the bleakness, he thought he began to understand Belilala's awe and delight, and he wished now that he had not spoken to her so sharply. The city was alive. Whether it was the actual Mohenjo-daro of thousands upon thousands of years ago, ripped from the past by some wondrous hook, or simply a cunning reproduction, did not matter at all. Real or not, this was the true Mohenjo-daro. It had been dead, and now, for the moment, it was alive again. These people, these *citizens*, might be trivial, but reconstructing Mohenjo-daro was no trivial achievement. And that the city that had been reconstructed was oppressive and sinister-looking was unimportant. No one was com-pelled to live in Mohenjo-daro any more. Its time had come and gone, long ago; those little dark-skinned peasants and craftsmen and merchants down there were mere temporaries, mere inanimate things, conjured up like zombies to enhance the illusion. They did not need his pity. Nor did he need to pity himself. He knew that he should be grateful for the chance to behold these things. Someday, when this dream had ended and his hosts had returned him to the world of subways and computers and income tax and television networks, he would think of Mohenjo-daro as he had once beheld it, lofty walls of tightly woven dark brick under a heavy sky, and he would remember only its beauty.

Glancing back, he searched for Belilala and could not for a moment find her. Then he caught sight of her carefully descending a narrow staircase that angled down the inner face of the citadel wall.

"Belilala!" he called.

She paused and looked his way, shading her eyes from the sun with her hand. "Are you all right?"

"Where are you going?"

"To the baths," she said "Do you want to come?"

He nodded. "Yes. Wait for me, will you? I'll be right there." He began to run toward her along the top of the wall.

The baths were attached to the citadel: a great open tank the size of a large swimming pool, lined with bricks set on edge in gypsum mortar and waterproofed with asphalt, and eight smaller tanks just north of it in a kind of covered arcade. He supposed that in ancient times the whole complex had had some ritual purpose, the large tank used by common folk and the small chambers set aside for the private ablutions of priests or nobles. Now the baths were maintained, it seemed, entirely for the pleasure of visiting citizens. As Phillips came up the passageway that led to the main bath he saw fifteen or twenty of them lolling in the water or padding languidly about, while temporaries of the dark-skinned Mohenjo-daro type served them drinks and pungent little morsels of spiced meat as though this were some sort of luxury resort. Which was, he realized, exactly what it was. The temporaries wore white cotton loincloths; the citizens were naked. In his former life he had encountered that sort of casual public nudity a few times on visits to California and the south of France, and it had made him mildly uneasy. But he was growing accustomed to it here.

The changing rooms were tiny brick cubicles connected by rows of closely placed steps to the courtyard that surrounded the central tank. They entered one and Belilala swiftly slipped out of the loose cotton robe that she had worn since their arrival that morning. With arms folded she stood leaning against the wall, waiting for him. After a moment he dropped his own robe and followed her outside. He felt a little giddy, sauntering around naked in the open like this.

On the way to the main bathing area they passed the private baths. None of them seemed to be occupied. They were elegantly constructed chambers, with finely jointed brick floors and carefully designed runnels to drain excess water into the passageway that led to the primary drain. Phillips was struck with admiration for the cleverness of the prehistoric engineers. He peered into this chamber and that to see how the conduits and ventilating ducts were arranged, and when he came to the last room in the sequence he was surprised and embarrassed to discover that it was in use. A brawny grinning man, big-muscled, deep-chested, with exuberantly flowing shoulder-length red hair and a flamboyant, sharply tapering beard was thrashing about merrily with two women in the small tank. Phillips had a quick glimpse of a lively tangle of arms, legs, breasts, buttocks.

"Sorry," he muttered. His cheeks reddened. Quickly he ducked out, blurting apologies as he went. "Didn't realize the room was occupied—no wish to intrude—"

Belilala had proceeded on down the passageway. Phillips hurried after her. From behind him came peals of cheerful raucous booming laughter and high-pitched giggling and the sound of splashing water. Probably they had not even noticed him.

He paused a moment, puzzled, playing back in his mind that one startling glimpse. Something was not right. Those women, he was fairly sure, were citizens: little slender elfin dark-haired girlish creatures, the standard model. But the man? That great curling sweep of red hair? Not a citizen. Citizens did not affect shoulder-length hair. And *red*? Nor had he ever seen a citizen so burly, so powerfully muscular. Or one with a beard. But he could hardly be a temporary, either. Phillips could conceive no reason why there would be so Anglo-Saxon-looking a temporary at Mohenjo-daro; and it was unthinkable for a temporary to be frolicking like that with citizens, anyway.

"Charles?"

He looked up ahead. Belilala stood at the end of the passageway, outlined in a nimbus of brilliant sunlight. "Charles?" she said again. "Did you lose your way?"

"I'm right here behind you," he said. "I'm coming."

"Who did you meet in there?"

"A man with a beard."

"With a what?"

"A beard," he said. "Red hair growing on his face. I wonder who he is."

"Nobody I know," said Belilala. "The only one I know with hair on his face is you. And yours is black, and you shave it off every

day." She laughed. "Come along, now! I see some friends by the
pool!"

He caught up with her, and they went hand in hand out into the
courtyard. Immediately a waiter glided up to them, an obsequious
little temporary with a tray of drinks. Phillips waved it away and
headed for the pool. He felt terribly exposed: he imagined that the
citizens disporting themselves here were staring intently at him,
studying his hairy primitive body as though he were some mythical
creature, a Minotaur, a werewolf, summoned up for their amusement. Belilala drifted off to talk to someone and he slipped into
the water, grateful for the concealment it offered. It was deep,
warm, comforting. With swift powerful strokes he breast-stroked
from one end to the other.

A citizen perched elegantly on the pool's rim smiled at him. "Ah,
so you've come at last, Charles!" *Char-less.* Two syllables. Someone
from Gioia's set: Stengard, Hawk, Aramayne? He could not remember which one. They were all so much alike.

Phillips returned the man's smile in a halfhearted, tentative way.
He searched for something to say and finally asked, "Have you
been here long?"

"Weeks. Perhaps months. What a splendid achievement this city
is, eh, Charles? Such utter unity of mood—such a total statement
of a uniquely single-minded esthetic—"

"Yes. Single-minded is the word," Phillips said dryly.

"Gioia's word, actually. Gioia's phrase. I was merely quoting."

Gioia. He felt as if he had been stabbed.

"You've spoken to Gioia lately?" he said.

"Actually, no. It was Hekna who saw her. You do remember
Hekna, eh?" He nodded toward two naked women standing on the
brick platform that bordered the pool, chatting, delicately nibbling
morsels of meat. They could have been twins. "There is Hekna,
with your Belilala." Hekna, yes. So this must be Hawk, Phillips
thought, unless there has been some recent shift of couples. "How
sweet she is, your Belilala," Hawk said. "Gioia chose very wisely
when she picked her for you."

Another stab: a much deeper one. "Is that how it was?" he said.
"Gioia *picked* Belilala for me?"

"Why, of course!" Hawk seemed surprised. It went without saying, evidently. "What did you think? That Gioia would merely go
off and leave you to fend for yourself?"

"Hardly. Not Gioia."

"She's very tender, very gentle, isn't she?"

"You mean Belilala? Yes, very," said Phillips carefully. "A dear
woman, a wonderful woman. But of course I hope to get together

with Gioia again soon." He paused. "They say she's been in Mohenjo-daro almost since it opened."

"She was here, yes."

"Was?"

"Oh, you know Gioia," Hawk said lightly. "She's moved along by now, naturally."

Phillips leaned forward. "Naturally," he said. Tension thickened his voice. "Where has she gone this time?"

"Timbuctoo, I think. Or New Chicago. I forget which one it was. She was telling us that she hoped to be in Timbuctoo for the closing-down party. But then Fenimon had some pressing reason for going to New Chicago. I can't remember what they decided to do." Hawk gestured sadly. "Either way, a pity that she left Mohenjo before the new visitor came. She had such a rewarding time with you, after all: I'm sure she'd have found much to learn from him also."

The unfamiliar term twanged an alarm deep in Phillips's consciousness. *"Visitor?"* he said, angling his head sharply toward Hawk. "What visitor do you mean?"

"You haven't met him yet? Oh, of course, you've only just arrived."

Phillips moistened his lips. "I think I may have seen him. Long red hair? Beard like this?"

"That's the one! Willoughby, he's called. He's—what?—a Viking, a pirate, something like that. Tremendous vigor and force. Remarkable person. We should have many more visitors, I think. They're far superior to temporaries, everyone agrees. Talking with a temporary is a little like talking to one's self, wouldn't you say? They give you no significant illumination. But a visitor—someone like this Willoughby—or like you, Charles—a visitor can be truly enlightening, a visitor can transform one's view of reality—"

"Excuse me," Phillips said. A throbbing began behind his forehead. "Perhaps we can continue this conversation later, yes?" He put the flats of his hands against the hot brick of the platform and hoisted himself swiftly from the pool. "At dinner, maybe—or afterward—yes? All right?" He set off at a quick half-trot back toward the passageway that led to the private baths.

As he entered the roofed part of the structure his throat grew dry, his breath suddenly came short. He padded quickly up the hall and peered into the little bath chamber. The bearded man was still there, sitting up in the tank, breast-high above the water, with one arm around each of the women. His eyes gleamed with fiery intensity in the dimness. He was grinning in marvelous self-satisfaction; he seemed to brim with intensity, confidence, gusto.

Let him be what I think he is, Phillips prayed. I have been alone among these people long enough.

"May I come in?" he asked.

"Aye, fellow!" cried the man in the tub thunderously. "By my troth, come ye in, and bring your lass as well! God's teeth, I wot there's room aplenty for more folk in this tub than we!"

At that great uproarious outcry Phillips felt a powerful surge of joy. What a joyous rowdy voice! How rich, how lusty, how totally uncitizenlike!

And those oddly archaic words! *God's teeth? By my troth?* What sort of talk was that? What else but the good pure sonorous Elizabethan diction! Certainly it had something of the roll and fervor of Shakespeare about it. And spoken with—an Irish brogue, was it? No, not quite: it was English, but English spoken in no manner Phillips had ever heard.

Citizens did not speak that way. But a *visitor* might.

So it was true. Relief flooded Phillips's soul. Not alone, then! Another relic of a former age—another wanderer—a companion in chaos, a brother in adversity—a fellow voyager, tossed even farther than he had been by the tempests of time—

The bearded man grinned heartily and beckoned to Phillips with a toss of his head. "Well, join us, join us, man! 'Tis good to see an English face again, amidst all these Moors and rogue Portugals! But what have ye done with thy lass? One can never have enough wenches, d'ye not agree?"

The force and vigor of him were extraordinary: almost too much so. He roared, he bellowed, he boomed. He was so very much what he ought to be that he seemed more a character out of some old pirate movie than anything else, so blustering, so real, that he seemed unreal. A stage Elizabethan, larger than life, a boisterous young Falstaff without the belly.

Hoarsely Phillips said, "Who are you?"

"Why, Ned Willoughby's son Francis am I, of Plymouth. Late of the service of Her Most Protestant Majesty, but most foully abducted by the powers of darkness and cast away among these blackamoor Hindus, or whatever they be. And thyself?"

"Charles Phillips." After a moment's uncertainty he added, "I'm from New York."

"*New* York? What place is that? In faith, man, I know it not!"

"A city in America."

"A city in America, forsooth! What a fine fancy that is! In America, you say, and not on the Moon, or perchance underneath the sea?" To the women Willoughby said, "D'ye hear him? He comes from a city in America! With the face of an Englishman, though not the manner of one, and not quite the proper sort of speech. A city in America! A *city*. God's blood, what will I hear next?"

Phillips trembled. Awe was beginning to take hold of him. This man had walked the streets of Shakespeare's London, perhaps. He had clinked canisters with Marlowe or Essex or Walter Raleigh; he had watched the ships of the Armada wallowing in the Channel. It strained Phillips's spirit to think of it. This strange dream in which he found himself was compounding its strangeness now. He felt like a weary swimmer assailed by heavy surf, winded, dazed. The hot close atmosphere of the baths was driving him toward vertigo. There could be no doubt of it any longer. He was not the only primitive—the only *visitor*—who was wandering loose in this fiftieth century. They were conducting other experiments as well. He gripped the sides of the door to steady himself and said, "When you speak of Her Most Protestant Majesty, it's Elizabeth the First you mean, is that not so?"

"Elizabeth, aye! As to the First, that is true enough, but why trouble to name her thus? There is but one. First and Last, I do trow, and God save her, there is no other!"

Phillips studied the other man warily. He knew that he must proceed with care. A misstep at this point and he would forfeit any chance that Willoughby would take him seriously. How much metaphysical bewilderment, after all, could this man absorb? What did he know, what had anyone of his time known, of past and present and future and the notion that one might somehow move from one to the other as readily as one would go from Surrey to Kent? That was a twentieth-century idea, late nineteenth at best, a fantastical speculation that very likely no one had even considered before Wells had sent his time traveler off to stare at the reddened sun of the earth's last twilight. Willoughby's world was a world of Protestants and Catholics, of kings and queens, of tiny sailing vessels, of swords at the hip and ox-carts on the road: that world seemed to Phillips far more alien and distant than was this world of citizens and temporaries. The risk that Willoughby would not begin to understand him was great.

But this man and he were natural allies against a world they had never made. Phillips chose to take the risk.

"Elizabeth the First is the queen you serve," he said. "There will be another of her name in England, in due time. Has already been, in fact."

Willoughby shook his head like a puzzled lion. "Another Elizabeth, d'ye say?"

"A second one, and not much like the first. Long after your

Virgin Queen, this one. She will reign in what you think of as the days to come. That I know without doubt."

The Englishman peered at him and frowned. "You see the future? Are you a soothsayer, then? A necromancer, mayhap? Or one of the very demons that brought me to this place?"

"Not at all," Phillips said gently. "Only a lost soul, like yourself." He stepped into the little room and crouched by the side of the tank. The two citizen-women were staring at him in bland fascination. He ignored them. To Willoughby he said, "Do you have any idea where you are?"

The Englishman had guessed, rightly enough, that he was in India: "I do believe these little brown Moorish folk are of the Hindu sort," he said. But that was as far as his comprehension of what had befallen him could go.

It had not occurred to him that he was no longer living in the sixteenth century. And of course he did not begin to suspect that this strange and somber brick city in which he found himself was a wanderer out of an era even more remote than his own. Was there any way, Phillips wondered, of explaining that to him?

He had been here only three days. He thought it was devils that had carried him off. "While I slept did they come for me," he said. "Mephistophilis Sathanas, his henchmen seized me—God alone can say why—and swept me in a moment out to this torrid realm from England, where I had reposed among friends and family. For I was between one voyage and the next, you must understand, awaiting Drake and his ship—you know Drake, the glorious Francis? God's blood, there's a mariner for ye! We were to go to the Main again, he and I, but instead here I be in this other place—" Willoughby leaned close and said, "I ask you, soothsayer, how can it be, that a man go to sleep in Plymouth and wake up in India? It is passing strange, is it not?"

"That it is," Phillips said.

"But he that is in the dance must needs dance on, though he do but hop, eh? So do I believe." He gestured toward the two citizen-women. "And therefore to console myself in this pagan land I have found me some sport among these little Portugal women—"

"Portugal?" said Phillips.

"Why, what else can they be, but Portugals? Is it not the Portugals who control all these coasts of India? See, the people are of two sorts here, the blackamoors and the others, the fair-skinned ones, the lords and masters who lie here in these baths. If they be not Hindus, and I think they are not, then Portugals is what they must be." He laughed and pulled the women against himself and rubbed his hands over their breasts as though they were fruits on a vine. "Is that not what you are, you little naked shameless Papist wenches? A pair of Portugals, eh?"

They giggled, but did not answer.

"No," Phillips said. "This is India, but not the India you think you know. And these women are not Portuguese."

"Not Portuguese?" Willoughby said, baffled.

"No more so than you. I'm quite certain of that."

Willoughby stroked his beard. "I do admit I found them very odd, for Portugals. I have heard not a syllable of their Portugee speech on their lips. And it is strange also that they run naked as Adam and Eve in these baths, and allow me free plunder of their women, which is not the way of Portugals at home, God wot. But I thought me, this is India, they choose to live in another fashion here—"

"No," Phillips said. "I tell you, these are not Portuguese, nor any other people of Europe who are known to you."

"Prithee, who are they, then?"

Do it delicately, now, Phillips warned himself. *Delicately.*

He said, "It is not far wrong to think of them as spirits of some kind—demons, even. Or sorcerers who have magicked us out of our proper places in the world." He paused, groping for some means to share with Willoughby, in a way that Willoughby might grasp, this mystery that had enfolded them. He drew a deep breath. "They've taken us not only across the sea," he said, "but across the years as well. We have both been hauled, you and I, far into the days that are to come."

Willoughby gave him a look of blank bewilderment.

"Days that are to come? Times yet unborn, d'ye mean? Why, I comprehend none of that!"

"Try to understand. We're both castaways in the same boat, man! But there's no way we can help each other if I can't make you see—"

Shaking his head, Willoughby muttered, "In faith, good friend, I find your words the merest folly. Today is today, and tomorrow is tomorrow, and how can a man step from one to t'other until tomorrow be turned into today?"

"I have no idea," said Phillips. Struggle was apparent on Willoughby's face; but plainly he could perceive no more than the haziest outline of what Phillips was driving at, if that much. "But this I know," he went on. "That your world and all that was in it is dead and gone. And so is mine, though I was born four hundred years after you, in the time of the second Elizabeth."

Willoughby snorted scornfully. "Four hundred—"

"You must believe me!"

"Nay! Nay!"

"It's the truth. Your time is only history to me. And mine and yours are history to *them*—ancient history. They call us visitors, but what we are is captives." Phillips felt himself quivering in the intensity of his effort. He was aware how insane this must sound to Willoughby. It was beginning to sound insane to him. "They've stolen us out of our proper times—seizing us like gypsies in the night—"

"Fie, man! You rave with lunacy!"

Phillips shook his head. He reached out and seized Willoughby tightly by the wrist. "I beg you, listen to me!" The citizen-women were watching closely, whispering to one another behind their hands, laughing. "Ask them!" Phillips cried. "Make them tell you what century this is! The sixteenth, do you think? Ask them!"

"What century could it be, but the sixteenth of our Lord?"

"They will tell you it is the fiftieth."

Willoughby looked at him pityingly. "Man, man, what a sorry thing thou art! The fiftieth, indeed!" He laughed. "Fellow, listen to me, now. There is but one Elizabeth, safe upon her throne in Westminster. This is India. The year is Anno 1591. Come, let us you and I steal a ship from these Portugals, and make our way back to England, and peradventure you may get from there to your America—"

"There is no England."

"Ah, can you say that and not be mad?"

"The cities and nations we knew are gone. These people live like magicians, Francis." There was no use holding anything back now, Phillips thought leadenly. He knew that he had lost. "They conjure up places of long ago, and build them here and there to suit their fancy, and when they are bored with them they destroy them, and start anew. There is no England. Europe is empty, featureless, void. Do you know what cities there are? There are only five in all the world. There is Alexandria of Egypt. There is Timbuctoo in Africa. There is New Chicago in America. There is a great city in China— in Cathay, I suppose you would say. And there is this place, which they call Mohenjo-daro, and which is far more ancient than Greece, than Rome, than Babylon."

Quietly Willoughby said, "Nay. This is mere absurdity. You say we are in some far tomorrow, and then you tell me we are dwelling in some city of long ago."

"A conjuration, only," Phillips said in desperation. "A likeness of that city. Which these folk have fashioned somehow for their own amusement. Just as we are here, you and I: to amuse them. Only to amuse them."

"You are completely mad."

"Come with me, then. Talk with the citizens by the great pool. Ask them what year this is; ask them about England; ask them how you come to be here." Once again Phillips grasped Willoughby's wrist. "We should be allies. If we work together, perhaps we can discover some way to get ourselves out of this place, and—"

"Let me be, fellow."

"Please—"

"Let me be!" roared Willoughby, and pulled his arm free. His eyes were stark with rage. Rising in the tank, he looked about furiously as though searching for a weapon. The citizen-women shrank back away from him, though at the same time they seemed captivated by the big man's fierce outburst. "Go to, get you to Bedlam! Let me be, madman! Let me be!"

Dismally Phillips roamed the dusty unpaved streets of Mohenjo-daro alone for hours. His failure with Willoughby had left him bleak-spirited and somber: he had hoped to stand back to back with the Elizabethan against the citizens, but he saw now that that was not to be. He had bungled things; or, more likely, it had been impossible ever to bring Willoughby to see the truth of their predicament.

In the stifling heat he went at random through the confusing congested lanes of flat-roofed windowless houses and blank featureless walls until he emerged into a broad marketplace. The life of the city swirled madly around him: the pseudo-life, rather, the intricate interactions of the thousands of temporaries who were nothing more than windup dolls set in motion to provide the illusion that pre-Vedic India was still a going concern. Here vendors sold beautiful little carved stone seals portraying tigers and monkeys and strange humped cattle, and women bargained vociferously with craftsmen for ornaments of ivory, gold, copper, and bronze. Weary-looking women squatted behind immense mounds of newly made pottery, pinkish red with black designs. No one paid any attention to him. He was the outsider here, neither citizen nor temporary. They belonged.

He went on, passing the huge granaries where workmen ceaselessly unloaded carts of wheat and others pounded grain on great circular brick platforms. He drifted into a public restaurant thronging with joyless silent people standing elbow to elbow at small brick counters, and was given a flat round piece of bread, a sort of tortilla or chapatti, in which was stuffed some spiced mincemeat that stung his lips like fire. Then he moved onward down a wide shallow timbered staircase into the lower part of the city, where the peasantry lived in cell-like rooms packed together as though in hives.

It was an oppressive city, but not a squalid one. The intensity of the concern with sanitation amazed him: wells and fountains and public privies everywhere, and brick drains running from each building, leading to covered cesspools. There was none of the open sewage and pestilent gutters that he knew still could be found in the India of his own time. He wondered whether ancient Mohenjo-daro had in truth been so fastidious. Perhaps the citizens had rede-signed the city to suit their own ideals of cleanliness. No: most likely what he saw was authentic, he decided, a function of the same obsessive discipline that had given the city its rigidity of form. If Mohenjo-daro had been a verminous filthy hole, the citizens proba-bly would have re-created it in just that way, and loved it for its fascinating reeking filth.

Not that he had ever noticed an excessive concern with authentic-ity on the part of the citizens; and Mohenjo-daro, like all the other restored cities he had visited, was full of the usual casual anachro-nisms. Phillips saw images of Shiva and Krishna here and there on the walls of buildings he took to be temples, and the benign face of the mother-goddess Kali loomed in the plazas. Surely those deities had arisen in India long after the collapse of the Mohenjo-daro civilization. Were the citizens indifferent to such matters of chronol-ogy? Or did they take a certain naughty pleasure in mixing the eras—a mosque and a church in Greek Alexandria, Hindu gods in prehistoric Mohenjo-daro? Perhaps their records of the past had become contaminated with errors over the thousands of years. He would not have been surprised to see banners bearing portraits of Gandhi and Nehru being carried in procession through the streets. And there were phantasms and chimeras at large here again, too, as if the citizens were untroubled by the boundary between history and myth: little fat elephant-headed Ganeshas blithely plunging their trunks into water fountains, a six-armed three-headed woman sunning herself on a brick terrace. Why not? Surely that was the motto of these people: *Why not, why not, why not?* They could do as they pleased, and they did. Yet Gioia had said to him, long ago, "Limits are very important." In what, Phillips wondered, did they limit themselves, other than the number of their cities? Was there a quota, perhaps, on the number of "visitors" they allowed them-selves to kidnap from the past? Until today he had thought he was the only one; now he knew there was at least one other; possibly there were more elsewhere, a step or two ahead or behind him, making the circuit with the citizens who traveled endlessly from New Chicago to Chang-an to Alexandria. We should join forces, he thought, and compel them to send us back to our rightful eras. *Compel?* How? File a class-action suit, maybe? Demonstrate in the streets? Sadly he thought of his failure to make common cause with Willoughby. We are natural allies, he thought. Together perhaps we might have won some compassion from these people. But to Willoughby it must be literally unthinkable that Good Queen Bess and her subjects were sealed away on the far side of a barrier hundreds of centuries thick. He would prefer to believe that England was just a few months' voyage away around the Cape of Good Hope, and that all he need do was commandeer a ship and set sail for home. Poor Willoughby: probably he would never see his home again.

The thought came to Phillips suddenly:

Neither will you.

And then, after it:

If you could go home, would you really want to?

One of the first things he had realized here was that he knew almost nothing substantial about his former existence. His mind was well stocked with details on life in twentieth-century New York, to be sure; but of himself he could say not much more than that he was Charles Phillips and had come from 1984. Profession? Age? Parents' names? Did he have a wife? Children? A cat, a dog, hobbies? No data: none. Possibly the citizens had stripped such things from him when they brought him here, to spare him from the pain of separation. They might be capable of that kindness. Knowing so little of what he had lost, could he truly say that he yearned for it? Willoughby seemed to remember much more of his former life, somehow, and longed for it all the more intensely. He was spared that. Why not stay here, and go on and on from city to city, sightseeing all of time past as the citizens conjured it back into being? Why not? Why not? The chances were that he had no choice about it, anyway.

He made his way back up toward the citadel and to the baths once more. He felt a little like a ghost, haunting a city of ghosts.

Belilala seemed unaware that he had been gone for most of the day. She sat by herself on the terrace of the baths, placidly sipping some thick milky beverage that had been sprinkled with a dark spice. He shook his head when she offered him some.

"Do you remember I mentioned that I saw a man with red hair and a beard this morning?" Phillips said. "He's a visitor. Hawk told me that."

"Is he?" Belilala asked.

"From a time about four hundred years before mine. I talked with him. He thinks he was brought here by demons." Phillips gave her a searching look. "I'm a visitor, too, isn't that so?"

"Of course, love."

"And how was I brought here? By demons also?"

Belilala smiled indifferently. "You'd have to ask someone else. Hawk, perhaps. I haven't looked into these things very deeply."

"I see. Are there many visitors here, do you know?"

A languid shrug. "Not many, no, not really. I've only heard of three or four besides you. There may be others by now, I suppose." She rested her hand lightly on his. "Are you having a good time in Mohenjo, Charles?"

He let her question pass as though he had not heard it.

"I asked Hawk about Gioia," he said.

"Oh?"

"He told me that she's no longer here, that she's gone on to Timbuctoo or New Chicago, he wasn't sure which."

"That's quite likely. As everybody knows, Gioia rarely stays in the same place very long."

Phillips nodded. "You said the other day that Gioia is a short-timer. That means she's going to grow old and die, doesn't it?"

"I thought you understood that, Charles."

"Whereas you will not age? Nor Hawk, nor Stengard, nor any of the rest of your set?"

"We will live as long as we wish," she said. "But we will not age, no."

"What makes a person a short-timer?"

"They're born that way, I think. Some missing gene, some extra gene—I don't actually know. It's extremely uncommon. Nothing can be done to help them. It's very slow, the aging. But it can't be halted."

Phillips nodded. "That must be very disagreeable," he said. "To find yourself one of the few people growing old in a world where everyone stays young. No wonder Gioia is so impatient. No wonder she runs around from place to place. No wonder she attached herself so quickly to the barbaric hairy visitor from the twentieth century, who comes from a time when *everybody* was a short-timer. She and I have something in common, wouldn't you say?"

"In a manner of speaking, yes."

"We understand aging. We understand death. Tell me: is Gioia likely to die very soon, Belilala?"

"Soon? Soon?" She gave him a wide-eyed childlike stare. "What is soon? How can I say? What you think of as soon and what I think of as soon are not the same things, Charles." Then her manner changed: she seemed to be hearing what he was saying for the first time. Softly she said, "No, no, Charles. I don't think she will die very soon."

"When she left me in Chang-an, was it because she had become bored with me?"

Belilala shook her head. "She was simply restless. It had nothing to do with you. She was never bored with you."

"Then I'm going to go looking for her. Wherever she may be, Timbuctoo, New Chicago, I'll find her. Gioia and I belong together."

"Perhaps you do," said Belilala. "Yes. Yes, I think you really do." She sounded altogether unperturbed, unrejected, unbereft. "By all means, Charles. Go to her. Follow her. Find her. Wherever she may be."

They had already begun dismantling Timbuctoo when Phillips got there. While he was still high overhead, his flitterflitter hovering above the dusty tawny plain where the River Niger met the sands of the Sahara, a surge of keen excitement rose in him as he looked down at the square gray flat-roofed mud brick buildings of the great desert capital. But when he landed he found gleaming metal-skinned robots swarming everywhere, a horde of them scuttling about like giant shining insects, pulling the place apart.

He had not known about the robots before. So that was how all these miracles were carried out, Phillips realized: an army of obliging machines. He imagined them bustling up out of the earth whenever their services were needed, emerging from some sterile subterranean storehouse to put together Venice or Thebes or Knossos or Houston or whatever place was required, down to the finest detail, and then at some later time returning to undo everything that they had fashioned. He watched them now, diligently pulling down the adobe walls, demolishing the heavy metal-studded gates, bulldozing the amazing labyrinth of alleyways and thoroughfares, sweeping away the market. On his last visit to Timbuctoo that market had been crowded with a horde of veiled Tuaregs and swaggering Moors, black Sudanese, shrewd-faced Syrian traders, all of them busily dickering for camels, horses, donkeys, slabs of salt, huge green melons, silver bracelets, splendid vellum Korans. They were all gone now, that picturesque crowd of swarthy temporaries. Nor were there any citizens to be seen. The dust of destruction choked the air. One of the robots came up to Phillips and said in a dry crackling insect-voice, "You ought not to be here. This city is closed."

He stared at the flashing, buzzing band of scanners and sensors across the creature's glittering tapered snout. "I'm trying to find someone, a citizen who may have been here recently. Her name is—"

"This city is closed," the robot repeated inexorably.

They would not let him stay as much as an hour. There is no food here, the robot said, no water, no shelter. This is not a place any longer. You may not stay. You may not stay. You may not stay. *This is not a place any longer.*

Perhaps he could find her in New Chicago, then. He took to the air again, soaring northward and westward over the vast emptiness. The land below him curved away into the hazy horizon, bare, sterile. What had they done with the vestiges of the world that had gone before? Had they turned their gleaming metal beetles loose to clean everything away? Were there no ruins of genuine antiquity anywhere? No scrap of Rome, no shard of Jerusalem, no stump of Fifth Avenue? It was all so barren down there: an empty stage, waiting for its next set to be built. He flew on a great arc across the jutting hump of Africa and on into what he supposed was southern Europe: the little vehicle did all the work, leaving him to doze or stare as he wished. Now and again he saw another flitterflitter pass by, far away, a dark distant winged teardrop outlined against the hard clarity of the sky. He wished there was some way of making radio contact with them, but he had no idea how to go about it. Not that he had anything he wanted to say; he wanted only to hear a human voice. He was utterly isolated. He might just as well have been the last living man on Earth. He closed his eyes and thought of Gioia.

"Like this?" Phillips asked. In an ivory-paneled oval room sixty stories above the softly glowing streets of New Chicago he touched a small cool plastic canister to his upper lip and pressed the stud at its base. He heard a foaming sound; and then blue vapor rose to his nostrils.

"Yes," Cantilena said. "That's right."

He detected a faint aroma of cinnamon, cloves, and something that might almost have been broiled lobster. Then a spasm of dizziness hit him and visions rushed through his head: Gothic cathedrals, the Pyramids, Central Park under fresh snow, the harsh brick warrens of Mohenjo-daro, and fifty thousand other places all at once, a wild roller-coaster ride through space and time. It seemed to go on for centuries. But finally his head cleared and he looked about, blinking, realizing that the whole thing had taken only a moment. Cantilena still stood at his elbow. The other citizens in the room—fifteen, twenty of them—had scarcely moved. The strange little man with the celadon skin over by the far wall continued to stare at him.

"Well?" Cantilena asked. "What did you think?"

"Incredible."

"And very authentic. It's an actual New Chicagoan drug. The exact formula. Would you like another?"

"Not just yet," Phillips said uneasily. He swayed and had to struggle for his balance. Sniffing that stuff might not have been such a wise idea, he thought.

He had been in New Chicago a week, or perhaps it was two, and he was still suffering from the peculiar disorientation that that city always aroused in him. This was the fourth time that he had come here, and it had been the same every time. New Chicago was the only one of the reconstructed cities of this world that in its original incarnation had existed *after* his own era. To him it was an outpost of the incomprehensible future; to the citizens it was a quaint simulacrum of the archaeological past. That paradox left him aswirl with impossible confusions and tensions.

What had happened to *old* Chicago was of course impossible for him to discover. Vanished without a trace, that was clear: no Water Tower, no Marina City, no Hancock Center, no Tribune building, not a fragment, not an atom. But it was hopeless to ask any of the million-plus inhabitants of New Chicago about their city's predecessor. They were only temporaries; they knew no more than they had to know, and all that they had to know was how to go through the motions of whatever it was that they did by way of creating the illusion that this was a real city. They had no need of knowing ancient history.

Nor was he likely to find out anything from a citizen, of course. Citizens did not seem to bother much about scholarly matters. Phillips had no reason to think that the world was anything other than an amusement park to them. Somewhere, certainly, there had to be those who specialized in the serious study of the lost civilizations of the past—for how, otherwise, would these uncanny reconstructed cities be brought into being? "The planners," he had once heard Nissandra or Aramayne say, "are already deep into their Byzantium research." But who were the planners? He had no idea. For all he knew, they were the robots. Perhaps the robots were the real masters of this whole era, who created the cities not primarily for the sake of amusing the citizens but in their own diligent attempt to comprehend the life of the world that had passed away. A wild speculation, yes; but not without some plausibility, he thought.

He felt oppressed by the party gaiety all about him. "I need some air," he said to Cantilena, and headed toward the window. It was the merest crescent, but a breeze came through. He looked out at the strange city below.

New Chicago had nothing in common with the old one but its

name. They had built it, at least, along the western shore of a large inland lake that might even be Lake Michigan, although when he had flown over it had seemed broader and less elongated than the lake he remembered. The city itself was a lacy fantasy of slender pastel-hued buildings rising at odd angles and linked by a webwork of gently undulating aerial bridges. The streets were long parentheses that touched the lake at their northern and southern ends and arched gracefully westward in the middle: Between each of the great boulevards ran a track for public transportation—sleek aquamarine bubble-vehicles gliding on soundless wheels—and flanking each of the tracks were lush strips of park. It was beautiful, astonishingly so, but insubstantial. The whole thing seemed to have been contrived from sunbeams and silk.

A soft voice beside him said, "Are you becoming ill?"

Phillips glanced around. The celadon man stood beside him: a compact, precise person, vaguely Oriental in appearance. His skin was of a curious gray-green hue like no skin Phillips had ever seen, and it was extraordinarily smooth in texture, as though he were made of fine porcelain.

He shook his head. "Just a little queasy," he said. "This city always scrambles me."

"I suppose it can be disconcerting," the little man replied. His tone was furry and veiled, the inflection strange. There was something feline about him. He seemed sinewy, unyielding, almost menacing. "Visitor, are you?"

Phillips studied him a moment. "Yes," he said.

"So am I, of course."

"Are you?"

"Indeed." The little man smiled. "What's your locus? Twentieth century? Twenty-first at the latest, I'd say."

"I'm from 1984. A.D. 1984."

Another smile, a self-satisfied one. "Not a bad guess, then." A brisk tilt of the head. "Y'ang-Yeovil."

"Pardon me?" Phillips said.

"Y'ang-Yeovil. It is my name. Formerly Colonel Y'ang-Yeovil of the Third Septentriad."

"Is that on some other planet?" asked Phillips, feeling a bit dazed.

"Oh, no, not at all," Y'ang-Yeovil said pleasantly. "This very world, I assure you. I am quite of human origin. Citizen of the Republic of Upper Han, native of the city of Port Ssu. And you— forgive me—your name—?"

"I'm sorry. Phillips. Charles Phillips. From New York City, once upon a time."

"Ah, New York!" Y'ang-Yeovil's face lit with a glimmer of recognition that quickly faded. "New York—New York—it was very famous, that I know—"

This is very strange, Phillips thought. He felt greater compassion for poor bewildered Francis Willoughby now. This man comes from a time so far beyond my own that he barely knows of New York—he must be a contemporary of the real New Chicago, in fact, I wonder whether he finds this version authentic—and yet to the citizens this Y'ang-Yeovil too is just a primitive, a curio out of antiquity—

"New York was the largest city of the United States of America," Phillips said.

"Of course. Yes. Very famous."

"But virtually forgotten by the time the Republic of Upper Han came into existence, I gather."

Y'ang-Yeovil said, looking uncomfortable, "There were disturbances between your time and mine. But by no means should you take from my words the impression that your city was—"

Sudden laughter resounded across the room. Five or six newcomers had arrived at the party. Phillips stared, gasped, gaped. Surely that was Stengard—and Aramayne beside him—and that other woman, half hidden behind them—

"If you'll pardon me a moment—" Phillips said, turning abruptly away from Y'ang-Yeovil. "Please excuse me. Someone just coming in—a person I've been trying to find ever since—"

He hurried toward her.

"Gioia?" he called. "Gioia, it's me! Wait! Wait!"

Stengard was in the way. Aramayne, turning to take a handful of the little vapor-sniffers from Cantilena, blocked him also. Phillips pushed through them as though they were not there. Gioia, halfway out the door, halted and looked toward him like a frightened deer.

"Don't go," he said. He took her hand in his.

He was startled by her appearance. How long had it been since their strange parting on that night of mysteries in Chang-an? A year? A year and a half? So he believed. Or had he lost all track of time? Were his perceptions of the passing of the months in this world that unreliable? She seemed at least ten or fifteen years older. Maybe she really was; maybe the years had been passing for him here as in a dream, and he had never known it. She looked strained, faded, worn. Out of a thinner and strangely altered face her eyes blazed at him almost defiantly, as though saying, *See? See how ugly I have become?*

He said, "I've been hunting for you for—I don't know how long it's been, Gioia. In Mohenjo, in Timbuctoo, now here. I want to be with you again."

"It isn't possible."

"Belilala explained everything to me in Mohenjo. I know that you're a short-timer—I know what that means, Gioia. But what of it? So you're beginning to age a little. So what? So you'll only have three or four hundred years, instead of forever. Don't you think I know what it means to be a short-timer? I'm just a simple ancient man of the twentieth century, remember? Sixty, seventy, eighty years is all we would get. You and I suffer from the same malady, Gioia. That's what drew you to me in the first place. I'm certain of that. That's why we belong with each other now. However much time we have, we can spend the rest of it together, don't you see?"

"You're the one who doesn't see, Charles," she said softly.

"Maybe. Maybe I still don't understand a damned thing about this place. Except that you and I—that I love you—that I think you love me—"

"I love you, yes. But you don't understand. It's precisely because I love you that you and I—you and I can't—"

With a despairing sigh she slid her hand free of his grasp. He reached for her again, but she shook him off and backed up quickly into the corridor.

"Gioia?"

"Please," she said. "No. I would never have come here if I knew you were here. Don't come after me. Please. Please."

She turned and fled.

He stood looking after her for a long moment. Cantilena and Aramayne appeared, and smiled at him as if nothing at all had happened. Cantilena offered him a vial of some sparkling amber fluid. He refused with a brusque gesture. Where do I go now, he wondered? What do I do? He wandered back into the party.

Y'ang-Yeovil glided to his side. "You are in great distress," the little man murmured.

Phillips glared. "Let me be."

"Perhaps I could be of some help."

"There's no help possible," said Phillips. He swung about and plucked one of the vials from a tray and gulped its contents. It made him feel as if there were two of him, standing on either side of Y'ang-Yeovil. He gulped another. Now there were four of him. "I'm in love with a citizen," he blurted. It seemed to him that he was speaking in chorus.

"Love. Ah. And does she love you?"

"So I thought. So I think. But she's a short-timer. Do you know what that means? She's not immortal like the others. She ages. She's beginning to look old. And so she's been running away from me. She doesn't want me to see her changing. She thinks it'll disgust me, I suppose. I tried to remind her just now that I'm not immortal either, that she and I could grow old together, but she—"

"Oh, no," Y'ang-Yeovil said quietly. "Why do you think you will age? Have you grown any older in all the time you have been here?"

Phillips was nonplussed. "Of course I have. I—I—"

"Have you?" Y'ang-Yeovil smiled. "Here. Look at yourself." He did something intricate with his fingers and a shimmering zone of mirrorlike light appeared between them. Phillips stared at his reflection. A youthful face stared back at him. It was true, then. He had simply not thought about it. How many years had he spent in this world? The time had simply slipped by: a great deal of time, though he could not calculate how much. They did not seem to keep close count of it here, nor had he. But it must have been many years, he thought. All that endless travel up and down the globe— so many cities had come and gone—Rio, Rome, Asgard, those were the first three that came to mind—and there were others; he could hardly remember every one. Years. His face had not changed at all. Time had worked its harshness on Gioia, yes, but not on him.

"I don't understand," he said. "Why am I not aging?"

"Because you are not real," said Y'ang-Yeovil. "Are you unaware of that?"

Phillips blinked. "Not—real?"

"Did you think you were lifted bodily out of your own time?" the little man asked. "Ah, no, no, there is no way for them to do such a thing. We are not actual time travelers: not you, not I, not any of the visitors. I thought you were aware of that. But perhaps your era is too early for a proper understanding of these things. We are very cleverly done, my friend. We are ingenious constructs, marvelously stuffed with the thoughts and attitudes and events of our own times. We are their finest achievement, you know: far more complex even than one of these cities. We are a step beyond the temporaries—more than a step, a great deal more. They do only what they are instructed to do, and their range is very narrow. They are nothing but machines, really. Whereas we are autonomous. We move about by our own will; we think, we talk, we even, so it seems, fall in love. But we will not age. How could we age? We are not real. We are mere artificial webworks of mental responses. We are mere illusions, done so well that we deceive even ourselves. You did not know that? Indeed, you did not know?"

* * *

He was airborne, touching destination buttons at random. Somehow he found himself heading back toward Timbuctoo. *This city is
closed. This is not a place any longer.* It did not matter to him. Why
should anything matter?

Fury and a choking sense of despair rose within him. I am software, Phillips thought. I am nothing but software.

Not real. Very cleverly done. An ingenious construct. A mere illusion.

No trace of Timbuctoo was visible from the air. He landed anyway. The gray sandy earth was smooth, unturned, as though there
had never been anything there. A few robots were still about, handling whatever final chores were required in the shutting-down of
a city. Two of them scuttled up to him. Huge bland gleaming silver-
skinned insects, not friendly.

"There is no city here," they said. "This is not a permissible
place."

"Permissible by whom?"

"There is no reason for you to be here."

"There's no reason for me to be anywhere," Phillips said. The
robots stirred, made uneasy humming sounds and ominous clicks,
waved their antennae about. They seemed troubled, he thought.
They seem to dislike my attitude. Perhaps I run some risk of being
taken off to the home for unruly software for debugging. "I'm
leaving now," he told them. "Thank you. Thank you very much."
He backed away from them and climbed into his flitterflitter. He
touched more destination buttons.

We move about by our own will. We think, we talk, we even fall in love.

He landed in Chang-an. This time there was no reception committee waiting for him at the Gate of Brilliant Virtue. The city
seemed larger and more resplendent: new pagodas, new palaces.
It felt like winter: a chilly cutting wind was blowing. The sky was
cloudless and dazzlingly bright. At the steps of the Silver Terrace
he encountered Francis Willoughby, a great hulking figure in magnificent brocaded robes, with two dainty little temporaries, pretty
as jade statuettes, engulfed in his arms. "Miracles and wonders!
The silly lunatic fellow is here, too!" Willoughby roared. "Look,
look, we are come to far Cathay, you and I!"

We are nowhere, Phillips thought. *We are mere illusions, done so well
that we deceive even ourselves.*

To Willoughby he said, "You look like an emperor in those robes,
Francis."

"Aye, like Prester John!" Willoughby cried. "Like Tamburlaine
himself! Aye, am I not majestic?" He slapped Phillips gaily on
the shoulder, a rough playful poke that spun him halfway about,

coughing and wheezing. "We flew in the air, as the eagles do, as the demons do, as the angels do! Soared like angels! Like angels!" He came close, looming over Phillips. "I would have gone to England, but the wench Belilala said there was an enchantment on me that would keep me from England just now; and so we voyaged to Cathay. Tell me this, fellow, will you go witness for me when we see England again? Swear that all that has befallen us did in truth befall? For I fear they will say I am as mad as Marco Polo, when I tell them of flying to Cathay."

"One madman backing another?" Phillips asked. "What can I tell you? You still think you'll reach England, do you?" Rage rose to the surface in him, bubbling hot. "Ah, Francis, Francis, do you know your Shakespeare? Did you go to the plays? We aren't real. *We aren't real.* We are such stuff as dreams are made on, the two of us. That's all we are. O brave new world! What England? Where? There's no England. There's no Francis Willoughby. There's no Charles Phillips. What we are is—"

"Let him be, Charles," a cool voice cut in.

He turned. Belilala, in the robes of an empress, coming down the steps of the Silver Terrace.

"I know the truth," he said bitterly. "Y'ang-Yeovil told me. The visitor from the twenty-fifth century. I saw him in New Chicago."

"Did you see Gioia there, too?" Belilala asked.

"Briefly. She looks much older."

"Yes. I know. She was here recently."

"And has gone on, I suppose?"

"To Mohenjo again, yes. Go after her, Charles. Leave poor Francis alone. I told her to wait for you. I told her that she needs you, and you need her."

"Very kind of you. But what good is it, Belilala? I don't even exist. And she's going to die."

"You exist. How can you doubt that you exist? You feel, don't you? You suffer. You love. You love Gioia: is that not so? And you are loved by Gioia. Would Gioia love what is not real?"

"You think she loves me?"

"I know she does. Go to her, Charles. Go. I told her to wait for you in Mohenjo."

Phillips nodded numbly. What was there to lose?

"Go to her," said Belilala again. "Now."

"Yes," Phillips said. "I'll go now." He turned to Willoughby. "If ever we meet in London, friend, I'll testify for you. Fear nothing. All will be well, Francis."

He left them and set his course for Mohenjo-daro, half expecting to find the robots already tearing it down. Mohenjo-daro was still there, no lovelier than before. He went to the baths, thinking he might find Gioia there. She was not; but he came upon Nissandra, Stengard, Fenimon. "She has gone to Alexandria," Fenimon told him. "She wants to see it one last time, before they close it."

"They're almost ready to open Constantinople," Stengard explained. "The capital of Byzantium, you know, the great city by the Golden Horn. They'll take Alexandria away, you understand, when Byzantium opens. They say it's going to be marvelous. We'll see you there for the opening, naturally?"

"Naturally," Phillips said.

He flew to Alexandria. He felt lost and weary. All this is hopeless folly, he told himself. I am nothing but a puppet jerking about on its strings. But somewhere above the shining breast of the Arabian Sea the deeper implications of something that Belilala had said to him started to sink in, and he felt his bitterness, his rage, his despair, all suddenly beginning to leave him. *You exist. How can you doubt that you exist? Would Gioia love what is not real?* Of course. Of course. Y'ang-Yeovil had been wrong: visitors were something more than mere illusions. Indeed, Y'ang-Yeovil had voiced the truth of their condition without understanding what he was really saying: *We think, we talk, we fall in love.* Yes. That was the heart of the situation. The visitors might be artificial, but they were not unreal. Belilala had been trying to tell him that just the other night. *You suffer. You love. You love Gioia. Would Gioia love what is not real?* Surely he was real, or at any rate real enough. What he was was something strange, something that would probably have been all but incomprehensible to the twentieth-century people whom he had been designed to simulate. But that did not mean that he was unreal. Did one have to be of woman born to be real? No. No. No. His kind of reality was a sufficient reality. He had no need to be ashamed of it. And, understanding that, he understood that Gioia did not need to grow old and die. There was a way by which she could be saved, if only she would embrace it. If only she would.

When he landed in Alexandria he went immediately to the hotel on the slopes of the Paneium where they had stayed on their first visit, so very long ago; and there she was, sitting quietly on a patio with a view of the harbor and the Lighthouse. There was something calm and resigned about the way she sat. She had given up. She did not even have the strength to flee from him any longer.

"Gioia," he said gently.

She looked older than she had in New Chicago. Her face was drawn and sallow and her eyes seemed sunken; and she was not even bothering these days to deal with the white strands that stood out in stark contrast against the darkness of her hair. He sat down beside her and put his hand over hers and looked out toward the obelisks, the palaces, the temples, the Lighthouse. At length he said, "I know what I really am now."

"Do you, Charles?" She sounded very far away.

"In my age we called it software. All I am is a set of commands, responses, cross-references, operating some sort of artificial body. It's infinitely better software then we could have imagined. But we were only just beginning to learn how, after all. They pumped me full of twentieth-century reflexes. The right moods, the right appetites, the right irrationalities, the right sort of combativeness. Somebody knows a lot about what it was like to be a twentieth-century man. They did a good job with Willoughby, too, all that Elizabethan rhetoric and swagger. And I suppose they got Y'ang-Yeovil right. *He* seems to think so: who better to judge? The twenty-fifth century, the Republic of Upper Han, people with gray-green skin, half Chinese and half Martian for all I know. *Somebody* knows. Somebody here is very good at programming, Gioia."

She was not looking at him.

"I feel frightened, Charles," she said in that same distant way.

"Of me? Of the things I'm saying?"

"No, not of you. Don't you see what has happened to me?"

"I see you. There are changes."

"I lived a long time wondering when the changes would begin. I thought maybe they wouldn't, not really. Who wants to believe they'll get old? But it started when we were in Alexandria that first time. In Chang-an it got much worse. And now—now—"

He said abruptly, "Stengard tells me they'll be opening Constantinople very soon."

"So?"

"Don't you want to be there when it opens?"

"I'm becoming old and ugly, Charles."

"We'll go to Constantinople together. We'll leave tomorrow, eh? What do you say? We'll charter a boat. It's a quick little hop, right across the Mediterranean. Sailing to Byzantium! There was a poem, you know, in my time. Not forgotten, I guess, because they've programmed it into me. All these thousands of years, and someone still remembers old Yeats. *The young in one another's arms, birds in the trees.* Come with me to Byzantium, Gioia."

She shrugged. "Looking like this? Getting more hideous every hour? While *they* stay young forever? While *you*—" She faltered; her voice cracked; she fell silent.

"Finish the sentence, Gioia."

"Please. Let me alone."

"You were going to say, 'While *you* stay young forever, too, Charles,' isn't that it? You knew all along that I was never going to change. I didn't know that, but you did."

"Yes. I knew. I pretended that it wasn't true—that as I aged, you'd age, too. It was very foolish of me. In Chang-an, when I first began to see the real signs of it—that was when I realized I couldn't stay with you any longer. Because I'd look at you, always young, always remaining the same age, and I'd look at myself, and—" She gestured, palms upward. "So I gave you to Belilala and ran away."

"All so unnecessary, Gioia."

"I didn't think it was."

"But you don't have to grow old. Not if you don't want to!"

"Don't be cruel, Charles," she said tonelessly. "There's no way of escaping what I have."

"But there is," he said.

"You know nothing about these things."

"Not very much, no," he said. "But I see how it can be done. Maybe it's a primitive simpleminded twentieth-century sort of solution, but I think it ought to work. I've been playing with the idea ever since I left Mohenjo. Tell me this, Gioia: Why can't you go to them, to the programmers, to the artificers, the planners, whoever they are, the ones who create the cities and the temporaries and the visitors. And have yourself made into something like me!"

She looked up, startled. "What are you saying?"

"They can cobble up a twentieth-century man out of nothing more than fragmentary records and make him plausible, can't they? Or an Elizabethan, or anyone else of any era at all, and he's authentic, he's convincing. So why couldn't they do an even better job with you? Produce a Gioia so real that even Gioia can't tell the difference? But a Gioia that will never age—a Gioia-construct, a Gioia-program, a visitor-Gioia! Why not? Tell me why not, Gioia."

She was trembling. "I've never heard of doing any such thing!"

"But don't you think it's possible?"

"How would I know?"

"Of course it's possible. If they can create visitors, they can take a citizen and duplicate her in such a way that—"

"It's never been done. I'm sure of it. I can't imagine any citizen agreeing to any such thing. To give up the body—to let yourself be turned into—into—"

She shook her head, but it seemed to be a gesture of astonishment as much as of negation.

He said, "Sure. To give up the body. Your natural body, your aging, shrinking, deteriorating short-timer body. What's so awful about that?"

She was very pale. "This is craziness, Charles. I don't want to talk about it any more."

"It doesn't sound crazy to me."

"You can't possibly understand."

"Can't I? I can certainly understand being afraid to die. I don't have a lot of trouble understanding what it's like to be one of the few aging people in a world where nobody grows old. What I can't understand is why you aren't even willing to consider the possibility that—"

"No," she said. "I tell you, it's crazy. They'd laugh at me."

"Who?"

"All of my friends. Hawk, Stengard, Aramayne—" Once again she would not look at him. "They can be very cruel, without even realizing it. They despise anything that seems ungraceful to them, anything sweaty and desperate and cowardly. Citizens don't do sweaty things, Charles. And that's how this will seem. Assuming it can be done at all. They'll be terribly patronizing. Oh, they'll be sweet to me, yes, dear Gioia, how wonderful for you, Gioia, but when I turn my back they'll laugh. They'll say the most wicked things about me. I couldn't bear that."

"They can afford to laugh," Phillips said. "It's easy to be brave and cool about dying when you know you're going to live forever. How very fine for them: but why should you be the only one to grow old and die? And they won't laugh, anyway. They're not as cruel as you think. Shallow, maybe, but not cruel. They'll be glad that you've found a way to save yourself. At the very least, they won't have to feel guilty about you any longer, and that's bound to please them. You can—"

"Stop it," she said.

She rose, walked to the railing of the patio, stared out toward the sea. He came up behind her. Red sails in the harbor, sunlight glittering along the sides of the Lighthouse, the palaces of the Ptolemies stark white against the sky. Lightly he rested his hand on her shoulder. She twitched as if to pull away from him, but remained where she was.

"Then I have another idea," he said quietly. "If you won't go to the planners, *I* will. Reprogram me, I'll say. Fix things so that I start to age at the same rate you do. It'll be more authentic, anyway, if I'm supposed to be playing the part of a twentieth-century man. Over the years I'll very gradually get some lines in my face, my hair will turn gray, I'll walk a little more slowly—we'll grow old together, Gioia. To hell with your lovely immortal friends. We'll have each other. We won't need them."

She swung around. Her eyes were wide with horror.

"Are you serious, Charles?"

"Of course."

"No," she murmured. "No. Everything you've said to me today is monstrous nonsense. Don't you realize that?"

He reached for her hand and enclosed her fingertips in his. "All I'm trying to do is find some way for you and me to—"

"Don't say any more," she said. "Please." Quickly, as though drawing back from a suddenly flaring flame, she tugged her fingers free of his and put her hand behind her. Though his face was just inches from hers he felt an immense chasm opening between them. They stared at one another for a moment; then she moved deftly to his left, darted around him, and ran from the patio.

Stunned, he watched her go, down the long marble corridor and out of sight. It was folly to give pursuit, he thought. She was lost to him: that was clear, that was beyond any question. She was terrified of him. Why cause her even more anguish? But somehow he found himself running through the halls of the hotel, along the winding garden path, into the cool green groves of the Paneium. He thought he saw her on the portico of Hadrian's palace, but when he got there the echoing stone halls were empty. To a temporary that was sweeping the steps he said, "Did you see a woman come this way?" A blank sullen stare was his only answer.

Phillips cursed and turned away.

"Gioia?" he called. "Wait! Come back!"

Was that her, going into the Library? He rushed past the startled mumbling librarians and sped through the stacks, peering beyond the mounds of double-handled scrolls into the shadowy corridors. "Gioia? *Gioia!*" It was a desecration, bellowing like that in this quiet place. He scarcely cared.

Emerging by a side door, he loped down to the harbor. The Lighthouse! Terror enfolded him. She might already be a hundred steps up that ramp, heading for the parapet from which she meant to fling herself into the sea. Scattering citizens and temporaries as if they were straws, he ran within. Up he went, never pausing for breath, though his synthetic lungs were screaming for respite, his ingeniously designed heart was desperately pounding. On the first balcony he imagined he caught a glimpse of her, but he circled it without finding her. Onward, upward. He went to the top, to the beacon chamber itself: no Gioia. Had she jumped? Had she gone down one ramp while he was ascending the other? He clung to the rim and looked out, down, searching the base of the Lighthouse, the rocks offshore, the causeway. No Gioia. I will find her somewhere, he thought. I will keep going until I find her. He went running down the ramp, calling her name. He reached ground level and sprinted back toward the center of town. Where next? The temple of Poseidon? The tomb of Cleopatra?

He paused in the middle of Canopus Street, groggy and dazed.
"Charles?" she said.

"Where are you?"

"Right here. Beside you." She seemed to materialize from the
air. Her face was unflushed, her robe bore no trace of perspiration.
Had he been chasing a phantom through the city? She came to him
and took his hand, and said, softly, tenderly, "Were you really
serious, about having them make you age?"

"If there's no other way, yes."

"The other way is so frightening, Charles."

"Is it?"

"You can't understand how much."

"More frightening than growing old? Than dying?"

"I don't know," she said. "I suppose not. The only thing I'm sure
of is that I don't want you to get old, Charles."

"But I won't have to. Will I?"

He stared at her.

"No," she said. "You won't have to. Neither of us will."

Phillips smiled. "We should get away from here," he said after a
while. "Let's go across to Byzantium, yes, Gioia? We'll show up in
Constantinople for the opening. Your friends will be there. We'll
tell them what you've decided to do. They'll know how to arrange
it. Someone will."

"It sounds so strange," said Gioia. "To turn myself into—into a
visitor? A visitor in my own world?"

"That's what you've always been, though."

"I suppose. In a way. But at least I've been *real* up to now."

"Whereas I'm not?"

"Are you, Charles?"

"Yes. Just as real as you. I was angry at first, when I found out
the truth about myself. But I came to accept it. Somewhere between
Mohenjo and here, I came to see that it was all right to be what I
am: that I perceive things, I form ideas, I draw conclusions. I am
very well designed, Gioia. I can't tell the difference between being
what I am and being completely alive, and to me that's being real
enough. I think, I feel, I experience joy and pain. I'm as real as I
need to be. And you will be, too. You'll never stop being Gioia, you
know. It's only your body that you'll cast away, the body that played
such a terrible joke on you anyway." He brushed her cheek with
his hand. "It was all said for us before, long ago:

'Once out of nature I shall never take
My bodily form from any natural thing,
But such a form as Grecian goldsmiths make

Of hammered gold and gold enamelling
To keep a drowsy Emperor awake—' "

"Is that the same poem?" she asked.

"The same poem, yes. The ancient poem that isn't quite forgotten yet."

"Finish it, Charles."

—*"Or set upon a golden bough to sing*
To lords and ladies of Byzantium
Of what is past, or passing, or to come."

"How beautiful. What does it mean?"

"That it isn't necessary to be mortal. That we can allow ourselves to be gathered into the artifice of eternity, that we can be transformed, that we can move on beyond the flesh. Yeats didn't mean it in quite the way I do—he wouldn't have begun to comprehend what we're talking about, not a word of it—and yet, and yet—the underlying truth is the same. Live, Gioia! With me!" He turned to her and saw color coming into her pallid cheeks. "It does make sense, what I'm suggesting, doesn't it? You'll attempt it, won't you? Whoever makes the visitors can be induced to remake you. Right? What do you think: can they, Gioia?"

She nodded in a barely perceptible way. "I think so," she said faintly. "It's very strange. But I think it ought to be possible. Why not, Charles? Why not?"

"Yes," he said. "Why not?"

In the morning they hired a vessel in the harbor, a low sleek pirogue with a blood-red sail, skippered by a rascally-looking temporary whose smile was irresistible. Phillips shaded his eyes and peered northward across the sea. He thought he could almost make out the shape of the great city sprawling on its seven hills, Constantine's New Rome beside the Golden Horn, the mighty dome of Hagia Sophia, the somber walls of the citadel, the palaces and churches, the Hippodrome, Christ in glory rising above all else in brilliant mosaic streaming with light.

"Byzantium," Phillips said. "Take us there the shortest and quickest way."

"It is my pleasure," said the boatman with unexpected grace.

Gioia smiled. He had not seen her looking so vibrantly alive since the night of the imperial feast in Chang-an. He reached for her hand—her slender fingers were quivering lightly—and helped her into the boat.

JAMES PATRICK KELLY

Mr. Boy

Like his friend and frequent collaborator John Kessel, James Patrick Kelly made his first sale in 1975, and has gone on to become one of the most respected and prominent writers of his generation. Although his most recent novel, *Look Into the Sun*, was generally well received, Kelly has had more impact as a writer of short fiction than as a novelist, and Kelly stories such as "Solstice," "The Prisoner of Chillon," "Glass Cloud," "Rat," "Home Front," and "Pogrom" rank among the most inventive and memorable short works of the eighties.

Mr. Boy, which was a Hugo and Nebula finalist, is widely considered to be Kelly's finest short work. F. Scott Fitzgerald told us long ago that the rich are not like you and me, but it takes the pyrotechnic and wildly inventive novella that follows to demonstrate just *how* unlike us they might eventually become. . . .

Kelly's first solo novel, the mostly-ignored *Planet of Whispers*, came out in 1984. It was followed by *Freedom Beach*, a novel written in collaboration with John Kessel, and then by the abovementioned solo novel, *Look Into the Sun*. Out soon will be a third solo novel, *Wildlife*, which features several of the characters from *Mr. Boy*. Born in Mineola, New York, Kelly now lives with his family in Portsmouth, New Hampshire.

I was already twitching by the time they strapped me down. Nasty pleasure and beautiful pain crackled through me, branching and rebranching like lightning. Extreme feelings are hard to tell apart when you have endorphins spilling across your brain. Another spasm shot down my legs and curled my toes. I moaned. The stiffs wore surgical masks that hid their mouths, but I knew that they were smiling. They hated me because my mom could afford to have me stunted. When I really was just a kid I did not understand that. Now I hated them back; it helped me get through the therapy. We had a very clean transaction going here. No secrets between us.

Even though it hurts, getting stunted is still the ultimate flash. As I unlived my life, I overdosed on dying feelings and experiences. My body was not big enough to hold them all; I thought I was going to explode. I must have screamed because I could see the laugh lines crinkling around the stiffs' eyes. You do not have to worry about laugh lines after they twank your genes and reset your mitotic limits. My face was smooth and I was going to be twelve years old forever, or at least as long as Mom kept paying for my rejuvenation.

I giggled as the short one leaned over me and pricked her catheter into my neck. Even through the mask, I could smell her breath. She reeked of dead meat.

Getting stunted always left me wobbly and thick, but this time I felt like last Tuesday's pizza. One of the stiffs had to roll me out of recovery in a wheelchair.

The lobby looked like a furniture showroom. Even the plants had been newly waxed. There was nothing to remind the clients that they were bags of blood and piss. You are all biological machines now, said the lobby, clean as space station lettuce. A scattering of people sat on the hard chairs. Stennie and Comrade were fidgeting by the elevators. They looked as if they were thinking of rearranging the furniture—like maybe into a pile in the middle of the room. Even before they waved, the stiff seemed to know that they were waiting for me.

Comrade smiled. *"Zdrast'ye."*

"You okay, Mr. Boy?" said Stennie. Stennie was a grapefruit yellow stenonychosaurus with a brown underbelly. His razor-clawed toes clicked against the slate floor as he walked.

"He's still a little weak," said the stiff, as he set the chair's parking brake. He strained to act nonchalant, not realizing that Stennie enjoys being stared at. "He needs rest. Are you his brother?" he said to Comrade.

Comrade appeared to be a teenaged spike neck with a head of silky black hair that hung to his waist. He wore a window coat on which twenty-three different talking heads chattered. He could pass for human, even though he was really a Panasonic. *"Nyet,"* said Comrade. "I'm just another one of his hallucinations."

The poor stiff gave him a dry nervous cough that might have been meant as a chuckle. He was probably wondering whether Stennie wanted to take me home or eat me for lunch. I always thought that the way Stennie got reshaped was more funny-looking than fierce—a python that had rear-ended an ostrich. But even though he was a head shorter than me, he did have enormous eyes and a mouthful of serrated teeth. He stopped next to the wheelchair and rose up to his full height. "I appreciate everything you've done." Stennie offered the stiff his spindly three-fingered hand to shake. "Sorry if he caused any trouble."

The stiff took it gingerly, then shrieked and flew backwards. I mean, he jumped almost a meter off the floor. Everyone in the lobby turned and Stennie opened his hand and waved the joy buzzer. He slapped his tail against the slate in triumph. Stennie's sense of humor was extreme, but then he was only thirteen years old.

Stennie's parents had given him the Nissan Alpha for his twelfth birthday and we had been customizing it ever since. We installed blue mirror glass and Stennie painted scenes from the Late Cretaceous on the exterior body armor. We ripped out all the seats, put in a wall-to-wall gel mat and a fridge and a microwave and a screen and a mini-dish. Comrade had even done an illegal operation on the carbrain so that we could override in an emergency and actually steer the Alpha ourselves with a joystick. It would have been cramped, but we would have lived in Stennie's car if our parents had let us.

"You okay there, Mr. Boy?" said Stennie.

"Mmm." As I watched the trees whoosh past in the rain, I pretended that the car was standing still and the world was passing me by.

"Think of something to do, okay?" Stennie had the car and all and he was fun to play with, but ideas were not his specialty. He was probably smart for a dinosaur. "I'm bored."

"Leave him alone, will you?" Comrade said.

"He hasn't said anything yet." Stennie stretched and nudged me with his foot. "Say something." He had legs like a horse; yellow skin stretched tight over long bones and stringy muscle.

"*Prosrees*! He just had his genes twanked, you jack." Comrade always took good care of me. Or tried to. "Remember what that's like? He's in damage control."

"Maybe I should go to socialization," Stennie said. "Aren't they having a dance this afternoon?"

"You're talking to me?" said the Alpha. "You haven't earned enough learning credits to socialize. You're a quiz behind and forty-five minutes short of E-class. You haven't linked since . . ."

"Just shut up and drive me over." Stennie and the Alpha did not get along. He thought the car was too strict. "I'll make up the plugging quiz, okay?" He probed a mess of empty juice boxes and snack wrappers with his foot. "Anyone see my comm anywhere?"

Stennie's schoolcomm was wedged behind my cushion. "You know," I said, "I can't take much more of this." I leaned forward, wriggled it free and handed it over.

"Of what, *poputchik?*" said Comrade. "Joyriding? Listening to the lizard here?"

"Being stunted."

Stennie flipped up the screen of his comm and went on line with the school's computer. "You guys help me, okay?" He retracted his claws and tapped at the oversized keyboard.

"It's extreme while you're on the table," I said, "but now I feel empty. Like I've lost myself."

"You'll get over it," said Stennie. "First question: Brand name of the first wiseguys sold for home use?"

"NEC-Bots, of course," said Comrade.

"Geneva? It got nuked, right?"

"*Da.*"

"Haile Selassie was that king of Egypt who the Marleys claim is god, right? Name the Cold Wars: Nicaragua, Angola . . . Korea was the first." Typing was hard work for Stennie; he did not have enough fingers for it. "One was something like Venezuela. Or something."

"Sure it wasn't Venice?"

"Or Venus?" I said, but Stennie was not paying attention.

"All right, I know that one. And that. The Sovs built the first space station. Ronald Reagan—he was the president who dropped the bomb?"

Comrade reached inside of his coat and pulled out an envelope. "I got you something, Mr. Boy. A get well present for your collection."

I opened it and scoped a picture of a naked dead fat man on a stainless steel table. The print had a DI verification grid on it, which meant this was the real thing, not a composite. Just above the corpse's left eye there was a neat hole. It was rimmed with purple which had faded to bruise blue. He had curly gray hair on his head and chest, skin the color of dried mayonnaise and a wonderfully complicated penis graft. He looked relieved to be dead. "Who was he?" I liked Comrade's present. It was extreme.

"CEO of Infoline. He had the wife, you know, the one who stole all the money so she could download herself into a computer."

I shivered as I stared at the dead man. I could hear myself breathing and feel the blood squirting through my arteries. "Didn't they turn her off?" I said. This was the kind of stuff we were not even supposed to imagine, much less look at. Too bad they had cleaned him up. "How much did this cost me?"

"You don't want to know."

"Hey!" Stennie thumped his tail against the side of the car. "I'm taking a quiz here and you guys are drooling over porn. When was the First World Depression?"

"Who cares?" I slipped the picture back into the envelope and grinned at Comrade.

"Well, let me see then." Stennie snatched the envelope. "You know what I think, Mr. Boy? I think this corpse jag you're on is kind of sick. Besides, you're going to get in trouble if you let Comrade keep breaking laws. Isn't this picture private?"

"Privacy is twentieth century thinking. It's all information, Stennie, and information should be accessible." I held out my hand. "But if *glasnost* bothers you, give it up." I wiggled my fingers.

Comrade snickered. Stennie pulled out the picture, glanced at it and hissed. "You're scaring me, Mr. Boy."

His schoolcomm beeped as it posted his score on the quiz and he sailed the envelope back across the car at me. "Not Venezuela, Viet Nam. Hey, *Truman* dropped the plugging bomb. Reagan was the one who spent all the money. What's wrong with you dumbscuts? Now I owe school another fifteen minutes."

"Hey, if you don't make it look good, they'll know you had help." Comrade laughed.

"What's with this dance anyway? You don't dance." I picked Comrade's present up and tucked it into my shirt pocket. "You find yourself a cush or something, lizard boy?"

"Maybe." Stennie could not blush but sometimes when he was embarrassed the loose skin under his jaw quivered. Even though he had been reshaped into a dinosaur, he was still growing up. "Maybe I am getting a little. What's it to you?"

"If you're getting it," I said, "it's got to be microscopic." This was a bad sign. I was losing him to his dick, just like all the other pals. No way I wanted to start over with someone new. I had been alive for twenty-five years now. I was running out of things to say to thirteen-year-olds.

As the Alpha pulled up to the school, I scoped the crowd waiting for the doors to open for third shift. Although there were a handful of stunted kids, a pair of gorilla brothers who were football stars and Freddy the Teddy, a bear who had furry hands instead of real paws, the majority of students at New Canaan High looked more or less normal. Most working stiffs thought that people who had their genes twanked were freaks.

"Come get me at 5:15," Stennie told the Alpha. "In the meantime, take these guys wherever they want to go." He opened the door. "You rest up, Mr. Boy, okay?"

"What?" I was not paying attention. "Sure." I had just seen the most beautiful girl in the world.

She leaned against one of the concrete columns of the portico, chatting with a couple other kids. Her hair was long and nut-colored and the ends twinkled. She was wearing a loose black robe over mirror skintights. Her schoolcomm dangled from a strap around her wrist. She appeared to be seventeen, maybe eighteen. But of course, appearances could be deceiving.

Girls had never interested me much, but I could not help but admire this one. "Wait, Stennie! Who's that?" She saw me point at her. "With the hair?"

"She's new—has one of those names you can't pronounce." He showed me his teeth as he got out. "Hey Mr. Boy, you're *stunted*. You haven't got what she wants."

He kicked the door shut, lowered his head and crossed in front of the car. When he walked he looked like he was trying to squash a bug with each step. His snaky tail curled high behind him for balance, his twiggy little arms dangled. When the new girl saw him, she pointed and smiled. Or maybe she was pointing at me.

"Where to?" said the car.

"I don't know." I sank low into my seat and pulled out Comrade's present again. "Home, I guess."

I was not the only one in my family with twanked genes. My mom was a three-quarters scale replica of the Statue of Liberty. Originally she wanted to be full-sized, but then she would have been the tallest thing in New Canaan, Connecticut. The town turned her down when she applied for a zoning variance. Her lawyers and their lawyers sued and countersued for almost two years. Mom's claim was that since she was born human, her freedom of form was protected by the Thirtieth Amendment. However, the form she wanted was a curtain of reshaped cells which would hang on a forty-two meter high ferroplastic skeleton. Her structure, said the planning board, was clearly subject to building codes and zoning laws. Eventually they reached an out-of-court settlement, which was why Mom was only as tall as an eleven story building.

She complied with the town's request for a setback of five hundred meters from Route 123. As Stennie's Alpha drove us down the long driveway, Comrade broadcast the recognition code which told the robot sentries that we were okay. One thing Mom and the town agreed on from the start: no tourists. Sure, she loved publicity, but she was also very fragile. In some places her skin was only a centimeter thick. Chunks of ice falling from her crown could punch holes in her.

The end of our driveway cut straight across the lawn to Mom's granite-paved foundation pad. To the west of the plaza, directly behind her, was a utility building faced in ashlar that housed her support systems. Mom had been bioengineered to be pretty much self-sufficient. She was green not only to match the real Statue of Liberty but also because she was photosynthetic. All she needed was a yearly truckload of fertilizer, water from the well, and a hundred and fifty kilowatts of electricity a day. Except for emergency surgery, the only time she required maintenance was in the fall, when her outer cells tended to flake off and had to be swept up and carted away.

Stennie's Alpha dropped us off by the doorbone in the right heel and then drove off to do whatever cars do when nobody is using them. Mom's greeter was waiting in the reception area inside the foot.

"Peter." She tried to hug me but I dodged out of her grasp. "How are you, Peter?"

"Tired." Even though Mom knew I did not like to be called that, I kissed the air near her cheek. Peter Cage was her name for me; I had given it up years ago.

"You poor boy. Here, let me see you." She held me at arm's length and brushed her fingers against my cheek. "You don't look a day over twelve. Oh, they do such good work—don't you think?" She squeezed my shoulder. "Are you happy with it?"

I think my mom meant well, but she never did understand me. Especially when she talked to me with her greeter remote. I wormed out of her grip and fell back onto one of the couches. "What's to eat?"

"Doboys, noodles, fries—whatever you want." She beamed at me and then bent over impulsively and gave me a kiss that I did not want. I never paid much attention to the greeter; she was lighter than air. She was always smiling and asking five questions in a row without waiting for an answer and flitting around the room. It wore me out just watching her. Naturally everything I said or did was cute, even if I was trying to be obnoxious. It was no fun being cute. Today Mom had her greeter wearing a dark blue dress and a very dumb white apron. The greeter's umbilical was too short to stretch up to the kitchen. So why was she wearing an apron? "I'm really, really glad you're home," she said.

"I'll take some cinnamon doboys." I kicked off my shoes and rubbed my bare feet through the dense black hair on the floor. "And a beer."

All of Mom's remotes had different personalities. I liked Nanny all right; she was simple but at least she listened. The lovers were a challenge because they were usually too busy looking into mirrors to notice me. Cook was as pretentious as a four star menu; the housekeeper had all the charm of a vacuum cleaner. I had always wondered what it would be like to talk directly to Mom's main brain up in the head, because then she would not be filtered through a remote. She would be herself.

"Cook is making you some nice broth to go with your doboys," said the greeter. "Nanny says you shouldn't be eating dessert all the time."

"Hey, did I ask for broth?"

At first Comrade had hung back while the greeter was fussing over me. Then he slid along the wrinkled pink walls of the reception room toward the plug where the greeter's umbilical was attached. When she started in about the broth I saw him lean against the plug. Carelessly, you know? At the same time he stepped on the greeter's umbilical, crimping the furry black cord. She gasped and the smile flattened horribly on her face as if her lips were two ropes someone had suddenly yanked taut. Her head jerked toward the umbilical plug.

"E-Excuse me." She was twitching.

"What?" Comrade glanced down at his foot as if it belonged to a stranger. "Oh, sorry." He pushed away from the wall and strolled across the room toward us. Although he seemed apologetic, about half the heads on his window coat were laughing.

The greeter flexed her cheek muscles. "You'd better watch out for your toy, Peter," she said. "It's going to get you in trouble someday."

Mom did not like Comrade much, even though she had given him to me when I was first stunted. She got mad when I snuck him down to Manhattan a couple of years ago to have a chop job done on his behavioral regulators. For a while after the operation, he used to ask me before he broke the law. Now he was on his own. He got caught once and she warned me he was out of control. But she still threw money at the people until they went away.

"Trouble?" I said. "Sounds like fun." I thought we were too rich for trouble. I was the trust baby of a trust baby; we had vintage money and lots of it. I stood and Comrade picked up my shoes for me. "And he's not a toy; he's my best friend." I put my arms around his shoulder. "Tell Cook I'll eat in my rooms."

I was tired after the long climb up the circular stairs to Mom's chest. When the roombrain sensed I had come in, it turned on all the electronic windows and blinked my message indicator. One reason I still lived in my mom was that she kept out of my rooms. She had promised me total security and I believed her. Actually I doubted that she cared enough to pry, although she could easily have tapped my windows. I was safe from her remotes up here, even the housekeeper. Comrade did everything for me.

I sent him for supper, perched on the edge of the bed, and cleared the nearest window of army ants foraging for meat through some Angolan jungle. The first message in the queue was from a gray-haired stiff wearing a navy blue corporate uniform. "Hello, Mr. Cage. My name is Weldon Montross and I'm with Datasafe. I'd like to arrange a meeting with you at your convenience. Call my DI number, 408-966-3286. I hope to hear from you soon."

"What the hell is Datasafe?"

The roombrain ran a search. "Datasafe offers services in encryption and information security. It was incorporated in the state of Delaware in 2013. Estimated billings last year were 340 million dollars. Headquarters are in San Jose, California, with branch offices in White Plains, New York and Chevy Chase, Maryland. Foreign offices. . . ."

"Are they trying to sell me something or what?"

The room did not offer an answer. "Delete," I said. "Next?"

Weldon Montross was back again, looking exactly as he had before. I wondered if he were using a virtual image. "Hello, Mr. Cage. I've just discovered that you've been admitted to the Thayer Clinic for rejuvenation therapy. Believe me when I say that I very much regret having to bother you during your convalescence and I would not do so if this were not a matter of importance. Would you please contact Department of Identification number 408-966-3286 as soon as you're able?"

"You're a pro, Weldon, I'll say that for you." Prying client information out of the Thayer Clinic was not easy, but then the guy was no doubt some kind of op. He was way too polite to be a salesman. What did Datasafe want with me? "Any more messages from him?"

"No," said the roombrain.

"Well, delete this one too and if he calls back tell him I'm too busy unless he wants to tell me what he's after." I stretched out on my bed. "Next?" The gel mattress shivered as it took my weight.

Happy Lurdane was having a smash party on the twentieth but Happy was a boring cush and there was a bill from the pet store for the iguanas that I paid and a warning from the SPCA that I deleted and a special offer for preferred customers from my favorite fireworks company that I saved to look at later and my dad was about to ask for another loan when I paused him and deleted and last of all there was a message from Stennie, time stamped ten minutes ago.

"Hey Mr. Boy, if you're feeling better I've lined up a VR party for tonight." He did not quite fit into the school's telelink booth; all I could see was his toothy face and the long yellow curve of his neck. "Bunch of us have reserved some time on Playroom. Come in disguise. That new kid said she'd link, so scope her yourself if you're so hot. I found out her name but it's kind of unpronounceable. Tree-something Joplin. Anyway it's at seven, meet on channel 17, password is warhead. Hey, did you send my car back yet? Later." He faded.

"Sounds like fun." Comrade kicked the doorbone open and backed through, balancing a tray loaded with soup and fresh doboys and a mug of cold beer. "Are we going?" He set it onto the nightstand next to my bed.

"Maybe." I yawned. It felt good to be in my own bed. "Flush the damn soup, would you?" I reached over for a doboy and felt something crinkle in my jacket pocket. I pulled out the picture of the dead CEO. About the only thing I did not like about it was that the eyes were shut. You feel dirtier when the corpse stares back. "This is one sweet hunk of meat, Comrade." I propped the picture beside the tray. "How did you get it, anyway? Must have taken some operating."

"Three days worth. Encryption wasn't all that tough but there was lots of it." Comrade admired the picture with me as he picked up the bowl of soup. "I ended up buying about ten hours from IBM to crack the file. Kind of pricey but since you were getting stunted, I had nothing else to do."

"You see the messages from that security op?" I bit into a doboy. "Maybe you were a little sloppy." The hot cinnamon scent tickled my nose.

"*Ya v'rot ego ebal!*" He laughed. "So some stiff is cranky? Plug him if he can't take a joke."

I said nothing. Comrade could be a pain sometimes. Of course I loved the picture, but he really should have been more careful. He had made a mess and left it for me to clean up. Just what I needed. I knew I would only get mad if I thought about it, so I changed the subject. "Well, do you think she's cute?"

"What's-her-face Joplin?" Comrade turned abruptly toward the bathroom. "Sure, for a *perdunya*," he said over his shoulder. "Why not?" Talking about girls made him snippy. I think he was afraid of them.

I brought my army ants back onto the window; they were swarming over a lump with brown fur. Thinking about him hanging on my elbow when I met this Tree-something Joplin made me feel weird. I listened as he poured the soup down the toilet. I was not myself at all. Getting stunted changes you; no one can predict how. I chugged the beer and rolled over to take a nap. It was the first time I had ever thought of leaving Comrade behind.

"VR party, Mr. Boy." Comrade nudged me awake. "Are we going or not?"

"Huh?" My gut still ached from the rejuvenation and I woke up mean enough to chew glass. "What do you mean *we*?"

"Nothing." Comrade had that blank look he always put on so I would not know what he was thinking. Still I could tell he was disappointed. "Are you going then?" he said.

I stretched—*ouch!* "Yeah, sure, get my joysuit." My bones felt brittle as candy. "And stop acting sorry for yourself." This nasty mood had momentum; it swept me past any regrets. "No way I'm going to lie here all night watching you pretend you have feelings to hurt."

"*Tak tochno.*" He saluted and went straight to the closet. I got out of bed and hobbled to the bathroom.

"This is a costume party, remember," Comrade called. "What are you wearing?"

"Whatever." Even his efficiency irked me; sometimes he did too much. "You decide." I needed to get away from him for a while.

Playroom was a new virtual reality service on our local net. If you wanted to throw an electronic party at Versailles or Monticello or San Simeon, all you had to do was link—if you could get a reservation.

I came back to the bedroom and Comrade stepped up behind me, holding the joysuit. I shrugged into it, velcroed the front seam and eyed myself in the nearest window. He had synthesized some kid-sized armor in the German Gothic style. My favorite. It was made of polished silver, with great fluting and scalloping. He had even programmed a little glow into the image so that on the window I looked like a walking night light. There was an armet helmet with a red ostrich plume; the visor was tipped up so I could see my face. I raised my arm and the joysuit translated the movement to the window so that my armored image waved back.

"Try a few steps," he said.

Although I could move easily in the lightweight joysuit, the motion interpreter made walking in the video armor seem realistically awkward. Comrade had scored the sound effects, too. Metal hinges rasped, chain mail rattled softly, and there was a satisfying *clunk* whenever my foot hit the floor.

"Great." I clenched my fist in approval. I was awake now and in control of my temper. I wanted to make up but Comrade was not taking the hint. I could never quite figure out whether he was just acting like a machine or whether he really did not care how I treated him.

"They're starting." All the windows in the room lit up with Playroom's welcome screen. "You want privacy, so I'm leaving. No one will bother you."

"Hey Comrade, you don't have to go . . ."

But he had already left the room. Playroom prompted me to identify myself. "Mr. Boy," I said, "Department of Identification number 203-966-2445. I'm looking for channel 17; the password is warhead."

A brass band started playing "Hail to the Chief" as the title screen lit the windows:

The White House
1600 Pennsylvania Avenue
Washington, DC, USA
copyright 2096, Playroom Presentations
REPRODUCTION OR REUSE STRICTLY PROHIBITED

and then I was looking at a wraparound view of a VR ballroom. A caption bar opened at the top of the windows and a message scrolled across. *This is the famous East Room, the largest room in the main house. It is used for press conferences, public receptions and entertainments.* I lowered my visor and entered the simulation.

The East Room was decorated in bone white and gold; three chandeliers hung like cut glass mushrooms above the huge parquet floor. A band played skitter at one end of the room but no one was dancing yet. The band was Warhead, according to their drum set. I had never heard of them. Someone's disguise? I turned and the joysuit changed the view on the windows. Just ahead Satan was chatting with a forklift and a rhinoceros. Beyond some blue cartoons were teasing Johnny America. There was not much furniture in the room, a couple of benches, an ugly piano, and some life-sized paintings of George and Martha. George looked like he had just been peeled off a cash card. I stared at him too long and the closed caption bar informed me that the painting had been painted by Gilbert Stuart and was the only White House object dating from the mansion's first occupancy in 1800.

"Hey," I said to a girl who was on fire. "How do I get rid of the plugging tour guide?"

"Can't," she said. "When Playroom found out we were kids they turned on all their educational crap and there's no override. I kind of don't think they want us back."

"Dumbscuts." I scoped the room for something that might be Stennie. No luck. "I like the way your hair is burning." Now that it was too late, I was sorry I had to make idle party chat.

"Thanks." When she tossed her head, sparks flared and crackled. "My mom helped me program it."

"So, I've never been to the White House. Is there more than this?"

"Sure," she said. "We're supposed to have pretty much the whole first floor. Unless they shorted us. You wouldn't be Stone Kinkaid in there, would you?"

"No, not really." Even though the voice was disguised, I could tell this was Happy Lurdane. I edged away from her. "I'm going to check the other rooms now. Later."

"If you run into Stone, tell him I'm looking for him."

I left the East Room and found myself in a long marble passageway with a red carpet. A dog skeleton trotted toward me. Or maybe it was supposed to be a sheep. I waved and went through a door on the other side.

Everyone in the Red Room was standing on the ceiling; I knew I had found Stennie. Even though what they see is only a simulation, most people lock into the perceptual field of a VR as if it were real. Stand on your head long enough—even if only in your imagination—and you get airsick. It took kilohours of practice to learn to compensate. Upside down was one of Stennie's trademark ways of showing off.

The Red Room is an intimate parlor in the American Empire style of 1815–20 . . .

"Hi," I said. I hopped over the wainscotting and walked up the silk-covered wall to join the three of them.

"You're wearing German armor." When the boy in blue grinned at me, his cheeks dimpled. He was wearing shorts and white knee socks, a navy sweater over a white shirt. "Augsburg?" said Little Boy Blue. Fine blond hair drooped from beneath his tweed cap.

"Try Wolf of Landshut," I said. Stennie and I had spent a lot of time fighting VR wars in full armor. "Nice shorts." Stennie's costume reminded me of Christopher Robin. Terminally cute.

"It's not fair," said the snowman, who I did not recognize. "He says this is what he actually looks like." The snowman was standing in a puddle which was dripping onto the rug below us. Great effect.

"No," said Stennie, "what I said was I would look like this if I hadn't done something about it, okay?"

I had not known Stennie before he was a dinosaur. "No wonder you got twanked." I wished I could have saved this image, but Playroom was copy-protected.

"You've been twanked? No joke?" The great horned owl ruffled in alarm. She had a girl's voice. "I know it's none of my business, but I don't understand why anyone would do it. Especially a kid. I mean, what's wrong with good old fashioned surgery? And you can be whoever you want in a VR." She paused, waiting for someone to agree with her. No help. "Okay, so I don't understand. But when you mess with your genes, you change who you are. I mean, don't you like who you are? *I* do."

"We're so happy for you." Stennie scowled. "What is this, mental health week?"

"We're rich," I said. "We can afford to hate ourselves."

"This may sound rude . . ." The owl's big blunt head swiveled from Stennie to me. ". . . but I think that's sad."

"Yeah well, we'll try to work up some tears for you, birdie," Stennie said.

Silence. In the East Room, the band turned the volume up.

"Anyway, I've got to be going." The owl shook herself. "Hanging upside-down is fine for bats, but not for me. Later." She let go of her perch and swooped out into the hall. The snowman turned to watch her go.

"You're driving them off, young man." I patted Stennie on the head. "Come on now, be nice."

"Nice makes me puke."

"You *do* have a bit of an edge tonight." I had trouble imagining this dainty little brat as my best friend. "Better watch out you don't cut someone."

The dog skeleton came to the doorway and called up to us. "We're supposed to dance now."

"About time." Stennie fell off the ceiling like a drop of water and splashed headfirst onto the beige Persian rug. His image went all muddy for a moment and then he re-formed, upright and unharmed. "Going to skitter, tin man?"

"I need to talk to you for a moment," the snowman murmured.

"You *need* to?" I said.

"Dance, dance, dance," sang Stennie. "Later." He swerved after the skeleton out of the room.

The snowman said, "It's about a possible theft of information."

Right then was when I should have slammed it into reverse. Caught up with Stennie or maybe faded from Playroom altogether. But all I did was raise my hands over my head. "You got me, snowman; I confess. But society is to blame, too, isn't it? You will tell the judge to go easy on me? I've had a tough life."

"This is serious."

"You're Weldon—what's your name?" Down the hall, I could hear the thud of Warhead's bass line. "Montross."

"I'll come to the point, Peter." The only acknowledgment he made was to drop the kid voice. "The firm I represent provides information security services. Last week someone operated on the protected database of one of our clients. We have reason to believe that a certified photograph was accessed and copied. What can you tell me about this?"

"Not bad, Mr. Montross sir. But if you were as good as you think you are, you'd know my name isn't Peter. It's Mr. Boy. And since nobody invited you to this party, maybe you'd better tell me now why I shouldn't just go ahead and have you deleted?"

"I know that you were undergoing genetic therapy at the time of the theft so you could not have been directly responsible. That's in your favor. However, I also know that you can help me clear this matter up. And you need to do that, son, just as quickly as you can. Otherwise there's big trouble coming."

"What are you going to do, tell my mommy?" My blood started to pump; I was coming back to life.

"This is my offer. It's not negotiable. You let me sweep your files for this image. You turn over any hardcopies you've made and you instruct your wiseguy to let me do a spot reprogramming, during which I will erase his memory of this incident. After that, we'll consider the matter closed."

"Why don't I just drop my pants and bend over while I'm at it?"

"Look, you can pretend if you want, but you're not a kid anymore. You're twenty-five years old. I don't believe for a minute that you're as thick as your friends out there. If you think about it, you'll realize that you can't fight us. The fact that I'm here and I know what I know means that all your personal information systems are already tapped. I'm an op, son. I could wipe your files clean any time and I will, if it comes to that. However, my orders are to be thorough. The only way I can be sure I have everything is if you cooperate."

"You're not even real, are you, Montross? I'll bet you're nothing but cheesy old code. I've talked to elevators with more personality."

"The offer is on the table."

"Stick it!"

The owl flew back into the room, braked with outstretched wings and caught onto the armrest of the Dolley Madison sofa. "Oh, you're still here," she said, noticing us. "I didn't mean to interrupt . . . ."

"Wait there," I said. "I'm coming right down."

"I'll be in touch," said the snowman. "Let me know just as soon as you change your mind." He faded.

I flipped backward off the ceiling and landed in front of her; my video armor rang from the impact. "Owl, you just saved the evening." I knew I was showing off, but just then I was willing to forgive myself. "Thanks."

"You're welcome, I guess." She edged away from me, moving with precise little birdlike steps toward the top of the couch. "But all I was trying to do was escape the band."

"Bad?"

"And loud." Her ear tufts flattened. "Do you think shutting the door would help?"

"Sure. Follow me. We can shut lots of doors." When she hesitated, I flapped my arms like silver wings. Actually, Montross had done me a favor; when he threatened me some inner clock had begun an adrenalin tick. If this was trouble, I wanted more. I felt twisted and dangerous and I did not care what happened next. Maybe that was why the owl flitted after me as I walked into the next room.

The sumptuous State Dining Room can seat about 130 for formal dinners. The white and gold decor dates from the administration of Theodore Roosevelt.

The owl glided over to the banquet table. I shut the door behind me. "Better?" Warhead still pounded on the walls.

"A little." She settled on a huge bronze doré centerpiece with a mirrored surface. "I'm going soon anyway."

"Why?"

"The band stinks, I don't know anyone and I hate these stupid disguises."

"I'm Mr. Boy." I raised my visor and grinned at her. "All right? Now you know someone."

She tucked her wings into place and fixed me with her owlish stare. "I don't like VRs much."

"They take some getting used to."

"Why bother?" she said. "I mean, if anything can happen in a simulation, nothing matters. And I feel dumb standing in a room all alone jumping up and down and flapping my arms. Besides, this joysuit is hot and I'm renting it by the hour."

"The trick is not to look at yourself," I said. "Just watch the screens and use your imagination."

"Reality is less work. You look like a little kid."

"Is that a problem?"

"Mr. Boy? What kind of name is that anyway?"

I wished she would blink. "A made up name. But then all names are made up, aren't they?"

"Didn't I see you at school Wednesday? You were the one who dropped off the dinosaur."

"My friend Stennie." I pulled out a chair and sat facing her. "Who you probably hate because he's twanked."

"That was him on the ceiling, wasn't it? Listen, I'm sorry about what I said. I'm new here. I'd never met anyone like him before I came to New Canaan. I mean, I'd heard of reshaping and all— getting twanked. But where I used to live, everybody was pretty much the same."

"Where was that, Squirrel Crossing, Nebraska?"

"Close." She laughed. "Elkhart; it's in Indiana."

The reckless ticking in my head slowed. Talking to her made it easy to forget about Montross. "You want to leave the party?" I said. "We could go into discreet."

"Just us?" She sounded doubtful. "Right now?"

"Why not? You said you weren't staying. We could get rid of these disguises. And the music."

She was silent for a moment. Maybe people in Elkhart, Indiana, did not ask one another into discreet unless they had met in Sunday school or the Four H Club.

"Okay," she said finally, "but I'll enable. What's your DI?"

I gave her my number.

"Be back in a minute."

I cleared Playroom from my screens. The message *Enabling discreet mode* flashed. I decided not to change out of the joysuit; instead I called up my wardrobe menu and chose an image of myself wearing black baggies. The loose folds and padded shoulders helped hide the scrawny little boy's body.

The message changed. *Discreet mode enabled. Do you accept, yes/no?*

"Sure," I said.

She was sitting naked in the middle of a room filled with tropical plants. Her skin was the color of cinnamon. She had freckles on her shoulders and across her breasts. Her hair tumbled down the curve of her spine; the ends glowed like embers in a breeze. She clutched her legs close to her and gave me a curious smile. Teenage still life. We were alone and secure. No one could tap us while we were in discreet. We could say anything we wanted. I was too croggled to speak.

"You *are* a little kid," she said.

I did not tell her that what she was watching was an enhanced image, a virtual me. "Uh . . . well, not really." I was glad Stennie could not see me. Mr. Boy at a loss—a first. "Sometimes I'm not sure what I am. I guess you're not going to like me either. I've been stunted a couple of times. I'm really twenty-five years old."

She frowned. "You keep deciding I won't like people. Why?"

"Most people are against genetic surgery. Probably because they haven't got the money."

"Myself, I wouldn't do it. Still, just because you did doesn't mean I hate you." She gestured for me to sit. "But my parents would probably be horrified. They're realists, you know."

"No fooling?" I could not help but chuckle. "That explains a lot." Like why she had an attitude about twanking. And why she thought VRs were dumb. And why she was naked and did not seem to care. According to hardcore realists, first came clothes, then jewelry, fashion, makeup, plastic surgery, skin tints, and *hey jack*, here we are up to our eyeballs in the delusions of 2096. Gene twanking, VR addicts, people downloading themselves into computers—better never to have started. They wanted to turn back to wornout twentieth century modes. "But you're no realist," I said. "Look at your hair."

She shook her head and the ends twinkled. "You like it?"

"It's extreme. But realists don't decorate!"

"Then maybe I'm not a realist. My parents let me try lots of stuff they wouldn't do themselves, like buying hairworks or linking to VRs. They're afraid I'd leave otherwise."

"Would you?"

She shrugged. "So what's it like to get stunted? I've heard it hurts."

I told her how sometimes I felt as if there were broken glass in my joints and how my bones ached and—more showing off—about the blood I would find on the toilet paper. Then I mentioned something about Mom. She had heard of Mom, of course. She asked about my dad and I explained how Mom paid him to stay away but that he kept running out of money. She wanted to know if I was working or still going to school and I made up some stuff about courses in history I was taking from Yale. Actually I had faded after my first semester. Couple of years ago. I did not have time to link to some boring college; I was too busy playing with Comrade and Stennie. But I still had an account at Yale.

"So that's who I am." I was amazed at how little I had lied. "Who are you?"

She told me that her name was Treemonisha but her friends called her Tree. It was an old family name; her great-great-grand-something-or-other had been a composer named Scott Joplin. Treemonisha was the name of his opera.

I had to force myself not to stare at her breasts when she talked. "You like *opera*?" I said.

"My dad says I'll grow into it." She made a face. "I hope not."

The Joplins were a franchise family; her mom and dad had just been transferred to the Green Dream, a plant shop in the Elm Street Mall. To hear her talk, you would think she had ordered them from the Good Fairy. They had been married for twenty-two years and were still together. She had a brother, Fidel, who was twelve. They all lived in the greenhouse next to the shop where they grew most of their food and where flowers were always in bloom and where everybody loved everyone else. Nice life for a bunch of mall drones. So why was she thinking of leaving?

"You should stop by sometime," she said.

"Sometime," I said. "Sure."

For hours after we faded, I kept remembering things about her I had not realized I had noticed. The fine hair on her legs. The curve of her eyebrows. The way her hands moved when she was excited.

It was Stennie's fault: after the Playroom party he started going to school almost every day. Not just linking to E-class with his comm, but actually showing up. We knew he had more than remedial reading on his mind, but no matter how much we teased, he would not talk about his mysterious new cush. Before he fell in love we used to joyride in his Alpha afternoons. Now Comrade and I had the car all to ourselves. Not as much fun.

We had already dropped Stennie off when I spotted Treemonisha waiting for the bus. I waved, she came over. The next thing I knew we had another passenger on the road to nowhere. Comrade stared vacantly out the window as we pulled onto South Street; he did not seem pleased with the company.

"Have you been out to the reservoir?" I said. "There are some extreme houses out there. Or we could drive over to Greenwich and look at yachts."

"I haven't been anywhere yet, so I don't care," she said. "By the way, you don't go to college." She was not accusing me or even asking—merely stating a fact.

"Why do you say that?" I said.

"Fidel told me."

I wondered how her twelve year old brother could know anything at all about me. Rumors maybe, or just guessing. Since she did not seem mad, I decided to tell the truth.

"He's right," I said, "I lied. I have an account at Yale but I haven't linked for months. Hey, you can't live without telling a few lies. At least I don't discriminate. I'll lie to anyone, even myself."

"You're bad." A smile twitched at the corners of her mouth. "So what *do* you do then?"

"I drive around a lot." I waved at the interior of Stennie's car. "Let's see . . . I go to parties. I buy stuff and use it."

"Fidel says you're rich."

"I'm going to have to meet this Fidel. Does money make a difference?"

When she nodded, her hairworks twinkled. Comrade gave me a knowing glance but I paid no attention. I was trying to figure out how she could make insults sound like compliments when I realized we were flirting. The idea took me by surprise. *Flirting.*

"Do you have any music?" Treemonisha said.

The Alpha asked what groups she liked and so we listened to some mindless dance hits as we took the circle route around the Laurel Reservoir. Treemonisha told me about how she was sick of her parents' store and rude customers and especially the dumb Green Dream uniform. "Back in Elkhart, Daddy used to make me wear it to school. Can you believe that? He said it was good advertising. When we moved, I told him either the khakis went or I did."

She had a yellow and orange dashiki over midnight blue skintights. "I like your clothes," I said. "You have taste."

"Thanks." She bobbed her head in time to the music. "I can't afford much because I can't get an outside job because I have to work for my parents. It makes me mad, sometimes. I mean, franchise life is fine for Mom and Dad; they're happy being tucked in every night by GD, Inc. But I want more. Thrills, chills—you know, adventure. No one has adventures in the mall."

As we drove, I showed her the log castle, the pyramids, the private train that pulled sleeping cars endlessly around a two mile track and the marble bunker where Sullivan, the assassinated president, still lived on in computer memory. Comrade kept busy acting bored.

"Can we go see your mom?" said Treemonisha. "All the kids at school tell me she's awesome."

Suddenly Comrade was interested in the conversation. I was not sure what the kids at school were talking about. Probably they wished they had seen Mom but I had never asked any of them over—except for Stennie.

"Not a good idea." I shook my head. "She's more flimsy than she looks, you know, and she gets real nervous if strangers just drop by. Or even friends."

"I just want to look. I won't get out of the car."

"Well," said Comrade, "if she doesn't get out of the car, who could she hurt?"

I scowled at him. He knew how paranoid Mom was. She was not going to like Treemonisha anyway, but certainly not if I brought her home without warning. "Let me work on her, okay?" I said to Treemonisha. "One of these days. I promise."

She pouted for about five seconds and then laughed at my expression. When I saw Comrade's smirk, I got angry. He was just sitting there watching us. Looking to cause trouble. Later there would be wisecracks. I had had about enough of him and his attitude.

By that time the Alpha was heading up High Ridge Road toward Stamford. "I'm hungry," I said. "Stop at the 7–11 up ahead." I pulled a cash card out and flipped it at him. "Go buy us some doboys."

I waited until he disappeared into the store and then ordered Stennie's car to drive on.

"Hey!" Treemonisha twisted in her seat and looked back at the store. "What are you doing?"

"Ditching him."

"Why? Won't he be mad?"

"He's got my card; he'll call a cab."

"But that's mean."

"So?"

Treemonisha thought about it. "He doesn't say much, does he?" She did not seem to know what to make of me—which I suppose was what I wanted. "At first I thought he was kind of like your teddy bear. Have you seen those big ones that keep little kids out of trouble?"

"He's just a wiseguy."

"Have you had him long?"

"Maybe too long."

I could not think of anything to say after that so we sat quietly listening to the music. Even though he was gone, Comrade was still aggravating me.

"Were you really hungry?" Treemonisha said finally. "Because I was. Think there's something in the fridge?"

I waited for the Alpha to tell us but it said nothing. I slid across the seat and opened the refrigerator door. Inside was a sheet of paper. "Dear Mr. Boy," it said. "If this was a bomb you and Comrade would be dead and the problem would be solved. Let's talk soon. Weldon Montross."

"What's that?"

I felt the warm flush that I always got from good corpse porn and for a moment I could not speak. "Practical joke," I said, crumpling the paper. "Too bad he doesn't have a sense of humor."

Push-ups. *Ten, eleven.*

"Uh-oh. Look at this," said Comrade.

"I'm busy!" *Twelve, thirteen, fourteen, fifteen . . . sixteen . . . seven. . . .* Dizzy, I slumped and rested my cheek against the warm floor. I could feel Mom's pulse beneath the tough skin. It was no good. I would never get muscles this way. There was only one fix for my skinny arms and bony shoulders. Grow up, Mr. Boy.

"*Ya yebou!* You really should scope this," said Comrade. "Very spooky."

I pulled myself onto the bed to see why he was bothering me; he had been pretty tame since I had stranded him at the 7–11. Most of the windows showed the usual: army ants next to old war movies next to feeding time from the Bronx Zoo's reptile house. But Firenet, which provided twenty-four hour coverage of killer fires from around the world, had been replaced with a picture of a morgue. There were three naked bodies, shrouds pulled back for identification: a fat gray-haired CEO with a purple hole over his left eye, Comrade, and me.

"You look kind of dead," said Comrade.

My tongue felt thick. "Where's it coming from?"

"Viruses all over the system," he said. "Probably Montross."

"You know about him?" The image on the window changed back to a *barridas* fire in Lima.

"He's been in touch." Comrade shrugged. "Made his offer."

Crying women watched as the straw walls of their huts peeled into flame and floated away.

"Oh." I did not know what to say. I wanted to reassure him, but this was serious. Montross was invading my life and I had no idea how to fight back. "Well, don't talk to him anymore."

"Okay." Comrade grinned. "He's dull as a spoon anyway."

"I bet he's a simulation. What else would a company like Datasafe use? You can't trust real people." I was still thinking about what I would look like dead. "Whatever, he's kind of scary." I shivered, worried and aroused at the same time. "He's slick enough to operate on Playroom. And now he's hijacking windows right here in my own mom." I should probably have told Comrade then about the note in the fridge, but we were still not talking about that day.

"He tapped into Playroom?" Comrade fitted input clips to the spikes on his neck, linked and played back the house files. "*Zayebees.* He was already here then. He piggybacked on with you." Comrade slapped his leg. "I can't understand how he beat my security so easily."

The roombrain flicked the message indicator. "Stennie's calling," it said.

"Pick up," I said.

"Hi, it's that time again." Stennie was alone in his car. "I'm on my way over to give you jacks a thrill." He pushed his triangular snout up to the camera and licked at the lens. "Doing anything?"

"Not really. Sitting around."

"I'll fix that. Five minutes." He faded.

Comrade was staring at nothing.

"Look Comrade, you did your best," I said. "I'm not mad at you."

"Too plugging easy." He shook his head as if I had missed the point.

"What I don't understand is why Montross is so cranky anyway. It's just a picture of meat."

"Maybe he's not really dead."

"Sure he is," I said. "You can't fake a verification grid."

"No, but you can fake a corpse."

"You know something?"

"If I did I wouldn't tell you," said Comrade. "You have enough problems already. Like how do we explain this to your mom?"

"We don't. Not yet. Let's wait him out. Sooner or later he's got to realize that we're not going to use his picture for anything. I mean if he's that nervous, I'll even give it back. I don't care anymore. You hear that Montross, you dumbscut? We're harmless. Get out of our lives!"

"It's more than the picture now," said Comrade. "It's me. I found the way in." He was careful to keep his expression blank.

I did not know what to say to him. No way Montross would be satisfied erasing only the memory of the operation. He would probably reconnect Comrade's regulators to bring him back under control. Turn him to pudding. He would be just another wiseguy, like anyone else could own. I was surprised that Comrade did not ask me to promise not to hand him over. Maybe he just assumed I would stand by him.

We did not hear Stennie coming until he sprang into the room.

"Have fun or die!" He was clutching a plastic gun in his spindly hand which he aimed at my head.

"Stennie, *no.*"

He fired as I rolled across the bed. The jellybee buzzed by me and squished against one of the windows. It was a purple and immediately I smelled the tang of artificial grape flavor. The splatter on the wrinkled wall pulsed and split in two, emitting a second burst of grapeness. The two halves oozed in opposite directions, shivered and divided again.

"Fun extremist!" He shot Comrade with a cherry as he dove for the closet. "Dance!"

I bounced up and down on the bed, timing my move. He fired a green at me that missed. Comrade, meanwhile, gathered himself up as zits of red jellybee squirmed across his window coat. He barreled out of the closet into Stennie, knocking him sideways. I sprang on top of them and wrestled the gun away. Stennie was paralyzed with laughter. I had to giggle too, in part because now I could put off talking to Comrade about Montross.

By the time we untangled ourselves, the jellybees had faded. "Set for twelve generations before they all die out," Stennie said as he settled himself on the bed. "So what's this my car tells me, you've been giving free rides? Is this the cush with the name?"

"None of your business. You never tell me about your cush."

"Okay. Her name is Janet Hoyt."

"Is it?" He caught me off guard again. Twice in one day, a record. "Comrade, let's see this prize."

Comrade linked to the roombrain and ran a search. "Got her." He called Janet Hoyt's DI file to screen and her face ballooned across an entire window.

She was a tanned blue-eyed blonde with the kind of off-the-shelf looks that med students slapped onto rabbits in genoplasty courses. Nothing on her face said she was different from any other ornamental moron fresh from the OR—not a dimple or a mole, not even a freckle. "You're ditching me for her?" It took all the imagination of a potato chip to be as pretty as Janet Hoyt. "Stennie, she's generic."

"Now wait a minute," said Stennie. "If we're going to play critic, let's scope your cush, too."

Without asking, Comrade put Tree's DI photo next to Janet's. I realized he was still mad at me because of her; he was only pretending not to care. "She's not my cush," I said, but no one was listening.

Stennie leered at her for a moment. "She's a stiff, isn't she?" he said. "She has that hungry look."

Seeing him standing there in front of the two huge faces on the wall, I felt like I was peeping on a stranger—that I was a stranger, too. I could not imagine how the two of us had come to this: Stennie and Mr. Boy with cushes. We were growing up. A frightening thought. Maybe next Stennie would get himself untwanked and really look like he had on Playroom. Then where would I be?

"Janet wants me to plug her," Stennie said.

"Right, and I'm the queen of Brooklyn."

"I'm old enough, you know." He thumped his tail against the floor.

"You're a dinosaur!"

"Hey, just because I got twanked doesn't mean *my* dick fell off."

"So do it then."

"I'm going to. I will, okay? But . . . this is no good." Stennie waved impatiently at Comrade. "I can't think with them watching me." He nodded at the windows. "Turn them off already."

"*N'ye pizdi!*" Comrade wiped the two faces from the windows, cleared all the screens in the room to blood red, yanked the input clips from his neck spikes and left them dangling from the room-brain's terminal. His expression empty, he walked from the room without asking permission or saying anything at all.

"What's his problem?" Stennie said.

"Who knows?" Comrade had left the door open; I shut it. "Maybe he doesn't like girls."

"Look, I want to ask a favor." I could tell Stennie was nervous; his head kept swaying. "This is kind of embarrassing but . . . okay, do you think maybe your mom would maybe let me practice on her lovers? I don't want Janet to know I've never done it before and there's some stuff I've got to figure out."

"I don't know," I said. "Ask her."

But I did know. She would be amused.

People claimed my mom did not have a sense of humor. Lovey was huge, an ocean of a woman. Her umbilical was as big around as my thigh. When she walked waves of flesh heaved and rolled. She had beautiful skin, flawless and moist. It did not take much to make her sweat. Peeling a banana would do it. Lovey was as oral as a baby; she would put anything into her mouth. And when she did not have a mouthful, she would babble on about whatever came into Mom's head. Dear hardly ever talked, although he could moan and growl and laugh. He touched Lovey whenever he could and shot her long smouldering looks. He was not furry, exactly, but he was covered with fine silver hair. Dear was a little guy, about my size. Although he had one of Upjohn's finest penises, elastic and over-loaded with neurons, he was one of the least convincing males I had ever met. I doubt Mom herself believed in him all that much.

Big chatty woman, squirrelly tongue-tied little man. It *was* funny in a bent sort of way to watch the two of them go at each other. Kind of like a tug churning against a supertanker. They did not get the chance that often. It was dangerous; Dear had to worry about getting crushed and poor Lovey's heart had stopped two or three times. Besides, I think Mom liked building up the pressure. Sometimes, as the days without sex stretched, you could almost feel lust sparkling off them like static electricity.

That was how they were when I brought Stennie up. Their suite took up the entire floor at the hips, Mom's widest part. Lovey was lolling in a tub of warm oil. She liked it flowery and laced with pheromones. Dear was prowling around her with a desperate expression, like he might jam his plug into a wall socket if he did not get taken care of soon. Stennie's timing was perfect.

"Look who's come to visit, Dear," said Lovey. "Peter and Stennie. How nice of you boys to stop by." She let Dear mop her forehead with a towel. "What can we do for you?"

The skin under Stennie's jaw quivered. He glanced at me, then at Dear and then at the thick red lips that served as the bathroom door. Never even looked at her. He was losing his nerve.

"Oh my, isn't this exciting, Dear? There's something going on." She sank into the bath until her chin touched the water. "It's a secret, isn't it, Peter? Share it with Lovey."

"No secret," I said, "he wants to ask a favor." And then I told her.

She giggled and sat up. "I love it." Honey-colored oil ran from her hair and slopped between her breasts. "Were you thinking of both of us, Stennie? Or just me?"

"Well, I . . ." Stennie's tail switched. "Maybe we just ought to forget it."

"No, no." She waved a hand at him. "Come here, Stennie. Come close, my pretty little monster."

He hesitated, then approached the tub. She reached for his right leg and touched him just above the heelknob. "You know, I've always wondered what scales would feel like." Her hand climbed; the oil made his yellow hide glisten. His eyes were the size of eggs.

The bedroom was all mattress. Beneath the transparent skin was a screen implant, so that Mom could project images not only on the walls but on the surface of the bed itself. Under the window was a layer of heavily vascular flesh, which could be stiffened with blood or drained until it was as soft as raw steak. A window dome arched over everything and could show slo-mo or thermographic fx across its span. The air was warm and wet and smelled like a chemical engineer's idea of a rose garden.

I settled by the lips. Dear ghosted along the edges of the room, dragging his umbilical like a chain, never coming quite near enough to touch anyone. I heard him humming as he passed me, a low moaning singsong, as if to block out what was happening. Stennie and Lovey were too busy with each other to care. As Lovey knelt in front of Stennie, Dear gave a mocking laugh. I did not understand how he could be jealous. He was with her, part of it. Lovey and Dear were Mom's remotes, two nodes of her nervous system. Yet his pain was as obvious as her pleasure. At last he squatted and rocked back and forth on his heels. I glanced up at the fx dome; yellow scales slid across oily rolls of flushed skin.

I yawned. I had always found sex kind of dull. Besides, this was all on the record. I could have Comrade replay it for me any time. Lovey stopped breathing—then came four or five shuddering gasps in a row. I wondered where Comrade had gone. I felt sorry for him. Stennie said something to her about rolling over. "Okay?" Feathery skin sounds. A grunt. The soft wet slap of flesh against flesh. I thought of my mother's brain, up there in the head where no one ever went. I had no idea how much attention she was paying. Was she quivering with Lovey and at the same time calculating insolation rates on her chloroplasts? Investing in soy futures on the Chicago Board of Trade? Fending off Weldon Montross's latest attack? *Plug Montross.* I needed to think about something fun. My collection. I started piling bodies up in my mind. The hangings and the open casket funerals and the stacks of dead at the camps and all those muddy soldiers. I shivered as I remembered the empty rigid faces. I liked it when their teeth showed. "Oh, oh, *oh!*" My greatest hits dated from the late twentieth century. The dead were everywhere back then, in vids and the news and even on T-shirts. They were not shy. That was what made Comrade's photo worth having; it was hard to find modern stuff that dirty. Dear brushed by me, his erection bobbing in front of him. It was as big around as my wrist. As he passed I could see Stennie's leg scratch across the mattress skin, which glowed with blood blue light. Lovey giggled beneath him and her umbilical twitched and suddenly I found myself wondering whether Tree was a virgin.

I came into the mall through the Main Street entrance and hopped the westbound slidewalk headed up Elm Street toward the train station. If I caught the 3:36 to Grand Central, I could eat dinner in Manhattan, far from my problems with Montross and Comrade. Running away had always worked for me before. Let someone else clean up the mess while I was gone.

The slidewalk carried me past a real estate agency, a flash bar, a jewelry store and a Baskin-Robbins. I thought about where I wanted to go after New York. San Francisco? Montreal? Maybe I should try Elkhart, Indiana—no one would think to look for me there. Just ahead, between a drugstore and a take-out Russian restaurant, was the wiseguy dealership where Mom had bought Comrade.

I did not want to think about Comrade waiting for me to come home, so I stepped into the drugstore and bought a dose of Carefree for $4.29. Normally I did not bother with drugs. I had been stunted; no over-the-counter flash could compare to that. But the propyl dicarbamates were all right. I fished the cash card out of my pocket and handed it to the stiff behind the counter. He did a doubletake when he saw the denomination, then carefully inserted the card into the reader to deduct the cost of the Carefree. It had my mom's name on it; he must have expected it would trip some alarm for counterfeit plastic or stolen credit. He stared at me for a moment, as if trying to remember my face so he could describe me to a cop, and then gave the cash card back. The denomination readout said it was still good for $16,381.18.

I picked out a bench in front of a specialty shop called The Happy Hippo, hiked up my shorts and poked Carefree into the widest part of my thigh. I took a short dreamy swim in the sea of tranquility and when I came back to myself, my guilt had been washed away. But so had my energy. I sat for a while and scoped the display of glass hippos and plastic hippos and fuzzy stuffed hippos, hippo vids and sheets and candles. Down the bench from me a homeless woman dozed. It was still pretty early in the season for a weather gypsy to have come this far north. She wore red shorts and droopy red socks with plastic sandals and four long-sleeved shirts, all unbuttoned, over a Funny Honey halter top. Her hair needed vacuuming and she smelled old. All grownups smelled that way to me; it was something I had never gotten used to. No perfume or deodorant could cover up the leathery stink of adulthood. Kids could smell bad, too, but usually from something they got on them. It did not come from a rotting body. I rubbed a finger in the dampness under my arm, slicked it and sniffed. There was a sweetness to kid sweat. I touched the drying finger to my tongue. You could even taste it. If I gave up getting stunted, stopped being Mr. Boy, I would smell like the woman at the end of the bench. I would start to die. I had never understood how grownups could live with that.

The gypsy woke up, stretched and smiled at me with gummy teeth. "You left Comrade behind?" she said.

I was startled. "What did you say?"

"You know what this is?" She twitched her sleeve and a penlight appeared in her hand.

My throat tightened. "I know what it looks like."

She gave me a wicked smile, aimed the penlight and burned a pinhole through the bench a few centimeters from my leg. "Maybe I could interest you in some free laser surgery?"

I could smell scorched plastic. "You're going to needle me here, in the middle of the Elm Street Mall?" I thought she was bluffing. Probably. I hoped.

"If that's the way you want it. Mr. Montross wants to know when you're delivering the wiseguy to us."

"Get away from me."

"Not until you do what needs to be done."

When I saw Happy Lurdane come out of The Happy Hippo, I waved. A desperation move, but then it was easy to be brave with a head full of Carefree.

"Mr. Boy." She veered over to us. "Hi!"

I scooted farther down the bench to make room for her between me and the gypsy. I knew she would stay to chat. Happy Lurdane was one of those chirpy lightweights who seemed to want lots of friends but did not really try to be one. We tolerated her because she did not mind being snubbed and she threw great parties.

"Where have you been?" She settled beside me. "Haven't seen you in ages." The penlight disappeared and the gypsy fell back into drowsy character.

"Around."

"Want to see what I just bought?"

I nodded. My heart was hammering.

She opened the bag and took out a fist-sized bundle covered with shipping plastic. She unwrapped a statue of a blue hippopotamus. "Be careful." She handed it to me.

"Cute." The hippo had crude flower designs drawn on its body; it was chipped and cracked.

"Ancient Egyptian. That means it's even *before* antique." She pulled a slip from the bag and read. "Twelfth Dynasty, 1991–1786 B.C. Can you believe you can just buy something like that here in the mall? I mean it must be like a thousand years old or something."

"Try four thousand."

"No wonder it cost so much. He wasn't going to sell it to me, so I had to spend some of next month's allowance." She took it from me and rewrapped it. "It's for the smash party tomorrow. You're coming, aren't you?"

"Maybe."

"Is something wrong?"

I ignored that.

"Hey, where's Comrade? I don't think I've ever seen you two apart before."

I decided to take a chance. "Want to get some doboys?"

"*Sure.*" She glanced at me with delighted astonishment. "Are you sure you're all right?"

I took her arm, maneuvering to keep her between me and the gypsy. If Happy got needled it would be no great loss to western civilization. She babbled on about her party as we stepped onto the westbound slidewalk. I turned to look back. The gypsy waved as she hopped the eastbound.

"Look Happy," I said, "I'm sorry, but I changed my mind. Later, okay?"

"But . . ."

I did not stop for an argument. I darted off the slidewalk and sprinted through the mall to the station. I went straight to a ticket window, shoved the cash card under the grille and asked the agent for a one way to Grand Central. Forty thousand people lived in New Canaan; most of them had heard of me because of my mom. Nine million strangers jammed New York City; it was a good place to disappear. The agent had my ticket in her hand when the reader beeped and spat the card out.

"No!" I slammed my fist on the counter. "Try it again." The cash card was guaranteed by AmEx to be secure. And it had just worked at the drugstore.

She glanced at the card, then slid it back under the grille. "No use." The denomination readout flashed alternating messages: *Voided* and *Bank recall*. "You've got trouble, son."

She was right. As I left the station, I felt the Carefree struggle one last time with my dread—and lose. I did not even have the money to call home. I wandered around for a while, dazed, and then I was standing in front of the flower shop in the Elm Street Mall.

Green Dream
Contemporary and Conventional Plants

I had telelinked with Tree every day since our drive and every day she had asked me over. But I was not ready to meet her family; I suppose I was still trying to pretend she was not a stiff. I wavered at the door now, breathing the cool scent of damp soil in clay pots. The gypsy could come after me again; I might be putting these people in danger. Using Happy as a shield was one thing, but I liked Tree. A lot. I backed away and peered through a window fringed with sweat and teeming with bizarre plants with flame-colored tongues. Someone wearing khaki moved. I could not tell if it was Tree or not. I thought of what she had said about no one having adventures in the mall.

The front of the showroom was a green cave, darker than I had expected. Baskets dripping with bright flowers hung like stalactites;

leathery-leaved understory plants formed stalagmites. As I threaded my way toward the back I came upon the kid I had seen wearing the Green Dream uniform, a khaki nightmare of pleats and flaps and brass buttons and about six too many pockets. He was misting leaves with a pump bottle filled with blue liquid. I decided he must be the brother.

"Hi," I said. "I'm looking for Treemonisha."

Fidel was shorter than me and darker than his sister. He had a wiry plush of beautiful black hair that I was immediately tempted to touch.

"Are you?" He eyed me as if deciding how hard I would be to beat up, then he smiled. He had crooked teeth. "You don't look like yourself."

"No?"

"What are you, scared? You're whiter than rice, cashman. Don't worry, the stiffs won't hurt you." Laughing, he feinted a punch at my arm; I was not reassured.

"You're Fidel."

"I've seen your DI files," he said. "I asked around, I know about you. So don't be telling my sister any more lies, understand?" He snapped his fingers in my face. "Behave yourself, cashman, and we'll be fine." He still had the boyish excitability I had lost after the first stunting. "She's out back, so first you have to get by the old man."

The rear of the store was brighter; sunlight streamed through the clear krylac roof. There was a counter and behind it a glass-doored refrigerator filled with cut flowers. A side entrance opened to the greenhouse. Mrs. Schlieman, one of Mom's lawyers who had an office in the mall, was deciding what to buy. She was shopping with her wiseguy secretary, who looked like he had just stepped out of a vodka ad.

"Wait." Fidel rested a hand on my shoulder. "I'll tell her you're here."

"But how long will they last?" Mrs. Schlieman sniffed a frilly yellow flower. "I should probably get the duraroses."

"Whatever you want, Mrs. Schlieman. Duraroses are a good product, I sell them by the truckload," said Mr. Joplin with a chuckle. "But these carnations are real flowers, raised here in my greenhouse. So maybe you can't stick them in your dishwasher, but put some where people can touch and smell them and I guarantee you'll get compliments."

"Why Peter Cage," said Mrs. Schlieman. "Is that you? I haven't seen you since the picnic. How's your mother?" She did not introduce her wiseguy.

"Extreme," I said.

She nodded absently. "That's nice. All right then, Mr. Joplin, give me a dozen of your carnations—and two dozen yellow duraroses."

Mrs. Schlieman chatted politely at me while Tree's father wrapped the order. He was a short, rumpled, balding man who smiled too much. He seemed to like wearing the corporate uniform. Anyone else would have fixed the hair and the wrinkles. Not Mr. Joplin; he was a museum-quality throwback. As he took Mrs. Schlieman's cash card from the wiseguy, he beamed at me over his glasses. Glasses!

When Mrs. Schlieman left, so did the smile. "Peter Cage?" he said. "Is that your name?"

"Mr. Boy is my name, sir."

"You're Tree's new friend." He nodded. "She's told us about you. She's doing chores just now. You know, we have to work for a living here."

Sure, and I knew what he left unsaid: *unlike you, you spoiled little freak.* It was always the same with these stiffs. I walked in the door and already they hated me. At least he was not pretending, like Mrs. Schlieman. I gave him two points for honesty and kept my mouth shut.

"What is it you want here, Peter?"

"Nothing, sir." If he was going to "Peter" me, I was going to "sir" him right back. "I just stopped by to say hello. Treemonisha did invite me, sir, but if you'd rather I left . . ."

"No, no. Tree warned us you might come."

She and Fidel raced into the room as if they were afraid their father and I would already be at each other's throats. "Oh hi, Mr. Boy," she said.

Her father snorted at the sound of my name.

"Hi." I grinned at her. It was the easiest thing I had done that day.

She was wearing her uniform. When she saw that I had noticed, she blushed. "Well, you asked for it." She tugged self-consciously at the waist of her fatigues. "You want to come in?"

"Just a minute." Mr. Joplin stepped in front of the door, blocking our escape. "You finished E-class?"

"Yes."

"Checked the flats?"

"I'm almost done."

"After that you'd better pick some dinner and get it started. Your mama called and said she wouldn't be home until six-fifteen."

"Sure."

"And you'll take orders for me on line two?"

She leaned against the counter and sighed. "Do I have a choice?"

He backed away and waved us through. "Sorry, sweetheart. I don't know how we would get along without you." He caught her brother by the shirt. "Not you, Fidel. You're misting, remember?"

A short tunnel ran from their mall storefront to the rehabbed furniture warehouse built over the Amtrak rails. Green Dream had installed a krylac roof and fans and a grolighting system; the Joplins squeezed themselves into the leftover spaces not filled with inventory. The air in the greenhouse was heavy and warm and it smelled like rain. No walls, no privacy other than that provided by the plants.

"Here's where I sleep." Tree sat on her unmade bed. Her space was formed by a cinder block wall painted yellow and a screen of palms. "Chinese fan, bamboo, lady, date, kentia," she said, naming them for me like they were her pets. "I grow them myself for spending money." Her school-comm was on top of her dresser. Several drawers hung open; pink skintights trailed from one. Clothes were scattered like piles of leaves across the floor. "I guess I'm kind of a slob," she said as she stripped off the uniform, wadded it and then banked it off the dresser into the top drawer. I could see her bare back in the mirror plastic taped to the wall. "Take your things off if you want."

I hesitated.

"Or not. But it's kind of muggy to stay dressed. You'll sweat."

I unvelcroed my shirt. I did not mind at all seeing Tree without clothes. But I did not undress for anyone except the stiffs at the clinic. I stepped out of my pants. Being naked somehow had got connected with being helpless. I had this puckery feeling in my dick, like it was going to curl up and die. I could imagine the gypsy popping out from behind a palm and laughing at me. No, I was not going to think about *that*. Not here.

"Comfortable?" said Tree.

"Sure." My voice was turning to dust in my throat. "Do all Green Dream employees run around the back room in the nude?"

"I doubt it." She smiled as if the thought tickled her. "We're not exactly your average mall drones. Come help me finish the chores."

I was glad to let her lead so that she was not looking at me, although I could still watch her. I was fascinated by the sweep of her buttocks, the curve of her spine. She strolled, flatfooted and at ease, through her private jungle. At first I scuttled along on the balls of my feet, ready to dart behind a plant if anyone came. But after a while I decided to stop being so skittish. I realized I would probably survive being naked.

Tree stopped in front of a workbench covered with potted seedlings in plastic trays and picked up a hose from the floor.

"What's this stuff?" I kept to the opposite side of the bench, using it to cover myself.

"Greens." She lifted a seedling to check the water level in the tray beneath.

"What are greens?"

"It's too boring." She squirted some water in and replaced the seedling.

"Tell me, I'm interested."

"In greens? You liar." She glanced at me and shook her head. "Okay." She pointed as she said the names. "Lettuce, spinach, pak choi, chard, kale, rocket—got that? And a few tomatoes over there. Peppers, too. GD is trying to break into the food business. They think people will grow more of their own if they find out how easy it is."

"Is it?"

"Greens are." She inspected the next tray. "Just add water."

"Yeah, sure."

"It's because they've been photosynthetically enhanced. Bigger leaves arranged better, low respiration rates. They teach us this stuff at GD Family Camp. It's what we do instead of vacation." She squashed something between her thumb and forefinger. "They mix all these bacteria that make their own fertilizer into the soil—fix nitrogen right out of the air. And then there's this other stuff that sticks to the roots, rhizobacteria and mycorrhizae." She finished the last tray and coiled the hose. "These flats will produce under candlelight in a closet. Bored yet?"

"How do they taste?"

"Pretty bland, most of them. Some stink, like kale and rocket. But we have to eat them for the good of the corporation." She stuck her tongue out. "You want to stay for dinner?"

Mrs. Joplin made me call home before she would feed me; she refused to understand that my mom did not care. So I linked, asked Mom to send a car to the back door at eight-thirty, and faded. No time to discuss the missing sixteen thousand.

Dinner was from the cookbook Tree had been issued at camp: a bowl of cold bean soup, fresh corn bread, and chard and cheese loaf. She let me help her make it, even though I had never cooked before. I was amazed at how simple corn bread was. Six ingredients: flour, corn meal, baking powder, milk, oil, and ovobinder. Mix and pour into a greased pan. Bake 20 minutes at 220 Celsius and serve! There is nothing magic or even very mysterious about homemade corn bread, except for the way its smell held me spellbound.

Supper was the Joplins' daily meal together. They ate in front of security windows near the tunnel to the store; when a customer came, someone ran out front. According to contract, they had to stay open twenty-four hours a day. Many of the suburban malls had gone to all-night operation; the competition from New York City was deadly. Mr. Joplin stood duty most of the time, but since they were a franchise family everybody took turns. Even Mrs. Joplin, who also worked part-time as a factfinder at the mall's DataStop.

Tree's mother was plump and graying and she had a smile that was almost bright enough to distract me from her naked body. She seemed harmless, except that she knew how to ask questions. After all, her job was finding out stuff for DataStop customers. She had this way of locking onto you as you talked; the longer the conversation, the greater her intensity. It was hard to lie to her. Normally that kind of aggressiveness in grownups made me jumpy.

No doubt she had run a search on me; I wondered just what she had turned up. Factfinders had to obey the law, so they only accessed public domain information—unlike Comrade, who would cheerfully operate on whatever I set him to. The Joplins' bank records, for instance. I knew that Mrs. Joplin had made about $11,000 last year at the Infomat in the Elkhart Mall, that the family borrowed $135,000 at 9.78 percent interest to move to their new franchise and that they lost $213 in their first two months in New Canaan.

I kept my research a secret, of course, and they acted innocent, too. I let them pump me about Mom as we ate. I was used to being asked; after all, Mom was famous. Fidel wanted to know how much it had cost her to get twanked, how big she was, what she looked like on the inside and what she ate, if she got cold in the winter. Stuff like that. The others asked more personal questions. Tree wondered if Mom ever got lonely and whether she was going to be the Statue of Liberty for the rest of her life. Mrs. Joplin was interested in Mom's remotes, of all things. Which ones I got along with, which ones I could not stand, whether I thought any of them was really her. Mr. Joplin asked if she liked being what she was. How was I supposed to know?

After dinner, I helped Fidel clear the table. While we were alone in the kitchen, he complained. "You think they eat this shit at GD headquarters?" He scraped his untouched chard loaf into the composter.

"I kind of liked the corn bread."

"If only he'd buy meat once in a while, but he's too cheap. Or doboys. Tree says you bought her doboys."

I told him to skip school some time and we would go out for lunch; he thought that was a great idea.

When we came back out, Mr. Joplin actually smiled at me. He had been losing his edge all during dinner. Maybe chard agreed with him. He pulled a pipe from his pocket, began stuffing something into it and asked me if I followed baseball. I told him no. Paintball? No. Basketball? I said I watched dino fights sometimes.

"His pal is the dinosaur that goes to our school," said Fidel.

"He may look like a dinosaur, but he's really a boy," said Mr. Joplin, as if making an important distinction. "The dinosaurs died out millions of years ago."

"Humans aren't allowed in dino fights," I said, just to keep the conversation going. "Only twanked dogs and horses and elephants."

Silence. Mr. Joplin puffed on his pipe and then passed it to his wife. She watched the glow in the bowl through half-lidded eyes as she inhaled. Fidel caught me staring.

"What's the matter? Don't you get twisted?" He took the pipe in his turn.

I was so croggled I did not know what to say. Even the Marleys had switched to THC inhalers. "But smoking is bad for you." It smelled like a dirty sock had caught fire.

"Hemp is ancient. Natural." Mr. Joplin spoke in a clipped voice as if swallowing his words. "Opens the mind to what's real." When he sighed, smoke poured out of his nose. "We grow it ourselves, you know."

I took the pipe when Tree offered it. Even before I brought the stem to my mouth, the world tilted and I watched myself slide into what seemed very much like an hallucination. Here I was sitting around naked, in the mall, with a bunch of stiffs, smoking antique drugs. And I was enjoying myself. Incredible. I inhaled and immediately the flash hit me; it was as if my brain were an enormous bud, blooming inside my head.

"Good stuff." I laughed smoke and then began coughing.

Fidel refilled my glass with ice water. "Have a sip, cashman."

"Customer." Tree pointed at the window.

"Leave!" Mr. Joplin waved impatiently at him. "Go away." The man on the screen knelt and turned over the price tag on a fern. "Damn." He jerked his uniform from the hook by the door, pulled on the khaki pants and was slithering into the shirt as he disappeared down the tunnel.

"So is Green Dream trying to break into the flash market, too?" I handed the pipe to Mrs. Joplin. There was a fleck of ash on her left breast.

"What we do back here is our business," she said. "We work hard so we can live the way we want." Tree was studying her fingerprints.

I realized I had said the wrong thing so I shut up. Obviously, the Joplins were drifting from the lifestyle taught at Green Dream Family Camp.

Fidel announced he was going to school tomorrow and Mrs. Joplin told him no, he could link to E-class as usual, and Fidel claimed he could not concentrate at home, and Mrs. Joplin said he was trying to get out of his chores. While they were arguing, Tree nudged my leg and shot me a *let's leave* look. I nodded.

"Excuse us." She pushed back her chair. "Mr. Boy has got to go home soon."

Mrs. Joplin pointed for her to stay. "You wait until your father gets back," she said. "Tell me, Mr. Boy, have you lived in New Canaan long?"

"All my life," I said.

"How old did you say you were?"

"Mama, he's twenty-five," said Tree. "I told you."

"And what do you do for a living?"

"*Mama*, you promised."

"Nothing," I said. "I'm lucky, I guess. I don't need to worry about money. If you didn't need to work, would you?"

"Everybody needs work to do," Mrs. Joplin said. "Work makes us real. Unless you have work to do and people who love you, you don't exist."

Talk about twentieth century humanist goop! At another time in another place, I probably would have snapped, but now the words would not come. My brain had turned into a flower; all I could think were daisy thoughts. The Joplins were such a strange combination of fast-forward and rewind. I could not tell what they wanted from me.

"Seventeen dollars and ninety-nine cents," said Mr. Joplin, returning from the storefront. "What's going on in here?" He glanced at his wife and some signal which I did not catch passed between them. He circled the table, came up behind me and laid his heavy hands on my shoulders. I shuddered; I thought for a moment he meant to strangle me.

"I'm not going to hurt you, Peter," he said. "Before you go I have something to say."

"*Daddy*." Tree squirmed in her chair. Fidel looked uncomfortable, too, as if he guessed what was coming.

"Sure." I did not have much choice.

The weight on my shoulders eased but did not entirely go away. "You should feel the ache in this boy, Ladonna."

"I know," said Mrs. Joplin.

"Hard as plastic." Mr. Joplin touched the muscles corded along my neck. "You get too hard, you snap." He set his thumbs at the base of my skull and kneaded with an easy circular motion. "Your body isn't some machine that you've downloaded into. It's alive. Real. You have to learn to listen to it. That's why we smoke. Hear these muscles? They're screaming." He let his hand slide down my shoulders. "Now listen." His fingertips probed along my upper spine. "Hear that? Your muscles stay tense because you don't trust anyone. You always have to be ready to take a hit and you can't tell where it's coming from. You're rigid and angry and scared. Reality . . . your body is speaking to you."

His voice was as big and warm as his hands. Tree was giving him a look that could boil water but the way he touched me made too much sense to resist.

"We don't mind helping you ease the strain. That's the way Mrs. Joplin and I are. That's the way we brought the kids up. But first you have to admit you're hurting. And then you have to respect us enough to take what we have to give. I don't feel that in you, Peter. You're not ready to give up your pain. You just want us poor stiffs to admire how hard it's made you. We haven't got time for that kind of shit, okay? You learn to listen to yourself and you'll be welcome around here. We'll even call you Mr. Boy, even though it's a damn stupid name."

No one spoke for a moment.

"Sorry, Tree," he said. "We've embarrassed you again. But we love you, so you're stuck with us." I could feel it in his hands when he chuckled. "I suppose I do get carried away sometimes."

"*Sometimes?*" said Fidel. Tree just smouldered.

"It's late," said Mrs. Joplin. "Let him go now, Jamaal. His mama's sending a car over."

Mr. Joplin stepped back and I almost fell off my chair from leaning back against him. I stood, shakily. "Thanks for dinner."

Tree stalked through the greenhouse to the rear exit, her hairworks glittering against her bare back. I had to trot to keep up with her. There was no car in sight so we waited at the doorway and I put on my clothes.

"I can't take much more of this." She stared through the little wire glass window in the door, like a prisoner plotting her escape. "I mean, he's *not* a psychologist or a great philosopher or whatever the hell he thinks he is. He's just a pompous mall drone."

"He's not that bad." Actually, I understood what her father had said to me; it was scary. "I like your family."

"You don't have to live with them!" She kept watching at the door. "They promised they'd behave with you; I should have known better. This happens every time I bring someone home." She

puffed an imaginary pipe, imitating her father. "Think what you're
doing to yourself, you poor fool, and say, isn't it just too bad about
modern life? Love, love, love—*fuck*!" She turned to me. "I'm sick
of it. People are going to think I'm as sappy and thickheaded as my
parents."

"I don't."

"You're lucky. You're rich and your mom leaves you alone.
You're New Canaan. My folks are Elkhart, Indiana."

"Being New Canaan is nothing to brag about. So what are you?"

"Not a Joplin." She shook her head. "Not much longer, anyway;
I'm eighteen in February. I think your car's here." She held out
her arms and hugged me goodbye. "Sorry you had to sit through
that. Don't drop me, okay? I like you, Mr. Boy." She did not let go
for a while.

Dropping her had never occurred to me; I was not thinking of
anything at all except the silkiness of her skin, the warmth of her
body. Her breath whispered through my hair and her nipples
brushed my ribs and then she kissed me. Just on the cheek but the
damage was done. I was stunted. I was not supposed to feel this
way about anyone.

Comrade was waiting in the back seat. We rode home in silence;
I had nothing to say to him. He would not understand—none of
my friends would. They would warn me that all she wanted was to
spend some of my money. Or they would make bad jokes about the
nudity or the Joplins' mushy realism. No way I could explain the
innocence of the way they touched one another. *The old man did
what to you?* Yeah, and if I wanted a hug at home who was I supposed
to ask? Comrade? Lovey? The greeter? Was I supposed to climb
up to the head and fall asleep against Mom's doorbone, waiting for
it to open, like I used to do when I was really a kid?

The greeter was her usual nonstick self when I got home. She
was so glad to see me and she wanted to know where I had been
and if I had a good time and if I wanted Cook to make me a snack?
Around. Yes. No.

She said the bank had called about some problem with one of
the cash cards she had given me, a security glitch which they had
taken care of and were very sorry about. Did I know about it and
did I need a new card and would twenty thousand be enough? Yes.
Please. Thanks.

And that was it. I found myself resenting Mom because she did
not have to care about losing sixteen or twenty or fifty thousand
dollars. And she had reminded me of my problems when all I
wanted to think of was Tree. She was no help to me, never had
been. I had things so twisted around that I almost told her about

Montross myself, just to get a reaction. Here some guy had tapped our files and threatened my life and she asked if I wanted a snack. Why keep me around if she was going to pay so little attention? I wanted to shock her, to make her take me seriously.

But I did not know how.

The roombrain woke me. "Stennie's calling."

"Mmm."

"Talk to me, Mr. Party Boy." A window opened; he was in his car. "You dead or alive?"

"Asleep." I rolled over. "Time is it?"

"Ten-thirty and I'm bored. Want me to come get you now or should I meet you there?"

"Wha . . . ?"

"Happy's. Don't tell me you forgot. They're doing a *piano*."

"Who cares?" I crawled out of bed and dropped into the bathroom.

"She says she's asking Tree Joplin," Stennie called after me.

"Asking her what?" I came out.

"To the party."

"Is she going?"

"She's your cush." He gave me a toothy smile. "Call back when you're ready. Later." He faded.

"She left a message," said the roombrain. "Half hour ago."

"Tree? You got me up for Stennie and not for her?"

"He's on the list, she's not. Happy called, too."

"Comrade should've told you. Where is he?" Now I was grouchy. "She's on the list, okay? Give me playback."

Tree seemed pleased with herself. "Hi, this is me. I got myself invited to a smash party this afternoon. You want to go?" She faded.

"That's all? Call her!"

"Both her numbers are busy; I'll set redial. I found Comrade; he's on another line. You want Happy's message?"

"No. Yes."

"You promised, Mr. Boy." Happy giggled. "Look, you really, really don't want to miss this. Stennie's coming and he said I should ask Joplin if I wanted you here. So you've got no excuse."

Someone tugged at her. "Stop that! Sorry, I'm being molested by a thick. . . ." She batted at her assailant. "Mr. Boy, did I tell you that this Japanese reporter is coming to shoot a vid? What?" She turned off camera. "Sure, just like on the nature channel. Wildlife of America. We're all going to be famous. In Japan! This is history, Mr. Boy. And you're . . ."

Her face froze as the redial program finally linked to the Green Dream. The roombrain brought Tree up in a new window. "Oh hi," she said. "You rich boys sleep late."

"What's this about Happy's?"

"She invited me." Tree was recharging her hairworks with a red brush. "I said yes. Something wrong?"

Comrade slipped into the room; I shushed him. "You sure you want to go to a smash party? Sometimes they get a little crazy."

She aimed the brush at me. "You've been to smash parties before. You survived."

"Sure, but . . ."

"Well, I haven't. All I know is that everybody at school is talking about this one and I want to see what it's about."

"You tell your parents you're going?"

"Are you kidding? They'd just say it was too dangerous. What's the matter, Mr. Boy, are you scared? Come on, it'll be extreme."

"She's right. You *should* go," said Comrade.

"Is that Comrade?" Tree said. "You tell him, Comrade!"

I glared at him. "Okay, okay, I guess I'm outnumbered. Stennie said he'd drive. You want us to pick you up?"

She did.

I flew at Comrade as soon as Tree faded. "Don't you ever do that again!" I shoved him and he bumped up against the wall. "I ought to throw you to Montross."

"You know, I just finished chatting with him." Comrade stayed calm and made no move to defend himself. "He wants to meet— the three of us, face to face. He suggested Happy's."

"He suggested . . . I told you not to talk to him."

"I know." He shrugged. "Anyway, I think we should do it."

"Who gave you permission to think?"

"You did. What if we give him the picture back and open our files and then I grovel, say I'm sorry, it'll never happen again, blah, blah, blah. Maybe we can even buy him off. What have we got to lose?"

"You can't bribe software. And what if he decides to snatch us?" I told Comrade about the gypsy with the penlight. "You want Tree mixed up in this?"

All the expression drained from his face. He did not say anything at first but I had watched his subroutines long enough to know that when he looked this blank, he was shaken. "So we take a risk, maybe we can get it over with," he said. "He's not interested in Tree and I won't let anything happen to you. Why do you think your mom bought me?"

* * *

Happy Lurdane lived on the former estate of Philip Johnson, a notorious twentieth century architect. In his will Johnson had arranged to turn his compound into the Philip Johnson Memorial Museum, but after he died his work went out of fashion. The glass skyscrapers in the cities did not age well; they started to fall apart or were torn down because they wasted energy. Nobody visited the museum and it went bankrupt. The Lurdanes had bought the property and made some changes.

Johnson had designed all the odd little buildings on the estate himself. The main house was a shoebox of glass with no inside walls; near it stood a windowless brick guest house. On a pond below was a dock that looked like a Greek temple. Past the circular swimming pool near the houses were two galleries which had once held Johnson's art collection, long since sold off. In Johnson's day, the scattered buildings had been connected only by paths, which made the compound impossible in the frosty Connecticut winters. The Lurdanes had enclosed the paths in clear tubes and commuted in a golf cart.

Stennie told his Alpha not to wait, since the lot was already full and cars were parked well down the driveway. Five of us squeezed out of the car: me, Tree, Comrade, Stennie, and Janet Hoyt. Janet wore a Yankees jersey over pinstriped shorts, Tree was a little overdressed in her silver jaunts, I had on baggies padded to make me seem bigger and Comrade wore his usual window coat. Stennie lugged a box with his swag for the party.

Freddy the Teddy let us in. "Stennie and Mr. Boy!" He reared back on his hindquarters and roared. "Glad I'm not going to be the only beastie here. Hi, Janet. Hi, I'm Freddy," he said to Tree. His pink tongue lolled. "Come in, this way. Fun starts right here. Some kids are swimming and there's sex in the guest house. Everybody else is with Happy having lunch in the sculpture gallery."

The interior of the Glass House was bright and hard. Dark wood block floor, some unfriendly furniture, huge panes of glass framed in black painted steel. The few kids in the kitchen were passing an inhaler around and watching a microwave fill up with popcorn.

"I'm hot." Janet stuck the inhaler into her face and pressed. "Anybody want to swim? Tree?"

"Okay." Tree breathed in a polite dose and breathed out a giggle. "You?" she asked me.

"I don't think so." I was too nervous: I kept expecting someone to jump out and throw a net over me. "I'll watch."

"I'd swim with you," said Stennie, "but I promised Happy I'd bring her these party favors as soon as I arrived." He nudged the box with his foot. "Can you wait a few minutes?"

"Comrade and I will take them over." I grabbed the box and headed for the door, glad for the excuse to leave Tree behind while I went to find Montross. "Meet you at the pool."

The golf cart was gone so we walked through the tube toward the sculpture gallery. "You have the picture?" I said.

Comrade patted the pocket of his window coat.

The tube was not air-conditioned and the afternoon sun pounded us through the optical plastic. There was no sound inside; even our footsteps were swallowed by the astroturf. The box got heavier. We passed the entrance to the old painting gallery, which looked like a bomb shelter. Finally I had to break the silence. "I feel strange, being here," I said. "Not just because of the thing with Montross. I really think I lost myself last time I got stunted. Not sure who I am anymore, but I don't think I belong with these kids."

"People change, *tovarisch*," said Comrade. "Even you."

"Have I changed?"

He smiled. "Now that you've got a cush, your own mother wouldn't recognize you."

"You know what your problem is?" I grinned and bumped up against him on purpose. "You're jealous of Tree."

"Shouldn't I be?"

"Oh, I don't know. I can't tell if Tree likes who I was or who I might be. She's changing, too. She's so hot to break away from her parents, become part of this town. Except that what she's headed for probably isn't worth the trip. I feel like I should protect her, but that means guarding her from people like me, except I don't think I'm Mom's Mr. Boy anymore. Does that make sense?"

"Sure." He gazed straight ahead but all the heads on his window coat were scoping me. "Maybe when you're finished changing, you won't need me."

The thought had occurred to me. For years he had been the only one I could talk to but, as we closed on the gallery, I did not know what to say. I shook my head. "I just feel strange."

And then we arrived. The sculpture gallery was designed for showoffs: short flights of steps and a series of stagy balconies descended around the white brick exterior walls to the central exhibition area. The space was open so you could chat with your little knot of friends and, at the same time, spy on everyone else. About thirty kids were eating pizza and crispex off paper plates. At the bottom of the stairs, as advertised, was a black upright piano. Piled beside it was the rest of the swag. A Boston rocker, a case of green

Coke bottles, a Virgin Mary in half a blue bathtub, a huge conch
shell, china and crystal and assorted smaller treasures, including a
four-thousand-year-old ceramic hippo. There were real animals,
too, in cages near the gun rack: a turkey, some stray dogs and cats,
turtles, frogs, assorted rodents.

I was threading my way across the first balcony when I was
stopped by the Japanese reporter, who was wearing microcam eyes.

"Excuse me, please," he said, "I am Matsuo Shikibu and I will be
recording this event today for Nippon Hoso Kyokai. Public telelink
of Japan." He smiled and bowed. When his head came up the red
light between his lenses was on. "You are . . . ?"

"Raskolnikov," said Comrade, edging between me and the camera. "Rodeo Raskolnikov." He took Shikibu's hand and pumped it.
"And my associate here, Mr. Peter Pan." He turned as if to introduce me but we had long since choreographed this dodge. As I
sidestepped past, he kept shielding me from the reporter with his
body. "We're friends of the bride," Comrade said, "and we're really
excited to be making new friends in your country. Banzai, Nippon!"

I slipped by them and scooted downstairs. Happy was basking by
the piano; she spotted me as I reached the middle landing.

"Mr. Boy!" It was not so much a greeting as an announcement.
She was wearing a body mike and her voice boomed over the sound
system. "You made it."

The stream of conversation rippled momentarily, a few heads
turned and then the party flowed on. Shikibu rushed to the edge
of the upper balcony and caught me with a long shot.

I set the box on the Steinway. "Stennie brought this."

She opened it eagerly. "Look everyone!" She held up a stack of
square cardboard albums, about thirty centimeters on a side. There
were pictures of musicians on the front, words on the back. "What
are they?" she asked me.

"Phonograph records," said the kid next to Happy. "It's how they
used to play music before digital."

"Erroll Garner *Soliloquy*," she read aloud. "What's this? D-j-a-n-g-o
Reinhardt and the American Jazz Giants. Sounds scary." She giggled
as she pawed quickly through the other albums. Handy, Ellington,
Hawkins, Parker, three Armstrongs. One was *Piano Rags By Scott
Joplin*. Stennie's bent idea of a joke? Maybe the lizard was smarter
than he looked. Happy pulled a black plastic record out of one sleeve
and scratched a fingernail across little ridges. "Oh, a non-slip surface."

The party had a limited attention span. When she realized she
had lost her audience, she shut off the mike and put the box with
the rest of the swag. "We have to start at four, no matter what.
There's so much stuff." The kid who knew about records wormed

into our conversation; Happy put her hand on his shoulder. "Mr. Boy, do you know my friend, Weldon?" she said. "He's new."

Montross grinned. "We met on Playroom."

"Where *is* Stennie, anyway?" said Happy.

"Swimming," I said. Montross appeared to be in his late teens. Bigger than me—everyone was bigger than me. He wore green shorts and a window shirt of surfers at Waimea. He looked like everybody; there was nothing about him to remember. I considered bashing the smirk off his face but it was a bad idea. If he was software he could not feel anything and I would probably break my hand on his temporary chassis. "Got to go. I promised Stennie I'd meet him back at the pool. Hey Weldon, want to tag along?"

"You come right back," said Happy. "We're starting at four. Tell everyone."

We avoided the tube and cut across the lawn for privacy. Comrade handed Montross the envelope. He slid the photograph out and I had one last glimpse. This time the dead man left me cold. In fact, I was embarrassed. Although he kept a straight face, I knew what Montross was thinking about me. Maybe he was right. I wished he would put the picture away. He was not one of us; he could not understand. I wondered if Tree had come far enough yet to appreciate corpse porn.

"It's the only copy," Comrade said.

"All right." Finally Montross crammed it into the pocket of his shorts.

"You tapped our files; you know it's true."

"So?"

"So enough!" I said. "You have what you wanted."

"I've already explained." Montross was being patient. "Getting this back doesn't close the case. I have to take preventive measures."

"Meaning you turn Comrade into a carrot."

"Meaning I repair him. You're the one who took him to the chop shop. Deregulated wiseguys are dangerous. Maybe not to you, but certainly to property and probably to other people. It's a straightforward procedure. He'll be fully functional afterward."

"Plug your procedure, jack. We're leaving."

Both wiseguys stopped. "I thought you agreed," said Montross.

"Let's go, Comrade." I grabbed his arm but he shook me off.

"Where?" he said.

"Anywhere! Just so I never have to listen to this again." I pulled again, angry at Comrade for stalling. Your wiseguy is supposed to anticipate your needs, do whatever you want.

"But we haven't even tried to . . ."

"Forget it then. I give up." I pushed him toward Montross. "You want to chat, fine, go right ahead. Let him rip the top of your head off while you're at it, but I'm not sticking around to watch."

I checked the pool but Tree, Stennie, and Janet had already gone. I went through the Glass House and caught up with them in the tube to the sculpture gallery.

"Can I talk to you?" I put my arm around Tree's waist, just like I had seen grownups do. "In private." I could tell she was annoyed to be separated from Janet. "We'll catch up." I waved Stennie on. "See you over there."

She waited until they were gone. "What?" Her hair, slick from swimming, left dark spots where it brushed her silver jaunts.

"I want to leave. We'll call my mom's car." She did not look happy. "I'll take you anywhere you want to go."

"But we just got here. Give it a chance."

"I've been to too many of these things."

"Then you shouldn't have come."

Silence. I wanted to tell her about Montross—everything—but not here. Anyone could come along and the tube was so hot. I was desperate to get her away, so I lied. "Believe me, you're not going to like this. I know." I tugged at her waist. "Sometimes even I think smash parties are too much."

"We've had this discussion before," she said. "Obviously you weren't listening. I don't need you to decide for me whether I'm going to like something, Mr. Boy. I have two parents too many; I don't need another." She stepped away from me. "Hey, I'm sorry if you're having a bad time. But do you really need to spoil it for me?" She turned and strode down the tube toward the gallery, her beautiful hair slapping against her back. I watched her go.

"But I'm in trouble," I muttered to the empty tube—and then was disgusted with myself because I did not have the guts to say it to Tree. I was too scared she would not care. I stood there, sweating. For a moment the stink of doubt filled my nostrils. Then I followed her in. I could not abandon her to the extremists.

The gallery was jammed now; maybe a hundred kids swarmed across the balconies and down the stairs. Some perched along the edges, their feet scuffing the white brick. Happy had turned up the volume.

". . . according to Guinness, was set at the University of Oklahoma in Norman, Oklahoma, in 2012. Three minutes and fourteen seconds." The crowd rumbled in disbelief. "The challenge states each piece must be small enough to pass through a hole thirty centimeters in diameter."

I worked my way to an opening beside a rubber tree. Happy

posed on the keyboard of the piano. Freddy the Teddy and the gorilla brothers, Mike and Bubba, lined up beside her. "No mechanical tools are allowed." She gestured at an armory of axes, sledgehammers, spikes, and crowbars laid out on the floor. A paper plate spun across the room. I could not see Tree.

"This piano is over two hundred years old," Happy continued, "which means the white keys are ivory." She plunked a note. "Dead elephants!" Everybody heaved a sympathetic *awww*. "The blacks are ebony, hacked from the rain forest." Another note, less reaction. "It deserves to die."

Applause. Comrade and I spotted each other at almost the same time. He and Montross stood toward the rear of the lower balcony. He gestured for me to come down; I ignored him.

"Do you boys have anything to say?" Happy said.

"Yeah." Freddy hefted an ax. "Let's make landfill."

I ducked around the rubber tree and heard the *crack* of splitting wood, the iron groan of a piano frame yielding its last music. The spectators hooted approval. As I bumped past kids, searching for Tree, the instrument's death cry made me think of taking a hammer to Montross. If fights broke out, no one would care if Comrade and I dragged him outside. I wanted to beat him until he shuddered and came unstrung and his works glinted in the thudding August light. It would make me feel extreme again. *Crunch!* Kids shrieked, "Go, go, go!" The party was lifting off and taking me with it.

"You are Mr. Boy Cage." Abruptly Shikibu's microcam eyes were in my face. "We know your famous mother." He had to shout to be heard. "I have a question."

"Go away."

"*Thirty seconds.*" A girl's voice boomed over the speakers.

"U.S. and Japan are very different, yes?" He pressed closer. "We honor ancestors, our past. You seem to hate so much." He gestured at the gallery. "Why?"

"Maybe we're spoiled." I barged past him.

I saw Freddy swing a sledgehammer at the exposed frame. *Clang!* A chunk of twisted iron clattered across the brick floor, trailing broken strings. Happy scooped the mess up and shoved it through a thirty centimeter hole drilled in an upright sheet of particle board.

The timekeeper called out again. "*One minute.*" I had come far enough around the curve of the stairs to see her.

"Treemonisha!"

She glanced up, her face alight with pleasure, and waved. I was frightened for her. She was climbing into the same box I needed to break out of. So I rushed down the stairs to rescue her—little boy knight in shining armor—and ran right into Comrade's arms.

"I've decided," he said. *"Mnye vcyaw ostoyeblo."*

"Great." I had to get to Tree. "Later, okay?" When I tried to go by, he picked me up. I started thrashing. It was the first fight of the afternoon and I lost. He carried me over to Montross. The gallery was in an uproar.

"All set," said Montross. "I'll have to borrow him for a while. I'll drop him off tonight at your mom. Then we're done."

"Done?" I kept trying to get free but Comrade crushed me against him.

"It's what you want." His body was so hard. "And what your mom wants."

"Mom? She doesn't even know."

"She knows everything," Comrade said. "She watches you constantly. What else does she have to do all day?" He let me go. "Remember you said I was sloppy getting the picture? I wasn't; it was a clean operation. Only someone tipped Datasafe off."

"But she promised. Besides that makes no . . ."

"Two minutes," Tree called.

". . . but he threatened me," I said. "He was going to blow me up. Needle me in the mall."

"We wouldn't do that." Montross spread his hands innocently. "It's against the law."

"Yeah? Well, then drop dead, jack." I poked a finger at him. "Deal's off."

"No, it's not," said Comrade. "It's too late. This isn't about the picture anymore, Mr. Boy; it's about you. You weren't supposed to change but you did. Maybe they botched the last stunting, maybe it's Treemonisha. Whatever, you've outgrown me, the way I am now. So I have to change, too, or else I'll keep getting in your way."

He always had everything under control; it made me crazy. He was too good at running my life. "You should have told me Mom turned you in." *Crash!* I felt like the crowd was inside my head, screaming.

"You could've figured it out, if you wanted to. Besides, if I had said anything, your mom wouldn't have bothered to be subtle. She would've squashed me. She still might, even though I'm being fixed. Only by then I won't care. *Rosproyebi tvayou mat!*"

I heard Tree finishing the count. *". . . twelve, thirteen, fourteen!"* No record today. Some kids began to boo, others laughed. "Time's up, you losers!"

I glared at the two wiseguys. Montross was busy emulating sincerity. Comrade found a way to grin for me, the same smirk he always wore when he tortured the greeter. "It's easier this way."

Easier. My life was too plugging easy. I had never done anything important by myself. Not even grow up. I wanted to smash something.

"Okay," I said. "You asked for it."

Comrade turned to Montross and they shook hands. I thought next they might clap one another on the shoulder and whistle as they strolled off into the sunset together. I felt like puking. "Have fun," said Comrade. *"Da svedanya."*

"Sure." Betraying Comrade, my best friend, brought me both pain and pleasure at once—but not enough to satisfy the shrieking wildness within me. The party was just starting.

Happy stood beaming beside the ruins of the Steinway. Although nothing of what was left was more than half a meter tall, Freddy, Mike and Bubba had given up now that the challenge was lost. Kids were already surging down the stairs to claim their share of the swag. I went along with them.

"Don't worry," announced Happy. "Plenty for everyone. Come take what you like. Remember, guns and animals outside, if you want to hunt. The safeties won't release unless you go through the door. Watch out for one another, people, we don't want anyone shot."

A bunch of kids were wrestling over the turkey cage; one of them staggered backwards and knocked into me. "Gobble, gobble," she said. I shoved her back.

"Mr. Boy! Over here." Tree, Stennie, and Janet were waiting on the far side of the gallery. As I crossed to them, Happy gave the sign and Stone Kinkaid hurled the four thousand year old ceramic hippo against the wall. It shattered. Everybody cheered. In the upper balconies, they were playing catch with a frog.

"You see who kept time?" said Janet.

"Didn't need to see," I said. "I could hear. They probably heard in Elkhart. So you like it, Tree?"

"It's about what I expected: dumb but fun. I don't think they . . ." The frog sailed from the top balcony and splatted at our feet. Its legs twitched and guts spilled from its open mouth. I watched Tree's smile turn brittle. She seemed slightly embarrassed, as if she had just been told the price of something she could not afford.

"This is going to be a war zone soon," Stennie said.

"Yeah, let's fade." Janet towed Stennie to the stairs, swerving around the three boys lugging Our Lady of the Bathtub out to the firing range.

"Wait." I blocked Tree. "You're here, so you have to destroy something. Get with the program."

"I have to?" She seemed doubtful. "Oh all right—but no animals."

A hail of antique Coke bottles crashed around Happy as she directed traffic at the dwindling swag heap. "Hey people, please be very careful where you throw things." Her amplified voice blasted us as we approached. The first floor was a graveyard of broken glass and piano bones and bloody feathers. Most of the good stuff was already gone.

"Any records left?" I said.

Happy wobbled closer to me. "What?" She seemed punchy, as if stunned by the success of her own party.

"The box I gave you. From Stennie." She pointed; I spotted it under some cages and grabbed it. Tree and the others were on the stairs. Outside I could hear the crackle of small arms fire. I caught up.

"Sir! Mr. Dinosaur, please." The press still lurked on the upper balcony. "Matsuo Shikibu, Japanese telelink NHK. Could I speak with you for a moment?"

"Excuse me, but this jack and I have some unfinished business." I handed Stennie the records and cut in front. He swayed and lashed his tail upward to counterbalance their weight.

"Remember me?" I bowed to Shikibu.

"My apologies if I offended . . ."

"Hey, Matsuo—can I call you Matsuo? This is your first smash party, right? Please, eyes on me. I want to explain why I was rude before. Help you understand the local customs. You see, we're kind of self-conscious here in the U.S. We don't like it when someone just watches while we play. You either join in or you're not one of us."

My little speech drew a crowd. "What's he talking about?" said Janet. She was shushed.

"So if you drop by our party and don't have fun, people resent you," I told him. "No one came here today to put on a show. This is who we are. What we believe in."

"Yeah!" Stennie was cheerleading for the extreme Mr. Boy of old. "Tell him." Too bad he did not realize it was his final appearance. What was Mr. Boy without his Comrade? "Make him feel some pain."

I snatched an album from the top of the stack, slipped the record out and held it close to Shikibu's microcam eyes. "What does this say?"

He craned his neck to read the label. "John Coltrane, *Giant Steps*."

"Very good." I grasped the record with both hands, and raised it over my head for all to see. "We're not picky, Matsuo. We welcome everyone. Therefore today it is my honor to initiate you—and the home audience back on NHK. If you're still watching, you're part of this too." I broke the record over his head.

He yelped and staggered backward and almost tripped over a dead cat. Stone Kinkaid caught him and propped him up. "Congratulations," said Stennie, as he waved his claws at Japan. "You're all extremists now."

Shikibu gaped at me, his microcam eyes askew. A couple of kids clapped.

"There's someone else here who has not yet joined us." I turned on Tree. "Another spectator." Her smile faded.

"You leave her alone," said Janet. "What are you, crazy?"

"I'm not going to touch her." I held up empty hands. "No, I just want her to ruin something. That's why you came, isn't it, Tree? To get a taste?" I rifled through the box until I found what I wanted. "How about this?" I thrust it at her.

"Oh yeah," said Stennie, "I meant to tell you . . ."

She took the record and scoped it briefly. When she glanced up at me, I almost lost my nerve.

"Matsuo Shikibu, meet Treemonisha Joplin." I clasped my hands behind my back so no one could see me tremble. "The great-great-great granddaughter of the famous American composer, Scott Joplin. Yes, Japan, we're all celebrities here in New Canaan. Now please observe." I read the record for him. "*Piano Rags by Scott Joplin*, Volume III. Who knows, this might be the last copy. We can only hope. So, what are you waiting for, Tree? You don't want to be a Joplin anymore? Just wait until your folks get a peek at this. We'll even send GD a copy. Go ahead, enjoy."

"Smash it!" The kids around us took up the chant. "Smash it!" Shikibu adjusted his lenses.

"You think I won't?" Tree pulled out the disc and threw the sleeve off the balcony. "This is a piece of junk, Mr. Boy." She laughed and then shattered the album against the wall. She held onto a shard. "It doesn't mean anything to me."

I heard Janet whisper. "What's going on?"

"I think they're having an argument."

"You want me to be your little dream cush." Tree tucked the piece of broken plastic into the pocket of my baggies. "The stiff from nowhere who knows nobody and does nothing without Mr. Boy. So you try to scare me off. You tell me you're so rich, you can afford to hate yourself. Stay home, you say, it's too dangerous, we're all crazy. Well, if you're so sure this is poison, how come you've still got your wiseguy and your cash cards? Are you going to move out of your mom, leave town, stop getting stunted? You're not giving it up, Mr. Boy, so why should I?"

Shikibu turned his camera eyes on me. No one spoke.

"You're right," I said. "She's right." I could not save anyone until

I saved myself. I felt the wildness lifting me to it. I leapt onto the balcony wall and shouted for everyone to hear. "Shut up and listen everybody! You're all invited to my place, okay?"

There was one last thing to smash.

"Stop this, Peter." The greeter no longer thought I was cute. "What're you doing?" She trembled as if the kids spilling into her were an infection.

"I thought you'd like to meet my friends," I said. A few had stayed behind with Happy, who had decided to sulk after I hijacked her guests. The rest had followed me home in a caravan so I could warn off the sentry robots. It was already a hall-of-fame bash. "Treemonisha Joplin, this is my mom. Sort of."

"Hi," Tree held out her hand uncertainly.

The greeter was no longer the human doormat. "Get them out of me." She was too jumpy to be polite. "Right now!"

Someone turned up a boombox. Skitter music filled the room like a siren. Tree said something I could not hear. When I put a hand to my ear, she leaned close and said, "Don't be so mean, Mr. Boy. I think she's really frightened."

I grinned and nodded. "I'll tell Cook to make us some snacks."

Bubba and Mike carried boxes filled with the last of the swag and set them on the coffee table. Kids fanned out, running their hands along her wrinkled blood-hot walls, bouncing on the furniture. Stennie waved at me as he led a bunch upstairs for a tour. A leftover cat had gotten loose and was hissing and scratching underfoot. Some twisted kids had already stripped and were rolling in the floor hair, getting ready to have sex.

"Get dressed, you." The greeter kicked at them as she coiled her umbilical to keep it from being trampled. She retreated to her wall plug. "You're *hurting* me." Although her voice rose to a scream, only half a dozen kids heard her. She went limp and sagged to the floor.

The whole room seemed to throb, as if to some great heartbeat, and the lights went out. It took a while for someone to kill the sound on the boombox. "What's wrong?" Voices called out. "Mr. Boy? Lights."

Both doorbones swung open and I saw a bughead silhouetted against the twilit sky. Shikibu in his microcams. "Party's over," Mom said over her speaker system. There was nervous laughter. "Leave before I call the cops. Peter, go to your room right now. I want to speak to you."

As the stampede began, I found Tree's hand. "Wait for me?" I pulled her close. "I'll only be a minute."

"What are you going to do?" She sounded frightened. It felt good to be taken so seriously.

"I'm moving out, chucking all this. I'm going to be a working stiff." I chuckled. "Think your dad would give me a job?"

"Look out, dumbscut! Hey, *hey*. Don't push!"

Tree dragged me out of the way. "You're crazy."

"I know. That's why I have to get out of Mom."

"Listen," she said, "you've never been poor, you have no idea. . . . Only a rich kid would think it's easy being a stiff. Just go up, apologize, tell her it won't happen again. Then change things later on, if you want. Believe me, life will be a lot simpler if you hang onto the money."

"I can't. Will you wait?"

"You want me to tell you it's okay to be stupid, is that it? Well, I've *been* poor, Mr. Boy, and still am, and I don't recommend it. So don't expect me to stand around and clap while you throw away something I've always wanted." She spun away from me and I lost her in the darkness. I wanted to catch up with her but I knew I had to do Mom now or I would lose my nerve.

As I was fumbling my way upstairs I heard stragglers coming down. "On your right," I called. Bodies nudged by me.

"Mr. Boy, is that you?" I recognized Stennie's voice.

"He's gone," I said.

Seven flights up, the lights were on. Nanny waited on the landing outside my rooms, her umbilical stretched nearly to its limit. She was the only remote which was physically able to get to my floor and this was as close as she could come.

It had been a while since I had seen her; Mom did not use her much anymore and I rarely visited, even though the nursery was only one flight down. But this was the remote who used to pick me up when I cried and who had changed my diapers and who taught me how to turn on my roombrain. She had skin so pale you could almost see veins and long black hair piled high on her head. I never thought of her as having a body because she always wore dark turtlenecks and long woolen skirts and silky panty hose. Nanny was a smile and warm hands and the smell of fresh pillowcases. Once upon a time I thought her the most beautiful creature in the world. Back then I would have done anything she said.

She was not smiling now. "I don't know how you expect me to trust you anymore, Peter." Nanny had never been a very good scold. "Those brats were out of control. I can't let you put me in danger this way."

"If you wanted someone to trust, maybe you shouldn't have had me stunted. You got exactly what you ordered, the neverending kid. Well, kids don't have to be responsible."

"What do you mean, what I ordered? It's what you wanted, too."

"Is it? Did you ever ask? I was only ten, the first time, too young to know better. For a long time I did it to please you. Getting stunted was the only thing I did that seemed important to you. But *you* never explained. You never sat me down and said 'This is the life you'll have and this is what you'll miss and this is how you'll feel about it.' "

"You want to grow up, is that it?" She was trying to threaten me. "You want to work and worry and get old and die someday?" She had no idea what we were talking about.

"I can't live this way anymore, Nanny."

At first she acted stunned, as if I had spoken in Albanian. Then her expression hardened when she realized she had lost her hold on me. She was ugly when she was angry. "They put you up to this." Her gaze narrowed in accusation. "That little black cush you've been seeing. Those realists!"

I had always managed to hide my anger from Mom. Right up until then. "How do you know about her?" I had never told her about Tree.

"Peter, they live in a mall!"

Comrade was right. "You've been spying on me." When she did not deny it, I went berserk. "You liar." I slammed my fist into her belly. "You said you wouldn't watch." She staggered and fell onto her umbilical, crimping it. As she twitched on the floor, I pounced. "You promised." I slapped her face. "Promised." I hit her again. Her hair had come undone and her eyes rolled back in their sockets and her face was slack. She made no effort to protect herself. Mom was retreating from this remote, too, but I was not going to let her get away.

"Mom!" I rolled off Nanny. "I'm coming up, Mom! You hear? Get ready." I was crying; it had been a long time since I had cried. Not something Mr. Boy did.

I scrambled up to the long landing at the shoulders. At one end another circular stairway wound up into the torch; in the middle four steps led into the neck. It was the only doorbone I had never seen open; I had no idea how to get through.

"Mom, I'm here." I pounded. "Mom! You hear me?"

Silence.

"Let me in, Mom." I smashed myself against the doorbone. Pain branched through my shoulder like lightning but it felt great because Mom shuddered from the impact. I backed up and, in a frenzy, hurled myself again. Something warm dripped on my cheek. She was bleeding from the hinges. I aimed a vicious kick at the doorbone and it banged open. I went through.

For years I had imagined that if only I could get into the head I could meet my real mother. Touch her. I had always wondered what she looked like; she got reshaped just after I was born. When I was little I used to think of her as a magic princess glowing with fairy light. Later I pictured her as one or another of my friends' moms, only better dressed. After I had started getting twanked, I was afraid she might be just a brain floating in nutrient solution, like in some pricey memory bank. All wrong.

The interior of the head was dark and absolutely freezing. There was no sound except for the hum of refrigeration units. "Mom?" My voice echoed in the empty space. I stumbled and caught myself against a smooth wall. Not skin, like everywhere else in Mom— metal. The tears froze on my face.

"There's nothing for you here," she said. "This is a clean room. You're compromising it. You must leave immediately."

Sterile environment, metal walls, the bitter cold that superconductors needed. I did not need to see. No one lived here. It had never occurred to me that there was no Mom to touch. She had downloaded, become an electron ghost tripping icy logic gates. "How long have you been dead?"

"This isn't where you belong," she said.

I shivered. "How long?"

"Go away," she said.

So I did. I had to. I could not stay very long in her secret place or I would die of the cold.

As I reeled down the stairs, Mom herself seemed to shift beneath my feet and I saw her as if she were a stranger. Dead—and I had been living in a tomb. I ran past Nanny; she still sprawled where I had left her. All those years I had loved her, I had been in love with death. Mom had been sucking life from me the way her refrigerators stole the warmth from my body.

Now I knew there was no way I could stay, no matter what anyone said. I knew it was not going to be easy leaving, and not just because of the money. For a long time Mom had been my entire world. But I could not let her use me to pretend she was alive, or I would end up like her.

I realized now that the door had always stayed locked because Mom had to hide what she had become. If I wanted, I could have destroyed her. Downloaded intelligences have no more rights than cars or wiseguys. Mom was legally dead and I was her only heir. I could have had her shut off, her body razed. But somehow it was enough to go, to walk away from my inheritance. I was scared and yet with every step I felt lighter. Happier. Extremely free.

I had not expected to find Tree waiting at the doorbone, chatting with Comrade as if nothing had happened. "I just had to see if you were really the biggest fool in the world," she said.

"Out." I pulled her through the door. "Before I change my mind."

Comrade started to follow us. "No, not you." I turned and stared back at the heads on his window coat. I had not intended to see him again; I had wanted to be gone before Montross returned him. "Look, I'm giving you back to Mom. She needs you more than I do."

If he had argued, I might have given in. The old, unregulated Comrade would have said something. But he just slumped a little and nodded and I knew that he was dead, too. The thing in front of me was another ghost. He and Mom were two of a kind. "Pretend you're her kid, maybe she'll like that." I patted his shoulder.

"Prekrassnaya ideya," he said. *"Spaceba."*

"You're welcome," I said.

Tree and I trotted together down the long driveway. Robot sentries crossed the lawn and turned their spotlights on us. I wanted to tell her she was right. I had probably just done the single most irresponsible thing of my life—and I had high standards. Still, I could not imagine how being poor could be worse than being rich and hating yourself. I had seen enough of what it was like to be dead. It was time to try living.

"Are we going someplace, Mr. Boy?" Tree squeezed my hand. "Or are we just wandering around in the dark?"

"Mr. Boy is a damn stupid name, don't you think?" I laughed. "Call me Pete." I felt like a kid again.

NANCY KRESS
And Wild for to Hold

Born in Buffalo, New York, Nancy Kress now lives in Brockport, New York. She began selling her elegant and incisive stories in 1976, and has since become a frequent contributor to *Asimov's Science Fiction*, *The Magazine of Fantasy & Science Fiction*, *Omni*, and others, as well as one of the most popular and critically acclaimed writers of her generation.

Although she sold her first novel in 1981, and followed it up with several more sales in subsequent years, her early books (*The Prince of Morning Bells*, *The Golden Grove*, and *The White Pipes*), all fantasy novels, went unnoticed for the most part within the science fiction field, and are still little read, even by fans of her SF work. What *did* gain her attention within the genre was her short work; Kress is prolific at shorter lengths, and even today, with a few exceptions, her reputation rests most solidly on her short fiction. This is not surprising, since she has published some of the best short work of the seventies and eighties (and right on into the nineties), including the provocative novella *Trinity*, the Nebula-winning "Out of All Them Bright Stars," "The Price of Oranges," "With the Original Cast," "Inertia," "Cannibals," "Night Win," "In Memoriam," "The Mountain to Mohammed," and literally dozens of other high-quality stories.

She made her biggest impact to date with her 1991 novella *Beggars in Spain*, which won her well-deserved Hugo and Nebula Awards, and was one of the most talked-about and acclaimed stories to have appeared in the field for some time. I was tempted to include *Beggars in Spain* in this anthology, but it had just recently received a great deal of exposure, and what was obscured by all the hoopla over *Beggars in Spain* was the fact that Kress had published *an-*

other exceptionally fine novella in 1991, one that had received far less attention than it deserved, the intricate, sly,
and surprising story you're about to read, the vivid and
compelling tale of a Queen cast adrift in time, *And Wild for
to Hold*.

   Some of Kress's stories have been gathered in *Trinity and
Other Stories*, and a second collection, *The Aliens of Earth*, is
due to appear shortly. Kress's other books include the science fiction novels *An Alien Light*, the well-received *Brain
Rose*, and the critically acclaimed novel version of *Beggars
in Spain*.

The demon came to her first in the long gallery at Hever Castle.
She had gone there to watch Henry ride away, magnificent on his
huge charger, the horse's legs barely visible through the summer
dust raised by the king's entourage. But Henry himself was visible.
He rose in his stirrups to half-turn his gaze back to the manor
house, searching its sun-glazed windows to see if she watched. The
spurned lover, riding off, watching over his shoulder the effect he
himself made. She knew just how his eyes would look, small blue
eyes under the curling red-gold hair. Mournful. Shrewd. Unde-
terred.

   Anne Boleyn was not moved. Let him ride. She had not wanted
him at Hever in the first place.

   As she turned from the gallery window, a glint of light in the far
corner caught her eye, and there for the first time was the demon.

   It was made all of light, which did not surprise her. Was not
Satan himself called Lucifer? The light was square, a perfectly
square box such as no light had ever been before. Anne crossed
herself and stepped forward. The box of light brightened, then
winked out.

   Anne stood perfectly still. She was not afraid; very little made
her afraid. But nonetheless she crossed herself again and uttered
a prayer. It would be unfortunate if a demon took up residence at
Hever. Demons could be dangerous.

   Like kings.

Lambert half-turned from her console toward Culhane, working
across the room. "Culhane—they said she was a witch."

   "Yes? So?" Culhane said. "In the 1500s they said any powerful
woman was a witch."

   "No, it was more. They said it *before* she became powerful." Culhane didn't answer. After a moment Lambert said quietly, "The
Rahvoli equations keep flagging her."

Culhane grew very still. Finally he said, "Let me see."

He crossed the bare, small room to Lambert's console. She stead-ied the picture on the central square. At the moment the console appeared in this location as a series of interlocking squares mount-ing from floor to ceiling. Some of the squares were solid real-time alloys; some were holo simulations; some were not there at all, neither in space nor time, although they appeared to be. The proj-ect focus square, which *was* there, said:

TIME RESCUE PROJECT
UNITED FEDERATION OF UPPER SLIB, EARTH
FOCUS: ANNE BOLEYN
  HEVER CASTLE, KENT, ENGLAND, EUROPE
  1525: 645:89:3
CHURCH OF THE HOLY HOSTAGE TEMPORARY
PERMIT #4592

In the time-jump square was framed a young girl, dark hair just visible below her coif, her hand arrested at her long, slender neck in the act of signing the cross.

Lambert said, as if to herself, "She considered herself a good Catholic."

Culhane stared at the image. His head had been freshly shaved, in honor of his promotion to project head. He wore, Lambert thought, his new importance as if it were a fragile implant, liable to be rejected. She found that touching.

Lambert said, "The Rahvoli probability is .798. She's a definite key."

Culhane sucked in his cheeks. The dye on them had barely dried. He said, "So is the other. I think we should talk to Brill."

The serving women had finally left. The priests had left, the doc-tors, the courtiers, the nurses, taking with them the baby. Even Henry had left, gone . . . where? To play cards with Harry Norris? To his latest mistress? Never mind—they had all at last left her alone.

A girl.

Anne rolled over in her bed and pounded her fists on the pillow. A girl. Not a prince, not the son that England needed, that *she* needed . . . a girl. And Henry growing colder every day, she could feel it, he no longer desired her, no longer loved her. He would bed with her—oh, that, most certainly, if it would get him his boy, but her power was going. Was gone. The power she had hated, despised, but had used nonetheless because it was there and Henry should feel it, as he had made her feel his power over and over again . . . her power was going. She was queen of England, but her power was slipping away like the Thames at ebb tide, and she just as helpless to stop it as to stop the tide itself. The only thing that could have preserved her power was a son. And she had borne a girl. Strong, lusty, with Henry's own red, curling hair . . . but a girl.

Anne rolled over on her back, painfully. Elizabeth was already a month old, but everything in Anne hurt. She had contracted white-leg, so much less dreaded than childbed fever but still weakening, and for the whole month had not left her bedchamber. Servants and ladies and musicians came and went, while Anne lay feverish, trying to plan . . . . Henry had as yet made no move. He had even seemed to take the baby's sex well: "She seems a lusty wench. I pray God will send her a brother in the same good shape." But Anne knew. She always knew. She had known when Henry's eye first fell upon her. Had known to a shade the exact intensity of his longing during the nine years she had kept him waiting: nine years of celibacy, of denial. She had known the exact moment when that hard mind behind the small blue eyes had decided: *It is worth it. I will divorce Katherine and make her queen.* Anne had known before he did when he decided it had all been a mistake. The price for making her queen had been too high. She was not worth it. Unless she gave him a son.

And if she did not . . .

In the darkness Anne squeezed her eyes shut. This was but an attack of childbed vapors; it signified nothing. She was never afraid, not she. This was only a night terror, and when she opened her eyes it would pass, because it must. She must go on fighting, must get herself heavy with a son, must safeguard her crown. And her daughter. There was no one else to do it for her, and there was no way out.

When she opened her eyes a demon, shaped like a square of light, glowed in the corner of the curtained bedchamber.

Lambert dipped her head respectfully as the high priest passed.

She was tall and wore no external augments. Eyes, arms, ears, shaved head, legs under the gray-green ceremonial robe—all were her own, as required by the charter of the Church of the Holy Hostage. Lambert had heard a rumor that before her election to high priest she had had brilliant, violet-augmented eyes and gamma-strength arms, but on her election had had both removed and the originals restored. The free representative of all the hostages in the solar system could not walk around enjoying high-maintenance augments. Hostages could, of course, but the person in charge of their spiritual and material welfare must appear human to any hostage she chose to visit. A four-handed spacer held in a free-fall chamber on Mars must find the high priest as human as did a genetically altered flier of Ipsu being held hostage by the New Trien Republic. The only way to do that was to forego external augments.

Internals, of course, were a different thing.

Beside the high priest walked the director of the Time Research Institute, Toshio Brill. No ban on externals for *him:* Brill wore gold-plated sensors in his shaved black head, a display Lambert found slightly ostentatious. Also puzzling: Brill was not ordinarily a flamboyant man. Perhaps he was differentiating himself from Her Holiness. Behind Brill his project heads, including Culhane, stood silent, not speaking unless spoken to. Culhane looked nervous: He was ambitious, Lambert knew. She sometimes wondered why she was not.

"So far I am impressed," the high priest said. "Impeccable hostage conditions on the material side."

Brill murmured, "Of course, the spiritual is difficult. The three hostages are so different from each other, and even for culture specialists and historians . . . the hostages arrive here very upset."

"As would you or I," the high priest said, not smiling, "in similar circumstances."

"Yes, Your Holiness."

"And now you wish to add a fourth hostage, from a fourth time stream."

"Yes."

The high priest looked slowly around at the main console; Lambert noticed that she looked right past the time-jump square itself. Not trained in peripheral vision techniques. But she looked a long time at the stasis square. They all did; outsiders were unduly fascinated by the idea that the whole building existed between time streams. Or maybe Her Holiness merely objected to the fact that the Time Research Institute, like some larger but hardly richer institutions, was exempt from the all-world taxation that supported the Church. Real-estate outside time was also outside taxation.

The high priest said, "I cannot give permission for such a political disruption without understanding fully every possible detail. Tell me again."

Lambert hid a grin. The high priest did not need to hear it again. She knew the whole argument, had pored over it for days, most likely, with her advisers. And she would agree; why wouldn't she? It could only add to her power. Brill knew that. He was being asked to explain only to show that the high priest could force him to do

it, again and again, until she—not he—decided the explanation was
sufficient and the Church of the Holy Hostage issued a permanent
hostage permit to hold one Anne Boleyn, of England Time Delta,
for the altruistic purpose of preventing a demonstrable, Class One
war.

Brill showed no outward recognition that he was being humbled.
"Your Holiness, this woman is a fulcrum. The Rahvoli equations,
developed in the last century by—"

"I know the Rahvoli equations," the high priest said. And smiled
sweetly.

"Then Your Holiness knows that any person identified by the
equations as a fulcrum is directly responsible for the course of
history. Even if he or she seems powerless in local time. Mistress
Boleyn was the second wife of Henry the Eighth of England. In
order to marry her, he divorced his first wife, Katharine of Aragon,
and in order to do that, he took all of England out of the Catholic
Church. Protestantism was—"

"And what again was that?" Her Holiness said, and even Culhane
glanced sideways at Lambert, appalled. The high priest was playing.
With a *research director*, Lambert hid her smile. Did Culhane know
that high seriousness opened one to the charge of pomposity? Probably not.

"Protestantism was another branch of 'Christianity,' " the director
said patiently. So far, by refusing to be provoked, he was winning.
"It was warlike, as was Catholicism. In 1642 various branches of
Protestantism were contending for political power within England,
as was a Catholic faction. King Charles was Catholic, in fact. Contention led to civil war. Thousands of people died fighting, starved
to death, were hung as traitors, were tortured as betrayers . . ."

Lambert saw Her Holiness wince. She must hear this all the time,
Lambert thought. What else was her office for? Yet the wince
looked genuine.

Brill pressed his point. "Children were reduced to eating rats to
survive. In Cornwall, rebels' hands and feet were cut off, gibbets were
erected in market squares and men hung on them alive, and—"

"Enough," the high priest said. "This is why the Church exists. To
promote the holy hostages that prevent war."

"And that is what we wish to do," Brill said swiftly, "in other time
streams, now that our own has been brought to peace. In Stream
Delta, which has only reached the sixteenth century—Your Holiness
knows that each stream progresses at a different relative rate—"

The high priest made a gesture of impatience.

"—the woman Anne Boleyn is the fulcrum. If she can be taken
hostage after the birth of her daughter Elizabeth, who will act

throughout a very long reign to preserve peace, and before Henry declares the Act of Supremacy that opens the door to religious divisiveness in England, we can prevent great loss of life. The Rahvoli equations show a 79.8 percent probability that history will be changed in the direction of greater peace, right up through the following two centuries. Religious wars often—"

"There are other, bloodier religious wars to prevent than the English civil war."

"True, Your Holiness," the director said humbly. At least it looked like humility to Lambert. "But ours is a young science. Identifying other time streams, focusing on one, identifying historical fulcra—it is such a new science. We do what we can, in the name of peace."

Everyone in the room looked pious. Lambert hid a smile. In the name of peace—and of prestigious scientific research, attended by rich financial support and richer academic reputations.

"And it is peace we seek," Brill pressed, "as much as the Church itself does. With a permanent permit to take Anne Boleyn hostage, we can save countless lives in this other time stream, just as the Church preserves peace in our own."

The high priest played with the sleeve of her robe. Lambert could not see her face. But when she looked up, she was smiling.

"I'll recommend to the All-World Forum that your hostage permit be granted, Director. I will return in two months to make an official check on the holy hostage."

Brill, Lambert saw, didn't quite stop himself in time from frowning. "Two months? But with the entire solar system of hostages to supervise—"

"Two months, Director," Her Holiness said. "The week before the All-World Forum convenes to vote on revenue and taxation."

"I—"

"Now I would like to inspect the three holy hostages you already hold for the altruistic prevention of war."

Later, Culhane said to Lambert, "He did not explain it very well. It could have been made so much more urgent . . . it *is* urgent. Those bodies rotting in Cornwall . . ." He shuddered.

Lambert looked at him. "You care. You genuinely do."

He looked back at her in astonishment. "And you don't? You must, to work on this project!"

"I care," Lambert said. "But not like that."

"Like what?"

She tried to clarify it for him, for herself. "The bodies rotting . . . I see them. But it's not our own history—"

"What does that matter? They're still human!"

He was so earnest. Intensity burned on him like skin tinglers. Did Culhane even use skin tinglers? Lambert wondered. Fellow researchers spoke of him as an ascetic, giving all his energy, all his time to the project. A woman in his domicile had told Lambert he even lived chaste, doing a voluntary celibacy mission for the entire length of his research grant. Lambert had never met anyone who actually did that. It was intriguing.

She said, "Are you thinking of the priesthood once the project is over, Culhane?"

He flushed. Color mounted from the dyed cheeks, light blue since he had been promoted to project head, to pink on the fine skin of his shaved temples.

"I'm thinking of it."

"And doing a celibacy mission now?"

"Yes. Why?" His tone was belligerent: A celibacy mission was slightly old-fashioned. Lambert studied his body: tall, well-made, strong. Augments? Muscular, maybe. He had beautiful muscles.

"No reason," she said, bending back to her console until she heard him walk away.

The demon advanced. Anne, lying feeble on her curtained bed, tried to call out. But her voice would not come, and who would hear her anyway? The bedclothes were thick, muffling sound; her ladies would all have retired for the night, alone or otherwise; the guards would be drinking the ale Henry had provided all of London to celebrate Elizabeth's christening. And Henry . . . he was not beside her. She had failed him of his son.

"Be gone," she said weakly to the demon. It moved closer.

They had called her a witch. Because of her little sixth finger, because of the dog named Urian, because she had kept Henry under her spell so long without bedding him. But if I were really a witch, she thought, I could send this demon away. More: I could hold Henry, could keep him from watching that whey-faced Jane Seymour, could keep him in my bed . . . . She was not a witch.

Therefore, it followed that there was nothing she could do about this demon. If it was come for her, it was come. If Satan, Master of Lies, was decided to have her, to punish her for taking the husband of another woman, and for . . . How much could demons know?

"This was all none of my wishing," she said aloud to the demon. "I wanted to marry someone else." The demon continued to advance.

Very well, then, let it take her. She would not scream. She never had—she prided herself on it. Not when they had told her she could not marry Harry Percy. Not when she had been sent home from the court, peremptorily and without explanation. Not when she had discovered the explanation: Henry wished to have her out of London so he could bed his latest mistress away from Katharine's eyes. She had not screamed when a crowd of whores had burst into the palace where she was supping, demanding Nan Bullen, who they said was one of them. She had escaped across the Thames in a barge, and not a cry had escaped her lips. They had admired her for her courage: Wyatt, Norris, Weston, Henry himself. She would not scream now.

The box of light grew larger as it approached. She had just time to say to it, "I have been God's faithful and true servant, and my husband, the king's," before it was upon her.

"The place where a war starts," Lambert said to the faces assembled below her in the Hall of Time, "is long before the first missile, or the first bullet, or the first spear."

She looked down at the faces. It was part of her responsibility as an intern researcher to teach a class of young, some of whom would become historians. The class was always taught in the Hall of Time. The expense was enormous: keeping the hall in stasis for nearly an hour, bringing the students in through the force field, activating all the squares at once. Her lecture would be replayed for them later, when they could pay attention to it. Lambert did not blame them for barely glancing at her now. Why should they? The walls of the circular room, which were only there in a virtual sense, were lined with squares that were not really there at all. The squares showed actual, local-time scenes from wars that had been there, were there now, somewhere, in someone's reality.

Men died writhing in the mud, arrows through intestines and neck and groin, at Agincourt.

Women lay flung across the bloody bodies of their children at Cawnpore.

In the hot sun the flies crawled thick upon the split faces of the heroes of Marathon.

Figures staggered, their faces burned off, away from Hiroshima.

Breathing bodies, their perfect faces untouched and their brains turned to mush by spekaline, sat in orderly rows under the ripped dome on Io-One.

Only one face turned toward Lambert, jerked as if on a string, a boy with wide violet eyes brimming with anguish. Lambert obligingly started again.

"The place where a war starts is long before the first missile, or the first bullet, or the first spear. There are always many forces causing a war: economic, political, religious, cultural. Nonetheless, it is the great historical discovery of our time that if you trace each of these back—through the records, through the eyewitness accounts, through the entire burden of data only Rahvoli equations can handle—you come to a fulcrum. A single event or act or person. It is like a decision tree with a thousand thousand generations of decisions: Somewhere there was one first yes/no. The place where the war started and where it could have been prevented.

"The great surprise of time rescue work has been how often that place was female.

"Men fought wars, when there were wars. Men controlled the gold and the weapons and the tariffs and sea rights and religions that have caused wars, and the men controlled the bodies of other men who did the actual fighting. But men are men. They acted at the fulcrum of history, but often what tipped their actions one way or another was what they loved. A woman. A child. She became the passive, powerless weight he chose to lift, and the balance tipped. She, not he, is the branching place, where the decision tree splits and the war begins."

The boy with the violet eyes was still watching her. Lambert stayed silent until he turned to watch the squares—which was the reason he had been brought here. Then she watched him. Anguished, passionate, able to feel what war meant—he might be a good candidate for the time rescue team when his preliminary studies were done. He reminded her a little of Culhane.

Who right now, as project head, was interviewing the new hostage, not lecturing to children.

Lambert stifled her jealousy. It was unworthy. And shortsighted: She remembered what this glimpse of human misery had meant to her three years ago, when she was an historian candidate. She had had nightmares for weeks. She had thought the event was pivotal to her life, a dividing point past which she would never be the same person again. How could she? She had been shown the depths to which humanity, without the Church of the Holy Hostage and the All-World Concordance, could descend. Burning eye sockets, mutilated genitals, a general who stood on a hill and said, "How I love to see the arms and legs fly!" It had been shattering. She had been shattered, as the orientation intended she should be.

The boy with the violet eyes was crying. Lambert wanted to step down from the platform and go to him. She wanted to put her arms around him and hold his head against her shoulder . . . but was that because of compassion, or was that because of his violet eyes?

She said silently to him, without leaving the podium, *you will be all right. Human beings are not as mutable as you think. When this is over, nothing permanent about you will have changed at all.*

* * *

Anne opened her eyes. Satan leaned over her.

His head was shaved, and he wore strange garb of an ugly blue-green. His cheeks were stained with dye. In one ear metal glittered and swung. Anne crossed herself.

"Hello," Satan said, and the voice was not human.

She struggled to sit up; if this be damnation, she would not lie prone for it. Her heart hammered in her throat. But the act of sitting brought the Prince of Darkness into focus, and her eyes widened. He looked like a man. Painted, made ugly, hung around with metal boxes that could be tools of evil—but a man.

"My name is Culhane."

A man. And she had faced men. Bishops, nobles, Chancellor Wolsey. She had outfaced Henry, Prince of England and France, Defender of the Faith.

"Don't be frightened, Mistress Boleyn. I will explain to you where you are and how you came to be here."

She saw now that the voice came not from his mouth, although his mouth moved, but from the box hung around his neck. How could that be? Was there then a demon in the box? But then she realized something else, something real to hold on to.

"Do not call me Mistress Boleyn. Address me as Your Grace. I am the queen."

The something that moved behind his eyes convinced her, finally, that he was a mortal man. She was used to reading men's eyes. But why should this one look at her like that? With pity? With admiration?

She struggled to stand, rising off the low pallet. It was carved of good English oak. The room was paneled in dark wood and hung with tapestries of embroidered wool. Small-paned windows shed brilliant light over carved chairs, table, chest. On the table rested a writing desk and a lute. Reassured, Anne pushed down the heavy cloth of her nightshift and rose.

The man, seated on a low stool, rose, too. He was taller than Henry—she had never seen a man taller than Henry—and superbly muscled. A soldier? Fright fluttered again, and she put her hand to her throat. This man, watching her—watching her *throat*. Was he then an executioner? Was she under arrest, drugged and brought by some secret method into the Tower of London? Had someone brought evidence against her? Or was Henry that disappointed that she had not borne a son that he was eager to supplant her already?

As steadily as she could, Anne walked to the window.

The Tower Bridge did not lie beyond in the sunshine. Nor the river, nor the gabled roofs of Greenwich Palace. Instead there was a sort of yard, with huge beasts of metal growling softly. On the grass naked young men and women jumped up and down, waving their arms, running in place and smiling and sweating as if they did not know either that they were uncovered or crazed.

Anne took firm hold of the windowsill. It was slippery in her hands, and she saw that it was not wood at all but some material made to resemble wood. She closed her eyes, then opened them. She was a queen. She had fought hard to become a queen, defending a virtue nobody believed she still had, against a man who claimed that to destroy that virtue was love. She had won, making the crown the price of her virtue. She had conquered a king, brought down a chancellor of England, outfaced a pope. She would not show fear to this executioner in this place of the damned, whatever it was.

She turned from the window, her head high. "Please begin your explanation, Master . . ."

"Culhane."

"Master Culhane. We are eager to hear what you have to say. And we do not like waiting."

She swept aside her long nightdress as if it were court dress and seated herself in the not-wooden chair carved like a throne.

"I am a hostage," Anne repeated. "In a time that has not yet happened."

From beside the window, Lambert watched. She was fascinated. Anne Boleyn had, according to Culhane's report, listened in silence to the entire explanation of the time rescue, that explanation so carefully crafted and revised a dozen times to fit what the sixteenth-century mind could understand of the twenty-second. Queen Anne had not become hysterical. She had not cried, nor fainted, nor professed disbelief. She had asked no questions. When Culhane had finished, she had requested, calmly and with staggering dignity, to see the ruler of this place, with his ministers. Toshio Brill, watching on monitor because the wisdom was that at first new hostages would find it easier to deal with one consistent researcher, had hastily summoned Lambert and two others. They had all dressed in the floor-length robes used for grand academic ceremonies and never else. And they had marched solemnly into the ersatz sixteenth-century room, bowing their heads.

Only their heads. No curtsies. Anne Boleyn was going to learn that no one curtsied anymore.

Covertly Lambert studied her, their fourth time hostage, so different from the other three. She had not risen from her chair, but even seated she was astonishingly tiny. Thin, delicate bones, great dark eyes, masses of silky black hair loose on her white nightdress. She was not pretty by the standards of this century; she had not even been counted pretty by the standards of her own. But she was compelling. Lambert had to give her that.

"And I am prisoner here," Anne Boleyn said. Lambert turned up her translator; the words were just familiar, but the accent so strange she could not catch them without electronic help.

"Not prisoner," the director said. "Hostage."

"Lord Brill, if I cannot leave, then I am a prisoner. Let us not mince words. I cannot leave this castle?"

"You cannot."

"Please address me as 'Your Grace.' Is there to be a ransom?"

"No, Your Grace. But because of your presence here thousands of men will live who would have otherwise died."

With a shock, Lambert saw Anne shrug; the deaths of thousands of men evidently did not interest her. It was true, then. They really were moral barbarians, even the women. The students should see this. That small shrug said more than all the battles viewed in squares. Lambert felt her sympathy for the abducted woman lessen, a physical sensation like the emptying of a bladder, and was relieved to feel it. It meant she, Lambert, still had her own moral sense.

"How long must I stay here?"

"For life, Your Grace," Brill said bluntly.

Anne made no reaction; her control was aweing.

"And how long will that be, Lord Brill?"

"No person knows the length of his or her life, Your Grace."

"But if you can read the future, as you claim, you must know what the length of mine would have been."

Lambert thought: We must not underestimate her. This hostage is not like the last one.

Brill said, with the same bluntness that honored Anne's comprehension—did she realize that?—"If we had not brought you here, you would have died May nineteenth, 1536."

"How?"

"It does not matter. You are no longer part of that future, and so now events there will—"

"*How?*"

Brill didn't answer.

Anne Boleyn rose and walked to the window, absurdly small, Lambert thought, in the trailing nightdress. Over her shoulder she said, "Is this castle in England?"

"No," Brill said. Lambert saw him exchange glances with Culhane.

"In France?"

"It is not in any place on Earth," Brill said, "although it can be entered from three places on Earth. It is outside of time."

She could not possibly have understood, but she said nothing, only went on staring out the window. Over her shoulder Lambert saw the exercise court, empty now, and the antimatter power generators. Two technicians crawled over them with a robot monitor. What did Anne Boleyn make of them?

"God alone knows if I had merited death," Anne said. Lambert saw Culhane start.

Brill stepped forward. "Your Grace—"

"Leave me now," she said without turning.

They did. Of course she would be monitored constantly—everything from brain scans to the output of her bowels. Although she would never know this. But if suicide was in that life-defying mind, it would not be possible. If Her Holiness ever learned of the suicide of a time hostage . . . Lambert's last glimpse before the door closed was of Anne Boleyn's back, still by the window, straight as a spear as she gazed out at antimatter power generators in a building in permanent stasis.

"Culhane, meeting in ten minutes," Brill said. Lambert guessed the time lapse was to let the director change into working clothes. Toshio Brill had come away from the interview with Anne Boleyn somehow diminished. He even looked shorter, although shouldn't her small stature have instead augmented his?

Culhane stood still in the corridor outside Anne's locked room (would she try the door?). His face was turned away from Lambert's. She said, "Culhane . . . You jumped a moment in there. When she said God alone knew if she had merited death."

"It was what she said at her trial," Culhane said. "When the verdict was announced. Almost the exact words."

He still had not moved so much as a muscle of that magnificent body. Lambert said, probing, "You found her impressive, then. Despite her scrawniness, and beyond the undeniable pathos of her situation."

He looked at her then, his eyes blazing: Culhane, the research engine. "I found her magnificent."

She never smiled. That was one of the things she knew they remarked upon among themselves: She had overheard them in the walled garden. *Anne Boleyn never smiles.* Alone, they did not call her Queen Anne, or Her Grace, or even the Marquis of Rochford, the title Henry had conferred upon her, the only female peeress in her own right in all of England. No, they called her Anne Boleyn, as if the marriage to Henry had never happened, as if she had never borne Elizabeth. And they said she never smiled.

What cause was there to smile, in this place that was neither life nor death?

Anne stitched deftly at a piece of amber velvet. She was not badly treated. They had given her a servant, cloth to make dresses—she had always been clever with a needle, and the skill had not deserted her when she could afford to order any dresses she chose. They had given her books, the writing Latin but the pictures curiously flat, with no raised ink or painting. They let her go into any unlocked room in the castle, out to the gardens, into the yards. She was a holy hostage.

When the amber velvet gown was finished, she put it on. They let her have a mirror. A lute. Writing paper and quills. Whatever she asked for, as generous as Henry had been in the early days of his passion, when he had divided her from her love Harry Percy and had kept her loving hostage to his own fancy.

Cages came in many sizes. Many shapes. And, if what Master Culhane and the Lady Mary Lambert said was true, in many times.

"I am not a lady," Lady Lambert had protested. She needn't have bothered. Of course she was not a lady—she was a commoner, like the others, and so perverted was this place that the woman sounded insulted to be called a lady. Lambert did not like her, Anne knew, although she had not yet found out why. The woman was unsexed, like all of them, working on her books and machines all day, exercising naked with men who thus no more looked at their bodies than they would those of fellow soldiers in the roughest camp. So it pleased Anne to call Lambert a lady when she did not want to be one, as Anne was now so many things she had never wanted to be. "Anne Boleyn." Who never smiled.

"I will create you a Lady," she said to Lambert. "I confer on you the rank of baroness. Who will gainsay me? I am the queen, and in this place there is no king."

And Mary Lambert had stared at her with the unsexed bad manners of a common drab.

Anne knotted her thread and cut it with silver scissors. The gown was finished. She slipped it over her head and struggled with the buttons in the back, rather than call the stupid girl who was her servant. The girl could not even dress hair. Anne smoothed her hair herself, then looked critically at her reflection in the fine mirror they had brought her.

For a woman a month and a half from childbed, she looked strong. They had put medicines in her food, they said. Her complexion, that creamy dark skin that seldom varied in color, was well set off by the amber velvet. She had often worn amber, or tawny. Her hair, loose since she had no headdress and did not know how to make one, streamed over her shoulders. Her hands, long and slim despite the tiny extra finger, carried a rose brought to her by Master Culhane. She toyed with the rose to show off the beautiful hands, and lifted her head high.

She was going to have an audience with Her Holiness, a female pope. And she had a request to make.

"She will ask, Your Holiness, to be told the future. Her future, the one Anne Boleyn experienced in her own time stream, after the point we took her hostage to ours. And the future of England." Brill's face had darkened; Lambert could see that he hated this. To forewarn his political rival that a hostage would complain about her treatment. A *hostage*, that person turned sacred object through the sacrifice of personal freedom to global peace. When Tullio Amaden Koyushi had been hostage from Mars Three to the Republic of China, he had told the Church official in charge of his case that he was not being allowed sufficient exercise. The resulting intersystem furor had lost the Republic of China two trade contracts, both important. There was no other way to maintain the necessary reverence for the hostage political system. The Church of the Holy Hostage was powerful because it must be, if the solar system was to stay at peace. Brill knew that.

So did Her Holiness.

She wore full state robes today, gorgeous with hundreds of tiny mirrors sent to her by the grateful across all worlds. Her head was newly shaved. Perfect, synthetic jewels glittered in her ears. Listening to Brill's apology-in-advance, Her Holiness smiled. Lambert saw the smile, and even across the room she felt Brill's polite, concealed frustration.

"Then if this is so," Her Holiness said, "why cannot Lady Anne Boleyn be told her future? Hers and England's?"

Lambert knew that the high priest already knew the answer. She wanted to make Brill say it.

Brill said, "It is not thought wise, Your Holiness. If you remember, we did that once before."

"Ah, yes, your last hostage. I will see her, too, of course, on this visit. Has Queen Helen's condition improved?"

"No," Brill said shortly.

"And no therapeutic brain drugs or electronic treatments have helped? She still is insane from the shock of finding herself with us?"

"Nothing has helped."

"You understand how reluctant I was to let you proceed with another time rescue at all," Her Holiness said, and even Lambert stifled a gasp. The high priest did not make those determinations; only the All-World Forum could authorize or disallow a hostage-taking—across space *or* time. The Church of the Holy Hostage was responsible only for the inspection and continuation of permits granted by the Forum. For the high priest to claim political power she did not possess . . .

The director's eyes gleamed angrily. But before he could reply, the door opened and Culhane escorted in Anne Boleyn.

Lambert pressed her lips together tightly. The woman had sewn herself a gown, a sweeping, ridiculous confection of amber velvet so tight at the breasts and waist she must hardly be able to breathe. How had women conducted their lives in such trappings? The dress narrowed her waist to nearly nothing; above the square neckline her collarbones were delicate as a bird's. Culhane hovered beside her, huge and protective. Anne walked straight to the high priest, knelt, and raised her face.

She was looking for a ring to kiss.

Lambert didn't bother to hide her smile. A high priest wore no jewelry except earrings, ever. The pompous little hostage had made a social error, no doubt significant in her own time.

Anne smiled up at Her Holiness, the first time anyone had seen her smile at all. It changed her face, lighting it with mischief, lending luster to the great dark eyes. A phrase came to Lambert, penned by the poet Thomas Wyatt to describe his cousin Anne: *And wild for to hold, though I seem tame.*

Anne said, in that sprightly yet aloof manner that Lambert was coming to associate with her, "It seems, Your Holiness, that we have reached for what is not there. But the lack is ours, not yours, and we hope it will not be repeated in the request we come to make of you."

Direct. Graceful, even through the translator and despite the ludicrous imperial plural. Lambert glanced at Culhane, who was gazing down at Anne as at a rare and fragile flower. How could he? That skinny body, without muscle tone let alone augments, that plain face, the mole on her neck . . . . This was not the sixteenth century. Culhane was a fool.

As Thomas Wyatt had been. And Sir Harry Percy. And Henry, king of England. All caught not by beauty but by that strange elusive charm.

Her Holiness laughed. "Stand up, Your Grace. We don't kneel

to officials here." *Your Grace.* The high priest always addressed
hostages by the honorifics of their own state, but in this case it could
only impede Anne's adjustment.

And what do I care about her adjustment? Lambert jeered at
herself. Nothing. What I care about is Culhane's infatuation, and
only because he rejected me first. Rejection, it seemed, was a great
whetter of appetite—in any century.

Anne rose. Her Holiness said, "I'm going to ask you some questions, Your Grace. You are free to answer any way you wish. My
function is to ensure that you are well treated and that the noble
science of the prevention of war, which has made you a holy hostage, is also well served. Do you understand?"

"We do."

"Have you received everything you need for your material comfort?"

"Yes," Anne said.

"Have you received everything you've requested for your mental
comfort? Books, objects of any description, company?"

"No," Anne said. Lambert saw Brill stiffen.

Her Holiness said, "No?"

"It is necessary for the comfort of our mind—and for our material comfort as well—to understand our situation as fully as possible. Any rational creature requires such understanding to reach
ease of mind."

Brill said, "You have been told everything related to your situation. What you ask is to know about situations that now, because
you are here, will never happen."

"Situations that *have* happened, Lord Brill, else no one could
know of them. You could not."

"In *your* time stream they will not happen," Brill said. Lambert
could hear the suppressed anger in his voice and wondered if the
high priest could. Anne Boleyn couldn't know how serious it was
to be charged by Her Holiness with a breach of hostage treatment.
If Brill was ambitious—and why wouldn't he be?—such charges
could hurt his future.

Anne said swiftly, "Our time is now your time. *You* have made it
so. The situation was none of our choosing. And if your time is
now ours, then surely we are entitled to the knowledge that accom-
panies our time." She looked at the high priest. "For the comfort
of our mind."

Brill said, "Your Holiness—"

"No, Queen Anne is correct. Her argument is valid. You will
designate a qualified researcher to answer any questions she has—

any at all—about the life she might have had, or the course of events England took when the queen did not become a sacred hostage."

Brill nodded stiffly.

"Good-bye, Your Grace," Her Holiness said. "I shall return in two weeks to inspect your situation again."

Two weeks? The high priest was not due for another inspection for six months. Lambert glanced at Culhane to see his reaction to this blatant political fault-hunting, but he was gazing at the floor, to which Anne Boleyn had sunk in another of her embarrassing curtesies, the amber velvet of her skirts spread around her like gold.

They sent a commoner to explain her life to her, and the life she had lost. A commoner. And he had as well the nerve to be besotted with her. Anne always knew. She tolerated such fellows, like that upstart musician Smeaton, when they were useful to her. If this Master Culhane dared to make any sort of declaration, he would receive the same sort of snub Smeaton once had. Inferior persons should not look to be spoken to as noblemen.

He sat on a straight-backed chair in her tower room, looking humble enough, while Anne sat in the great carved chair with her hands tightly folded to keep them from shaking.

"Tell me how I came to die in 1536." God's blood! Had ever before there been such a sentence uttered?

Culhane said, "You were beheaded. Found guilty of treason." He stopped and flushed.

She knew, then. In a queen, there was one cause for a charge of treason. "He charged me with adultery. To remove me, so he could marry again."

"Yes."

"To Jane Seymour."

"Yes."

"Had I first given him a son?"

"No," Culhane said.

"Did Jane Seymour give him a son?"

"Yes. Edward the Sixth. But he died at sixteen, a few years after Henry."

There was vindication in that, but not enough to stem the sick feeling in her gut. Treason. And no son . . . . There must have been more than desire for the Seymour bitch. Henry must have hated her. Adultery . . .

"With whom?"

Again the oaf flushed. "With five men, Your Grace. Everyone knew the charges were false, created merely to excuse his own cuckoldry—even your enemies admitted such."

"Who were they?"

"Sir Henry Norris. Sir Francis Weston. William Brereton. Mark Smeaton. And . . . and your brother George."

For a moment she thought she would be sick. Each name fell like a blow, the last like the ax itself. George. Her beloved brother, 'so talented at music, so high-spirited and witty . . . Harry Norris, the king's friend. Weston and Brereton, young and lighthearted but always, to her, respectful and careful . . . and Mark Smeaton, the oaf made courtier because he could play the virginals.

The long, beautiful hands clutched the sides of the chair. But the moment passed, and she could say with dignity, "They denied the charges?"

"Smeaton confessed, but he was tortured into it. The others denied the charges completely. Harry Norris offered to defend your honor in single combat."

Yes, that was like Harry: so old-fashioned, so principled. She said, "They all died." It was not a question: If she had died for treason, they would have, too. And not alone; no one died alone. "Who else?"

Culhane said, "Maybe we should wait for the rest of this, Your—"

"Who else? My father?"

"No. Sir Thomas More, John Fisher—"

"More? For my . . ." She could not say *adultery*.

"Because he would not swear to the Oath of Supremacy, which made the king and not the pope head of the church in England. That act opened the door to religious dissension in England."

"It did not. The heretics were already strong in England. History cannot fault that to me!"

"Not as strong as they would become," Culhane said almost apologetically. "Queen Mary was known as Bloody Mary for burning heretics who used the Act of Supremacy to break from Rome— Your Grace! Are you all right . . . Anne?"

"Do not touch me," she said. Queen Mary. Then her own daughter Elizabeth had been disinherited, or killed. . . . Had Henry become so warped that he would kill a child? His own child? Unless he had come to believe . . .

She whispered, "Elizabeth?"

Comprehension flooded his eye. "Oh. No, Anne! No! Mary ruled first, as the elder, but when she died heirless, Elizabeth was only twenty-five. Elizabeth became the greatest ruler England had ever known! She ruled for forty-four years, and under her England became a great power."

The greatest ruler. Her baby Elizabeth. Anne could feel her hands unknotting on the ugly artificial chair. Henry had not repudiated Elizabeth, nor had her killed. She had become the greatest ruler England had ever known.

Culhane said, "This is why we thought it best not to tell you all this."

She said coldly, "I will be the judge of that."

"I'm sorry." He sat stiffly, hands dangling awkwardly between his knees. He looked like a plowman, like that oaf Smeaton. . . . She remembered what Henry had done, and rage returned.

"I stood accused. With five men . . . with George. And the charges were false." Something in his face changed. Anne faced him steadily. "Unless . . . were they false, Master Culhane? You who know so much of history. Does history say . . ." She could not finish. To beg for history's judgment from a man like this . . . no humiliation had ever been greater. Not even the Spanish ambassador, referring to her as "the concubine," had ever humiliated her so.

Culhane said carefully, "History is silent on the subject, Your Grace. What your conduct was . . . would have been . . . is known only to you."

"As it should be. It was . . . would have been . . . mine," she said viciously, mocking his tones perfectly. He looked at her like a wounded puppy, like that lout Smeaton when she had snubbed him. "Tell me this, Master Culhane. You have changed history as it would have been, you tell me. Will my daughter Elizabeth still become the greatest ruler England has ever seen—in *my* 'time stream'? Or will that be altered, too, by your quest for peace at any cost?"

"We don't know. I explained to you . . . We can only watch your time stream now as it unfolds. It had only reached October 1533, which is why after analyzing our own history we—"

"You have explained all that. It will be sixty years from now before you know if my daughter will still be great. Or if you have changed that as well by abducting me and ruining my life."

"Abducting! You were going to be killed! Accused, beheaded—"

"And you have prevented that." She rose, in a greater fury than ever she had been with Henry, with Wolsey, with anyone. "You have also robbed me of my remaining three years as surely as Henry would have robbed me of my old age. And you have mayhap robbed my daughter as well, as Henry sought to do with his Seymour-get prince. So what is the difference between you, Master Culhane,

that you are a saint and Henry a villain? He held me in the Tower
until my soul could be commended to God; you hold me here in
this castle you say I can never leave where time does not exist, and
mayhap God neither. Who has done me the worse injury? Henry
gave me the crown. You—all you and my Lord Brill have given me
is a living death, and then given my daughter's crown a danger and
uncertainty that without you she would not have known! Who has
done to Elizabeth and me the worse turn? And in the name of
preventing war! You have made war upon *me*! Get out, get out!"

"Your—"

"Get out! I never want to see you again! If I am in hell, let there
be one less demon!"

Lambert slipped from her monitor to run down the corridor. Culhane flew from the room; behind him the sound of something
heavy struck the door. Culhane slumped against it, his face pasty
around his cheek dye. Lambert could almost find it in herself to
pity him. Almost.

She said softly, "I told you so."

"She's like a wild thing."

"You knew she could be. It's documented enough, Culhane. I've
put a suicide watch on her."

"Yes. Good. I . . . she was like a wild thing."

Lambert peered at him. "You still want her! After that!"

That sobered him; he straightened and looked at her coldly. "She
is a holy hostage, Lambert."

"I remember that. Do you?"

"Don't insult me, intern."

He moved angrily away; she caught his sleeve. "Culhane—don't
be angry. I only meant that the sixteenth century was so different
from our own, but—"

"Do you think I don't know that? I was doing historical research
while you were learning to read, Lambert. Don't instruct me."

He stalked off. Lambert bit down hard on her own fury and
stared at Anne Boleyn's closed door. No sound came from behind
it. To the soundless door she finished her sentence: "—but some
traps don't change."

The door didn't answer. Lambert shrugged. It had nothing to
do with her. She didn't care what happened to Anne Boleyn, in
this century or that other one. Or to Culhane, either. Why should
she? There were other men. She was no Henry VIII, to bring down
her world for passion. What was the good of being a time researcher
if you could not even learn from times past?

She leaned thoughtfully against the door, trying to remember the name of the beautiful boy in her orientation lecture, the one with the violet eyes.

She was still there, thinking, when Toshio Brill called a staff meeting to announce, his voice stiff with anger, that Her Holiness of the Church of the Holy Hostage had filed a motion with the All-World Forum that the Time Research Institute, because of the essentially reverent nature of the time rescue program, be removed from administration by the Forum and placed instead under the direct control of the Church.

She had to think. It was important to think, as she had thought through her denial of Henry's ardor, and her actions when that ardor waned. Thought was all.

She could not return to her London, to Elizabeth. They had told her that. But did she know beyond doubt that it was true?

Anne left her apartments. At the top of the stairs she usually took to the garden, she instead turned and opened another door. It opened easily. She walked along a different corridor. Apparently even now no one was going to stop her.

And if they did, what could they do to her? They did not use the scaffold or the rack; she had determined this from talking to that oaf Culhane and that huge ungainly woman, Lady Mary Lambert. They did not believe in violence, in punishment, in death. (How could you not believe in death? Even they must one day die.) The most they could do to her was shut her up in her rooms, and there the female pope would come to see she was well treated.

Essentially they were powerless.

The corridor was lined with doors, most set with small windows. She peered in: rooms with desks and machines, rooms without desks and machines, rooms with people seated around a table talking, kitchens, still rooms. No one stopped her. At the end of the corridor she came to a room without a window and tried the door. It was locked, but as she stood there, her hand still on the knob, the door opened from within.

"Lady Anne! Oh!"

Could no one in this accursed place get her name right? The woman who stood there was clearly a servant, although she wore the same ugly gray-green tunic as everyone else. Perhaps, like Lady Mary, she was really an apprentice. She was of no interest, but behind her was the last thing Anne expected to see in this place; a child.

She pushed past the servant and entered the room. It was a little boy, his dress strange but clearly a uniform of some sort. He had dark eyes, curling dark hair, a bright smile. How old? Perhaps four.

There was an air about him that was unmistakable; she would have wagered her life this child was royal.

"Who are you, little one?"

He answered her with an outpouring of a language she did not know. The servant scrambled to some device on the wall; in a moment Culhane stood before her.

"You said you didn't want to see me, Your Grace. But I was closest to answer Kiti's summons . . ."

Anne looked at him. It seemed to her that she looked clear through him, to all that he was: Desire, and pride of his pitiful strange learning, and smugness of his holy mission that had brought her life to wreck. Hers, and perhaps Elizabeth's as well. She saw Culhane's conviction, shared by Lord Director Brill and even by such as Lady Mary, that what they did was right because they did it. She knew that look well: It had been Cardinal Wolsey's, Henry's right-hand man and chancellor of England, the man who had advised Henry to separate Anne from Harry Percy. And advised Henry against marrying her. Until she, Anne Boleyn, upstart Tom Boleyn's powerless daughter, had turned Henry against Wolsey and had the cardinal brought to trial. She.

In that minute she made her decision.

"I was wrong, Master Culhane. I spoke in anger. Forgive me." She smiled and held out her hand, and she had the satisfaction of watching Culhane turn color.

How old was he? Not in his first youth. But neither had Henry.

He said, "Of course, Your Grace. Kiti said you talked to the Tsarevitch."

She made a face, still smiling at him. She had often mocked Henry thus. Even Harry Percy, so long ago, a lifetime ago . . . No. Two lifetimes ago. "The what?"

"The Tsarevitch." He indicated the child.

Was the dye on his face permanent, or would it wash off?

She said, not asking, "He is another time hostage. He, too, in his small person, prevents a war."

Culhane nodded, clearly unsure of her mood. Anne looked wonderingly at the child, then winningly at Culhane. "I would have you tell me about him. What language does he speak? Who is he?"

"Russian. He is—was—the future emperor. He suffers from a terrible disease: You called it the bleeding sickness. Because his mother, the empress, was so driven with worry over him, she fell under the influence of a holy man who led her to make some disastrous decisions while she was acting for her husband, the emperor, who was away at war."

Anne said, "And the bad decisions brought about another war."

"They made more bloody than necessary a major rebellion."

"You prevent rebellions as well as wars? Rebellions against a monarchy?"

"Yes, it—history did not go in the direction of monarchies."

That made little sense. How could history go other than in the direction of those who were divinely anointed, those who held the power? Royalty won. In the end, they always won.

But there could be many casualties before the end.

She said, with that combination of liquid dark gaze and aloof body that had so intrigued Henry—and Norris, and Wyatt, and even presumptuous Smeaton, God damn his soul—"I find I wish to know more about this child and his country's history. Will you tell me?"

"Yes," Culhane said. She caught the nature of his smile: relieved, still uncertain how far he had been forgiven, eager to find out. Familiar, all so familiar.

She was careful not to let her body touch his as they passed through the doorway. But she went first, so he could catch the smell of her hair.

"Master Culhane—you are listed on the demon machine as 'M. Culhane.' "

"The . . . oh, the computer. I didn't know you ever looked at one."

"I did. Through a window."

"It's not a demon, Your Grace."

She let the words pass; what did she care what it was? But his tone told her something. He liked reassuring her. In this world where women did the same work as men and where female bodies were to be seen uncovered in the exercise yard so often that even turning your head to look must become a bore, this oaf nonetheless liked reassuring her.

She said, "What does the 'M' mean?"

He smiled. "Michael. Why?"

As the door closed, the captive royal child began to wail.

Anne smiled, too. "An idle fancy. I wondered if it stood for Mark."

"What argument has the church filed with the All-World Forum?" a senior researcher asked.

Brill said irritably, as it were an answer, "Where is Mahjoub?"

Lambert spoke up promptly. "He is with Helen of Troy, Director, and the doctor. The queen had another seizure last night." Enzio Mahjoub was the unfortunate project head for their last time rescue.

Brill ran his hand over the back of his neck. His skull needed shaving, and his cheek dye was sloppily applied. He said, "Then we will begin without Mahjoub. The argument of Her Holiness is that the primary function of this institute is no longer pure time research but practical application, and that the primary practical application is time rescue. As such, we exist to take hostages, and thus should come under the direct control of the Church of the Holy Hostage. Her secondary argument is that the time hostages are not receiving treatment up to intersystem standards as specified by the All-World Accord of 2154."

Lambert's eyes darted around the room. Cassia Kohambu, project head for the institute's greatest success, sat up straight, looking outraged. "Our hostages are—on what are these charges allegedly based?"

Brill said, "No formal charges as yet. Instead, she has requested an investigation. She claims we have hundreds of potential hostages pinpointed by the Rahvoli equations, and the ones we have chosen do not meet standards for either internal psychic stability or benefit accrued to the hostages themselves, as specified in the All-World Accord. We have chosen to please ourselves, with flagrant disregard for the welfare of the hostages."

"Flagrant disregard!" It was Culhane, already on his feet. Beneath the face dye his cheeks flamed. Lambert eyed him carefully. "How can Her Holiness charge flagrant disregard when without us the Tsarevitch Alexis would have been in constant pain from hemophiliac episodes, Queen Helen would have been abducted and raped, Herr Hitler blown up in an underground bunker, and Queen Anne Boleyn beheaded!"

Brill said bluntly, "Because the Tsarevitch cries constantly for his mother, the Lady Helen is mad, and Mistress Boleyn tells the church she has been made war upon!"

Well, Lambert thought, that still left Herr Hitler. She was just as appalled as anyone at Her Holiness's charges, but Culhane had clearly violated both good manners and good sense. Brill never appreciated being upstaged.

Brill continued,—"An investigative committee from the All-World Forum will arrive here next month. It will be small: Delegates Soshiru, Vlakhav, and Tullio. In three days the institute staff will meet again at oh-seven hundred, and by that time I want each project group to have prepared an argument in favor of the hostage you hold. Use the prepermit justifications, including all the mathematical models, but go far beyond that in documenting benefits to the hostages themselves since they arrived here. Are there any questions?"

Only one, Lambert thought. She stood. "Director—were the three delegates who will investigate us chosen by the All-World Forum or requested by Her Holiness? To whom do they already owe their allegiance?"

Brill looked annoyed. He said austerely, "I think we can rely upon the All-World delegates to file a fair report, Intern Lambert," and Lambert lowered her eyes. Evidently she still had much to learn. The question should not have been asked aloud.

Would Mistress Boleyn have known that?

Anne took the hand of the little boy. "Come, Alexis," she said. "We walk now."

The prince looked up at her. How handsome he was, with his thick, curling hair and beautiful eyes almost as dark as her own. If she had given Henry such a child . . . She pushed the thought away. She spoke to Alexis in her rudimentary Russian, without using the translator box hung like a peculiarly ugly pendant around her neck. He answered with a stream of words she couldn't follow, and she waited for the box to translate.

"Why should we walk? I like it here in the garden."

"The garden is very beautiful," Anne agreed. "But I have something interesting to show you."

Alexis trotted beside her obediently then. It had not been hard to win his trust—had no one here ever passed time with children? Wash off the scary cheek paint, play for him songs on the lute—an instrument he could understand, not like the terrifying sounds coming without musicians from yet another box—learn a few phrases of his language. She had always been good at languages.

Anne led the child through the far gate of the walled garden, into the yard. Machinery hummed; naked men and women "exercised" together on the grass. Alexis watched them curiously, but Anne ignored them. Servants. Her long, full skirts, tawny silk, trailed on the ground.

At the far end of the yard she started down the short path to that other gate, the one that ended at nothing.

Queen Isabella of Spain, Henry had told Anne once, had sent an expedition of sailors to circumnavigate the globe. They were supposed to find a faster way to India. They had not done so, but neither had they fallen off the edge of the world, which many had prophesied for them. Anne had not shown much interest in the story, because Isabella had, after all, been Katharine's mother. The edge of the world.

The gate ended with a wall of nothing. Nothing to see, or smell, or taste—Anne had tried. To the touch the wall was solid enough, and faintly tingly. A "force field," Culhane said. Out of time as we experience it; out of space. The gate, one of three, led to a place called Upper Slib, in what had once been Egypt.

Anne lifted Alexis. He was heavier than even a month ago; since she had been attending him every day he had begun to eat better, play more, cease crying for his mother. Except at night. "Look, Alexis, a gate. Touch it."

The little boy did, then drew back his hand at the tingling. Anne laughed, and after a moment Alexis laughed, too.

The alarms sounded.

"Why, Your Grace?" Culhane said. "Why again?"

"I wished to see if the gate was unlocked," Anne said coolly. "We both wished to see." This was a lie. She knew it. Did he? Not yet perhaps.

"I told you, Your Grace, it is not a gate that can be left locked or unlocked, as you understand the terms. It must be activated by the stasis square."

"Then do so; the prince and I wish for an outing."

Culhane's eyes darkened; each time he was in more anguish. And each time, he came running. However much he might wish to avoid her, commanding his henchmen to talk to her most of the time, he must come when there was an emergency because he was her gaoler, appointed by Lord Brill. So much had Anne discovered in a month of careful trials. He said now, "I told you, Your Grace, you can't move past the force field, no more than I could move into your palace at Greenwich. In the time stream beyond that gate— *my* time stream—you don't exist. The second you crossed the force field you'd disintegrate into nothingness."

Nothingness again. To Alexis she said sadly in Russian, "He will never let us out. Never, never."

The child began to cry. Anne held him closer, looking reproachfully at Culhane, who was shifting toward anger. She caught him just before the shift was complete, befuddling him with unlooked-for wistfulness: "It is just that there is so little we can do here, in this time we do not belong. You can understand that, can you not, Master Culhane? Would it not be the same for you, in my court of England?"

Emotions warred on his face. Anne put her free hand gently on his arm. He looked down: the long, slim fingers with their delicate tendons, the tawny silk against his drab uniform. He choked out, "Anything in my power, anything within the rules, Your Grace . . ."

She had not yet gotten him to blurt out "Anne," as he had the day she'd thrown a candlestick after him at the door.

She removed her hand, shifted the sobbing child against her neck, spoke so softly he could not hear her.

He leaned forward, toward her. "What did you say, Your Grace?"

"Would you come again tonight to accompany my lute on your guitar? For Alexis and me?"

Culhane stepped back. His eyes looked trapped.

"Please, Master Culhane?"

Culhane nodded.

Lambert stared at the monitor. It showed the hospital suite, barred windows and low white pallets, where Helen of Troy was housed. The queen sat quiescent on the floor, as she usually did, except for the brief and terrifying periods when she erupted, shrieking and tearing at her incredible hair. There had never been a single coherent word in the eruptions, not since the first moment they had told Helen where she was, and why. Or maybe that fragile mind, already quivering under the strain of her affair with Paris, had snapped too completely even to hear them. Helen, Lambert thought, was no Anne Boleyn.

Anne sat close to the mad Greek queen, her silk skirts overlapping Helen's white tunic, her slender body leaning so far forward that her hair, too, mingled with Helen's, straight black waterfall with masses of springing black curls. Before she could stop herself, Lambert had run her hand over her own shaved head.

What was Mistress Anne trying to say to Helen? The words were too low for the microphones to pick up, and the double curtain of hair hid Anne's lips. Yet Lambert was as certain as death that Anne was talking. And Helen, quiescent—was she nonetheless hearing? What could it matter if she were, words in a tongue that from her point of view would not exist for another two millennia?

Yet the Boleyn woman visited her every day, right after she left the Tsarevitch. How good was Anne, from a time almost as barbaric as Helen's own, at nonverbal coercion of the crazed?

Culhane entered, glanced at the monitor, and winced.

Lambert said levelly, "You're a fool, Culhane."

He didn't answer.

"You go whenever she summons. You—"

He suddenly strode across the room, two strides at a time. Grabbing Lambert, he pulled her from her chair and yanked her to her feet. For an astonished moment she thought he was actually going to hit her—researchers *hitting* each other. She tensed to slug him back. But abruptly he dropped her, giving a little shove so that she tumbled gracelessly back into her chair.

"You feel like a fat stone."

Lambert stared at him. Indifferently he activated his own console and began work. Something rose in her, so cold the vertebrae of her back felt fused in ice. Stiffly she rose from the chair, left the room, and walked along the corridor.

A fat stone. Heavy, stolid yet doughy, the flesh yielding like a slug or a maggot. Bulky, without grace, without beauty, almost without individuality, as stones were all alike. A fat stone.

Anne Boleyn was just leaving Helen's chamber. In the corridor, back to the monitor, Lambert faced her. Her voice was low, like a subterranean growl. "Leave him alone."

Anne looked at her coolly. She did not ask whom Lambert meant.

"Don't you know you are watched every minute? That you can't so much as use your chamberpot without being taped? How do you ever expect to get him to your bed? Or to do anything with poor Helen?"

Anne's eyes widened. She said loudly, "Even when I use the chamberpot? Watched? Have I not even the privacy of the beasts in the field?"

Lambert clenched her fists. Anne was acting. Someone had already told her, or she had guessed, about the surveillance. Lambert could see that she was acting—but not *why*. A part of her mind noted coolly that she had never wanted to kill anyone before. So this, finally, was what it felt like, all those emotions she had researched throughout time: fury and jealousy and the desire to destroy. The emotions that started wars.

Anne cried, even more loudly, "I had been better had you never told me!" and rushed toward her own apartments.

Lambert walked slowly back to her work area, a fat stone.

Anne lay on the grass between the two massive power generators. It was a poor excuse for grass; although green enough, it had no smell. No dew formed on it, not even at night. Culhane had explained that it was bred to withstand disease, and that no dew formed because the air had little moisture. He explained, too, that the night was as man-bred as the grass; there was no natural night here. Henry would have been highly interested in such things; she was not. But she had listened carefully, as she listened to everything Michael said.

She lay completely still, waiting. Eventually the head of a researcher thrust around the corner of the towering machinery: a purposeful thrust. "Your Grace? What are you doing?"

Anne did not answer. Getting to her feet, she walked back toward the castle. The place between the generators was no good: The woman had already known where Anne was.

* * *

The three delegates from the All-World Forum arrived at the Time Research Institute looking apprehensive. Lambert could understand this; for those who had never left their own time-space continuum, it probably seemed significant to step through a force field to a place that did not exist in any accepted sense of the word. The delegates looked at the ground, and inspected the facilities, and asked the same kinds of questions visitors always asked, before they settled down actually to investigate anything.

They were given an hour's overview of the time rescue program, presented by the director himself. Lambert, who had not helped write this, listened to the careful sentiments about the prevention of war, the nobility of hostages, the deep understanding the Time Research Institute held of the All-World Accord of 2154, the altruistic extension of the Holy Mission of Peace into other time streams. Brill then moved on to discuss the four time hostages, dwelling heavily on the first. In the four years since Herr Hitler had become a hostage, the National Socialist Party had all but collapsed in Germany. President Paul von Hindenburg had died on schedule, and the new moderate chancellors were slowly bringing order to Germany. The economy was still very bad and unrest was widespread, but no one was arresting Jews or Gypsies or homosexuals or Jehovah's Witnesses or . . . Lambert stopped listening. The delegates knew all this. The entire solar system knew all this. Hitler had been a tremendous popular success as a hostage, the reason the Institute had obtained permits for the next three. Herr Hitler was kept in his locked suite, where he spent his time reading power-fantasy novels whose authors had not been born when the bunker under Berlin was detonated.

"Very impressive, Director," Goro Soshiru said. He was small, thin, elongated, a typical free-fall spacer, with a sharp mind and a reputation for incorruptibility. "May we now talk to the hostages, one at a time?"

"Without any monitors. That is our instruction," said Anna Vlakhav. She was the senior member of the investigative team, a sleek, gray-haired Chinese who refused all augments. Her left hand, Lambert noticed, trembled constantly. She belonged to the All-World Forum's Inner Council and had once been a hostage herself for three years.

"Please," Soren Tullio said with a smile. He was young, handsome, very wealthy. Disposable, added by the Forum to fill out the committee, with few recorded views of his own. Insomuch as they existed, however, they were not tinged with any bias toward the

Church. Her Holiness had not succeeded in naming the members of the investigative committee—if indeed she had tried.

"Certainly," Brill said. "We've set aside the private conference room for your use. As specified by the Church, it is a sanctuary: There are no monitors of any kind. I would recommend, however, that you allow the bodyguard to remain with Herr Hitler, although, of course, you will make up your own minds."

Delegate Vlakhav said, "The bodyguard may stay. Herr Hitler is not our concern here."

Surprise, Lambert thought. Guess who is?

The delegates kept Hitler only ten minutes, the catatonic Helen only three. They said the queen did not speak. They talked to the little Tsarevitch a half hour. They kept Anne Boleyn in the sanctuary/conference room four hours and twenty-three minutes.

She came out calm, blank-faced, and proceeded to her own apartments. Behind her the three delegates were tight-lipped and silent. Anna Vlakhav, the former hostage, said to Toshio Brill, "We have no comment at this time. You will be informed."

Brill's eyes narrowed. He said nothing.

The next day, Director Toshio Brill was subpoenaed to appear before the All-World Forum on the gravest of all charges: mistreating holy hostages detained to keep peace. The tribunal would consist of the full Inner Council of the All-World Forum. Since Director Brill had the right to confront those who accused him, the investigation would be held at the Time Research Institute.

How? Lambert wondered. They would not take her unsupported word. How had the woman done it?

She said to Culhane, "The delegates evidently make no distinction between political hostages on our own world and time hostages snatched from shadowy parallel ones."

"Why should they?" coldly said Culhane. The idealist. And where had it brought him?

Lambert was assigned that night to monitor the tsarevitch, who was asleep in his crib. She sat in her office, her screen turned to Anne Boleyn's chambers, watching her play on the lute and sing softly to herself the songs written for her by Henry VIII when his passion was new and fresh six hundred years before.

Anne sat embroidering a sleeve cover of cinnamon velvet. In strands of black silk she worked intertwined H and A: Henry and Anne. Let their spying machines make of that what they would.

The door opened and, without permission, Culhane entered. He stood by her chair and looked down into her face. "Why, Anne? Why?"

She laughed. He had finally called her by her Christian name. Now, when it could not possibly matter.

When he saw that she would not answer, his manner grew formal. "A lawyer has been assigned to you. He arrives tomorrow."

A lawyer. Thomas Cromwell had been a lawyer, and Sir Thomas More. Dead, both of them, at Henry's hand. So had Master Culhane told her, and yet he still believed that protection was afforded by the law.

"The lawyer will review all the monitor records. What you did, what you said, every minute."

She smiled at him mockingly. "Why tell me this now?"

"It is your right to know."

"And you are concerned with rights. Almost as much as with death." She knotted the end of her thread and cut it. "How is it that you command so many machines and yet do not command the knowledge that every man must die?"

"We know that," Culhane said evenly. His desire for her had at last been killed; she could feel its absence, like an empty well. The use of her name had been but the last drop of living water. "But we try to prevent death when we can."

"Ah, but you can't. 'Prevent death'—as if it were a fever. You can only postpone it, Master Culhane, and you never even ask if that is worth doing."

"I only came to tell you about the lawyer," Culhane said stiffly. "Good night, Mistress Boleyn."

"Good night, Michael," she said, and started to laugh. She was still laughing when the door closed behind him.

The Hall of Time, designed to hold three hundred, was packed.

Lambert remembered the day she had given the orientation lecture to the history candidates, among them what's-his-name of the violet eyes. Twenty young people huddled together against horror in the middle of squares, virtual and simulated but not really present. Today the squares were absent and the middle of the floor was empty, while all four sides were lined ten-deep with All-World Inner Council members on high polished benches, archbishops and lamas and shamans of the Church of the Holy Hostage, and reporters from every major newsgrid in the solar system. Her Holiness the high priest sat among her followers, pretending she wanted to be inconspicuous, Toshio Brill sat in a chair alone, facing the current premier of the All-World Council, Dagar Krenya of Mars.

Anne Boleyn was led to a seat. She walked with her head high, her long black skirts sweeping the floor.

Lambert remembered that she had worn black to her trial for treason, in 1536.

"This investigation will begin," Premier Krenya said. He wore his hair to his shoulders; fashions must have changed again on Mars. Lambert looked at the shaved heads of her colleagues, at the long, loose black hair of Anne Boleyn. To Culhane, seated beside her, she whispered, "We'll be growing our hair again soon." He looked at her as if she were crazy.

It *was* a kind of crazy, to live everything twice: once in research, once in the flesh. Did it seem so to Anne Boleyn? Lambert knew her frivolity was misplaced, and she thought of the frivolity of Anne in the Tower, awaiting execution: "They will have no trouble finding a name for me. I shall be Queen Anne Lackhead." At the memory, Lambert's hatred burst out fresh. She had the memory, and now Anne never would. But in bequeathing it forward in time to Lambert, the memory had become secondhand. That was Anne Boleyn's real crime, for which she would never be tried: She had made this whole proceeding, so important to Lambert and Brill and Culhane, a mere reenactment. Prescripted. Secondhand. She had robbed them of their own, unused time.

Krenya said, "The charges are as follows: That the Time Research Institute has mistreated the holy hostage Anne Boleyn, held hostage against war. Three counts of mistreatment are under consideration this day: First, that researchers willfully increased a hostage's mental anguish by dwelling on the pain of those left behind by the hostage's confinement, and on those aspects of confinement that cause emotional unease. Second, that researchers failed to choose a hostage who would truly prevent war. Third, that researchers willfully used a hostage for sexual gratification."

Lambert felt herself go very still. Beside her, Culhane rose to his feet, then sat down again slowly, his face rigid. Was it possible he had . . . No. He had been infatuated, but not to the extent of throwing away his career. He was not Henry, any more than Lambert had been over him.

The spectators buzzed, an uneven sound like malfunctioning equipment. Krenya rapped for order. "Director Brill: How do you answer these charges?"

"False, Premier. Every one."

"Then let us hear the evidence against the Institute."

Anne Boleyn was called. She took the chair in which Brill had been sitting. *"She made an entry as though she were going to a great triumph and sat down with elegance"* . . . But that was the other time, the first time. Lambert groped for Culhane's hand. It felt limp.

"Mistress Boleyn," Krenya said—he had evidently not been told that she insisted on being addressed as a queen, and the omission gave Lambert a mean pleasure—"in what ways was your anguish willfully increased by researchers at this Institute?"

Anne held out her hand. To Lambert's astonishment, her lawyer put into it a lute. At an official All-World Forum investigation—a *lute*. Anne began to play, the tune high and plaintive. Her unbound black hair fell forward; her slight body made a poignant contrast to the torment in the words:

> *Defiled is my name, full sore,*
> *Through cruel spite and false report,*
> *That I may say forever more,*
> *Farewell to joy,* adieu *comfort.*

> *Oh, death, rock me asleep,*
> *Bring on my quiet rest,*
> *Let pass my very guiltless ghost*
> *Out of my careful breast.*

> *Ring out the doleful knell,*
> *Let its sound my death tell,*
> *For I must die,*
> *There is no remedy,*
> *For now I die!*

The last notes faded. Anne looked directly at Krenya. "I wrote that, my Lords, in my other life. Master Culhane of this place played it for me, along with death songs written by my . . . my brother . . ."

"Mistress Boleyn . . ."

"No, I recover myself. George's death tune was hard for me to hear, my Lords. Accused and condemned because of me, who always loved him well."

Krenya said to the lawyer whose staff had spent a month reviewing every moment of monitor records, "Culhane made her listen to these?"

"Yes," the lawyer said. Beside Lambert, Culhane sat unmoving.

"Go on," Krenya said to Anne.

"He told me that I was made to suffer watching the men accused with me die. How I was led to a window overlooking the block, how my brother George kneeled, putting his head on the block, how the ax was raised . . ." She stopped, shuddering. A murmur ran over the room. It sounded like cruelty, Lambert thought. But whose?

"Worst of all, my Lords," Anne said, "was that I was told I had bastardized my own child. I chose to sign a paper declaring no valid marriage had ever existed because I had been precontracted to Sir Henry Percy, so my daughter Elizabeth was illegitimate and thus barred from her throne. I was taunted with the fact that I had done this, ruining the prospects of my own child. He said it over and over, Master Culhane did . . ."

Krenya said to the lawyer, "Is this in the visuals?"

"Yes."

Krenya turned back to Anne. "But Mistress Boleyn—these are things that because of your time rescue did *not* happen. Will not happen in your time stream. How can they thus increase your anguish for relatives left behind?"

Anne stood. She took one step forward, then stopped. Her voice was low and passionate. "My good Lord—do you not understand? It is because you took me here that these things did not happen. Left to my own time, I *would have been responsible for them all.* For my brother's death, for the other four brave men, for my daughter's bastardization, for the torment in my own music . . . I have escaped them only because of *you.* To tell me them in such detail, not the mere provision of facts that I myself requested but agonizing detail of mind and heart—is to tell me that I alone, in my own character, am evil, giving pain to those I love most. And that in this time stream you have brought me to, I *did* these things, felt them, feel them still. You have made me guilty of them. My Lord Premier, have you ever been a hostage yourself? Do you know, or can you imagine, the torment that comes from imagining the grief of those who love you? And to know you have caused this grief, not merely loss but death, blood, the pain of disinheritance—that you have caused it, and are now being told of the anguish you cause? Told over and over? In words, in song even—can you imagine what that feels like to one such as I, who cannot return at will and comfort those hurt by my actions?"

The room was silent. Who, Lambert wondered, had told Anne Boleyn that Premier Krenya had once served as a holy hostage?

"Forgive me, my Lords," Anne said dully, "I forget myself."

"Your testimony may take whatever form you choose," Krenya said, and it seemed to Lambert that there were shades and depths in his voice.

The questioning continued. A researcher, said Anne, had taunted her with being spied on even at her chamberpot—Lambert leaned slowly forward—which had made Anne cry out, "It had been better had you never told me!" Since then, modesty had made her reluctant even to answer nature, "so that there is every hour a most wretched twisting and churning in my bowels."

Asked why she thought the Institute had chosen the wrong hostage, Anne said she had been told so by my Lord Brill. The room exploded into sound, and Krenya rapped for quiet. "That visual now, please." On a square created in the center of the room, the visuals replayed on three sides:

> "*My Lord Brill . . . was there no other person you could take but I to prevent this war you say is a hundred years off? This civil war in England?*"
> "*The mathematics identified you as the best hostage, Your Grace.*"
> "*The best? Best for what, my Lord? If you had taken Henry himself, then he could not have issued the Act of Supremacy. His supposed death would have served the purpose as well as mine.*"
> "*Yes. But for Henry the Eighth to disappear from history while his heir is but a month old . . . we did not know if that might not have started a civil war in itself. Between the factions supporting Elizabeth and those for Queen Katharine, who was still alive.*"
> "*What did your mathematical learning tell you?*"
> "*That it probably would not,*" Brill said.
> "*And yet choosing me instead of Henry left him free to behead yet another wife, as you yourself have told me, my cousin Catherine Howard!*"
> Brill shifted on his chair. "*That is true, Your Grace.*"
> "*Then why not Henry instead of me?*"
> "*I'm afraid Your Grace does not have sufficient grasp of the science of probabilities for me to explain, Your Grace.*"
> Anne was silent. Finally she said, "*I think that the probability is that you would find it easier to deal with a deposed woman than with Henry of England, whom no man can withstand in either a passion or a temper.*"
> Brill did not answer. The visual rolled—ten seconds, fifteen— and he did not answer.

"Mr. Premier," Brill said in a choked voice, "Mr. Premier—"

"You will have time to address these issues soon, Mr. Director," Krenya said. "Mistress Boleyn, this third charge—sexual abuse . . ."

The term had not existed in the sixteenth century, thought Lambert. Yet Anne understood it. She said, "I was frightened, my Lord, by the strangeness of this place. I was afraid for my life. I didn't know then that a woman may refuse those in power, may—"

"That is why sexual contact with hostages is universally forbidden," Krenya said. "Tell us what you think happened."

Not what *did* happen—what you *think* happened. Lambert took heart.

Anne said, "Master Culhane bade me meet him at a place . . . it is a small alcove beside a short flight of stairs near the kitchens. . . . He bade me meet him there at night. Frightened, I went."

"Visuals," Krenya said in a tight voice.

The virtual square reappeared. Anne, in the same white night-dress in which she had been taken hostage, crept from her chamber, along the corridor, her body heat registering in infrared. Down the stairs, around to the kitchens, into the cubbyhole formed by the flight of steps, themselves oddly angled as if they had been added, or altered, after the main structure was built, after the monitoring system installed. . . . Anne dropped to her knees and crept forward beside the isolated stairs. And disappeared.

Lambert gasped. A time hostage was under constant surveillance. That was a basic condition of their permit; there was no way the Boleyn bitch could escape constant monitoring. But she had.

"Master Culhane was already there," Anne said in a dull voice. "He . . . he used me ill there."

The room was awash with sound. Krenya said over it, "Mistress Boleyn—there is no visual evidence that Master Culhane was there. He has sworn he was not. Can you offer any proof that he met you there? Anything at all?"

"Yes. Two arguments, my Lord. First: How would I know there were not spying devices in but this one hidden alcove? I did not design this castle; it is not mine."

Krenya's face showed nothing. "And the other argument?"

"I am pregnant with Master Culhane's child."

Pandemonium. Krenya rapped for order. When it was finally restored, he said to Brill, "Did you know of this?"

"No, I . . . it was a hostage's right by the Accord to refuse intrusive medical treatment. . . . She has been healthy. . . ."

"Mistress Boleyn, you will be examined by a doctor immediately."

She nodded assent. Watching her, Lambert knew it was true. Anne Boleyn was pregnant, and had defeated herself thereby. But she did not know it yet.

Lambert fingered the knowledge, seeing it as a tangible thing, cold as steel.

"How do we know," Krenya said, "that you were not pregnant before you were taken hostage?"

"It was but a month after my daughter Elizabeth's birth, and I had the white-leg. Ask one of your experts if a woman would bed a man then. Ask a woman expert in the women of my time. Ask Lady Mary Lambert."

Heads in the room turned. Ask whom? Krenya said, "Ask

whom?" An aide leaned toward him and whispered something. He said, "We will have her put on the witness list."

Anne said, "I carry Michael Culhane's child. I, who could not carry a prince for the king."

Krenya said, almost powerlessly, "That last has nothing to do with this investigation, Mistress Boleyn."

She only looked at him.

They called Brill to testify, and he threw up clouds of probability equations that did nothing to clarify the choice of Anne over Henry as holy hostage. Was the woman right? Had there been a staff meeting to choose between the candidates identified by the Rahvoli applications, and had someone said of two very close candidates, "We should think about the effect on the Institute as well as on history . . ."? Had someone been developing a master theory based on a percentage of women influencing history? Had someone had an infatuation with the period, and chosen by that what should be altered? Lambert would never know. She was an intern.

Had been an intern.

Culhane was called. He denied seducing Anne Boleyn. The songs on the lute, the descriptions of her brother's death, the bastardization of Elizabeth—all done to convince her that what she had been saved from was worse than where she had been saved to. Culhane felt so much that he made a poor witness, stumbling over his words, protesting too much.

Lambert was called. As neutrally as possible she said, "Yes, Mr. Premier, historical accounts show that Queen Anne was taken with white-leg after Elizabeth's birth. It is a childbed illness. The legs swell up and ache painfully. It can last from a few weeks to months. We don't know how long it lasted—would have lasted—for Mistress Boleyn."

"And would a woman with this disease be inclined to sexual activity?"

" 'Inclined'—no."

"Thank you, Researcher Lambert."

Lambert returned to her seat. The committee next looked at visuals, hours of visuals—Culhane, flushed and tender, making a fool of himself with Anne. Anne with the little tsarevitch, an exile trying to comfort a child torn from his mother. Helen of Troy, mad and pathetic. Brill, telling newsgrids around the solar system that the time rescue program, savior of countless lives, was run strictly in conformance with the All-World Accord of 2154. And all the time, through all the visuals, Lambert waited for what was known to everyone in that room except Anne Boleyn: She could not pull off in this century what she might have in Henry's. The paternity of a child could be genotyped in the womb.

Who? Mark Smeaton, after all? Another miscarriage from Henry, precipitately gotten and unrecorded by history? Thomas Wyatt, her most faithful cousin and cavalier?

After the committee had satisfied itself that it had heard enough, everyone but Forum delegates was dismissed. Anne, Lambert saw, was led away by a doctor. Lambert smiled to herself. It was already over. The Boleyn bitch was defeated.

The All-World Forum investigative committee deliberated for less than a day. Then it issued a statement: The child carried by holy hostage Anne Boleyn had not been sired by Researcher Michael Culhane. Its genotypes matched no one's at the Institute for Time Research. The Institute, however, was guilty of two counts of hostage mistreatment. The Institute's charter as an independent, tax-exempt organization was revoked. Toshio Brill was released from his position, as were Project Head Michael Culhane and intern Mary Lambert. The Institute stewardship was reassigned to the Church of the Holy Hostage under the direct care of Her Holiness the high priest.

Lambert slipped through the outside door to the walled garden. It was dusk. On a seat at the far end a figure sat, skirts spread wide, a darker shape against the dark wall. As Lambert approached, Anne looked up without surprise.

"Culhane's gone. I leave tomorrow. Neither of us will ever work in time research again."

Anne went on gazing upward. Those great dark eyes, that slim neck, so vulnerable. . . . Lambert clasped her hands together hard.

"Why?" Lambert said. "Why do it all again? Last time use a king to bring down the power of the church, this time use a church to—before, at least you gained a crown. Why do it here, when you gain nothing?"

"You could have taken Henry. He deserved it; I did not."

"But we didn't take Henry!" Lambert shouted. "So why?"

Anne did not answer. She put out one hand to point behind her. Her sleeve fell away, and Lambert saw clearly the small sixth finger that had marked her as a witch. A tech came running across the half-lit garden. "Researcher Lambert—"

"What is it?"

"They want you inside. Everybody. The queen—the other one, Helen—she's killed herself."

The garden blurred, straightened. "How?"

"Stabbed with a silver sewing scissors hidden in her tunic. It was so quick, the researchers saw it on the monitor but couldn't get there in time."

"Tell them I'm coming."

Lambert looked at Anne Boleyn. "You did this."

Anne laughed. *This lady*, wrote the Tower constable, *hath much joy in death*. Anne said, "Lady Mary—every birth is a sentence of death. Your age has forgotten that."

"Helen didn't need to die yet. And the Time Research Institute didn't need to be dismantled—it *will* be dismantled. Completely. But somewhere, sometime, you will be punished for this. I'll see to that!"

"Punished, Lady Mary? And mayhap beheaded?"

Lambert looked at Anne: the magnificent black eyes, the sixth finger, the slim neck. Lambert said slowly, "You want your own death. As you had it before."

"What else did you leave me?" Anne Boleyn said. "Except the power to live the life that is mine?"

"You will never get it. We don't kill here!"

Anne smiled. "Then how will you 'punish' me—'sometime, somehow'?"

Lambert didn't answer. She walked back across the walled garden, toward the looming walls gray in the dusk, toward the chamber where lay the other dead queen.